CW01072561

R.D. Blackmore

Mary Anerley

outlook

R.D. Blackmore

Mary Anerley

1st Edition | ISBN: 978-3-73408-943-5

Place of Publication: Frankfurt am Main, Germany

Year of Publication: 2019

Outlook Verlag GmbH, Germany.

Reproduction of the original.

MARY ANERLEY

by R. D. Blackmore

1880

Contents

CHAPTER I

HEADSTRONG AND HEADLONG

Far from any house or hut, in the depth of dreary moor-land, a road, unfenced and almost unformed, descends to a rapid river. The crossing is called the "Seven Corpse Ford," because a large party of farmers, riding homeward from Middleton, banded together and perhaps well primed through fear of a famous highwayman, came down to this place on a foggy evening, after heavy rain-fall. One of the company set before them what the power of the water was, but they laughed at him and spurred into it, and one alone spurred out of it. Whether taken with fright, or with too much courage, they laid hold of one another, and seven out of eight of them, all large farmers, and thoroughly understanding land, came never upon it alive again; and their bodies, being found upon the ridge that cast them up, gave a dismal name to a place that never was merry in the best of weather.

However, worse things than this had happened; and the country is not chary of its living, though apt to be scared of its dead; and so the ford came into use again, with a little attempt at improvement. For those farmers being beyond recall, and their families hard to provide for, Richard Yordas, of Scargate Hall, the chief owner of the neighborhood, set a long heavy stone up on either brink, and stretched a strong chain between them, not only to mark out the course of the shallow, whose shelf is askew to the channel, but also that any one being washed away might fetch up, and feel how to save himself. For the Tees is a violent water sometimes, and the safest way to cross it is to go on till you come to a good stone bridge.

Now forty years after that sad destruction of brave but not well-guided men, and thirty years after the chain was fixed, that their sons might not go after them, another thing happened at "Seven Corpse Ford," worse than the drowning of the farmers. Or, at any rate, it made more stir (which is of wider spread than sorrow), because of the eminence of the man, and the length and width of his property. Neither could any one at first believe in so quiet an end to so turbulent a course. Nevertheless it came to pass, as lightly as if he were a reed or a bubble of the river that belonged to him.

It was upon a gentle evening, a few days after Michaelmas of 1777. No flood was in the river then, and no fog on the moor-land, only the usual course of time, keeping the silent company of stars. The young moon was down, and the hover of the sky (in doubt of various lights) was gone, and the equal spread of obscurity soothed the eyes of any reasonable man.

But the man who rode down to the river that night had little love of reason. Headstrong chief of a headlong race, no will must depart a hair's-breadth from his; and fifty years of arrogant port had stiffened a neck too stiff at birth. Even now in the dim light his large square form stood out against the sky like a cromlech, and his heavy arms swung like gnarled boughs of oak, for a storm of wrath was moving him. In his youth he had rebelled against his father; and now his own son was a rebel to him.

"Good, my boy, good!" he said, within his grizzled beard, while his eyes shone with fire, like the flints beneath his horse; "you have had your own way, have you, then? But never shall you step upon an acre of your own, and your timber shall be the gallows. Done, my boy, once and forever."

Philip, the squire, the son of Richard, and father of Duncan Yordas, with fierce satisfaction struck the bosom of his heavy Bradford riding-coat, and the crackle of parchment replied to the blow, while with the other hand he drew rein on the brink of the Tees sliding rapidly.

The water was dark with the twinkle of the stars, and wide with the vapor of the valley, but Philip Yordas in the rage of triumph laughed and spurred his reflecting horse.

"Fool!" he cried, without an oath—no Yordas ever used an oath except in playful moments—"fool! what fear you? There hangs my respected father's chain. Ah, he was something like a man! Had I ever dared to flout him so, he would have hanged me with it."

Wild with his wrong, he struck the rowel deep into the flank of his wading horse, and in scorn of the depth drove him up the river. The shoulders of the swimming horse broke the swirling water, as he panted and snorted against it; and if Philip Yordas had drawn back at once, he might even now have crossed safely. But the fury of his blood was up, the stronger the torrent the fiercer his will, and the fight between passion and power went on. The poor horse was fain to swerve back at last; but he struck him on the head with a carbine, and shouted to the torrent:

"Drown me, if you can. My father used to say that I was never born to drown. My own water drown me! That would be a little too much insolence."

"Too much insolence" were his last words. The strength of the horse was exhausted. The beat of his legs grew short and faint, the white of his eyes rolled piteously, and the gurgle of his breath subsided. His heavy head dropped under water, and his sodden crest rolled over, like sea-weed where a wave breaks. The stream had him all at its mercy, and showed no more than his savage master had, but swept him a wallowing lump away, and over the reef of the crossing. With both feet locked in the twisted stirrups, and right arm broken at the elbow, the rider was swung (like the mast of a wreck) and flung with his head upon his father's chain. There he was held by his great square chin—for the jar of his backbone stunned him—and the weight of the swept-away horse broke the neck which never had been known to bend. In the morning a peasant found him there, not drowned but hanged, with eyes wide open, a swaying corpse upon a creaking chain. So his father (though long in the grave) was his death, as he often had promised to be to him; while he (with the habit of his race) clutched fast with dead hand on dead bosom the instrument securing the starvation of his son.

Of the Yordas family truly was it said that the will of God was nothing to their will—as long as the latter lasted—and that every man of them scorned all Testament, old or new, except his own.

CHAPTER II

SCARGATE HALL

Nearly twenty-four years had passed since Philip Yordas was carried to his last (as well as his first) repose, and Scargate Hall had enjoyed some rest from the turbulence of owners. For as soon as Duncan (Philip's son, whose marriage had maddened his father) was clearly apprised by the late squire's lawyer of his disinheritance, he collected his own little money and his wife's, and set sail for India. His mother, a Scotchwoman of good birth but evil fortunes, had left him something; and his bride (the daughter of his father's greatest foe) was not altogether empty-handed. His sisters were forbidden by the will to help him with a single penny; and Philippa, the elder, declaring and believing that Duncan had killed her father, strictly obeyed the injunction. But Eliza, being of a softer kind, and herself then in love with Captain Carnaby, would gladly have aided her only brother, but for his stern refusal. In such a case, a more gentle nature than ever endowed a Yordas might have grown hardened and bitter; and Duncan, being of true Yordas fibre (thickened and toughened with slower Scotch sap), was not of the sort to be ousted lightly and grow at the feet of his supplanters.

Therefore he cast himself on the winds, in search of fairer soil, and was not heard of in his native land; and Scargate Hall and estates were held by the sisters in joint tenancy, with remainder to the first son born of whichever it might be of them. And this was so worded through the hurry of their father to get some one established in the place of his own son.

But from paltry passions, turn away a little while to the things which excite, but are not excited by them.

Scargate Hall stands, high and old, in the wildest and most rugged part of the wild and rough North Riding. Many are the tales about it, in the few and humble cots, scattered in the modest distance, mainly to look up at it. In spring and summer, of the years that have any, the height and the air are not only fine, but even fair and pleasant. So do the shadows and the sunshine wander, elbowing into one another on the moor, and so does the glance of smiling foliage soothe the austerity of crag and scaur. At such time, also, the restless torrent (whose fury has driven content away through many a short day and long night) is not in such desperate hurry to bury its troubles in the breast of Tees, but spreads them in language that sparkles to the sun, or even makes leisure to turn into corners of deep brown-study about the people on its banks —especially, perhaps, the miller.

But never had this impetuous water more reason to stop and reflect upon people of greater importance, who called it their own, than now when it was at the lowest of itself, in August of the year 1801.

From time beyond date the race of Yordas had owned and inhabited this old place. From them the river, and the river's valley, and the mountain of its birth, took name, or else, perhaps, gave name to them; for the history of the giant Yordas still remains to be written, and the materials are scanty. His present descendants did not care an old song for his memory, even if he ever had existence to produce it. Piety (whether in the Latin sense or English) never had marked them for her own; their days were long in the land, through a long inactivity of the Decalogue.

And yet in some manner this lawless race had been as a law to itself throughout. From age to age came certain gifts and certain ways of management, which saved the family life from falling out of rank and land and lot. From deadly feuds, exhausting suits, and ruinous profusion, when all appeared lost, there had always arisen a man of direct lineal stock to retrieve the estates and reprieve the name. And what is still more conducive to the longevity of families, no member had appeared as yet of a power too large and an aim too lofty, whose eminence must be cut short with axe, outlawry, and attainder. Therefore there ever had been a Yordas, good or bad (and by his own showing more often of the latter kind), to stand before heaven, and hold the land, and harass them that dwelt thereon. But now at last the world seemed to be threatened with the extinction of a fine old name.

When Squire Philip died in the river, as above recorded, his death, from one point of view, was dry, since nobody shed a tear for him, unless it was his child Eliza. Still, he was missed and lamented in speech, and even in eloquent speeches, having been a very strong Justice of the Peace, as well as the foremost of riotous gentlemen keeping the order of the county. He stood above them in his firm resolve to have his own way always, and his way was so crooked that the difficulty was to get out of it and let him have it. And when he was dead, it was either too good or too bad to believe in; and even after he was buried it was held that this might be only another of his tricks.

But after his ghost had been seen repeatedly, sitting on the chain and swearing, it began to be known that he was gone indeed, and the relief afforded by his absence endeared him to sad memory. Moreover, his good successors enhanced the relish of scandal about him by seeming themselves to be always so dry, distant, and unimpeachable. Especially so did "My Lady Philippa," as the elder daughter was called by all the tenants and dependents, though the family now held no title of honor.

Mistress Yordas, as she was more correctly styled by usage of the period, was a maiden lady of fine presence, uncumbered as yet by weight of years, and only dignified thereby. Stately, and straight, and substantial of figure, firm but not coarse of feature, she had reached her forty-fifth year without an ailment or a wrinkle. Her eyes were steadfast, clear, and bright, well able to second her distinct calm voice, and handsome still, though their deep blue had waned into a quiet, impenetrable gray; while her broad clear forehead, straight nose, and red lips might well be considered as comely as ever, at least by those who loved her. Of these, however, there were not many; and she was content to have it so.

Mrs. Carnaby, the younger sister, would not have been content to have it so. Though not of the weak lot which is enfeoffed to popularity, she liked to be regarded kindly, and would rather win a smile than exact a courtesy. Continually it was said of her that she was no genuine Yordas, though really she had all the pride and all the stubbornness of that race, enlarged, perhaps, but little weakened, by severe afflictions. This lady had lost a beloved husband, Colonel Carnaby, killed in battle; and after that four children of the five she had been so proud of. And the waters of affliction had not turned to bitterness in her soul.

Concerning the outward part—which matters more than the inward at first hand—Mrs. Carnaby had no reason to complain of fortune. She had started well as a very fine baby, and grown up well into a lovely maiden, passing through wedlock into a sightly matron, gentle, fair, and showing reason. For generations it had come to pass that those of the Yordas race who deserved to be cut off for their doings out-of-doors were followed by ladies of decorum, self-restraint, and regard for their neighbor's landmark. And so it was now with these two ladies, the handsome Philippa and the fair Eliza leading a peaceful and reputable life, and carefully studying their rent-roll.

It was not, however, in the fitness of things that quiet should reign at Scargate Hall for a quarter of a century; and one strong element of disturbance grew already manifest. Under the will of Squire Philip the heir-apparent was the one surviving child of Mrs. Carnaby.

If ever a mortal life was saved by dint of sleepless care, warm coddling, and perpetual doctoring, it was the precious life of Master Lancelot Yordas Carnaby. In him all the mischief of his race revived, without the strong substance to carry it off. Though his parents were healthy and vigorous, he was of weakly constitution, which would not have been half so dangerous to him if his mind also had been weakly. But his mind (or at any rate that rudiment thereof which appears in the shape of self-will even before the teeth appear) was a piece of muscular contortion, tough as oak and hard as iron. "Pet" was his name with his mother and his aunt; and his enemies (being the rest of mankind) said that pet was his name and his nature.

For this dear child could brook no denial, no slow submission to his wishes; whatever he wanted must come in a moment, punctual as an echo. In him re-appeared not the stubbornness only, but also the keen ingenuity of Yordas in finding out the very thing that never should be done, and then the unerring perception of the way in which it could be done most noxiously. Yet any one looking at his eyes would think how tender and bright must his nature be! "He favoreth his forebears; how can he help it?" kind people exclaimed, when they knew him. And the servants of the house excused themselves when condemned for putting up with him, "Yo know not what 'a is, yo that talk so. He maun get 's own gait, lestwise yo wud chok' un."

Being too valuable to be choked, he got his own way always.

CHAPTER III

A DISAPPOINTING APPOINTMENT

For the sake of Pet Carnaby and of themselves, the ladies of the house were disquieted now, in the first summer weather of a wet cold year, the year of our Lord 1801. And their trouble arose as follows:

There had long been a question between the sisters and Sir Walter Carnaby, brother of the late colonel, about an exchange of outlying land, which would have to be ratified by "Pet" hereafter. Terms being settled and agreement signed, the lawyers fell to at the linked sweetness of deducing title. The abstract of the Yordas title was nearly as big as the parish Bible, so in and out had their dealings been, and so intricate their pugnacity.

Among the many other of the Yordas freaks was a fatuous and generally fatal one. For the slightest miscarriage they discharged their lawyer, and leaped into the office of a new one. Has any man moved in the affairs of men, with a grain of common-sense or half a pennyweight of experience, without being taught that an old tenter-hook sits easier to him than a new one? And not only that, but in shifting his quarters he may leave some truly fundamental thing behind.

Old Mr. Jellicorse, of Middleton in Teesdale, had won golden opinions every where. He was an uncommonly honest lawyer, highly incapable of almost any trick, and lofty in his view of things, when his side of them was the legal one. He had a large collection of those interesting boxes which are to a lawyer and his family better than caskets of silver and gold; and especially were his shelves furnished with what might be called the library of the Scargate title-deeds. He had been proud to take charge of these nearly thirty years ago, and had married on the strength of them, though warned by the rival from whom they were wrested that he must not hope to keep them long. However, through the peaceful incumbency of ladies, they remained in his office all those years.

This was the gentleman who had drawn and legally sped to its purport the will of the lamented Squire Philip, who refused very clearly to leave it, and took horse to flourish it at his rebellious son. Mr. Jellicorse had done the utmost, as behooved him, against that rancorous testament; but meeting with silence more savage than words, and a bow to depart, he had yielded; and the squire stamped about the room until his job was finished.

A fact accomplished, whether good or bad, improves in character with every revolution of this little world around the sun, that heavenly example of subservience. And now Mr. Jellicorse was well convinced, as nothing had occurred to disturb that will, and the life of the testator had been sacrificed to it, and the devisees under it were his own good clients, and some of his finest turns of words were in it, and the preparation, execution, and attestation, in an hour and ten minutes of the office clock, had never been equalled in Yorkshire before, and perhaps never honestly in London—taking all these things into conscious or unconscious balance, Mr. Jellicorse grew into the clear conviction that "righteous and wise" were the words to be used whenever this will was spoken of.

With pleasant remembrance of the starveling fees wherewith he used to charge the public, ere ever his golden spurs were won, the prosperous lawyer now began to run his eye through a duplicate of an abstract furnished upon some little sale about forty years before. This would form the basis of the abstract now to be furnished to Sir Walter Carnaby, with little to be added but the will of Philip Yordas, and statement of facts to be verified. Mr. Jellicorse was fat, but very active still; he liked good living, but he liked to earn it, and could not sit down to his dinner without feeling that he had helped the Lord to provide these mercies. He carried a pencil on his chain, and liked to use it ere ever he began with knife and fork. For the young men in the office, as he always said, knew nothing.

The day was very bright and clear, and the sun shone through soft lilac leaves on more important folios, while Mr. Jellicorse, with happy sniffs—for his dinner was roasting in the distance—drew a single line here, or a double line there, or a gable on the margin of the paper, to show his head clerk what to cite, and in what letters, and what to omit, in the abstract to be rendered. For the good solicitor had spent some time in the chambers of a famous conveyancer in London, and prided himself upon deducing title, directly, exhaustively, and yet tersely, in one word, scientifically, and not as the mere quill-driver. The title to the hereditaments, now to be given in exchange, went back for many generations; but as the deeds were not to pass, Mr. Jellicorse, like an honest man, drew a line across, and made a star at one quite old enough to begin with, in which the little moorland farm in treaty now was specified. With hum and ha of satisfaction he came down the records, as far as the settlement made upon the marriage of Richard Yordas, of Scargate Hall, Esquire, and Eleanor, the daughter of Sir Fursan de Roos. This document created no entail, for strict settlements had never been the manner of the race; but the property assured in trust, to satisfy the jointure, was then declared subject to joint and surviving powers of appointment limited to the issue of the marriage, with remainder to the uses of the will of the aforesaid Richard Yordas, or, failing such will, to his right heirs forever.

All this was usual enough, and Mr. Jellicorse heeded it little, having never heard of any appointment, and knowing that Richard, the grandfather of his clients, had died, as became a true Yordas, in a fit of fury with a poor tenant, intestate, as well as unrepentant. The lawyer, being a slightly pious man, afforded a little sigh to this remembrance, and lifted his finger to turn the leaf, but the leaf stuck a moment, and the paper being raised at the very best angle to the sun, he saw, or seemed to see, a faint red line, just over against that appointment clause. And then the yellow margin showed some faint red marks.

"Well, I never," Mr. Jellicorse exclaimed—"certainly never saw these marks before. Diana, where are my glasses?"

Mrs. Jellicorse had been to see the potatoes on (for the new cook simply made "kettlefuls of fish" of every thing put upon the fire), and now at her husband's call she went to her work-box for his spectacles, which he was not allowed to wear except on Sundays, for fear of injuring his eyesight. Equipped with these, and drawing nearer to the window, the lawyer gradually made out this: first a broad faint line of red, as if some attorney, now a ghost, had cut his finger, and over against that in small round hand the letters "v. b. c." Mr. Jellicorse could swear that they were "v. b. c."

"Don't ask me to eat any dinner to-day," he exclaimed, when his wife came to fetch him. "Diana, I am occupied; go and eat it up without me."

"Nonsense, James," she answered, calmly; "you never get any clever thoughts by starving."

Moved by this reasoning, he submitted, fed his wife and children and own good self, and then brought up a bottle of old Spanish wine to strengthen the founts of discovery. Whose writing was that upon the broad marge of verbosity? Why had it never been observed before? Above all, what was meant by "v. b. c."?

Unaided, he might have gone on forever, to the bottom of a butt of Xeres wine; but finding the second glass better than the first, he called to Mrs. Jellicorse, who was in the garden gathering striped roses, to come and have a sip with him, and taste the yellow cherries. And when she came promptly, with the flowers in her hand, and their youngest little daughter making sly eyes at the fruit, bothered as he was, he could not help smiling and saying, "Oh, Diana, what is 'v. b. c.'?"

"Very black currants, papa!" cried Emily, dancing a long bunch in the air.

"Hush, dear child, you are getting too forward," said her mother, though proud of her quickness. "James, how should I know what 'v. b. c.' is? But I wish most heartily that you would rid me of my old enemy, box C. I want to put a hanging press in that corner, instead of which you turn the very passages into office."

"Box C? I remember no box C."

"You may not have noticed the letter C upon it, but the box you must know as well as I do. It belongs to those proud Yordas people, who hold their heads so high, forsooth, as if nobody but themselves belonged to a good old county family! That makes me hate the box the more."

"I will take it out of your way at once. I may want it. It should be with the others. I know it as well as I know my snuff-box. It was Aberthaw who put it in that corner; but I had forgotten that it was lettered. The others are all numbered."

Of course Mr. Jellicorse was not weak enough to make the partner of his bosom the partner of his business; and much as she longed to know why he had put an unusual question to her, she trusted to the future for discovery of that point. She left him, and he with no undue haste—for the business, after all, was not his own—began to follow out his train of thought, in manner much as follows:

"This is that old Duncombe's writing—'Dunder-headed Duncombe,' as he used to be called in his lifetime, but 'Long-headed Duncombe' afterward. None but his wife knew whether he was a wise man, or a wiseacre. Perhaps either, according to the treatment he received. Richard Yordas treated him badly; that may have made him wiser. V. b. c. means 'vide box C,' unless I am greatly mistaken. He wrote those letters as plainly and clearly as he could against this power of appointment as recited here. But afterward, with knife and pounce, he scraped them out, as now becomes plain with this magnifying-glass; probably he did so when all these archives, as he used to call them, were rudely ordered over to my predecessor. A nice bit of revenge, if my suspicions are correct; and a pretty confusion will follow it."

The lawyer's suspicions proved too correct. He took that box to his private room, and with some trouble unlocked it. A damp and musty smell came forth, as when a man delves a potato-bury; and then appeared layers of parchment yellow and brown, in and out with one another, according to the curing of the sheep-skin, perhaps, or the age of the sheep when he began to die; skins much older than any man's who handled them, and drier than the brains of any lawyer.

"Anno Jacobi tertio, and Quadragesimo Elisabethae! How nice it sounds!" Mr. Jellicorse exclaimed; "they ought all to go in, and be charged for. People to be satisfied with sixty years' title! Why, bless the Lord, I am sixty-eight myself, and could buy and sell the grammar school at eight years old. It is no security, no security at all. What did the learned Bacupiston say—'If a rogue only lives to be a hundred and eleven, he may have been for ninety years disseized, and nobody alive to know it!'"

Older and older grew the documents as the lawyer's hand travelled downward; any flaw or failure must have been healed by lapse of time long and long ago; dust and grime and mildew thickened, ink became paler, and contractions more contorted; it was rather an antiquary's business now than a lawyer's to decipher them.

"What a fool I am!" the solicitor thought. "My cuffs will never wash white again, and all I have found is a mare's-nest. However, I'll go to the bottom now. There may be a gold seal—they used to put them in with the deeds three hundred years ago. A charter of Edward the Fourth, I declare! Ah, the Yordases were Yorkists—halloa! what is here? By the Touchstone of Shepherd, I was right after all! Well done, Long-headed Duncombe!"

From the very bottom of the box he took a parchment comparatively fresh and new, indorsed "Appointment by Richard Yordas, Esquire, and Eleanor his wife, of lands and heredits at Scargate and elsewhere in the county of York, dated Nov. 15th, A.D. 1751." Having glanced at the signatures and seals, Mr. Jellicorse spread the document, which was of moderate compass, and soon convinced himself that his work of the morning had been wholly thrown away. No title could be shown to Whitestone Farm, nor even to Scargate Hall itself, on the part of the present owners.

The appointment was by deed-poll, and strictly in accordance with the powers of the settlement. Duly executed and attested, clearly though clumsily expressed, and beyond all question genuine, it simply nullified (as concerned the better half of the property) the will which had cost Philip Yordas his life. For under this limitation Philip held a mere life-interest, his father and mother giving all men to know by those presents that they did thereby from and after the decease of their said son Philip grant limit and appoint &c. all and singular the said lands &c. to the heirs of his body lawfully begotten &c. &c. in tail general, with remainder over, and final remainder to the right heirs of the said Richard Yordas forever. From all which it followed that while Duncan Yordas, or child, or other descendant of his, remained in the land of the living, or even without that if he having learned it had been enabled to bar the entail and then sell or devise the lands away, the ladies in possession could show no title, except a possessory one, as yet unhallowed by the lapse of time.

Mr. Jellicorse was a very pleasant-looking man, also one who took a pleasant view of other men and things; but he could not help pulling a long and sad face as he thought of the puzzle before him. Duncan Yordas had not been heard of among his own hills and valleys since 1778, when he embarked for India. None of the family ever had cared to write or read long letters, their correspondence (if any) was short, without being sweet by any means. It might be a subject for prayer and hope that Duncan should be gone to a better world, without leaving hostages to fortune here; but sad it is to say that neither prayer nor hope produces any faith in the counsel who prepares "requisitions upon title."

On the other hand, inquiry as to Duncan's history since he left his native land would be a delicate and expensive work, and perhaps even dangerous, if he should hear of it, and inquire about the inquirers. For the last thing to be done from a legal point of view—though the first of all from a just one—was to apprise the rightful owner of his unexpected position. Now Mr. Jellicorse was a just man; but his justice was due to his clients first.

After a long brown-study he reaped his crop of meditation thus: "It is a ticklish job; and I will sleep three nights upon it."

CHAPTER IV

DISQUIETUDE

The ladies of Scargate Hall were uneasy, although the weather was so fine, upon this day of early August, in the year now current. It was a remarkable fact, that in spite of the distance they slept asunder, which could not be less than five-and-thirty yards, both had been visited by a dream, which appeared to be quite the same dream until examined narrowly, and being examined, grew more surprising in its points of difference. They were much above paying any heed to dreams, though instructed by the patriarchs to do so; and they seemed to be quite getting over the effects, when the lesson and the punishment astonished them.

Lately it had been established (although many leading people went against it, and threatened to prosecute the man for trespass) that here in these quiet and reputable places, where no spy could be needed, a man should come twice every week with letters, and in the name of the king be paid for them. Such things were required in towns, perhaps, as corporations and gutters were; but to bring them where people could mind their own business, and charge them two groats for some fool who knew their names, was like putting a tax upon their christening. So it was the hope of many, as well as every one's belief, that the postman, being of Lancastrian race, would very soon be bogged, or famished, or get lost in a fog, or swept off by a flood, or go and break his own neck from a precipice.

The postman, however, was a wiry fellow, and as tough as any native, and he rode a pony even tougher than himself, whose cradle was a marsh, and whose mother a mountain, his first breath a fog, and his weaning meat wire-grass, and his form a combination of sole-leather and corundum. He wore no shoes for fear of not making sparks at night, to know the road by, and although his bit had been a blacksmith's rasp, he would yield to it only when it suited him. The postman, whose name was George King (which confounded him with King George, in the money to pay), carried a sword and blunderbuss, and would use them sooner than argue.

Now this man and horse had come slowly along, without meaning any mischief, to deliver a large sealed packet, with sixteen pence to pay put upon it, "to Mistress Philippa Yordas, etc., her own hands, and speed, speed, speed;" which they carried out duly by stop, stop, stop, whensoever they were hungry, or saw any thing to look at. None the less for that, though with certainty much later, they arrived in good trim, by the middle of the day, and ready for the comfort which they both deserved.

As yet it was not considered safe to trust any tidings of importance to the post in such a world as this was; and even were it safe, it would be bad manners from a man of business. Therefore Mr. Jellicorse had sealed up little, except his respectful consideration and request to be allowed to wait upon his honored clients, concerning a matter of great moment, upon the afternoon of Thursday then next ensuing. And the post had gone so far, to give good distance for the money, that the Thursday of the future came to be that very day.

The present century opened with a chilly and dark year, following three bad seasons of severity and scarcity. And in the northwest of Yorkshire, though the summer was now so far advanced, there had been very little sunshine. For the last day or two, the sun had labored to sweep up the mist and cloud, and was beginning to prevail so far that the mists drew their skirts up and retired into haze, while the clouds fell away to the ring of the sky, and there lay down to abide their time. Wherefore it happened that "Yordas House" (as the ancient building was in old time called) had a clearer view than usual of the valley, and the river that ran away, and the road that tried to run up to it. Now this was considered a wonderful road, and in fair truth it was wonderful, withstanding all efforts of even the Royal Mail pony to knock it to pieces. In its rapidity down hill it surpassed altogether the river, which galloped along by the side of it, and it stood out so boldly with stones of no shame that even by moonlight nobody could lose it, until it abruptly lost itself. But it never did that, until the house it came from was two miles away, and no other to be seen; and so why should it go any further?

At the head of this road stood the old gray house, facing toward the south of east, to claim whatever might come up the valley, sun, or storm, or columned fog. In the days of the past it had claimed much more—goods, and cattle, and tribute of the traffic going northward—as the loop-holed quadrangle for impounded stock, and the deeply embrasured tower, showed. At the back of the house rose a mountain spine, blocking out the westering sun, but cut with one deep portal where a pass ran into Westmoreland—the scaur-gate whence the house was named; and through this gate of mountain often, when the day was waning, a bar of slanting sunset entered, like a plume of golden dust, and hovered on a broad black patch of weather-beaten fir-trees. The day was waning now, and every steep ascent looked steeper, while down the valley light and shade made longer cast of shuttle, and the margin of the west began to glow with a deep wine-color, as the sun came down—the tinge of many mountains and the distant sea—until the sun himself settled quietly into it, and there grew richer and more ripe (as old bottled wine is fed by the crust), and bowed his rubicund farewell, through the postern of the scaur-gate, to the old Hall, and the valley, and the face of Mr. Jellicorse.

That gentleman's countenance did not, however, reply with its usual brightness to the mellow salute of evening. Wearied and shaken by the long, rough ride, and depressed by the heavy solitude, he hated and almost feared the task which every step brought nearer. As the house rose higher and higher against the red sky, and grew darker, and as the sullen roar of blood-hounds (terrors of the neighborhood) roused the slow echoes of the crags, the lawyer was almost fain to turn his horse's head, and face the risks of wandering over the moor by night. But the hoisting of a flag, the well-known token (confirmed by large letters on a rock) that strangers might safely approach, inasmuch as the savage dogs were kennelled—this, and the thought of such an entry for his day-book, kept Mr. Jellicorse from ignominious flight. He was in for it now, and must carry it through.

In a deep embayed window of leaded glass Mistress Yordas and her widowed sister sat for an hour, without many words, watching the zigzag of shale and rock which formed their chief communication with the peopled world. They did not care to improve their access, or increase their traffic; not through cold morosity, or even proud indifference, but because they had been so brought up, and so confirmed by circumstance. For the Yordas blood, however hot and wild and savage in the gentlemen, was generally calm and good, though steadfast, in the weaker vessels. For the main part, however, a family takes it character more from the sword than the spindle; and their sword hand had been like Esau's.

Little as they meddled with the doings of the world, of one thing at least these stately Madams—as the baffled squires of the Riding called them— were by no means heedless. They dressed themselves according to their rank, or perhaps above it. Many a nobleman's wife in Yorkshire had not such apparel; and even of those so richly gifted, few could have come up to the purpose better. Nobody, unless of their own sex, thought of their dresses when looking at them.

"He rides very badly," Philippa said; "the people from the lowlands always do. He may not have courage to go home tonight. But he ought to have thought of that before."

"Poor man! We must offer him a bed, of course," Mrs. Carnaby answered; "but he should have come earlier in the day. What shall we do with him, when he has done his business?"

"It is not our place to amuse our lawyer. He might go and smoke in the Justice-room, and then Welldrum could play bagatelle with him."

"Philippa, you forget that the Jellicorses are of a good old county stock. His wife is a stupid, pretentious thing; but we need not treat him as we must treat her. And it may be as well to make much of him, perhaps, if there really is any trouble coming."

"You are thinking of Pet. By-the-bye, are you certain that Pet can not get at Saracen? You know how he let him loose last Easter, when the flag was flying, and the poor man has been in his bed ever since."

"Jordas will see to that. He can be trusted to mind the dogs well, ever since you fined him in a fortnight's wages. That was an excellent thought of yours."

Jordas might have been called the keeper, or the hind, or the henchman, or the ranger, or the porter, or the bailiff, or the reeve, or some other of some fifty names of office, in a place of more civilization, so many and so various were his tasks. But here his professional name was the "dogman;" and he held that office according to an ancient custom of the Scargate race, whence also his surname (if such it were) arose. For of old time and in outlandish parts a finer humanity prevailed, and a richer practical wisdom upon certain questions. Irregular offsets of the stock, instead of being cast upon the world as waifs and strays, were allowed a place in the kitchen-garden or stable-yard, and flourished there without disgrace, while useful and obedient. Thus for generations here the legitimate son was Yordas, and took the house and manors; the illegitimate became Jordas, and took to the gate, and the minding of the dogs, and any other office of fidelity.

The present Jordas was, however, of less immediate kin to the owners, being only the son of a former Jordas, and in the enjoyment of a Christian name, which never was provided for a first-hand Jordas; and now as his mistress looked out on the terrace, his burly figure came duly forth, and his keen eyes ranged the walks and courts, in search of Master Lancelot, who gave him more trouble in a day, sometimes, than all the dogs cost in a twelvemonth. With a fine sense of mischief, this boy delighted to watch the road for visitors, and then (if barbarously denied his proper enjoyment and that of the dogs) he still had goodly devices of his own for producing little tragedies.

Mr. Jellicorse knew Jordas well, and felt some pity for him, because, if his grandmother had been wiser, he might have been the master now; and the lawyer, having much good feeling, liked not to make a groom of him. Jordas, however, knew his place, and touched his hat respectfully, then helped the solicitor to dismount, the which was sorely needed.

"You came not by the way of the ford, Sir?" the dogman asked, while considering the leathers. "The water is down; you might have saved three miles."

"Better lose thirty than my life. Will any of your men, Master Jordas, show me a room, where I may prepare to wait upon your ladies?"

Mr. Jellicorse walked through the old arched gate of the reever's court, and was shown to a room, where he unpacked his valise, and changed his riding clothes, and refreshed himself. A jug of Scargate ale was brought to him, and a bottle of foreign wine, with the cork drawn, lest he should hesitate; also a cold pie, bread and butter, and a small case-bottle of some liqueur. He was not hungry, for his wife had cared to victual him well for the journey; but for fear of offense he ate a morsel, found it good, and ate some more. Then after a sip or two of the liqueur, and a glance or two at his black silk stockings, buckled shoes, and best small-clothes, he felt himself fit to go before a duchess, as once upon a time he had actually done, and expressed himself very well indeed, according to the dialogue delivered whenever he told the story about it every day.

Welldrum, the butler, was waiting for him—a man who had his own ideas, and was going to be put upon by nobody. "If my father could only come to life for one minute, he would spend it in kicking that man," Mrs. Carnaby had exclaimed, about him, after carefully shutting the door; but he never showed airs before Miss Yordas.

"Come along, Sir," Welldrum said, after one professional glance at the tray, to ascertain his residue. "My ladies have been waiting this half hour; and for sure, Sir, you looks wonderful! This way, Sir, and have a care of them oak fagots. My ladies, Lawyer Jellicorse!"

CHAPTER V

DECISION

The sun was well down and away behind the great fell at the back of the house, and the large and heavily furnished room was feebly lit by four wax candles, and the glow of the west reflected as a gleam into eastern windows. The lawyer was pleased to have it so, and to speak with a dimly lighted face. The ladies looked beautiful; that was all that Mr. Jellicorse could say, when cross-examined by his wife next day concerning their lace and velvet. Whether they wore lace or net was almost more than he could say, for he did not heed such trifles; but velvet was within his knowledge (though not the color or the shape), because he thought it hot for summer, until he remembered what the climate was. Really he could say nothing more, except that they looked beautiful; and when Mrs. Jellicorse jerked her head, he said that he only meant, of course, considering their time of life.

The ladies saw his admiration, and felt that it was but natural. Mrs. Carnaby came forward kindly, and offered him a nice warm hand; while the elder sister was content to bow, and thank him for coming, and hope that he was well. As yet it had not become proper for a gentleman, visiting ladies, to yawn, and throw himself into the nearest chair, and cross his legs, and dance one foot, and ask how much the toy-terrier cost. Mr. Jellicorse made a fine series of bows, not without a scrape or two, which showed his goodly calf; and after that he waited for the gracious invitation to sit down.

"If I understood your letter clearly," Mistress Yordas began, when these little rites were duly accomplished, "you have something important to tell us concerning our poor property here. A small property, Mr. Jellicorse, compared with that of the Duke of Lunedale, but perhaps a little longer in one family."

"The duke is a new-fangled interloper," replied hypocritical Jellicorse, though no other duke was the husband of the duchess of whom he indited daily; "properties of that sort come and go, and only tradesmen notice it. Your estates have been longer in the seisin of one family, madam, than any other in the Riding, or perhaps in Yorkshire."

"We never seized them!" cried Mrs. Carnaby, being sensitive as to ancestral thefts, through tales about cattle-lifting. "You must be aware that they came to us by grant from the Crown, or even before there was any Crown to grant them."

"I beg your pardon for using a technical word, without explaining it. Seisin is a legal word, which simply means possession, or rather the bodily holding of a thing, and is used especially of corporeal hereditaments. You ladies have seisin of this house and lands, although you never seized them."

"The last thing we would think of doing," answered Mrs. Carnaby, who was more impulsive than her sister, also less straightforward. "How often we have wished that our poor lost brother had not been deprived of them! But our father's will was sacred, and you told us we were helpless. We struggled, as you know; but we could do nothing."

"That is the question which brought me here," the lawyer said, very quietly, at the same time producing a small roll of parchment sealed in cartridge paper. "Last week I discovered a document which I am forced to submit to your judgment. Shall I read it to you, or tell its purport briefly?"

"Whatever it may be, it can not in any way alter our conclusions. Our conclusions have never varied, however deeply they may have grieved us. We were bound to do justice to our dear father."

"Certainly, madam; and you did it. Also, as I know, you did it as kindly as possible toward other relatives, and you only met with perversity. I had the honor of preparing your respected father's will, a model of clearness and precision, considering—considering the time afforded, and other disturbing influences. I know for a fact that a copy was laid before the finest draftsman in London, by—by those who were displeased with it, and his words were: 'Beautiful! beautiful! Every word of it holds water.' Now that, madam, can not be said of many; indeed, of not one in—"

"Pardon, me for interrupting you, but I have always understood you to speak highly of it. And in such a case, what can be the matter?"

"The matter of all matters, madam, is that the testator should have disposing power."

"He could dispose of his own property as he was disposed, you mean."

"You misapprehend me." Mr. Jellicorse now was in his element, for he loved to lecture—an absurdity just coming into vogue. "Indulge me one moment. I take this silver dish, for instance; it is in my hands, I have the use of it; but can I give it to either of you ladies?"

"Not very well, because it belongs to us already."

"You misapprehend me. I can not give it because it is not mine to give." Mrs. Carnaby looked puzzled.

"Eliza, allow me," said Mistress Yordas, in her stiffer manner, and now for the first time interfering. "Mr. Jellicorse assures us that his language is a

27

model of clearness and precision; perhaps he will prove it by telling us now, in plain words, what his meaning is."

"What I mean, madam, is that your respected father could devise you a part only of this property, because the rest was not his to devise. He only had a life-interest in it."

"His will, therefore, fails as to some part of the property? How much, and what part, if you please?"

"The larger and better part of the estates, including this house and grounds, and the home-farm."

Mrs. Carnaby started and began to speak; but her sister moved only to stop her, and showed no signs of dismay or anger.

"For fear of putting too many questions at once," she said, with a slight bow and a smile, "let me beg you to explain, as shortly as possible, this very surprising matter."

Mr. Jellicorse watched her with some suspicion, because she called it so surprising, yet showed so little surprise herself. For a moment he thought that she must have heard of the document now in his hands; but he very soon saw that it could not be so. It was only the ancient Yordas pride, perversity, and stiffneckedness. And even Mrs. Carnaby, strengthened by the strength of her sister, managed to look as if nothing more than a tale of some tenant were pending. But this, or ten times this, availed not to deceive Mr. Jellicorse. That gentleman, having seen much of the world, whispered to himself that this was all "high jinks," felt himself placed on the stool of authority, and even ventured upon a pinch of snuff. This was unwise, and cost him dear, for the ladies would not have been true to their birth if they had not stored it against him.

He, however, with a friendly mind, and a tap now and then upon his document, to give emphasis to his story, recounted the whole of it, and set forth how much was come of it already, and how much it might lead to. To Scargate Hall, and the better part of the property always enjoyed therewith, Philippa Yordas and Eliza Carnaby had no claim whatever, except on the score of possession, until it could be shown that their brother Duncan was dead, without any heirs or assignment (which might have come to pass through a son adult), and even so, his widow might come forward and give trouble. Concerning all that, there was time enough to think; but something must be done at once to cancel the bargain with Sir Walter Carnaby, without letting his man of law get scent of the fatal defect in title. And now that the ladies knew all, what did they say?

28

In answer to this, the ladies were inclined to put the whole blame upon him, for not having managed matters better; and when he had shown that the whole of it was done before he had any thing to do with it, they were firmly convinced that he ought to have known it, and found a proper remedy. And in the finished manner of well-born ladies they gave him to know, without a strong expression, that such an atrocity was a black stain on every legal son of Satan, living, dead, or still to issue from Gerizim.

"That can not affect the title now—I assure you, madam, that it can not," the unfortunate lawyer exclaimed at last; "and as for damages, poor old Duncombe has left no representatives, even if an action would lie now, which is simply out of the question. On my part no neglect can be shown, and indeed for your knowledge of the present state of things, if humbly I may say so, you are wholly indebted to my zeal."

"Sir, I heartily wish," Mrs. Carnaby replied, "that your zeal had been exhausted on your own affairs."

"Eliza, Mr. Jellicorse has acted well, and we can not feel too much obliged to him." Miss Yordas, having humor of a sort, smiled faintly at the double meaning of her own words, which was not intended. "Whatever is right must be done, of course, according to the rule of our family. In such a case it appears to me that mere niceties of laws, and quips and quirks, are entirely subordinate to high sense of honor. The first consideration must be thoroughly unselfish and pure justice."

The lawyer looked at her with admiration. He was capable of large sentiments. And yet a faint shadow of disappointment lingered in the folios of his heart—there might have been such a very grand long suit, upon which his grandson (to be born next month) might have been enabled to settle for life, and bring up a legal family. Justice, however, was justice, and more noble than even such prospects. So he bowed his head, and took another pinch of snuff.

But Mrs. Carnaby (who had wept a little, in a place beyond the candle-light) came back with a passionate flush in her eyes, and a resolute bearing of her well-formed neck.

"Philippa, I am amazed at you," she said, "Mr. Jellicorse, my share is equal with my sister's, and more, because my son comes after me. Whatever she may do, I will never yield a pin's point of my rights, and leave my son a beggar. Philippa, would you make Pet a beggar? And his turtle in bed, before the sun is on the window, and his sturgeon jelly when he gets out of bed! There never was any one, by a good Providence, less sent into the world to be a beggar."

Mrs. Carnaby, having discharged her meaning, began to be overcome by it. She sat down, in fear of hysteria, but with her mind made up to stop it; while the gallant Jellicorse was swept away by her eloquence, mixed with professional views. But it came home to him, from experience with his wife, that the less he said the wiser. But while he moved about, and almost danced, in his strong desire to be useful, there was another who sat quite still, and meant to have the final say.

"From some confusion of ideas, I suppose, or possibly through my own fault," Philippa Yordas said, with less contempt in her voice than in her mind, "it seems that I can not make my meaning clear, even to my own sister. I said that we first must do the right, and scorn all legal subtleties. That we must maintain unselfish justice, and high sense of honor. Can there be any doubt what these dictate? What sort of daughters should we be if we basely betrayed our own father's will?"

"Excellent, madam," the lawyer said; "that view of the case never struck me. But there is a great deal in it."

"Oh, Philippa, how noble you are!" her sister Eliza cried; and cried no more, so far as tears go, for a long time afterward.

CHAPTER VI

ANERLEY FARM

On the eastern coast of the same great county, at more than ninety miles of distance for a homing pigeon, and some hundred and twenty for a carriage from the Hall of Yordas, there was in those days, and there still may be found, a property of no vast size—snug, however, and of good repute—and called universally "Anerley Farm." How long it has borne that name it knows not, neither cares to moot the question; and there lives no antiquary of enough antiquity to decide it. A place of smiling hope, and comfort, and content with quietude; no memory of man about it runneth to the contrary; while every ox, and horse, and sheep, and fowl, and frisky porker, is full of warm domestic feeling and each homely virtue.

For this land, like a happy country, has escaped, for years and years, the affliction of much history. It has not felt the desolating tramp of lawyer or land-agent, nor been bombarded by fine and recovery, lease and release, bargain and sale, Doe and Roe and Geoffrey Styles, and the rest of the pitiless shower of slugs, ending with a charge of Demons. Blows, and blights, and plagues of that sort have not come to Anerley, nor any other drain of nurture to exhaust the green of meadow and the gold of harvest. Here stands the homestead, and here lies the meadow-land; there walk the kine (having no call to run), and yonder the wheat in the hollow of the hill, bowing to the silvery stroke of the wind, is touched with the promise of increasing gold.

As good as the cattle and the crops themselves are the people that live upon them; or at least, in a fair degree, they try to be so; though not of course so harmless, or faithful, or peaceful, or charitable. But still, in proportion, they may be called as good; and in fact they believe themselves much better. And this from no conceit of any sort, beyond what is indispensable; for nature not only enables but compels a man to look down upon his betters.

From generation to generation, man, and beast, and house, and land, have gone on in succession here, replacing, following, renewing, repairing and being repaired, demanding and getting more support, with such judicious give-and-take, and thoroughly good understanding, that now in the August of this year, when Scargate Hall is full of care, and afraid to cart a load of dung, Anerley farm is quite at ease, and in the very best of heart, man, and horse, and land, and crops, and the cock that crows the time of day. Nevertheless, no acre yet in Yorkshire, or in the whole wide world, has ever been so farmed or fenced as to exclude the step of change.

32

From father to son the good lands had passed, without even a will to disturb them, except at distant intervals; and the present owner was Stephen Anerley, a thrifty and well-to-do Yorkshire farmer of the olden type. Master Anerley was turned quite lately of his fifty-second year, and hopeful (if so pleased the Lord) to turn a good many more years yet, as a strong horse works his furrow. For he was strong and of a cheerful face, ruddy, square, and steadfast, built up also with firm body to a wholesome stature, and able to show the best man on the farm the way to swing a pitchfork. Yet might he be seen, upon every Lord's day, as clean as a new-shelled chestnut; neither at any time of the week was he dirtier than need be. Happy alike in the place of his birth, his lot in life, and the wisdom of the powers appointed over him, he looked up with a substantial faith, yet a solid reserve of judgment, to the Church, the Justices of the Peace, spiritual lords and temporal, and above all His Majesty George the Third. Without any reserve of judgmemt, which could not deal with such low subjects, he looked down upon every Dissenter, every pork-dealer, and every Frenchman. What he was brought up to, that he would abide by; and the sin beyond repentance, to his mind, was the sin of the turncoat.

With all these hard-set lines of thought, or of doctrine (the scabbard of thought, which saves its edge, and keeps it out of mischief), Stephen Anerley was not hard, or stern, or narrow-hearted. Kind, and gentle, and good to every one who knew "how to behave himself," and dealing to every man full justice —meted by his own measure—he was liable even to generous acts, after being severe and having his own way. But if any body ever got the better of him by lies, and not fair bettering, that man had wiser not begin to laugh inside the Riding. Stephen Anerley was slow but sure; not so very keen, perhaps, but grained with kerns of maxim'd thought, to meet his uses as they came, and to make a rogue uneasy. To move him from such thoughts was hard; but to move him from a spoken word had never been found possible.

The wife of this solid man was solid and well fitted to him. In early days, by her own account, she had possessed considerable elegance, and was not devoid of it even now, whenever she received a visitor capable of understanding it. But for home use that gift had been cut short, almost in the honey-moon, by a total want of appreciation on the part of her husband. And now, after five-and-twenty years of studying and entering into him, she had fairly earned his firm belief that she was the wisest of women. For she always agreed with him, when he wished it; and she knew exactly when to contradict him, and that was before he had said a thing at all, and while he was rolling it slowly in his mind, with a strong tendency against it. In out-door matters she never meddled, without being specially consulted by the master; but in-doors she governed with watchful eyes, a firm hand, and a quiet tongue.

This good woman now was five-and-forty years of age, vigorous, clean, and of a very pleasant look, with that richness of color which settles on fair women when the fugitive beauty of blushing is past. When the work of the morning was done, and the clock in the kitchen was only ten minutes from twelve, and the dinner was fit for the dishing, then Mistress Anerley remembered as a rule the necessity of looking to her own appearance. She went up stairs, with a quarter of an hour to spare, but not to squander, and she came down so neat that the farmer was obliged to be careful in helping the gravy. For she always sat next to him, as she had done before there came any children, and it seemed ever since to be the best place for her to manage their plates and their manners as well.

Alas! that the kindest and wisest of women have one (if not twenty) blind sides to them; and if any such weakness is pointed out, it is sure to have come from their father. Mistress Anerley's weakness was almost conspicuous to herself—she worshipped her eldest son, perhaps the least worshipful of the family.

Willie Anerley was a fine young fellow, two inches taller than his father, with delicate features, and curly black hair, and cheeks as bright as a maiden's. He had soft blue eyes, and a rich clear voice, with a melancholy way of saying things, as if he were above all this. And yet he looked not like a fool; neither was he one altogether, when he began to think of things. The worst of him was that he always wanted something new to go on with. He never could be idle; and yet he never worked to the end which crowns the task. In the early stage he would labor hard, be full of the greatness of his aim, and demand every body's interest, exciting, also, mighty hopes of what was safe to come of it. And even after that he sometimes carried on with patience; but he had not perseverance. Once or twice he had been on the very nick of accomplishing something, and had driven home his nail; but then he let it spring back without clinching. "Oh, any fool can do that!" he cried, and never stood to it, to do it again, or to see that it came not undone. In a word, he stuck to nothing, but swerved about, here, there, and every where.

His father, being of so different a cast, and knowing how often the wisest of men must do what any fool can do, was bitterly vexed at the flighty ways of Willie, and could do no more than hope, with a general contempt, that when the boy grew older he might be a wiser fool. But Willie's dear mother maintained, with great consistency, that such a perfect wonder could never be expected to do any thing not wonderful. To this the farmer used to listen with a grim, decorous smile; then grumbled, as soon as he was out of hearing, and fell to and did the little jobs himself.

Sore jealousy of Willie, perhaps, and keen sense of injustice, as well as high spirit and love of adventure, had driven the younger son, Jack, from home, and launched him on a sea-faring life. With a stick and a bundle he had departed from the ancestral fields and lanes, one summer morning about three years since, when the cows were lowing for the milk pail, and a royal cutter was cruising off the Head. For a twelvemonth nothing was heard of him, until there came a letter beginning, "Dear and respected parents," and ending, "Your affectionate and dutiful son, Jack." The body of the letter was of three lines only, occupied entirely with kind inquiries as to the welfare of every body, especially his pup, and his old pony, and dear sister Mary.

Mary Anerley, the only daughter and the youngest child, well deserved the best remembrance of the distant sailor, though Jack may have gone too far in declaring (as he did till he came to his love-time) that the world contained no other girl fit to hold a candle to her. No doubt it would have been hard to find a girl more true and loving, more modest and industrious; but hundreds and hundreds of better girls might be found perhaps even in Yorkshire.

For this maiden had a strong will of her own, which makes against absolute perfection; also she was troubled with a strenuous hate of injustice—which is sure, in this world, to find cause for an outbreak—and too active a desire to rush after what is right, instead of being well content to let it come occasionally. And so firm could she be, when her mind was set, that she would not take parables, or long experience, or even kindly laughter, as a power to move her from the thing she meant. Her mother, knowing better how the world goes on, promiscuously, and at leisure, and how the right point slides away when stronger forces come to bear, was very often vexed by the crotchets of the girl, and called her wayward, headstrong, and sometimes nothing milder than "a saucy miss."

This, however, was absurd, and Mary scarcely deigned to cry about it, but went to her father, as she always did when any weight lay on her mind. Nothing was said about any injustice, because that might lead to more of it, as well as be (from a proper point of view) most indecorous. Nevertheless, it was felt between them, when her pretty hair was shed upon his noble waistcoat, that they two were in the right, and cared very little who thought otherwise.

Now it was time to leave off this; for Mary (without heed almost of any but her mother) had turned into a full-grown damsel, comely, sweet, and graceful. She was tall enough never to look short, and short enough never to seem too tall, even when her best feelings were outraged; and nobody, looking at her face, could wish to do any thing but please her—so kind was the gaze of her deep blue eyes, so pleasant the frankness of her gentle forehead, so playful the readiness of rosy lips for a pretty answer or a lovely smile. But if any could be found so callous and morose as not to be charmed or nicely cheered by this, let him only take a longer look, not rudely, but simply in a spirit of polite inquiry; and then would he see, on the delicate rounding of each soft and dimpled cheek, a carmine hard to match on palette, morning sky, or flower bed.

Lovely people ought to be at home in lovely places; and though this can not be so always, as a general rule it is. At Anerley Farm the land was equal to the stock it had to bear, whether of trees, or corn, or cattle, hogs, or mushrooms, or mankind. The farm was not so large or rambling as to tire the mind or foot, yet wide enough and full of change—rich pasture, hazel copse, green valleys, fallows brown, and golden breast-lands pillowing into nooks of fern, clumps of shade for horse or heifer, and for rabbits sandy warren, furzy cleve for hare and partridge, not without a little mere for willows and for wild-ducks. And the whole of the land, with a general slope of liveliness and rejoicing, spread itself well to the sun, with a strong inclination toward the morning, to catch the cheery import of his voyage across the sea.

The pleasure of this situation was the more desirable because of all the parts above it being bleak and dreary. Round the shoulders of the upland, like the arch of a great arm-chair, ran a barren scraggy ridge, whereupon no tree could stand upright, no cow be certain of her own tail, and scarcely a crow breast the violent air by stooping ragged pinions, so furious was the rush of wind when any power awoke the clouds; or sometimes, when the air was jaded with continual conflict, a heavy settlement of brackish cloud lay upon a waste of chalky flint.

By dint of persevering work there are many changes for the better now, more shelter and more root-hold; but still it is a battle-ground of winds, which rarely change their habits, for this is the chump of the spine of the Wolds, which hulks up at last into Flamborough Head.

Flamborough Head, the furthest forefront of a bare and jagged coast, stretches boldly off to eastward—a strong and rugged barrier. Away to the north the land falls back, with coving bends, and some straight lines of precipice and shingle, to which the German Ocean sweeps, seldom free from sullen swell in the very best of weather. But to the southward of the Head a different spirit seems to move upon the face of every thing. For here is spread a peaceful bay, and plains of brighter sea more gently furrowed by the wind, and cliffs that have no cause to be so steep, and bathing-places, and scarcely freckled sands, where towns may lay their drain-pipes undisturbed. In short, to have rounded that headland from the north is as good as to turn the corner of a garden wall in March, and pass from a buffeted back, and bare shivers, to a sunny front of hope all as busy as a bee, with pears spurring forward into creamy buds of promise, peach-trees already in a flush of tasselled pink, and the green lobe of the apricot shedding the snowy bloom.

Below this point the gallant skipper of the British collier, slouching with a heavy load of grime for London, or waddling back in ballast to his native North, alike is delighted to discover storms ahead, and to cast his tarry anchor into soft gray calm. For here shall he find the good shelter of friends like-minded with himself, and of hospitable turn, having no cause to hurry any more than he has, all too wise to command their own ships; and here will they all jollify together while the sky holds a cloud or the locker a drop. Nothing here can shake their ships, except a violent east wind, against which they wet the other eye; lazy boats visit them with comfort and delight, while white waves are leaping, in the offing; they cherish their well-earned rest, and eat the lotus—or rather the onion—and drink ambrosial grog; they lean upon the bulwarks, and contemplate their shadows—the noblest possible employment for mankind—and lo! if they care to lift their eyes, in the south shines the quay of Bridlington, inland the long ridge of Priory stands high, and westward in a nook, if they level well a clear glass (after holding on the slope so many steamy ones), they may espy Anerley Farm, and sometimes Mary Anerley herself.

For she, when the ripple of the tide is fresh, and the glance of the summer morn glistening on the sands, also if a little rocky basin happens to be fit for shrimping, and only some sleepy ships at anchor in the distance look at her, fearless she—because all sailors are generally down at breakfast—tucks up her skirt and gayly runs upon the accustomed play-ground, with her pony left to wait for her. The pony is old, while she is young (although she was born before him), and now he belies his name, "Lord Keppel," by starting at every soft glimmer of the sea. Therefore now he is left to roam at his leisure above high-water mark, poking his nose into black dry weed, probing the winnow casts of yellow drift for oats, and snorting disappointment through a gritty dance of sand-hoppers.

Mary has brought him down the old "Dane's Dike" for society rather than service, and to strengthen his nerves with the dew of the salt, for the sake of her Jack who loved him. He may do as he likes, as he always does. If his conscience allows him to walk home, no one will think the less of him. Having very little conscience at his time of life (after so much contact with mankind), he considers convenience only. To go home would suit him very well, but his crib would be empty till his young mistress came; moreover, there is a little dog that plagues him when his door is open; and in spite of old age, it is something to be free, and in spite of all experience, to hope for something good. Therefore Lord Keppel is as faithful as the rocks; he lifts his long heavy head, and gazes wistfully at the anchored ships, and Mary is sure that the darling pines for his absent master.

But she, with the multitudinous tingle of youth, runs away rejoicing. The buoyant power and brilliance of the morning are upon her, and the air of the bright sea lifts and spreads her, like a pillowy skate's egg. The polish of the wet sand flickers like veneer of maple-wood at every quick touch of her dancing feet. Her dancing feet are as light as nature and high spirits made them, not only quit of spindle heels, but even free from shoes and socks left high and dry on the shingle. And lighter even than the dancing feet the merry heart is dancing, laughing at the shadows of its own delight; while the radiance of blue eyes springs like a fount of brighter heaven; and the sunny hair falls, flows, or floats, to provoke the wind for playmate.

Such a pretty sight was good to see for innocence and largeness. So the buoyancy of nature springs anew in those who have been weary, when they see her brisk power inspiring the young, who never stand still to think of her, but are up and away with her, where she will, at the breath of her subtle encouragement.

CHAPTER VII

A DANE IN THE DIKE

Now, whether spy-glass had been used by any watchful mariner, or whether only blind chance willed it, sure it is that one fine morning Mary met with somebody. And this was the more remarkable, when people came to think of it, because it was only the night before that her mother had almost said as much.

"Ye munna gaw doon to t' sea be yersell," Mistress Anerley said to her daughter; "happen ye mought be one too many."

Master Anerley's wife had been at "boarding-school," as far south as Suffolk, and could speak the very best of Southern English (like her daughter Mary) upon polite occasion. But family cares and farm-house life had partly cured her of her education, and from troubles of distant speech she had returned to the ease of her native dialect.

"And if I go not to the sea by myself," asked Mary, with natural logic, "why, who is there now to go with me?" She was thinking of her sadly missed comrade, Jack.

"Happen some day, perhaps, one too many."

The maiden was almost too innocent to blush; but her father took her part as usual.

"The little lass sall gaw doon," he said, "wheniver sha likes." And so she went down the next morning.

A thousand years ago the Dane's Dike must have been a very grand intrenchment, and a thousand years ere that perhaps it was still grander; for learned men say that it is a British work, wrought out before the Danes had even learned to build a ship. Whatever, however, may be argued about that, the wise and the witless do agree about one thing—the stronghold inside it has been held by Danes, while severed by the Dike from inland parts; and these Danes made a good colony of their own, and left to their descendants distinct speech and manners, some traces of which are existing even now. The Dike, extending from the rough North Sea to the calmer waters of Bridlington Bay, is nothing more than a deep dry trench, skillfully following the hollows of the ground, and cutting off Flamborough Head and a solid cantle of high land from the rest of Yorkshire. The corner, so intercepted, used to be and is still called "Little Denmark;" and the in-dwellers feel a large contempt for all their outer neighbors. And this is sad, because Anerley Farm lies wholly outside of the Dike, which for a long crooked distance serves as its eastern boundary.

Upon the morning of the self-same day that saw Mr. Jellicorse set forth upon his return from Scargate Hall, armed with instructions to defy the devil, and to keep his discovery quiet—upon a lovely August morning of the first year of a new century, Mary Anerley, blithe and gay, came riding down the grassy hollow of this ancient Dane's Dike. This was her shortest way to the sea, and the tide would suit (if she could only catch it) for a take of shrimps, and perhaps even prawns, in time for her father's breakfast. And not to lose this, she arose right early, and rousing Lord Keppel, set forth for the spot where she kept her net covered with sea-weed. The sun, though up and brisk already upon sea and foreland, had not found time to rout the shadows skulking in the dingles. But even here, where sap of time had breached the turfy ramparts, the hover of the dew-mist passed away, and the steady light was unfolded.

For the season was early August still, with beautiful weather come at last; and the green world seemed to stand on tiptoe to make the extraordinary acquaintance of the sun. Humble plants which had long lain flat stood up with a sense of casting something off; and the damp heavy trunks which had trickled for a twelvemonth, or been only sponged with moss, were hailing the fresher light with keener lines and dove-colored tints upon their smoother boles. Then, conquering the barrier of the eastern land crest, rose the glorious sun himself, strewing before him trees and crags in long steep shadows down the hill. Then the sloping rays, through furze and brush-land, kindling the sparkles of the dew, descended to the brink of the Dike, and scorning to halt at petty obstacles, with a hundred golden hurdles bridged it wherever any opening was.

Under this luminous span, or through it where the crossing gullies ran, Mary Anerley rode at leisure, allowing her pony to choose his pace. That privilege he had long secured, in right of age, wisdom, and remarkable force of character. Considering his time of life, he looked well and sleek, and almost sprightly; and so, without any reservation, did his gentle and graceful rider. The maiden looked well in a place like that, as indeed in almost any place; but now she especially set off the color of things, and was set off by them. For instance, how could the silver of the dew-cloud, and golden weft of sunrise, playing through the dapples of a partly wooded glen, do better (in the matter of variety) than frame a pretty moving figure in a pink checked frock, with a skirt of russet murrey, and a bright brown hat? Not that the hat itself was bright, even under the kiss of sunshine, simply having seen already too much of the sun, but rather that its early lustre seemed to be revived by a sense of the happy position it was in; the clustering hair and the bright eyes beneath it answering the sunny dance of life and light. Many a handsomer face, no doubt, more perfect, grand, and lofty, received—at least if it was out of bed—the greeting of that morning sun; but scarcely any prettier one, or kinder, or more pleasant, so gentle without being weak, so good-tempered without looking void of all temper at all.

Suddenly the beauty of the time and place was broken by sharp angry sound. Bang! bang! came the roar of muskets fired from the shore at the mouth of the Dike, and echoing up the winding glen. At the first report the girl, though startled, was not greatly frightened; for the sound was common enough in the week when those most gallant volunteers entitled the "Yorkshire Invincibles" came down for their annual practice of skilled gunnery against the French. Their habit was to bring down a red cock, and tether him against a chalky cliff, and then vie with one another in shooting at him. The same cock had tested their skill for three summers, but failed hitherto to attest it, preferring to return in a hamper to his hens, with a story of moving adventures.

Mary had watched those Invincibles sometimes from a respectful distance, and therefore felt sure (when she began to think) that she had not them to thank for this little scare. For they always slept soundly in the first watch of the morning; and even supposing they had jumped up with nightmare, where was the jubilant crow of the cock? For the cock, being almost as invincible as they were, never could deny himself the glory of a crow when the bullet came into his neighborhood. He replied to every volley with an elevated comb, and a flapping of his wings, and a clarion peal, which rang along the foreshore ere the musket roar died out. But before the girl had time to ponder what it was, or wherefore, round the corner came somebody, running very swiftly.

In a moment Mary saw that this man had been shot at, and was making for his life away; and to give him every chance she jerked her pony aside, and called and beckoned; and without a word he flew to her. Words were beyond him, till his breath should come back, and he seemed to have no time to wait for that. He had outstripped the wind, and his own wind, by his speed.

"Poor man!" cried Mary Anerley, "what a hurry you are in! But I suppose you can not help it. Are they shooting at you?"

The runaway nodded, for he could not spare a breath, but was deeply inhaling for another start, and could not even bow without hinderance. But to show that he had manners, he took off his hat. Then he clapped it on his head and set off again.

"Come back!" cried the maid; "I can show you a place. I can hide you from your enemies forever."

The young fellow stopped. He was come to that pitch of exhaustion in which a man scarcely cares whether he is killed or dies. And his face showed not a sign of fear.

"Look! That little hole—up there—by the fern. Up at once, and this cloth over you!"

He snatched it, and was gone, like the darting lizard, up a little puckering side issue of the Dike, at the very same instant that three broad figures and a long one appeared at the lip of the mouth. The quick-witted girl rode on to meet them, to give the poor fugitive time to get into his hole and draw the brown skirt over him. The dazzle of the sun, pouring over the crest, made the hollow a twinkling obscurity; and the cloth was just in keeping with the dead stuff around. The three broad men, with heavy fusils cocked, came up from the sea mouth of the Dike, steadily panting, and running steadily with a long-enduring stride. Behind them a tall bony man with a cutlass was swinging it high in the air, and limping, and swearing with great velocity.

"Coast-riders," thought Mary, "and he a free-trader! Four against one is cowardice."

"Halt!" cried the tall man, while the rest were running past her; "halt! ground arms; never scare young ladies." Then he flourished his hat, with a grand bow to Mary. "Fair young Mistress Anerley, I fear we spoil your ride. But his Majesty's duty must be done. Hats off, fellows, at the name of your king! Mary, my dear, the most daring villain, the devil's own son, has just run up here—scarcely two minutes—you must have seen him. Wait a minute; tell no lies—excuse me, I mean fibs. Your father is the right sort. He hates those scoundrels. In the name of his Majesty, which way is he gone?"

"Was it—oh, was it a man, if you please? Captain Carroway, don't say so."

"A man? Is it likely that we shot at a woman? You are trifling. It will be the worse for you. Forgive me—but we are in such a hurry. Whoa! whoa! pony."

"You always used to be so polite, Sir, that you quite surprise me. And those guns look so dreadful! My father would be quite astonished to see me not even allowed to go down to the sea, but hurried back here, as if the French had landed."

"How can I help it, if your pony runs away so?" For Mary all this time had been cleverly contriving to increase and exaggerate her pony's fear, and so brought the gunners for a long way up the Dike, without giving them any time to spy at all about. She knew that this was wicked from a loyal point of view;

not a bit the less she did it. "What a troublesome little horse it is!" she cried. "Oh, Captain Carroway, hold him just a moment. I will jump down, and then you can jump up, and ride after all his Majesty's enemies."

"The Lord forbid! He slews all out of gear, like a carronade with rotten lashings. If I boarded him, how could I get out of his way? No, no, my dear, brace him up sharp, and bear clear."

"But you wanted to know about some enemy, captain. An enemy as bad as my poor Lord Keppel?"

"Mary, my dear, the very biggest villain! A hundred golden guineas on his head, and half for you. Think of your father, my dear, and Sunday gowns. And you must have a young man by-and-by, you know—such a beautiful maid as you are. And you might get a leather purse, and give it to him. Mary, on your duty, now?"

"Captain, you drive me so, what can I say? I can not bear the thought of betraying any body."

"Of course not, Mary dear; nobody asks you. He must be half a mile off by this time. You could never hurt him now; and you can tell your father that you have done your duty to the king."

"Well, Captain Carroway, if you are quite sure that it is too late to catch him, I can tell you all about him. But remember your word about the fifty guineas."

"Every farthing, every farthing, Mary, whatever my wife may say to it. Quick! quick! Which way did he run, my dear?"

"He really did not seem to me to be running at all; he was too tired."

"To be sure, to be sure, a worn-out fox! We have been two hours after him; he could not run; no more can we. But which way did he go, I mean?"

"I will not say any thing for certain, Sir; even for fifty guineas. But he may have come up here—mind, I say not that he did—and if so, he might have set off again for Sewerby. Slowly, very slowly, because of being tired. But perhaps, after all, he was not the man you mean."

"Forward, double-quick! We are sure to have him!" shouted the lieutenant —for his true rank was that—flourishing his cutlass again, and setting off at a wonderful pace, considering his limp. "Five guineas every man Jack of you. Thank you, young mistress—most heartily thank you. Dead or alive, five guineas!"

With gun and sword in readiness, they all rushed off; but one of the party, named John Cadman, shook his head and looked back with great mistrust at

Mary, having no better judgment of women than this, that he never could believe even his own wife. And he knew that it was mainly by the grace of womankind that so much contraband work was going on. Nevertheless, it was out of his power to act upon his own low opinions now.

The maiden, blushing deeply with the sense of her deceit, was informed by her guilty conscience of that nasty man's suspicions, and therefore gave a smack with her fern whip to Lord Keppel, impelling him to join, like a loyal little horse, the pursuit of his Majesty's enemies. But no sooner did she see all the men dispersed, and scouring the distance with trustful ardor, than she turned her pony's head toward the sea again, and rode back round the bend of the hollow. What would her mother say if she lost the murrey skirt, which had cost six shillings at Bridlington fair? And ten times that money might be lost much better than for her father to discover how she lost it. For Master Stephen Anerley was a straight-backed man, and took three weeks of training in the Land Defense Yeomanry, at periods not more than a year apart, so that many people called him "Captain" now; and the loss of his suppleness at knee and elbow had turned his mind largely to politics, making him stiffly patriotic, and especially hot against all free-traders putting bad bargains to his wife, at the cost of the king and his revenue. If the bargain were a good one, that was no concern of his.

Not that Mary, however, could believe, or would even have such a bad mind as to imagine, that any one, after being helped by her, would be mean enough to run off with her property. And now she came to think of it, there was something high and noble, she might almost say something downright honest, in the face of that poor persecuted man. And in spite of all his panting, how brave he must have been, what a runner, and how clever, to escape from all those cowardly coast-riders shooting right and left at him! Such a man steal that paltry skirt that her mother made such a fuss about! She was much more likely to find it in her clothes-press filled with golden guineas.

Before she was as certain as she wished to be of this (by reason of shrewd nativity), and while she believed that the fugitive must have seized such a chance and made good his escape toward North Sea or Flamborough, a quick shadow glanced across the long shafts of the sun, and a bodily form sped after it. To the middle of the Dike leaped a young man, smiling, and forth from the gully which had saved his life. To look at him, nobody ever could have guessed how fast he had fled, and how close he had lain hid. For he stood there as clean and spruce and careless as even a sailor can be wished to be. Limber yet stalwart, agile though substantial, and as quick as a dart while as strong as a pike, he seemed cut out by nature for a true blue-jacket; but condition had made him a smuggler, or, to put it more gently, a free-trader.

45

Britannia, being then at war with all the world, and alone in the right (as usual), had need of such lads, and produced them accordingly, and sometimes one too many. But Mary did not understand these laws.

This made her look at him with great surprise, and almost doubt whether he could be the man, until she saw her skirt neatly folded in his hand, and then she said, "How do you do, Sir?"

The free-trader looked at her with equal surprise. He had been in such a hurry, and his breath so short, and the chance of a fatal bullet after him so sharp, that his mind had been astray from any sense of beauty, and of every thing else except the safety of the body. But now he looked at Mary, and his breath again went from him.

"You can run again now; I am sure of it," said she; "and if you would like to do any thing to please me, run as fast as possible."

"What have I to run away from now?" he answered, in a deep sweet voice. "I run from enemies, but not from friends."

"That is very wise. But your enemies are still almost within call of you. They will come back worse than ever when they find you are not there."

"I am not afraid, fair lady, for I understand their ways. I have led them a good many dances before this; though it would have been my last, without your help. They will go on, all the morning, in the wrong direction, even while they know it. Carroway is the most stubborn of men. He never turns back; and the further he goes, the better his bad leg is. They will scatter about, among the fields and hedges, and call one another like partridges. And when they can not take another step, they will come back to Anerley for breakfast."

"I dare say they will; and we shall be glad to see them. My father is a soldier, and his duty is to nourish and comfort the forces of the king."

"Then you are young Mistress Anerley? I was sure of it before. There are no two such. And you have saved my life. It is something to owe it so fairly."

The young sailor wanted to kiss Mary's hand; but not being used to any gallantry, she held out her hand in the simplest manner to take back her riding skirt; and he, though longing in his heart to keep it, for a token or pretext for another meeting, found no excuse for doing so. And yet he was not without some resource.

For the maiden was giving him a farewell smile, being quite content with the good she had done, and the luck of recovering her property; and that sense of right which in those days formed a part of every good young woman said to her plainly that she must be off. And she felt how unkind it was to keep him any longer in a place where the muzzle of a gun, with a man behind it, might appear at any moment. But he, having plentiful breath again, was at home with himself to spend it.

"Fair young lady," he began, for he saw that Mary liked to be called a lady, because it was a novelty, "owing more than I ever can pay you already, may I ask a little more? Then it is that, on your way down to the sea, you would just pick up (if you should chance to see it) the fellow ring to this, and perhaps you will look at this to know it by. The one that was shot away flew against a stone just on the left of the mouth of the Dike, but I durst not stop to look for it, and I must not go back that way now. It is more to me than a hatful of gold, though nobody else would give a crown for it."

"And they really shot away one of your ear-rings? Careless, cruel, wasteful men! What could they have been thinking of?"

"They were thinking of getting what is called 'blood-money.' One hundred pounds for Robin Lyth. Dead or alive—one hundred pounds."

"It makes me shiver, with the sun upon me. Of course they must offer money for—for people. For people who have killed other people, and bad things—but to offer a hundred pounds for a free-trader, and fire great guns at him to get it—I never should have thought it of Captain Carroway."

"Carroway only does his duty. I like him none the worse for it. Carroway is a fool, of course. His life has been in my hands fifty times; but I will never take it. He must be killed sooner or later, because he rushes into every thing. But never will it be my doing."

"Then are you the celebrated Robin Lyth—the new Robin Hood, as they call him? The man who can do almost any thing?"

"Mistress Anerley, I am Robin Lyth; but, as you have seen, I can not do much. I can not even search for my own earring."

"I will search for it till I find it. They have shot at you too much. Cowardly, cowardly people! Captain Lyth, where shall I put it, if I find it?"

"If you could hide it for a week, and then—then tell me where to find it, in the afternoon, toward four o'clock, in the lane toward Bempton Cliffs. We are off tonight upon important business. We have been too careless lately, from laughing at poor Carroway."

"You are very careless now. You quite frighten me almost. The coast-riders might come back at any moment. And what could you do then?"

"Run away gallantly, as I did before; with this little difference, that I should be fresh, while they are as stiff as nut-cracks. They have missed the best chance they ever had at me; it will make their temper very bad. If they shot at me again, they could do no good. Crooked mood makes crookedmode."

"You forget that I should not see such things. You may like very much to be shot at; but—but you should think of other people."

"I shall think of you only—I mean of your great kindness, and your promise to keep my ring for me. Of course you will tell nobody, Carroway will have me like a tiger if you do. Farewell, young lady—for one week farewell."

With a wave of his hat he was gone, before Mary had time to retract her promise; and she thought of her mother, as she rode on slowly to look for the smuggler's trinket.

49

CHAPTER VIII

CAPTAIN CARROWAY

Fame, that light-of-love trusted by so many, and never a wife till a widow —fame, the fair daughter of fuss and caprice, may yet take the phantom of bold Robin Lyth by the right hand, and lead it to a pedestal almost as lofty as Robin Hood's, or she may let it vanish like a bat across Lethe—a thing not bad enough for eminence.

However, at the date and in the part of the world now dealt with, this great free-trader enjoyed the warm though possibly brief embrace of fame, having no rival, and being highly respected by all who were unwarped by a sense of duty. And blessed as he was with a lively nature, he proceeded happily upon his path in life, notwithstanding a certain ticklish sense of being shot at undesirably. This had befallen him now so often, without producing any tangible effect, that a great many people, and especially the shooters (convinced of the accuracy of their aim), went far to believe that he possessed some charm against wholesome bullet and gunpowder. And lately even a crooked sixpence dipped in holy water (which was still to be had in Yorkshire) confirmed and doubled the faith of all good people, by being declared upon oath to have passed clean through him, as was proved by its being picked up quite clean.

This strong belief was of great use to him; for, like many other beliefs, it went a very long way to prove itself. Steady left hands now grew shaky in the level of the carbine, and firm forefingers trembled slightly upon draught of trigger, and the chief result of a large discharge was a wale upon the marksman's shoulder. Robin, though so clever and well practiced in the world, was scarcely old enough yet to have learned the advantage of misapprehension, which, if well handled by any man, helps him, in the cunning of paltry things, better than a truer estimate. But without going into that, he was pleased with the fancy of being invulnerable, which not only doubled his courage, but trebled the discipline of his followers, and secured him the respect of all tradesmen. However, the worst of all things is that just when they are establishing themselves, and earning true faith by continuance, out of pure opposition the direct contrary arises, and begins to prove itself. And to Captain Lyth this had just happened in the shot which carried off his left ear-ring.

Not that his body, or any fleshly member, could be said directly to have parted with its charm, but that a warning and a diffidence arose from so near a visitation. All genuine sailors are blessed with strong faith, as they must be, by nature's compensation. Their bodies continually going up and down upon perpetual fluxion, they never could live if their minds did the same, like the minds of stationary landsmen. Therefore their minds are of stanch immobility, to restore the due share of firm element. And not only that, but these men have compressed (through generations of circumstance), from small complications, simplicity. Being out in all weathers, and rolling about so, how can they stand upon trifles? Solid stays, and stanchions, and strong bulwarks are their need, and not a dance of gnats in gossamer; hating all fogs, they blow not up with their own breath misty mysteries, and gazing mainly at the sky and sea, believe purely in God and the devil. In a word, these sailors have religion.

Some of their religion is not well pronounced, but declares itself in overstrong expressions. However, it is in them, and at any moment waiting opportunity of action—a shipwreck or a grape-shot; and the chaplain has good hopes of them when the doctor has given them over.

Now one of their principal canons of faith, and the one best observed in practice, is (or at any rate used to be) that a man is bound to wear ear-rings. For these, as sure tradition shows, and no pious mariner would dare to doubt, act as a whetstone in all weathers to the keen edge of the eyes. Semble—as the lawyers say—that this idea was born of great phonetic facts in the days when a seaman knew his duty better than the way to spell it; and when, if his outlook were sharpened by a friendly wring from the captain of the watch, he never dreamed of a police court.

But Robin Lyth had never cared to ask why he wore ear-rings. His nature was not meditative. Enough for him that all the other men of Flamborough did so; and enough for them that their fathers had done it. Whether his own father had done so, was more than he could say, because he knew of no such parent; and of that other necessity, a mother, he was equally ignorant. His first appearance at Flamborough, though it made little stir at the moment in a place of so many adventures, might still be considered unusual, and in some little degree remarkable. So that Mistress Anerley was not wrong when she pressed upon Lieutenant Carroway how unwise it might be to shoot him, any more than Carroway himself was wrong in turning in at Anerley gate for breakfast.

This he had not done without good cause of honest and loyal necessity. Free-trading Robin had predicted well the course of his pursuers. Rushing eagerly up the Dike, and over its brim, with their muskets, that gallant force of revenue men steadily scoured the neighborhood; and the further they went, the worse they fared. There was not a horse standing down by a pool, with his stiff legs shut up into biped form, nor a cow staring blandly across an old rail, nor a sheep with a pectoral cough behind a hedge, nor a rabbit making rustle at the eyebrow of his hole, nor even a moot, that might either be a man or hold a man inside it, whom or which those active fellows did not circumvent and poke into. In none of these, however, could they find the smallest breach of the strictest laws of the revenue; until at last, having exhausted their bodies by great zeal both of themselves and of mind, they braced them again to the duty of going, as promptly as possible, to breakfast.

For a purpose of that kind few better places, perhaps, could be found than this Anerley Farm, though not at the best of itself just now, because of the denials of the season. It is a sad truth about the heyday of the year, such as August is in Yorkshire—where they have no spring—that just when a man would like his victuals to rise to the mark of the period, to be simple yet varied, exhilarating yet substantial, the heat of the summer day defrauds its increased length for feeding. For instance, to cite a very trifling point—at least in some opinions—August has banished that bright content and most devout resignation which ensue the removal of a petted pig from this troublous world of grunt. The fat pig rolls in wallowing rapture, defying his friends to make pork of him yet, and hugs with complacence unpickleable hams. The partridge among the pillared wheat, tenderly footing the way for his chicks, and teaching little balls of down to hop, knows how sacred are their lives to others as well as to himself; and the less paternal cock-pheasant scratches the ridge of green-shouldered potatoes, without fear of keeping them company at table.

But though the bright glory of the griddle remains in suspense for the hoary mornings, and hooks that carried woodcocks once, and hope to do so yet again, are primed with dust instead of lard, and the frying-pan hangs on the cellar nail with a holiday gloss of raw mutton suet, yet is there still some comfort left, yet dappled brawn, and bacon streaked, yet golden-hearted eggs, and mushrooms quilted with pink satin, spiced beef carded with pellucid fat, buckstone cake, and brown bread scented with the ash of gorse bloom—of these, and more that pave the way into the good-will of mankind, what lack have fine farm-houses?

And then, again, for the liquid duct, the softer and more sensitive, the one that is never out of season, but perennially clear—here we have advantage of the gentle time that mellows thirst. The long ride of the summer sun makes men who are in feeling with him, and like him go up and down, not forego the moral of his labor, which is work and rest. Work all day, and light the rounded land with fruit and nurture, and rest at evening, looking through bright fluid, as the sun goes down.

But times there are when sun and man, by stress of work, or clouds, or light, or it may be some Process of the Equinox, make draughts upon the untilted day, and solace themselves in the morning. For lack of dew the sun draws lengthy sucks of cloud quite early, and men who have labored far and dry, and scattered the rime of the night with dust, find themselves ready about 8 A.M. for the golden encouragement of gentle ale.

The farm-house had an old porch of stone, with a bench of stone on either side, and pointed windows trying to look out under brows of ivy; and this porch led into the long low hall, where the breakfast was beginning. To say what was on the table would be only waste of time, because it has all been eaten so long ago; but the farmer was vexed because there were no shrimps. Not that he cared half the clip of a whisker for all the shrimps that ever bearded the sea, only that he liked to seem to love them, to keep Mary at work for him. The flower of his flock, and of all the flocks of the world of the universe to his mind, was his darling daughter Mary: the strength of his love was upon her, and he liked to eat any thing of her cooking.

His body was too firm to fidget; but his mind was out of its usual comfort, because the pride of his heart, his Mary, seemed to be hiding something from him. And with the justice to be expected from far clearer minds than his, being vexed by one, he was ripe for the relief of snapping at fifty others. Mary, who could read him, as a sailor reads his compass, by the corner of one eye, awaited with good content the usual result—an outbreak of words upon the indolent Willie, whenever that young farmer should come down to breakfast, then a comforting glance from the mother at her William, followed by a plate kept hot for him, and then a fine shake of the master's shoulders, and a stamp of departure for business. But instead of that, what came to pass was this.

In the first place, a mighty bark of dogs arose; as needs must be, when a man does his duty toward the nobler animals; for sure it is that the dogs will not fail of their part. Then an inferior noise of men, crying, "Good dog! good dog!" and other fulsome flatteries, in the hope of avoiding any tooth-mark on their legs; and after that a shaking down and settlement of sounds, as if feet were brought into good order, and stopped. Then a tall man, with a body full of corners, and a face of grim temper, stood in the doorway.

"Well, well, captain, now!" cried Stephen Anerley, getting up after waiting to be spoken to, "the breath of us all is hard to get, with doing of our duty, Sir. Come ye in, and sit doon to table, and his Majesty's forces along o' ye."

"Cadman, Ellis, and Dick, be damned!" the lieutenant shouted out to them; "you shall have all the victuals you want, by-and-by. Cross legs, and get your winds up. Captain of the coast-defense, I am under your orders, in your own house." Carroway was starving, as only a man with long and active jaws can starve; and now the appearance of the farmer's mouth, half full of a kindly relish, made the emptiness of his own more bitter. But happen what might, he resolved, as usual, to enforce strict discipline, to feed himself first, and his men in proper order.

"Walk in gentlemen, all walk in," Master Anerley shouted, as if all men were alike, and coming to the door with a hospitable stride; "glad to see all of ye, upon my soul I am. Ye've hit upon the right time for coming, too; though there might 'a been more upon the table. Mary, run, that's a dear, and fetch your grandfather's big Sabbath carver. Them peaky little clams a'most puts out all my shoulder-blades, and wunna bite through a twine of gristle. Plates for all the gentlemen, Winnie lass! Bill, go and drah the black jarge full o' yell."

The farmer knew well enough that Willie was not down yet; but this was his manner of letting people see that he did not approve of such hours.

"My poor lad Willie," said the mistress of the house, returning with a courtesy the brave lieutenant's scrape, "I fear he hath the rheum again, overheating of himself after sungate."

"Ay, ay, I forgot. He hath to heat himself in bed again, with the sun upon his coverlid. Mary lof, how many hours was ye up?"

"Your daughter, Sir," answered the lieutenant, with a glance at the maiden over the opal gleam of froth, which she had headed up for him—"your daughter has been down the Dike before the sun was, and doing of her duty by the king and by his revenue. Mistress Anerley, your good health! Master Anerley, the like to you, and your daughter, and all of your good household." Before they had finished their thanks for this honor, the quart pot was set down empty. "A very pretty brew, Sir—a pretty brew indeed! Fall back, men! Have heed of discipline. A chalked line is what they want, Sir. Mistress Anerley, your good health again. The air is now thirsty in the mornings. If those fellows could be given a bench against the wall—a bench against the wall is what they feel for with their legs. It comes so natural to their—yes, yes, their legs, and the crook of their heels, ma'am, from what they were brought up to sit upon. And if you have any beer brewed for washing days, ma'am, that is what they like, and the right thing for their bellies. Cadman, Ellis, and Dick Hackerbody, sit down and be thankful."

"But surely, Captain Carroway, you would never be happy to sit down without them. Look at their small-clothes, the dust and the dirt! And their mouths show what you might make of them."

"Yes, madam, yes; the very worst of them is that. They are always looking out, here, there, and every where, for victuals everlasting. Let them wait their proper time, and then they do it properly."

"Their proper time is now, Sir. Winnie, fill their horns up. Mary, wait you upon the officer. Captain Carroway, I will not have any body starve in my house."

"Madam, you are the lawgiver in your own house. Men of the coast-guard, fall to upon your victuals."

The lieutenant frowned horribly at his men, as much as to say, "Take no advantage, but show your best manners;" and they touched their forelocks with a pleasant grin, and began to feed rapidly; and verily their wives would have said that it was high time for them. Feeding, as a duty, was the order of the day, and discipline had no rank left. Good things appeared and disappeared, with the speedy doom of all excellence. Mary, and Winnie the maid, flitted in and out like carrier-pigeons.

"Now when the situation comes to this," said the farmer at last, being heartily pleased with the style of their feeding and laughing, "his Majesty hath made an officer of me, though void of his own writing. Mounted Fencibles, Filey Briggers, called in the foreign parts 'Brigadiers.' Not that I stand upon sermonry about it, except in the matter of his Majesty's health, as never is due without ardent spirits. But my wife hath a right to her own way, and never yet I knowed her go away from it."

"Not so, by any means," the mistress said, and said it so quietly that some believed her; "I never was so much for that. Captain, you are a married man. But reason is reason, in the middle of us all, and what else should I say to my husband? Mary lass, Mary lof, wherever is your duty? The captain hath the best pot empty!"

With a bright blush Mary sprang up to do her duty. In those days no girl was ashamed to blush; and the bloodless cheek savored of small-pox.

"Hold up your head, my lof," her father said aloud, with a smile of tidy pride, and a pat upon her back; "no call to look at all ashamed, my dear. To my mind, captain, though I may be wrong, however, but to my mind, this little maid may stan' upright in the presence of downright any one."

"There lies the very thing that never should be said. Captain, you have seven children, or it may be eight of them justly. And the pride of life—Mary, you be off!"

Mary was glad to run away, for she liked not to be among so many men. But her father would not have her triumphed over.

"Speak for yourself, good wife," he said. "I know what you have got behind, as well as rooks know plough-tail. Captain, you never heard me say that the lass were any booty, but the very same as God hath made her, and thankful for straight legs and eyes. Howsoever, there might be worse-favored maidens, without running out of the Riding."

"You may ride all the way to the city of London," the captain exclaimed, with a clinch of his fist, "or even to Portsmouth, where my wife came from, and never find a maid fit to hold a candle for Mary to curl her hair by."

The farmer was so pleased that he whispered something; but Carroway put his hand before his mouth, and said, "Never, no, never in the morning!" But in spite of that, Master Anerley felt in his pocket for a key, and departed.

"Wicked, wicked, is the word I use," protested Mrs. Anerley, "for all this fribble about rooks and looks, and holding of candles, and curling of hair. When I was Mary's age—oh dear! It may not be so for your daughters, captain; but evil for mine was the day that invented those proud swinging-glasses."

"That you may pronounce, ma'am, and I will say Amen. Why, my eldest daughter, in her tenth year now—"

"Come, Captain Carroway," broke in the farmer, returning softly with a square old bottle, "how goes the fighting with the Crappos now? Put your legs up, and light your pipe, and tell us all the news."

"Cadman, and Ellis, and Dick Hackerbody," the lieutenant of the coast-guard shouted, "you have fed well. Be off, men; no more neglect of duty! Place an outpost at fork of the Sewerby road, and strictly observe the enemy, while I hold a council of war with my brother officer, Captain Anerley. Half a crown for you, if you catch the rogue, half a crown each, and promotion of twopence. Attention, eyes right, make yourselves scarce! Well, now the rogues are gone, let us make ourselves at home. Anerley, your question is a dry one. A dry one; but this is uncommonly fine stuff! How the devil has it slipped through our fingers? Never mind that, inter amicos—Sir, I was at school at Shrewsbury—but as to the war, Sir, the service is going to the devil, for the want of pure principle."

The farmer nodded; and his looks declared that to some extent he felt it. He had got the worst side of some bargains that week; but his wife had another way of thinking.

"Why, Captain Carroway, whatever could be purer? When you were at sea, had you ever a man of the downright principles of Nelson?"

"Nelson has done very well in his way; but he is a man who has risen too fast, as other men rise too slowly. Nothing in him; no substance, madam; I knew him as a youngster, and I could have tossed him on a marling-spike. And instead of feeding well, Sir, he quite wore himself away. To my firm knowledge, he would scarcely turn the scale upon a good Frenchman of half of the peas. Every man should work his own way up, unless his father did it for him. In my time we had fifty men as good, and made no fuss about them."

"And you not the last of them, captain, I dare say. Though I do love to hear of the Lord's Lord Nelson, as the people call him. If ever a man fought his own way up—"

"Madam, I know him, and respect him well. He would walk up to the devil, with a sword between his teeth, and a boarder's pistol in each hand. Madam, I leaped, in that condition, a depth of six fathoms and a half into the starboard mizzen-chains of the French line-of-battle ship Peace and Thunder."

"Oh, Captain Carroway, how dreadful! What had you to lay hold with?"

"At such times a man must not lay hold. My business was to lay about; and I did it to some purpose. This little slash, across my eyes struck fire, and it does the same now by moonlight."

One of the last men in the world to brag was Lieutenant Carroway. Nothing but the great thirst of this morning, and strong necessity of quenching it, could ever have led him to speak about himself, and remember his own little exploits. But the farmer was pleased, and said, "Tell us some more, Sir."

"Mistress Anerley," the captain answered, shutting up the scar, which he was able to expand by means of a muscle of excitement, "you know that a man should drop these subjects when he has got a large family. I have been in the Army and the Navy, madam, and now I am in the Revenue; but my duty is first to my own house."

"Do take care, Sir; I beg you to be careful. Those free-traders now are come to such a pitch that any day or night they may shoot you."

"Not they, madam. No, they are not murderers. In a hand-to-hand conflict they might do it, as I might do the same to them. This very morning my men shot at the captain of all smugglers, Robin Lyth, of Flamborough, with a hundred guineas upon his head. It was no wish of mine; but my breath was short to stop them, and a man with a family like mine can never despise a hundred guineas."

"Why, Sophy," said the farmer, thinking slowly, with a frown, "that must have been the noise come in at window, when I were getting up this morning. I said, 'Why, there's some poacher fellow popping at the conies!' and out I went straight to the warren to see. Three gun-shots, or might 'a been four. How many men was you shooting at?"

"The force under my command was in pursuit of one notorious criminal—that well-known villain, Robin Lyth."

"Captain, your duty is to do your duty. But without your own word for it, I never would believe that you brought four gun muzzles down upon one man."

"The force under my command carried three guns only. It was not in their power to shoot off four."

"Captain, I never would have done it in your place. I call it no better than unmanly. Now go you not for to stir yourself amiss. To look thunder at me is what I laugh at. But many things are done in a hurry, Captain Carroway, and I take it that this was one of them."

"As to that, no! I will not have it. All was in thorough good order. I was never so much as a cable's length behind, though the devil, some years ago, split my heel up, like his own, Sir."

"Captain, I see it, and I ask your pardon. Your men were out of reach of hollering. At our time of life the wind dies quick, from want of blowing oftener."

"Stuff!" cried the captain. "Who was the freshest that came to your hospitable door, Sir? I will foot it with any man for six leagues, but not for half a mile, ma'am. I depart from nothing. I said, 'Fire!' and fire they did, and they shall again. What do Volunteers know of the service?"

"Stephen, you shall not say a single other word;" Mistress Anerley stopped her husband thus; "these matters are out of your line altogether; because you have never taken any body's blood. The captain here is used to it, like all the sons of Belial, brought up in the early portions of the Holy Writ."

Lieutenant Carroway's acquaintance with the Bible was not more extensive than that of other officers, and comprised little more than the story of Joseph, and that of David and Goliath; so he bowed to his hostess for her comparison, while his gaunt and bristly countenance gave way to a pleasant smile. For this officer of the British Crown had a face of strong features, and upon it whatever he thought was told as plainly as the time of day is told by the clock in the kitchen. At the same time, Master Anerley was thinking that he might have said more than a host should say concerning a matter which, after all, was no particular concern of his; whereas it was his special place to be kind to any visitor. All this he considered with a sound grave mind, and then stretched forth his right hand to the officer.

Carroway, being a generous man, would not be outdone in apologies. So these two strengthened their mutual esteem, without any fighting—which generally is the quickest way of renewing respect—and Mistress Anerley, having been a little frightened, took credit to herself for the good words she had used. Then the farmer, who never drank cordials, although he liked to see other people do it, set forth to see a man who was come about a rick, and sundry other business. But Carroway, in spite of all his boasts, was stiff, though he bravely denied that he could be; and when the good housewife insisted on his stopping to listen to something that was much upon her mind, and of great importance to the revenue, he could not help owning that duty compelled him to smoke another pipe, and hearken.

CHAPTER IX

ROBIN COCKSCROFT

Nothing ever was allowed to stop Mrs. Anerley from seeing to the bedrooms. She kept them airing for about three hours at this time of the sunstitch—as she called all the doings of the sun upon the sky—and then there was pushing, and probing, and tossing, and pulling, and thumping, and kneading of knuckles, till the rib of every feather was aching; and then (like dough before the fire) every well-belabored tick was left to yeast itself a while. Winnie, the maid, was as strong as a post, and wore them all out in bed-making. Carroway heard the beginning of this noise, but none of it meddled at all with his comfort; he lay back nicely in a happy fit of chair, stretched his legs well upon a bench, and nodded, keeping slow time with the breathings of his pipe, and drawing a vapory dream of ease. He had fared many stony miles afoot that morning; and feet, legs, and body were now less young than they used to be once upon a time. Looking up sleepily, the captain had idea of a pretty young face hanging over him, and a soft voice saying, "It was me who did it all," which was very good grammar in those days; "will you forgive me? But I could not help it, and you must have been sorry to shoot him."

"Shoot every body who attempts to land," the weary man ordered, drowsily. "Mattie, once more, you are not to dust my pistols."

"I could not be happy without telling you the truth," the soft voice continued, "because I told you such a dreadful story. And now—Oh! here comes mother!"

"What has come over you this morning, child? You do the most extraordinary things, and now you can not let the captain rest. Go round and look for eggs this very moment. You will want to be playing fine music next. Now, captain, I am at your service, if you please, unless you feel too sleepy."

"Mistress Anerley, I never felt more wide-awake in all my life. We of the service must snatch a wink whenever we can, but with one eye open; and it is not often that we see such charming sights."

The farmer's wife having set the beds to "plump," had stolen a look at the glass, and put on her second-best Sunday cap, in honor of a real officer; and she looked very nice indeed, especially when she received a compliment. But she had seen too much of life to be disturbed thereby.

"Ah, Captain Carroway, what ways you have of getting on with simple people, while you are laughing all the time at them! It comes of the foreign war experience, going on so long that in the end we shall all be foreigners. But one place there is that you never can conquer, nor Boneypart himself, to my belief."

"Ah, you mean Flamborough—Flamborough, yes! It is a nest of cockatrices."

"Captain, it is nothing of the sort. It is the most honest place in all the world. A man may throw a guinea on the crossroads in the night, and have it back from Dr. Upandown any time within seven years. You ought to know by this time what they are, hard as it is to get among them."

"I only know that they can shut their mouths; and the devil himself—I beg your pardon, madam—Old Nick himself never could unscrew them."

"You are right, Sir. I know their manner well. They are open as the sky with one another, but close as the grave to all the world outside them, and most of all to people of authority like you."

"Mistress Anerley, you have just hit it. Not a word can I get out of them. The name of the king—God bless him!—seems to have no weight among them."

"And you can not get at them, Sir, by any dint of money, or even by living in the midst of them. The only way to do it is by kin of blood, or marriage. And that is how I come to know more about them than almost any body else outside. My master can scarcely win a word of them even, kind as he is, and well-spoken; and neither might I, though my tongue was tenfold, if it were not for Joan Cockscroft. But being Joan's cousin, I am like one of themselves."

"Cockscroft! Cockscroft? I have heard that name. Do they keep the public-house there?"

The lieutenant was now on the scent of duty, and assumed his most knowing air, the sole effect of which was to put every body upon guard against him. For this was a man of no subtlety, but straightforward, downright, and ready to believe; and his cleverest device was to seem to disbelieve.

"The Cockscrofts keep no public-house," Mrs. Anerley answered, with a little flush of pride. "Why, she was half-niece to my own grandmother, and never was beer in the family. Not that it would have been wrong, if it was. Captain, you are thinking of Widow Precious, licensed to the Cod with the hook in his gills. I should have thought, Sir, that you might have known a little more of your neighbors having fallen below the path of life by reason of bad bank-tokens. Banking came up in her parts like dog-madness, as it might have done here, if our farmers were the fools to handle their cash with gloves on. And Joan became robbed by the fault of her trustees, the very best bakers in Scarborough, though Robin never married her for it, thank God! Still it was very sad, and scarcely bears describing of, and pulled them in the crook of this world's swing to a lower pitch than if they had robbed the folk that robbed and ruined them. And Robin so was driven to the fish again, which he always had hankered after. It must have been before you heard of this coast, captain, and before the long war was so hard on us, that every body about these parts was to double his bags by banking, and no man was right to pocket his own guineas, for fear of his own wife feeling them. And bitterly such were paid out for their cowardice and swindling of their own bosoms."

"I have heard of it often, and it served them right. Master Anerley knew where his money was safe, ma'am!"

"Neither Captain Robin Cockscroft nor his wife was in any way to blame," answered Mrs. Anerley. "I have framed my mind to tell you about them; and I will do it truly, if I am not interrupted. Two hammers never yet drove a nail straight, and I make a rule of silence when my betters wish to talk."

"Madam, you remind me of my own wife. She asks me a question, and she will not let me answer."

"That is the only way I know of getting on. Mistress Carroway must understand you, captain. I was at the point of telling you how my cousin Joan was married, before her money went, and when she was really good-looking. I was quite a child, and ran along the shore to see it. It must have been in the high summer-time, with the weather fit for bathing, and the sea as smooth as a duck-pond. And Captain Robin, being well-to-do, and established with every thing except a wife, and pleased with the pretty smile and quiet ways of Joan —for he never had heard of her money, mind—put his oar into the sea and rowed from Flamborough all the way to Filey Brigg, with thirty-five fishermen after him; for the Flamborough people make a point of seeing one another through their troubles. And Robin was known for the handsomest man and the uttermost fisher of the landing, with three boats of his own, and good birth, and long sea-lines. And there at once they found my cousin Joan, with her trustees, come overland, four wagons and a cart in all of them; and after they were married, they burned sea-weed, having no fear in those days of invasions. And a merry day they made of it, and rowed back by the moonshine. For every one liked and respected Captain Cockscroft on account of his skill with the deep-sea lines, and the openness of his hands when full— a wonderful quiet and harmless man, as the manner is of all great fishermen. They had bacon for breakfast whenever they liked, and a guinea to lend to any body in distress.

"Then suddenly one morning, when his hair was growing gray and his eyes getting weary of the night work, so that he said his young Robin must grow big enough to learn all the secrets of the fishes, while his father took a spell in the blankets, suddenly there came to them a shocking piece of news. All his wife's bit of money, and his own as well, which he had been putting by from year to year, was lost in a new-fangled Bank, supposed as faithful as the Bible. Joan was very nearly crazed about it; but Captain Cockscroft never heaved a sigh, though they say it was nearly seven hundred guineas. 'There are fish enough still in the sea,' he said; 'and the Lord has spared our children. I will build a new boat, and not think of feather-beds.'

"Captain Carroway, he did so, and every body knows what befell him. The new boat, built with his own hands, was called the Mercy Robin, for his only son and daughter, little Mercy and poor Robin. The boat is there as bright as ever, scarlet within and white outside; but the name is painted off, because the little dears are in their graves. Two nicer children were never seen, clever, and sprightly, and good to learn; they never even took a common bird's nest, I have heard, but loved all the little things the Lord has made, as if with a foreknowledge of going early home to Him. Their father came back very tired one morning, and went up the hill to his breakfast, and the children got into the boat and pushed off, in imitation of their daddy. It came on to blow, as it does down there, without a single whiff of warning; and when Robin awoke for his middle-day meal, the bodies of his little ones were lying on the table. And from that very day Captain Cockscroft and his wife began to grow old very quickly. The boat was recovered without much damage; and in it he sits by the hour on dry land, whenever there is no one on the cliffs to see him, with his hands upon his lap, and his eyes upon the place where his dear little children used to sit. Because he has always taken whatever fell upon him gently; and of course that makes it ever so much worse when he dwells upon the things that come inside of him."

"Madam, you make me feel quite sorry for him," the lieutenant exclaimed, as she began to cry, "If even one of my little ones was drowned, I declare to you, I can not tell what I should be like. And to lose them all at once, and as his own wife perhaps would say, because he was thinking of his breakfast! And when he had been robbed, and the world all gone against him! Madam, it is a long time, thank God, since I heard so sad a tale."

"Now you would not, captain, I am sure you would not," said Mistress Anerley, getting up a smile, yet freshening his perception of a tear as well —"you would never have the heart to destroy that poor old couple by striking the last prop from under them. By the will of the Lord they are broken down enough. They are quietly hobbling to their graves, and would you be the man to come and knock them on their heads at once?"

"Mistress Anerley, have you ever heard that I am a brute and inhuman? Madam, I have no less than seven children, and I hope to have fourteen."

"I hope with all my heart you may. And you will deserve them all, for promising so very kindly not to shoot poor Robin Lyth."

"Robin Lyth! I never spoke of him, madam. He is outlawed, condemned, with a fine reward upon him. We shot at him to-day; we shall shoot at him again; and before very long we must hit him. Ma'am, it is my duty to the king, the Constitution, the service I belong to, and the babes I have begotten."

"Blood-money poisons all innocent mouths, Sir, and breaks out for generations. And for it you will have to take three lives—Robin's, the captain's, and my dear old cousin Joan's."

"Mistress Anerley, you deprive me of all satisfaction. It is just my luck, when my duty was so plain, and would pay so well for doing of."

"Listen now, captain. It is my opinion, and I am generally borne out by the end, that instead of a hundred pounds for killing Robin Lyth, you may get a thousand for preserving him alive. Do you know how he came upon this coast, and how he has won his extraordinary name?"

"I have certainly heard rumors; scarcely any two alike. But I took no heed of them. My duty was to catch him; and it mattered not a straw to me who or what he was. But now I must really beg to know all about him, and what makes you think such things of him. Why should that excellent old couple hang upon him? and what can make him worth such a quantity of money? Honestly, of course, I mean; honestly worth it, ma'am, without any cheating of his Majesty."

"Captain Carroway," his hostess said, not without a little blush, as she thought of the king and his revenue, "cheating of his Majesty is a thing we leave for others. But if you wish to hear the story of that young man, so far as known, which is not so even in Flamborough, you must please to come on Sunday, Sir; for Sunday is the only day that I can spare for clacking, as the common people say. I must be off now; I have fifty things to see to. And on Sunday my master has his best things on, and loves no better than to sit with his legs up, and a long clay pipe lying on him down below his waist (or, to speak more correctly, where it used to be, as he might, indeed, almost say the very same to me), and then not to speak a word, but hear other folk tell stories, that might not have made such a dinner as himself. And as for dinner, Sir, if you will do the honor to dine with them that are no more than in the

Volunteers, a saddle of good mutton fit for the Body-Guards to ride upon, the men with the skins around them all turned up, will be ready just at one o'clock, if the parson lets us out."

"My dear madam, I shall scarcely care to look at any slice of victuals until one o'clock on Sunday, by reason of looking forward."

After all, this was not such a gross exaggeration, Anerley Farm being famous for its cheer; whereas the poor lieutenant, at the best of times, had as much as he could do to make both ends meet; and his wife, though a wonderful manager, could give him no better than coarse bread, and almost coarser meat.

"And, Sir, if your good lady would oblige us also—"

"No, madam, no!" he cried, with vigorous decision, having found many festive occasions spoiled by excess of loving vigilance; "we thank you most truly; but I must say 'no.' She would jump at the chance; but a husband must consider. You may have heard it mentioned that the Lord is now considering about the production of an eighth little Carroway."

"Captain, I have not, or I should not so have spoken. But with all my heart I wish you joy."

"I have pleasure, I assure you, in the prospect, Mistress Anerley. My friends make wry faces, but I blow them away, 'Tush,' I say, 'tush, Sir; at the rate we now are fighting, and exhausting all British material, there can not be too many, Sir, of mettle such as mine!' What do you say to that, madam?"

"Sir, I believe it is the Lord's own truth. And true it is also that our country should do more to support the brave hearts that fight for it."

Mrs. Anerley sighed, for she thought of her younger son, by his own perversity launched into the thankless peril of fighting England's battles. His death at any time might come home, if any kind person should take the trouble even to send news of it; or he might lie at the bottom of the sea unknown, even while they were talking. But Carroway buttoned up his coat and marched, after a pleasant and kind farewell. In the course of hard service he had seen much grief, and suffered plenty of bitterness, and he knew that it is not the part of a man to multiply any of his troubles but children. He went about his work, and he thought of all his comforts, which need not have taken very long to count, but he added to their score by not counting them, and by the self-same process diminished that of troubles. And thus, upon the whole, he deserved his Sunday dinner, and the tale of his hostess after it, not a word of which Mary was allowed to hear, for some subtle reason of her mother's. But the farmer heard it all, and kept interrupting so, when his noddings and the joggings of his pipe allowed, or, perhaps one should say, compelled him, that merely for the courtesy of saving common time it is better now to set it down without them. Moreover, there are many things well worthy of production which she did not produce, for reasons which are now no hinderance. And the foremost of those reasons is that the lady did not know the things; the second that she could not tell them clearly as a man might; and the third, and best of all, that if she could, she would not do so. In which she certainly was quite right; for it would have become her very badly, as the cousin of Joan Cockscroft (half removed, and upon the mother's side), and therefore kindly received at Flamborough, and admitted into the inner circle, and allowed to buy fish at wholesale prices, if she had turned round upon all these benefits, and described all the holes to be found in the place, for the teaching of a revenue officer.

Still, it must be clearly understood that the nature of the people is fishing. They never were known to encourage free-trading, but did their very utmost to protect themselves; and if they had produced the very noblest free-trader, born before the time of Mr. Cobden, neither the credit nor the blame was theirs.

CHAPTER X

ROBIN LYTH

Half a league to the north of bold Flamborough Head the billows have carved for themselves a little cove among cliffs which are rugged, but not very high. This opening is something like the grain shoot of a mill, or a screen for riddling gravel, so steep is the pitch of the ground, and so narrow the shingly ledge at the bottom. And truly in bad weather and at high tides there is no shingle ledge at all, but the crest of the wave volleys up the incline, and the surf rushes on to the top of it. For the cove, though sheltered from other quarters, receives the full brunt of northeasterly gales, and offers no safe anchorage. But the hardy fishermen make the most of its scant convenience, and gratefully call it "North Landing," albeit both wind and tide must be in good humor, or the only thing sure of any landing is the sea. The long desolation of the sea rolls in with a sound of melancholy, the gray fog droops its fold of drizzle in the leaden-tinted troughs, the pent cliffs overhang the flapping of the sail, and a few yards of pebble and of weed are all that a boat may come home upon harmlessly. Yet here in the old time landed men who carved the shape of England; and here even in these lesser days, are landed uncommonly fine cod.

The difficulties of the feat are these: to get ashore soundly, and then to make it good; and after that to clinch the exploit by getting on land, which is yet a harder step. Because the steep of the ground, like a staircase void of stairs, stands facing you, and the cliff upon either side juts up close, to forbid any flanking movement, and the scanty scarp denies fair start for a rush at the power of the hill front. Yet here must the heavy boats beach themselves, and wallow and yaw in the shingly roar, while their cargo and crew get out of them, their gunwales swinging from side to side, in the manner of a porpoise rolling, and their stem and stern going up and down like a pair of lads at seesaw.

But after these heavy boats have endured all that, they have not found their rest yet without a crowning effort. Up that gravelly and gliddery ascent, which changes every groove and run at every sudden shower, but never grows any the softer—up that the heavy boats must make clamber somehow, or not a single timber of their precious frames is safe. A big rope from the capstan at the summit is made fast as soon as the tails of the jackasses (laden with three cwt. of fish apiece) have wagged their last flick at the brow of the steep; and then with "yo-heave-ho" above and below, through the cliffs echoing over the dull sea, the groaning and grinding of the stubborn tug begins. Each boat has her own special course to travel up, and her own special berth of safety, and she knows every jag that will gore her on the road, and every flint from which she will strike fire. By dint of sheer sturdiness of arms, legs, and lungs, keeping true time with the pant and the shout, steadily goes it with hoist and haul, and cheerily undulates the melody of call that rallies them all with a strong will together, until the steep bluff and the burden of the bulk by masculine labor are conquered, and a long row of powerful pinnaces displayed, as a mounted battery, against the fishful sea. With a view to this clambering ruggedness of life, all of these boats receive from their cradle a certain limber rake and accommodating curve, instead of a straight pertinacity of keel, so that they may ride over all the scandals of this arduous world. And happen what may to them, when they are at home, and gallantly balanced on the brow line of the steep, they make a bright show upon the dreariness of coast-land, hanging as they do above the gullet of the deep. Painted outside with the brightest of scarlet, and inside with the purest white, at a little way off they resemble gay butterflies, preening their wings for a flight into the depth.

Here it must have been, and in the middle of all these, that the very famous Robin Lyth—prophetically treating him, but free as yet of fame or name, and simply unable to tell himself—shone in the doubt of the early daylight (as a tidy-sized cod, if forgotten, might have shone) upon the morning of St. Swithin, A.D. 1782.

The day and the date were remembered long by all the good people of Flamborough, from the coming of the turn of a long bad luck and a bitter time of starving. For the weather of the summer had been worse than usual—which is no little thing to say—and the fish had expressed their opinion of it by the eloquent silence of absence. Therefore, as the whole place lives on fish, whether in the fishy or the fiscal form, goodly apparel was becoming very rare, even upon high Sundays; and stomachs that might have looked well beneath it, sank into unobtrusive grief. But it is a long lane that has no turning; and turns are the essence of one very vital part.

Suddenly over the village had flown the news of a noble arrival of fish. From the cross-roads, and the public-house, and the licensed head-quarters of pepper and snuff, and the loop-hole where a sheep had been known to hang, in times of better trade, but never could dream of hanging now; also from the window of the man who had had a hundred heads (superior to his own) shaken at him because he set up for making breeches in opposition to the women, and showed a few patterns of what he could do if any man of legs would trade with him—from all these head-centres of intelligence, and others not so prominent but equally potent, into the very smallest hole it went (like the thrill in a troublesome tooth) that here was a chance come of feeding, a chance at last of feeding. For the man on the cliff, the despairing watchman, weary of fastening his eyes upon the sea, through constant fog and drizzle, at length had discovered the well-known flicker, the glassy flaw, and the hovering of gulls, and had run along Weighing Lane so fast, to tell his good news in the village, that down he fell and broke his leg, exactly opposite the tailor's shop. And this was on St. Swithin's Eve.

There was nothing to be done that night, of course, for mackerel must be delicately worked; but long before the sun arose, all Flamborough, able to put leg in front of leg, and some who could not yet do that, gathered together where the land-hold was, above the incline for the launching of the boats. Here was a medley, not of fisher-folk alone, and all their bodily belongings, but also of the thousand things that have no soul, and get kicked about and sworn at much because they can not answer. Rollers, buoys, nets, kegs, swabs, fenders, blocks, buckets, kedges, corks, buckie-pots, oars, poppies, tillers, sprits, gaffs, and every kind of gear (more than Theocritus himself could tell) lay about, and rolled about, and upset their own masters, here and there and everywhere, upon this half acre of slip and stumble, at the top of the boat channel down to the sea, and in the faint rivalry of three vague lights, all making darkness visible.

For very ancient lanterns, with a gentle horny glimmer, and loop-holes of large exaggeration at the top, were casting upon anything quite within their reach a general idea of the crinkled tin that framed them, and a shuffle of inconstant shadows, but refused to shed any light on friend or stranger, or clear up suspicions, more than three yards off. In rivalry with these appeared the pale disk of the moon, just setting over the western highlands, and "drawing straws" through summer haze; while away in the northeast over the sea, a slender irregular wisp of gray, so weak that it seemed as if it were being blown away, betokened the intention of the sun to restore clear ideas of number and of figure by-and-by. But little did anybody heed such things; every one ran against everybody else, and all was eagerness, haste, and bustle for the first great launch of the Flamborough boats, all of which must be taken in order.

But when they laid hold of the boat No. 7, which used to be the Mercy Robin, and were jerking the timber shores out, one of the men stooping under her stern beheld something white and gleaming. He put his hand down to it, and, lo! it was a child, in imminent peril of a deadly crush, as the boat came heeling over. "Hold hard!" cried the man, not in time with his voice, but in time with his sturdy shoulder, to delay the descent of the counter. Then he stooped underneath, while they steadied the boat, and drew forth a child in a white linen dress, heartily asleep and happy.

There was no time to think of any children now, even of a man's own fine breed, and the boat was beginning much to chafe upon the rope, and thirty or forty fine fellows were all waiting, loath to hurry Captain Robin (because of the many things he had dearly lost), yet straining upon their own hearts to stand still. And the captain could not find his wife, who had slipped aside of the noisy scene, to have her own little cry, because of the dance her children would have made if they had lived to see it.

There were plenty of other women running all about to help, and to talk, and to give the best advice to their husbands and to one another; but most of them naturally had their own babies, and if words came to action, quite enough to do to nurse them. On this account, Cockscroft could do no better, bound as he was to rush forth upon the sea, than lay the child gently aside of the stir, and cover him with an old sail, and leave word with an ancient woman for his wife when found. The little boy slept on calmly still, in spite of all the din and uproar, the song and the shout, the tramp of heavy feet, the creaking of capstans, and the thump of bulky oars, and the crush of ponderous rollers. Away went these upon their errand to the sea, and then came back the grating roar and plashy jerks of launching, the plunging, and the gurgling, and the quiet murmur of cleft waves.

That child slept on, in the warm good luck of having no boat keel launched upon him, nor even a human heel of bulk as likely to prove fatal. And the ancient woman fell asleep beside him, because at her time of life it was unjust that she should be astir so early. And it happened that Mrs. Cockscroft followed her troubled husband down the steep, having something in her pocket for him, which she failed to fetch to hand. So everybody went about its own business (according to the laws of nature), and the old woman slept by the side of the child, without giving him a corner of her scarlet shawl.

But when the day was broad and brave, and the spirit of the air was vigorous, and every cliff had a color of its own, and a character to come out with; and beautiful boats, upon a shining sea, flashed their oars, and went up waves which clearly were the stairs of heaven; and never a woman, come to watch her husband, could be sure how far he had carried his obedience in the matter of keeping his hat and coat on; neither could anybody say what next those very clever fishermen might be after—nobody having a spy-glass—but only this being understood all round, that hunger and salt were the victuals for the day, and the children must chew the mouse-trap baits until their dads came home again; and yet in spite of all this, with lightsome hearts (so hope outstrips the sun, and soars with him behind her) and a strong will, up the hill they went, to do without much breakfast, but prepare for a glorious supper. For mackerel are good fish that do not strive to live forever, but seem glad to support the human race.

Flamburians speak a rich burr of their own, broadly and handsomely distinct from that of outer Yorkshire. The same sagacious contempt for all hot haste and hurry (which people of impatient fibre are too apt to call "a drawl") may here be found, as in other Yorkshire, guiding and retarding well that headlong instrument the tongue. Yet even here there is advantage on the side of Flamborough—a longer resonance, a larger breadth, a deeper power of melancholy, and a stronger turn up of the tail of discourse, by some called the end of a sentence. Over and above all these there dwell in "Little Denmark" many words foreign to the real Yorkshireman. But, alas! these merits of their speech can not be embodied in print without sad trouble, and result (if successful) still more saddening. Therefore it is proposed to let them speak in our inferior tongue, and to try to make them be not so very long about it. For when they are left to themselves entirely, they have so much solid matter to express, and they ripen it in their minds and throats with a process so deliberate, that strangers might condemn them briefly, and be off without hearing half of it. Whenever this happens to a Flamborough man, he finishes what he proposed to say, and then says it all over again to the wind.

When the "lavings" of the village (as the weaker part, unfit for sea, and left behind, were politely called, being very old men, women, and small children), full of conversation, came, upon their way back from the tide, to the gravel brow now bare of boats, they could not help discovering there the poor old woman that fell asleep because she ought to have been in bed, and by her side a little boy, who seemed to have no bed at all. The child lay above her in a tump of stubbly grass, where Robin Cockscroft had laid him; he had tossed the old sail off, perhaps in a dream, and he threatened to roll down upon the granny. The contrast between his young, beautiful face, white raiment, and readiness to roll, and the ancient woman's weary age (which it would be ungracious to describe), and scarlet shawl which she could not spare, and satisfaction to lie still—as the best thing left her now to do—this difference between them was enough to take anybody's notice, facing the well-established sun.

"Nanny Pegler, get oop wi' ye!" cried a woman even older, but of tougher constitution. "Shame on ye to lig aboot so. Be ye browt to bed this toime o' loife?"

"A wonderful foine babby for sich an owd moother," another proceeded with the elegant joke; "and foine swaddles too, wi' solid gowd upon 'em!"

"Stan' ivery one o' ye oot o' the way," cried ancient Nanny, now as wide-awake as ever; "Master Robin Cockscroft gie ma t' bairn, an' nawbody sall hev him but Joan Cockscroft."

Joan Cockscroft, with a heavy heart, was lingering far behind the rest, thinking of the many merry launches, when her smart young Robin would have been in the boat with his father, and her pretty little Mercy clinging to her hand upon the homeward road, and prattling of the fish to be caught that day; and inasmuch as Joan had not been able to get face to face with her husband on the beach, she had not yet heard of the stranger child. But soon the women sent a little boy to fetch her, and she came among them, wondering what it could be. For now a debate of some vigor was arising upon a momentous and exciting point, though not so keen by a hundredth part as it would have been twenty years afterward. For the eldest old woman had pronounced her decision.

"Tell ye wat, ah dean't think bud wat yon bairn mud he a Frogman."

This caused some panic and a general retreat; for though the immortal Napoleon had scarcely finished changing his teeth as yet, a chronic uneasiness about Crappos haunted that coast already, and they might have sent this little boy to pave the way, being capable of almost everything.

"Frogman!" cried the old woman next to her by birth, and believed to have higher parts, though not yet ripe. "Na, na; what Frogman here? Frogmen ha' skinny shanks, and larks' heels, and holes down their bodies like lamperns. No sign of no frog aboot yon bairn. As fair as a wench, and as clean as a tyke. A' mought a'most been born to Flaambro'. And what gowd ha' Crappos got, poor divils?"

This opened the gate for a clamor of discourse; for there surely could be no denial of her words. And yet while her elder was alive and out of bed, the habit of the village was to listen to her say, unless any man of equal age arose to countervail it. But while they were thus divided, Mrs. Cockscroft came, and they stood aside. For she had been kind to everybody when her better chances were; and now in her trouble all were grieved because she took it so to heart. Joan Cockscroft did not say a word, but glanced at the child with some contempt. In spite of white linen and yellow gold, what was he to her own dead Robin?

But suddenly this child, whatever he was, and vastly soever inferior, opened his eyes and sent home their first glance to the very heart of Joan Cockscroft. It was the exact look—or so she always said—of her dead angel, when she denied him something, for the sake of his poor dear stomach. With an outburst of tears, she flew straight to the little one, snatched him in her arms, and tried to cover him with kisses.

The child, however, in a lordly manner, did not seem to like it. He drew away his red lips, and gathered up his nose, and passion flew out of his beautiful eyes, higher passion than that of any Cockscroft. And he tried to say something which no one could make out. And women of high consideration, looking on, were wicked enough to be pleased at this, and say that he must be a young lord, and they had quite foreseen it. But Joan knew what children are, and soothed him down so with delicate hands, and a gentle look, and a subtle way of warming his cold places, that he very soon began to cuddle into her, and smile. Then she turned round to the other people, with both of his arms flung round her neck, and his cheek laid on her shoulder, and she only said, "The Lord hath sent him."

CHAPTER XI

DR. UPANDOWN

The practice of Flamborough was to listen fairly to anything that might be said by any one truly of the native breed, and to receive it well into the crust of the mind, and let it sink down slowly. But even after that, it might not take root, unless it were fixed in its settlement by their two great powers—the law, and the Lord.

They had many visitations from the Lord, as needs must be in such a very stormy place; whereas of the law they heard much less; but still they were even more afraid of that; for they never knew how much it might cost.

Balancing matters (as they did their fish, when the price was worth it, in Weigh Lane), they came to the set conclusion that the law and the Lord might not agree concerning the child cast among them by the latter. A child or two had been thrown ashore before, and trouble once or twice had come of it; and this child being cast, no one could say how, to such a height above all other children, he was likely enough to bring a spell upon their boats, if anything crooked to God's will were done; and even to draw them to their last stocking, if anything offended the providence of law.

In any other place it would have been a point of combat what to say and what to do in such a case as this. But Flamborough was of all the wide world happiest in possessing an authority to reconcile all doubts. The law and the Lord—two powers supposed to be at variance always, and to share the week between them in proportions fixed by lawyers—the holy and unholy elements of man's brief existence, were combined in Flamborough parish in the person of its magisterial rector. He was also believed to excel in the arts of divination and medicine too, for he was a full Doctor of Divinity. Before this gentleman must be laid, both for purse and conscience' sake, the case of the child just come out of the fogs.

And true it was that all these powers were centred in one famous man, known among the laity as "Parson Upandown." For the Reverend Turner Upround, to give him his proper name, was a doctor of divinity, a justice of the peace, and the present rector of Flamborough. Of all his offices and powers, there was not one that he overstrained; and all that knew him, unless they were thorough-going rogues and vagabonds, loved him. Not that he was such a soft-spoken man as many were, who thought more evil; but because of his deeds and nature, which were of the kindest. He did his utmost, on demand of duty, to sacrifice this nature to his stern position as pastor and master of an up-hill parish, with many wrong things to be kept under. But while he succeeded in the form now and then, he failed continually in the substance.

This gentleman was not by any means a fool, unless a kind heart proves folly. At Cambridge he had done very well, in the early days of the tripos, and was chosen fellow and tutor of Gonville and Caius College. But tiring of that dull round in his prime, he married, and took to a living; and the living was one of the many upon which a perpetual faster can barely live, unless he can go naked also, and keep naked children. Now the parsons had not yet discovered the glorious merits of hard fasting, but freely enjoyed, and with gratitude to God, the powers with which He had blessed them. Happily Dr. Upround had a solid income of his own, and (like a sound mathematician) he took a wife of terms coincident. So, without being wealthy, they lived very well, and helped their poorer neighbors.

Such a man generally thrives in the thriving of his flock, and does not harry them. He gives them spiritual food enough to support them without daintiness, and he keeps the proper distinction between the Sunday and the poorer days. He clangs no bell of reproach upon a Monday, when the squire is leading the lady in to dinner, and the laborer sniffing at his supper pot; and he lets the world play on a Saturday, while he works his own head to find good ends for the morrow. Because he is a wise man who knows what other men are, and how seldom they desire to be told the same thing more than a hundred and four times in a year. Neither did his clerical skill stop here; for Parson Upround thought twice about it before he said anything to rub sore consciences, even when he had them at his mercy, and silent before him, on a Sunday. He behaved like a gentleman in this matter, where so much temptation lurks, looking always at the man whom he did not mean to hit, so that the guilty one received it through him, and felt himself better by comparison. In a word, this parson did his duty well, and pleasantly for all his flock; and nothing imbittered him, unless a man pretended to doctrine without holy orders.

For the doctor reasoned thus—and sound it sounds—if divinity is a matter for Tom, Dick, or Harry, how can there be degrees in it? He held a degree in it, and felt what it had cost; and not the parish only, but even his own wife, was proud to have a doctor every Sunday. And his wife took care that his rich red hood, kerseymere small-clothes, and black silk stockings upon calves of dignity, were such that his congregation scorned the surgeons all the way to Beverley.

Happy in a pleasant nature, kindly heart, and tranquil home, he was also happy in those awards of life in which men are helpless. He was blessed with a good wife and three good children, doing well, and vigorous and hardy as the air and clime and cliffs. His wife was not quite of his own age, but old enough to understand and follow him faithfully down the slope of years. A wife with mind enough to know that a husband is not faultless, and with heart enough to feel that if he were, she would not love him so. And under her were comprised their children—two boys at school, and a baby-girl at home.

So far, the rector of this parish was truly blessed and blessing. But in every man's lot must be some crook, since this crooked world turned round. In Parson Upround's lot the crook might seem a very small one; but he found it almost too big for him. His dignity and peace of mind, large good-will of ministry and strong Christian sense of magistracy, all were sadly pricked and wounded by a very small thorn in the flesh of his spirit.

Almost every honest man is the rightful owner of a nickname. When he was a boy at school he could not do without one, and if the other boys valued him, perhaps he had a dozen. And afterward, when there is less perception of right and wrong and character, in the weaker time of manhood, he may earn another, if the spirit is within him.

But woe is him if a nasty foe, or somebody trying to be one, annoyed for the moment with him, yet meaning no more harm than pepper, smite him to the quick, at venture, in his most retired and privy-conscienced hole. And when this is done by a Nonconformist to a Doctor of Divinity, and the man who does it owes some money to the man he does it to, can the latter gentleman take a large and genial view of his critics.

This gross wrong and ungrateful outrage was inflicted thus. A leading Methodist from Filey town, who owed the doctor half a guinea, came one summer and set up his staff in the hollow of a limekiln, where he lived upon fish for change of diet, and because he could get it for nothing. This was a man of some eloquence, and his calling in life was cobbling, and to encourage him therein, and keep him from theology, the rector not only forgot his half guinea, but sent him three or four pairs of riding-boots to mend, and let him charge his own price, which was strictly heterodox. As a part of the bargain, this fellow came to church, and behaved as well as could be hoped of a man who had received his money. He sat by a pillar, and no more than crossed his legs at the worst thing that disagreed with him. And it might have done him good, and made a decent cobbler of him, if the parson had only held him when he got him on the hook. But this is the very thing which all great preachers are too benevolent to do. Dr. Upround looked at this sinner, who was getting into a fright upon his own account, though not a bad preacher when he could afford it; and the cobbler could no more look up to the doctor than when he charged him a full crown beyond the contract. In his kindness for all who seemed convinced of sin, the good preacher halted, and looked at Mr. Jobbins with a soft, relaxing gaze. Jobbins appeared as if he would come to church forever, and never cheat any sound clergyman again; whereupon the generous divine omitted a whole page of menaces prepared for him, and passed prematurely to the tender strain which always winds up a good sermon.

Now what did Jobbins do in return for all this magnanimous mercy? Invited to dine with the senior church-warden upon the strength of having been at church, and to encourage him for another visit, and being asked, as soon as ever decency permitted, what he thought of Parson Upround's doctrine, between two crackles of young griskin (come straight from the rectory pig-sty), he was grieved to express a stern opinion long remembered at Flamborough:

"Ca' yo yon mon 'Dr. Uproond?' I ca' un 'Dr. Upandoon.'"

From that day forth the rector of the parish was known far and wide as "Dr. Upandown," even among those who loved him best. For the name well described his benevolent practice of undoing any harsh thing he might have said, sometimes by a smile, and very often with a shilling, or a basket of spring cabbages. So that Mrs. Upround, when buttoning up his coat—which he always forgot to do for himself—did it with the words, "My dear, now scold no one; really it is becoming too expensive." "Shall I abandon duty," he would answer, with some dignity, "while a shilling is sufficient to enforce it?"

Dr. Upround's people had now found out that their minister and magistrate discharged his duty toward his pillow, no less than to his pulpit. His parish had acquired, through the work of generations, a habit of getting up at night, and being all alive at cock-crow; and the rector (while very new amongst them) tried to bow—or rather rise—to night-watch. But a little of that exercise lasted him for long; and he liked to talk of it afterward, but for the present was obliged to drop it. For he found himself pale, when his wife made him see himself; and his hours of shaving were so dreadful; and scarcely a bit of fair dinner could be got, with the whole of the day thrown out so. In short, he settled it wisely that the fishers of fish must yield to the habits of fish, which can not be corrected; but the fishers of men (who can live without catching them) need not be up to all their hours, but may take them reasonably.

His parishioners—who could do very well without him, as far as that goes, all the week, and by no means wanted him among their boats—joyfully left him to his own time of day, and no more worried him out of season than he worried them so. It became a matter of right feeling with them not to ring a big bell, which the rector had put up to challenge everybody's spiritual need, until the stable clock behind the bell had struck ten and finished gurgling.

For this reason, on St. Swithin's morn, in the said year 1782, the grannies, wives, and babes of Flamborough, who had been to help the launch, but could not pull the laboring oar, nor even hold the tiller, spent the time till ten o'clock in seeing to their own affairs—the most laudable of all pursuits for almost any woman. And then, with some little dispute among them (the offspring of the merest accident), they arrived in some force at the gate of Dr. Upround, and no woman liked to pull the bell, and still less to let another woman do it for her. But an old man came up who was quite deaf, and every one asked him to do it.

In spite of the scarcity of all good things, Mrs. Cockscroft had thoroughly fed the little stranger, and washed him, and undressed him, and set him up in her own bed, and wrapped him in her woollen shawl, because he shivered sadly; and there he stared about with wondering eyes, and gave great orders— so far as his new nurse could make out—but speaking gibberish, as she said, and flying into a rage because it was out of Christian knowledge. But he seemed to understand some English, although he could only pronounce two words, both short, and in such conjunction quite unlawful for any except the highest Spiritual Power. Mrs. Cockscroft, being a pious woman, hoped that her ears were wrong, or else that the words were foreign and meant no harm, though the child seemed to take in much of what was said, and when asked his name, answered, wrathfully, and as if everybody was bound to know, "Izunsabe! Izunsabe!"

But now, when brought before Dr. Upround, no child of the very best English stock could look more calm and peaceful. He could walk well enough, but liked better to be carried; and the kind woman who had so taken him up was only too proud to carry him. Whatever the rector and magistrate might say, her meaning was to keep this little one, with her husband's good consent, which she was sure of getting.

"Set him down, ma'am," the doctor said, when he had heard from half a dozen good women all about him; "Mistress Cockscroft, put him on his legs, and let me question him."

But the child resisted this proceeding. With nature's inborn and just loathing of examination, he spun upon his little heels, and swore with all his might, at the same time throwing up his hands and twirling his thumbs in a very odd and foreign way.

"What a shocking child!" cried Mrs. Upround, who was come to know all about it. "Jane, run away with Miss Janetta."

"The child is not to blame," said the rector, "but only the people who have brought him up. A prettier or more clever little head I have never seen in all my life; and we studied such things at Cambridge. My fine little fellow, shake hands with me."

The boy broke off his vicious little dance, and looked up at this tall gentleman with great surprise. His dark eyes dwelt upon the parson's kindly face, with that power of inquiry which the very young possess, and then he put both little hands into the gentleman's, and burst into a torrent of the most heart-broken tears.

"Poor little man!" said the rector, very gently, taking him up in his arms and patting the silky black curls, while great drops fell, and a nose was rubbed on his shoulder; "it is early for you to begin bad times. Why, how old are you, if you please?"

The little boy sat up on the kind man's arm, and poked a small investigating finger into the ear that was next to him, and the locks just beginning to be marked with gray; and then he said, "Sore," and tossed his chin up, evidently meaning, "Make your best of that." And the women drew a long breath, and nudged at one another.

"Well done! Four years old, my dear. You see that he understands English well enough," said the parson to his parishioners: "he will tell us all about himself by-and-by, if we do not hurry him. You think him a French child. I do not, though the name which he gives himself, 'Izunsabe,' has a French aspect about it. Let me think. I will try him with a French interrogation: 'Parlez-vous Francais, mon enfan?'"

Dr. Upround watched the effect of his words with outward calm, but an inward flutter. For if this clever child should reply in French, the doctor could never go on with it, but must stand there before his congregation in a worse position than when he lost his place, as sometimes happened, in a sermon. With wild temerity he had given vent to the only French words within his knowledge; and he determined to follow them up with Latin if the worst came to the worst.

But luckily no harm came of this, but, contrariwise, a lasting good. For the child looked none the wiser, while the doctor's influence was increased.

"Aha!" the good parson cried. "I was sure that he was no Frenchman. But we must hear something about him very soon, for what you tell me is impossible. If he had come from the sea, he must have been wet; it could never be otherwise. Whereas, his linen clothes are dry, and even quite lately fullered—ironed you might call it."

"Please your worship," cried Mrs. Cockscroft, who was growing wild with jealousy, "I did up all his little things, hours and hours ere your hoose was up."

"Ah, you had night-work! To be sure! Were his clothes dry or wet when you took them off?"

"Not to say dry, your worship; and yet not to say very wet. Betwixt and between, like my good master's, when he cometh from a pour of rain, or a heavy spray. And the color of the land was upon them here and there. And the gold tags were sewn with something wonderful. My best pair of scissors would not touch it. I was frightened to put them to the tub, your worship; but they up and shone lovely like a tailor's buttons. My master hath found him, Sir; and it lies with him to keep him. And the Lord hath taken away our Bob."

"It is true," said Dr. Upround, gently, and placing the child in her arms again, "the Almighty has chastened you very sadly. This child is not mine to dispose of, nor yours; but if he will comfort you, keep him till we hear of him. I will take down in writing the particulars of the case, when Captain Robin has come home and had his rest—say, at this time to-morrow, or later; and then you will sign them, and they shall be published. For you know, Mrs. Cockscroft, however much you may be taken with him, you must not turn kidnapper. Moreover, it is needful, as there may have been some wreck (though none of you seem to have heard of any), that this strange occurrence should be made known. Then, if nothing is heard of it, you can keep him, and may the Lord bless him to you!"

Without any more ado, she kissed the child, and wanted to carry him straight away, after courtesying to his worship; but all the other women insisted on a smack of him, for pity's sake, and the pleasure of the gold, and to confirm the settlement. And a settlement it was, for nothing came of any publication of the case, such as in those days could be made without great expense and exertion.

So the boy grew up, tall, brave, and comely, and full of the spirit of adventure, as behooved a boy cast on the winds. So far as that goes, his foster-parents would rather have found him more steady and less comely, for if he was to step into their lost son's shoes, he might do it without seeming to outshine him. But they got over that little jealousy in time, when the boy began to be useful, and, so far as was possible, they kept him under by quoting against him the character of Bob, bringing it back from heaven of a much higher quality than ever it was upon the earth. In vain did this living child aspire to such level; how can an earthly boy compare with one who never did a wrong thing, as soon as he was dead?

Passing that difficult question, and forbearing to compare a boy with angels, be he what he will, his first need (after that of victuals) is a name whereby his fellow-boys may know him. Is he to be shouted at with, "Come here, what's your name?" or is he to be called (as if in high rebuke), "Boy?" And yet there are grown-up folk who do all this without hesitation, failing to remember their own predicament at a by-gone period. Boys are as useful, in their way, as any other order; and if they can be said to do some mischief, they can not be said to do it negligently. It is their privilege and duty to be truly active; and their Maker, having spread a dull world before them, has provided them with gifts of play while their joints are supple.

The present boy, having been born without a father or a mother (so far as could yet be discovered), was driven to do what our ancestors must have done when it was less needful. That is to say, to work his own name out by some distinctive process. When the parson had clearly shown him not to be a Frenchman, a large contumely spread itself about, by reason of his gold, and eyes, and hair, and name (which might be meant for Isaak), that he was sprung from a race more honored now than a hundred years ago. But the women declared that it could not be; and the rector desiring to christen him, because it might never have been done before, refused point-blank to put any "Isaac" in, and was satisfied with "Robin" only, the name of the man who had saved him.

The rector showed deep knowledge of his flock, which looked upon Jews as the goats of the Kingdom; for any Jew must die for a world of generations ere ever a Christian thinks much of him. But finding him not to be a Jew, the other boys, instead of being satisfied, condemned him for a Dutchman.

Whatever he was, the boy throve well, and being so flouted by his playmates, took to thoughts and habits and amusements of his own. In-door life never suited him at all, nor too much of hard learning, although his capacity was such that he took more advancement in an hour than the thick heads of young Flamborough made in a whole leap-year of Sundays. For any Flamburian boy was considered a "Brain Scholar," and a "Head-Languager," when he could write down the parson's text, and chalk up a fish on the weigh-board so that his father or mother could tell in three guesses what manner of fish it was. And very few indeed had ever passed this trial.

For young Robin it was a very hard thing to be treated so by the other boys. He could run, or jump, or throw a stone, or climb a rock with the best of them; but all these things he must do by himself, simply because he had no name. A feeble youth would have moped, but Robin only grew more resolute. Alone he did what the other boys would scarcely in competition dare. No crag was too steep for him, no cave too dangerous and wave-beaten, no race of the tide so strong and swirling as to scare him of his wits. He seemed to rejoice in danger, having very little else to rejoice in; and he won for himself by nimble ways and rapid turns on land and sea, the name of "Lithe," or "Lyth," and made it famous even far inland.

For it may be supposed that his love of excitement, versatility, and daring demanded a livelier outlet than the slow toil of deep-sea fishing. To the most patient, persevering, and long-suffering of the arts, Robin Lyth did not take kindly, although he was so handy with a boat. Old Robin vainly strove to cast his angling mantle over him. The gifts of the youth were brighter and higher; he showed an inborn fitness for the lofty development of free trade. Eminent powers must force their way, as now they were doing with Napoleon; and they did the same with Robin Lyth, without exacting tithe in kind of all the foremost human race.

CHAPTER XII

IN A LANE, NOT ALONE

Stephen Anerley's daughter was by no means of a crooked mind, but open as the day in all things, unless any one mistrusted her, and showed it by cross-questioning. When this was done, she resented it quickly by concealing the very things which she would have told of her own accord; and it so happened that the person to whom of all she should have been most open, was the one most apt to check her by suspicious curiosity. And now her mother already began to do this, as concerned the smuggler, knowing from the revenue officer that Mary must have seen him. Mary, being a truthful damsel, told no lies about it; but, on the other hand, she did not rush forth with all the history, as she probably would have done if left unexamined. And so she said nothing about the ear-ring, or the run that was to come off that week, or the riding-skirt, or a host of little things, including her promise to visit Bempton Lane.

On the other hand, she had a mind to tell her father, and take his opinion about it all. But he was a little cross that evening, not with her, but with the world at large; and that discouraged her; and then she thought that being an officer of the king—as he liked to call himself sometimes—he might feel bound to give information about the impending process of free trade; which to her would be a breach of honor, considering how she knew of it.

Upon the whole, she heartily wished that she never had seen that Robin Lyth; and then she became ashamed of herself for indulging such a selfish wish. For he might have been lying dead but for her; and then what would become of the many poor people whose greatest comfort he was said to be? And what good could arise from his destruction, if cruel people compassed it? Free trade must be carried on, for the sake of everybody, including Captain Carroway himself; and if an old and ugly man succeeded a young and generous one as leader of the free-trade movement, all the women in the country would put the blame on her.

Looking at these things loftily, and with a strong determination not to think twice of what any one might say who did not understand the subject, Mary was forced at last to the stern conclusion that she must keep her promise. Not only because it was a promise—although that went a very long way with her —but also because there seemed no other chance of performing a positive duty. Simple honesty demanded that she should restore to the owner a valuable, and beyond all doubt important, piece of property. Two hours had she spent in looking for it, and deprived her dear father of his breakfast shrimps; and was all this trouble to be thrown away, and herself, perhaps, accused of theft, because her mother was so short and sharp in wanting to know everything, and to turn it her own way?

The trinket, which she had found at last, seemed to be a very uncommon and precious piece of jewelry; it was made of pure gold, minutely chased and threaded with curious workmanship, in form like a melon, and bearing what seemed to be characters of some foreign language: there might be a spell, or even witchcraft, in it, and the sooner it was out of her keeping the better. Nevertheless she took very good care of it, wrapping it in lamb's-wool, and peeping at it many times a day, to be sure that it was safe, until it made her think of the owner so much, and the many wonders she had heard about him, that she grew quite angry with herself and it, and locked it away, and then looked at it again.

As luck would have it, on the very day when Mary was to stroll down Bempton Lane (not to meet any one, of course, but simply for the merest chance of what might happen), her father had business at Driffield corn market, which would keep him from home nearly all the day. When his daughter heard of it she was much cast down; for she hoped that he might have been looking about on the northern part of the farm, as he generally was in the afternoon; and although he could not see Bempton Lane at all, perhaps, without some newly acquired power of seeing round sharp corners, still it would have been a comfort and a strong resource for conscience to have felt that he was not so very far away. And this feeling of want made his daughter resolve to have some one at any rate near her. If Jack had only been at home, she need have sought no further, for he would have entered into all her thoughts about it, and obeyed her orders beautifully. But Willie was quite different, and hated any trouble, being spoiled so by his mother and the maidens all around them.

However, in such a strait, what was there to do but to trust in Willie, who was old enough, being five years in front of Mary, and then to try to make him sensible? Willie Anerley had no idea that anybody—far less his own sister—could take such a view of him. He knew himself to be, and all would say the same of him, superior in his original gifts, and his manner of making use of them, to the rest of the family put together. He had spent a month in Glasgow, when the whole place was astir with the ferment of many great inventions, and another month in Edinburgh, when that noble city was aglow with the dawn of large ideas; also, he had visited London, foremost of his family, and seen enough new things there to fill all Yorkshire with surprise; and the result of such wide experience was that he did not like hard work at all. Neither could he even be content to accept and enjoy, without labor of his own, the many good things provided for him. He was always trying to discover something which never seemed to answer, and continually flying after something new, of which he never got fast hold. In a word, he was spoiled, by nature first, and then by circumstances, for the peaceful life of his ancestors, and the unacknowledged blessings of a farmer.

"Willie dear, will you come with me?" Mary said to him that day, catching him as he ran down stairs to air some inspiration. "Will you come with me for just one hour? I wish you would; and I would be so thankful."

"Child, it is quite impossible," he answered, with a frown which set off his delicate eyebrows and high but rather narrow forehead; "you always want me at the very moment when I have the most important work in hand. Any childish whim of yours matters more than hours and hours of hard labor."

"Oh, Willie, but you know how I try to help you, and all the patterns I cut out last week! Do come for once, Willie; if you refuse, you will never, never forgive yourself."

Willie Anerley was as good-natured as any self-indulged youth can be; he loved his sister in his way, and was indebted to her for getting out of a great many little scrapes. He saw how much she was in earnest now, and felt some desire to know what it was about. Moreover—which settled the point—he was getting tired of sticking to one thing for a time unusually long with him. But he would not throw away the chance of scoring a huge debt of gratitude.

"Well, do what you like with me," he answered, with a smile; "I never can have my own way five minutes. It serves me quite right for being so good-natured."

Mary gave him a kiss, which must have been an object of ambition to anybody else; but it only made him wipe his mouth; and presently the two set forth upon the path toward Bempton.

Robin Lyth had chosen well his place for meeting Mary. The lane (of which he knew every yard as well as he knew the rocks themselves) was deep and winding, and fringed with bushes, so that an active and keen-eyed man might leap into thicket almost before there was a fair chance of shooting him. He knew well enough that he might trust Mary; but he never could be sure that the bold "coast-riders," despairing by this time of catching him at sea, and longing for the weight of gold put upon his head, might not be setting privy snares to catch him in his walks abroad. They had done so when they pursued him up the Dike; and though he was inclined to doubt the strict legality of that proceeding, he could not see his way to a fair discussion of it, in case of their putting a bullet through him. And this consideration made him careful.

The brother and sister went on well by the foot-path over the uplands of the farm, and crossing the neck of the Flamburn peninsula, tripped away merrily northward. The wheat looked healthy, and the barley also, and a four-acre patch of potatoes smelled sweetly (for the breeze of them was pleasant in their wholesome days), and Willie, having overworked his brain, according to his own account of it, strode along loftily before his sister, casting over his shoulder an eddy of some large ideas with which he had been visited before she interrupted him. But as nothing ever came of them, they need not here be stated. From a practical point of view, however, as they both had to live upon the profits of the farm, it pleased them to observe what a difference there was when they had surmounted the chine and began to descend toward the north upon other people's land. Here all was damp and cold and slow; and chalk looked slimy instead of being clean; and shadowy places had an oozy cast; and trees (wherever they could stand) were facing the east with wrinkled visage, and the west with wiry beards. Willie (who had, among other great inventions, a scheme for improvement of the climate) was reminded at once of all the things he meant to do in that way; and making, as he always did, a great point of getting observations first—a point whereon he stuck fast mainly —without any time for delay he applied himself to a rapid study of the subject. He found some things just like other things which he had seen in Scotland, yet differing so as to prove, more clearly than even their resemblance did, the value of his discovery.

"Look!" he cried; "can anything be clearer? The cause of all these evils is not (as an ignorant person might suppose) the want of sunshine, or too much wet, but an inadequate movement of the air—"

"Why, I thought it was always blowing up here. The very last time I came, my bonnet strings were split."

"You do not understand me; you never do. When I say inadequate, I mean, of course, incorrect, inaccurate, unequable. Now the air is a fluid; you may stare as you like, Mary, but the air has been proved to be a fluid. Very well; no fluid in large bodies moves with an equal velocity throughout. Part of it is rapid and part quite stagnant. The stagnant places of the air produce this green scum, this mossy, unwholesome, and injurious stuff; while the overrapid motion causes this iron appearance, this hard surface, and general sterility. By the simplest of simple contrivances, I make this evil its own remedy. An equable impulse given to the air produces an adequate uniform flow, preventing stagnation in one place, and excessive vehemence in another. And the beauty of it is that by my new invention I make the air itself correct and regulate its own inequalities."

"How clever you are, to be sure!" exclaimed Mary, wondering that her father could not see it. "Oh, Willie, you will make your fortune by it! However do you do it?"

"The simplicity of it is such that even you can understand it. All great discoveries are simple. I fix in a prominent situation a large and vertically revolving fan, of a light and vibrating substance. The movement of the air causes this to rotate by the mere force of the impact. The rotation and the vibration of the fan convert an irregular impulse into a steady and equable undulation; and such is the elasticity of the fluid called, in popular language, 'the air,' that for miles around the rotation of this fan regulates the circulation, modifies extremes, annihilates sterility, and makes it quite impossible for moss and green scum and all this sour growth to live. Even you can see, Mary, how beautiful it is."

"Yes, that I can," she answered, simply, as they turned the corner upon a large windmill, with arms revolving merrily; "but, Willie dear, would not Farmer Topping's mill, perpetually going as it is, answer the same purpose? And yet the moss seems to be as thick as ever here, and the ground as naked."

"Tush!" cried Willie. "Stuff and nonsense! When will you girls understand? Good-by! I will throw away no more time on you."

Without stopping to finish his sentence he was off and out of sight both of the mill and Mary, before the poor girl, who had not the least intention of offending him, could even beg his pardon, or say how much she wanted him; for she had not dared as yet to tell him what was the purpose of her walk, his nature being such that no one, not even his own mother, could tell what conclusion he might come to upon any practical question. He might rush off at once to put the revenue men on the smuggler's track, or he might stop his sister from going, or he might (in the absence of his father) order a feast to be prepared, and fetch the outlaw to be his guest. So Mary had resolved not to tell him until the last moment, when he could do none of these things.

But now she must either go on all alone, or give up her purpose and break her promise. After some hesitation she determined to go on, for the place would scarcely seem so very lonely now with the windmill in view, which would always remind her henceforth of her dear brother William. It was perfectly certain that Captain Robert Lyth, whose fame for chivalry was everywhere, and whose character was all in all to him with the ladies who bought his silks and lace, would see her through all danger caused by confidence in him; and really it was too bad of her to admit any paltry misgivings. But reason as she might, her young conscience told her that this was not the proper thing to do, and she made up her mind not to do it again. Then she laughed at the notion of being ever even asked, and told herself that she was too conceited; and to cut the matter short, went very bravely down the hill.

The lane, which came winding from the beach up to the windmill, was as pretty a lane as may anywhere be found in any other county than that of Devon. With a Devonshire lane it could not presume to vie, having little of the glorious garniture of fern, and nothing of the crystal brook that leaps at every corner; no arches of tall ash, keyed with dog-rose, and not much of honeysuckle, and a sight of other wants which people feel who have lived in the plenitude of everything. But in spite of all that, the lane was very fine for Yorkshire.

On the other hand, Mary had prettier ankles, and a more graceful and lighter walk, than the Devonshire lanes, which like to echo something, for the most part seem accustomed to; and the short dress of the time made good such favorable facts when found. Nor was this all that could be said, for the maiden (while her mother was so busy pickling cabbage, from which she drove all intruders) had managed to forget what the day of the week was, and had opened the drawer that should be locked up until Sunday. To walk with such a handsome tall fellow as Willie compelled her to look like something too, and without any thought of it she put her best hat on, and a very pretty thing with some French name, and made of a delicate peach-colored silk, which came down over her bosom, and tied in the neatest of knots at the small of her back, which at that time of life was very small. All these were the gifts of her dear uncle Popplewell, upon the other side of Filey, who might have been married for forty years, but nobody knew how long it was, because he had no children, and so he made Mary his darling. And this ancient gentleman had leanings toward free trade.

Whether these goods were French or not—which no decent person could think of asking—no French damsel could have put them on better, or shown a more pleasing appearance in them; for Mary's desire was to please all people who meant no harm to her—as nobody could—and yet to let them know that her object was only to do what was right, and to never think of asking whether she looked this, that, or the other. Her mother, as a matter of duty, told her how plain she was almost every day; but the girl was not of that opinion; and when Mrs. Anerley finished her lecture (as she did nine times in ten) by turning the glass to the wall, and declaring that beauty was a snare skin-deep, with a frown of warning instead of a smile of comfort, then Mary believed in her looking-glass again, and had the smile of comfort on her own face.

However, she never thought of that just now, but only of how she could do her duty, and have no trouble in her own mind with thinking, and satisfy her father when she told him all, as she meant to do, when there could be no harm done to any one; and this, as she heartily hoped, would be to-morrow. And truly, if there did exist any vanity at all, it was not confined to the sex in which it is so much more natural and comely.

For when a very active figure came to light suddenly, at a little elbow of the lane, and with quick steps advanced toward Mary, she was lost in surprise at the gayety, not to say grandeur, of its apparel. A broad hat, looped at the side, and having a pointed black crown, with a scarlet feather and a dove-colored brim, sat well upon the mass of crisp black curls. A short blue jacket of the finest Flemish cloth, and set (not too thickly) with embossed silver buttons, left properly open the strong brown neck, while a shirt of pale blue silk, with a turned-down collar of fine needle-work, fitted, without a wrinkle or a pucker, the broad and amply rounded chest. Then a belt of brown leather, with an anchor clasp, and empty loops for either fire-arm or steel, supported true sailor's trousers of the purest white and the noblest man-of-war cut; and where these widened at the instep shone a lovely pair of pumps, with buckles radiant of best Bristol diamonds. The wearer of all these splendors smiled, and seemed to become them as they became him.

"Well," thought Mary, "how free trade must pay! What a pity that he is not in the Royal Navy!"

With his usual quickness, and the self-esteem which added such lustre to his character, the smuggler perceived what was passing in her mind, but he was not rude enough to say so.

"Young lady," he began—and Mary, with all her wisdom, could not help being fond of that—"young lady, I was quite sure that you would keep your word."

"I never do anything else," she answered, showing that she scarcely looked at him. "I have found this for you, and then good-by."

"Surely you will wait to hear my thanks, and to know what made me dare to ask you, after all you had done for me already, to begin again for me. But I am such an outcast that I never should have done it."

"I never saw any one look more thoroughly unlike an outcast," Mary said; and then she was angry with herself for speaking, and glancing, and, worst of all, for smiling,

"Ladies who live on land can never understand what we go through," Robin replied, in his softest voice, as rich as the murmur of the summer sea. "When we expect great honors, we try to look a little tidy, as any one but a common boor would do; and we laugh at ourselves for trying to look well, after all the knocking about we get. Our time is short—we must make the most of it."

"Oh, please not to talk in such a dreadful way," said Mary.

"You remind me of my dear friend Dr. Upround—the very best man in the whole world, I believe. He always says to me, 'Robin, Robin—'"

"What! is Dr. Upandown a friend of yours?" Mary exclaimed, in amazement, and with a stoppage of the foot that was poised for quick departure.

"Dr. Upandown, as many people call him," said the smuggler, with a tone of condemnation, "is the best and dearest friend I have, next to Captain and Mistress Cockscroft, who may have been heard of at Anerley Manor. Dr. Upround is our magistrate and clergyman, and he lets people say what they like against me, while he honors me with his friendship. I must not stay long to thank you even, because I am going to the dear old doctor's for supper at seven o'clock and a game of chess."

"Oh dear! oh dear! And he is such a Justice! And yet they shot at you last week! It makes me wonder when I hear such things."

"Young lady, it makes everybody wonder. In my opinion there never could be a more shameful murder than to shoot me; and yet but for you it would surely have been done."

"You must not dwell upon such things," said Mary; "they may have a very bad effect upon your mind. But good-by, Captain Lyth; I forgot that I was robbing Dr. Upround of your society."

"Shall I be so ungrateful as not to see you safe upon your own land after all your trouble? My road to Flamborough lies that way. Surely you will not refuse to hear what made me so anxious about this bauble, which now will be worth ten times as much. I never saw it look so bright before."

"It—it must be the sand has made it shine," the maiden stammered, with a fine bright blush; "it does the same to my shrimping net."

"Ah, shrimping is a very fine pursuit! There is nothing I love better; what pools I could show you, if I only might; pools where you may fill a sack with large prawns in a single tide—pools known to nobody but myself. When do you think of going shrimping next?"

"Perhaps next summer I may try again, if Captain Carroway will come with me."

"That is too unkind of you. How very harsh you are to me! I could hardly have believed it after all that you have done. And you really do not care to hear the story of this relic?"

"If I could stop, I should like it very much. But my brother, who came with me, may perhaps be waiting for me." Mary knew that this was not very likely; still, it was just possible, for Willie's ill tempers seldom lasted very long; and she wanted to let the smuggler know that she had not come all alone to meet him.

"I shall not be two minutes," Robin Lyth replied; "I have been forced to learn short talking. May I tell you about this trinket?"

"Yes, if you will only begin at once, and finish by the time we get to that corner."

"That is very short measure for a tale," said Robin, though he liked her all the better for such qualities; "however, I will try; only walk a little slower. Nobody knows where I was born, any more than they know how or why. Only when I came upon this coast as a very little boy, and without knowing anything about it, they say that I had very wonderful buttons of gold upon a linen dress, adorned with gold-lace, which I used to wear on Sundays. Dr. Upround ordered them to keep those buttons, and was to have had them in his own care; but before that, all of them were lost save two. My parents, as I call them from their wonderful goodness, kinder than the ones who have turned me on the world (unless themselves went out of it), resolved to have my white coat done up grandly, when I grew too big for it, and to lay it by in lavender; and knowing of a great man in the gold-lace trade, as far away as Scarborough, they sent it by a fishing-smack to him, with people whom they knew thoroughly. That was the last of it ever known here. The man swore a manifest that he never saw it, and threatened them with libel; and the smack was condemned, and all her hands impressed, because of some trifle she happened to carry; and nobody knows any more of it. But two of the buttons had fallen off, and good mother had put them by, to give a last finish to the coat herself; and when I grew up, and had to go to sea at night, they were turned into a pair of ear-rings. There, now, Miss Anerley, I have not been long, and you know all about it."

"How very lonesome it must be for you," said Mary, with a gentle gaze, which, coming from such lovely eyes, went straight into his heart, "to have no one belonging to you by right, and to seem to belong to nobody! I am sure I can not tell whatever I should do without any father, or mother, or uncle, or even a cousin to be certain of."

"All the ladies seem to think that it is rather hard upon me," Robin answered, with an excellent effort at a sigh; "but I do my very best to get on without them. And one thing that helps me most of all is when kind ladies, who have good hearts, allow me to talk to them as if I had a sister. This makes me forget what I am sometimes."

"You never should try to forget what you are. Everybody in the world speaks well of you. Even that cruel Lieutenant Carroway can not help admiring you. And if you have taken to free trade, what else could you do, when you had no friends, and even your coat was stolen?"

"High-minded people take that view of it, I know. But I do not pretend to any such excuse. I took to free trade for the sake of my friends—to support the old couple who have been so good to me."

"That is better still; it shows such good principle. My uncle Popplewell has studied the subject of what they call 'political economy,' and he says that the country requires free trade, and the only way to get it is to go on so that the government must give way at last. However, I need not instruct you about that; and you must not stop any longer."

"Miss Anerley, I will not encroach upon your kindness. You have said things that I never shall forget. On the Continent I meet very many ladies who tell me good things, and make me better; but not at all as you have done. A minute of talk with you is worth an hour with anybody else. But I fear that you laugh at me all the while, and are only too glad to be rid of me. Good-by. May I kiss your hand? God bless you!"

Mary had no time to say a single word, or even to express her ideas by a look, before Robin Lyth, with all his bright apparel, was "conspicuous by his absence." As a diving bird disappears from a gun, or a trout from a shadow on his hover, or even a debtor from his creditor, so the great free-trader had vanished into lightsome air, and left emptiness behind him.

The young maid, having been prepared to yield him a few yards more of good advice, if he held out for another corner, now could only say to herself that she never had met such a wonderful man. So active, strong, and astonishingly brave; so thoroughly acquainted with foreign lands, yet superior to their ladies; so able to see all the meaning of good words, and to value them when offered quietly; so sweet in his manner, and voice, and looks; and with all his fame so unpretending, and—much as it frightened her to think it—really seeming to be afraid of her.

CHAPTER XIII

GRUMBLING AND GROWLING

While these successful runs went on, and great authorities smiled at seeing the little authorities set at naught, and men of the revenue smote their breasts for not being born good smugglers, and the general public was well pleased, and congratulated them cordially upon their accomplishment of naught, one man there was whose noble spirit chafed and knew no comfort. He strode up and down at Coast-guard Point, and communed with himself, while Robin held sweet converse in the lane.

"Why was I born?" the sad Carroway cried; "why was I thoroughly educated and trained in both services of the king, expected to rise, and beginning to rise, till a vile bit of splinter stopped me, and then sent down to this hole of a place to starve, and be laughed at, and baffled by a boy? Another lucky run, and the revenue bamboozled, and the whole of us sent upon a wild-goose chase! Every gapper-mouth zany grinning at me, and scoundrels swearing that I get my share! And the only time I have had my dinner with my knees crook'd, for at least a fortnight, was at Anerley Farm on Sunday. I am not sure that even they wouldn't turn against me; I am certain that pretty girl would. I've a great mind to throw it up—a great mind to throw it up. It is hardly the work for a gentleman born, and the grandson of a rear-admiral. Tinkers' and tailors' sons get the luck now; and a man of good blood is put on the back shelf, behind the blacking-bottles. A man who has battled for his country—"

"Charles, are you coming to your dinner, once more?"

"No, I am not. There's no dinner worth coming to. You and the children may eat the rat pie. A man who has battled for his country, and bled till all his veins were empty, and it took two men to hold him up, and yet waved his Sword at the head of them—it is the downright contradiction of the world in everything for him to poke about with pots and tubs, like a pig in a brewery, grain-hunting."

"Once more, Charles, there is next to nothing left. The children are eating for their very lives. If you stay out there another minute, you must take the consequence."

"Alas, that I should have so much stomach, and so little to put into it! My dear, put a little bit under a basin, if any of them has no appetite. I wanted just to think a little."

"Charles, they have all got tremendous appetites. It is the way the wind is. You may think by-and-by, but if you want to eat, you must do it now, or never."

"'Never' never suits me in that matter," the brave lieutenant answered. "Matilda, put Geraldine to warm the pewter plate for me. Geraldine darling, you can do it with your mouth full."

The commander of the coast-guard turned abruptly from his long indignant stride, and entered the cottage provided for him, and which he had peopled so speedily.

Small as it was, it looked beautifully clean and neat, and everybody used to wonder how Mrs. Carroway kept it so. But in spite of all her troubles and many complaints, she was very proud of this little house, with its healthful position and beautiful outlook over the bay of Bridlington. It stood in a niche of the low soft cliff, where now the sea-parade extends from the northern pier of Bridlington Quay; and when the roadstead between that and the point was filled with a fleet of every kind of craft, or, better still, when they all made sail at once—as happened when a trusty breeze arose—the view was lively, and very pleasant, and full of moving interest. Often one of his Majesty's cutters, Swordfish, Kestrel, or Albatross, would swoop in with all sail set, and hover, while the skipper came ashore to see the "Ancient Carroway," as this vigilant officer was called; and sometimes even a sloop of war, armed brigantine, or light corvette, prowling for recruits, or cruising for their training, would run in under the Head, and overhaul every wind-bound ship with a very high hand.

"Ancient Carroway"—as old friends called him, and even young people who had never seen him—was famous upon this coast now for nearly three degrees of latitude. He had dwelled here long, and in highly good content, hospitably treated by his neighbors, and himself more hospitable than his wife could wish, until two troubles in his life arose, and from year to year grew worse and worse. One of these troubles was the growth of mouths in number and size, that required to be filled; and the other trouble was the rampant growth of smuggling, and the glory of that upstart Robin Lyth. Now let it be lawful to take that subject first.

Fair Robin, though not at all anxious for fame, but modestly willing to decline it, had not been successful—though he worked so much by night—in preserving sweet obscurity. His character was public, and set on high by fortune, to be gazed at from wholly different points of view. From their narrow and lime-eyed outlook the coast-guard beheld in him the latest incarnation of Old Nick; yet they hated him only in an abstract manner, and as men feel toward that evil one. Magistrates also, and the large protective powers, were arrayed against him, yet happy to abstain from laying hands, when their hands were their own, upon him. And many of the farmers, who should have been his warmest friends and best customers, were now so attached to their king and country, by bellicose warmth and army contracts, that instead of a guinea for a four-gallon anker, they would offer three crowns, or the exciseman. And not only conscience, but short cash, after three bad harvests, constrained them.

Yet the staple of public opinion was sound, as it must be where women predominate. The best of women could not see why they should not have anything they wanted for less than it cost the maker. To gaze at a sister woman better dressed at half the money was simply to abjure every lofty principle. And to go to church with a counterfeit on, when the genuine lace was in the next pew on a body of inferior standing, was a downright outrage to the congregation, the rector, and all religion. A cold-blooded creature, with no pin-money, might reconcile it with her principles, if any she had, to stand up like a dowdy and allow a poor man to risk his life by shot and storm and starvation, and then to deny him a word or a look, because of his coming with the genuine thing at a quarter the price fat tradesmen asked, who never stirred out of their shops when it rained, for a thing that was a story and an imposition. Charity, duty, and common honesty to their good husbands in these bad times compelled them to make the very best of bargains; of which they got really more and more, as those brave mariners themselves bore witness, because of the depression in the free trade now and the glorious victories of England. Were they bound to pay three times the genuine value, and then look a figure, and be laughed at?

And as for Captain Carroway, let him scold, and threaten, and stride about, and be jealous, because his wife dare not buy true things, poor creature— although there were two stories also about that, and the quantities of things that he got for nothing, whenever he was clever enough to catch them, which scarcely ever happened, thank goodness! Let Captain Carroway attend to his own business; unless he was much belied, he had a wife who would keep him to it. Who was Captain Carroway to come down here, without even being born in Yorkshire, and lay down the law, as if he owned the manor?

Lieutenant Carroway had heard such questions, but disdained to answer them. He knew who he was, and what his grandfather had been, and he never cared a—short word—what sort of stuff long tongues might prate of him. Barbarous broad-drawlers, murderers of his Majesty's English, could they even pronounce the name of an officer highly distinguished for many years in both of the royal services? That was his description, and the Yorkshire yokels might go and read it—if read they could—in the pages of authority.

Like the celebrated calf that sucked two cows, Carroway had drawn royal pay, though in very small drains, upon either element, beginning with a skeleton regiment, and then, when he became too hot for it, diving off into a frigate as a recommended volunteer. Here he was more at home, though he never ceased longing to be a general; and having the credit of fighting well ashore, he was looked at with interest when he fought a fight at sea. He fought it uncommonly well, and it was good, and so many men fell that he picked up his commission, and got into a fifty-two-gun ship. After several years of service, without promotion—for his grandfather's name was worn out now, and the wars were not properly constant—there came a very lively succession of fights, and Carroway got into all of them, or at least into all the best of them. And he ought to have gone up much faster than he did, and he must have done so but for his long lean jaws, the which are the worst things that any man can have. Not only because of their own consumption and slow length of leverage, but mainly on account of the sadness they impart, and the timid recollection of a hungry wolf, to the man who might have lifted up a fatter individual.

But in Rodney's great encounter with the Spanish fleet, Carroway showed such a dauntless spirit, and received such a wound, that it was impossible not to pay him some attention. His name was near the bottom of a very long list, but it made a mark on some one's memory, depositing a chance of coming up some day, when he should be reported hit again. And so good was his luck that he soon was hit again, and a very bad hit it was; but still he got over it without promotion, because that enterprise was one in which nearly all our men ran away, and therefore required to be well pushed up for the sake of the national honor. When such things happen, the few who stay behind must be left behind in the Gazette as well. That wound, therefore, seemed at first to go against him, but he bandaged it, and plastered it, and hoped for better luck. And his third wound truly was a blessed one, a slight one, and taken in the proper course of things, without a slur upon any of his comrades. This set him up again with advancement and appointment, and enabled him to marry and have children seven.

The lieutenant was now about fifty years of age, gallant and lively as ever, and resolute to attend to his duty and himself as well. His duty was now along shore, in command of the Coast-guard of the East District; for the loss of a good deal of one heel made it hard for him to step about as he should do when afloat. The place suited him, and he was fond of it, although he grumbled sometimes about his grandfather, and went on as if his office was beneath him. He abused all his men, and all the good ones liked him, and respected him for his clear English. And he enjoyed this free exercise of language out-of-doors, because inside his threshold he was on his P's and Q's. To call him "ugly Carroway," as coarse people did, because of a scar across his long bold nose, was petty and unjust, and directly contradicted by his own and his wife's opinion. For nobody could have brighter eyes, or a kindlier smile, and more open aspect in the forepart of the week, while his Sunday shave retained its influence, so far as its limited area went, for he kept a long beard always. By Wednesday he certainly began to look grim, and on Saturday ferocious, pending the advent of the Bridlington barber, who shaved all the Quay every Sunday. But his mind was none the worse, and his daughters liked him better when he rasped their young cheeks with his beard, and paid a penny. For to his children he was a loving and tender-hearted father, puzzled at their number, and sometimes perplexed at having to feed and clothe them, yet happy to give them his last and go without, and even ready to welcome more, if Heaven should be pleased to send them.

But Mrs. Carroway, most fidgety of women, and born of a well-shorn family, was unhappy from the middle to the end of the week that she could not scrub her husband's beard off. The lady's sense of human crime, and of everything hateful in creation, expressed itself mainly in the word "dirt." Her rancor against that nobly tranquil and most natural of elements inured itself into a downright passion. From babyhood she had been notorious for kicking her little legs out at the least speck of dust upon a tiny red shoe. Her father—a clergyman—heard so much of this, and had so many children of a different stamp, that when he came to christen her, at six months of age (which used to be considered quite an early time of life), he put upon her the name of "Lauta," to which she thoroughly acted up; but people having ignorance of foreign tongues said that he always meant "Matilda."

Such was her nature, and it grew upon her; so that when a young and gallant officer, tall and fresh, and as clean as a frigate, was captured by her neat bright eyes, very clean run, and sharp cut-water, she began to like to look at him. Before very long, his spruce trim ducks, careful scrape of Brunswick-leather boots, clean pocket-handkerchiefs, and fine specklessness, were making and keeping a well-swept path to the thoroughly dusted store-room of her heart. How little she dreamed, in those virgin days, that the future could ever contain a week when her Charles would decline to shave more than once, and then have it done for him on a Sunday!

She hesitated, for she had her thoughts—doubts she disdained to call them —but still he forgot once to draw his boots sideways, after having purged the toe and heel, across the bristle of her father's mat. With the quick eye of love he perceived her frown, and the very next day he conquered her. His scheme was unworthy, as it substituted corporate for personal purity; still it succeeded, as unworthy schemes will do. On the birthday of his sacred

Majesty, Charles took Matilda to see his ship, the 48-gun frigate Immaculate, commanded by a well-known martinet. Her spirit fell within her, like the Queen of Sheba's, as she gazed, but trembled to set down foot upon the trim order and the dazzling choring. She might have survived the strict purity of all things, the deck lines whiter than Parian marble, the bulwarks brighter than the cheek-piece of a grate, the breeches of the guns like goodly gold, and not a whisker of a rope's end curling the wrong way, if only she could have espied a swab, or a bucket, or a flake of holy-stone, or any indicament of labor done. "Artis est celare artem;" this art was unfathomable.

Matilda was fain to assure herself that the main part of this might be superficial, like a dish-cover polished with the spots on, and she lost her handkerchief on purpose to come back and try a little test-work of her own. This was a piece of unstopped knotting in the panel of a hatchway, a resinous hole that must catch and keep any speck of dust meandering on the wayward will of wind. Her cambric came out as white as it went in!

She surrendered at discretion, and became the prize of Carroway.

Now people at Bridlington Quay declared that the lieutenant, though he might have carried off a prize, was certainly not the prize-master; and they even went so far as to say that "he could scarcely call his soul his own." The matter was no concern of theirs, neither were their conclusions true. In little things the gallant officer, for the sake of discipline and peace, submitted to due authority; and being so much from home, he left all household matters to a firm control. In return for this, he was always thought of first, and the best of everything was kept for him, and Mrs. Carroway quoted him to others as a wonder, though she may not have done so to himself. And so, upon the whole, they got on very well together.

Now on this day, when the lieutenant had exhausted a grumble of unusual intensity, and the fair Geraldine (his eldest child) had obeyed him to the letter, by keeping her mouth full while she warmed a plate for him, it was not long before his usual luck befell the bold Carroway. Rap, rap, came a knock at the side door of his cottage—a knock only too familiar; and he heard the gruff voice of Cadman—"Can I see his honor immediately?"

"No, you can not," replied Mrs. Carroway. "One would think you were all in a league to starve him. No sooner does he get half a mouthful—"

"Geraldine, put it on the hob, my dear, and a basin over it. Matilda, my love, you know my maxim—'Duty first, dinner afterward.' Cadman, I will come with you."

The revenue officer took up his hat (which had less time now than his dinner to get cold) and followed Cadman to the usual place for holding privy councils. This was under the heel of the pier (which was then about half as long as now) at a spot where the outer wall combed over, to break the crest of the surges in the height of a heavy eastern gale. At neap tides, and in moderate weather, this place was dry, with a fine salt smell; and with nothing in front of it but the sea, and nothing behind it but solid stone wall, any one would think that here must be commune sacred, secret, and secluded from eavesdroppers. And yet it was not so, by reason of a very simple reason.

Upon the roadway of the pier, and over against a mooring-post, where the parapet and the pier itself made a needful turn toward the south, there was an equally needful thing, a gully-hole with an iron trap to carry off the rain that fell, or the spray that broke upon the fabric; and the outlet of this gully was in the face of the masonry outside. Carroway, not being gifted with a crooked mind, had never dreamed that this little gut might conduct the pulses of the air, like the Tyrant's Ear, and that the trap at the end might be a trap for him. Yet so it was; and by gently raising the movable iron frame at the top, a well-disposed person might hear every word that was spoken in the snug recess below. Cadman was well aware of this little fact, but left his commander to find it out.

The officer, always thinly clad (both through the state of his wardrobe and his dread of effeminate comfort), settled his bony shoulders against the rough stonework, and his heels upon a groyne, and gave his subordinate a nod, which meant, "Make no fuss, but out with it." Cadman, a short square fellow with crafty eyes, began to do so.

"Captain, I have hit it off at last. Hackerbody put me wrong last time, through the wench he hath a hankering after. This time I got it, and no mistake, as right as if the villain lay asleep 'twixt you and me, and told us all about it with his tongue out; and a good thing for men of large families like me."

"All that I have heard such a number of times," his commander answered, crustily, "that I whistle, as we used to do in a dead calm, Cadman. An old salt like you knows how little comes of that."

"There I don't quite agree with your honor. I have known a hurricane come from whistling. But this time there is no woman about it, and the penny have come down straightforrard. New moon Tuesday next, and Monday we slips first into that snug little cave. He hath a' had his last good run."

"How much is coming this time, Cadman? I am sick and tired of those three caves. It is all old woman's talk of caves, while they are running south, upon the open beach."

"Captain, it is a big venture—the biggest of all the summer, I do believe.

Two thousand pounds, if there is a penny, in it. The schooner, and the lugger, and the ketch, all to once, of purpose to send us scattering. But your honor knows what we be after most. No woman in it this time, Sir. The murder has been of the women, all along. When there is no woman, I can see my way. We have got the right pig by the ear this time."

"John Cadman, your manner of speech is rude. You forget that your commanding officer has a wife and family, three-quarters of which are female. You will give me your information without any rude observations as to sex, of which you, as a married man, should be ashamed. A man and his wife are one flesh, Cadman, and therefore you are a woman yourself, and must labor not to disgrace yourself. Now don't look amazed, but consider these things. If you had not been in a flurry, like a woman, you would not have spoiled my dinner so. I will meet you at the outlook at six o'clock. I have business on hand of importance."

With these words Carroway hastened home, leaving Cadman to mutter his wrath, and then to growl it, when his officer was out of ear-shot.

"Never a day, nor an hour a'most, without he insulteth of me. A woman, indeed! Well, his wife may be a man, but what call hath he to speak of mine so? John Cadman a woman, and one flesh with his wife! Pretty news that would be for my missus!"

CHAPTER XIV

SERIOUS CHARGES

"Stephen, if it was anybody else, you would listen to me in a moment," said Mrs. Anerley to her lord, a few days after that little interview in the Bempton Lane; "for instance, if it was poor Willie, how long would you be in believing it? But because it is Mary, you say 'pooh! pooh!' And I may as well talk to the old cracked churn."

"First time of all my born days," the farmer answered, with a pleasant smile, "that ever I was resembled to a churn. But a man's wife ought to know best about un."

"Stephen, it is not the churn—I mean you; and you never should attempt to ride off in that sort of way. I tell you Mary hath a mischief on her mind; and you never ought to bring up old churns to me. As long as I can carry almost anything in mind, I have been considered to be full of common-sense. And what should I use it upon, Captain Anerley, without it was my own daughter?"

The farmer was always conquered when she called him "Captain Anerley." He took it to point at him as a pretender, a coxcomb fond of titles, a would-be officer who took good care to hold aloof from fighting. And he knew in his heart that he loved to be called "Captain Anerley" by every one who meant it.

"My dear," he said, in a tone of submission, and with a look that grieved her, "the knowledge of such things is with you. I can not enter into young maids' minds, any more than command a company."

"Stephen, you could do both, if you chose, better than ten of eleven who do it. For, Stephen, you have a very tender mind, and are not at all like a churn, my dear. That was my manner of speech, you ought to know, because from my youngest days I had a crowd of imagination. You remember that, Stephen, don't you?"

"I remember, Sophy, that in the old time you never resembled me to a churn, let alone a cracked one. You used to christen me a pillar, and a tree, and a rock, and a polished corner; but there, what's the odds, when a man has done his duty? The names of him makes no difference."

"'Twist you and me, my dear," she said, "nothing can make any difference. We know one another too well for that. You are all that I ever used to call you, before I knew better about you, and when I used to dwell upon your hair and your smile. You know what I used to say of them, now, Stephen?"

"Most complimentary—highly complimentary! Another young woman brought me word of it, and it made me stick firm when my mind was doubtful."

"And glad you ought to be that you did stick firm. And you have the Lord to thank for it, as well as your own sense. But no time to talk of our old times now. They are coming up again, with those younkers, I'm afraid. Willie is like a Church; and Jack—no chance of him getting the chance of it; but Mary, your darling of the lot, our Mary—her mind is unsettled, and a worry coming over her; the same as with me when I saw you first."

"It is the Lord that directs those things," the farmer answered, steadfastly; "and Mary hath the sense of her mother, I believe. That it is maketh me so fond on her. If the young maid hath taken a fancy, it will pass, without a bit of substance to settle on. Why, how many fancies had you, Sophy, before you had the good luck to clap eyes on me?"

"That is neither here nor there," his wife replied, audaciously; "how many times have you asked such questions, which are no concern of yours? You could not expect me, before ever I saw you, not to have any eyes or ears. I had plenty to say for myself; and I was not plain; and I acted accordingly."

Master Anerley thought about this, because he had heard it and thought of it many times before. He hated to think about anything new, having never known any good come of it; and his thoughts would rather flow than fly, even in the fugitive brevity of youth. And now, in his settled way, his practice was to tread thought deeper into thought, as a man in deep snow keeps the track of his own boots, or as a child writes ink on pencil in his earliest copy-books. "You acted according," he said; "and Mary might act according to you, mother."

"How can you talk so, Stephen? That would be a different thing altogether. Young girls are not a bit like what they used to be in my time. No steadiness, no diligence, no duty to their parents. Gadding about is all they think of, and light-headed chatter, and saucy ribbons."

"May be so with some of them. But I never see none of that in Mary."

"Mary is a good girl, and well brought up," her mother could not help admitting, "and fond of her home, and industrious. But for all that, she must be looked after sharply. And who can look after a child like her mother? I can tell you one thing, Master Stephen: your daughter Mary has more will of her own than the rest of your family all put together, including even your own good wife."

"Prodigious!" cried the farmer, while he rubbed his hands and laughed —"prodigious, and a man might say impossible. A young lass like Mary, such a coaxing little poppet, as tender as a lambkin, and as soft as wool!"

"Flannel won't only run one way; no more won't Mary," said her mother. "I know her better a long sight than you do; and I say if ever Mary sets her heart on any one, have him she will, be he cowboy, thief, or chimney-sweep. So now you know what to expect, Master Anerley."

Stephen Anerley never made light of his wife's opinions in those few cases wherein they differed from his own. She agreed with him so generally that in common fairness he thought very highly of her wisdom, and the present subject was one upon which she had an especial right to be heard.

"Sophy," he said, as he set up his coat to be off to a cutting of clover on the hill—for no reaping would begin yet for another month—"the things you have said shall abide in my mind. Only you be a-watching of the little wench. Harry Tanfield is the man I would choose for her of all others. But I never would force any husband on a lass; though stern would I be to force a bad one off, or one in an unfit walk of life. No inkle in your mind who it is, or wouldst have told me?"

"Well, I may, or I may not. I never like to speak promiscuous. You have the first right to know what I think. But I beg you to let me be a while. Not even to you, Steve, would I say it, without more to go upon than there is yet. I might do the lass a great wrong in my surmising; and then you would visit my mistake on me, for she is the apple of your eye, no doubt."

"There is never such another maid in all York County, nor in England, to my thinking."

"She is my daughter as well as yours, and I would be the last to make cheap of her. I will not say another word until I know. But if I am right—which the Lord forbid—we shall both be ashamed of her, Stephen."

"The Lord forbid! The Lord forbid! Amen. I will not hear another word." The farmer snatched up his hat, and made off with a haste unusual for him, while his wife sat down, and crossed her arms, and began to think rather bitterly. For, without any dream of such a possibility, she was jealous sometimes of her own child. Presently the farmer rushed back again, triumphant with a new idea. His eyes were sparkling, and his step full of spring, and a brisk smile shone upon his strong and ruddy face.

"What a pair of stupes we must be to go on so!" he cried, with a couple of bright guineas in his hand. "Mary hath not had a new frock even, going on now for a year and a half. Sophy, it is enough to turn a maid into thinking of any sort of mischief. Take you these and make everything right. I was saving them up for her birthday, but maybe another will turn up by that. My dear, you take them, and never be afeared."

"Stephen, you may leave them, if you like. I shall not be in any haste to let them go. Either give them to the lass yourself, or leave it to me purely. She shall not have a sixpence, unless it is deserved."

"Of course I leave it in your hands, wife. I never come between you and your children. But young folk go piping always after money now; and even our Mary might be turning sad without it."

He hastened off again, without hearing any more; for he knew that some hours of strong labor were before him, and to meet them with a heavy heart would be almost a new thing for him. Some time ago he had begun to hold the plough of heaviness, through the difficult looseness of Willie's staple, and the sudden maritime slope of Jack; yet he held on steadily through all this, with the strength of homely courage. But if in the pride of his heart, his Mary, he should find no better than a crooked furrow, then truly the labor of his latter days would be the dull round of a mill horse.

Now Mary, in total ignorance of that council held concerning her, and even of her mother's bad suspicions, chanced to come in at the front porch door soon after her father set off to his meadows by way of the back yard. Having been hard at work among her flowers, she was come to get a cupful of milk for herself, and the cheery content and general goodwill encouraged by the gardener's gentle craft were smiling on her rosy lips and sparkling in her eyes. Her dress was as plain as plain could be—a lavender twill cut and fitted by herself—and there was not an ornament about her that came from any other hand than Nature's. But simple grace of movement and light elegance of figure, fair curves of gentle face and loving kindness of expression, gladdened with the hope of youth—what did these want with smart dresses, golden brooches, and two guineas? Her mother almost thought of this when she called Mary into the little parlor. And the two guineas lay upon the table.

"Mary, can you spare a little time to talk with me? You seem wonderfully busy, as usual."

"Mother, will you never make allowance for my flowers? They depend upon the weather, and they must have things accordingly."

"Very well; let them think about what they want next, while you sit down a while and talk with me."

The girl was vexed; for to listen to a lecture, already manifest in her mother's eyes, was a far less agreeable job than gardening. And the lecture would have done as well by candle-light, which seldom can be said of any gardening. However, she took off her hat, and sat down, without the least sign of impatience, and without any token of guilt, as her mother saw, and yet stupidly proceeded just the same.

"Mary," she began, with a gaze of stern discretion, which the girl met steadfastly and pleasantly, "you know that I am your own mother, and bound to look after you well, while you are so very young; for though you are sensible some ways, Mary, in years and in experience what are you but a child? Of the traps of the world and the wickedness of people you can have no knowledge. You always think the best of everybody; which is a very proper thing to do, and what I have always brought you up to, and never would dream of discouraging. And with such examples as your father and your mother, you must be perverse to do otherwise. Still, it is my duty to warn you, Mary—and you are getting old enough to want it—that the world is not made up of fathers and mothers, brothers and sisters, and good uncles. There are always bad folk who go prowling about like wolves in—wolves in—what is it —"

"Sheep's clothing," the maiden suggested, with a smile, and then dropped her eyes maliciously.

"How dare you be pert, miss, correcting your own mother? Do I ever catch you reading of your Bible? But you seem to know so much about it, perhaps you have met some of them?"

"How can I tell, mother, when you won't tell me?"

"I tell you, indeed! It is your place to tell me, I think. And what is more, I insist at once upon knowing all about it. What makes you go on in the way that you are doing? Do you take me for a drumledore, you foolish child? On Tuesday afternoon I saw you sewing with a double thread. Your father had potato-eyes upon his plate on Sunday; and which way did I see you trying to hang up a dish-cover? But that is nothing; fifty things you go wandering about in; and always out, on some pretense, as if the roof you were born under was not big enough for you. And then your eyes—I have seen your eyes flash up, as if you were fighting; and the bosom of your Sunday frock was loose in church two buttons; it was not hot at all to speak of, and there was a wasp next pew. All these things make me unhappy, Mary. My darling, tell me what it is."

Mary listened with great amazement to this catalogue of crimes. At the time of their commission she had never even thought of them, although she was vexed with herself when she saw one eye—for in verity that was all—of a potato upon her father's plate. Now she blushed when she heard of the buttons of her frock—which was only done because of tightness, and showed how long she must have worn it; but as to the double thread, she was sure that nothing of that sort could have happened.

"Why, mother dear," she said, quite softly, coming up in her coaxing way, which nobody could resist, because it was true and gentle lovingness, "you know a hundred times more than I do. I have never known of any of the sad mistakes you speak of, except about the potato-eye, and then I had a round-pointed knife. But I want to make no excuses, mother; and there is nothing the matter with me. Tell me what you mean about the wolves."

"My child," said her mother, whose face she was kissing, while they both went on with talking, "it is no good trying to get over me. Either you have something on your mind, or you have not—which is it?"

"Mother, what can I have on my mind? I have never hurt any one, and never mean to do it. Every one is kind to me, and everybody likes me, and of course I like them all again. And I always have plenty to do, in and out, as you take very good care, dear mother. My father loves me, and so do you, a great deal more than I deserve, perhaps. I am happy in a Sunday frock that wants more stuff to button; and I have only one trouble in all the world. When I think of the other girls I see—"

"Never mind them, my dear. What is your one trouble?"

"Mother, as if you could help knowing! About my dear brother Jack, of course. Jack was so wonderfully good to me! I would walk on my hands and knees all the way to York to get a single glimpse of him."

"You would never get as far as the rick-yard hedge. You children talk such nonsense. Jack ran away of his own free-will, and out of downright contrariness. He has repented of it only once, I dare say, and that has been ever since he did it, and every time he thought of it. I wish he was home again, with all my heart, for I can not bear to lose my children. And Jack was as good a boy as need be, when he got everything his own way. Mary, is that your only trouble? Stand where I can see you plainly, and tell me every word the truth. Put your hair back from your eyes now, like the catechism."

"If I were saying fifty catechisms, what more could I do than speak the truth?" Mary asked this with some little vexation, while she stood up proudly before her mother, and clasped her hands behind her back. "I have told you everything I know, except one little thing, which I am not sure about."

"What little thing, if you please? and how can you help being sure about it, positive as you are about everything?"

"Mother, I mean that I have not been sure whether I ought to tell you; and I meant to tell my father first, when there could be no mischief."

"Mary, I can scarcely believe my ears. To tell your father before your mother, and not even him until nothing could be done to stop it, which you call 'mischief!' I insist upon knowing at once what it is. I have felt that you were hiding something. How very unlike you, how unlike a child of mine!"

"You need not disturb yourself, mother dear. It is nothing of any importance to me, though to other people it might be. And that is the reason why I kept it to myself."

"Oh, we shall come to something by-and-by! One would really think you were older than your mother. Now, miss, if you please, let us judge of your discretion. What is it that you have been hiding so long?"

Mary's face grew crimson now, but with anger rather than with shame; she had never thought twice about Robin Lyth with anything warmer than pity, but this was the very way to drive her into dwelling in a mischievous manner upon him.

"What I have been hiding," she said, most distinctly, and steadfastly looking at her mother, "is only that I have had two talks with the great free-trader Robin Lyth."

"That arrant smuggler! That leader of all outlaws! You have been meeting him on the sly!"

"Certainly not. But I met him once by chance; and then, as a matter of business, I was forced to meet him again, dear mother."

"These things are too much for me," Mrs. Anerley said, decisively. "When matters have come to such a pass, I must beg your dear father to see to them."

"Very well, mother; I would rather have it so. May I go now and make an end of my gardening?"

"Certainly—as soon as you have made an end of me, as you must quite have laid your plans to do. I have seen too much to be astonished any more. But to think that a child of mine, my one and only daughter, who looks as if butter wouldn't melt in her mouth, should be hand in glove with the wickedest smuggler of the age, the rogue everybody shoots at—but can not hit him, because he was born to be hanged—-the by-name, the by-word, the by-blow, Robin Lyth!" Mrs. Anerley covered her face with both hands.

"How would you like your own second cousin," said Mary, plucking up her spirit, "your own second cousin, Mistress Cockscroft, to hear you speak so of the man that supports them at the risk of his life, every hour of it? He may be doing wrong—it is not for me to say—but he does it very well, and he does it nobly. And what did you show me in your drawer, dear mother? And what did you wear when that very cruel man, Captain Carroway, came here to dine on Sunday?"

"You wicked, undutiful child! Go away! I wish to have nothing more to say to you."

"No, I will not go away," cried Mary, with her resolute spirit in her eyes and brow; "when false and cruel charges are brought against me, I have the right to speak, and I will use it. I am not hand in glove with Robin Lyth, or any other Robin. I think a little more of myself than that. If I have done any wrong, I will meet it, and be sorry, and submit to any punishment. I ought to have told you before, perhaps; that is the worst you can say of it. But I never attached much importance to it; and when a man is hunted so, was I to join his enemies? I have only seen him twice: the first time by purest accident, and the second time to give him back a piece of his own property. And I took my brother with me; but he ran away, as usual."

"Of course, of course. Every one to blame but you, miss. However, we shall see what your father has to say. You have very nearly taken all my breath away; but I shall expect the whole sky to tumble in upon us if Captain Anerley approves of Robin Lyth as a sweetheart for his daughter."

"I never thought of Captain Lyth; and Captain Lyth never thought of me. But I can tell you one thing, mother—if you wanted to make me think of him, you could not do it better than by speaking so unjustly."

"After that perhaps you will go back to your flowers. I have heard that they grow very fine ones in Holland. Perhaps you have got some smuggled tulips, my dear."

Mary did not condescend to answer, but said to herself, as she went to work again, "Tulips in August! That is like the rest of it. However, I am not going to be put out, when I feel that I have not done a single bit of harm." And she tried to be happy with her flowers, but could not enter into them as before.

Mistress Anerley was as good as her word, at the very first opportunity. Her husband returned from the clover-stack tired and hungry, and angry with a man who had taken too much beer, and ran at him with a pitchfork; angry also with his own son Willie for not being anywhere in the way to help. He did not complain; and his wife knew at once that he ought to have done so, to obtain relief. She perceived that her own discourse about their daughter was still on his mind, and would require working off before any more was said about it. And she felt as sure as if she saw it that in his severity against poor Willie— for not doing things that were beneath him—her master would take Mary's folly as a joke, and fall upon her brother, who was so much older, for not going on to protect and guide her. So she kept till after supper-time her mouthful of bad tidings.

And when the farmer heard it all, as he did before going to sleep that night, he had smoked three pipes of tobacco, and was calm; he had sipped (for once in a way) a little Hollands, and was hopeful. And though he said nothing about it, he felt that without any order of his, or so much as the faintest desire to be told of it, neither of these petty comforts would bear to be rudely examined of its duty. He hoped for the best, and he believed the best, and if the king was cheated, why, his loyal subject was the same, and the women were their masters.

"Have no fear, no fear," he muttered back through the closing gate of sleep; "Mary knows her business—business—" and he buzzed it off into a snore.

In the morning, however, he took a stronger and more serious view of the case, pronouncing that Mary was only a young lass, and no one could ever tell about young lasses. And he quite fell into his wife's suggestion, that the maid could be spared till harvest-time, of which (even with the best of weather) there was little chance now for another six weeks, the season being late and backward. So it was resolved between them both that the girl should go on the following day for a visit to her uncle Popplewell, some miles the other side of Filey. No invitation was required; for Mr. and Mrs. Popplewell, a snug and comfortable pair, were only too glad to have their niece, and had often wanted to have her altogether; but the farmer would never hear of that.

CHAPTER XV

CAUGHT AT LAST

While these little things were doing thus, the coast from the mouth of the Tees to that of Humber, and even the inland parts, were in a great stir of talk and work about events impending. It must not be thought that Flamborough, although it was Robin's dwelling-place—so far as he had any—was the principal scene of his operations, or the stronghold of his enterprise. On the contrary, his liking was for quiet coves near Scarborough, or even to the north of Whitby, when the wind and tide were suitable. And for this there were many reasons which are not of any moment now.

One of them showed fine feeling and much delicacy on his part. He knew that Flamborough was a place of extraordinary honesty, where every one of his buttons had been safe, and would have been so forever; and strictly as he believed in the virtue of his own free importation, it was impossible for him not to learn that certain people thought otherwise, or acted as if they did so. From the troubles which such doubts might cause, he strove to keep the natives free.

Flamburians scarcely understood this largeness of good-will to them. Their instincts told them that free trade was every Briton's privilege; and they had the finest set of donkeys on the coast for landing it. But none the more did any of them care to make a movement toward it. They were satisfied with their own old way—to cast the net their father cast, and bait the hook as it was baited on their good grandfather's thumb.

Yet even Flamborough knew that now a mighty enterprise was in hand. It was said, without any contradiction, that young Captain Robin had laid a wager of one hundred guineas with the worshipful mayor of Scarborough and the commandant of the castle, that before the new moon he would land on Yorkshire coast, without firing pistol or drawing steel, free goods to the value of two thousand pounds, and carry them inland safely. And Flamborough believed that he would do it.

Dr. Upround's house stood well, as rectories generally contrive to do. No place in Flamborough parish could hope to swindle the wind of its vested right, or to embezzle much treasure of the sun, but the parsonage made a good effort to do both, and sometimes for three days together got the credit of succeeding. And the dwellers therein, who felt the edge of the difference outside their own walls, not only said but thoroughly believed that they lived in a little Goshen.

For the house was well settled in a wrinkle of the hill expanding southward, and encouraging the noon. From the windows a pleasant glimpse might be obtained of the broad and tranquil anchorage, peopled with white or black, according as the sails went up or down; for the rectory stood to the southward of the point, as the rest of Flamborough surely must have stood, if built by any other race than armadillos. But to see all those vessels, and be sure what they were doing, the proper place was a little snug "gazebo," chosen and made by the doctor himself, near the crest of the gully he inhabited.

Here upon a genial summer day—when it came, as it sometimes dared to do—was the finest little nook upon the Yorkshire coast for watching what Virgil calls "the sail-winged sea." Not that a man could see round the Head, unless his own were gifted with very crooked eyes; but without doing that (which would only have disturbed the tranquillity of his prospect) there was plenty to engage him in the peaceful spread of comparatively waveless waters. Here might he see long vessels rolling, not with great misery, but just enough to make him feel happy in the firmness of his bench, and little jolly-boats it was more jolly to be out of, and faraway heads giving genial bobs, and sea-legs straddled in predicaments desirable rather for study than for practice. All was highly picturesque and nice, and charming for the critic who had never got to do it.

"Now, papa, you must come this very moment," cried Miss Janetta Upround, the daughter of the house, and indeed the only daughter, with a gush of excitement, rushing into the study of this deeply read divine; "there is something doing that I can not understand. You must bring up the spy-glass at once and explain. I am sure that there is something very wrong."

"In the parish, my dear?" the rector asked, with a feeble attempt at malice, for he did not want to be disturbed just now, and for weeks he had tried (with very poor success) to make Janetta useful; for she had no gift in that way.

"No, not in the parish at all, papa, unless it runs out under water, as I am certain it ought to do, and make every one of those ships pay tithe. If the law was worth anything, they would have to do it. They get all the good out of our situation, and they save whole thousands of pounds at a time, and they never pay a penny, nor even hoist a flag, unless the day is fine, and the flag wants drying. But come along, papa, now. I really can not wait; and they will have done it all without us."

"Janetta, take the glass and get the focus. I will come presently, presently. In about two minutes—by the time that you are ready."

"Very well, papa. It is very good of you. I see quite clearly what you want to do; and I hope you will do it. But you promise not to play another game now?"

"My dear, I will promise that with pleasure. Only do please be off about your business."

The rector was a most inveterate and insatiable chess-player. In the household, rather than by it, he was, as a matter of lofty belief, supposed to be deeply engaged with theology, or magisterial questions of almost equal depth, or (to put it at the lowest) parochial affairs, the while he was solidly and seriously engaged in getting up the sound defense to some Continental gambit. And this, not only to satisfy himself upon some point of theory, but from a nearer and dearer point of view—for he never did like to be beaten.

At present he was laboring to discover the proper defense to a new and slashing form of the Algaier gambit, by means of which Robin Lyth had won every game in which he had the move, upon their last encounter. The great free-trader, while a boy, had shown an especial aptitude for chess, and even as a child he had seemed to know the men when first, by some accident, he saw them. The rector being struck by this exception to the ways of childhood— whose manner it is to take chess-men for "dollies," or roll them about like nine-pins—at once included in the education of "Izunsabe," which he took upon himself, a course of elemental doctrine in the one true game. And the boy fought his way up at such a pace that he jumped from odds of queen and rook to pawn and two moves in less than two years. And now he could almost give odds to his tutor, though he never presumed to offer them; and trading as he did with enlightened merchants of large Continental sea-ports, who had plenty of time on their hands and played well, he imported new openings of a dash and freedom which swallowed the ground up under the feet of the steady-going players, who had never seen a book upon their favorite subject. Of course it was competent to all these to decline such fiery onslaught; but chivalry and the true love of analysis (which without may none play chess) compelled the acceptance of the challenge, even with a trembling forecast of the taste of dust.

"Never mind," said Dr. Upround, as he rose and stretched himself, a good straight man of threescore years, with silver hair that shone like silk; "it has not come to me yet; but it must, with a little more perseverance. At Cambridge I beat everybody; and who is this uncircumcised—at least, I beg his pardon, for I did myself baptize him—but who is Robin Lyth, to mate his pastor and his master? All these gambits are like a night attack. If once met properly and expelled, you are in the very heart of the enemy's camp. He has left his own watch-fires to rush at yours. The next game I play, I shall be sure to beat him."

Fully convinced of this great truth, he took a strong oak staff and hastened to obey his daughter. Miss Janetta Upround had not only learned by nature, but also had been carefully taught by her parents, and by every one, how to get her own way always, and to be thanked for taking it. But she had such a happy nature, full of kindness and good-will, that other people's wishes always seemed to flow into her own, instead of being swept aside. Over her father her government was in no sort constitutional, nor even a quiet despotism sweetened with liberal illusions, but as pure a piece of autocracy as the Continent could itself contain, in the time of this first Napoleon.

"Papa, what a time you have been, to be sure!" she exclaimed, as the doctor came gradually up, probing his way in perfect leisure, and fragrant still of that gambit; "one would think that your parish was on dry land altogether, while the better half of it, as they call themselves—though the women are in righteousness the better half a hundredfold—"

"My dear, do try to talk with some little sense of arithmetic, if no other. A hundredfold the half would be the unit multiplied by fifty. Not to mention that there can be no better half—"

"Yes, there can, papa, ever so many; and you may see one in mamma every day. Now you put one eye to this glass, and the half is better than the whole. With both, you see nothing; with one, you see better, fifty times better, than with both before. Don't talk of arithmetic after that. It is algebra now, and quod demonstrandum."

"To reason with the less worthy gender is degeneration of reason. What would they have said in the Senate-house, Janetta? However, I will obey your orders. What am I to look at?"

"A tall and very extraordinary man, striking his arms out, thus and thus. I never saw any one looking so excited; and he flourishes a long sword now and again, as if he would like to cut everybody's head off. There he has been going from ship to ship, for an hour or more, with a long white boat, and a lot of men jumping after him. Every one seems to be scared of him, and he stumps along the deck just as if he were on springs, and one spring longer than the other. You see that heavy brig outside the rest, painted with ten port-holes; well, she began to make sail and run away, but he fired a gun—quite a real cannon—and she had to come back again and drop her colors. Oh, is it some very great admiral, papa? Perhaps Lord Nelson himself; I would go and be seasick for three days to see Lord Nelson. Papa, it must be Lord Nelson."

"My dear, Lord Nelson is a little, short man, with a very brisk walk, and one arm gone. Now let me see who this can be. Whereabout is he now, Janetta?"

"Do you see that clumsy-looking schooner, papa, just behind a pilot-boat? He is just in front of her foremast—making such a fuss—"

"What eyes you have got, my child! You see better without the glass than I do with it.—Oh, now I have him! Why, I might have guessed. Of course it is that very active man and vigilant officer Lieutenant Carroway."

"Captain Carroway from Bridlington, papa? Why, what can he be doing with such authority? I have often heard of him, but I thought he was only a coast-guard."

"He is, as you say, showing great authority, and, I fear, using very bad language, for which he is quite celebrated. However, the telescope refuses to repeat it, for which it is much to be commended. But every allowance must be made for a man who has to deal with a wholly uncultivated race, and not of natural piety, like ours."

"Well, papa, I doubt if ours have too much, though you always make the best of them. But let me look again, please; and do tell me what he can be doing there."

"You know that the revenue officers must take the law into their own hands sometimes. There have lately been certain rumors of some contraband proceedings on the Yorkshire coast. Not in Flamborough parish, of course, and perhaps—probably, I may say—a long way off—-"

"Papa dear, will you never confess that free trade prevails and flourishes greatly even under your own dear nose?"

"Facts do not warrant me in any such assertion. If the fact were so, it must have been brought officially before me. I decline to listen to uncharitable rumors. But however that matter may be, there are officers on the spot to deal with it. My commission as a justice of the peace gives me no cognizance of offenses—if such there are—upon the high seas. Ah! you see something particular; my dear, what is it?"

"Captain Carroway has found something, or somebody, of great importance. He has got a man by the collar, and he is absolutely dancing with delight. Ah! there he goes, dragging him along the deck as if he were a cod-fish or a conger. And now, I declare, he is lashing his arms and legs with a great thick rope. Papa, is that legal, without even a warrant?"

"I can hardly say how far his powers may extend, and he is just the man to extend them farther. I only hope not to be involved in the matter. Maritime law is not my province."

"But, papa, it is much within three miles of the shore, if that has got anything to do with it. My goodness me! They are all coming here; I am almost sure that they will apply to you. Yes, two boat-loads of people, racing to get their oars out, and to be here first. Where are your spectacles, dear papa? You had better go and get up the law before they come. You will scarcely have time, they are coming so fast—a white boat and a black boat. The prisoner is in the white boat, and the officer has got him by the collar still. The men in the white boat will want to commit him, and the men in the black boat are his friends, no doubt, coming for a habeas corpus—"

"My dear, what nonsense you do talk! What has a simple justice of the peace—"

"Never mind that, papa; my facts are sound—sounder than yours about smuggling, I fear. But do hurry in, and get up the law. I will go and lock both gates, to give you more time."

"Do nothing of the kind, Janetta. A magistrate should be accessible always; and how can I get up the law, without knowing what it is to be about—or even a clerk to help me? And perhaps they are not coming here at all. They may be only landing their prisoner."

"If that were it, they would not be coming so, but rowing toward the proper place, Bridlington Quay, where their station-house is. Papa, you are in for it, and I am getting eager. May I come and hear all about it? I should be a great support to you, you know. And they would tell the truth so much better!"

"Janetta, what are you dreaming of? It may even be a case of secrecy."

"Secrecy, papa, with two boat-loads of men and about thirty ships involved in it! Oh, do let me hear all about it!"

"Whatever it may be, your presence is not required, and would be improper. Unless I should happen to want a book; and in that case I might ring for you."

"Oh, do, papa, do! No one else can ever find them. Promise me now that you will want a book. If I am not there, there will be no justice done. I wish you severely to reprimand, whatever the facts of the case may be, and even to punish, if you can, that tall, lame, violent, ferocious man, for dragging the poor fellow about like that, and cutting him with ropes, when completely needless, and when he was quite at his mercy. It is my opinion that the other man does not deserve one bit of it; and whatever the law may be, papa, your duty is to strain it benevolently, and question every syllable upon the stronger side."

"Perhaps I had better resign, my dear, upon condition that you shall be appointed in the stead of me. It might be a popular measure, and would secure universal justice."

"Papa, I would do justice to myself—which is a thing you never do. But here, they are landing; and they hoist him out as if he were a sack, or a thing without a joint. They could scarcely be harder with a man compelled to be hanged to-morrow morning."

"Condemned is what you mean, Janetta. You never will understand the use of words. What a nice magistrate you would make!"

"There can be no more correct expression. Would any man be hanged if he were not compelled? Papa, you say the most illegal things sometimes. Now please to go in and get up your legal points. Let me go and meet those people for you. I will keep them waiting till you are quite ready."

"My dear, you will go to your room, and try to learn a little patience. You begin to be too pat with your own opinions, which in a young lady is ungraceful. There, you need not cry, my darling, because your opinions are always sensible, and I value them very highly; but still you must bear in mind that you are but a girl."

"And behave accordingly, as they say. Nobody can do more so. But though I am only a girl, papa, can you put your hand upon a better one?"

"Certainly not, my dear; for going down hill, I can always depend on you."

Suiting the action to the word, Dr. Upround, whose feet were a little touched with gout, came down from his outlook to his kitchen-garden, and thence through the shrubbery back to his own study, where, with a little sigh, he put away his chess-men, and heartily hoped that it might not be his favorite adversary who was coming before him to be sent to jail. For although the good rector had a warm regard, and even affection, for Robin Lyth, as a waif cast into his care, and then a pupil wonderfully apt (which breeds love in the teacher), and after that a most gallant and highly distinguished young parishioner—with all this it was a difficulty for him to be ignorant that the law was adverse. More than once he had striven hard to lead the youth into some better path of life, and had even induced him to "follow the sea" for a short time in the merchant service. But the force of nature and of circumstances had very soon prevailed again, and Robin returned to his old pursuits with larger experience, and seamanship improved.

A violent ringing at the gate bell, followed by equal urgency upon the front door, apprised the kind magistrate of a sharp call on his faculties, and perhaps a most unpleasant one. "The poor boy!" he said to himself—"poor boy! From Carroway's excitement I greatly fear that it is indeed poor Robin. How many a grand game have we had! His new variety of that fine gambit scarcely beginning to be analyzed; and if I commit him to the meeting next week, when shall we ever meet again? It will seem as if I did it because he won three games; and I certainly was a little vexed with him. However, I must be stern, stern, stern. Show them in, Betsy; I am quite prepared."

A noise, and a sound of strong language in the hall, and a dragging of something on the oil-cloth, led up to the entry of a dozen rough men, pushed on by at least another dozen.

"You will have the manners to take off your hats," said the magistrate, with all his dignity; "not from any undue deference to me, but common respect to his Majesty."

"Off with your covers, you sons of"—something, shouted a loud voice; and then the lieutenant, with his blade still drawn, stood before them.

"Sheathe your sword, Sir," said Dr. Upround, in a voice which amazed the officer.

"I beg your Worship's pardon," he began, with his grim face flushing purple, but his sword laid where it should have been; "but if you knew half of the worry I have had, you would not care to rebuke me. Cadman, have you got him by the neck? Keep your knuckles into him, while I make my deposition."

"Cast that man free, I receive no depositions with a man half strangled before me."

The men of the coast-guard glanced at their commander, and receiving a surly nod, obeyed. But the prisoner could not stand as yet; he gasped for breath, and some one set him on a chair.

"Your Worship, this is a mere matter of form," said Carroway, still keeping eyes on his prey; "if I had my own way, I would not trouble you at all, and I believe it to be quite needless. For this man is an outlaw felon, and not entitled to any grace of law; but I must obey my orders."

"Certainly you must, Lieutenant Carroway, even though you are better acquainted with the law. You are ready to be sworn? Take this book, and follow me."

This being done, the worthy magistrate prepared to write down what the gallant officer might say, which, in brief, came to this, that having orders to seize Robin Lyth wherever he might find him, and having sure knowledge that said Robin was on board of a certain schooner vessel, the Elizabeth, of Goole, the which he had laden with goods liable to duty, he, Charles Carroway, had gently laid hands on him, and brought him to the nearest justice of the peace, to obtain an order of commitment.

All this, at fifty times the length here given, Lieutenant Carroway deposed on oath, while his Worship, for want of a clerk, set it down in his own very neat handwriting. But several very coaly-looking men, who could scarcely be taught to keep silence, observed that the magistrate smiled once or twice; and this made them wait a bit, and wink at one another.

"Very clear indeed, Lieutenant Carroway," said Dr. Upround, with spectacles on nose. "Good Sir, have the kindness to sign your deposition. It may become my duty to commit the prisoner, upon identification. Of that I must have evidence, confirmatory evidence. But first we will hear what he has to say. Robin Lyth, stand forward."

"Me no Robin Lyth, Sar; no Robin man or woman," cried the captive, trying very hard to stand; "me only a poor Francais, make liberty to what you call—row, row, sweem, sweem, sail, sail, from la belle France; for why, for why, there is no import to nobody."

"Your Worship, he is always going on about imports," Cadman said, respectfully; "that is enough to show who he is."

"You may trust me to know him," cried Lieutenant Carroway. "My fine fellow, no more of that stuff! He can pass himself off for any countryman whatever. He knows all their jabber, Sir, better than his own. Put a cork between his teeth, Hackerbody. I never did see such a noisy rogue. He is Robin Lyth all over."

"I'll be blest if he is, nor under nayther," cried the biggest of the coaly men; "this here froggy come out of a Chaise and Mary as had run up from Dunkirk. I know Robin Lyth as well as our own figure-head. But what good to try reason with that there revenue hofficer?"

At this, all his friends set a good laugh up, and wanted to give him a cheer for such a speech; but that being hushed, they were satisfied with condemning his organs of sight and their own quite fairly.

"Lieutenant Carroway," his Worship said, amidst an impressive silence, "I greatly fear that you have allowed zeal, my dear Sir, to outrun discretion. Robin Lyth is a young, and in many ways highly respected, parishioner of mine. He may have been guilty of casual breaches of the laws concerning importation—laws which fluctuate from year to year, and require deep knowledge of legislation both to observe and to administer. I heartily trust that you may not suffer from having discharged your duty in a manner most truly exemplary, if only the example had been the right one. This gentleman is no more Robin Lyth than I am."

CHAPTER XVI

DISCIPLINE ASSERTED

As soon as his troublesome visitors were gone, the rector sat down in his deep arm-chair, laid aside his spectacles, and began to think. His face, while he thought, lost more and more of the calm and cheerful expression which made it so pleasant a face to gaze upon; and he sighed, without knowing it, at some dark ideas, and gave a little shake of his grand old head. The revenue officer had called his favorite pupil and cleverest parishioner "a felon outlaw;" and if that were so, Robin Lyth was no less than a convicted criminal, and must not be admitted within his doors. Formerly the regular penalty for illicit importation had been the forfeiture of the goods when caught, and the smugglers (unless they made resistance or carried fire-arms) were allowed to escape and retrieve their bad luck, which they very soon contrived to do. And as yet, upon this part of the coast, they had not been guilty of atrocious crimes, such as the smugglers of Sussex and Hampshire—who must have been utter fiends—committed, thereby raising all the land against them. Dr. Upround had heard of no proclamation, exaction, or even capias issued against this young free-trader; and he knew well enough that the worst offenders were not the bold seamen who contracted for the run, nor the people of the coast who were hired for the carriage, but the rich indwellers who provided all the money, and received the lion's share of all the profits. And with these the law never even tried to deal. However, the magistrate-parson resolved that, in spite of all the interest of tutorship and chess-play, and even all the influence of his wife and daughter (who were hearty admirers of brave smuggling), he must either reform this young man, or compel him to keep at a distance, which would be very sad.

Meanwhile the lieutenant had departed in a fury, which seemed to be incapable of growing any worse. Never an oath did he utter all the way to the landing where his boat was left; and his men, who knew how much that meant, were afraid to do more than just wink at one another. Even the sailors of the collier schooner forbore to jeer him, until he was afloat, when they gave him three fine rounds of mock cheers, to which the poor Frenchman contributed a shriek. For this man had been most inhospitably treated, through his strange but undeniable likeness to a perfidious Briton.

"Home!" cried the officer, glowering at those fellows, while his men held their oars, and were ready to rush at them. "Home, with a will! Give way, men!" And not another word he spoke, till they touched the steps at

Bridlington. Then he fixed stern eyes upon Cadman, who vainly strove to meet them, and he said, "Come to me in one hour and a half." Cadman touched his hat without an answer, saw to the boat, and then went home along the quay.

Carroway, though of a violent temper, especially when laughed at, was not of that steadfast and sedentary wrath which chews the cud of grievances, and feeds upon it in a shady place. He had a good wife—though a little overclean—and seven fine-appetited children, who gave him the greatest pleasure in providing victuals. Also, he had his pipe, and his quiet corners, sacred to the atmosphere and the private thoughts of Carroway. And here he would often be ambitious even now, perceiving no good reason why he might not yet command a line-of-battle ship, and run up his own flag, and nobly tread his own lofty quarter-deck. If so, he would have Mrs. Carroway on board, and not only on the boards, but at them; so that a challenge should be issued every day for any other ship in all the service to display white so wholly spotless, and black so void of streakiness. And while he was dwelling upon personal matters—which, after all, concerned the nation most—he had tried very hard to discover any reason (putting paltry luck aside) why Horatio Nelson should be a Lord, and what was more to the purpose, an admiral, while Charles Carroway (his old shipmate, and in every way superior, who could eat him at a mouthful, if only he were good enough) should now be no more than a 'long-shore lieutenant, and a Jonathan Wild of the revenue. However, as for envying Nelson, the Lord knew that he would not give his little Geraldine's worst frock for all the fellow's grand coat of arms, and freedom in a snuff-box, and golden shields, and devices, this, that, and the other, with Bona Robas to support them.

To this conclusion he was fairly come, after a good meal, and with the second glass of the finest Jamaica pine-apple rum—which he drank from pure principle, because it was not smuggled—steaming and scenting the blue curls of his pipe, when his admirable wife came in to say that on no account would she interrupt him.

"My dear, I am busy, and am very glad to hear it. Pish! where have I put all those accounts?"

"Charles, you are not doing any accounts. When you have done your pipe and glass, I wish to say a quiet word or two. I am sure that there is not a woman in a thousand—"

"Matilda, I know it. Nor one in fifty thousand. You are very good at figures: will you take this sheet away with you? Eight o'clock will be quite time enough for it."

128

"My dear, I am always too pleased to do whatever I can to help you. But I must talk to you now; really I must say a few words about something, tired as you may be, Charles, and well deserving of a little good sleep, which you never seem able to manage in bed. You told me, you know, that you expected Cadman, that surly, dirty fellow, who delights to spoil my stones, and would like nothing better than to take the pattern out of our drawing-room Kidderminster. Now I have a reason for saying something. Charles, will you listen to me once, just once?"

"I never do anything else," said the husband, with justice, and meaning no mischief.

"Ah! how very seldom you hear me talk; and when I do, I might just as well address the winds! But for once, my dear, attend, I do implore you. That surly, burly Cadman will be here directly, and I know that you are much put out with him. Now I tell you he is dangerous, savagely dangerous; I can see it in his unhealthy skin. Oh, Charles, where have you put down your pipe? I cleaned that shelf this very morning! How little I thought when I promised to be yours that you ever would knock out your ashes like that! But do bear in mind, dear, whatever you do, if anything happened to you, what ever would become of all of us? All your sweet children and your faithful wife—I declare you have made two great rings with your tumbler upon the new cover of the table."

"Matilda, that has been done ever so long. But I am almost certain this tumbler leaks."

"So you always say; just as if I would allow it. You never will think of simply wiping the rim every time you use it; when I put you a saucer for your glass, you forget it; there never was such a man, I do believe. I shall have to stop the rum and water altogether."

"No, no, no. I'll do anything you like. I'll have a tumbler made with a saucer to it—I'll buy a piece of oil-cloth the size of a foretop-sail—I'll—"

"Charles, no nonsense, if you please: as if I were ever unreasonable! But your quickness of temper is such that I dread what you may say to that Cadman. Remember what opportunities he has, dear. He might shoot you in the dark any night, my darling, and put it upon the smugglers. I entreat you not to irritate the man, and make him your enemy. He is so spiteful; and I should be in terror the whole night long."

"Matilda, in the house you may command me as you please—even in my own cuddy here. But as regards my duty, you know well that I permit no interference. And I should have expected you to have more sense. A pretty officer I should be if I were afraid of my own men! When a man is to blame, I tell him so, in good round language, and shall do so now. This man is greatly to blame, and I doubt whether to consider him a fool or a rogue. If it were not that he has seven children, as we have, I would discharge him this very night."

"Charles, I am very sorry for his seven children, but our place is to think of our own seven first. I beg you, I implore you, to discharge the man; for he has not the courage to harm you, I believe, except with the cowardly advantage he has got. Now promise me either to say nothing to him, or to discharge him, and be done with him."

"Matilda, of such things you know nothing; and I can not allow you to say any more."

"Very well, very well. I know my duty. I shall sit up and pray every dark night you are out, and the whole place will go to the dogs, of course. Of the smugglers I am not afraid one bit, nor of any honest fighting, such as you are used to. But oh, my dear Charles, the very bravest man can do nothing against base treachery."

"To dream of such things shows a bad imagination," Carroway answered, sternly; but seeing his wife's eyes fill with tears, he took her hand gently, and begged her pardon, and promised to be very careful, "I am the last man to be rash," he said, "after getting so many more kicks than coppers. I never had a fellow under my command who would lift a finger to harm me. And you must remember, my darling Tilly, that I command Englishmen, not Lascars."

With this she was forced to be content, to the best of her ability; and Geraldine ran bouncing in from school to fill her father's pipe for him; so that by the time John Cadman came, his commander had almost forgotten the wrath created by the failure of the morning. But unluckily Cadman had not forgotten the words and the look he received before his comrades.

"Here I am, Sir, to give an account of myself," he said, in an insolent tone, having taken much liquor to brace him for the meeting. "Is it your pleasure to say out what you mean?"

"Yes, but not here. You will follow me to the station." The lieutenant took his favorite staff, and set forth, while his wife, from the little window, watched him with a very anxious gaze. She saw her husband stride in front with the long rough gait she knew so well, and the swing of his arms which always showed that his temper was not in its best condition; and behind him Cadman slouched along, with his shoulders up and his red hands clinched. And the poor wife sadly went back to work, for her life was a truly anxious one.

130

The station, as it was rather grandly called, was a hut, about the size of a four-post bed, upon the low cliff, undermined by the sea, and even then threatened to be swept away. Here was a tall flag-staff for signals, and a place for a beacon-light when needed, and a bench with a rest for a spy-glass. In the hut itself were signal flags, and a few spare muskets, and a keg of bullets, with maps and codes hung round the wall, and flint and tinder, and a good many pipes, and odds and ends on ledges. Carroway was very proud of this place, and kept the key strictly in his own pocket, and very seldom allowed a man to pass through the narrow doorway. But he liked to sit inside, and see them looking desirous to come in.

"Stand there, Cadman," he said, as soon as he had settled himself in the one hard chair; and the man, though thoroughly primed for revolt, obeyed the old habit, and stood outside.

"Once more you have misled me, Cadman, and abused my confidence. More than that, you have made me a common laughing-stock for scores of fools, and even for a learned gentleman, magistrate of divinity. I was not content with your information until you confirmed it by letters you produced from men well known to you, as you said, and even from the inland trader who had contracted for the venture. The schooner Elizabeth, of Goole, disguised as a collier, was to bring to, with Robin Lyth on board of her, and the goods in her hold under covering of coal, and to run the goods at the South Flamborough landing this very night. I have searched the Elizabeth from stem to stern, and the craft brought up alongside of her; and all I have found is a wretched Frenchman, who skulked so that I made sure of him, and not a blessed anker of foreign brandy, nor even a forty-pound bag of tea. You had that packet of letters in your neck-tie. Hand them to me this moment—"

"If your Honor has made up your mind to think that a sailor of the Royal Navy—"

"Cadman, none of that! No lick-spittle lies to me; those letters, that I may establish them! You shall have them back, if they are right. And I will pay you a half crown for the loan."

"If I was to leave they letters in your hand, I could never hold head up in Burlington no more."

"That is no concern of mine. Your duty is to hold up your head with me, and those who find you in bread and butter."

"Precious little butter I ever gets, and very little bread to speak of. The folk that does the work gets nothing. Them that does nothing gets the name and game."

"Fellow, no reasoning, but obey me!" Carroway shouted, with his temper rising. "Hand over those letters, or you leave the service."

"How can I give away another man's property?" As he said these words, the man folded his arms, as who should say, "That is all you get out of me."

"Is that the way you speak to your commanding officer? Who owns those letters, then, according to your ideas?"

"Butcher Hewson; and he says that you shall have them as soon as he sees the money for his little bill."

This was a trifle too much for Carroway. Up he jumped with surprising speed, took one stride through the station door, and seizing Cadman by the collar, shook him, wrung his ear with the left hand, which was like a pair of pincers, and then with the other flung him backward as if he were an empty bag. The fellow was too much amazed to strike, or close with him, or even swear, but received the vehement impact without any stay behind him. So that he staggered back, hat downward, and striking one heel on a stone, fell over the brink of the shallow cliff to the sand below.

The lieutenant, who never had thought of this, was terribly scared, and his wrath turned cold. For although the fall was of no great depth, and the ground at the bottom so soft, if the poor man had struck it poll foremost, as he fell, it was likely that his neck was broken. Without any thought of his crippled heel, Carroway took the jump himself.

As soon as he recovered from the jar, which shook his stiff joints and stiffer back, he ran to the coast-guardsman and raised him, and found him very much inclined to swear. This was a good sign, and the officer was thankful, and raised him in the gravelly sand, and kindly requested him to have it out, and to thank the Lord as soon as he felt better. But Cadman, although he very soon came round, abstained from every token of gratitude. Falling with his mouth wide open in surprise, he had filled it with gravel of inferior taste, as a tidy sewer pipe ran out just there, and at every execration he discharged a little.

"What can be done with a fellow so ungrateful?" cried the lieutenant, standing stiffly up again; "nothing but to let him come back to his manners. Hark you, John Cadman, between your bad words, if a glass of hot grog will restore your right wits, you can come up and have it, when your clothes are brushed."

With these words Carroway strode off to his cottage, without even deigning to look back, for a minute had been enough to show him that no very serious harm was done.

The other man did not stir until his officer was out of sight; and then he arose and rubbed himself, but did not care to go for his rummer of hot grog.

"I must work this off," the lieutenant said, as soon as he had told his wife, and received his scolding; "I can not sit down; I must do something. My mind is becoming too much for me, I fear. Can you expect me to be laughed at? I shall take a little sail in the boat; the wind suits, and I have a particular reason. Expect me, my dear, when you see me."

In half an hour the largest boat, which carried a brass swivel-gun in her bows, was stretching gracefully across the bay, with her three white sails flashing back the sunset. The lieutenant steered, and he had four men with him, of whom Cadman was not one, that worthy being left at home to nurse his bruises and his dudgeon. These four men now were quite marvellously civil, having heard of their comrade's plight, and being pleased alike with that and with their commander's prowess. For Cadman was by no means popular among them, because, though his pay was the same as theirs, he always tried to be looked up to; the while his manners were not distinguished, and scarcely could be called polite, when a supper required to be paid for. In derision of this, and of his desire for mastery, they had taken to call him "Boatswain Jack," or "John Boatswain," and provoked him by a subscription to present him with a pig-whistle. For these were men who liked well enough to receive hard words from their betters who were masters of their business, but saw neither virtue nor value in submitting to superior airs from their equals.

The Royal George, as this boat was called, passed through the fleet of quiet vessels, some of which trembled for a second visitation; but not deigning to molest them, she stood on, and rounding Flamborough Head, passed by the pillar rocks called King and Queen, and bore up for the North Landing cove. Here sail was taken in, and oars were manned; and Carroway ordered his men to pull in to the entrance of each of the well-known caves.

To enter these, when any swell is running, requires great care and experience; and the Royal George had too much beam to do it comfortably, even in the best of weather. And now what the sailors call a "chopping sea" had set in with the turn of the tide, although the wind was still off-shore; so that even to lie to at the mouth made rather a ticklish job of it. The men looked at one another, and did not like it, for a badly handled oar would have cast them on the rocks, which are villainously hard and jagged, and would stave in the toughest boat, like biscuit china. However, they durst not say that they feared it; and by skill and steadiness they examined all three caves quite enough to be certain that no boat was in them.

The largest of the three, and perhaps the finest, was the one they first came to, which already was beginning to be called the cave of Robin Lyth. The dome is very high, and sheds down light when the gleam of the sea strikes inward. From the gloomy mouth of it, as far as they could venture, the lapping of the wavelets could be heard all round it, without a boat, or even a balk of wood to break it. Then they tried echo, whose clear answer hesitates where any soft material is; but the shout rang only of hard rock and glassy water. To make assurance doubly sure, they lit a blue-light, and sent it floating through the depths, while they held their position with two boat-hooks and a fender. The cavern was lit up with a very fine effect, but not a soul inside of it to animate the scene. And to tell the truth, the bold invaders were by no means grieved at this; for if there had been smugglers there, it would have been hard to tackle them.

Hauling off safely, which was worse than running in, they pulled across the narrow cove, and rounding the little headland, examined the Church Cave and the Dovecote likewise, and with a like result. Then heartily tired, and well content with having done all that man could do, they set sail again in the dusk of the night, and forged their way against a strong ebb-tide toward the softer waters of Bridlington, and the warmer comfort of their humble homes.

CHAPTER XVII

DELICATE INQUIRIES

A genuine summer day pays a visit nearly once in the season to Flamborough; and when it does come, it has a wonderful effect. Often the sun shines brightly there, and often the air broods hot with thunder; but the sun owes his brightness to sweep of the wind, which sweeps away his warmth as well; while, on the other hand, the thunder-clouds, like heavy smoke capping the headland, may oppress the air with heat, but are not of sweet summer's beauty.

For once, however, the fine day came, and the natives made haste to revile it. Before it was three hours old they had found a hundred and fifty faults with it. Most of the men truly wanted a good sleep, after being lively all the night upon the waves, and the heat and the yellow light came in upon their eyes, and set the flies buzzing all about them. And even the women, who had slept out their time, and talked quietly, like the clock ticking, were vexed with the sun, which kept their kettles from good boiling, and wrote upon their faces the years of their life. But each made allowance for her neighbor's appearance, on the strength of the troubles she had been through. For the matter of that, the sun cared not the selvage of a shadow what was thought of him, but went his bright way with a scattering of clouds and a tossing of vapors anywhere. Upon the few fishermen who gave up hope of sleep, and came to stand dazed in their doorways, the glare of white walls and chalky stones, and dusty roads, produced the same effect as if they had put on their fathers' goggles. Therefore they yawned their way back to their room, and poked up the fire, without which, at Flamborough, no hot weather would be half hot enough.

The children, however, were wide-awake, and so were the washer-women, whose turn it had been to sleep last night for the labors of the morning. These were plying hand and tongue in a little field by the three cross-roads, where gaffers and gammers of by-gone time had set up troughs of proven wood, and the bilge of a long storm-beaten boat, near a pool of softish water. Stout brown arms were roped with curd, and wedding rings looked slippery things, and thumb-nails bordered with inveterate black, like broad beans ripe for planting, shone through a hubbub of snowy froth; while sluicing and wringing and rinsing went on over the bubbled and lathery turf; and every handy bush or stub, and every tump of wiry grass, was sheeted with white, like a ship in full sail, and shining in the sun-glare.

From time to time these active women glanced back at their cottages, to see that the hearth was still alive, or at their little daughters squatting under the low wall which kept them from the road, where they had got all the babies to nurse, and their toes and other members to compare, and dandelion chains to make. But from their washing ground the women could not see the hill that brings to the bottom of the village the crooked road from Sewerby. Down that hill came a horseman slowly, with nobody to notice him, though himself on the watch for everybody; and there in the bottom below the first cottage he allowed his horse to turn aside and cool hot feet and leathery lips, in a brown pool spread by Providence for the comfort of wayworn roadsters.

The horse looked as if he had labored far, while his rider was calmly resting; for the cross-felled sutures of his flank were crusted with gray perspiration, and the runnels of his shoulders were dabbled; and now it behooved him to be careful how he sucked the earthy-flavored water, so as to keep time with the heaving of his barrel. In a word, he was drinking as if he would burst—as his hostler at home often told him—but the clever old roadster knew better than that, and timing it well between snorts and coughs, was tightening his girths with deep pleasure.

"Enough, my friend, is as good as a feast," said his rider to him, gently, yet strongly pulling up the far-stretched head, "and too much is worse than a famine."

The horse, though he did not belong to this gentleman, but was hired by him only yesterday, had already discovered that, with him on his back, his own judgment must lie dormant, so that he quietly whisked his tail and glanced with regret at the waste of his drip, and then, with a roundabout step, to prolong the pleasure of this little wade, sadly but steadily out he walked, and, after the necessary shake, began his first invasion of the village. His rider said nothing, but kept a sharp look-out.

Now this was Master Geoffrey Mordacks, of the ancient city of York, a general factor and land agent. What a "general factor" is, or is not, none but himself can pretend to say, even in these days of definition, and far less in times when thought was loose; and perhaps Mr. Mordacks would rather have it so. But any one who paid him well could trust him, according to the ancient state of things. To look at him, nobody would even dare to think that money could be a consideration to him, or the name of it other than an insult. So lofty and steadfast his whole appearance was, and he put back his shoulders so manfully. Upright, stiff, and well appointed with a Roman nose, he rode with the seat of a soldier and the decision of a tax-collector. From his long steel spurs to his hard coned hat not a soft line was there, nor a feeble curve. Stern honesty and strict purpose stamped every open piece of him so strictly that a man in a hedge-row fostering devious principles, and resolved to try them, could do no more than run away, and be thankful for the chance of it.

But in those rough and dangerous times, when thousands of people were starving, the view of a pistol-butt went further than sternest aspect of strong eyes. Geoffrey Mordacks well knew this, and did not neglect his knowledge. The brown walnut stock of a heavy pistol shone above either holster, and a cavalry sword in a leathern scabbard hung within easy reach of hand. Altogether this gentleman seemed not one to be rashly attacked by daylight.

No man had ever dreamed as yet of coming to this outlandish place for pleasure of the prospect. So that when this lonely rider was descried from the washing field over the low wall of the lane, the women made up their minds at once that it must be a justice of the peace, or some great rider of the Revenue, on his way to see Dr. Upandown, or at the least a high constable concerned with some great sheep-stealing. Not that any such crime was known in the village itself of Flamborough, which confined its operations to the sea; but in the outer world of land that malady was rife just now, and a Flamborough man, too fond of mutton, had farmed some sheep on the downs, and lost them, which was considered a judgment on him for willfully quitting ancestral ways.

But instead of turning at the corner where the rector was trying to grow some trees, the stranger kept on along the rugged highway, and between the straggling cottages, so that the women rinsed their arms, and turned round to take a good look at him, over the brambles and furze, and the wall of chalky flint and rubble.

"This is just what I wanted," thought Geoffrey Mordacks: "skill makes luck, and I am always lucky. Now, first of all, to recruit the inner man."

At this time Mrs. Theophila Precious, generally called "Tapsy," the widow of a man who had been lost at sea, kept the "Cod with a Hook in his Gills," the only hostelry in Flamborough village, although there was another toward the Landing. The cod had been painted from life—or death—by a clever old fisherman who understood him, and he looked so firm, and stiff, and hard, that a healthy man, with purse enough to tire of butcher's-meat, might grow in appetite by gazing. Mr. Mordacks pulled up, and fixed steadfast eyes upon this noble fish, the while a score of sharp eyes from the green and white meadow were fixed steadfastly on him.

"How he shines with salt-water! How firm he looks, and his gills as bright as a rose in June! I have never yet tasted a cod at first hand. It is early in the day, but the air is hungry. My expenses are paid, and I mean to live well, for a strong mind will be required. I will have a cut out of that fish, to begin with."

Inditing of this, and of matters even better, the rider turned into the yard of the inn, where an old boat (as usual) stood for a horse-trough, and sea-tubs served as buckets. Strong sunshine glared upon the oversaling tiles, and white buckled walls, and cracky lintels; but nothing showed life, except an old yellow cat, and a pair of house-martins, who had scarcely time to breathe, such a number of little heads flipped out with a white flap under the beak of each, demanding momentous victualling. At these the yellow cat winked with dreamy joyfulness, well aware how fat they would be when they came to tumble out.

"What a place of vile laziness!" grumbled Mr. Mordacks, as he got off his horse, after vainly shouting "Hostler!" and led him to the byre, which did duty for a stable. "York is a lazy hole enough, but the further you go from it, the lazier they get. No energy, no movement, no ambition, anywhere. What a country! what a people! I shall have to go back and enlist the washerwomen."

A Yorkshireman might have answered this complaint, if he thought it deserving of an answer, by requesting Master Mordacks not to be so overquick, but to bide a wee bit longer before he made so sure of the vast superiority of his own wit, for the long heads might prove better than the sharp ones in the end of it. However, the general factor thought that he could not have come to a better place to get all that he wanted out of everybody. He put away his saddle, and the saddlebags and sword, in a rough old sea-chest with a padlock to it, and having a sprinkle of chaff at the bottom. Then he calmly took the key, as if the place were his, gave his horse a rackful of long-cut grass, and presented himself, with a lordly aspect, at the front door of the silent inn. Here he made noise enough to stir the dead; and at the conclusion of a reasonable time, during which she had finished a pleasant dream to the simmering of the kitchen pot, the landlady showed herself in the distance, feeling for her keys with one hand, and rubbing her eyes with the other. This was the head-woman of the village, but seldom tyrannical, unless ill-treated, Widow Precious, tall and square, and of no mean capacity.

"Young mon," with a deep voice she said, "what is tha' deein' wi' aw that clatter?"

"Alas, my dear madam, I am not a young man; and therefore time is more precious to me. I have lived out half my allotted span, and shall never complete it unless I get food."

"T' life o' mon is aw a hoory," replied Widow Precious, with slow truth. "Young mon, what 'll ye hev?"

"Dinner, madam; dinner at the earliest moment. I have ridden far, and my back is sore, and my substance is calling for renewal."

"Ate, ate, ate, that's t' waa of aw menkins. Bud ye maa coom in, and crack o' it."

"Madam, you are most hospitable; and the place altogether seems to be of that description. What a beautiful room! May I sit down? I perceive a fine smell of most delicate soup. Ah, know how to do things at Flamborough."

"Young mon, ye can ha' nune of yon potty. Yon's for mesell and t' childer."

"My excellent hostess, mistake me not. I do not aspire to such lofty pot-luck. I simply referred to it as a proof of your admirable culinary powers."

"Yon's beeg words. What 'll ye hev te ate?"

"A fish like that upon your sign-post, madam, or at least the upper half of him; and three dozen oysters just out of the sea, swimming in their own juice, with lovely melted butter."

"Young mon, hast tha gotten t' brass? Them 'at ates offens forgets t' reck'nin'."

"Yes, madam, I have the needful in abundance. Ecce signum! Which is Latin, madam, for the stamps of the king upon twenty guineas. One to be deposited in your fair hand for a taste, for a sniff, madam, such as I had of your pot."

"Na, na. No tokkins till a' airned them. What ood your Warship be for ating when a' boileth?"

The general factor, perceiving his way, was steadfast to the shoulder cut of a decent cod; and though the full season was scarcely yet come, Mrs. Precious knew where to find one. Oysters there were none, but she gave him boiled limpets, and he thought it the manner of the place that made them tough. After these things he had a duck of the noblest and best that live anywhere in England. Such ducks were then, and perhaps are still, the most remarkable residents of Flamborough. Not only because the air is fine, and the puddles and the dabblings of extraordinary merit, and the wind fluffs up their pretty feathers while alive, as the eloquent poulterer by-and-by will do; but because they have really distinguished birth, and adventurous, chivalrous, and bright blue Norman blood. To such purpose do the gay young Vikings of the world of quack pour in (when the weather and the time of year invite), equipped with red boots and plumes of purple velvet, to enchant the coy lady ducks in soft water, and eclipse the familiar and too legal drake. For a while they revel in the change of scene, the luxury of unsalted mud and scarcely rippled water, and the sweetness and culture of tame dilly-ducks, to whom their brilliant bravery, as well as an air of romance and billowy peril, commends them too seductively. The responsible sire of the pond is grieved, sinks his unappreciated bill into his back, and vainly reflects upon the vanity of love.

From a loftier point of view, however, this is a fine provision; and Mr. Mordacks always took a lofty view of everything.

"A beautiful duck, ma'am; a very grand duck!" in his usual loud and masterful tone, he exclaimed to Widow Precious. "I understand your question now as to my ability to pay for him. Madam, he is worth a man's last shilling. A goose is a smaller and a coarser bird. In what manner do you get them?"

"They gets their own sells, wi' the will of the Lord. What will your Warship be for ating, come after?"

"None of your puddings and pies, if you please, nor your excellent jellies and custards. A red Dutch cheese, with a pat of fresh butter, and another imperial pint of ale."

"Now yon is what I call a man," thought Mrs. Precious, having neither pie nor pudding, as Master Mordacks was well aware; "aisy to please, and a' knoweth what a' wants. A' mought 'a been born i' Flaambro. A' maa baide for a week, if a' hath the tokkins."

Mr. Mordacks felt that he had made his footing; but he was not the man to abide for a week where a day would suit his purpose. His rule was never to beat about the bush when he could break through it, and he thought that he saw his way to do so now. Having finished his meal, he set down his knife with a bang, sat upright in the oaken chair, and gazed in a bold yet pleasant manner at the sturdy hostess.

"You are wondering what has brought me here. That I will tell you in a very few words. Whatever I do is straightforward, madam; and all the world may know it. That has been my character throughout life; and in that respect I differ from the great bulk of mankind. You Flamborough folk, however, are much of the very same nature as I am. We ought to get on well together. Times are very bad—very bad indeed. I could put a good trifle of money in your way; but you tell the truth without it, which is very, very noble. Yet people with a family have duties to discharge to them, and must sacrifice their feelings to affection. Fifty guincas is a tidy little figure, ma'am. With the famine growing in the land, no parent should turn his honest back upon fifty guineas. And to get the gold, and do good at the same time, is a very rare chance indeed."

This speech was too much for Widow Precious to carry to her settled judgment, and get verdict in a breath. She liked it, on the whole, but yet there might be many things upon the other side; so she did what Flamborough generally does, when desirous to consider things, as it generally is. That is to say, she stood with her feet well apart, and her arms akimbo, and her head thrown back to give the hinder part a rest, and no sign of speculation in her eyes, although they certainly were not dull. When these good people are in this frame of mind and body, it is hard to say whether they look more wise or foolish. Mr. Mordacks, impatient as he was, even after so fine a dinner, was not far from catching the infection of slow thought, which spreads itself as pleasantly as that of slow discourse.

"You are heeding me, madam; you have quick wits," he said, without any sarcasm, for she rescued the time from waste by affording a study of the deepest wisdom; "you are wondering how the money is to come, and whether it brings any risk with it. No, Mistress Precious, not a particle of risk. A little honest speaking is the one thing needed."

"The money cometh scores of times more freely fra wrong-doing."

"Your observation, madam, shows a deep acquaintance with the human race. Too often the money does come so; and thus it becomes mere mammon. On such occasions we should wash our hands, and not forget the charities. But the beauty of money, fairly come by, is that we can keep it all. To do good in getting it, and do good with it, and to feel ourselves better in every way, and our dear children happier—this is the true way of considering the question. I saw some pretty little dears peeping in, and wanted to give them a token or two, for I do love superior children. But you called them away, madam. You are too stern."

Widow Precious had plenty of sharp sense to tell her that her children were by no means "pretty dears" to anybody but herself, and to herself only when in a very soft state of mind; at other times they were but three gew-mouthed lasses, and two looby loons with teeth enough for crunching up the dripping-pan.

"Your Warship spaketh fair," she said; "a'most too fair, I'm doubting. Wad ye say what the maning is, and what name goeth pledge for the fafty poon, Sir?"

"Mistress Precious, my meaning always is plainer than a pikestaff; and as to pledges, the pledge is the hard cash down upon the nail, ma'am."

"Bank-tokkins, mayhap, and I prummeese to paa, with the sign of the Dragon, and a woman among sheeps."

"Madam, a bag of solid gold that can be weighed and counted. Fifty new guineas from the mint of King George, in a water-proof bag just fit to be buried at the foot of a tree, or well under the thatch, or sewn up in the sacking of your bedstead, ma'am. Ah, pretty dreams, what pretty dreams, with a virtuous knowledge of having done the right! Shall we say it is a bargain, ma'am, and wet it with a glass, at my expense, of the crystal spring that comes under the sea?"

"Naw, Sir, naw!—not till I knaw what. I niver trafficks with the divil, Sir. There wur a chap of Flaambro deed—"

"My good madam, I can not stop all day. I have far to ride before night-fall. All that I want is simply this, and having gone so far, I must tell you all, or make an enemy of you. I want to match this; and I have reason to believe that it can be matched in Flamborough. Produce me the fellow, and I pay you fifty guineas."

With these words Mr. Mordacks took from an inner pocket a little pill-box, and thence produced a globe, or rather an oblate spheroid, of bright gold, rather larger than a musket-ball, but fluted or crenelled like a poppy-head, and stamped or embossed with marks like letters. Widow Precious looked down at it, as if to think what an extraordinary thing it was, but truly to hide from the stranger her surprise at the sudden recognition. For Robin Lyth was a foremost favorite of hers, and most useful to her vocation; and neither fifty guineas nor five hundred should lead her to do him an injury. At a glance she had known that this bead must belong to the set from which Robin's ear-rings came; and perhaps it was her conscience which helped her to suspect that a trap was being laid for the free-trade hero. To recover herself, and have time to think, as well as for closer discretion, she invited Master Mordacks to the choice guest-chamber.

"Set ye doon, Sir, hereaboot," she said, opening a solid door into the inner room; "neaver gain no fear at aw o' crackin' o' the setties; fairm, fairm anoo' they be, thoo sketterish o' their lukes, Sir. Set ye doon, your Warship; fafty poons desarveth a good room, wi'oot ony lugs o' anemees."

"What a beautiful room!" exclaimed Mr. Mordacks; "and how it savors of the place! I never should have thought of finding art and taste of such degree in a little place like Flamborough. Why, madam, you must have inherited it direct from the Danes themselves."

"Naw, Sir, naw. I fetched it aw oop fra the breck of the say and the cobbles. Book-folk tooneth naw heed o' what we do."

"Well, it is worth a great deal of heed. Lovely patterns of sea-weed on the floor—no carpet can compare with them; shelves of—I am sure I don't know what—fished up from the deep, no doubt; and shells innumerable, and stones that glitter, and fish like glass, and tufts like lace, and birds with most wonderful things in their mouths: Mistress Precious, you are too bad. The whole of it ought to go to London, where they make collections!"

"Lor, Sir, how ye da be laffin' at me. But purty maa be said of 'em wi'out ony lees."

The landlady smiled as she set for him a chair, toward which he trod gingerly, and picking every step, for his own sake as well as of the garniture. For the black oak floor was so oiled and polished, to set off the pattern of the sea-flowers on it (which really were laid with no mean taste and no small sense of color), that for slippery boots there was some peril.

"This is a sacred as well as beautiful place," said Mr. Mordacks. "I may finish my words with safety here. Madam, I commend your prudence as well as your excellent skill and industry. I should like to bring my daughter Arabella here: what a lesson she would gain for tapestry! But now, again, for business. What do you say? Unless I am mistaken, you have some knowledge of the matter depending on this bauble. You must not suppose that I came to you at random. No, madam, no; I have heard far away of your great intelligence, caution, and skill, and influence in this important town. 'Mistress Precious is the Mayor of Flamborough,' was said to me only last Saturday; 'if you would study the wise people there, hang up your hat in her noble hostelry.' Madam, I have taken that advice, and heartily rejoice at doing so. I am a man of few words, very few words—as you must have seen already— but of the strictest straightforwardness in deeds. And now again, what do you say, ma'am?"

"Your Warship hath left ma nowt to saa. Your Warship hath had the mooth aw to yosell."

"Now Mistress, Mistress Precious, truly that is a little too bad of you. It is out of my power to help admiring things which are utterly beyond me to describe, and a dinner of such cooking may enlarge the tongue, after all the fine things it has been rolling in. But business is my motto, in the fewest words that may be. You know what I want; you will keep it to yourself, otherwise other people might demand the money. Through very simple channels you will find out whether the fellow thing to this can be found here or elsewhere; and if so, who has got it, and how it was come by, and everything else that can be learned about it; and when you know all, you just make a mark on this piece of paper, ready folded and addressed; and then you will seal it, and give it to the man who calls for the letters nearly twice a week. And when I get that, I come and eat another duck, and have oysters with my cod-fish, which to-day we could not have, except in the form of mussels, ma'am."

"Naw, not a moosel—they was aw gude flithers."

144

"Well, ma'am, they may have been unknown animals; but good they were, and as fresh as the day. Now, you will remember that my desire is to do good. I have nothing to do with the revenue, nor the magistrates, nor his Majesty. I shall not even go to your parson, who is the chief authority, I am told; for I wish this matter to be kept quiet, and beside the law altogether. The whole credit of it shall belong to you, and a truly good action you will have performed, and done a little good for your own good self. As for this trinket, I do not leave it with you, but I leave you this model in wax, ma'am, made by my daughter, who is very clever. From this you can judge quite as well as from the other. If there are any more of these things in Flamborough, as I have strong reason to believe, you will know best where to find them, and I need not tell you that they are almost certain to be in the possession of a woman. You know all the women, and you skillfully inquire, without even letting them suspect it. Now I shall just stretch my legs a little, and look at your noble prospect, and in three hours' time a little more refreshment, and then, Mistress Precious, you see the last of your obedient servant, until you demand from him fifty gold guineas."

After seeing to his horse again, he set forth for a stroll, in the course of which he met with Dr. Upround and his daughter. The rector looked hard at this distinguished stranger, as if he desired to know his name, and expected to be accosted by him, while quick Miss Janetta glanced with undisguised suspicion, and asked her father, so that Mr. Mordacks overheard it, what business such a man could have, and what could he come spying after, in their quiet parish? The general factor raised his hat, and passed on with a tranquil smile, taking the crooked path which leads along and around the cliffs, by way of the light-house, from the north to the southern landing. The present light-house was not yet built, but an old round tower, which still exists, had long been used as a signal station, for semaphore by day, and at night for beacon, in the times of war and tumult; and most people called it the "Monument." This station was now of very small importance, and sometimes did nothing for a year together; but still it was very good and useful, because it enabled an ancient tar, whose feet had been carried away by a cannon-ball, to draw a little money once a month, and to think himself still a fine British bulwark.

In the summer-time this hero always slung his hammock here, with plenty of wind to rock him off to sleep, but in winter King AEolus himself could not have borne it. "Monument Joe," as almost everybody called him, was a queer old character of days gone by. Sturdy and silent, but as honest as the sun, he made his rounds as regularly as that great orb, and with equally beneficent object. For twice a day he stumped to fetch his beer from Widow Precious, and the third time to get his little pannikin of grog. And now the time was growing for that last important duty, when a stranger stood before him with a crown piece in his hand.

"Now don't get up, captain, don't disturb yourself," said Mr. Mordacks, graciously; "your country has claimed your activity, I see, and I hope it makes amends to you. At the same time I know that it very seldom does. Accept this little tribute from the admiration of a friend."

Old Joe took the silver piece and rung it on his tin tobacco-box, then stowed it inside, and said, "Gammon! What d'ye want of me?"

"Your manners, my good Sir, are scarcely on a par with your merits. I bribe no man; it is the last thing I would ever dream of doing. But whenever a question of memory arises, I have often observed a great failure of that power without—without, if you will excuse the expression, the administration of a little grease."

"Smooggling? Aught about smooggling?" Old Joe shut his mouth sternly; for he hated and scorned the coast-guards, whose wages were shamefully above his own, and who had the impudence to order him for signals; while, on the other hand, he found free trade a policy liberal, enlightening, and inspiriting.

"No, captain, no; not a syllable of that. You have been in this place about sixteen years. If you had only been here four years more, your evidence would have settled all I want to know. No wreck can take place here, of course, without your knowledge?"

"Dunno that. B'lieve one have. There's a twist of the tide here—but what good to tell landlubbers?"

"You are right. I should never understand such things. But I find them wonderfully interesting. You are not a native of this place, and knew nothing of Flamborough before you came here?"

Monument Joe gave a grunt at this, and a long squirt of tobacco juice. "And don't want," he said.

"Of course, you are superior, in every way superior. You find these people rough, and far inferior in manners. But either, my good friend, you will re-open your tobacco-box, or else you will answer me a few short questions, which trespass in no way upon your duty to the king, or to his loyal smugglers."

Old Joe looked up, with weather-beaten eyes, and saw that he had no fool to deal with, in spite of all soft palaver. The intensity of Mr. Mordacks's eyes made him blink, and mutter a bad word or two, but remain pretty much at his service. And the last intention he could entertain was that of restoring this fine crown piece. "Spake on, Sir," he said; "and I will spake accordin'."

"Very good. I shall give you very little trouble. I wish to know whether there was any wreck here, kept quiet perhaps, but still some ship lost, about three or four years before you came to this station. It does not matter what ship, any ship at all, which may have gone down without any fuss at all. You know of none such? Very well. You were not here; and the people of this place are wonderfully close. But a veteran of the Royal Navy should know how to deal with them. Make your inquiries without seeming to inquire. The question is altogether private, and can not in any way bring you into trouble. Whereas, if you find out anything, you will be a made man, and live like a gentleman. You hate the lawyers? All the honest seamen do. I am not a lawyer, and my object is to fire a broadside into them. Accept this guinea; and if it would suit you to have one every week for the rest of your life, I will pledge you my word for it, paid in advance, if you only find out for me one little fact, of which I have no doubt whatever, that a merchant ship was cast away near this Head just about nineteen years agone."

That ancient sailor was accustomed to surprises; but this, as he said, when he came to think of it, made a clean sweep of him, fore and aft. Nevertheless, he had the presence of mind required for pocketing the guinea, which was too good for his tobacco-box; and as one thing at a time was quite enough upon his mind, he probed away slowly, to be sure there was no hole. Then he got up from his squatting form, with the usual activity of those who are supposed to have none left, and touched his brown hat, standing cleverly. "What be I to do for all this?" he asked.

"Nothing more than what I have told you. To find out slowly, and without saying why, in the way you sailors know how to do, whether such a thing came to pass, as I suppose. You must not be stopped by the lies of anybody. Of course they will deny it, if they got some of the wrecking; or it is just possible that no one even heard of it; and yet there may be some traces. Put two and two together, my good friend, as you have the very best chance of doing; and soon you may put two to that in your pocket, and twenty, and a hundred, and as much as you can hold."

"When shall I see your good honor again, to score log-run, and come to a reckoning?"

"Master Joseph, work a wary course. Your rating for life will depend upon that. You may come to this address, if you have anything important. Otherwise you shall soon hear of me again. Good-by."

CHAPTER XVIII

GOYLE BAY

While all the world was at cross-purposes thus—Mr. Jellicorse uneasy at some rumors he had heard; Captain Carroway splitting his poor heel with indignation at the craftiness of free-traders; Farmer Anerley vexed at being put upon by people, without any daughter to console him, or catch shrimps; Master Mordacks pursuing a noble game, strictly above-board, as usual; Robin Lyth troubled in his largest principles of revolt against revenue by a nasty little pain that kept going to his heart, with an emptiness there, as for another heart; and last, and perhaps of all most important, the rector perpetually pining for his game of chess, and utterly discontented with the frigid embraces of analysis—where was the best, and most simple, and least selfish of the whole lot, Mary Anerley?

Mary was in as good a place as even she was worthy of. A place not by any means so snug and favored by nature as Anerley Farm, but pretty well sheltered by large trees of a strong and hardy order. And the comfortable ways of good old folk, who needed no labor to live by spread a happy leisure and a gentle ease upon everything under their roof-tree. Here was no necessity for getting up until the sun encouraged it; and the time for going to bed depended upon the time of sleepiness. Old Johnny Popplewell, as everybody called him, without any protest on his part, had made a good pocket by the tanning business, and having no children to bring up to it, and only his wife to depend upon him, had sold the good-will, the yard, and the stock as soon as he had turned his sixtieth year. "I have worked hard all my life," he said, "and I mean to rest for the rest of it."

At first he was heartily miserable, and wandered about with a vacant look, having only himself to look after. And he tried to find a hole in his bargain with the man who enjoyed all the smells he was accustomed to, and might even be heard through a gap in the fence rating the men as old Johnny used to do, at the same time of day, and for the same neglect, and almost in the self-same words which the old owner used, but stronger. Instead of being happy, Master Popplewell lost more flesh in a month than he used to lay on in the most prosperous year; and he owed it to his wife, no doubt, as generally happens, that he was not speedily gathered to the bosom of the hospitable Simon of Joppa. For Mrs. Popplewell said, "Go away; Johnny, go away from this village; smell new smells, and never see a hide without a walking thing inside of it. Sea-weed smells almost as nice as tan; though of course it is not so wholesome." The tanner obeyed, and bought a snug little place about ten miles from the old premises, which he called, at the suggestion of the parson, "Byrsa Cottage."

Here was Mary, as blithe as a lark, and as petted as a robin-redbreast, by no means pining, or even hankering, for any other robin. She was not the girl to give her heart before it was even asked for; and hitherto she had regarded the smuggler with pity more than admiration. For in many points she was like her father, whom she loved foremost of the world; and Master Anerley was a law-abiding man, like every other true Englishman. Her uncle Popplewell was also such, but exerted his principles less strictly. Moreover, he was greatly under influence of wife, which happens more freely to a man without children, the which are a source of contradiction. And Mistress Popplewell was a most thorough and conscientious free-trader.

Now Mary was from childhood so accustomed to the sea, and the relish of salt breezes, and the racy dance of little waves that crowd on one another, and the tidal delivery of delightful rubbish, that to fail of seeing the many works and plays and constant variance of her never wearying or weary friend was more than she could long put up with. She called upon Lord Keppel almost every day, having brought him from home for the good of his health, to gird up his loins, or rather get his belly girths on, and come along the sands with her, and dig into new places. But he, though delighted for a while with Byrsa stable, and the social charms of Master Popplewell's old cob, and a rick of fine tan-colored clover hay and bean haulm, when the novelty of these delights was passed, he pined for his home, and the split in his crib, and the knot of hard wood he had polished with his neck, and even the little dog that snapped at him. He did not care for retired people—as he said to the cob every evening—he liked to see farm-work going on, or at any rate to hear all about it, and to listen to horses who had worked hard, and could scarcely speak, for chewing, about the great quantity they had turned of earth, and how they had answered very bad words with a bow. In short, to put it in the mildest terms, Lord Keppel was giving himself great airs, unworthy of his age, ungrateful to a degree, and ungraceful, as the cob said repeatedly; considering how he was fed, and bedded, and not a thing left undone for him. But his arrogance soon had to pay its own costs.

For, away to the right of Byrsa Cottage, as you look down the hollow of the ground toward the sea, a ridge of high scrubby land runs up to a forefront of bold cliff, indented with a dark and narrow bay. "Goyle Bay," as it is called, or sometimes "Basin Bay," is a lonely and rugged place, and even dangerous for unwary visitors. For at low spring tides a deep hollow is left dry, rather more than a quarter of a mile across, strewn with kelp and oozy stones, among which may often be found pretty shells, weeds richly tinted and of subtle workmanship, stars, and flowers, and love-knots of the sea, and sometimes carnelians and crystals. But anybody making a collection here should be able to keep one eye upward and one down, or else in his pocket to have two things—a good watch and a trusty tide-table.

John and Deborah Popplewell were accustomed to water in small supplies, such as that of a well, or a road-side pond, or their own old noble tan-pits; but to understand the sea it was too late in life, though it pleased them, and gave them fine appetites now to go down when it was perfectly calm, and a sailor assured them that the tide was mild. But even at such seasons they preferred to keep their distance, and called out frequently to one another. They looked upon their niece, from all she told them, as a creature almost amphibious; but still they were often uneasy about her, and would gladly have kept her well inland. She, however, laughed at any such idea; and their discipline was to let her have her own way. But now a thing happened which proved forever how much better old heads are than young ones.

For Mary, being tired of the quiet places, and the strands where she knew every pebble, resolved to explore Goyle Bay at last, and she chose the worst possible time for it. The weather had been very fine and gentle, and the sea delightfully plausible, without a wave—tide after tide—bigger than the furrow of a two-horse plough; and the maid began to believe at last that there never were any storms just here. She had heard of the pretty things in Goyle Bay, which was difficult of access from the land, but she resolved to take opportunity of tide, and thus circumvent the position; she would rather have done it afoot, but her uncle and aunt made a point of her riding to the shore, regarding the pony as a safe companion, and sure refuge from the waves. And so, upon the morning of St. Michael, she compelled Lord Keppel, with an adverse mind, to turn a headland they had never turned before.

The tide was far out and ebbing still, but the wind had shifted, and was blowing from the east rather stiffly, and with increasing force. Mary knew that the strong equinoctial tides were running at their height; but she had timed her visit carefully, as she thought, with no less than an hour and a half to spare. And even without any thought of tide, she was bound to be back in less time than that, for her uncle had been most particular to warn her to be home without fail at one o'clock, when the sacred goose, to which he always paid his duties, would be on the table. And if anything marred his serenity of mind, it was to have dinner kept waiting.

Without any misgivings, she rode into Basin Bay, keeping within the black barrier of rocks, outside of which wet sands were shining. She saw that these rocks, like the bar of a river, crossed the inlet of the cove; but she had not been told of their peculiar frame and upshot, which made them so treacherous a rampart. At the mouth of the bay they formed a level crescent, as even as a set of good teeth, against the sea, with a slope of sand running up to their outer front, but a deep and long pit inside of them. This pit drained itself very nearly dry when the sea went away from it, through some stony tubes which only worked one way, by the closure of their mouths when the tide returned; so that the volume of the deep sometimes, with tide and wind behind it, leaped over the brim into the pit, with tenfold the roar, a thousandfold the power, and scarcely less than the speed, of a lion.

Mary Anerley thought what a lovely place it was, so deep and secluded from anybody's sight, and full of bright wet colors. Her pony refused, with his usual wisdom, to be dragged to the bottom of the hole, but she made him come further down than he thought just, and pegged him by the bridle there. He looked at her sadly, and with half a mind to expostulate more forcibly, but getting no glimpse of the sea where he stood, he thought it as well to put up with it; and presently he snorted out a tribe of little creatures, which puzzled him and took up his attention.

Meanwhile Mary was not only puzzled, but delighted beyond description. She never yet had come upon such treasures of the sea, and she scarcely knew what to lay hands upon first. She wanted the weeds of such wonderful forms, and colors yet more exquisite, and she wanted the shells of such delicate fabric that fairies must have made them, and a thousand other little things that had no names; and then she seemed most of all to want the pebbles. For the light came through them in stripes and patterns, and many of them looked like downright jewels. She had brought a great bag of strong canvas, luckily, and with both hands she set to to fill it.

So busy was the girl with the vast delight of sanguine acquisition—this for her father, and that for her mother, and so much for everybody she could think of—that time had no time to be counted at all, but flew by with feathers unheeded. The mutter of the sea became a roar, and the breeze waxed into a heavy gale, and spray began to sputter through the air like suds; but Mary saw the rampart of the rocks before her, and thought that she could easily get back around the point. And her taste began continually to grow more choice, so that she spent as much time in discarding the rubbish which at first she had prized so highly as she did in collecting the real rarities, which she was learning to distinguish. But unluckily the sea made no allowance for all this.

For just as Mary, with her bag quite full, was stooping with a long stretch to get something more—a thing that perhaps was the very best of all, and therefore had got into a corner—there fell upon her back quite a solid lump of wave, as a horse gets the bottom of the bucket cast at him. This made her look up, not a minute too soon; and even then she was not at all aware of danger, but took it for a notice to be moving. And she thought more of shaking that saltwater from her dress than of running away from the rest of it.

But as soon as she began to look about in earnest, sweeping back her salted hair, she saw enough of peril to turn pale the roses and strike away the smile upon her very busy face. She was standing several yards below the level of the sea, and great surges were hurrying to swallow her. The hollow of the rocks received the first billow with a thump and a slush, and a rush of pointed hillocks in a fury to find their way back again, which failing, they spread into a long white pool, taking Mary above her pretty ankles. "Don't you think to frighten me," said Mary; "I know all your ways, and I mean to take my time."

But even before she had finished her words, a great black wall (doubled over at the top with whiteness, that seemed to race along it like a fringe) hung above the rampart, and leaped over, casting at Mary such a volley that she fell. This quenched her last audacity, although she was not hurt; and jumping up nimbly, she made all haste through the rising water toward her pony. But as she would not forsake her bag, and the rocks became more and more slippery, towering higher and higher surges crashed in over the barrier, and swelled the yeasty turmoil which began to fill the basin; while a scurry of foam flew like pellets from the rampart, blinding even the very best young eyes.

Mary began to lose some of her presence of mind and familiar approval of the sea. She could swim pretty well, from her frequent bathing; but swimming would be of little service here, if once the great rollers came over the bar, which they threatened to do every moment. And when at length she fought her way to the poor old pony, her danger and distress were multiplied. Lord Keppel was in a state of abject fear; despair was knocking at his fine old heart; he was up to his knees in the loathsome brine already, and being so twisted up by his own exertions that to budge another inch was beyond him, he did what a horse is apt to do in such condition—he consoled himself with fatalism. He meant to expire; but before he did so he determined to make his mistress feel what she had done. Therefore, with a sad nudge of white old nose, he drew her attention to his last expression, sighed as plainly as a man could sigh, and fixed upon her meek eyes, telling volumes.

"I know, I know that it is all my fault," cried Mary, with the brine almost smothering her tears, as she flung her arms around his neck; "but I never will do it again, my darling. And I never will run away and let you drown. Oh, if I only had a knife! I can not even cast your bridle off; the tongue has stuck fast, and my hands are cramped. But, Keppel, I will stay, and be drowned with you."

This resolve was quite unworthy of Mary's common-sense; for how could her being drowned with Keppel help him? However, the mere conception showed a spirit of lofty order; though the body might object to be ordered under. Without any thought of all that, she stood, resolute, tearful, and thoroughly wet through, while she hunted in her pocket for a penknife.

The nature of all knives is, not to be found; and Mary's knife was loyal to its kind. Then she tugged at her pony, and pulled out his bit, and labored again at the obstinate strap; but nothing could be done with it. Keppel must be drowned, and he did not seem to care, but to think that the object of his birth was that. If the stupid little fellow would have only stepped forward, the hands of his mistress, though cramped and benumbed, might perhaps have unbuckled his stiff and sodden reins, or even undone their tangle; on the other hand, if he would have jerked with all his might, something or other must have given way; but stir he would not from one fatuous position, which kept all his head-gear on the strain, but could not snap it. Mary even struck him with her heavy bag of stones, to make him do something; but he only looked reproachful.

"Was there ever such a stupid?" the poor girl cried, with the water rising almost to her waist, and the inner waves beginning to dash over her, while the outer billows threatened to rush in and crush them both. "But I will not abuse you any more, poor Keppel. What will dear father say? Oh, what will he think of it?"

Then she burst into a fit of sobs, and leaned against the pony, to support her from a rushing wave which took her breath away, and she thought that she would never try to look up any more, but shut her eyes to all the rest of it. But suddenly she heard a loud shout and a splash, and found herself caught up and carried like an infant.

"Lie still. Never mind the pony: what is he? I will go for him afterward. You first, you first of all the world, my Mary."

She tried to speak, but not a word would come; and that was all the better. She was carried quick as might be through a whirl of tossing waters, and gently laid upon a pile of kelp; and then Robin Lyth said, "You are quite safe here, for at least another hour. I will go and get your pony."

"No, no; you will be knocked to pieces," she cried; for the pony, in the drift and scud, could scarcely be seen but for his helpless struggles. But the young man was half way toward him while she spoke, and she knelt upon the kelp, and clasped her hands.

Now Robin was at home in a matter such as this. He had landed many kegs in a sea as strong or stronger, and he knew how to deal with the horses in a surf. There still was a break of almost a fathom in the level of the inner and the outer waves, for the basin was so large that it could not fill at once; and so long as this lasted, every roller must comb over at the entrance, and mainly spend itself. "At least five minutes to spare," he shouted back, "and there is no such thing as any danger." But the girl did not believe him.

Rapidly and skillfully he made his way, meeting the larger waves sideways, and rising at their onset; until he was obliged to swim at last where the little horse was swimming desperately. The leather, still jammed in some crevice at the bottom, was jerking his poor chin downward; his eyes were screwed up like a new-born kitten's, and his dainty nose looked like a jelly-fish. He thought how sad it was that he should ever die like this, after all the good works of his life—the people he had carried, and the chaise that he had drawn, and all his kindness to mankind. Then he turned his head away to receive the stroke of grace, which the next wave would administer.

No! He was free. He could turn his honest tail on the sea, which he always had detested so; he could toss up his nose and blow the filthy salt out, and sputter back his scorn, while he made off for his life. So intent was he on this that he never looked twice to make out who his benefactor was, but gave him just a taste of his hind-foot on the elbow, in the scuffle of his hurry to be round about and off. "Such is gratitude!" the smuggler cried; but a clot of salt-water flipped into his mouth, and closed all cynical outlet. Bearing up against the waves, he stowed his long knife away, and then struck off for the shore with might and main.

Here Mary ran into the water to meet him, shivering as she was with fright and cold, and stretched out both hands to him as he waded forth; and he took them and clasped them, quite as if he needed help. Lord Keppel stood afar off, recovering his breath, and scarcely dared to look askance at the execrable sea.

"How cold you are!" Robin Lyth exclaimed. "You must not stay a moment. No talking, if you please—though I love your voice so. You are not safe yet. You can not get back round the point. See the waves dashing up against it! You must climb the cliff, and that is no easy job for a lady, in the best of weather. In a couple of hours the tide will be over the whole of this beach a fathom deep. There is no boat nearer than Filey; and a boat could scarcely live over that bar. You must climb the cliff, and begin at once, before you get any colder."

"Then is my poor pony to be drowned, after all? If he is, he had better have been drowned at once."

The smuggler looked at her with a smile, which meant, "Your gratitude is about the same as his;" but he answered, to assure her, though by no means

155

sure himself:

"There is time enough for him; he shall not be drowned. But you must be got out of danger first. When you are off my mind, I will fetch up pony. Now you must follow me step by step, carefully and steadily. I would carry you up if I could; but even a giant could scarcely do that, in a stiff gale of wind, and with the crag so wet."

Mary looked up with a shiver of dismay. She was brave and nimble generally, but now so wet and cold, and the steep cliff looked so slippery, that she said: "It is useless; I can never get up there. Captain Lyth, save yourself, and leave me."

"That would be a pretty thing to do!" he replied; "and where should I be afterward? I am not at the end of my devices yet. I have got a very snug little crane up there. It was here we ran our last lot, and beat the brave lieutenant so. But unluckily I have no cave just here. None of my lads are about here now, or we would make short work of it. But I could hoist you very well, if you would let me."

"I would never think of such a thing. To come up like a keg! Captain Lyth, you must know that I never would be so disgraced."

"Well, I was afraid that you might take it so, though I can not see why it should be any harm. We often hoist the last man so."

"It is different with me," said Mary. "It may be no harm; but I could not have it."

The free-trader looked at her bright eyes and color, and admired her spirit, which his words had roused.

"I pray your forgiveness, Miss Anerley," he said; "I meant no harm. I was thinking of your life. But you look now as if you could do anything almost."

"Yes, I am warm again. I have no fear. I will not go up like a keg, but like myself. I can do it without help from anybody."

"Only please to take care not to cut your little hands," said Robin, as he began the climb; for he saw that her spirit was up to do it.

"My hands are not little; and I will cut them if I choose. Please not even to look back at me. I am not in the least afraid of anything."

The cliff was not of the soft and friable stuff to be found at Bridlington, but of hard and slippery sandstone, with bulky ribs oversaling here and there, and threatening to cast the climber back. At such spots nicks for the feet had been cut, or broken with a hammer, but scarcely wider than a stirrup-iron, and far less inviting. To surmount these was quite impossible except by a process of crawling; and Mary, with her heart in her mouth, repented of her rash contempt for the crane sling. Luckily the height was not very great, or, tired as she was, she must have given way; for her bodily warmth had waned again in the strong wind buffeting the cliff. Otherwise the wind had helped her greatly by keeping her from swaying outward; but her courage began to fail at last, and very near the top she called for help. A short piece of lanyard was thrown to her at once, and Robin Lyth landed her on the bluff, panting, breathless, and blushing again.

"Well done!" he cried, gazing as she turned her face away. "Young ladies may teach even sailors to climb. Not every sailor could get up this cliff. Now back to Master Popplewell's as fast as you can run, and your aunt will know what to do with you."

"You seem well acquainted with my family affairs," said Mary, who could not help smiling. "Pray how did you even know where I am staying?"

"Little birds tell me everything, especially about the best, and most gentle, and beautiful of all birds."

The maiden was inclined to be vexed; but remembering how much he had done, and how little gratitude she had shown, she forgave him, and asked him to come to the cottage.

"I will bring up the little horse. Have no fear," he replied. "I will not come up at all unless I bring him. But it may take two or three hours."

With no more than a wave of his hat, he set off, as if the coast-riders were after him, by the path along the cliffs toward Filey, for he knew that Lord Keppel must be hoisted by the crane, and he could not manage it without another man, and the tide would wait for none of them. Upon the next headland he found one of his men, for the smugglers maintained a much sharper look-out than did the forces of his Majesty, because they were paid much better; and returning, they managed to strap Lord Keppel, and hoist him like a big bale of contraband goods. For their crane had been left in a brambled hole, and they very soon rigged it out again. The little horse kicked pretty freely in the air, not perceiving his own welfare; but a cross-beam and pulley kept him well out from the cliff, and they swung him in over handsomely, and landed him well up on the sward within the brink. Then they gave him three cheers for his great adventure, which he scarcely seemed to appreciate.

CHAPTER XIX

A FARM TO LET

That storm on the festival of St. Michael broke up the short summer weather of the north. A wet and tempestuous month set in, and the harvest, in all but the very best places, lay flat on the ground, without scythe or sickle. The men of the Riding were not disturbed by this, as farmers would have been in Suffolk; for these were quite used to walk over their crops, without much occasion to lift their feet. They always expected their corn to be laid, and would have been afraid of it if it stood upright. Even at Anerley Farm this salam of the wheat was expected in bad seasons; and it suited the reapers of the neighborhood, who scarcely knew what to make of knees unbent, and upright discipline of stiff-cravated ranks.

In the northwest corner of the county, where the rocky land was mantled so frequently with cloud, and the prevalence of western winds bore sway, an upright harvest was a thing to talk of, as the legend of a century, credible because it scarcely could have been imagined. And this year it would have been hard to imagine any more prostrate and lowly position than that of every kind of crop. The bright weather of August and attentions of the sun, and gentle surprise of rich dews in the morning, together with abundance of moisture underneath, had made things look as they scarcely ever looked—clean, and straight, and elegant. But none of them had found time to form the dry and solid substance, without which neither man nor his staff of life can stand against adversity.

"My Lady Philippa," as the tenants called her, came out one day to see how things looked, and whether the tenants were likely to pay their Michaelmas rents at Christmas. Her sister, Mrs. Carnaby, felt like interest in the question, but hated long walks, being weaker and less active, and therefore rode a quiet pony. Very little wheat was grown on their estates, both soil and climate declining it; but the barley crop was of more importance, and flourished pretty well upon the southern slopes. The land, as a rule, was poor and shallow, and nourished more grouse than partridges; but here and there valleys of soft shelter and fair soil relieved the eye and comforted the pocket of the owner. These little bits of Goshen formed the heart of every farm; though oftentimes the homestead was, as if by some perversity, set up in bleak and barren spots, outside of comfort's elbow.

The ladies marched on, without much heed of any other point than one—would the barley crop do well? They had many tenants who trusted chiefly to that, and to the rough hill oats, and wool, to make up in coin what part of their rent they were not allowed to pay in kind. For as yet machinery and reeking factories had not besmirched the country-side.

"How much further do you mean to go, Philippa?" asked Mrs. Carnaby, although she was not travelling by virtue of her own legs. "For my part, I think we have gone too far already."

"Your ambition is always to turn back. You may turn back now if you like. I shall go on." Miss Yordas knew that her sister would fail of the courage to ride home all alone.

Mrs. Carnaby never would ride without Jordas or some other serving-man behind her, as was right and usual for a lady of her position; but "Lady Philippa" was of bolder strain, and cared for nobody's thoughts, words, or deeds. And she had ordered her sister's servant back for certain reasons of her own.

"Very well, very well. You always will go on, and always on the road you choose yourself. Although it requires a vast deal of knowledge to know that there is any road here at all."

The widow, who looked very comely for her age, and sat her pony prettily, gave way (as usual) to the stronger will; though she always liked to enter protest, which the elder scarcely ever deigned to notice. But hearing that Eliza had a little cough at night, and knowing that her appetite had not been as it ought to be, Philippa (who really was wrapped up in her sister, but never or seldom let her dream of such a fact) turned round graciously and said:

"I have ordered the carriage here for half past three o'clock. We will go back by the Scarbend road, and Heartsease can trot behind us."

"Heartsease, uneasy you have kept my heart by your shufflings and trippings perpetual. Philippa, I want a better-stepping pony. Pet has ruined Heartsease."

"Pet ruins everything and everybody; and you are ruining him, Eliza. I am the only one who has the smallest power over him. And he is beginning to cast off that. If it comes to open war between us, I shall be sorry for Lancelot."

"And I shall be sorry for you, Philippa. In a few years Pet will be a man. And a man is always stronger than a woman; at any rate in our family."

"Stronger than such as you, Eliza. But let him only rebel against me, and he will find himself an outcast. And to prove that, I have brought you here."

Mistress Yordas turned round, and looked in a well-known manner at her sister, whose beautiful eyes filled with tears, and fell.

"Philippa," she said, with a breath like a sob, "sometimes you look harder than poor dear papa, in his very worst moments, used to look. I am sure that I do not at all deserve it. All that I pray for is peace and comfort; and little do I get of either."

"And you will get less, as long as you pray for them, instead of doing something better. The only way to get such things is to make them."

"Then I think that you might make enough for us both, if you had any regard for them, or for me, Philippa."

Mistress Yordas smiled, as she often did, at her sister's style of reasoning. And she cared not a jot for the last word, so long as the will and the way were left to her. And in this frame of mind she turned a corner from the open moor track into a little lane, or rather the expiring delivery of a lane, which was leading a better existence further on.

Mrs. Carnaby followed dutifully, and Heartsease began to pick up his feet, which he scorned to do upon the negligence of sward. And following this good lane, they came to a gate, corded to an ancient tree, and showing up its foot, as a dog does when he has a thorn in it. This gate seemed to stand for an ornament, or perhaps a landmark; for the lane, instead of submitting to it, passed by upon either side, and plunged into a dingle, where a gray old house was sheltering. The lonely moorside farm—if such a wild and desolate spot could be a farm—was known as "Wallhead," from the relics of some ancient wall; and the folk who lived there, or tried to live, although they possessed a surname—which is not a necessary consequence of life—very seldom used it, and more rarely still had it used for them. For the ancient fashion still held ground of attaching the idea of a man to that of things more extensive and substantial. So the head of the house was "Will o' the Wallhead;" his son was "Tommy o' Will o' the Wallhead;" and his grandson, "Willy o' Tommy o' Will o' the Wallhead." But the one their great lady desired to see was the unmarried daughter of the house, "Sally o' Will o' the Wallhead."

Mistress Yordas knew that the men of the house would be out upon the land at this time of day, while Sally would be full of household work, and preparing their homely supper. So she walked in bravely at the open door, while her sister waited with the pony in the yard. Sally was clumping about in clog-shoes, with a child or two sprawling after her (for Tommy's wife was away with him at work), and if the place was not as clean as could be, it seemed as clean as need be.

The natives of this part are rough in manner, and apt to regard civility as the same thing with servility. Their bluntness does not proceed from thickness, as in the south of England, but from a surety of their own worth, and inferiority to no one. And to deal with them rightly, this must be entered into.

Sally o' Will o' the Wallhead bobbed her solid and black curly head, with a clout like a jelly on the poll of it, to the owner of their land, and a lady of high birth; but she vouchsafed no courtesy, neither did Mistress Yordas expect one. But the active and self-contained woman set a chair in the low dark room, which was their best, and stood waiting to be spoken to.

"Sally," said the lady, who also possessed the Yorkshire gift of going to the point, "you had a man ten years ago; you behaved badly to him, and he went into the Indian Company."

"A' deed," replied the maiden, without any blush, because she had been in the right throughout; "and noo a' hath coom in a better moind."

"And you have come to know your own mind about him. You have been steadfast to him for ten years. He has saved up some money, and is come back to marry you."

"I heed nane o' the brass. But my Jack is back again."

"His father held under us for many years. He was a thoroughly honest man, and paid his rent as often as he could. Would Jack like to have his father's farm? It has been let to his cousin, as you know; but they have been going from bad to worse; and everything must be sold off, unless I stop it."

Sally was of dark Lancastrian race, with handsome features and fine brown eyes. She had been a beauty ten years ago, and could still look comely, when her heart was up.

"My lady," she said, with her heart up now, at the hope of soon having a home of her own, and something to work for that she might keep, "such words should not pass the mouth wi' out bin meant."

What she said was very different in sound, and not to be rendered in echo by any one born far away from that country, where three dialects meet and find it hard to guess what each of the others is up to. Enough that this is what Sally meant to say, and that Mistress Yordas understood it.

"It is not my custom to say a thing without meaning it," she answered; "but unless it is taken up at once, it is likely to come to nothing. Where is your man Jack?"

"Jack is awaa to the minister to tell of us cooming tegither." Sally made no blush over this, as she might have done ten years ago.

"He must be an excellent and faithful man. He shall have the farm if he

162

wishes it, and can give some security at going in. Let him come and see Jordas tomorrow."

After a few more words, the lady left Sally full of gratitude, very little of which was expressed aloud, and therefore the whole was more likely to work, as Mistress Yordas knew right well.

The farm was a better one than Wallhead, having some good barley land upon it; and Jack did not fail to present himself at Scargate upon the following morning. But the lady of the house did not think fit herself to hold discourse with him. Jordas was bidden to entertain him, and find out how he stood in cash, and whether his character was solid; and then to leave him with a jug of ale, and come and report proceedings. The dogman discharged this duty well, being as faithful as the dogs he kept, and as keen a judge of human nature.

"The man hath no harm in him," he said, touching his hair to the ladies, as he entered the audit-room. "A' hath been knocked aboot a bit in them wars i' Injury, and hath only one hand left; but a' can lay it upon fifty poon, and get surety for anither fifty."

"Then tell him, Jordas, that he may go to Mr. Jellicorse to-morrow, to see about the writings, which he must pay for. I will write full instructions for Mr. Jellicorse, and you go and get your dinner; and then take my letter, that he may have time to consider it. Wait a moment. There are other things to be done in Middleton, and it would be late for you to come back to-night, the days are drawing in so. Sleep at our tea-grocer's; he will put you up. Give your letter at once into the hands of Mr. Jellicorse, and he will get forward with the writings. Tell this man Jack that he must be there before twelve o'clock to-morrow, and then you can call about two o'clock, and bring back what there may be for signature; and be careful of it. Eliza, I think I have set forth your wishes."

"But, my lady, lawyers do take such a time; and who will look after Master Lancelot? I fear to have my feet two moiles off here—"

"Obey your orders, without reasoning; that is for those who give them. Eliza, I am sure that you agree with me. Jordas, make this man clearly understand, as you can do when you take the trouble. But you first must clearly understand the whole yourself. I will repeat it for you."

Philippa Yordas went through the whole of her orders again most clearly, and at every one of them the dogman nodded his large head distinctly, and counted the nods on his fingers to make sure; for this part is gifted with high mathematics. And the numbers stick fast like pegs driven into clay.

"Poor Jordas! Philippa, you are working him too hard. You have made great wrinkles in his forehead. Jordas, you must have no wrinkles until you are married."

While Mrs. Carnaby spoke so kindly, the dogman took his fingers off their numeral scale, and looked at her. By nature the two were first cousins, of half blood; by law and custom, and education, and vital institution, they were sundered more widely than black and white. But, for all that, the dogman loved the lady, at a faithful distance.

"You seem to me now to have it clearly, Jordas," said the elder sister, looking at him sternly, because Eliza was so soft; "you will see that no mischief can be done with the dogs or horses while you are away; and Mr. Jellicorse will give you a letter for me, to say that everything is right. My desire is to have things settled promptly, because your friend Jack has been to set the banns up; and the Church is more speedy in such matters than the law. Now the sooner you are off, the better."

Jordas, in his steady but by no means stupid way, considered at his leisure what such things could mean. He knew all the property, and the many little holdings, as well as, and perhaps a great deal better than, if they had happened to be his own. But he never had known such a hurry made before, or such a special interest shown about the letting of any tenement, of perhaps tenfold the value. However, he said, like a sensible man (and therefore to himself only), that the ways of women are beyond compute, and must be suitably carried out, without any contradiction.

CHAPTER XX

AN OLD SOLDIER

Now Mr. Jellicorse had been taking a careful view of everything. He wished to be certain of placing himself both on the righteous side and the right one; and in such a case this was not to be done without much circumspection. He felt himself bound to his present clients, and could not even dream of deserting them; but still there are many things that may be done to conciliate the adversary of one's friend, without being false to the friend himself. And some of these already were occurring to the lawyer.

It was true that no adversary had as yet appeared, nor even shown token of existence; but some little sign of complication had arisen, and one serious fact was come to light. The solicitors of Sir Ulphus de Roos (the grandson of Sir Fursan, whose daughter had married Richard Yordas) had pretty strong evidence, in some old letters, that a deed of appointment had been made by the said Richard, and Eleanor his wife, under the powers of their settlement. Luckily they had not been employed in the matter, and possessed not so much as a draft or a letter of instructions; and now it was no concern of theirs to make, or meddle, or even move. Neither did they know that any question could arise about it; for they were a highly antiquated firm, of most rigid respectability, being legal advisers to the Chapter of York, and clerks of the Prerogative Court, and able to charge twice as much as almost any other firm, and nearly three times as much as poor Jellicorse.

Mr. Jellicorse had been most skillful and wary in sounding these deep and silent people; for he wanted to find out how much they knew, without letting them suspect that there was anything to know. And he proved an old woman's will gratis, or at least put it down to those who could afford it—because nobody meant to have it proved—simply for the sake of getting golden contact with Messrs. Akeborum, Micklegate, and Brigant. Right craftily then did he fetch a young member of the firm, who delighted in angling, to take his holiday at Middleton, and fish the goodly Tees; and by gentle and casual discourse of gossip, in hours of hospitality, out of him he hooked and landed all that his firm knew of the Yordas race. Young Brigant thought it natural enough that his host, as the lawyer of that family, and their trusted adviser for five-and-twenty years, should like to talk over things of an elder date, which now could be little more than trifles of genealogical history. He got some fine fishing and good dinners, and found himself pleased with the river and the town, and his very kind host and hostess; and it came into his head that if

Miss Emily grew up as pretty and lively as she promised to be, he might do worse than marry her, and open a connection with such a fishing station. At any rate he left her as a "chose in action," which might be reduced into possession some fine day.

Such was the state of affairs when Jordas, after a long and muddy ride, sent word that he would like to see the master, for a minute or two, if convenient. The days were grown short, and the candles lit, and Mr. Jellicorse was fast asleep, having had a good deal to get through that day, including an excellent supper. The lawyer's wife said: "Let him call in the morning. Business is over, and the office is closed. Susanna, your master must not be disturbed." But the master awoke, and declared that he would see him.

Candles were set in the study, while Jordas was having a trifle of refreshment; and when he came in, Mr. Jellicorse was there, with his spectacles on, and full of business.

"Asking of your pardon. Sir, for disturbing of you now," said the dogman, with the rain upon his tarred coat shining, in a little course of drainage from his great brown beard, "my orders wur to lay this in your own hand, and seek answer to-morrow by dinner-time, if may be."

"Master Jordas, you shall have it, if it can be. Do you know anybody who can promise more than that?"

"Plenty, Sir, to promise it, as you must know by this time; but never a body to perform so much as half. But craving of your pardon again, and separate, I wud foin spake a word or two of myself."

"Certainly, Jordas, I shall listen with great pleasure. A fine-looking fellow like you must have affairs. And the lady ought to make some settlement. It shall all be done for you at half price."

"No, Sir, it is none o' that kind of thing," the dogman answered, with a smile, as if he might have had such opportunities, but would trouble no lawyer about them; "and I get too much of half price at home. It is about my ladies I desire to make speech. They keep their business too tight, master."

"Jordas, you have been well taught and trained; and you are a man of sagacity. Tell me faithfully what you mean. It shall go no further. And it may be of great service to your ladies."

"It is not much, Master Jellicoose; and you may make less than that of it. But a lie shud be met and knocked doon, Sir, according to my opinion."

"Certainly, Jordas, when an action will not lie; and sometimes even where it does, it is wise to commit a defensible assault, and so to become the defendant. Jordas, you are big enough to do that."

"Master Jellicoose, you are a pleasant man; but you twist my maning, as a lawyer must. They all does it, to keep their hand in. I am speaking of the stories, Sir, that is so much about. And I think that my ladies should be told of them right out, and come forward, and lay their hands on them. The Yordases always did wrong, of old time; but they never was afraid to jump on it."

"My friend, you speak in parables. What stories have arisen to be jumped upon?"

"Well, Sir, for one thing, they do tell that the proper owner of the property is Sir Duncan, now away in India. A man hath come home who knows him well, and sayeth that he is like a prince out there, with command of a country twice as big as Great Britain, and they up and made 'Sir Duncan' of him, by his duty to the king. And if he cometh home, all must fall before him."

"Even the law of the land, I suppose, and the will of his own father. Pretty well, so far, Jordas. And what next?"

"Nought, Sir, nought. But I thought I wur duty-bound to tell you that. What is women before a man Yordas?"

"My good friend, we will not despair. But you are keeping back something; I know it by your feet. You are duty-bound to tell me every word now, Jordas."

"The lawyers is the devil," said the dogman to himself; and being quite used to this reflection, Mr. Jellicorse smiled and nodded; "but if you must have it all, Sir, it is no more than this. Jack o' the Smithies, as is to marry Sally o' Will o' the Wallhead, is to have the lease of Shipboro' farm, and he is the man as hath told it all."

"Very well. We will wish him good luck with his farm," Mr. Jellicorse answered, cheerfully; "and what is even rarer nowadays, I fear, good luck of his wife, Master Jordas."

But as soon as the sturdy retainer was gone, and the sound of his heavy boots had died away, Mr. Jellicorse shook his head very gravely, and said, as he opened and looked through his packet, which confirmed the words of Jordas, "Sad indiscretion—want of legal knowledge—headstrong women— the very way to spoil it all! My troubles are beginning, and I had better go to bed."

His good wife seconded this wise resolve; and without further parley it was put into effect, and proclaimed to be successful by a symphony of snores. For this is the excellence of having other people's cares to carry (with the carriage well paid), that they sit very lightly on the springs of sleep. That well-balanced vehicle rolls on smoothly, without jerk, or jar, or kick, so long as it travels over alien land.

In the morning Mr. Jellicorse was up to anything, legitimate, legal, and likely to be paid for. Not that he would stir half the breadth of one wheat corn, even for the sake of his daily bread, from the straight and strict line of integrity. He had made up his mind about that long ago, not only from natural virtue, strong and dominant as that was, but also by dwelling on his high repute, and the solid foundations of character. He scarcely knew anybody, when he came to think of it, capable of taking such a lofty course; but that simply confirmed him in his stern resolve to do what was right and expedient.

It was quite one o'clock before Jack o' the Smithies rang the bell to see about his lease. He ought to have done it two hours sooner, if he meant to become a humble tenant; and the lawyer, although he had plenty to do of other people's business, looked upon this as a very bad sign. Then he read his letter of instructions once more, and could not but admire the nice brevity of these, and the skillful style of hinting much and declaring very little.

For after giving full particulars about the farm, and the rent, and the covenants required, Mistress Yordas proceeded thus:

"The new tenant is the son of a former occupant, who proved to be a remarkably honest man, in a case of strong temptation. As happens too often with men of probity, he was misled and made bankrupt, and died about twelve years ago, I think. Please to verify this by reference. The late tenant was his nephew, and has never perceived the necessity of paying rent. We have been obliged to distrain, as you know; and I wish John Smithies to buy in what he pleases. He has saved some capital in India, where I am told that he fought most gallantly. Singular to say, he has met with, and perhaps served under, our lamented and lost brother Duncan, of whom and his family he may give us interesting particulars. You know how this neighborhood excels in idle talk, and if John Smithies becomes our tenant, his discourse must be confined to his own business. But he must not hesitate to impart to you any facts you may think it right to ask about. Jordas will bring us your answer, under seal."

"Skillfully put, up to that last word, which savors too much of teaching me my own business. Aberthaw, are you quite ready with that lease? It is wanted rather in a hurry."

As Mr. Jellicorse thought the former, and uttered the latter part of these words, it was plain to see that he was fidgety. He had put on superior clothes to get up with; and the clerks had whispered to one another that it must be his wedding day, and ought to end in a half-holiday all round, and be chalked thenceforth on the calendar; but instead of being joyful and jocular, like a man who feels a saving Providence over him, the lawyer was as dismal, and unsettled and splenetic, as a prophet on the brink of wedlock. But the very last thing that he ever dreamed of doubting was his power to turn this old soldier inside out.

Jack o' the Smithies was announced at last; and the lawyer, being vexed with him for taking such a time, resolved to let him take a little longer, and kept him waiting, without any bread and cheese, for nearly half an hour. The wisdom of doing this depended on the character of the man, and the state of his finances. And both of these being strong enough to stand, to keep him so long on his legs was unwise. At last he came in, a very sturdy sort of fellow, thinking no atom the less of himself because some of his anatomy was honorably gone.

"Servant, Sir," he said, making a salute; "I had orders to come to you about a little lease."

"Right, my man, I remember now. You are thinking of taking to your father's farm, after knocking about for some years in foreign parts. Ah, nothing like old England after all. And to tread the ancestral soil, and cherish the old associations, and to nurture a virtuous family in the fear of the Lord, and to be ready with the rent—"

"Rent is too high, Sir; I must have five pounds off. It ought to be ten, by right. Cousin Joe has taken all out, and put nought in."

"John o' the Smithies, you astonish me. I have strong reason for believing that the rent is far too low. I have no instructions to reduce it."

"Then I must try for another farm, Sir. I can have one of better land, under Sir Walter; only I seemed to hold on to the old place; and my Sally likes to be under the old ladies."

"Old ladies! Jack, what are you come to? Beautiful ladies in the prime of life—but perhaps they would be old in India. I fear that you have not learned much behavior. But at any rate you ought to know your own mind. Is it your intention to refuse so kind an offer (which was only made for your father's sake, and to please your faithful Sally) simply because another of your family has not been honest in his farming?"

"I never have took it in that way before," the steady old soldier answered, showing that rare phenomenon, the dawn of a new opinion upon a stubborn face. "Give me a bit to turn it over in my mind, Sir. Lawyers be so quick, and so nimble, and all-cornered."

"Turn it over fifty times, Master Smithies. We have no wish to force the farm upon you. Take a pinch of snuff, to help your sense of justice. Or if you would like a pipe, go and have it in my kitchen. And if you are hungry, cook will give you eggs and bacon."

"No, Sir; I am very much obliged to you. I never make much o' my thinking. I go by what the Lord sends right inside o' me, whenever I have decent folk to deal with. And spite of your cloth, Sir, you have a honest look."

"You deserve another pinch of snuff for that. Master Smithies, you have a gift of putting hard things softly. But this is not business. Is your mind made up?"

"Yes, Sir. I will take the farm, at full rent, if the covenants are to my liking. They must be on both sides—both sides, mind you."

Mr. Jellicorse smiled as he began to read the draft prepared from a very ancient form which was firmly established on the Scargate Hall estates. The covenants, as usual, were all upon one side, the lessee being bound to a multitude of things, and the lessor to little more than acceptance of the rent. But such a result is in the nature of the case. Yet Jack o' the Smithies was not well content. In him true Yorkshire stubbornness was multiplied by the dogged tenacity of a British soldier, and the aggregate raised to an unknown power by the efforts of shrewd ignorance; and at last the lawyer took occasion to say,

"Master John Smithies, you are worthy to serve under the colors of a Yordas."

"That I have, Sir, that I have," cried the veteran, taken unawares, and shaking the stump of his arm in proof; "I have served under Sir Duncan Yordas, who will come home some day and claim his own; and he won't want no covenants of me."

"You can not have served under Duncan Yordas," Mr. Jellicorse answered, with a smile of disbelief, craftily rousing the pugnacity of the man; "because he was not even in the army of the Company, or any other army. I mean, of course, unless there was some other Duncan Yordas."

"Tell me!" Jack o' Smithies almost shouted—"tell me about Duncan Yordas, indeed! Who he was, and what he wasn't! And what do lawyers know of such things? Why, you might have to command a regiment, and read covenants to them out there! Sir Duncan was not our colonel, nor our captain; but we was under his orders all the more; and well he knew how to give them. Not one in fifty of us was white; but he made us all as good as white men; and the enemy never saw the color of our backs. I wish I was out there again, I do, and would have staid, but for being hoarse of combat; though the fault was never in my throat, but in my arm."

"There is no fault in your throat, John Smithies, except that it is a great deal too loud. I am sorry for Sally, with a temper such as yours."

"That shows how much you know about it. I never lose my temper, without I hearken lies. And for you to go and say that I never saw Sir Duncan—"

"I said nothing of the kind, my friend. But you did not come here to talk about Duncan, or Captain, or Colonel, or Nabob, or Rajah, or whatever potentate he may be—of him we desire to know nothing more—a man who ran away, and disgraced his family, and killed his poor father, knows better than ever to set his foot on Scargate land again. You talk about having a lease from him, a man with fifty wives, I dare say, and a hundred children! We all know what they are out there."

There are very few tricks of the human face divine more forcibly expressive of contempt than the lowering of the eyelids so that only a narrow streak of eye is exposed to the fellow-mortal, and that streak fixed upon him steadfastly; and the contumely is intensified when (as in the present instance) the man who does it is gifted with yellow lashes on the under lid. Jack o' the Smithies treated Mr. Jellicorse to a gaze of this sort; and the lawyer, whose wrath had been feigned, to rouse the other's, and so extract full information, began to feel his own temper rise. And if Jack had known when to hold his tongue, he must have had the best of it. But the lawyer knew this, and the soldier did not.

"Master Jellicorse," said the latter, with his forehead deeply wrinkled, and his eyes now opened to their widest, "in saying of that you make a liar of yourself. Lease or no lease—that you do. Leasing stands for lying in the Bible, and a' seemeth to do the same thing in Yorkshire. Fifty wives, and a hundred children! Sir Duncan hath had one wife, and lost her, through the Neljan fever and her worry; and a Yorkshire lady, as you might know—and never hath he cared to look at any woman since. There now, what you make of that—you lawyers that make out every man a rake, and every woman a light o' love? Get along! I hate the lot o' you."

"What a strange character you are! You must have had jungle fever, I should think. No, Diana, there is no danger"—for Jack o' the Smithies had made such a noise that Mrs. Jellicorse got frightened and ran in: "this poor man has only one arm; and if he had two, he could not hurt me, even if he wished it. Be pleased to withdraw, Diana. John Smithies, you have simply made a fool of yourself. I have not said a word against Sir Duncan Yordas, or his wife, or his son—"

"He hath no son, I tell you; and that was partly how he lost his wife."

"Well, then, his daughters, I have said no harm of them."

"And very good reason—because he hath none. You lawyers think you are so clever; and you never know anything rightly. Sir Duncan hath himself alone to see to, and hundreds of thousands of darkies to manage, with a score of British bayonets. But he never heedeth of the bayonets, not he."

"I have read of such men, but I never saw them," Mr. Jellicorse said, as if thinking to himself; "I always feel doubt about the possibility of them."

"He hath ten elephants," continued Soldier Smithies, resolved to crown the pillar of his wonders while about it—"ten great elephants that come and kneel before him, and a thousand men ready to run to his thumb; and his word is law—better law than is in England—for scores and scores of miles on the top of hundreds."

"Why did you come away, John Smithies? Why did you leave such a great prince, and come home?"

"Because it was home, Sir. And for sake of Sally."

"There is some sense in that, my friend. And now if you wish to make a happy life for Sally, you will do as I advise you. Will you take my advice? My time is of value; and I am not accustomed to waste my words."

"Well, Sir, I will hearken to you. No man that meaneth it can say more than that."

"Jack o' the Smithies, you are acute. You have not been all over the world for nothing. But if you have made up your mind to settle, and be happy in your native parts, one thing must be attended to. It is a maxim of law, time-honored and of the highest authority, that the tenant must never call in question the title of his landlord. Before attorning, you may do so; after that you are estopped. Now is it or is it not your wish to become the tenant of the Smithies farm, which your father held so honorably? Farm produce is fetching great prices now; and if you refuse this offer, we can have a man, the day after to-morrow, who will give my ladies 10 pounds more, and who has not been a soldier, but a farmer all his life."

"Lawyer Jellicorse, I will take it; for Sally hath set her heart on it; and I know every crumple of the ground better than the wisest farmer doth. Sir, I will sign the articles."

"The lease will be engrossed by next market day; and the sale will be stopped until you have taken whatever you wish at a valuation. But remember what I said—you are not to go prating about this wonderful Sir Duncan, who is never likely to come home, if he lives in such grand state out there, and who is forbidden by his father's will from taking an acre of the property. And as he has no heirs, and is so wealthy, it can not matter much to him."

"That is true," said the soldier; "but he might love to come home, as all our folk in India do; and if he doth, I will not deny him. I tell you fairly, Master Jellicorse."

"I like you for being an outspoken man, and true to those who have used you well. You could do him no good, and you might do harm to others, and unsettle simple minds, by going on about him among the tenants."

"His name hath never crossed my lips till now, and shall not again without good cause. Here is my hand upon it, Master Lawyer."

The lawyer shook hands with him heartily, for he could not but respect the man for his sturdiness and sincerity. And when Jack was gone, Mr. Jellicorse played with his spectacles and his snuff-box for several minutes before he could make up his mind how to deal with the matter. Then hearing the solid knock of Jordas, who was bound to take horse for Scargate House pretty early at this time of year (with the weakening of the day among the mountains), he lost a few moments in confusion. The dogman could not go without any answer; and how was any good answer to be given in half an hour, at the utmost? A time had been when the lawyer studied curtness and precision under minds of abridgment in London. But the more he had labored to introduce rash brevity into Yorkshire, and to cut away nine words out of ten, when all the ten meant one thing only, the more of contempt for his ignorance he won, and the less money he made out of it. And no sooner did he marry than he was forced to give up that, and, like a respectable butcher, put in every pennyweight of fat that could be charged for. Thus had he thriven and grown like a goodly deed of fine amplification; and if he had made Squire Philip's will now, it would scarcely have gone into any breast pocket. Unluckily it is an easier thing to make a man's will than to carry it out, even though fortune be favorable.

In the present case obstacles seemed to be arising which might at any moment require great skill and tact to surmount them; and the lawyer, hearing Jordas striding to and fro impatiently in the waiting-room, was fain to win time for consideration by writing a short note to say that he proposed to wait upon the ladies the very next day. For he had important news which seemed expedient to discuss with them. In the mean time he begged them not to be at all uneasy, for his news upon the whole was propitious.

CHAPTER XXI

JACK AND JILL GO DOWN THE GILL

Upon a little beck that runs away into the Lune, which is a tributary of the Tees, there stood at this time a small square house of gray stone, partly greened with moss, or patched with drip, and opening to the sun with small dark windows. It looked as if it never could be warm inside, by sunshine or by fire-glow, and cared not, although it was the only house for miles, whether it were peopled or stood empty. But this cold, hard-looking place just now was the home of some hot and passionate hearts.

The people were poor; and how they made their living would have been a mystery to their neighbors, if there had been any. They rented no land, and they followed no trade, and they took no alms by land or post; for the begging-letter system was not yet invented. For the house itself they paid a small rent, which Jordas received on behalf of his ladies, and always found it ready; and that being so, he had nothing more to ask, and never meddled with them. They had been there before he came into office, and it was not his place to seek into their history; and if it had been, he would not have done it. For his sympathies were (as was natural and native to a man so placed) with all outsiders, and the people who compress into one or two generations that ignorance of lineage which some few families strive to defer for centuries, showing thereby unwise insistence, if latter-day theories are correct.

But if Master Jordas knew little of these people, somebody else knew more about them, and perhaps too much about one of them. Lancelot Carnaby, still called "Pet," in one of those rushes after random change which the wildness of his nature drove upon him, had ridden his pony to a stand-still on the moor one sultry day of that August. No pity or care for the pony had he, but plenty of both for his own dear self. The pony might be left for the crows to pick his bones, so far as mattered to Pet Carnaby; but it mattered very greatly to a boy like him to have to go home upon his own legs. Long exertion was hateful to him, though he loved quick difficulty; for he was one of the many who combine activity with laziness. And while he was wondering what he should do, and worrying the fine little animal, a wave of the wind carried into his ear the brawling of a beck, like the humming of a hive. The boy had forgotten that the moor just here was broken by a narrow glen, engrooved with sliding water.

Now with all his strength, which was not much, he tugged the panting and limping little horse to the flat breach, and then down the steep of the gill, and let him walk into the water and begin to slake off a little of the crust of thirst. But no sooner did he see him preparing to rejoice in large crystal draughts (which his sobs had first forbidden) than he jerked him with the bit, and made a bad kick at him, because he could bear to see nothing happy. The pony had sense enough to reply, weary as he was, with a stronger kick, which took Master Lancelot in the knee, and discouraged him for any further contest. Bully as he was, the boy had too much of ancient Yordas pith in him to howl, or cry, or even whimper, but sat down on a little ridge to nurse his poor knee, and meditate revenge against the animal with hoofs. Presently pain and wrath combined became too much for the weakness of his frame, and he fell back and lay upon the hard ground in a fainting fit.

At such times, as everybody said (especially those whom he knocked about in his lively moments), this boy looked wonderfully lovely. His features were almost perfect; and he had long eyelashes like an Andalusian girl, and cheeks more exquisite than almost any doll's, a mouth of fine curve, and a chin of pert roundness, a neck of the mould that once was called "Byronic," and curly dark hair flying all around, as fine as the very best peruke. In a word, he was just what a boy ought not to be, who means to become an Englishman.

Such, however, was not the opinion of a creature even more beautiful than he, in the truer points of beauty. Coming with a pitcher for some water from the beck, Insie of the Gill (the daughter of Bat and Zilpie of the Gill) was quite amazed as she chanced round a niche of the bank upon this image. An image fallen from the sun, she thought it, or at any rate from some part of heaven, until she saw the pony, who was testing the geology of the district by the flavor of its herbage. Then Insie knew that here was a mortal boy, not dead, but sadly wounded; and she drew her short striped kirtle down, because her shapely legs were bare.

Lancelot Carnaby, coming to himself (which was a poor return for him), opened his large brown eyes, and saw a beautiful girl looking at him. As their eyes met, his insolent languor fell—for he generally awoke from these weak lapses into a slow persistent rage—and wonder and unknown admiration moved something in his nature that had never moved before. His words, however, were scarcely up to the high mark of the moment. "Who are you?" was all he said.

"I am called 'Insie of the Gill.' My father is Bat of the Gill, and my mother Zilpie of the Gill. You must be a stranger, not to know us."

"I never heard of you in all my life; although you seem to be living on my land. All the land about here belongs to me; though my mother has it for a little time."

177

"I did not know," she answered, softly, and scarcely thinking what she said, "that the land belonged to anybody, besides the birds and animals. And is the water yours as well?"

"Yes; every drop of it, of course. But you are quite welcome to a pitcherful." This was the rarest affability of Pet; and he expected extraordinary thanks.

But Insie looked at him with surprise. "I am very much obliged to you," she said; "but I never asked any one to give it me, unless it is the beck itself; and the beck never seems to grudge it."

"You are not like anybody I ever saw. You speak very different from the people about here; and you look very different ten times over."

Insie reddened at his steadfast gaze, and turned her sweet soft face away. And yet she wanted to know more. "Different means a great many things. Do you mean that I look better, or worse?"

"Better, of course; fifty thousand times better! Why, you look like a beautiful lady. I tell you, I have seen hundreds of ladies; perhaps you haven't, but I have. And you look better than all of them."

"You say a great deal that you do not think," Insie answered, quietly, yet turning round to show her face again. "I have heard that gentlemen always do; and I suppose that you are a young gentleman."

"I should hope so indeed. Don't you know who I am? I am Lancelot Yordas Carnaby."

"Why, you look quite as if you could stop the river," she answered, with a laugh, though she felt his grandeur. "I suppose you consider me nobody at all. But I must get my water."

"You shall not carry water. You are much too pretty. I will carry it for you."

Pet was not "introspective;" otherwise he must have been astonished at himself. His mother and aunt would have doubted their own eyes if they had beheld this most dainty of the dainty, and mischievous of the mischievous (with pain and passion for the moment vanquished), carefully carrying an old brown pitcher. Yet this he did, and wonderfully well, as he believed; though Insie only laughed to see him. For he had on the loveliest gaiters in the world, of thin white buckskin with agate buttons, and breeches of silk, and a long brocaded waistcoat, and a short coat of rich purple velvet, also a riding hat with a gray ostrich plume. And though he had very little calf inside his gaiters, and not much chest to fill out his waistcoat, and narrower shoulders than a velvet coat deserved, it would have been manifest, even to a tailor, that the boy had lineal, if not lateral, right to his rich habiliments.

Insie of the Gill (who seemed not to be of peasant birth, though so plainly dressed), came gently down the steep brook-side to see what was going to be done for her.

She admired Lancelot, both for bravery of apparel and of action; and she longed to know how he would get a good pitcher of water without any splash upon his clothes. So she stood behind a little bush, pretending not to be at all concerned, but amused at having her work done for her. But Pet was too sharp to play cat's-paw for nothing.

"Smile, and say 'thank you,'" he cried, "or I won't do it. I am not going up to my middle for nothing; I know that you want to laugh at me."

"You must have a very low middle," said Insie; "why, it never comes half way to my knees."

"You have got no stockings, and no new gaiters," Lancelot answered, reasonably; and then, like two children, they set to and laughed, till the gill almost echoed with them.

"Why, you're holding the mouth of the pitcher down stream!" Insie could hardly speak for laughing. "Is that how you go to fill a pitcher?"

"Yes, and the right way too," he answered; "the best water always comes up the eddies. You ought to be old enough to know that."

"I don't know anything at all—except that you are ruining your best clothes."

"I don't care twopence for such rubbish. You ought to see me on a Sunday, Insie, if you want to know what is good. There, you never drew such a pitcher as that. And I believe there is a fish in the bottom of it."

"Oh, if there is a fish, let me have him in my hands. I can nurse a fish on dry land, until he gets quite used to it. Are you sure that there is a little fish?"

"No, there is no fish; and I am soaking wet. But I never care what anybody thinks of me. If they say what I don't like, I kick them."

"Ah, you are accustomed to have your own way. That any one might know by looking at you. But I have got a quantity of work to do. You can see that by my fingers."

The girl made a courtesy, and took the pitcher from him, because he was knocking it against his legs; but he could not be angry when he looked into her eyes, though the habit of his temper made him try to fume.

"Do you know what I think?" she said, fixing bright hazel eyes upon him;

"I think that you are very passionate sometimes."

"Well, if I am, it is my own business. Who told you anything about it? Whoever it was shall pay out for it."

"Nobody told me, Sir. You must remember that I never even heard of your name before."

"Oh, come, I can't quite take down that. Everybody knows me for fifty miles or more; and I don't care what they think of me."

"You may please yourself about believing me," she answered, without concern about it. "No one who knows me doubts my word, though I am not known for even five miles away."

"What an extraordinary girl you are! You say things on purpose to provoke me. Nobody ever does that; they are only too glad to keep me in a good temper."

"If you are like that, Sir, I had better run away. My father will be home in about an hour, and he might think that you had no business here."

"I! No business upon my own land! This place must be bewitched, I think. There is a witch upon the moors, I know, who can take almost any shape; but —but they say she is three hundred years of age, or more."

"Perhaps, then, I am bewitched," said Insie; "or why should I stop to talk with you, who are only a rude boy, after all, even according to your own account?"

"Well, you can go if you like. I suppose you live in that queer little place down there?"

"The house is quite good enough for me and my father and mother and brother Maunder. Good-by; and please never to come here again."

"You don't understand me. I have made you cry. Oh, Insie, let me have hold of your hand. I would rather make anybody cry than you. I never liked anybody so before."

"Cry, indeed! Who ever heard me cry? It is the way you splashed the water up. I am not in the habit of crying for a stranger. Good-by, now; and go to your great people. You say that you are bad; and I fear it is too true."

"I am not bad at all. It is only what everybody says, because I never want to please them. But I want to please you. I would give anything to do it; if you would only tell me how."

The girl having cleverly dried her eyes, poured all their bright beauty upon him, and the heart of the youth was enlarged with a new, very sweet, and most timorous feeling. Then his dark eyes dropped, and he touched her gently, and only said, "Don't go away."

"But I must go away," Insie answered, with a blush, and a look as of more tears lurking in her eyes. "I have stopped too long; I must go away at once."

"But when may I come again? I will hold you, and fight for you with everybody in the world, unless you tell me when to come again."

"Hush! I am quite ashamed to hear you talk so. I am a poor girl, and you a great young gentleman."

"Never mind that. That has nothing to do with it. Would you like to make me miserable, and a great deal more wicked than I ever was before? Do you hate me so much as all that, Insie?"

"No. You have been very kind to me. Only my father would be angry, I am sure; and my brother Maunder is dreadful. They all go away every other Friday, and that is the only free time I have."

"Every other Friday! What a long time, to be sure! Won't you come again for water this day fortnight?"

"Yes; I come for water three or four times every day. But if they were to see you, they would kill you first, and then lock me up forever. The only wise plan is for you to come no more."

"You can not be thinking for a moment what you say. I will tell you what; if you don't come, I will march up to the house, and beat the door in. The landlord can do that, according to law."

"If you care at all for me," said Insie, looking as if she had known him for ten years, "you will do exactly what I tell you. You will think no more about me for a fortnight; and then if you fancy that I can do you good by advice about your bad temper, or by teaching you how to plait reeds for a bat, and how to fill a pitcher—perhaps I might be able to come down the gill again."

"I wish it was to-morrow. I shall count the days. But be sure to come early, if they go away all day. I shall bring my dinner with me; and you shall have the first help, and I will carve. But I should like one thing before I go; and it is the first time I ever asked anybody, though they ask me often enough, I can tell you."

"What would you like? You seem to me to be always wanting something."

"I should like very much—very much indeed—just to give you one kiss, Insie."

"It can not be thought of for a moment," she replied; "and the first time of my ever seeing you, Sir!"

Before he could reason in favor of a privilege which goes proverbially by favor, the young maid was gone upon the winding path, with the pitcher truly balanced on her well-tressed head. Then Pet sat down and watched her; and she turned round in the distance, and waved him a kiss at decorous interval.

Not more than three days after this, Mrs. Carnaby came into the drawing-room with a hasty step, and a web of wrinkles upon her generally smooth, white forehead.

"Eliza," asked her sister, "what has put you out so? That chair is not very strong, and you are rather heavy. Do you call that gracefully sinking on a seat, as we used to learn the way to do at school?"

"No, I do not call it anything of the kind. And if I am heavy, I only keep my heart in countenance, Philippa. You know not the anxieties of a mother."

"I am thankful to say that I do not. I have plenty of larger cares to attend to, as well as the anxieties of an aunt and sister. But what is this new maternal care?"

"Poor Pet's illness—his serious illness. I am surprised that you have not noticed it, Philippa; it seems so unkind of you."

"There can not be anything much amiss with him. I never saw any one eat a better breakfast. What makes you fancy that the boy must be unwell?"

"It is no fancy. He must be very ill. Poor dear! I can not bear to think of it. He has done no mischief for quite three days."

"Then he must indeed be at the point of death. Oh, if we could only keep him always so, Eliza!"

"My dear sister, you will never understand him. He must have his little playful ways. Would you like him to be a milksop?"

"Certainly not. But I should like him first to be a manly boy, and then a boyish man. The Yordases always have been manly boys; instead of puling, and puking, and picking this, that, and the other."

"The poor child can not help his health, Philippa. He never had the Yordas constitution. He inherits his delicate system from his poor dear gallant father."

Mrs. Carnaby wiped away a tear; and her sister (who never was hard to her) spoke gently, and said there were many worse boys than he, and she liked him for many good and brave points of character, and especially for hating medicine.

"Philippa, you are right; he does hate medicine," the good mother answered, with a soft, sad sigh; "and he kicked the last apothecary in the stomach, when he made certain of its going down. But such things are trifles, dear, in comparison with now. If he would only kick Jordas, or Welldrum, or almost any one who would take it nicely, I should have some hope that he was coming to himself. But to see him sit quiet is so truly sad. He gets up a tree with his vast activity, and there he sits moping by the hour, and gazing in one fixed direction. I am almost sure that he has knocked his leg; but he flew into a fury when I wanted to examine it; and when I made a poultice, there was Saracen devouring it; and the nasty dog swallowed one of my lace handkerchiefs."

"Then surely you are unjust, Eliza, in lamenting all lack of mischief. But I have noticed things as well as you. And yesterday I saw something more portentous than anything you have told me. I came upon Lancelot suddenly, in the last place where I should have looked for him. He was positively in the library, and reading—reading a real book."

"A book, Phillppa! Oh, that settles everything. He must have gone altogether out of his sane mind."

"Not only was it a book, but even a book of what people call poetry. You have heard of that bold young man over the mountains, who is trying to turn poetry upside down, by making it out of every single thing he sees; and who despises all the pieces that we used to learn at school. I can not remember his name; but never mind. I thought that we ought to encourage him, because he might know some people in this neighborhood; and so I ordered a book of his. Perhaps I told you; and that is the very book your learned boy was reading."

"Philippa, it seems to me impossible almost. He must have been looking at the pictures. I do hope he was only looking at the pictures."

"There is not a picture in the hook of any sort. He was reading it, and saying it quite softly to himself; and I felt that if you saw him, you would send for Dr. Spraggs."

"Ring the bell at once, dear, if you will be kind enough. I hope there is a fresh horse in the stable. Or the best way would be to send the jumping-car; then he would be certain to come back at once."

"Do as you like. I begin to think that we ought to take proper precautions. But when that is done, I will tell you what I think he may be up the tree for."

A man with the jumping-car was soon dispatched, by urgency of Jordas, for Dr. Spraggs, who lived several miles away, in a hamlet to the westward, inaccessible to anything that could not jump right nimbly. But the ladies made a slight mistake: they caught the doctor, but no patient.

For Pet being well up in his favorite tree—poring with great wonder over Lyrical Ballads, which took his fancy somehow—thence descried the hateful form of Dr. Spraggs, too surely approaching in the seat of honor of the jumping-car. Was ever any poesy of such power as to elevate the soul above the smell of physic? The lofty poet of the lakes and fells fell into Pet's pocket anyhow, and down the off side of the tree came he, with even his bad leg ready to be foremost in giving leg-bail to the medical man. The driver of the jumping-car espied this action; but knowing that he would have done the like, grinned softly, and said nothing. And long after Dr. Spraggs was gone, leaving behind him sage advice, and a vast benevolence of bottles, Pet returned, very dirty and hungry, and cross, and most unpoetical.

CHAPTER XXII

YOUNG GILLY FLOWERS

"Drum," said Pet, in his free and easy style, about ten days after that escape, to a highly respected individual, Mr. Welldrum, the butler—"Drum, you have heard perhaps about my being poorly."

"Ay, that I have, and too much of it," replied the portly butler, busy in his office with inferior work, which he never should have had to do, if rightly estimated. "What you wants, Master Lancelot, is a little more of this here sort of thing—sleeves up—elbow grease—scrub away at hold ancient plate, and be blowed up if you puts a scratch on it; and the more you sweats, the less thanks you gets."

"Drum, when you come to be my butler, you shall have all the keys allowed you, and walk about with them on a great gold ring, with a gold chain down to your breeches pocket. You shall dine when you like, and have it cooked on purpose, and order it directly after breakfast; and you shall have the very best hot-water plates; because you hate grease, don't you, Drum?"

"That I do; especial from young chaps as wants to get something out of me."

"I am always as good as my word; come, now."

"That you are, Sir; and nothing very grand to say, considering the hepithets you applies to me sometimes. But you han't insulted me for three days now; and that proves to my mind that you can't be quite right."

"But you would like to see me better. I am sure you would. There is nobody so good to you as I am, Drum; and you are very crusty at times, you know. Your daughter shall be the head cook; and then everything must be to your liking."

"Master Lancelot, you speaks fair. What can I have the honor of doing for you, Sir, to set you up again in your poor dear 'ealth?"

"Well, you hate physic, don't you, Drum? And you make a strict point of never taking it."

"I never knew no good to come out of no bottle, without it were a bottle of old crusted port-wine. Ah! you likes that, Master Lancelot."

"I'll tell you what it is, Drum; I am obliged to be very careful. The reason why I don't get on is from taking my meals too much in-doors. There is no fresh air in these old rooms. I have got a man who says—I could read it to you; but perhaps you don't care to hear poetry, Drum?" The butler made a face, and put the leather to his ears. "Very well, then; I am only just beginning; and it's like claret, you must learn to come to it. But from what he says, and from my own stomach, I intend to go and dine out-of-doors to-day."

"Lord! Master Lancelot, you must be gone clean daft. How ever could you have hot gravy, Sir? And all the Yordases hales cold meat. Your poor dear grandfather—ah! he was a man."

"So am I. And I have got half a guinea. Now, Drum, you do just what I tell you; and mind, not a word to any one. It will be the last coin you ever see of mine, either now or in all my life, remember, if you let my mamma ever hear of it. You slip down to the larder and get me a cold grouse, and a cold partridge, and two of the hearth-stone cakes, and a pat of butter, and a pinch of salt, and put them in my army knapsack Aunt Philippa gave me; also a knife and fork and plate; and—let me see—what had I better have to drink?"

"Well, Sir, if I might offer an opinion, a pint bottle of dry port, or your grandfather's Madeira."

"Young ladies—young gentlemen I mean, of course—never take strong wines in the middle of the day. Bucellas, Drum—Bucellas is the proper thing. And when you have got it all together, turn the old cat into the larder, and get away cleverly by your little door, and put my knapsack in the old oak-tree, the one that was struck by lightning. Now do you understand all about it? It must all be ready in half an hour. And if I make a good dinner out on the moor, why, you might get another half guinea before long." And with these words away strode Pet.

"Well, well," the butler began muttering to himself; "what wickedness are you up to next? A lassie in his head, and his dear mammy thought he was sickening over his wisdom-teeth! He is beginning airly, and no mistake. But the gals are a coarse ugly lot about here"—Master Welldrum was not a Yorkshireman—"and the lad hath good taste in the matter of wine; although he is that contrairy, Solomon's self could not be upsides with him. Fall fair, fall foul, I must humor the boy, or out of this place I go, neck and crop."

Accordingly, Pet found all that he had ordered, and several little things which he had not thought of, especially a corkscrew and a glass; and forgetting half his laziness, he set off briskly, keeping through the trees where no window could espy him, and down a little side glen, all afoot; for it seemed to him safer to forego his pony.

The gill (or "ghyll," as the poet writes it), from which the lonely family that dwelt there took their name, was not upon the bridle-road from Scargate Hall toward Middleton, nor even within eye or reach of any road at all; but overlooked by kites alone, and tracked with thoroughfare of nothing but the mountain streamlet. The four who lived there—"Bat and Zilpic, Maunder and Insie, of the Gill"—had nothing to do with, and little to say to, any of the scatterling folk about them, across the blue distance of the moor. They ploughed no land, they kept no cattle, they scarcely put spade in the ground, except for about a fortnight in April, when they broke up a strip of alluvial soil new every season, and abutting on the brook; and there sowed or planted their vegetable crop, and left it to the clemency of heaven. Yet twice every year they were ready with their rent when it suited Master Jordas to come for it, since audits at the hall, and tenants' dinners, were not to their liking. The rent was a trifle; but Jordas respected them highly for handing it done up in white paper, without even making him leave the saddle. How many paid less, or paid nothing at all, yet came to the dinners under rent reservation of perhaps one mark, then strictly reserved their rent, but failed not to make the most punctual and liberal marks upon roast beef and plum-pudding!

But while the worthy dogman got his little bit of money, sealed up and so correct that (careful as he was) he never stopped now to count it, even his keen eyes could make nothing of these people, except that they stood upon their dignity. To him they appeared to be of gypsy race; or partly of wild and partly perhaps of Lancastrian origin; for they rather "featured" the Lancashire than the Yorkshire type of countenance, yet without any rustic coarseness, whether of aspect, voice, or manners. The story of their settlement in this glen had flagged out of memory of gossip by reason of their calm obscurity, and all that survived was the belief that they were queer, and the certainty that they would not be meddled with.

Lancelot Yordas Carnaby was brave, both in the outward and the inward boy, when he struck into the gill from a trackless spread of moor, not far from the source of the beck that had shaped or been shaped by this fissure. He had made up his mind to learn all about the water that filled sweet Insie's pitcher; and although the great poet of nature as yet was only in early utterance, some of his words had already touched Pet as he had never been touched before; but perhaps that fine effect was due to the sapping power of first love.

Yet first love, however it may soften and enlarge a petulant and wayward nature, instead of increasing, cuts short and crisp the patience of the patient. When Lancelot was as near as manners and prudence allowed to that lonesome house, he sat down quietly for a little while in a little niche of scrubby bush whence he could spy the door. For a short time this was very well; also it was well to be furnishing his mind with a form for the beautiful expressions in it, and prepare it for the order of their coming out. And when he was sure that these were well arranged, and could not fail at any crisis, he found a further pastime in considering his boots, then his gaiters and small-clothes (which were of lofty type), and his waistcoat, elegant for anybody's bosom. But after a bit even this began to pall; and when one of his feet went fast asleep, in spite of its beautiful surroundings, he jumped up and stamped, and was not so very far from hot words as he should have been. For his habit was not so much to want a thing as to get it before he wanted it, which is very poor training for the trials of the love-time.

But just as he was beginning to resolve to be wise, and eat his victuals, now or never, and be sorry for any one who came too late—there came somebody by another track, whose step made the heart rise, and the stomach fall. Lancelot's mind began to fail him all at once; and the spirit that was ready with a host of words fluttered away into a quaking depth of silence. Yet Insie tripped along as if the world held no one to cast a pretty shadow from the sun beside her own.

Even the youngest girls are full of little tricks far beyond the oldest boy's comprehension. But the wonder of all wonders is, they have so pure a conscience as never to be thinking of themselves at all, far less of any one who thinks too much of them. "I declare, she has forgotten that she ever saw me!" Lancelot muttered to the bush in which he trembled. "It would serve her right, if I walked straight away." But he looked again, and could not help looking more than many times again, so piercing (as an ancient poet puts it) is the shaft from the eyes of the female women. And Insie was especially a female girl—which has now ceased to be tautology—so feminine were her walk, and way, and sudden variety of unreasonable charm.

"Dear me! I never thought to see you any more, Sir;" said she, with a bright blush, perhaps at such a story, as Pet jumped out eagerly, with hands stretched forth. "It is the most surprising thing. And we might have done very well with rain-water."

"Oh, Insie! don't be so cold-hearted. Who can drink rain-water? I have got something very good for you indeed. I have carried it all the way myself; and only a strong man could have done it. Why, you have got stockings on, I declare; but I like you much better without them."

"Then, Master Lancelot Yordas Carnaby, you had better go home with all your good things."

"You are totally mistaken about that. I could never get these things into the house again, without being caught out to a certainty. It shows how little girls know of anything."

"A girl can not be expected," she answered, looking most innocently at

189

him, "to understand anything sly or cunning. Why should anything of that sort be?"

"Well, if it comes to that," cried Pet, who (like all unreasonable people) had large rudiments of reasoning, "why should not I come up to your door, and knock, and say, 'I want to see Miss Insie; I am fond of Miss Insie, and have got something good for her'? That is what I shall do next time."

"If you do, my brother Maunder will beat you dreadfully—so dreadfully that you will never walk home. But don't let us talk of such terrible things. You must never come here, if you think of such things. I would not have you hurt for all the world; for sometimes I think that I like you very much."

The lovely girl looked at the handsome boy, as if they were at school together, learning something difficult, which must be repeated to the other's eyes, with a nod, or a shake of the head, as may be. A kind, and pure, and soft gaze she gave him, as if she would love his thoughts, if he could explain them. And Pet turned away, because he could not do so.

"I'll tell you what it is," he said, bravely, while his heart was thrilling with desire to speak well; "we will set to at once, and have a jolly good spread. I told my man to put up something very good, because I was certain that you would be very hungry."

"Surely you were not so foolish as to speak of me?"

"No, no, no; I know a trick worth two of that. I was not such a fool as to speak of you, of course. But—"

"But I would never condescend to touch one bit. You were ashamed to say a word about me, then, were you?"

"Insie, now, Insie, too bad of you it is. You can have no idea what those butlers and footmen are, if ever you tell them anything. They are worse than the maids; they go down stairs, and they get all the tidbits out of the cook, and sit by the girl they like best, on the strength of having a secret about their master."

"Well, you are cunning!" cried the maiden, with a sigh. "I thought that your nature was loftier than that. No, I do not know anything of butlers and footmen; and I think that the less I know of you the better."

"Oh, Insie, darling Insie, if you run away like that—I have got both your hands, and you shall not run away. Do you want to kill me, Insie? They have had the doctor for me."

"Oh, how very dreadful! that does sound dreadful. I am not at all crying, and you need not look. But what did he say? Please to tell me what he said."

"He said, 'Salts and senna.' But I got up a high tree. Let us think of nicer things. It is enough to spoil one's dinner. Oh, Insie, what is anything to eat or drink, compared with looking at you, when you are good? If I could only tell you the things that I have felt, all day and all night, since this day fortnight, how sorry you would be for having evil thoughts of me!"

"I have no evil thoughts; I have no thoughts at all. But it puzzles me to think what on earth you have been thinking. There, I will sit down, and listen for a moment."

"And I may hold one of your hands? I must, or you would never understand me. Why, your hands are much smaller than mine, I declare! And mine are very small; because of thinking about you. Now you need not laugh—it does spoil everything to laugh so. It is more than a fortnight since I laughed at all. You make me feel so miserable. But would you like to know how I felt? Mind, I would rather cut my head off than tell it to any one in the world but you."

"Now I call that very kind of you. If you please, I should like to know how you have been feeling." With these words Insie came quite close up to his side, and looked at him so that he could hardly speak. "You may say it in a whisper, if you like," she said; "there is nobody coming for at least three hours, and so you may say it in a whisper."

"Then I will tell you; it was just like this. You know that I began to think how beautiful you were at the very first time I looked at you. But you could not expect me so to love you all at once as I love you now, dear Insie."

"I can not understand any meaning in such things." But she took a little distance, quite as if she did.

"Well, I went away without thinking very much, because I had a bad place in my knee—a blue place bigger than the new half crown, where you saw that the pony kicked me. I had him up, and thrashed him, when I got home; but that has got nothing to do with it—only that I made him know who was his master. And then I tried to go on with a lot of things as usual; but somehow I did not care at all. There was a great rat hunt that I had been thinking of more than three weeks, when they got the straddles down, to be ready for the new ricks to come instead. But I could not go near it; and it made them think that the whole of my inside was out of order. And it must have been. I can see by looking back; it must have been so, without my knowing it. I hit several people with my holly on their shins, because they knew more than I did. But that was no good; nor was anything else. I only got more and more out of sorts, and could not stay quiet anywhere; and yet it was no good to me to try to make a noise. All day I went about as if I did not care whether people contradicted me or not, or where I was, or what time I should get back, or whether there would be any dinner. And I tucked up my feet in my nightgown every night; but instead of stopping there, as they always used to do, they were down in cold places immediately; and instead of any sleep, I bit holes by the hundred in the sheets, with thinking. I hated to be spoken to, and I hated everybody; and so I do now, whenever I come to think about them!"

"Including even poor me, I suppose?" Insie had wonderfully pretty eyebrows, and a pretty way of raising them, and letting more light into her bright hazel eyes.

"No, I never seemed to hate you; though I often was put out, because I could never make your face come well. I was thinking of you always, but I could not see you. Now tell me whether you have been like that."

"Not at all; but I have thought of you once or twice, and wondered what could make you want to come and see me. If I were a boy, perhaps I could understand it."

"I hate boys; I am a man all over now. I am old enough to have a wife; and I mean to have you. How much do you suppose my waistcoat cost? Well, never mind, because you are not rich. But I have got money enough for both of us to live well, and nobody can keep me out of it. You know what a road is, I suppose—a good road leading to a town? Have you ever seen one? A brown place, with hedges on each side, made hard and smooth for horses to go upon, and wheels that make a rumble. Well, if you will have me, and behave well to me, you shall sit up by yourself in a velvet dress, with a man before you and a man behind, and believe that you are flying."

"But what would become of my father, and my mother, and my brother Maunder?"

"Oh, they must stop here, of course. We shouldn't want them. But I would give them all their house rent-free, and a fat pig every Christmas. Now you sit there and spread your lap, that I may help you properly. I want to see you eat; you must learn to eat like a lady of the highest quality; for that you are going to be, I can tell you."

The beautiful maid of the gill smiled sweetly, sitting on the low bank with the grace of simple nature and the playfulness of girlhood. She looked up at Lancelot, the self-appointed man, with a bright glance of curious contemplation; and contemplation (of any other subject than self) is dangerously near contempt. She thought very little of his large, free brag, of his patronizing manner, and fine self-content, reference of everything to his own standard, beauty too feminine, and instead of female gentleness, highly cultivated waywardness. But in spite of all that, she could not help liking, and sometimes admiring him, when he looked away. And now he was very busy with the high feast he had brought.

"To begin with," he said, when his good things were displayed, "you must remember that nothing is more vulgar than to be hungry. A gentleman may have a tremendous appetite, but a lady never."

"But why? but why? That does seem foolish. I have read that the ladies are always helped first. That must be because of their appetites."

"Insie, I tell you things, not the reasons of them. Things are learned by seeing other people, and not by arguing about them."

"Then you had better eat your dinner first, and let me sit and watch you. And then I can eat mine by imitation; that is to say, if there is any left."

"You are one of the oddest people I have ever seen. You go round the corner of all that I say, instead of following properly. When we are married, you will always make me laugh. At one time they kept a boy to make me laugh; but I got tired of him. Now I help you first, although I am myself so hungry. I do it from a lofty feeling, which my aunt Philippa calls 'chivalry.' Ladies talk about it when they want to get the best of us. I have given you all the best part, you see; and I only keep the worst of it for myself."

If Pet had any hope that his self-denial would promptly be denied to him, he made a great mistake; for the damsel of the gill had a healthy moorland appetite, and did justice to all that was put before her; and presently he began, for the first time in his life, to find pleasure in seeing another person pleased. But the wine she would not even taste, in spite of persuasion and example; the water from the brook was all she drank, and she drank as prettily as a pigeon. Whatever she did was done gracefully and well.

"I am very particular," he said at last; "but you are fit to dine with anybody. How have you managed to learn it all? You take the best of everything, without a word about it, as gently as great ladies do. I thought that you would want me to eat the nicest pieces; but instead of that, you have left me bones and drumsticks."

He gave such a melancholy look at these that Insie laughed quite merrily. "I wanted to see you practice chivalry," she said.

"Well, never mind; I shall know another time. Instead of two birds, I shall order four, and other things in proportion. But now I want to know about your father and your mother. They must be respectable people, to judge by you. What is their proper name, and how much have they got to live upon?"

"More than you—a great deal more than you," she answered, with such a roguish smile that he forgot his grievances, or began to lose them in the mist of beauty.

"More than me! And they live in such a hole, where only the crows come near them?"

"Yes, more than you, Sir. They have their wits to live upon, and industry, and honesty."

Pet was not old enough yet in the world to say, "What is the use of all those? All their income is starvation." He was young enough to think that those who owned them had advantage of him, for he knew that he was very lazy. Moreover, he had heard of such people getting on—through the striking power of exception, so much more brilliant than the rule—when all the blind virtues found luck to lead them. Industry, honesty, and ability always get on in story-books, and nothing is nicer than to hear a pretty story. But in some ways Pet was sharp enough.

"Then they never will want that house rent-free, nor the fat pig, nor any other presents. Oh, Insie, how very much better that will be! I find it so much nicer always to get thing's than to give them. And people are so good-natured, when they have done it, and can talk of it. Insie, they shall give me something when I marry you, and as often as they like afterward."

"They will give you something you will not like," she answered, with a laugh, and a look along the moor, "if you stay here too long chattering with me. Do you know what o'clock it is? I know always, whether the sun is out or in. You need show no gold watch to me."

"Oh, that comes of living in a draught all day. The out-door people grow too wise. What do you see about ten miles off? It must be ten miles to that hill."

"That hill is scarcely five miles off, and what I see is not half of that. I brought you up here to be quite safe. Maunder's eyes are better than mine. But he will not see us, for another mile, if you cover your grand waistcoat, because we are in the shadows. Slip down into the gill again, and keep below the edge of it, and go home as fast as possible."

Lancelot felt inclined to do as he was told, and keep to safe obscurity. The long uncomfortable loneliness of prospect, and dim airy distance of the sinking sun, and deeply silent emptiness of hollows, where great shadows began to crawl—in the waning of the day, and so far away from home—all these united to impress upon the boy a spiritual influence, whose bodily expression would be the appearance of a clean pair of heels. But, to meet this sensible impulse, there arose the stubborn nature of his race, which hated to be told to do anything, and the dignity of his new-born love—such as it was—and the thought of looking small.

"Why should I go?" he said. "I will meet them, and tell them that I am their landlord, and have a right to know all about them. My grandfather never ran away from anybody. And they have got a donkey with them."

"They will have two, if you stop," cried Insie, although she admired his spirit. "My father is a very quiet man. But Maunder would take you by the throat and cast you down into the beck."

"I should like to see him try to do it. I am not so very strong, but I am active as a cat. I have no idea of being threatened."

"Then will you be coaxed? I do implore you, for my sake, to go, or it will be too late. Never, never, will you see me again, unless you do what I beseech of you."

"I will not stir one peg, unless you put your arms round my neck and kiss me, and say that you will never have anybody else."

Insie blushed deeply, and her bright eyes flashed with passion not of loving kind. But it went to her heart that he was brave, and that he loved her truly. She flung her comely arms round his neck, and touched her rosy lips with his; and before he could clasp her she was gone, with no more comfort than these words:

"Now if you are a gentleman, you must go, and never come near this place again."

Not a moment too soon he plunged into the gill, and hurried up its winding course; but turning back at the corner, saw a sweet smile in the distance, and a wave of the hand, that warmed his heart.

CHAPTER XXIII

LOVE MILITANT

So far so good. But that noble and exalted condition of the youthful mind which is to itself pure wisdom's zenith, but to folk of coarse maturity and tough experience "calf-love," superior as it is to words and reason, must be left to its own course. The settled resolve of a middle-aged man, with seven large-appetited children, and an eighth approaching the shores of light, while baby-linen too often transmitted betrays a transient texture, and hose has ripened into holes, and breeches verify their name, and a knock at the door knocks at the heart—the fixed resolution of such a man to strike a bold stroke, for the sake of his home, is worthier of attention than the flitting fancy of boy and girl, who pop upon one another, and skip through zigzag vernal ecstasy, like the weathery dalliance of gnats.

Lieutenant Carroway had dealt and done with amorous grace and attitude, soaring rapture, and profundity of sigh, suspense (more agonizing than suspension), despair, prostration, grinding of the teeth, the hollow and spectral laugh of a heart forever broken, and all the other symptoms of an annual bill of vitality; and every new pledge of his affections sped him toward the pledge-shop. But never had he crossed that fatal threshold; the thought of his uniform and dignity prevailed; and he was not so mean as to send a child to do what the father was ashamed of.

So it was scarcely to be expected that even as a man he should sympathize deeply with the tender passion, and far less, as a coast-guardsman, with the wooing of a smuggler. Master Robin Lyth, by this time, was in the contraband condition known to the authorities as love; Carroway had found out this fact; but instead of indulging in generous emotion, he made up his mind to nab him through it. For he reasoned as follows; and granting that reason has any business on such premises, the process does not seem amiss.

A man in love has only got one-eighth part of his wits at home to govern the doings of his arms, legs, and tongue. A large half is occupied with his fancy, in all the wanderings of that creature, dreamy, flimsy, anchoring with gossamer, climbing the sky with steps of fog, cast into abysms (as great writers call it) by imaginary demons, and even at its best in a queer condition, pitiful, yet exceeding proud. A quarter of the mental power is employed in wanting to know what the other people think; an eighth part ought to be dwelling upon the fair distracting object; and only a small eighth can remain to attend to the business of the solid day. But in spite of all this, such lads get on about as well as usual. If Bacchus has a protective power, Venus has no less of it, and possibly is more active, as behooves a female.

And surely it was a cold-blooded scheme, which even the Revenue should have excised from an honest scale of duties, to catch a poor fellow in the meshes of love, because he was too sharp otherwise. This, however, was the large idea ripening in the breast of Carroway.

"To-night I shall have him," he said to his wife, who was inditing of softer things, her eighth confinement, and the shilling she had laid that it would be a boy this time. "The weather is stormy, yet the fellow makes love between the showers in a barefaced way. That old fool of a tanner knows it, and has no more right feeling than if he were a boy. Aha, my Robin, fine robin as you are, I shall catch you piping with your Jenny Wren tonight!" The lieutenant shared the popular ignorance of simplest natural history.

"Charles, you never should have told me of it. Where is your feeling for the days gone by? And as for his coming between the showers, what should I have thought of you if you had made a point of bringing your umbrella? My dear, it is wrong. And I beg you, for my sake, not to catch him with his true love, but only with his tubs."

"Matilda, your mind is weakened by the coming trial of your nerves. I would rather have him with his tubs, of course; they would set us up for several years, and his silks would come in for your churching. But everything can not be as we desire. And he carries large pistols when he is not courting. Do you wish me to be shot, Matilda?"

"Captain Carroway, how little thought you have, to speak to me in that way! And I felt before dinner that I never should get over it. Oh, who would have the smugglers on her mind, at such a time?"

"My dear, I beg your pardon. Pray exert your strength of mind, and cast such thoughts away from you—or perhaps it will be a smuggler. And yet if it were, how much better it would pay!"

"Then I hope it will, Charles; I heartily hope it will be. It would serve you quite right to be snaring your own son, after snaring a poor youth through his sweetheart."

"Well, well, time will show. Put me up the flat bottle, Tilly, and the knuckle of pork that was left last night. Goodness knows when I shall be back; and I never like to rack my mind upon an empty stomach."

The revenue officer had far to go, and was wise in providing provender. And the weather being on the fall toward the equinox, and the tides running strong and uncertain, he had made up his mind to fare inland, instead of attempting the watery ways. He felt that he could ride, as every sailor always feels; and he had a fine horse upon hire from his butcher, which the king himself would pay for. The inferior men had been sent ahead on foot, with orders to march along and hold their tongues. And one of these men was John Cadman, the self-same man who had descended the cliff without any footpath. They were all to be ready, with hanger and pistol, in a hole toward Byrsa Cottage.

Lieutenant Carroway enjoyed his ride. There are men to whom excitement is an elevation of the sad and slow mind, which otherwise seems to have nothing to do. And what finer excitement can a good mind have than in balancing the chances of its body tumbling out of the saddle, and evicting its poor self?

The mind of Charles Carroway was wide awake to this, and tenderly anxious about the bad foot in which its owner ended—because of the importance of the stirrups—and all the sanguine vigor of the heart (which seemed to like some thumping) conveyed to the seat of reason little more than a wish to be well out of it. The brave lieutenant holding place, and sticking to it through a sense of duty, and of the difficulty of getting off, remembered to have heard, when quite a little boy, that a man who gazes steadily between his horse's ears can not possibly tumble off the back. The saying in its wisdom is akin to that which describes the potency of salt upon a sparrow's tail.

While Carroway gloomily pounded the road, with reflection a dangerous luxury, things of even deeper interest took their course at the goal of his endeavors. Mary Anerley, still an exile in the house of the tanner, by reason of her mother's strict coast-guard, had long been thinking that more injustice is done in the world than ought to be; and especially in the matter of free trade she had imbibed lax opinions, which may not be abhorrent to a tanner's nature, but were most unbecoming to the daughter of a farmer orthodox upon his own land, and an officer of King's Fencibles. But how did Mary make this change, and upon questions of public policy chop sides, as quickly as a clever journal does? She did it in the way in which all women think, whose thoughts are of any value, by allowing the heart to go to work, being the more active organ, and create large scenery, into which the tempted mind must follow. To anybody whose life has been saved by anybody else, there should arise not only a fine image of the preserver, but a high sense of the service done to the universe, which must have gone into deepest mourning if deprived of No. One. And then, almost of necessity, succeeds the investment of this benefactor to the world at large with all the great qualities needed for an exploit so stupendous. He has done a great deed, he has proved himself to be gallant, generous, magnanimous; shall I, who exist through his grand nobility, listen to his very low enemies? Therefore Robin was an angel now, and his persecutors must be demons.

Captain Lyth had not been slow to enter into his good luck. He knew that Master Popplewell had a cultivated taste for rare old schnapps, while the partner of his life, and labor, and repose, possessed a desire for the finer kinds of lace. Attending to these points, he was always welcome; and the excellent couple encouraged his affection and liberal goodwill toward them. But Mary would accept no presents from him, and behaved for a long time very strangely, and as if she would rather keep out of his way. Yet he managed to keep on running after her, as much as she managed to run away; for he had been down now into the hold of his heart, searching it with a dark lantern, and there he had discovered "Mary," "Mary," not only branded on the hullage of all things, but the pith and pack of everything; and without any fraud upon charter-party, the cargo entire was "Mary."

Who can tell what a young maid feels, when she herself is doubtful? Somehow she has very large ideas, which only come up when she begins to think; and too often, after some very little thing, she exclaims that all is rubbish. The key-note of her heart is high, and a lot of things fall below harmony, and notably (if she is not a stupe), some of her own dear love's expressions before she has made up her soul to love him. This is a hard time for almost any man, who feels his random mind dipped into with a spirit-gauge and a saccharometer. But in spite of all these indications, Robin Lyth stuck to himself, which is the right way to get credit for sticking.

"Johnny, my dear," said Deborah Popplewell to her valued husband, just about the time when bold Carroway was getting hot and sore upon the Filey Road, yet steadily enlarging all the penance of return, "things ought to be coming to a point, I think. We ought not to let them so be going on forever. Young people like to be married in the spring; the birds are singing, and the price of coal goes down. And they ought to be engaged six months at least. We were married in the spring, my dear, the Tuesday but one that comes next from Easter-day. There was no lilac out, but there ought to have been, because it was not sunny. And we have never repented it, you know."

"Never as long as I live shall I forget that day," said Popplewell; "they sent me home a suit of clothes as were made for kidney-bean sticks. I did want to look nice at church, and crack, crack, crack they went, and out came all the lining. Debby, I had good legs in those days, and could crunch down bark like brewers' grains."

"And so you could now, my dear, every bit as well. Scarcely any of the young men have your legs. How thankful we ought to be for them—and teeth! But everything seems to be different now, and nobody has any dignity of mind. We sowed broad beans, like a pigeon's foot-tread, out and in, all the way to church."

"The folk can never do such things now; we must not expect it of such times, my dear. Five-and-forty years ago was ninety times better than these days, Debby, except that you and I was steadfast, and mean to be so to the end, God willing. Lord! what are the lasses that He makes now?"

"Johnny, they try to look their best; and we must not be hard upon them. Our Mary looks well enow, when she hath a color, though my eyes might 'a been a brighter blue if I never hadn't took to spectacles. Johnny, I am sure a'most that she is in her love-time. She crieth at night, which is nobody's business; the strings of her night-cap run out of their starch; and there looks like a channel on the pillow, though the sharp young hussy turns it upside down. I shall be upsides with her, if you won't."

"Certainly it shall be left to you; you are the one to do it best. You push her on, and I will stir him up. I will smuggle some schnapps into his tea to-night, to make him look up bolder; as mild as any milk it is. When I was taken with your cheeks, Debby, and your bit of money, I was never that long in telling you."

"That's true enow, Johnny; you was sarcy. But I'm thinking of the trouble we may get into over at Anerley about it."

"I'll carry that, lass. My back's as broad as Stephen's. What more can they want for her than a fine young fellow, a credit to his business and the country? Lord! how I hate them rough coast-riders! it wouldn't be good for them to come here."

"Then they are here, I tell you, and much they care. You seem to me to have shut your eyes since ever you left off tanning. How many times have I told you, John, that a sneaking fellow hath got in with Sue? I saw him with my own eyes last night skulking past the wicket-gate; and the girl's addle-pate is completely turned. You think her such a wonder, that you won't hearken. But I know the women best, I do."

"Out of this house she goes, neck and crop, if what you say is true, Deb. Don't say it again, that's a kind, good soul; it spoils my pipe to think of it."

Toward sundown Robin Lyth appeared, according to invitation. Dandy as he generally was, he looked unusually smart this time, with snow-white ducks and a velvet waistcoat, pumps like a dressing-glass, lace to his shirt, and a blue coat with gold buttons. His keen eyes glanced about for Mary, and sparkled as soon as she came down; and when he took her hand she blushed, and was half afraid to look at him; for she felt in her heart that he meant to say something, if he could find occasion; but her heart did not tell her what answer she would make, because of her father's grief and wrath; so she tried to hope that nothing would be said, and she kept very near her good aunt's apron-string. Such tactics, however, were doomed to defeat. The host and hostess of Byrsa Cottage were very proud of the tea they gave to any distinguished visitor. Tea was a luxury, being very dear, and although large quantities were smuggled, the quality was not, like that of other goods so imported, equal or superior to the fair legitimate staple. And Robin, who never was shy of his profession, confessed that he could not supply a cup so good.

"You shall come and have another out-of-doors, my friend," said his entertainer, graciously. "Mary, take the captain's cup to the bower; the rain has cleared off, and the evening will be fine. I will smoke my pipe, and we will talk adventures. Things have happened to me that would make you stare, if I could bring myself to tell them. Ah yes, I have lived in stirring times. Fifty years ago men and women knew their minds; and a dog could eat his dinner without a damask napkin."

Master Popplewell, who was of a good round form, and tucked his heels over one another as he walked (which indicates a pleasant self-esteem), now lit his long pipe and marched ahead, carefully gazing to the front and far away; so that the young folk might have free boot and free hand behind him. That they should have flutters of loving-kindness, and crafty little breaths of whispering, and extraordinary gifts of just looking at each other in time not to be looked at again, as well as a strange sort of in and out of feeling, as if they were patterned with the same zigzag—as the famous Herefordshire graft is made—and above all the rest, that they should desire to have no one in the world to look at them, was to be expected by a clever old codger, a tanner who had realized a competence, and eaten many "tanner's pies." The which is a good thing; and so much the better because it costs nothing save the crust and the coal. But instead of any pretty little goings on such as this worthy man made room for, to tell the stupid truth, this lad and lass came down the long walk as far apart and as independent of one another as two stakes of an espalier. There had not been a word gone amiss between them, nor even a thought the wrong way of the grain; but the pressure of fear and of prickly expectation was upon them both, and kept them mute. The lad was afraid that he would get "nay," and the lass was afraid that she could not give it.

The bower was quite at the end of the garden, through and beyond the pot-herb part, and upon a little bank which overhung a little lane. Here in this corner a good woman had contrived what women nearly always understand the best, a little nook of pleasure and of perfume, after the rank ranks of the kitchen-stuff. Not that these are to be disdained; far otherwise; they indeed are the real business; and herein lies true test of skill. But still the flowers may declare that they do smell better. And not only were there flowers here, and little shrubs planted sprucely, but also good grass, which is always softness, and soothes the impatient eyes of men. And on this grass there stood, or hung, or flowered, or did whatever it was meant to do, a beautiful weeping-ash, the only one anywhere in that neighborhood.

"I can't look at skies, and that—have seen too many of them. You young folk, go and chirp under the tree. What I want is a little rum and water."

With these words the tanner went into his bower, where he kept a good store of materials in moss; and the plaited ivy of the narrow entrance shook with his voice, and steps, and the decision of his thoughts. For he wanted to see things come to a point, and his only way to do it was to get quite out of sight. Such fools the young people of the age were now!

While his thoughts were such, or scarcely any better, his partner in life came down the walk, with a heap of little things which she thought needful for the preservation of the tanner, and she waddled a little and turned her toes out, for she as well was roundish.

"Ah, you ought to have Sue. Where is Sue?" said Master Popplewell. "Now come you in out of the way of the wind, Debby; you know how your back-sinew ached with the darning before last wash."

Mrs. Popplewell grumbled, but obeyed; for she saw that her lord had his reasons. So Mary and Robin were left outside, quite as if they were nothing to any but themselves. Mary was aware of all this manoeuvring, and it brought a little frown upon her pretty forehead, as if she were cast before the feet of Robin Lyth; but her gentleness prevailed, because they meant her well. Under the weeping-ash there was a little seat, and the beauty of it was that it would not hold two people. She sat down upon it, and became absorbed in the clouds that were busy with the sunset.

These were very beautiful, as they so often are in the broken weather of the autumn; but sailors would rather see fair sky, and Robin's fair heaven was in Mary's eyes. At these he gazed with a natural desire to learn what the symptoms of the weather were; but it seemed as if little could be made out there, because everything seemed so lofty: perhaps Mary had forgotten his existence.

Could any lad of wax put up with this, least of all a daring mariner? He resolved to run the cargo of his heart right in, at the risk of all breakers and drawn cutlasses; and to make a good beginning he came up and took her hand. The tanner in the bower gave approval with a cough, like Cupid with a sneeze; then he turned it to a snore.

"Mary, why do you carry on like this?" the smuggler inquired, in a very gentle voice. "I have done nothing to offend you, have I? That would be the last thing I would ever do."

"Captain Lyth, you are always very good; you never should think such things of me. I am just looking at a particular cloud. And who ever said that you might call me 'Mary'?"

"Perhaps the particular cloud said so; but you must have been the cloud yourself, for you told me only yesterday."

"Then I will never say another word about it; but people should not take advantage."

"Who are people? How you talk! quite as if I were somebody you never saw before. I should like you just to look round now, and let me see why you are so different from yourself."

Mary Anerley looked round; for she always did what people liked, without good reason otherwise; and if her mind was full of clouds, her eyes had little sign of them.

"You look as lovely as you always do," said the smuggler, growing bolder as she looked at something else. "You know long ago what my opinion of you is, and yet you seem to take no notice. Now I must be off, as you know, to-night; not for any reason of my own, as I told you yesterday, but to carry out a contract. I may not see you for many months again; and you may fall in love with a Preventive man."

"I never fall in love with anybody. Why should I go from one extreme to the other? Captain Carroway has seven children, as well as a very active wife."

"I am not afraid of Carroway, in love or in war. He is an honest fellow, with no more brains than this ash-tree over us. I mean the dashing captains who come in with their cutters, and would carry you off as soon as look."

"Captain Lyth, you are not at all considering what you say: those officers do not want me—they want you."

"Then they shall get neither; they may trust me for that. But, Mary, do tell me how your heart is; you know well how mine has been for ever such a time. I tell you downright that I have thought of girls before—"

"Oh, I was not at all aware of that; surely you had better go on with thinking of them."

"You have not heard me out. I have only thought of them; nothing more than thinking, in a foolish sort of way. But of you I do not think; I seem to feel you all through me."

"What sort of a sensation do I seem to be? A foolish one, I suppose, like all those many others."

"No, not at all. A very wise one; a regular knowledge that I can not live without you; a certainty that I could only mope about a little—"

"And not run any more cargoes on the coast?"

"Not a single tub, nor a quarter bale of silk; except, of course, what is under contract now; and, if you should tell me that you can not care about me—"

"Hush! I am almost sure that I hear footsteps. Listen, just a moment."

"No, I will not listen to any one in the world but you. I beg you not to try to put me off. Think of the winter, and the long time coming; say if you will think of me. I must allow that I am not, like you, of a respectable old family. The Lord alone knows where I came from, or where I may go to. My business is a random and up-and-down one, but no one can call it disreputable; and if you went against it, I would throw it up. There are plenty of trades that I can turn my hand to; and I will turn it to anything you please, if you will only put yours inside it. Mary, only let me have your hand; and you need not say anything unless you like."

"But I always do like to say something, when things are brought before me so. I have to consider my father, and my mother, and others belonging to me. It is not as if I were all alone, and could do exactly as I pleased. My father bears an ill-will toward free trade; and my mother has made bad bargains, when she felt sure of very good ones."

"I know that there are rogues about," Robin answered, with a judicial frown; "but foul play never should hurt fair play; and we haul them through the water when we catch them. Your father is terribly particular, I know, and that is the worst thing there can be; but I do not care a groat for all objections, Mary, unless the objection begins with you. I am sure by your eyes, and your pretty lips and forehead, that you are not the one to change. If once any lucky fellow wins your heart, he will have it—unless he is a fool—forever. I can do most things, but not that, or you never would be thinking about the other people. What would anybody be to me in comparison with you, if I only had the chance? I would kick them all to Jericho. Can you see it in that way? can you get hot every time you think of me?"

"Really," said Mary, looking very gently at him, because of his serious excitement, "you are very good, and very brave, and have done wonders for me; but why should I get hot?"

"No, I suppose it is not to be expected. When I am in great peril I grow hot, and tingle, and am alive all over. Men of a loftier courage grow cold; it depends upon the constitution; but I enjoy it more than they do, and I can see things ten times quicker. Oh, how I wish I was Nelson! how he must enjoy himself!"

"But if you have love of continual danger, and eagerness to be always at it," said Mary, with wide Yorkshire sense, much as she admired this heroic type, "the proper thing for you to do is to lead a single life. You might be enjoying all the danger very much; but what would your wife at home be doing? Only to knit, and sigh, and lie awake."

Mary made a bad hit here. This picture was not at all deterrent; so daring are young men, and so selfish.

"Nothing of that sort should ever come to pass," cried Robin, with the gaze of the head of a household, "supposing only that my wife was you. I would be home regularly every night before the kitchen clock struck eight. I would always come home with an appetite, and kiss you, and do both my feet upon the scraper. I would ask how the baby was, and carry him about, and go 'one, two, three,' as the nurses do, I would quite leave the government to put on taxes, and pay them—if I could—without a word of grumble. I would keep every rope about the house in order, as only a sailor knows how to do, and fettle my own mending, and carry out my orders, and never meddle with the kitchen, at least unless my opinion was sought for concerning any little thing that might happen to be meant for me."

"Well," exclaimed Mary, "you quite take my breath away. I had no idea that you were so clever. In return for all these wonders, what should poor I have to do?"

"Poor I would only have to say just once, 'Robin, I will have you, and begin to try to love you.'"

"I am afraid that it has been done long ago; and the thing that I ought to do is to try and help it."

What happened upon this it would be needless to report, and not only needless, but a vast deal worse—shabby, interloping, meddlesome and mean, undignified, unmanly, and disreputably low; for even the tanner and his wife (who must have had right to come forward, if anybody had) felt that their right was a shadow, and kept back as if they were a hundred miles away, and took one another by the hand and nodded, as much as to say: "You remember how we did it; better than that, my dear. Here is your good health."

This being so, and the time so sacred to the higher emotions, even the boldest intruder should endeavor to check his ardor for intrusion. Without any inkling of Preventive Force, Robin and Mary, having once done away with all that stood between them, found it very difficult to be too near together; because of all the many things that each had for to say. They seemed to get into an unwise condition of longing to know matters that surely could not matter. When did each of them first feel sure of being meant only for the other nobler one? At first sight, of course, and with a perfect gift of seeing how much loftier each was than the other; and what an extraordinary fact it was that in everything imaginable they were quite alike, except in the palpable certainty possessed by each of the betterness of the other. What an age it seemed since first they met, positively without thinking, and in the very middle of a skirmish, yet with a remarkable drawing out of perceptions one anotherward! Did Mary feel this, when she acted so cleverly, and led away those vile pursuers? and did Robin, when his breath came back, discover why his heart was glowing in the rabbit-hole? Questions of such depth can not be fathomed in a moment; and even to attempt to do any justice to them, heads must be very long laid together. Not only so, but also it is of prime necessity to make sure that every whisper goes into the proper ear, and abides there only, and every subtlety of glance, and every nicety of touch, gets warm with exclusive reciprocity. It is not too much to say that in so sad a gladness the faculties of self-preservation are weak, when they ought to be most active; therefore it should surprise nobody (except those who are so far above all surprise) to become aware that every word they said, and everything (even doubly sacred) that they did, was well entered into, and thoroughly enjoyed, by a liberal audience of family-minded men, who had been through pretty scenes like this, and quietly enjoyed dry memory.

Cadman, Ellis, and Dick Hackerbody were in comfortable places of retirement, just under the combing of the hedge; all waiting for a whistle, yet at leisure to enjoy the whisper, the murmur, or even the sigh, of a genuine piece of "sweet-hearting." Unjust as it may be, and hard, and truly narrow, there does exist in the human mind, or at least in the masculine half of it, a strong conviction that a man in love is a man in a scrape, in a hole, in a pitfall, in a pitiful condition, untrue for the moment to the brotherhood of man, and cast down among the inferior vessels. And instead of being sorry for him, those who are all right look down, and glory over him, with very ancient gibes. So these three men, instead of being touched at heart by soft confessions, laid hard hands to wrinkled noses.

"Mary, I vow to you, as I stand here," said Robin, for the fiftieth time, leading her nearer to the treacherous hedge, as he pressed her trembling hand, and gazed with deep ecstasy into her truthful eyes, "I will live only to deserve you, darling. I will give up everything and everybody in the world, and start afresh. I will pay king's duty upon every single tub; and set up in the tea and spirit line, with his Majesty's arms upon the lintel. I will take a large contract for the royal navy, who never get anything genuine, and not one of them ever knows good from bad—"

"That's a dirty lie, Sir. In the king's name I arrest you."

Lieutenant Carroway leaped before them, flourishing a long sword, and dancing with excitement, in this the supreme moment of his life. At the same instant three men came bursting through the hedge, drew hangers, and waited for orders. Robin Lyth, in the midst of his love, was so amazed, that he stood like a boy under orders to be caned.

"Surrender, Sir! Down with your arms; you are my prisoner. Strike to his Majesty. Hands to your side! or I run you through like Jack Robinson! Keep back, men. He belongs to me."

But Carroway counted his chicks too soon; or at any rate he overlooked a little chick. For while he was making fine passes (having learned the rudiments of swordsmanship beyond other British officers), and just as he was executing a splendid flourish, upon his bony breast lay Mary. She flung her arms round him, so that move he could not without grievously tearing her; and she managed, in a very wicked way, to throw the whole weight of two bodies on his wounded heel. A flash of pain shot up to his very sword; and down he went, with Mary to protect him, or at any rate to cover him. His three men, like true Britons, stood in position, and waited for their officer to get up and give orders.

These three men showed such perfect discipline that Robin was invited to knock them down, as if they had simply been three skittles in a row; he recovered his presence of mind and did it; and looking back at Mary, received signal to be off. Perceiving that his brave love would take no harm—for the tanner was come forth blustering loudly, and Mrs. Popplewell with shrieks and screams enough to prevent the whole Preventive Service—the free-trader kissed his hand to Mary, and was lost through the bushes, and away into the dark.

CHAPTER XXIV

LOVE PENITENT

"I tell you, Captain Anerley, that she knocked me down. Your daughter there, who looks as if butter would not melt in her mouth, knocked down Commander Carroway of his Majesty's coastguard, like a royal Bengal tiger, Sir. I am not come to complain; such an action I would scorn; and I admire the young lady for her spirit, Sir. My sword was drawn; no man could have come near me; but before I could think, Sir, I was lying on my back. Do you call that constitutional?"

"Mary, lof, however could you think it—to knock down Captain Carroway?"

"Father, I never did. He went down of himself, because he was flourishing about so. I never thought what I was doing of at all. And with all my heart I beg his pardon. What right had you, Sir, to come spying after me?"

This interview was not of the common sort. Lieutenant Carroway, in full uniform, was come to Anerley Farm that afternoon; not for a moment to complain of Mary, but to do his duty, and to put things straight; while Mary had insisted upon going home at once from the hospitable house of Uncle Popplewell, who had also insisted upon going with her, and taking his wife to help the situation.

A council had been called immediately, with Mistress Anerley presiding; and before it had got beyond the crying stage, in marched the brave lieutenant.

Stephen Anerley was reserving his opinion—which generally means that there is none yet to reserve—but in his case there would be a great deal by-and-by. Master Popplewell had made up his mind and his wife's, long ago, and confirmed it in the one-horse shay, while Mary was riding Lord Keppel in the rear; and the mind of the tanner was as tough as good oak bark. His premises had been intruded upon—the property which he had bought with his own money saved by years of honest trade, his private garden, his ornamental bower, his wife's own pleasure-plot, at a sacred moment invaded, trampled, and outraged by a scurvy preventive-man and his low crew. The first thing he had done to the prostrate Carroway was to lay hold of him by the collar, and shake his fist at him and demand his warrant—a magistrate's warrant, or from the crown itself. The poor lieutenant having none to show, "Then I will have the law of you, Sir," the tanner shouted; "if it costs me two hundred and fifty pounds. I am known for a man, Sir, who sticks to his word; and my attorney is a genuine bulldog."

This had frightened Carroway more than fifty broadsides. Truly he loved fighting; but the boldest sailor bears away at prospect of an action at law. Popplewell saw this, and stuck to his advantage, and vowed, until bed-time, satisfaction he would have; and never lost the sight of it until he fell asleep.

Even now it was in his mind, as Carroway could see; his eyebrows meant it, and his very surly nod, and the way in which he put his hands far down into his pockets. The poor lieutenant, being well aware that zeal had exceeded duty (without the golden amnesty of success), and finding out that Popplewell was rich and had no children, did his very best to look with real pleasure at him, and try to raise a loftier feeling in his breast than damages. But the tanner only frowned, and squared his elbows, and stuck his knuckles sharply out of both his breeches pockets. And Mrs. Popplewell, like a fat and most kind-hearted lady, stared at the officer as if she longed to choke him.

"I tell you again, Captain Anerley," cried the lieutenant, with his temper kindling, "that no consideration moved me, Sir, except that of duty. As for my spying after any pretty girls, my wife, who is now down with her eighth baby, would get up sooner than hear of it. If I intruded upon your daughter, so as to justify her in knocking me down, Captain Anerley, it was because—well I won't say, Mary, I won't say; we have all been young; and our place is to know better."

"Sir, you are a gentleman," cried Popplewell with heat; "here is my hand, and you may trespass on my premises, without bringing any attorney."

"Did you say her eighth baby? Oh, Commander Carroway," Mrs. Popplewell began to whisper; "what a most interesting situation! Oh, I see why you have such high color, Sir."

"Madam, it is enough to make me pale. At the same time I do like sympathy; and my dear wife loves the smell of tan."

"We have retired, Sir, many years ago, and purchased a property near the seaside; and from the front gate you must have seen—But oh, I forgot, captain, you came through the hedge, or at any rate down the row of kidney-beans."

"I want to know the truth," shouted Stephen Anerley, who had been ploughing through his brow into his brain, while he kept his eyes fixed upon his daughter's, and there found abashment, but no abasement; "naught have I to do with any little goings on, or whether an action was a gentleman's or not. That question belongs to the regulars, I wand, or to the folk who have retired.

Nobbut a farmer am I, in little business; but concerning of my children I will have my say. All of you tell me what is this about my Mary."

As if he would drag their thoughts out of them, he went from one to another with a hard quick glance, which they all tried to shun; for they did not want to tell until he should get into a better frame of mind. And they looked at Mistress Anerley, to come forth and take his edge off; but she knew that when his eyes were so, to interfere was mischief. But Carroway did not understand the man.

"Come, now, Anerley," the bold lieutenant said; "what are you getting into such a way about? I would sooner have lost the hundred pounds twice over, and a hundred of my own—if so be I ever had it—than get little Mary into such a row as this. Why, Lord bless my heart, one would think that there was murder in a little bit of sweethearting. All pretty girls do it; and the plain ones too. Come and smoke a pipe, my good fellow, and don't terrify her."

For Mary was sobbing in a corner by herself, without even her mother to come up and say a word.

"My daughter never does it," answered Stephen Anerley; "my daughter is not like the foolish girls and women. My daughter knows her mind; and what she does she means to do. Mary, lof, come to your father, and tell him that every one is lying of you. Sooner would I trust a single quiet word of yours, than a pile, as big as Flambro Head, sworn by all the world together against my little Mary."

The rest of them, though much aggrieved by such a bitter calumny, held their peace, and let him go with open arms toward his Mary. The farmer smiled, that his daughter might not have any terror of his public talk; and because he was heartily expecting her to come and tell him some trifle, and be comforted, and then go for a good happy cry, while he shut off all her enemies.

But instead of any nice work of that nature, Mary Anerley arose and looked at the people in the room—which was their very best, and by no means badly furnished—and after trying to make out, as a very trifling matter, what their unsettled minds might be, her eyes came home to her father's, and did not flinch, although they were so wet.

Master Anerley, once and forever, knew that his daughter was gone from him. That a stronger love than one generation can have for the one before it—pure and devoted and ennobling as that love is—now had arisen, and would force its way. He did not think it out like that, for his mind was not strictly analytic—however his ideas were to that effect, which is all that need be said about them.

"Every word of it is true," the girl said, gently; "father, I have done every word of what they say, except about knocking down Captain Carroway. I have promised to marry Robin Lyth, by-and-by, when you agree to it."

Stephen Anerley's ruddy cheeks grew pale, and his blue eyes glittered with amazement. He stared at his daughter till her gaze gave way; and then he turned to his wife, to see whether she had heard of it. "I told you so," was all she said; and that tended little to comfort him. But he broke forth into no passion, as he might have done with justice and some benefit, but turned back quietly and looked at his Mary, as if he were saying, once for all, "good-by."

"Oh, don't, father, don't," the girl answered with a sob; "revile me, or beat me, or do anything but that. That is more than I can bear."

"Have I ever reviled you? Have I ever beaten you?"

"Never—never once in all my life. But I beg you—I implore of you to do it now. Oh, father, perhaps I have deserved it."

"You know best what you deserve. But no bad word shall you have of me. Only you must be careful for the future never to call me 'father.'"

The farmer forgot all his visitors, and walked, without looking at anybody, toward the porch. Then that hospitable spot re-awakened his good manners, and he turned and smiled as if he saw them all sitting down to something juicy.

"My good friends, make yourselves at home," he said; "the mistress will see to you while I look round. I shall be back directly, and we will have an early supper."

But when he got outside, and was alone with earth and sky, big tears arose into his brave blue eyes, and he looked at his ricks, and his workmen in the distance, and even at the favorite old horse that whinnied and came to have his white nose rubbed, as if none of them belonged to him ever any more. "A' would sooner have heard of broken bank," he muttered to himself and to the ancient horse, "fifty times sooner, and begin the world anew, only to have Mary for a little child again."

As the sound of his footsteps died away, the girl hurried out of the room, as if she were going to run after him; but suddenly stopped in the porch, as she saw that he scarcely even cared to feel the cheek of Lightfoot, who made a point of rubbing up his master's whiskers with it, "Better wait, and let him come round," thought Mary; "I never did see him so put out." Then she ran up the stairs to the window on the landing, and watched her dear father grow dimmer and dimmer up the distance of the hill, with a bright young tear for every sad old step.

CHAPTER XXV

DOWN AMONG THE DEAD WEEDS

Can it be supposed that all this time Master Geoffrey Mordacks, of the city of York, land agent, surveyor, and general factor, and maker and doer of everything whether general or particular, was spending his days in doing nothing, and his nights in dreaming? If so, he must have had a sunstroke on that very bright day of the year when he stirred up the minds of the washer-women, and the tongue of Widow Precious. But Flamborough is not at all the place for sunstroke, although it reflects so much in whitewash; neither had Mordacks the head to be sunstruck, but a hard, impenetrable, wiry poll, as weather-proof as felt asphalted. At first sight almost everybody said that he must have been a soldier, at a time when soldiers were made of iron, whalebone, whip-cord, and ramrods. Such opinions he rewarded with a grin, and shook his straight shoulders straighter. If pride of any sort was not beneath him, as a matter of strict business, it was the pride which he allowed his friends to take in his military figure and aspect.

This gentleman's place of business was scarcely equal to the expectations which might have been formed from a view of the owner. The old King's Staith, on the right hand after crossing Ouse Bridge from the Micklegate, is a passageway scarcely to be called a street, but combining the features of an alley, a lane, a jetty, a quay, and a barge-walk, and ending ignominiously. Nevertheless, it is a lively place sometimes, and in moments of excitement. Also it is a good place for business, and for brogue of the broadest; and a man who is unable to be happy there, must have something on his mind unusual. Geoffrey Mordacks had nothing on his mind except other people's business; which (as in the case of Lawyer Jellicorse) is a very favorable state of the human constitution for happiness.

But though Mr. Mordacks attended so to other people's business, he would not have anybody to attend to his. No partner, no clerk, no pupil, had a hand in the inner breast pockets of his business; there was nothing mysterious about his work, but he liked to follow it out alone. Things that were honest and wise came to him to be carried out with judgment; and he knew that the best way to carry them out is to act with discreet candor. For the slug shall be known by his slime; and the spider who shams death shall receive it.

Now here, upon a very sad November afternoon, when the Northern day was narrowing in; and the Ouse, which is usually of a ginger-color, was nearly as dark as a nutmeg; and the bridge, and the staith, and the houses, and the people, resembled one another in tint and tone; while between the Minster and the Clifford Tower there was not much difference of outline—here and now Master Geoffrey Mordacks was sitting in the little room where strangers were received. The live part of his household consisted of his daughter, and a very young Geoffrey, who did more harm than good, and a thoroughly hard-working country maid, whose slowness was gradually giving way to pressure.

The weather was enough to make anybody dull, and the sap of every human thing insipid; and the time of day suggested tea, hot cakes, and the crossing of comfortable legs. Mordacks could well afford all these good things, and he never was hard upon his family; but every day he liked to feel that he had earned the bread of it, and this day he had labored without seeming to earn anything. For after all the ordinary business of the morning, he had been devoting several hours to the diligent revisal of his premises and data, in a matter which he was resolved to carry through, both for his credit and his interest. And this was the matter which had cost him two days' ride, from York to Flamborough, and three days on the road home, as was natural after such a dinner as he made in little Denmark. But all that trouble he would not have minded, especially after his enjoyment of the place, if it had only borne good fruit. He had felt quite certain that it must do this, and that he would have to pay another visit to the Head, and eat another duck, and have a flirt with Widow Precious.

But up to the present time nothing had come of it, and so far as he could see he might just as well have spared himself that long rough ride. Three months had passed, and that surely was enough for even Flamborough folk to do something, if they ever meant to do it. It was plain that he had been misled for once, that what he suspected had not come to pass, and that he must seek elsewhere the light which had gleamed upon him vainly from the Danish town. To this end he went through all his case again, while hope (being very hard to beat, as usual) kept on rambling over everything unsettled, with a very sage conviction that there must be something there, and doubly sure, because there was no sign of it.

Men at the time of life which he had reached, conducting their bodies with less suppleness of joint, and administering food to them with greater care, begin to have doubts about their intellect as well, whether it can work as briskly as it used to do. And the mind, falling under this discouragement of doubt, asserts itself amiss, in making futile strokes, even as a gardener can never work his best while conscious of suspicious glances through the window-blinds. Geoffrey Mordacks told himself that it could not be the self it used to be, in the days when no mistakes were made, but everything was evident at half a glance, and carried out successfully with only half a hand. In this Flamborough matter he had felt no doubt of running triumphantly through, and being crowned with five hundred pounds in one issue of the case, and five thousand in the other. But lo! here was nothing. And he must reply, by the next mail, that he had made a sad mistake.

Suddenly, while he was rubbing his wiry head with irritation, and poring over his letters for some clew, like a dunce going back through his pot-hooks, suddenly a great knock sounded through the house—one, two, three—like the thumping of a mallet on a cask, to learn whether any beer may still be hoped for.

"This must be a Flamborough man," cried Master Mordacks, jumping up; "that is how I heard them do it; they knock the doors, instead of knocking at them. It would be a very strange thing just now if news were to come from Flamborough; but the stranger a thing is, the more it can be trusted, as often is the case with human beings. Whoever it is, show them up at once," he shouted down the narrow stairs; for no small noise was arising in the passage.

"A' canna coom oop. I wand a' canna," was the answer in Kitty's well-known brogue; "how can a', when a' hanna got naa legs?"

"Oh ho! I see," said Mr. Mordacks to himself; "my veteran friend from the watch-tower, doubtless. A man with no legs would not have come so far for nothing. Show the gentleman into the parlor, Kitty; and Miss Arabella may bring her work up here."

The general factor, though eager for the news, knew better than to show any haste about it; so he kept the old mariner just long enough in waiting to damp a too covetous ardor, and then he complacently locked Arabella in her bedroom, and bolted off Kitty in the basement; because they both were sadly inquisitive, and this strange arrival had excited them.

"Ah, mine ancient friend of the tower! Veteran Joseph, if my memory is right," Mr. Mordacks exclaimed, in his lively way, as he went up and offered the old tar both hands, to seat him in state upon the sofa; but the legless sailor condemned "them swabs," and crutched himself into a hard-bottomed chair. Then he pulled off his hat, and wiped his white head with a shred of old flag, and began hunting for his pipe.

"First time I ever was in York city; and don't think much of it, if this here is a sample."

"Joseph, you must not be supercilious," his host replied, with an amiable smile; "you will see things better through a glass of grog; and the state of the weather points to something dark. You have had a long journey, and the scenery is new. Rum shall it be, my friend? Your countenance says 'yes.'

Rum, like a ruby of the finest water, have I; and no water shall you have with it. Said I well? A man without legs must keep himself well above water."

"First time I ever was in York city," the ancient watchman answered, "and grog must be done as they does it here. A berth on them old walls would suit me well; and no need to travel such a distance for my beer."

"And you would be the man of all the world for such a berth," said Master Mordacks, gravely, as he poured the sparkling liquor into a glass that was really a tumbler; "for such a post we want a man who is himself a post; a man who will not quit his duty, just because he can not, which is the only way of making sure. Joseph, your idea is a very good one, and your beer could be brought to you at the middle of each watch. I have interest; you shall be appointed."

"Sir, I am obligated to you," said the watchman; "but never could I live a month without a wink of sea-stuff. The coming of the clouds, and the dipping of the land, and the waiting of the distance for what may come to be in it; let alone how they goes changing of their color, and making of a noise that is always out of sight: it is the very same as my beer is to me. Master, I never could get on without it."

"Well, I can understand a thing like that," Mordacks answered, graciously; "my water-butt leaked for three weeks, pat, pat, all night long upon a piece of slate, and when a man came and caulked it up, I put all the blame upon the pillow; but the pillow was as good as ever. Not a wink could I sleep till it began to leak again; and you may trust a York workman that it wasn't very long. But, Joseph, I have interest at Scarborough also. The castle needs a watchman for fear of tumbling down; and that is not the soldiers' business, because they are inside. There you could have quantities of sea-stuff, my good friend; and the tap at the Hooked Cod is nothing to it there. Cheer up, Joseph, we will land you yet. How the devil did you manage, now, to come so far?"

"Well, now, your honor, I had rare luck for it, as I must say, ever since I set eyes on you. There comes a son of mine as I thought were lost at sea; but not he, blow me! nearly all of him come back, with a handful of guineas, and the memory of his father. Lord! I could have cried; and he up and blubbered fairly, a trick as he learned from ten Frenchmen he had killed. Ah! he have done his work well, and aimed a good conduck—fourpence-halfpenny a day, so long as ever he shall live hereafter."

"In this world you mean, I suppose, my friend; but be not overcome; such things will happen. But what did you do with all that money, Joseph?"

"We never wasted none of it, not half a groat, Sir. We finished out the cellar at the Hooked Cod first; and when Mother Precious made a grumble of it, we gave her the money for to fill it up again, upon the understanding to come back when it was ready; and then we went to Burlington, and spent the rest in poshays like two gentlemen; and when we was down upon our stumps at last, for only one leg there is between us both, your honor, my boy he ups and makes a rummage in his traps; which the Lord he put it into his mind to do so, when he were gone a few good sheets in the wind; and there sure enough he finds five good guineas in the tail of an old hankercher he had clean forgotten; and he says, 'Now, father, you take care of them. Let us go and see the capital, and that good gentleman, as you have picked up a bit of news for.' So we shaped a course for York, on board the schooner Mary Anne, and from Goole in a barge as far as this here bridge; and here we are, high and dry, your honor. I was half a mind to bring in my boy Bob; but he saith, 'Not without the old chap axes;' and being such a noisy one, I took him at his word; though he hath found out what there was to find—not me."

"How noble a thing is parental love!" cried the general factor, in his hard, short way, which made many people trust him, because it was unpleasant; "and filial duty of unfathomable grog! Worthy Joseph, let your narrative proceed."

"They big words is beyond me, Sir. What use is any man to talk over a chap's head?"

"Then, dash your eyes, go on, Joe. Can you understand that, now?"

"Yes, Sir, I can, and I likes a thing put sensible. If the gentlemen would always speak like that, there need be no difference atween us. Well, it was all along of all that money-bag of Bob's that he and I found out anything. What good were your guinea? Who could stand treat on that more than a night or two, and the right man never near you? But when you keep a good shop open for a month, as Bob and me did with Widow Tapsy, it standeth to reason that you must have everybody, to be called at all respectable, for miles and miles around. For the first few nights or so some on 'em holds off—for an old chalk against them, or for doubt of what is forrard, or for cowardliness of their wives, or things they may have sworn to stop, or other bad manners. But only go on a little longer, and let them see that you don't care, and send everybody home a-singing through the lanes as merry as a voting-time for Parliament, and the outer ones begins to shake their heads, and to say that they are bound to go, and stop the racket of it. And so you get them all, your honor, saints as well as sinners, if you only keeps the tap turned long enough."

"Your reasoning is ingenious, Joseph, and shows a deep knowledge of human nature. But who was this tardy saint that came at last for grog?"

"Your honor, he were as big a sinner as ever you clap eyes on. Me and my son was among the sawdust, spite of our three crutches, and he spreading hands at us, sober as a judge, for lumps of ungenerous iniquity. Mother Tapsy told us of it, the very next day, for it was not in our power to be ackirate when he done it, and we see everybody laffing at us round the corner. But we took the wind out of his sails the next night, captain, you may warrant us. Here's to your good health, Sir, afore I beats to win'ard."

"Why, Joseph, you seem to be making up lost way for years of taciturnity in the tower. They say there is a balance in all things."

"We had the balance of him next night, and no mistake, your honor. He was one of them 'longshore beggars as turns up here, there, and everywhere, galley-raking, like a stinking ray-fish when the tide goes out; thundering scoundrels that make a living of it, pushing out for roguery with their legs tucked up; no courage for smuggling, nor honest enough, they goes on anyhow with their children paid for. We found out what he were, and made us more ashamed, for such a sneaking rat to preach upon us, like a regular hordinated chaplain, as might say a word or two and mean no harm, with the license of the Lord to do it. So my son Bob and me called a court-martial in the old tower, so soon as we come round; and we had a red herring, because we was thirsty, and we chawed a bit of pigtail to keep it down. At first we was glum; but we got our peckers up, as a family is bound to do when they comes together. My son Bob was a sharp lad in his time, and could read in Holy Scripter afore he chewed a quid; and I see'd a good deal of it in his mind now, remembering of King Solomon. 'Dad,' he says, 'fetch out that bottle as was left of French white brandy, and rouse up a bit of fire in the old port-hole. We ain't got many toes to warm between us'—only five, you see, your worship —'but,' says he, 'we'll warm up the currents where they used to be.'

"According to what my son said, I done; for he leadeth me now, being younger of the two, and still using half of a shoemaker. However, I says to him, 'Warm yourself; it don't lay in my power to do that for you.' He never said nothing; for he taketh after me, in tongue and other likings; but he up with the kettle on the fire, and put in about a fathom and a half of pigtail. 'So?' says I; and he says, 'So!' and we both of us began to laugh, as long and as gentle as a pair of cockles, with their tongues inside their shells.

"Well, your honor understands; I never spake so much before since ever I pass my coorting-time. We boiled down the pigtail to a pint of tidy soup, and strained it as bright as sturgeon juice; then we got a bottle with 'Navy Supply' on a bull's-eye in the belly of it; and we filled it with the French white brandy, and the pigtail soup, and a noggin of molasses, and shook it all up well together; and a better contract-rum, your honor, never come into high admiral's stores."

"But, Joseph, good Joseph," cried Mr. Mordacks, "do forge ahead a little faster. Your private feelings, and the manufacture of them, are highly interesting to you; but I only want to know what came of it."

"Your honor is like a child hearing of a story; you wants the end first, and the middle of it after; but I bowls along with a hitch and a squirt, from habit of fo'castle: and the more you crosses hawse, the wider I shall head about, or down helm and bear off, mayhap. I can hear my Bob a-singing: what a voice he hath! They tell me it cometh from the timber of his leg; the same as a old Cremony. He tuned up a many times in yonder old barge, and shook the brown water, like a frigate's wake. He would just make our fortin in the Minister, they said, with Black-eyed Susan and Tom Bowline."

"Truly, he has a magnificent voice: what power, what compass, what a rich clear tone! In spite of the fog I will have the window up."

Geoffrey Mordacks loved good singing, the grandest of all melody, and, impatient as he was, he forgot all hurry; while the river, and the buildings, and the arches of the bridge, were ringing, and echoing, and sweetly embosoming the mellow delivery of the one-legged tar. And old Joe was highly pleased, although he would not show it, at such an effect upon a man so hard and dry.

"Now, your honor, it is overbad of you," he continued, with a softening grin, "to hasten me so, and then to hear me out o' window, because Bob hath a sweeter pipe. Ah, he can whistle like a blackbird, too, and gain a lot of money; but there, what good? He sacrifices it all to the honor of his heart, first maggot that cometh into it; and he done the very same with Rickon Goold, the Methody galley-raker. We never was so softy when I were afloat. But your honor shall hear, and give judgment for yourself.

"Mother Precious was ready in her mind to run out a double-shotted gun at Rickon, who liveth down upon the rabbit-warren, to the other side of Bempton, because he scarcely ever doth come nigh her; and when he do come, he putteth up both bands, to bless her for hospitality, but neither of them into his breeches pocket. And being a lone woman, she doth feel it. Bob and me gave her sailing orders—'twould amaze you, captain; all was carried out as ship-shape as the battle of the Nile. There was Rickon Goold at anchor, with a spring upon his cable, having been converted; and he up and hailed that he would slip, at the very first bad word we used. My son hath such knowledge of good words that he, answered, 'Amen, so be it.'

"Well, your honor, we goes on decorous, as our old quartermaster used to give the word; and we tried him first with the usual tipple, and several other hands dropped in. But my son and me never took a blessed drop, except from a gin-bottle full of cold water, till we see all the others with their scuppers well awash. Then Bob he findeth fault—Lor' how beautiful he done it!—with the scantling of the stuff; and he shouteth out, 'Mother, I'm blest if I won't stand that old guinea bottle of best Jamaica, the one as you put by, with the cobwebs on it, for Lord Admiral. No Lord Admiral won't come now. Just you send away, and hoist it up.'

"Rickon Goold pricked up his ugly ears at this; and Mother Tapsy did it bootiful. And to cut a long yarn short, we spliced him, captain, with never a thought of what would come of it; only to have our revenge, your honor. He showed himself that greedy of our patent rum, that he never let the bottle out of his own elbow, and the more he stowed away, the more his derrick chains was creaking; but if anybody reasoned, there he stood upon his rights, and defied every way of seeing different, until we was compelled to take and spread him down, in the little room with sea-weeds over it.

"With all this, Bob and me was as sober as two judges, though your honor would hardly believe it, perhaps; but we left him in the dark, to come round upon the weeds, as a galley-raker ought to do. And now we began to have a little drop ourselves, after towing the prize into port, and recovering the honor of the British navy; and we stood all round to every quarter of the compass, with the bottom of the locker still not come to shallow soundings. But sudden our harmony was spoiled by a scream, like a whistle from the very bottom of the sea.

"We all of us jumped up, as if a gun had broke its lashings; and the last day of judgment was the thoughts of many bodies; but Bob he down at once with his button-stump gun-metal, and takes the command of the whole of us. 'Bear a hand, all on you,' he saith, quite steadfast; 'Rickon Goold is preaching to his own text to-night.' And so a' was, sure enough; so a' was, your honor.

"We thought he must have died, although he managed to claw off of it, with confessing of his wickedness, and striking to his Maker. All of us was frightened so, there was no laugh among us, till we come to talk over it afterward. There the thundering rascal lay in the middle of that there mangerie of sea-stuff, as Mother Precious is so proud of, that the village calleth it the 'Widow's Weeds.' Blest if he didn't think that he were a-lying at the bottom of the sea, among the stars and cuttles, waiting for the day of judgment!

"'Oh, Captain McNabbins, and Mate Govery,' he cries, 'the hand of the Lord hath sent me down to keep you company down here. I never would 'a done it, captain, hard as you was on me, if only I had knowed how dark and cold and shivery it would be down here. I cut the plank out; I'll not lie; no lies is any good down here, with the fingers of the deep things pointing to me, and the black devil's wings coming over me—but a score of years agone it were,

223

and never no one dreamed of it—oh, pull away, pull! for God's sake, pull!—the wet woman and the three innocent babbies crawling over me like congers!'

"This was the shadows of our legs, your honor, from good Mother Tapsy's candle; for she was in a dreadful way by this time about her reputation and her weeds, and come down with her tongue upon the lot of us. 'Enter all them names upon the log,' says I to Bob, for he writeth like a scholar. But Bob says, 'Hold hard, dad; now or never.' And with that, down he goeth on the deck himself, and wriggleth up to Rickon through the weeds, with a hiss like a great sea-snake, and grippeth him. 'Name of ship, you sinner!' cried Bob, in his deep voice, like Old Nick a-hailing from a sepulchre. 'Golconda, of Calcutta,' says the fellow, with a groan as seemed to come out of the whites of his eyes; and down goes his head again, enough to split a cat-head. And that was the last of him we heard that night.

"Well, now, captain, you scarcely would believe, but although my nob is so much older of the pair, and white where his is as black as any coal, Bob's it was as first throwed the painter up, for a-hitching of this drifty to the starn of your consarns. And it never come across him till the locker was run out, and the two of us pulling longer faces than our legs is. Then Bob, by the mercy of the Lord, like Peter, found them guineas in the corner of his swab—some puts it round their necks, and some into their pockets; I never heard of such a thing till chaps run soft and watery—and so we come to this here place to change the air and the breeding, and spin this yarn to your honor's honor, as hath a liberal twist in it; and then to take orders, and draw rations, and any 'rears of pay fallen due, after all dibs gone in your service; and for Bob to tip a stave in the Minister."

"You have done wisely and well in coming here," said Mr, Mordacks, cheerfully; "but we must have further particulars, my friend. You seem to have hit upon the clew I wanted, but it must be followed very cautiously. You know where to lay your hand upon this villain? You have had the sense not to scare him off?"

"Sarten, your honor. I could clap the irons on him any hour you gives that signal."

"Capital! Take your son to see the sights, and both of you come to me at ten to-morrow morning. Stop: you may as well take this half guinea. But when you get drunk, drink inwards."

CHAPTER XXVI

MEN OF SOLID TIMBER

Mr. Mordacks was one of those vivacious men who have strong faith in their good luck, and yet attribute to their merits whatever turns out well. In the present matter he had done as yet nothing at all ingenious, or even to be called sagacious. The discovery of "Monument Joe," or "Peg-leg Joe," as he was called at Flamborough, was not the result of any skill whatever, either his own or the factor's, but a piece of as pure luck as could be. For all that, however, Mr. Mordacks intended to have the whole credit as his sole and righteous due.

"Whenever I am at all down-hearted, samples of my skill turn up," he said to himself as soon as Joe was gone; "and happy results come home, on purpose to rebuke my diffidence. Would any other man have got so far as I have got by simple, straightforward, yet truly skillful action, without a suspicion being started? Old Jellicorse lies on his bed of roses, snoring folios of long words, without a dream of the gathering cloud. Those insolent ladies are revelling in the land from which they have ousted their only brother; they are granting leases not worth a straw; they are riding the high horse; they are bringing up that cub (who set the big dog at me) in every wanton luxury. But wait a bit—wait a bit, my ladies; as sure as I live I shall have you.

"In the first place, it is clear that my conclusion was correct concerning that poor Golconda; and why not also in the other issue? The Indiaman was scuttled—I had never thought of that, but only of a wreck. It comes to the same thing, only she went down more quietly; and that explains a lot of things. She was bound for Leith, with the boy to be delivered into the hands of his Scotch relatives. She was spoken last off Yarmouth Roads, all well, and under easy sail. Very good so far. I have solved her fate, which for twenty years has been a mystery. We shall have all particulars in proper time, by steering on one side of the law, which always huddles up everything. A keen eye must be kept upon that scoundrel, but he must never dream that he is watched at all; he has committed a capital offense. But as yet there is nothing but his own raving to convict him of barratry. The truth must be got at by gentle means. I must not claim the 500 pounds as yet, but I am sure of getting it. And I have excellent hopes of the 5000 pounds."

Geoffrey Mordacks never took three nights to sleep upon his thoughts (as the lawyer of Middleton loved to do), but rather was apt to overdrive his purport, with the goad of hasty action. But now he was quite resolved to be most careful; for the high hand would never do in such a ticklish matter, and the fewer the hands introduced at all into it, the better the chance of coming out clear and clean. The general factor had never done anything which, in his opinion, was not thoroughly upright; and now, with his reputation made, and his conscience stiffened to the shape of it, even a large sum of money must be clean, and cleanly got at, to make it pay for handling.

This made him counsel with himself just now. For he was a superior man upon the whole, and particular always in feeling sure that the right word in anything would be upon his side. Not that he cared a groat for anybody's gossip; only that he kept a lofty tenor of good opinion. And sailors who made other sailors tipsy, and went rolling about on the floor all together, whether with natural legs or artificial, would do no credit to his stairs of office on a fine market-day in the morning. On the other hand, while memory held sway, no instance could be cited of two jolly sailors coming to see the wonders of this venerable town, and failing to be wholly intoxicated with them, before the Minster bell struck one.

This was to be avoided, or rather forestalled, as a thing inevitable should be. Even in York city, teeming as it is with most delightful queerities, the approach of two sailors with three wooden legs might be anticipated at a distant offing, so abundant are boys there, and everywhere. Therefore it was well provided, on the part of Master Mordacks, that Kitty, or Koity, the maid-of-all-work, a damsel of muscular power and hard wit, should hold tryst with these mariners in the time of early bucket, and appoint a little meeting with her master by-and-by. This she did cleverly, and they were not put out; because they were to dine at his expense at a snug little chop-house in Parliament Street, and there to remain until he came to pay the score.

All this happened to the utmost of desires; and before they had time to get thick-witted, Mordacks stood before them. His sharp eyes took in Sailor Bob before the poor fellow looked twice at him, and the general factor saw that he might be trusted not to think much for himself. This was quite as Mr. Mordacks hoped; he wanted a man who could hold his tongue, and do what he was told to do.

After a few words about their dinner, and how they got on, and so forth, the principal came to the point by saying: "Now both of you must start to-morrow morning; such clever fellows can not be spared to go to sleep. You shall come and see York again, with free billet, and lashings of money in your pockets, as soon as you have carried out your sailing orders. To-night you may jollify; but after that you are under strict discipline, for a month at least. What do you say to that, my men?"

Watchman Joe looked rather glum; he had hoped for a fortnight of stumping about, with a tail of admiring boys after him, and of hailing every public-house the cut of whose jib was inviting; however, he put his knife into his mouth, with a bit of fat, saved for a soft adieu to dinner, and nodded for his son to launch true wisdom into the vasty deep of words.

Now Bob, the son of Joe, had striven to keep himself up to the paternal mark. He cited his father as the miracle of the age, when he was a long way off; and when he was nigh at hand, he showed his sense of duty, nearly always, by letting him get tipsy first. Still, they were very sober fellows in the main, and most respectable, when they had no money.

"Sir," began Bob, after jerking up his chin, as a sailor always does when he begins to think (perhaps for hereditary counsel with the sky), "my father and I have been hauling of it over, to do whatever is laid down by duty, without going any way again' ourselves. And this is the sense we be come to, that we should like to have something handsome down, to lay by again' chances; also a dokkyment in black and white, to bear us harmless of the law, and enter the prize-money."

"What a fine councillor a' would have made!" old Joe exclaimed, with ecstasy. "He hath been round the world three times—excuseth of him for only one leg left."

"My friend, how you condemn yourself! You have not been round the world at all, and yet you have no leg at all." So spake Mr. Mordacks, wishing to confuse ideas; for the speech of Bob misliked him.

"The corners of the body is the Lord's good-will," old Joe answered, with his feelings hurt; "He calleth home a piece to let the rest bide on, and giveth longer time to it—so saith King David."

"It may be so; but I forget the passage. Now what has your son Bob to say?"

Bob was a sailor of the fine old British type, still to be found even nowadays, and fit to survive forever. Broad and resolute of aspect, set with prejudice as stiff as his own pigtail, truthful when let alone, yet joyful in a lie, if anybody doubted him, peaceable in little things through plenty of fight in great ones, gentle with women and children, and generous with mankind in general, expecting to be cheated, yet not duly resigned at being so, and subject to unaccountable extremes of laziness and diligence. His simple mind was now confused by the general factor's appeal to him to pronounce his opinion, when he had just now pronounced it, after great exertion.

"Sir," he said, "I leave such things to father's opinion; he hath been ashore some years; and I almost forget how the land lays."

"Sea-faring Robert, you are well advised. A man may go round the world till he has no limbs left, yet never overtake his father. So the matter is left to my decision. Very good; you shall have no reason to repent it. To-night you have liberty to splice the main-brace, or whatever your expression is for getting jolly drunk; in the morning you will be sobriety itself, sad, and wise, and aching. But hear my proposal, before you take a gloomy view of things, such as to-morrow's shades may bring. You have been of service to me, and I have paid you with great generosity; but what I have done, including dinner, is dust in the balance to what I shall do, provided only that you act with judgment, discipline, and self-denial, never being tipsy more than once a week, which is fair naval average, and doing it then with only one another. Hard it may be; but it must be so. Now before I go any further, let me ask whether you, Joseph, as a watchman under government, have lost your position by having left it for two months upon a private spree?"

"Lor', no, your honor! Sure you must know more than that. I gived a old 'ooman elevenpence a week, and a pot of beer a Sunday, to carry out the dooties of the government."

"You farmed out your appointment at a low figure. My opinion of your powers and discretion is enhanced; you will return to your post with redoubled ardor, and vigor renewed by recreation; you will be twice the man you were, and certainly ought to get double pay. I have interest; I may be enabled to double your salary—if you go on well."

This made both of them look exceeding downcast, and chew the bitter quid of disappointment. They had laid their heads together over glass number one, and resolved upon asking for a guinea a week; over glass number two, they had made up their minds upon getting two guineas weekly; and glass number three had convinced them that they must be poor fools to accept less than three. Also they felt that the guineas they had spent, in drinking their way up to a great discovery, should without hesitation be made good ere ever they had another pint of health. In this catastrophe of large ideas, the father gazed sadly at the son, and the son reproachfully reflected the paternal gaze. How little availed it to have come up here, wearily going on upon yellow waters, in a barge where the fleas could man the helm, without aid of the stouter insect, and where a fresh run sailor was in more demand than salmon; and even without that (which had largely enhanced the inestimable benefit of having wooden legs), this pair of tars had got into a state of mind to return the whole way upon horseback. No spurs could they wear, and no stirrups could they want, and to get up would be difficult; but what is the use of living, except to conquer difficulties? They rejoiced all the more in the four legs of a horse, by reason of the paucity of their own; which approves a liberal mind. But now, where was the horse to come from, or the money to make him go?

"You look sad," proceeded Mr. Mordacks. "It grieves me when any good man looks sad; and doubly so when a brace of them do it. Explain your feelings, Joe and Bob; if it lies in a human being to relieve them, I will do it."

"Captain, we only wants what is our due," said Bob, with his chin up, and his strong eyes stern. "We have been on the loose; and it is the manner of us, and encouraged by the high authorities. We have come across, by luck of drink, a thing as seems to suit you; and we have told you all our knowledge without no conditions. If you takes us for a pair of fools, and want no more of us, you are welcome, and it will be what we are used to; but if your meaning is to use us, we must have fair wages; and even so, we would have naught to do with it if it was against an honest man; but a rogue who has scuttled a ship —Lor', there!"

Bob cast out the juice of his chew into the fire, as if it were the life-blood of such a villain, and looked at his father, who expressed approval by the like proceeding. And Geoffrey Mordacks was well content at finding them made of decent stuff. It was not his manner to do things meanly; and he had only spoken so to moderate their minds and keep them steady.

"Mariner Bob, you speak well and wisely," he answered, with a superior smile. "Your anxiety as to ways and means does credit to your intellect. That subject has received my consideration. I have studied the style of life at Flamborough, and the prices of provisions—would that such they were in York!—and to keep you in temperate and healthy comfort, without temptation, and with minds alert, I am determined to allow for the two of you, over and above all your present income from a grateful country (which pays a man less when amputation has left less of him), the sum of one guinea and a half per week. But remember that, to draw this stipend, both of you must be in condition to walk one mile and a half on a Saturday night, which is a test of character. You will both be fitted up with solid steel ends, by the cutler at the end of Ouse Bridge, to-morrow morning, so that the state of the roads will not affect you, and take note of one thing, mutual support (graceful though it always is in paternal and filial communion) will not be allowed on a Saturday night. Each man must stand on his own stumps."

"Sir," replied Bob, who had much education, which led him to a knowledge of his failings, "never you fear but what we shall do it. Sunday will be the day of standing with a shake to it; for such, is the habit of the navy. Father, return thanks; make a leg—no man can do it better. Master Mordacks, you shall have our utmost duty; but a little brass in hand would be convenient."

"You shall have a fortnight in advance; after that you must go every

Saturday night to a place I will appoint for you. Now keep your own counsel; watch that fellow; by no means scare him at first, unless you see signs of his making off; but rather let him think that you know nothing of his crime. Labor hard to make him drink again; then terrify him like Davy Jones himself; and get every particular out of him, especially how he himself escaped, where he landed, and who was with him. I want to learn all about a little boy (at least, he may be a big man now), who was on board the ship Golconda, under the captain's special charge. I can not help thinking that the child escaped; and I got a little trace of something connected with him at Flamborough. I durst not make much inquiry there, because I am ordered to keep things quiet. Still, I did enough to convince me almost that my suspicion was an error; for Widow Precious—"

"Pay you no heed, Sir, to any manoeuvring of Widow Precious. We find her no worse than the other women; but not a blamed bit better."

"I think highly of the female race; at least, in comparison with the male one. I have always found reason to believe that a woman, put upon her mettle by a secret, will find it out, or perish."

"Your honor, everybody knows as much as that; but it doth not follow that she tells it on again, without she was ordered not to do so."

"Bob, you have not been round the world for nothing. I see my blot, and you have hit it; you deserve to know all about the matter now. Match me that button, and you shall have ten guineas."

The two sailors stared at the bead of Indian gold which Mordacks pulled out of his pocket. Buttons are a subject for nautical contempt and condemnation; perhaps because there is nobody to sew them on at sea; while ear-rings, being altogether useless, are held in good esteem and honor.

"I have seen a brace of ear-rings like it," said old Joe, wading through deep thought. "Bob, you knows who was a-wearing of 'em."

"A score of them fishermen, like enough," cautious Bob answered; for he knew what his father meant, but would not speak of the great free-trader; for Master Mordacks might even be connected with the revenue. "What use to go on about such gear? His honor wanteth to hear of buttons, regulation buttons by the look of it, and good enough for Lord Nelson. Will you let us take the scantle, and the rig of it, your honor?"

"By all means, if you can do so, my friend; but what have you to do it with?"

"Hold on a bit, Sir, and you shall see." With these words Bob clapped a piece of soft York bread into the hollow of his broad brown palm, moistened it with sugary dregs of ale, such as that good city loves, and kneading it firmly with some rapid flits of thumb, tempered and enriched it nobly with the mellow juice of quid. Treated thus, it took consistence, plastic, docile, and retentive pulp; and the color was something like that of gold which had passed, according to its fate, through a large number of unclean hands.

"Now the pattern, your honor," said Bob, with a grin; "I could do it from memory, but better from the thing." He took the bauble, and set it on the foot of a rummer which stood on the table; and in half a minute he had the counterpart in size, shape, and line; but without the inscription. "A sample of them in the hollow will do, and good enough for the nigger-body words—heathen writing, to my mind." With lofty British intolerance, he felt that it might be a sinful thing to make such marks; nevertheless he impressed one side, whereon the characters were boldest, into the corresponding groove of his paste model; then he scooped up the model on the broad blade of his knife, and set it in the oven of the little fire-place, in a part where the heat was moderate.

"Well done, indeed!" cried Mr. Mordacks; "you will have a better likeness of it than good Mother Precious. Robert, I admire your ingenuity. But all sailors are ingenious."

"At sea, in the trades, or in a calm, Sir, what have we to do but to twiddle our thumbs, and practice fiddling with them? A lively tune is what I like, and a-serving of the guns red-hot; a man must act according to what nature puts upon him. And nature hath taken one of my legs from me with a cannon-shot from the French line-of-battle ship—Rights of Mankind the name of her."

CHAPTER XXVII

THE PROPER WAY TO ARGUE

Alas, how seldom is anything done in proper time and season! Either too fast, or too slow, is the clock of all human dealings; and what is the law of them, when the sun (the regulator of works and ways) has to be allowed for very often on his own meridian? With the best intention every man sets forth to do his duty, and to talk of it; and he makes quite sure that he has done it, and to his privy circle boasts, or lets them do it better for him; but before his lips are dry, his ears apprise him that he was a stroke too late.

So happened it with Master Mordacks, who of all born men was foremost, with his wiry fingers spread, to pass them through the scattery forelock of that mettlesome horse, old Time. The old horse galloped by him unawares, and left him standing still, to hearken the swish of the tail, and the clatter of the hoofs, and the spirited nostrils neighing for a race, on the wide breezy down at the end of the lane. But Geoffrey Mordacks was not to blame. His instructions were to move slowly, until he was sure of something worth moving for. And of this he had no surety yet, and was only too likely to lose it altogether by any headlong action. Therefore, instead of making any instant rush, or belting on his pistols, and hiring the sagacious quadruped that understood his character, content he was to advance deliberately upon one foot and three artificial legs.

Meanwhile, at Anerley Farm, the usual fatness of full garners, and bright comfort of the evening hearth, the glow of peace, which labor kindles in the mind that has earned its rest, and the pleasant laziness of heart which comes where family love lies careless, confident, and unassailed—the pleasure also of pitying the people who never can get in their wheat, and the hot benevolence of boiling down the bones for the man who has tumbled off one's own rick—all these blisses, large and little, were not in their usual prime.

The master of the house was stern and silent, heavy and careless of his customary victuals, neglectful also of his customary jokes. He disliked the worse side of a bargain as much as in his most happy moments; and the meditation (which is generally supposed to be going on where speech is scarce) was not of such loftiness as to overlook the time a man stopped round the corner. As a horse settles down to strong collar-work better when the gloss of the stable takes the ruffle of the air, so this man worked at his business all the harder, with the brightness of the home joys fading. But it went very hard with him more than once, when he made a good stroke of salesmanship, to have to put the money in the bottom of his pocket, without even rubbing a bright half crown, and saying to himself, "I have a'most a mind to give this to Mary."

Now if this settled and steadfast man (with three-quarters of his life gone over him, and less and less time every year for considering soft subjects), in spite of all that, was put out of his way by not being looked at as usual—though for that matter, perhaps, himself failed to look in search of those looks as usual—what, on the other hand, was likely to remain of mirth and light-heartedness in a weaker quarter? Mary, who used to be as happy as a bird where worms abound and cats are scarce, was now in a grievous plight of mind, restless, lonely, troubled in her heart, and doubtful of her conscience. Her mother had certainly shown kind feeling, and even a readiness to take her part, which surprised the maiden, after all her words; and once or twice they had had a cry together, clearing and strengthening their intellects desirably. For the more Mistress Anerley began to think about it, the more she was almost sure that something could be said on both sides. She never had altogether approved of the farmer's volunteering, which took him away to drill at places where ladies came to look at him; and where he slept out of his own bed, and got things to eat that she had never heard of; and he never was the better afterward. If that was the thing which set his mind against free trade so bitterly, it went far to show that free trade was good, and it made all the difference of a blanket. And more than that, she had always said from the very first, and had even told the same thing to Captain Carroway, in spite of his position, that nobody knew what Robin Lyth might not turn out in the end to be. He had spoken most highly of her, as Mary had not feared to mention; and she felt obliged to him for doing so, though of course he could not do otherwise. Still, there were people who would not have done that, and it proved that he was a very promising young man.

Mary was pleased with this conclusion, and glad to have some one who did not condemn her; hopeful, moreover, that her mother's influence might have some effect by-and-by. But for the present it seemed to do more harm than good; because the farmer, having quite as much jealousy as justice, took it into silent dudgeon that the mother of his daughter, who regularly used to be hard upon her for next to nothing, should now turn round and take her part, from downright womanism, in the teeth of all reason, and of her own husband! Brave as he was, he did not put it to his wife in so strong a way as that; but he argued it so to himself, and would let it fly forth, without thinking twice about it, if they went on in that style much longer, quite as if he were nobody, and they could do better without him. Little he knew, in this hurt state of mind—for which he should really have been too old—how the heart of his child was slow and chill, stupid with the strangeness he had made, waiting for him to take the lead, or open some door for entrance, and watching for the humors of the elder body, as the young of past generations did. And sometimes, faithful as she was to plighted truth and tenderness, one coaxing word would have brought her home to the arms that used to carry her.

But while such things were waiting to be done till they were thought of, the time for doing them went by; and to think of them was memory. Master Popplewell had told Captain Anerley continually what his opinions were, fairly giving him to know on each occasion that they were to be taken for what they were worth; that it did not follow, from his own success in life, that he might not be mistaken now; and that he did not care a d—n, except for Christian feeling, whether any fool hearkened to him twice or not. He said that he never had been far out in any opinion he had formed in all his life; but none the more for that would he venture to foretell a thing with cross-purposes about it. A man of sagacity and dealings with the world might happen to be right ninety-nine times in a hundred, and yet he might be wrong the other time. Therefore he would not give any opinion, except that everybody would be sorry by-and-by, when things were too late for mending.

To this the farmer listened with an air of wisdom, not put forward too severely; because Brother Popplewell had got a lot of money, and must behave handsomely when in a better world. The simplest way of treating him was just to let him talk—for it pleased him, and could do no harm—and then to recover self-content by saying what a fool he was when out of hearing. The tanner partly suspected this; and it put his nature upon edge; for he always drove his opinions in as if they were so many tenpenny nails, which the other man must either clinch or strike back into his teeth outright. He would rather have that than flabby silence, as if he were nailing into dry-rot.

"I tell you what it is," he said, the third time he came over, which was well within a week—for nothing breeds impatience faster than retirement from work—"you are so thick-headed in your farmhouse ways, sometimes I am worn out with you. I do not expect to be thought of any higher because I have left off working for myself; and Deborah is satisfied to be called 'Debby,' and walks no prouder than if she had got to clean her own steps daily. You can not enter into what people think of me, counting Parson Beloe; and therefore it is no good saying anything about it. But, Stephen, you may rely upon it that you will be sorry afterward. That poor girl, the prettiest girl in Yorkshire, and the kindest, and the best, is going off her victuals, and consuming of her substance, because you will not even look at her. If you don't want the child, let me have her. To us she is welcome as the flowers in May."

"If Mary wishes it, she can go with you," the farmer answered, sternly; and hating many words, he betook himself to work, resolving to keep at it until the tanner should be gone. But when he came home after dusk, his steadfast heart was beating faster than his stubborn mind approved. Mary might have taken him at his word, and flown for refuge from displeasure, cold voice, and dull comfort, to the warmth, and hearty cheer, and love of the folk who only cared to please her, spoil her, and utterly ruin her. Folk who had no sense of fatherly duty, or right conscience; but, having piled up dirty money, thought that it covered everything: such people might think it fair to come between a father and his child, and truckle to her, by backing her up in whims that were against her good, and making light of right and wrong, as if they turned on money; but Mary (such a prudent lass, although she was a fool just now) must see through all such shallow tricks, such rigmarole about Parson Beloe, who must be an idiot himself to think so much of Simon Popplewell—for Easter offerings, no doubt—but there, if Mary had the heart to go away, what use to stand maundering about it? Stephen Anerley would be dashed if he cared which way it was.

Meaning all this, Stephen Anerley, however, carried it out in a style at variance with such reckless vigor. Instead of marching boldly in at his own door, and throwing himself upon a bench, and waiting to be waited upon, he left the narrow gravel-walk (which led from the horse gate to the front door) and craftily fetched a compass through the pleasure beds and little shrubs, upon the sward, and in the dusk, so that none might see or hear him. Then, priding himself upon his stealth, as a man with whom it is rare may do, yet knowing all the time that he was more than half ashamed of it, he began to peep in at his own windows, as if he were planning how to rob his own house. This thought struck him, but instead of smiling, he sighed very sadly; for his object was to learn whether house and home had been robbed of that which he loved so fondly. There was no Mary in the kitchen, seeing to his supper; the fire was bright, and the pot was there, but only shadows round it. No Mary in the little parlor; only Willie half asleep, with a stupid book upon his lap, and a wretched candle guttering. Then, as a last hope, he peered into the dairy, where she often went at fall of night, to see things safe, and sang to keep the ghosts away. She would not be singing now of course, because he was so cross with her; but if she were there, it would be better than the merriest song for him. But no, the place was dark and cold; tub and pan, and wooden skimmer, and the pails hung up to drain, all were left to themselves, and the depth of want of life was over them. "She hathn't been there for an hour," thought he; "a reek o' milk, and not my lassie."

Very few human beings have such fragrance of good-will as milk. The farmer knew that he had gone too far in speaking coarsely of the cow, whose children first forego their food for the benefit of ours, and then become veal to please us. "My little maid is gone," said the lord of many cows, and who had robbed some thousand of their dear calves. "I trow I must make up my mind to see my little maid no more."

Without compunction for any mortal cow (though one was bellowing sadly in the distance, that had lost her calf that day), and without even dreaming of a grievance there, Master Anerley sat down to think upon a little bench hard by. His thoughts were not very deep or subtle; yet to him they were difficult, because they were so new and sad. He had always hoped to go through life in the happiest way there is of it, with simply doing common work, and heeding daily business, and letting other people think the higher class of thought for him. To live as Nature, cultivated quite enough for her own content, enjoys the round of months and years, the changes of the earth and sky, and gentle slope of time subsiding to softer shadows and milder tones. And, most of all, to see his children, dutiful, good, and loving, able and ready to take his place —when he should be carried from farm to church—to work the land he loved so well, and to walk in his ways, and praise him.

But now he thought, like Job in his sorrow, "All these things are against me." The air was laden with the scents of autumn, rich and ripe and soothing —the sweet fulfillment of the year. The mellow odor of stacked wheat, the stronger perfume of clover, the brisk smell of apples newly gathered, the distant hint of onions roped, and the luscious waft of honey, spread and hung upon the evening breeze. "What is the good of all this," he muttered, "when my little lassie is gone away, as if she had no father?"

"Father, I am not gone away. Oh, father, I never will go away, if you will love me as you did."

Here Mary stopped; for the short breath of a sob was threatening to catch her words; and her nature was too like her father's to let him triumph over her. The sense of wrong was in her heart, as firm and deep as in his own, and her love of justice quite as strong; only they differed as to what it was. Therefore Mary would not sob until she was invited. She stood in the arch of trimmed yew-tree, almost within reach of his arms; and though it was dark, he knew her face as if the sun was on it.

"Dearie, sit down here," he said; "there used to be room for you and me, without two chairs, when you was my child."

"Father, I am still your child," she answered, softly, sitting by him. "Were you looking for me just now? Say it was me you were looking for."

"There is such a lot of rogues to look for; they skulk about so, and they fire the stacks—"

238

"Now, father, you never could tell a fib," she answered, sidling closer up, and preparing for his repentance.

"I say that I was looking for a rogue. If the cap fits—" here he smiled a little, as much as to say, "I had you there;" and then, without meaning it, from simple force of habit, he did a thing equal to utter surrender. He stroked his chin, as he always used to do when going to kiss Mary, that the bristles might lie down for her.

"The cap doesn't fit; nothing fits but you; you—you—you, my own dear father," she cried, as she kissed him again and again, and put her arms round to protect him. "And nobody fits you, but your own Mary. I knew you were sorry. You needn't say it. You are too stubborn, and I will let you off. Now don't say a word, father, I can do without it. I don't want to humble you, but only to make you good; and you are the very best of all people, when you please. And you never must be cross again with your darling Mary. Promise me immediately; or you shall have no supper."

"Well," said the farmer, "I used to think that I was gifted with the gift of argument. Not like a woman, perhaps; but still pretty well for a man, as can't spare time for speechifying, and hath to earn bread for self and young 'uns."

"Father, it is that arguing spirit that has done you so much harm. You must take things as Heaven sends them; and not go arguing about them. For instance, Heaven has sent you me."

"So a' might," Master Anerley replied; "but without a voice from the belly of a fish, I wunna' believe that He sent Bob Lyth."

240

CHAPTER XXVIII

FAREWELL, WIFE AND CHILDREN DEAR

Now Robin Lyth held himself in good esteem; as every honest man is bound to do, or surely the rogues will devour him. Modesty kept him silent as to his merits very often; but the exercise of self-examination made them manifest to himself. As the Yorkshireman said to his minister, when pressed to make daily introspection, "I dare na do it, sir; it sets me up so, and leaveth no chance for my neighbors;" so the great free-trader, in charity for others, forbore to examine himself too much. But without doing that, he was conscious of being as good as Master Anerley; and intended, with equal mind and manner, to state his claim to the daughter's hand.

It was not, therefore, as the farmer thought, any deep sense of illegality which kept him from coming forward now, as a gallant sailor always does; but rather the pressure of sterner business, and the hard necessity of running goods, according to honorable contract. After his narrow escape from outrage upon personal privilege—for the habeas corpus of the Constitution should at least protect a man while making love—it was clear that the field of his duties as a citizen was padlocked against him, until next time. Accordingly he sought the wider bosom of the ever-liberal sea; and leaving the noble Carroway to mourn—or in stricter truth, alas! to swear—away he sailed, at the quartering of the moon, for the land of the genial Dutchman.

Now this was the time when the forces of the realm were mightily gathered together against him. Hitherto there had been much fine feeling on the part of his Majesty's revenue, and a delicate sense of etiquette. All the commanders of the cutters on the coast, of whom and of which there now were three, had met at Carroway's festive board; and, looking at his family, had one and all agreed to let him have the first chance of the good prize-money. It was All-saints' Day of the year gone by when they met and thus enjoyed themselves; and they bade their host appoint his time; and he said he should not want three months. At this they laughed, and gave him twelve; and now the twelve had slipped away.

"I would much rather never have him caught at all," said Carroway, to his wife, when his year of precaption had expired, "than for any of those fellows to nab him; especially that prig last sent down."

"So would I, dear; so would I, of course," replied Mrs. Carroway, who had been all gratitude for their noble self-denial when they made the promise;

"what airs they would give themselves! And what could they do with the money? Drink it out! I am sure that the condition of our best tumblers, after they come, is something. People who don't know anything about it always fancy that glass will clean. Glass won't clean, after such men as those; and as for the table—don't talk of it."

"Two out of the three are gone"—the lieutenant's conscience was not void of offense concerning tables—"gone upon promotion. Everybody gets promotion, if he only does his very best never to deserve it. They ought to have caught Lyth long and long ago. What are such dummies fit for?"

"But, Charles, you know that they would have acted meanly and dishonestly if they had done so. They promised not to catch him; and they carried out their promise."

"Matilda, such questions are beyond you altogether. You can not be expected to understand the service. One of those trumpery, half-decked craft —or they used to be half-deckers in my time—has had three of those fresh-meat Jemmies over her in a single twelvemonth. But of course they were all bound by the bargain they had made. As for that, small thanks to them. How could they catch him, when I couldn't? They chop and they change so, I forget their names; my head is not so good as it was, with getting so much moonlight."

"Nonsense, Charles; you know them like your fingers. But I know what you want; you want Geraldine, you are so proud to hear her tell it."

"Tilly, you are worse. You love to hear her say it. Well, call her in, and let her do it. She is making an oyster-shell cradle over there, with two of the blessed babies."

"Charles, how very profane you are! All babes are blest by the Lord, in an independent parable, whether they can walk, or crawl, or put up their feet and take nourishment. Jerry, you come in this very moment. What are you doing with your two brothers there, and a dead skate—bless the children! Now say the cutters and their captains."

Geraldine, who was a pretty little girl, as well as a good and clever one, swept her wind-tossed hair aside, and began to repeat her lesson; for which she sometimes got a penny when her father had made a good dinner.

"His Majesty's cutter Swordfish, Commander Nettlebones, senior officer of the eastern division after my papa, although a very young man still, carries a swivel-gun and two bow-chasers. His Majesty's cutter Kestrel, commanded by Lieutenant Bowler, is armed with three long-John's, or strap-guns, capable of carrying a pound of shrapnel. His Majesty's cutter Albatross, Lieutenant

Corkoran Donovan, carries no artillery yet—"

"Not artillery—guns, child; your mother calls them 'artillery.'"

"Carries no guns yet, because she was captured from the foreign enemy; and as yet she has not been reported stanch, since the British fire made a hole in her. It is, however, expected that those asses at the dock-yard——"

"Geraldine, how often must I tell you that you are not to use that word? It is your father's expression."

"It is, however, expected that those donkeys at the dock-yard will recommend her to be fitted with two brass howisyers."

"Howitzers, my darling. Spell that word, and you shall have your penny. Now you may run out and play again. Give your old father a pretty kiss for it. I often wish," continued the lieutenant, as his daughter flew back to the dead skate and the babies, "that I had only got that child's clear head. Sometimes the worry is too much for me. And now if Nettlebones catches Robin Lyth, to a certainty I shall be superseded, and all of us go to the workhouse. Oh, Tilly, why won't your old aunt die? We might be so happy afterward."

"Charles, it is not only sinful, but wicked, to show any wish to hurry her. The Lord knows best what is good for us; and our prayers upon such matters should be silent."

"Well, mine would be silent and loud too, according to the best chance of being heard. Not that I would harm the poor old soul; I wish her every heavenly blessing; and her time is come for all of them. But I never like to think of that, because one's own time might come first. I have felt very much out of spirits to-day, as my poor father did the day before he got his billet. You know, Matilda, he was under old Boscawen, and was killed by the very first shot fired; it must be five-and-forty years ago. How my mother did cry, to be sure! But I was too young to understand it. Ah, she had a bad time with us all! Matilda, what would you do without me?"

"Why, Charles, you are not a bit like yourself. Don't go to-night; stay at home for once. And the weather is very uncertain, too. They never will attempt their job to-night. Countermand the boats, dear; I will send word to stop them. You shall not even go out of the house yourself."

"As if it were possible! I am not an old woman, nor even an old man yet, I hope. In half an hour I must be off. There will be good time for a pipe. One more pipe in the old home, Tilly. After all I am well contented with it, although now and then I grumble; and I don't like so much cleaning."

"The cleaning must be done; I could never leave off that. Your room is going to be turned out to-morrow, and before you go you must put away your papers, unless you wish me to do it. You really never seem to understand when things are really important. Do you wish me to have a great fever in the house? It is a fortnight since your boards were scrubbed; and how can you think of smoking?"

"Very well, Tilly, I can have it by-and-by, 'upon the dancing waves,' as little Tommy has picked up the song. Only I can not let the men on duty; and to see them longing destroys my pleasure. Lord, how many times I should like to pass my pipe to Dick, or Ellis, if discipline allowed of it! A thing of that sort is not like feeding, which must be kept apart by nature; but this by custom only."

"And a very good custom, and most needful," answered Mrs. Carroway. "I never can see why men should want to do all sorts of foolish things with tobacco—dirty stuff, and full of dust. No sooner do they begin, like a tinder-box, than one would think that it made them all alike. They want to see another body puffing two great streams of reeking smoke from pipe and from mouth, as if their own was not enough; and their good resolutions to speak truth of one another float away like so much smoke; and they fill themselves with bad charity. Sir Walter Raleigh deserved his head off, and Henry the Eighth knew what was right."

"My dear, I fancy that your history is wrong. The king only chopped off his own wives' heads. But the moral of the lesson is the same. I will go and put away my papers. It will very soon be dark enough for us to start."

"Charles, I can not bear your going. The weather is so dark, and the sea so lonely, and the waves are making such a melancholy sound. It is not like the summer nights, when I can see you six miles off, with the moon upon the sails, and the land out of the way. Let anybody catch him that has the luck. Don't go this time, Charley."

Carroway kissed his wife, and sent her to the baby, who was squalling well up stairs. And when she came down he was ready to start, and she brought the baby for him to kiss.

"Good-by, little chap—good-by, dear wife." With his usual vigor and flourish, he said, "I never knew how to kiss a baby, though I have had such a lot of them."

"Good-by, Charley dear. All your things are right; and here is the key of the locker. You are fitted out for three days; but you must on no account make that time of it. To-morrow I shall be very busy, but you must be home by the evening. Perhaps there will be a favorite thing of yours for supper. You are going a long way; but don't be long."

"Good-by, Tilly darling—good-by, Jerry dear—good-by, Tommy boy, and all my countless family. I am coming home to-morrow with a mint of money."

CHAPTER XXIX

TACTICS OF DEFENSE

The sea at this time was not pleasant, and nobody looking at it longed to employ upon it any members of a shorter reach than eyes.

It was not rushing upon the land, nor running largely in the offing, nor making white streaks on the shoals; neither in any other places doing things remarkable. No sign whatever of coming storm or gathering fury moved it; only it was sullen, heavy, petulant, and out of sorts. It went about its business in a state of lumps irregular, without long billows or big furrows, as if it took the impulse more of distant waters than of wind; and its color was a dirty green. Ancient fishermen hate this, and ancient mariners do the same; for then the fish lie sulking on their bellies, and then the ship wallows without gift of sail.

"Bear off, Tomkins, and lay by till the ebb. I can only say, dash the whole of it!"

Commander Nettlebones, of the Swordfish, gave this order in disgust at last; for the tide was against her, with a heavy pitch of sea, and the mainsail scarcely drew the sheet. What little wind there was came off the land, and would have been fair if it had been firm; but often it dropped altogether where the cliffs, or the clouds that lay upon them, held it. The cutter had slipped away from Scarborough, as soon as it was dark last night, under orders for Robin Hood's Bay, where the Albatross and Kestrel were to meet her, bring tidings, and take orders. Partly by coast-riding, and partly by coast signals, it had been arranged that these three revenue cruisers should come together in a lonely place during the haze of November morning, and hold privy council of importance. From Scarborough, with any wind at all, or even with ordinary tide-run, a coal barge might almost make sure of getting to Robin Hood's Bay in six hours, if the sea was fit to swim in. Yet here was a cutter that valued herself upon her sailing powers already eighteen hours out, and headed back perpetually, like a donkey-plough. Commander Nettlebones could not understand it, and the more impatient he became, the less could he enter into it. The sea was nasty, and the wind uncertain, also the tide against him; but how often had such things combined to hinder, and yet he had made much fairer way! Fore and aft he bestrode the planks, and cast keen eyes at everything, above, around, or underneath, but nothing showed him anything. Nettlebones was a Cornishman, and Cornishmen at that time had a reverent faith in witchcraft. "Robin Lyth has bought the powers, or ancient Carroway has done it," he said to himself, in stronger language than is now reportable. "Old Carroway is against us, I know, from his confounded jealousy; and this cursed delay will floor all my plans."

He deserved to have his best plans floored for such vile suspicion of Carroway. Whatever the brave lieutenant did was loyal, faithful, and well above-board. Against the enemy he had his plans, as every great commander must, and he certainly did not desire to have his glory stolen by Nettlebones. But that he would have suffered, with only a grin at the bad luck so habitual; to do any crooked thing against it was not in his nature. The cause of the grief of Commander Nettlebones lay far away from Carroway; and free trade was at the bottom of it.

For now this trim and lively craft was doing herself but scanty credit, either on or off a wind. She was like a poor cat with her tail in a gin, which sadly obstructs her progress; even more was she like to the little horse of wood, which sits on the edge of a table and gallops, with a balance weight limiting his energies. None of the crew could understand it, if they were to be believed; and the more sagacious talked of currents and mysterious "under-tow." And sure enough it was under-tow, the mystery of which was simple. One of the very best hands on board was a hardy seaman from Flamborough, akin to old Robin Cockscroft, and no stranger to his adopted son. This gallant seaman fully entered into the value of long leverage, and he made fine use of a plug-hole which had come to his knowledge behind his berth. It was just above the water-line, and out of sight from deck, because the hollow of the run was there. And long ere the lights of Scarborough died into the haze of night, as the cutter began to cleave watery way, the sailor passed a stout new rope from a belaying-pin through this hole, and then he betrayed his watch on deck by hauling the end up with a clew, and gently returning it to the deep with a long grappling-iron made fast to it. This had not fluke enough to lay fast hold and bring the vessel up; for in that case it would have been immediately discovered; but it dragged along the bottom like a trawl, and by its weight, and a hitch every now and then in some hole, it hampered quite sufficiently the objectionable voyage. Instead of meeting her consorts in the cloud of early morning, the Swordfish was scarcely abreast of the Southern Cheek by the middle of the afternoon. No wonder if Commander Nettlebones was in a fury long ere that, and fitted neither to give nor take the counsel of calm wisdom; and this condition of his mind, as well as the loss of precious time, should have been taken into more consideration by those who condemned him for the things that followed.

"Better late than never, as they say," he cried, when the Kestrel and the Albatross hove in sight. "Tomkins, signal to make sail and close. We seem to

be moving more lively at last. I suppose we are out of that infernal under-
tow."

"Well, sir, she seems like herself a little more. She've had a witch on board
of her, that's where it is. When I were a younker, just joined his Majesty's
forty-two-gun frigate—"

"Stow that, Tomkins. No time now. I remember all about it, and very good
it is. Let us have it all again when this job is done with. Bowler and Donovan
will pick holes if they can, after waiting for us half a day. Not a word about
our slow sailing, mind; leave that to me. They are framptious enough. Have
everything trim, and all hands ready. When they range within hail, sing out
for both to come to me."

It was pretty to see the three cutters meet, all handled as smartly as
possible; for the Flamborough man had cast off his clog, and the Swordfish
again was as nimble as need be. Lieutenants Bowler and Donovan were soon
in the cabin of their senior officer, and durst not question him very strictly as
to his breach of rendezvous, for his manner was short and sharp with them.

"There is plenty of time, if we waste it not in talking," he said, when they
had finished comparing notes. "All these reports we are bound to receive and
consider; but I believe none of them. The reason why poor Carroway has
made nothing but a mess of it is that he will listen to the country people's
tales. They are all bound together, all tarred with one brush—all stuffed with a
heap of lies, to send us wrong; and as for the fishing-boats, and what they see,
I have been here long enough already to be sure that their fishing is a sham
nine times in ten, and their real business is to help those rogues. Our plan is to
listen, and pretend to be misled."

"True for you, captain," cried the ardent Donovan. "You 'bout ship as soon
as you can see them out of sight."

"My own opinion is this," said Bowler, "that we never shall catch any
fellow until we have a large sum of money placed at our disposal. The general
feeling is in their favor, and against us entirely. Why is it in their favor?
Because they are generally supposed to run great risks, and suffer great
hardships. And so they do; but not half so much as we do, who keep the sea in
all sorts of weather, while they can choose their own. Also because they
outrun the law, which nature makes everybody long to do, and admire the
lucky ones who can. But most of all because they are free-handed, and we can
be only niggards. They rob the king with impunity, because they pay well for
doing it; and he pays badly, or not at all, to defend himself from robbery. If
we had a thousand pounds apiece, with orders to spend it on public service,
take no receipt, and give no account, I am sure that in three months we could

stop all contraband work upon this coast."

"Upon me sowl and so we could; and it's meself that would go into the trade, so soon as it was stopped with the thousand pounds."

"We have no time for talking nonsense;" answered Nettlebones, severely, according to the universal law that the man who has wasted the time of others gets into a flurry about his own. "Your suggestion, Bowler, is a very wise one, and as full as possible of common-sense. You also, Donovan, have shown with great sagacity what might come of it thereafter. But unluckily we have to get on as we can, without sixpence to spare for anybody. We know that the fishermen and people on the coast, and especially the womankind, are all to a man—as our good friend here would say—banded in league against us. Nevertheless, this landing shall not be, at least upon our district. What happens north of Teesmouth is none of our business; and we should have the laugh of the old Scotchman there, if they pay him a visit, as I hope they may; for he cuts many jokes at our expense. But, by the Lord Harry, there shall be no run between the Tees and Yare, this side of Christmas. If there is, we may call ourselves three old women. Shake hands, gentlemen, upon that point; and we will have a glass of grog to it."

This was friendly, and rejoiced them all; for Nettlebones had been stiff at first. Readily enough they took his orders, which seemed to make it impossible almost for anything large to slip between them, except in case of a heavy fog; and in that case they were to land, and post their outlooks near the likely places.

"We have shed no blood yet, and I hope we never shall," said the senior officer, pleasantly. "The smugglers of this coast are too wise, and I hope too kind-hearted, for that sort of work. They are not like those desperate scoundrels of Sussex. When these men are nabbed, they give up their venture as soon as it goes beyond cudgel-play, and they never lie in wait for a murderous revenge. In the south I have known a very different race, who would jump on an officer till he died, or lash him to death with their long cart-whips; such fellows as broke open Poole Custom-house, and murdered poor Galley and Cator, and the rest, in a manner that makes human blood run cold. It was some time back; but their sons are just as bad. Smuggling turns them all to devils."

"My belief is," said Bowler, who had a gift of looking at things from an outer point of view, "that these fellows never propose to themselves to transgress the law, but to carry it out according to their own interpretation. One of them reasoned with me some time ago, and he talked so well about the Constitution that I was at a loss to answer him."

"Me jewel, forbear," shouted Donovan; "a clout on the head is the only answer for them Constitutionals. Niver will it go out of my mind about the time I was last in Cark; shure, thin, and it was holiday-time; and me sister's wife's cousin, young Tim O'Brady—Tim says to me, 'Now, Corkoran, me lad —'"

"Donovan," Nettlebones suddenly broke in, "we will have that story, which I can see by the cut of your jib is too good to be hurried, when first we come together after business done. The sun will be down in less than half an hour, and by that time we all must be well under way. We are watched from the land, as I need not tell you, and we must not let them spy for nothing. They shall see us all stand out to sea to catch them in the open, as I said in the town-hall of Scarborough yesterday, on purpose. Everybody laughed; but I stuck to it, knowing how far the tale would go. They take it for a crotchet of mine, and will expect it, especially after they have seen us standing out; and their plans will be laid accordingly."

"The head-piece ye have is beyont me inthirely. And if ye stand out, how will ye lay close inshore?"

"By returning, my good friend, before the morning breaks; each man to his station, lying as close as can be by day, with proper outlooks hidden at the points, but standing along the coast every night, and communicating with sentries. Have nothing to say to any fishing-boats—they are nearly all spies—and that puzzles them. This Robin Hood's Bay is our centre for the present, unless there comes change of weather. Donovan's beat is from Whitby to Teesmouth, mine from Whitby to Scarborough, and Bowler's thence to Flamborough. Carroway goes where he likes, of course, as the manner of the man is. He is a little in the doldrums now, and likely enough to come meddling. From Flamborough to Hornsea is left to him, and quite as much as he can manage. Further south there is no fear; our Yarmouth men will see to that. Now I think that you quite understand. Good-by; we shall nab some of them to a certainty this time; they are trying it on too large a scale."

"If they runs any goods through me, then just ye may reckon the legs of me four times over."

"And if they slip in past me," said Bowler, "without a thick fog, or a storm that drives me off, I will believe more than all the wonders told of Robin Lyth."

"Oh! concerning that fellow, by-the-bye," Commander Nettlebones stopped his brother officers as they were making off; "you know what a point poor Carroway has made, even before I was sent down here, of catching the celebrated Robin for himself. He has even let his fellows fire at him once or twice when he was quietly departing, although we are not allowed to shoot except upon strenuous resistance. Cannon we may fire, but no muskets, according to wise ordinance. Luckily, he has not hit him yet; and, upon the whole, we should be glad of it, for the young fellow is a prime sailor, as you know, and would make fine stuff for Nelson. Therefore we must do one thing of two—let Carroway catch him, and get the money to pay for all the breeches and the petticoats we saw; or if we catch him ourselves, say nothing, but draft him right off to the Harpy. You understand me. It is below us to get blood-money upon the man. We are gentlemen, not thief-catchers."

The Irishman agreed to this at once, but Bowler was not well pleased with it. "Our duty is to give him up," he said.

"Your duty is to take my orders," answered Nettlebones, severely. "If there is a fuss about it, lay the blame on me. I know what I am about in what I say. Gentlemen, good-by, and good luck to you."

After long shivers in teeth of the wind and pendulous labor of rolling, the three cutters joyfully took the word to go. With a creak, and a cant, and a swish of canvas, upon their light heels they flew round, and trembled with the eagerness of leaping on their way. The taper boom dipped toward the running hills of sea, and the jib-foreleech drew a white arc against the darkness of the sky to the bowsprit's plunge. Then, as each keen cut-water clove with the pressure of the wind upon the beam, and the glistening bends lay over, green hurry of surges streaked with gray began the quick dance along them. Away they went merrily, scattering the brine, and leaving broad tracks upon the closing sea.

Away also went, at a rapid scamper, three men who had watched them from the breast-work of the cliffs—one went northward, another to the south, and the third rode a pony up an inland lane. Swiftly as the cutters flew over the sea, the tidings of their flight took wing ashore, and before the night swallowed up their distant sails, everybody on the land whom it concerned to know, knew as well as their steersmen what course they had laid.

CHAPTER XXX

INLAND OPINION

Whatever may be said, it does seem hard, from a wholly disinterested point of view, that so many mighty men, with swift ships, armed with villainous saltpetre and sharp steel, should have set their keen faces all together and at once to nip, defeat, and destroy as with a blow, liberal and well-conceived proceedings, which they had long regarded with a larger mind. Every one who had been led to embark soundly and kindly in this branch of trade felt it as an outrage and a special instance of his own peculiar bad luck that suddenly the officers should become so active. For long success had encouraged enterprise; men who had made a noble profit nobly yearned to treble it; and commerce, having shaken off her shackles, flapped her wings and began to crow; so at least she had been declared to do at a public banquet given by the Mayor of Malton, and attended by a large grain factor, who was known as a wholesale purveyor of illicit goods.

This man, Thomas Rideout, long had been the head-master of the smuggling school. The poor sea-faring men could not find money to buy, or even hire, the craft (with heavy deposit against forfeiture) which the breadth and turbulence of the North Sea made needful for such ventures. Across the narrow English Channel an open lobster boat might run, in common summer weather, without much risk of life or goods. Smooth water, sandy coves, and shelfy landings tempted comfortable jobs; and any man owning a boat that would carry a sail as big as a shawl might smuggle, with heed of the weather, and audacity. It is said that once upon the Sussex coast a band of haymakers, when the rick was done, and their wages in hand on a Saturday night, laid hold of a stout boat on the beach, pushed off to sea in tipsy faith of luck, and hit upon Dieppe with a set-fair breeze, having only a fisherman's boy for guide. There on the Sunday they heartily enjoyed the hospitality of the natives; and the dawn of Tuesday beheld them rapt in domestic bliss and breakfast, with their money invested in old Cognac; and glad would they have been to make such hay every season. But in Yorkshire a good solid capital was needed to carry on free importation. Without broad bottoms and deep sides, the long and turbulent and often foggy voyage, and the rocky landing, could scarcely be attempted by sane folk; well-to-do people found the money, and jeopardized neither their own bodies, consciences, nor good repute. And perhaps this fact had more to do with the comparative mildness of the men than difference of race, superior culture, or a loftier mould of mind; for what man will fight for his employer's goods with the ferocity inspired by his own? A thorough good ducking, or a tow behind a boat, was the utmost penalty generally exacted by the victors from the vanquished.

Now, however, it seemed too likely that harder measures must be meted. The long success of that daring Lyth, and the large scale of his operations, had compelled the authorities to stir at last. They began by setting a high price upon him, and severely reprimanding Carroway, who had long been doing his best in vain, and becoming flurried, did it more vainly still; and now they had sent the sharp Nettlebones down, who boasted largely, but as yet without result. The smugglers, however, were aware of added peril, and raised their wages accordingly.

When the pending great venture was resolved upon, as a noble finish to the season, Thomas Rideout would intrust it to no one but Robin Lyth himself; and the bold young mariner stipulated that after succeeding he should be free, and started in some more lawful business. For Dr. Upround, possessing as he did great influence with Robin, and shocked as he was by what Carroway had said, refused to have anything more to do with his most distinguished parishioner until he should forsake his ways. And for this he must not be thought narrow-minded, strait-laced, or unduly dignified. His wife quite agreed with him, and indeed had urged it as the only proper course; for her motherly mind was uneasy about the impulsive nature of Janetta; and chess-men to her were dolls, without even the merit of encouraging the needle. Therefore, with a deep sigh, the worthy magistrate put away his board— which came out again next day—and did his best to endure for a night the arithmetical torture of cribbage; while he found himself supported by a sense of duty, and capable of preaching hard at Carroway if he would only come for it on Sunday.

From that perhaps an officer of revenue may abstain, through the pressure of his duty and his purity of conscience; but a man of less correctness must behave more strictly. Therefore, when a gentleman of vigorous aspect, resolute step, and successful-looking forehead marched into church the next Sunday morning, showed himself into a prominent position, and hung his hat against a leading pillar, after putting his mouth into it, as if for prayer, but scarcely long enough to say "Amen," behind other hats low whispers passed that here was the great financier of free trade, the Chancellor of the Exchequer of smuggling, the celebrated Master Rideout.

That conclusion was shared by the rector, whose heart immediately burned within him to have at this man, whom he had met before and suspiciously glanced at in Weighing Lane, as an interloper in his parish. Probably this was the very man whom Robin Lyth served too faithfully; and the chances were that the great operations now known to be pending had brought him hither, spying out all Flamborough. The corruption of fish-folk, the beguiling of women with foreign silks and laces, and of men with brandy, the seduction of Robin from lawful commerce, and even the loss of his own pet pastime, were to be laid at this man's door. While donning his surplice, Dr. Upround revolved these things with gentle indignation, quickened, as soon as he found himself in white, by clerical and theological zeal. These feelings impelled him to produce a creaking of the heavy vestry door, a well-known signal for his daughter to slip out of the chancel pew and come to him.

"Now, papa, what is it?" cried that quick young lady; "that miserable Methodist that ruined your boots, has he got the impudence to come again? Oh, please do say so, and show me where he is; after church nobody shall stop me—"

"Janetta, you quite forget where you are, as well as my present condition. Be off like a good girl, as quick as you can, and bring No. 27 of my own handwriting—'Render unto Caesar'—and put my hat upon it. My desire is that Billyjack should not know that a change has been made in my subject of discourse."

"Papa, I see; it shall be done to perfection, while Billyjack is at his very loudest roar in the chorus of the anthem. But do tell me who it is; or how can I enjoy it? And lemon drops—lemon drops—"

"Janetta, I must have some very serious talk with you. Now don't be vexed, darling; you are a thoroughly good girl, only thoughtless and careless; and remember, dear, church is not a place for high spirits."

The rector, as behooved him, kissed his child behind the vestry door, to soothe all sting, and then he strode forth toward the reading-desk; and the tuning of fiddles sank to deferential scrape.

It was not at all a common thing, as one might know, for Widow Precious to be able to escape from casks and taps, and the frying pan of eggs demanded by some half-drowned fisherman, also the reckoning of notches on the bench for the pints of the week unpaid for, and then to put herself into her two best gowns (which she wore in the winter, one over the other—a plan to be highly commended to ladies who never can have dress enough), and so to enjoy, without losing a penny, the warmth of the neighborhood of a congregation. In the afternoon she could hardly ever do it, even if she had so wished, with knowledge that this was common people's time; so if she went at all, it must —in spite of the difference of length—be managed in the morning. And this very morning here she was, earnest, humble, and devout, with both the tap keys in her pocket, and turning the leaves with a smack of her thumb, not only to show her learning, but to get the sweet approval of the rector's pew.

Now if the good rector had sent for this lady, instead of his daughter Janetta, the sermon which he brought would have been the one to preach, and that about Caesar might have stopped at home; for no sooner did the widow begin to look about, taking in the congregation with a dignified eye, and nodding to her solvent customers, than the wrath of perplexity began to gather on her goodly countenance. To see that distinguished stranger was to know him ever afterward; his power of eating, and of paying, had endeared his memory; and for him to put up at any other house were foul shame to the "Cod Fish."

"Hath a' put up his beastie?" she whispered to her eldest daughter, who came in late.

"Naa, naa, no beastie," the child replied, and the widow's relish of her thumb was gone; for, sooth to say, no Master Rideout, nor any other patron of free trade was here, but Geoffrey Mordacks, of York city, general factor, and universal agent.

It was beautiful to see how Dr. Upround, firmly delivering his text, and stoutly determined to spare nobody, even insisted in the present case upon looking at the man he meant to hit, because he was not his parishioner. The sermon was eloquent, and even trenchant. The necessity of duties was urged most sternly; if not of directly Divine institution (though learned parallels were adduced which almost proved them to be so), yet to every decent Christian citizen they were synonymous with duty. To defy or elude them, for the sake of paltry gain, was a dark crime recoiling on the criminal; and the preacher drew a contrast between such guilty ways and the innocent path of the fisherman. Neither did he even relent and comfort, according to his custom, toward the end; that part was there, but he left it out; and the only consolation for any poor smuggler in all the discourse was the final Amen.

But to the rector's great amazement, and inward indignation, the object of his sermon seemed to take it as a personal compliment. Mr. Mordacks not only failed to wince, but finding himself particularly fixed by the gaze of the eloquent divine, concluded that it was from his superior intelligence, and visible gifts of appreciation. Delighted with this—for he was not free from vanity—what did he do but return the compliment, not indecorously, but nodding very gently, as much as to say, "That was very good indeed, you were quite right, sir, in addressing that to me; you perceive that it is far above these common people. I never heard a better sermon."

"What a hardened rogue you are!" thought Dr. Upround; "how feebly and incapably I must have put it! If you ever come again, you shall have my Ahab sermon."

But the clergyman was still more astonished a very few minutes afterward. For, as he passed out of the church-yard gate, receiving, with his wife and daughter, the kindly salute of the parish, the same tall stranger stood before him, with a face as hard as a statue's, and, making a short, quick flourish with his hat, begged for the honor of shaking his hand.

"Sir, it is to thank you for the very finest sermon I ever had the privilege of hearing. My name is Mordacks, and I flatter nobody—except myself—that I know a good thing when I get it."

"Sir, I am obliged to you," said Dr. Upround, stiffly, and not without suspicion of being bantered, so dry was the stranger's countenance, and his manner so peculiar; "and if I have been enabled to say a good word in season, and its season lasts, it will be a source of satisfaction to me."

"Yes, I fear there are many smugglers here. But I am no revenue officer, as your congregation seemed to think. May I call upon business to-morrow, sir? Thank you; then may I say ten o'clock—your time of beginning, as I hear? Mordacks is my name, sir, of York city, not unfavorably known there. Ladies, my duty to you!"

"What an extraordinary man, my dear!" Mrs. Upround exclaimed, with some ingratitude, after the beautiful bow she had received. "He may talk as he likes, but he must be a smuggler. He said that he was not an officer; that shows it, for they always run into the opposite extreme. You have converted him, my dear; and I am sure that we ought to be so much obliged to him. If he comes to-morrow morning to give up all his lace, do try to remember how my little all has been ruined in the wash, and I am sick of working at it."

"My dear, he is no smuggler. I begin to recollect. He was down here in the summer, and I made a great mistake. I took him for Rideout; and I did the same to-day. When I see him to-morrow, I shall beg his pardon. One gets so hurried in the vestry always; they are so impatient with their fiddles! A great deal of it was Janetta's fault."

"It always is my fault, papa, somehow or other," the young lady answered, with a faultless smile: and so they went home to the early Sunday dinner.

"Papa, I am in such a state of excitement; I am quite unfit to go to church this afternoon," Miss Upround exclaimed, as they set forth again. "You may put me in stocks made out of hassocks—you may rope me to the Flodden Field man's monument, of the ominous name of 'Constable;' but whatever you do, I shall never attend; and I feel that it is so sinful."

"Janetta, your mamma has that feeling sometimes; for instance, she has it this afternoon; and there is a good deal to be said for it. But I fear that it would grow with indulgence."

"I can firmly fancy that it never would; though one can not be sure without trying. Suppose that I were to try it just once, and let you know how it feels at tea-time?"

"My dear, we are quite round the corner of the lane. The example would be too shocking."

"Now don't you make any excuses, papa. Only one woman can have seen us yet; and she is so blind she will think it was her fault. May I go? Quick, before any one else comes."

"If you are quite sure, Janetta, of being in a frame of mind which unfits you for the worship of your Maker—"

"As sure as a pike-staff, dear papa."

"Then, by all means, go before anybody sees you, for whom it might be undesirable; and correct your thoughts, and endeavor to get into a befitting state of mind by tea-time."

"Certainly, papa. I will go down on the stones, and look at the sea. That always makes me better; because it is so large and so uncomfortable."

The rector went on to do his duty, by himself. A narrow-minded man might have shaken solemn head, even if he had allowed such dereliction. But Dr. Upround knew that the girl was good, and he never put strain upon her honesty. So away she sped by a lonely little foot-path, where nobody could take from her contagion of bad morals; and avoiding the incline of boats, she made off nicely for the quiet outer bay, and there, upon a shelfy rock, she sat and breathed the sea.

Flamborough, excellent place as it is, and delightful, and full of interest for people who do not live there, is apt to grow dull perhaps for spirited youth, in the scanty and foggy winter light. There is not so very much of that choice product generally called "society" by a man who has a house to let in an eligible neighborhood, and by ladies who do not heed their own. Moreover, it is vexatious not to have more rogues to talk about.

That scarcity may be less lamentable now, being one that takes care to redress itself, and perhaps any amateur purchaser of fish may find rogues enough now for his interest. But the rector's daughter pined for neither society nor scandal: she had plenty of interest in her life, and in pleasing other people, whenever she could do it with pleasure to herself, and that was nearly always. Her present ailment was not languor, weariness, or dullness, but rather the want of such things; which we long for when they happen to be scarce, and declare them to be our first need, under the sweet name of repose.

Her mind was a little disturbed by rumors, wonders, and uncertainty. She was not at all in love with Robin Lyth, and laughed at his vanity quite as much as she admired his gallantry. She looked upon him also as of lower rank, kindly patronized by her father, but not to be treated as upon an equal footing. He might be of any rank, for all that was known; but he must be taken to belong to those who had brought him up and fed him. Janetta was a lively girl, of quick perception and some discretion, though she often talked much nonsense. She was rather proud of her position, and somewhat disdainful of uneducated folk; though (thanks to her father) Lyth was not one of these. Possibly love (if she had felt it) would have swept away such barriers; but Robin was grateful to his patron, and, knowing his own place in life, would rightly have thought it a mean return to attempt to inveigle the daughter. So they liked one another—but nothing more. It was not, therefore, for his sake only, but for her father's, and that of the place, that Miss Upround now was anxious. For days and days she had watched the sea with unusual forebodings, knowing that a great importation was toward, and pretty sure to lead to blows, after so much preparation. With feminine zeal, she detested poor Carroway, whom she regarded as a tyrant and a spy; and she would have clapped her hands at beholding the three cruisers run upon a shoal, and there stick fast. And as for King George, she had never believed that he was the proper King of England. There were many stanch Jacobites still in Yorkshire, and especially the bright young ladies.

To-night, at least, the coast was likely to be uninvaded. Smugglers, even if their own forces would make breach upon the day of rest, durst not outrage the piety of the land, which would only deal with kegs in-doors. The coast-guard, being for the most part southerns, splashed about as usual—a far more heinous sin against the Word of God than smuggling. It is the manner of Yorkshiremen to think for themselves, with boldness, in the way they are brought up to: and they made it a point of serious doubt whether the orders of the king himself could set aside the Fourth Commandment, though his arms were over it.

Dr. Upround's daughter, as she watched the sea, felt sure that, even if the goods were ready, no attempt at landing would be made that night, though something might be done in the morning. But even that was not very likely, because (as seemed to be widely known) the venture was a very large one, and the landers would require a whole night's work to get entirely through with it.

"I wish it was over, one way or the other," she kept on saying to herself, as she gazed at the dark, weary lifting of the sea; "it keeps one unsettled as the waves themselves. Sunday always makes me feel restless, because there is so little to do. It is wicked, I suppose; but how can I help it? Why, there is a boat, I do declare! Well, even a boat is welcome, just to break this gray monotony. What boat can it be? None of ours, of course. And what can they want with our Church Cave? I hope they understand its dangers."

Although the wind was not upon the shore, and no long rollers were setting in, short, uncomfortable, clumsy waves were lolloping under the steep gray cliffs, and casting up splashes of white here and there. To enter that cave is a risky thing, except at very favorable times, and even then some experience is needed, for the rocks around it are like knives, and the boat must generally be backed in, with more use of fender and hook than of oars. But the people in the boat seemed to understand all that. There were two men rowing, and one steering with an oar, and a fourth standing up, as if to give directions; though in truth he knew nothing about it, but hated even to seem to play second fiddle.

"What a strange thing!" Janetta thought, as she drew behind a rock, that they might not see her, "I could almost declare that the man standing up is that most extraordinary gentleman papa preached quite the wrong sermon at. Truly he deserves the Ahab one, for spying our caves out on a Sunday. He must be a smuggler, after all, or a very crafty agent of the Revenue. Well, I never! That old man steering, as sure as I live, is Robin Cockscroft, by the scarlet handkerchief round his head. Oh, Robin! Robin! could I ever have believed that you would break the Sabbath so? But the boat is not Robin's. What boat can it be? I have not staid away from church for nothing. One of the men rowing has got no legs, when the boat goes up and down. It must be that villain of a tipsy Joe, who used to keep the 'Monument.' I heard that he was come back again, to stump for his beer as usual: and his son, that sings like the big church bell, and has such a very fine face and one leg—why, he is the man that pulls the other oar. Was there ever such a boat-load? But they know what they are doing."

Truly it was, as the young lady said, an extraordinary boat's crew. Old Robin Cockscroft, with a fringe of silver hair escaping from the crimson silk, which he valued so much more than it, and his face still grand (in spite of wrinkles and some weakness of the eyes), keenly understanding every wave, its character, temper, and complexity of influence, as only a man can understand who has for his life stood over them. Then tugging at the oars, or rather dipping them with a short well-practiced plunge, and very little toil of body, two ancient sailors, one considerably older than the other, inasmuch as he was his father, yet chips alike from a sturdy block, and fitted up with jury-stumps. Old Joe pulled rather the better oar, and called his son "a one-legged fiddler" when he missed the dip of wave; while Mordacks stood with his leg's apart, and playing the easy part of critic, had his sneers at both of them. But they let him gibe to his liking; because they knew their work, and he did not. And, upon the whole, they went merrily.

The only one with any doubt concerning the issue of the job was the one who knew most about it, and that was Robin Cockscroft. He doubted not about want of strength, or skill, or discipline of his oars, but because the boat was not Flamburian, but borrowed from a collier round the Head. No Flamborough boat would ever think of putting to sea on a Sunday, unless it were to save human life; and it seemed to him that no strange boat could find her way into the native caves. He doubted also whether, even with the pressure of strong motive put upon him, which was not of money, it was a godly thing on his part to be steering in his Sunday clothes; and he feared to hear of it thereafter. But being in for it, he must do his utmost.

With genuine skill and solid patience, the entrance of the cave was made, and the boat was lost to Janetta's view. She as well was lost in the deeper cavern of great wonder, and waited long, and much desired to wait even longer, to see them issue forth again, and learn what they could have been after. But the mist out of which they had come, and inside of which they would rather have remained perhaps, now thickened over land and sea, and groping dreamily for something to lay hold of, found a solid stay and rest-hold in the jagged headlands here. Here, accordingly, the coilings of the wandering forms began to slide into strait layers, and soft settlement of vapor. Loops of hanging moisture marked the hollows of the land-front, or the alleys of the waning light; and then the mass abandoned outline, fused its shades to pulp, and melted into one great blur of rain. Janetta thought of her Sunday frock, forgot the boat, and sped away for home.

CHAPTER XXXI

TACTICS OF ATTACK

"I am sorry to be troublesome, Mynheer Van Dunck, but I can not say good-by without having your receipt in full for the old bilander."

"Goot, it is vere good, Meester Lyth; you are te goot man for te pisness."

With these words the wealthy merchant of the Zuyder-Zee drew forth his ancient inkhorn, smeared with the dirt of countless contracts, and signed an acquittance which the smuggler had prepared. But he signed it with a sigh, as a man declares that a favorite horse must go at last; sighing, not for the money, but the memories that go with it. Then, as the wind began to pipe, and the roll of the sea grew heavier, the solid Dutchman was lowered carefully into his shore boat, and drew the apron over his great and gouty legs.

"I vos married in dat zhips," he shouted back, with his ponderous fist wagging up at Robin Lyth, "Dis taime you will have de bad luck, sir."

"Well, mynheer, you have only to pay the difference, and the ketch will do; the bilander sails almost as fast."

But Master Van Dunck only heaved another sigh, and felt that his leather bag was safe and full in his breeches pocket. Then he turned his eyes away, and relieved his mind by swearing at his men.

Now this was off the Isle of Texel, and the time was Sunday morning, the very same morning which saw the general factor sitting to be preached at. The flotilla of free trade was putting forth upon its great emprise, and Van Dunck (who had been ship's husband) came to speed them from their moorings.

He took no risk, and to him it mattered little, except as a question of commission; but still he enjoyed the relish of breaking English law most heartily. He hated England, as a loyal Dutchman, for generations, was compelled to do; and he held that a Dutchman was a better sailor, a better ship-builder, and a better fighter than the very best Englishman ever born. However, his opinions mattered little, being (as we must feel) absurd. Therefore let him go his way, and grumble, and reckon his guilders. It was generally known that he could sink a ship with money; and when such a man is insolent, who dares to contradict him?

The flotilla in the offing soon ploughed hissing furrows through the misty waves. There were three craft, all of different rig—a schooner, a ketch, and the said bilander. All were laden as heavily as speed and safety would allow, and all were thoroughly well manned. They laid their course for the Dogger Bank, where they would receive the latest news of the disposition of the enemy. Robin Lyth, high admiral of smugglers, kept to his favorite schooner, the Glimpse, which had often shown a fading wake to fastest cutters. His squadron was made up by the ketch, Good Hope, and the old Dutch coaster, Crown of Gold. This vessel, though built for peaceful navigation and inland waters, had proved herself so thoroughly at home in the roughest situations, and so swift of foot, though round of cheek, that the smugglers gloried in her and the good luck which sat upon her prow. They called her "the lugger," though her rig was widely different from that, and her due title was "bilander." She was very deeply laden now, and, having great capacity, appeared an unusually tempting prize.

This grand armada of invasion made its way quite leisurely. Off the Dogger Bank they waited for the last news, and received it, and the whole of it was to their liking, though the fisherman who brought it strongly advised them to put back again. But Captain Lyth had no such thought, for the weather was most suitable for the bold scheme he had hit upon. "This is my last run," he said, "and I mean to make it a good one." Then he dressed himself as smartly as if he were going to meet Mary Anerley, and sent a boat for the skippers of the Good Hope, and the Crown of Gold, who came very promptly and held counsel in his cabin.

"I'm thinking that your notion is a very good one, captain," said the master of the bilander, Brown, a dry old hand from Grimsby.

"Capital, capital; there never was a better," the master of the ketch chimed in, "Nettlebones and Carroway—they will knock their heads together!"

"The plan is clever enough," replied Robin, who was free from all mock-modesty, "But you heard what that old Van Dunck said. I wish he had not said it."

"Ten tousan' tuyfels—as the stingy old thief himself says—he might have held his infernal croak. I hate to make sail with a croak astern; 'tis as bad as a crow on forestay-sail."

"All very fine for you to talk," grumbled the man of the bilander to the master of the ketch; "but the bad luck is saddled upon me this voyage. You two get the gilgoes, and I the bilboes!"

"Brown, none of that!" Captain Lyth said, quietly, but with a look which the other understood; "you are not such a fool as you pretend to be. You may get a shot or two fired at you; but what is that to a Grimsby man? And who will look at you when your hold is broached? Your game is the easiest that any man can play—to hold your tongue and run away."

"Brown, you share the profits, don't you see?" the ketch man went on, while the other looked glum; "and what risk do you take for it? Even if they collar you, through your own clumsiness, what is there for them to do? A Grimsby man is a grumbling man, I have heard ever since I was that high. I'll change berths with you, if you choose, this minute."

"You could never do it," said the Grimsby man, with that high contempt which abounds where he was born—"a boy like you! I should like to see you try it."

"Remember, both of you," said Robin Lyth, "that you are not here to do as you please, but to obey my orders. If the coast-guard quarrel, we do not; and that is why we beat them. You will both do exactly as I have laid it down; and the risk of failure falls on me. The plan is very simple, and can not fail, if you will just try not to think for yourselves, which always makes everything go wrong. The only thing you have to think about at all is any sudden change of weather. If a gale from the east sets in, you both run north, and I come after you. But there will not be any easterly gale for the present week, to my belief; although I am not quite sure of it."

"Not a sign of it. Wind will hold with sunset, up to next quarter of the moon."

"The time I ha' been on the coast," said Brown, "and to hear the young chaps talking over my head! Never you mind how I know, but I'll lay a guinea with both of you—easterly gale afore Friday."

"Brown, you may be right," said Robin; "I have had some fear of it, and I know that you carry a weather eye. No man under forty can pretend to that. But if it will only hold off till Friday, we shall have the laugh of it. And even if it come on, Tom and I shall manage. But you will be badly off in that case, Brown. After all, you are right; the main danger is for you."

Lyth, knowing well how important it was that each man should play his part with true good-will, shifted his ground thus to satisfy the other, who was not the man to shrink from peril, but liked to have his share acknowledged.

"Ay, ay, captain, you see clear enough, though Tom here has not got the gumption," the man of Grimsby answered, with a lofty smile. "Everybody knows pretty well what William Brown is. When there is anything that needs a bit of pluck, it is sure to be put upon old Bill Brown. And never you come across the man, Captain Lyth, as could say that Bill Brown was not all there. Now orders is orders, lad. Tip us your latest."

"Then latest orders are to this effect. Toward dusk of night you stand in first, a league or more ahead of us, according to the daylight, Tom to the north of you, and me to the south, just within signaling distance. The Kestrel and Albatross will come to speak the Swordfish off Robin Hood's Bay, at that very hour, as we happen to be aware. You sight them, even before they sight you, because you know where to look for them, and you keep a sharper look-out, of course. Not one of them will sight us, so far off in the offing. Signal immediately, one, two, or three; and I heartily hope it will be all three. Then you still stand in, as if you could not see them; and they begin to laugh, and draw inshore; knowing the Inlander as they do, they will hug the cliffs for you to run into their jaws. Tom and I bear off, all sail, never allowing them to sight us. We crack on to the north and south, and by that time it will be nearly dark. You still carry on, till they know that you must see them; then 'bout ship, and crowd sail to escape. They give chase, and you lead them out to sea, and the longer you carry on, the better. Then, as they begin to fore-reach, and threaten to close, you 'bout ship again, as in despair, run under their counters, and stand in for the bay. They may fire at you; but it is not very likely, for they would not like to sink such a valuable prize; though nobody else would have much fear of that."

"Captain, I laugh at their brass kettle-pots. They may blaze away as blue as verdigris. Though an Englishman haven't no right to be shot at, only by a Frenchman."

"Very well, then, you hold on, like a Norfolk man, through the thickest of the enemy. Nelson is a Norfolk man; and you charge through as he does. You bear right on, and rig a gangway for the landing, which puts them all quite upon the scream. All three cutters race after you pell-mell, and it is much if they do not run into one another. You take the beach, stem on, with the tide upon the ebb, and by that time it ought to be getting on for midnight. What to do then, I need not tell you; but make all the stand you can to spare us any hurry. But don't give the knock-down blow if you can help it; the lawyers make such a point of that, from their intimacy with the prize-fighters."

Clearly perceiving their duty now, these three men braced up loin, and sailed to execute the same accordingly. For invaders and defenders were by this time in real earnest with their work, and sure alike of having done the very best that could be done. With equal confidence on either side, a noble triumph was expected, while the people on the dry land shook their heads and were thankful to be out of it. Carroway, in a perpetual ferment, gave no peace to any of his men, and never entered his own door; but riding, rowing, or sailing up and down, here and there and everywhere, set an example of unflagging zeal, which was largely admired and avoided. And yet he was not the only remarkably active man in the neighborhood; for that great fact, and universal factor, Geoffrey Mordacks, was entirely here. He had not broken the heart of Widow Precious by taking up his quarters at the Thornwick Inn, as she at first imagined, but loyally brought himself and his horse to her sign-post for their Sunday dinner. Nor was this all, but he ordered the very best bedroom, and the "coral parlor"—as he elegantly called the sea-weedy room—gave every child, whether male or female, sixpence of new mintage, and created such impression on her widowed heart that he even won the privilege of basting his own duck. Whatever this gentleman did never failed to reflect equal credit on him and itself. But thoroughly well as he basted his duck, and efficiently as he consumed it, deeper things were in his mind, and moving with every mouthful. If Captain Carroway labored hard on public and royal service, no less severely did Mordacks work, though his stronger sense of self-duty led him to feed the labor better. On the Monday morning he had a long and highly interesting talk with the magisterial rector, to whom he set forth certain portions of his purpose, loftily spurning entire concealment, according to the motto of his life. "You see, sir," he said, as he rose to depart, "what I have told you is very important, and in the strictest confidence, of course, because I never do anything on the sly."

"Mr. Mordacks, you have surprised me," answered Dr. Upround; "though I am not so very much wiser at present. I really must congratulate you upon your activity, and the impression you create."

"Not at all, sir, not at all. It is my manner of doing business, now for thirty years or more. Moles and fools, sir, work under-ground, and only get traps set for them; I travel entirely above-ground, and go ten miles for their ten inches. My strategy, sir, is simplicity. Nothing puzzles rogues so much, because they can not believe it."

"The theory is good; may the practice prove the same! I should be sorry to be against you in any case you undertake. In the present matter I am wholly with you, so far as I understand what it is. Still, Flamborough is a place of great difficulties—"

"The greatest difficulty of all would be to fail, as I look at it. Especially with your most valuable aid."

"What little I can do shall be most readily forth-coming. But remember there is many a slip—If you had interfered but one month ago, how much easier it might have been!"

"Truly. But I have to grope my way; and it is a hard people, as you say, to deal with. But I have no fear, sir; I shall overcome all Flamborough, unless—unless, what I fear to think of, there should happen to be bloodshed."

"There will be none of that, Mr. Mordacks; we are too skillful, and too gentle, for anything more than a few cracked crowns."

"Then everything is as it ought to be. But I must be off; I have many points to see to. How I find time for this affair is the wonder."

"But you will not leave us, I suppose, until—until what appears to be expected has happened!"

"When I undertake a thing, Dr. Upround, my rule is to go through with it. You have promised me the honor of an interview at any time. Good-by, sir; and pray give the compliments of Mr. Mordacks to the ladies."

With even more than his usual confidence and high spirits the general factor mounted horse and rode at once to Bridlington, or rather to the quay thereof, in search of Lieutenant Carroway. But Carroway was not at home, and his poor wife said, with a sigh, that now she had given up expecting him. "Have no fear, madam; I will bring him back," Mordacks answered, as if he already held him by the collar. "I have very good news, madam, very grand news for him, and you, and all those lovely and highly intelligent children. Place me, madam, under the very deepest obligation by allowing these two little dears to take the basket I see yonder, and accompany me to that apple stand. I saw there some fruit of a sort which used to fit my teeth most wonderfully when they were just the size of theirs. And here is another little darling, with a pin-before infinitely too spotless. If you will spare her also, we will do our best to take away that reproach, ma'am."

"Oh, sir, you are much too kind. But to speak of good news does one good. It is so long since there has been any, that I scarcely know how to pronounce the words."

"Mistress Carroway, take my word for it, that such a state of things shall be shortly of the past. I will bring back Captain Carroway, madam, to his sweet and most beautifully situated home, and with tidings which shall please you."

"It is kind of you not to tell me the good news now, sir. I shall enjoy it so much more, to see my husband hear it. Good-by, and I hope that you will soon be back again."

While Mr. Mordacks was loading the children with all that they made soft mouths at, he observed for the second time three men who appeared to be taking much interest in his doings. They had sauntered aloof while he called at the cottage, as if they had something to say to him, but would keep it until he had finished there. But they did not come up to him as he expected; and when he had seen the small Carroways home, he rode up to ask what they wanted with him. "Nothing, only this, sir," the shortest of them answered, while the others pretended not to hear; "we was told that yon was Smuggler's house, and we thought that your Honor was the famous Captain Lyth."

"If I ever want a man," said the general factor, "to tell a lie with a perfect face, I shall come here and look for you, my friend." The man looked at him, and smiled, and nodded, as much as to say, "You might get it done worse," and then carelessly followed his comrades toward the sea. And Mr. Mordacks, riding off with equal jauntiness, cocked his hat, and stared at the Priory Church as if he had never seen any such building before.

"I begin to have a very strong suspicion," he said to himself as he put his horse along, "that this is the place where the main attack will be. Signs of a well-suppressed activity are manifest to an experienced eye like mine. All the grocers, the bakers, the candlestick-makers, and the women, who always precede the men, are mightily gathered together. And the men are holding counsel in a milder way. They have got three jugs at the old boat-house for the benefit of holloaing in the open air. Moreover, the lane inland is scored with a regular market-day of wheels, and there is no market this side of the old town. Carroway, vigilant captain of men, why have you forsaken your domestic hearth? Is it through jealousy of Nettlebones, and a stern resolve to be ahead of him? Robin, my Robin, is a genius in tactics, a very bright Napoleon of free trade. He penetrates the counsels, or, what is more, the feelings, of those who camp against him. He means to land this great emprise at Captain Carroway's threshold. True justice on the man for sleeping out of his own bed so long! But instead of bowing to the blow, he would turn a downright maniac, according to all I hear of him. Well, it is no concern of mine, so long as nobody is killed, which everybody makes such a fuss about."

CHAPTER XXXII

CORDIAL ENJOYMENT

The poise of this great enterprise was hanging largely in the sky, from which come all things, and to which resolved they are referred again. The sky, to hold an equal balance, or to decline all troublesome responsibility about it, went away, or (to put it more politely) retired from the scene. Even as nine men out of ten, when a handsome fight is toward, would rather have no opinion on the merits, but abide in their breeches, and there keep their hands till the fist of the victor is opened, so at this period the upper firmament nodded a strict neutrality. And yet, on the whole, it must have indulged a sneaking proclivity toward free trade; otherwise, why should it have been as follows?

November now was far advanced; and none but sanguine Britons hoped, at least in this part of the world, to know (except from memory and predictions of the almanac) whether the sun were round or square, until next Easter-day should come. It was not quite impossible that he might appear at Candlemas, when he is supposed to give a dance, though hitherto a strictly private one; but even so, this premature frisk of his were undesirable, if faith in ancient rhyme be any. But putting him out of the question, as he had already put himself, the things that were below him, and, from length of practice, manage well to shape their course without him, were moving now and managing themselves with moderation.

The tone of the clouds was very mild, and so was the color of the sea. A comely fog involved the day, and a decent mist restrained the night from ostentatious waste of stars. It was not such very bad weather; but a captious man might find fault with it, and only a thoroughly cheerful one could enlarge upon its merits. Plainly enough these might be found by anybody having any core of rest inside him, or any gift of turning over upon a rigidly neutral side, and considerably outgazing the color of his eyes.

Commander Nettlebones was not of poetic, philosophic, or vague mind. "What a ——- fog!" he exclaimed in the morning; and he used the same words in the afternoon, through a speaking-trumpet, as the two other cutters ranged up within hail. This they did very carefully, at the appointed rendezvous, toward the fall of the afternoon, and hauled their wind under easy sail, shivering in the southwestern breeze.

"Not half so bad as it was," returned Bowler, being of a cheerful mind. "It is lifting every minute, sir. Have you had sight of anything?"

"Not a blessed stick, except a fishing-boat. What makes you ask, lieutenant?"

"Why, sir, as we rounded in, it lifted for a moment, and I saw a craft some two leagues out, standing straight in for us."

"The devil you did! What was she like? and where away, lieutenant?"

"A heavy lugger, under all sail, about E.N.E, as near as may be. She is standing for Robin Hood's Bay, I believe. In an hour's time she will be upon us, if the weather keeps so thick."

"She may have seen you, and sheered off. Stand straight for her, as nigh as you can guess. The fog is lifting, as you say. If you sight her, signal instantly. Lieutenant Donovan, have you heard Bowler's news?"

"Sure an' if it wasn't for the fog, I would. Every word of it come to me, as clear as seeing."

"Very well. Carry on a little to the south, half a league or so, and then stand out, but keep within sound of signal. I shall bear up presently. It is clearing every minute, and we must nab them."

The fog began to rise in loops and alleys, with the upward pressure of the evening breeze, which freshened from the land in lines and patches, according to the run of cliff. Here the water darkened with the ruffle of the wind, and there it lay quiet, with a glassy shine, or gentle shadows of variety. Soon the three cruisers saw one another clearly; and then they all sighted an approaching sail.

This was a full-bowed vessel, of quaint rig, heavy sheer, and extraordinary build—a foreigner clearly, and an ancient one. She differed from a lugger as widely as a lugger differs from a schooner, and her broad spread of canvas combined the features of square and of fore-and-aft tackle. But whatever her build or rig might be, she was going through the water at a strapping pace, heavily laden as she was, with her long yards creaking, and her broad frame croaking, and her deep bows driving up the fountains of the sea. Her enormous mainsail upon the mizzenmast—or mainmast, for she only carried two—was hung obliquely, yet not as a lugger's, slung at one-third of its length, but bent to a long yard hanging fore and aft, with a long fore-end sloping down to midship. This great sail gave her vast power, when close hauled; and she carried a square sail on the foremast, and a square sail on either topmast.

"Lord, have mercy! She could run us all down if she tried!" exclaimed

Commander Nettlebones; "and what are my pop-guns against such beam?"

For a while the bilander seemed to mean to try it, for she carried on toward the central cruiser as if she had not seen one of them. Then, beautifully handled, she brought to, and was scudding before the wind in another minute, leading them all a brave stern-chase out to sea.

"It must be that dare-devil Lyth himself," Nettlebones said, as the Swordfish strained, with all canvas set, but no gain made; "no other fellow in all the world would dare to beard us in this style. I'd lay ten guineas that Donovan's guns won't go off, if he tries them. Ah, I thought so—a fizz, and a stink—trust an Irishman."

For this gallant lieutenant, slanting toward the bows of the flying bilander, which he had no hope of fore-reaching, trained his long swivel-gun upon her, and let go—or rather tried to let go—at her. But his powder was wet, or else there was some stoppage; for the only result was a spurt of smoke inward, and a powdery eruption on his own red cheeks.

"I wish I could have heard him swear," grumbled Nettlebones; "that would have been worth something. But Bowler is further out. Bowler will cross her bows, and he is not a fool. Don't be in a hurry, my fine Bob Lyth. You are not clear yet, though you crack on like a trooper. Well done, Bowler, you have headed him! By Jove, I don't understand these tactics. Stand by there! She is running back again."

To the great amazement of all on board the cruisers, except perhaps one or two, the great Dutch vessel, which might haply have escaped by standing on her present course, spun round like a top, and bore in again among her three pursuers. She had the heels of all of them before the wind, and might have run down any intercepter, but seemed not to know it, or to lose all nerve. "Thank the Lord in heaven, all rogues are fools! She may double as she will, but she is ours now. Signal Albatross and Kestrel to stand in."

In a few minutes all four were standing for the bay; the Dutch vessel leading with all sail set, the cruisers following warily, and spreading, to head her from the north or south. It was plain that they had her well in the toils; she must either surrender or run ashore; close hauled as she was, she could not run them down, even if she would dream of such an outrage.

So far from showing any sign of rudeness was the smuggling vessel, that she would not even plead want of light as excuse for want of courtesy. For running past the royal cutters, who took much longer to come about, she saluted each of them with deep respect for the swallowtail of his Majesty. And then she bore on, like the admiral's ship, with signal for all to follow her.

"Such cursed impudence never did I see," cried every one of the revenue skippers, as they all were compelled to obey her. "Surrender she must, or else run upon the rocks. Does the fool know what he is driving at?"

The fool, who was Master James Brown of Grimsby, knew very well what he was about. Every shoal, and sounding, and rocky gut, was thoroughly familiar to him, and the spread of faint light on the waves and alongshore told him all his bearings. The loud cackle of laughter, which Grimsby men (at the cost of the rest of the world) enjoy, was carried by the wind to the ears of Nettlebones.

The latter set fast his teeth, and ground them; for now in the rising of the large full moon he perceived that the beach of the cove was black with figures gathering rapidly. "I see the villain's game; it is all clear now," he shouted, as he slammed his spy-glass. "He means to run in where we dare not follow: and he knows that Carroway is out of hail. The hull may go smash for the sake of the cargo; and his flat-bottomed tub can run where we can not. I dare not carry after him—court-martial if I do: that is where those fellows beat us always. But, by the Lord Harry, he shall not prevail! Guns are no good—the rogue knows that. We will land round the point, and nab him."

By this time the moon was beginning to open the clouds, and strew the waves with light; and the vapors, which had lain across the day, defying all power of sun ray, were gracefully yielding, and departing softly, at the insinuating whisper of the gliding night. Between the busy rolling of the distant waves, and the shining prominence of forward cliffs, a quiet space was left for ships to sail in, and for men to show activity in shooting one another. And some of these were hurrying to do so, if they could.

"There is little chance of hitting them in this bad light; but let them have it, Jakins; and a guinea for you, if you can only bring that big mainsail down."

The gunner was yearning for this, and the bellow of his piece responded to the captain's words. But the shot only threw up a long path of fountains, and the bilander ploughed on as merrily as before.

"Hard aport! By the Lord, I felt her touch! Go about! So, so—easy! Now lie to, for Kestrel and Albatross to join. My certy! but that was a narrow shave. How the beggar would have laughed if we had grounded! Give them another shot. It will do the gun good; she wants a little exercise."

Nothing loath was master gunner, as the other bow-gun came into bearing, to make a little more noise in the world, and possibly produce a greater effect. And therein he must have had a grand success, and established a noble reputation, by carrying off a great Grimsby head, if he only had attended to a little matter. Gunner Jakins was a celebrated shot, and the miss he had made stirred him up to shoot again. If the other gun was crooked, this one should be straight; and dark as it was inshore, he got a patch of white ground to sight by. The bilander was a good sizable object, and not to hit her anywhere would be too bad. He considered these things carefully, and cocked both eyes, with a twinkling ambiguity between them; then trusting mainly to the left one, as an ancient gunner for the most part does, he watched the due moment, and fired. The smoke curled over the sea, and so did the Dutchman's maintop-sail, for the mast beneath it was cut clean through. Some of the crew were frightened, as may be the bravest man when for the first time shot at; but James Brown rubbed his horny hands.

"Now this is a good judgment for that younker Robin Lyth," he shouted aloud, with the glory of a man who has verified his own opinions. "He puts all the danger upon his elders, and tells them there is none of it. A' might just as well have been my head, if a wave hadn't lifted the muzzle when that straight-eyed chap let fire. Bear a hand, boys, and cut away the wreck. He hathn't got never another shot to send. He hath saved us trouble o' shortening that there canvas. We don't need too much way on her."

This was true enough, as all hands knew; for the craft was bound to take the beach, without going to pieces yet awhile. Jem Brown stood at the wheel himself, and carried her in with consummate skill.

"It goeth to my heart to throw away good stuff," he grumbled at almost every creak. "Two hunder pound I would 'a paid myself for this here piece of timber. Steady as a light-house, and as handy as a mop; but what do they young fellows care? There, now, my lads, hold your legs a moment; and now make your best of that."

"With a crash, and a grating, and a long sad grind, the nuptial ark of the wealthy Dutchman cast herself into her last bed and berth.

"I done it right well," said the Grimsby man.

The poor old bilander had made herself such a hole in the shingle that she rolled no more, but only lifted at the stern and groaned, as the quiet waves swept under her. The beach was swarming with men, who gave her a cheer, and flung their hats up; and in two or three minutes as many gangways of timber and rope were rigged to her hawse-holes, or fore-chains, or almost anywhere. And then the rolling of puncheons began, and the hoisting of bales, and the thump and the creak, and the laughter, and the swearing.

"Now be you partiklar, uncommon partiklar; never start a stave nor fray a bale. Powerful precious stuff this time. Gold every bit of it, if it are a penny. They blessed coast-riders will be on us round the point. But never you hurry, lads, the more for that. Better a'most to let 'em have it, than damage a drop or a thread of such goods."

"All right, Cappen Brown. Don't you be so wonnerful unaisy. Not the first time we have handled such stuff."

"I'm not so sure of that," replied Brown, as he lit a short pipe and began to puff. "I've a-run some afore, but never none so precious."

Then the men of the coast and the sailors worked with a will, by the broad light of the moon, which showed their brawny arms and panting chests, with the hoisting, and the heaving, and the rolling. In less than an hour three-fourths of the cargo was landed, and some already stowed inland, where no Preventive eye could penetrate. Then Captain Brown put away his pipe, and was busy, in a dark empty part of the hold, with some barrels of his own, which he covered with a sailcloth.

Presently the tramp of marching men was heard in a lane on the north side of the cove, and then the like sound echoed from the south. "Now never you hurry," said the Grimsby man. The others, however, could not attain such standard of equanimity. They fell into sudden confusion, and babble of tongues, and hesitation—everybody longing to be off, but nobody liking to run without something good. And to get away with anything at all substantial, even in the dark, was difficult, because there were cliffs in front, and the flanks would be stopped by men with cutlasses.

"Ston' you still," cried Captain Brown; "never you budge, ne'er a one of ye. I stands upon my legitimacy; and I answer for the consekence. I takes all responsibility."

Like all honest Britons, they loved long words, and they knew that if the worst came to the worst, a mere broken head or two would make all straight; so they huddled together in the moonlight waiting, and no one desired to be the outside man. And while they were striving for precedence toward the middle, the coast-guards from either side marched upon them, according to their very best drill and in high discipline, to knock down almost any man with the pommel of the sword.

But the smugglers also showed high discipline under the commanding voice of Captain Brown.

"Every man ston' with his hands to his sides, and ask of they sojjers for a pinch of bacca."

This made them laugh, till Captain Nettlebones strode up.

"In the name of his Majesty, surrender, all you fellows. You are fairly caught in the very act of landing a large run of goods contraband. It is high time to make an example of you. Where is your skipper, lads? Robin Lyth, come forth."

"May it please your good honor and his Majesty's commission," said Brown, in his full, round voice, as he walked down the broadest of the gangways leisurely, "my name is not Robin Lyth, but James Brown, a family man of Grimsby, and an honest trader upon the high seas. My cargo is medical water and rags, mainly for the use of the revenue men, by reason they han't had their new uniforms this twelve months."

Several of the enemy began to giggle, for their winter supply of clothes had failed, through some lapse of the department. But Nettlebones marched up, and collared Captain Brown, and said, "You are my prisoner, sir. Surrender, Robin Lyth, this moment." Brown made no resistance, but respectfully touched his hat, and thought.

"I were trying to call upon my memory," he said, as the revenue officer led him aside, and promised him that he should get off easily if he would only give up his chief. "I am not going to deny, your honor, that I have heard tell of that name 'Robin Lyth.' But my memory never do come in a moment. Now were he a man in the contraband line?"

"Brown, you want to provoke me. It will only be ten times worse for you. Now give him up like an honest fellow, and I will do my best for you. I might even let a few tubs slip by."

"Sir, I am a stranger round these parts; and the lingo is beyond me. Tubs is a bucket as the women use for washing. Never I heared of any other sort of tubs. But my mate he knoweth more of Yorkshire talk. Jack, here his honor is a-speaking about tubs; ever you hear of tubs, Jack?"

"Make the villain fast to yonder mooring-post," shouted Nettlebones, losing his temper; "and one of you stand by him, with a hanger ready. Now, Master Brown, we'll see what tubs are, if you please; and what sort of rags you land at night. One chance more for you—will you give up Robin Lyth?"

"Yes, sir, that I will, without two thoughts about 'un. Only too happy, as the young women say, to give 'un up, quick stick—so soon as ever I ha' got 'un."

"If ever there was a contumacious rogue! Roll up a couple of those puncheons, Mr. Avery; and now light half a dozen links. Have you got your spigot-heels—and rummers? Very good; Lieutenant Donovan, Mr. Avery, and Senior Volunteer Brett, oblige me by standing by to verify. Gentlemen, we will endeavor to hold what is judicially called an assay—a proof of the purity of substances. The brand on these casks is of the very highest order—the renowned Mynheer Van Dunck himself. Donovan, you shall be our foreman; I have heard you say that you understood ardent spirits from your birth."

"Faix, and I quite forget, commander, whether I was weaned on or off of them. But the foine judge me father was come down till me—honey, don't be narvous; slope it well, then—a little thick, is it? All the richer for that same, me boy. Commander, here's the good health of his Majesty—Oh Lord!"

Mr. Corkoran Donovan fell down upon the shingle, and rolled and bellowed: "Sure me inside's out! 'Tis poisoned I am, every mortial bit o' me. A docthor, a docthor, and a praste, to kill me! That ever I should live to die like this! Ochone, ochone, every bit of me; to be brought forth upon good whiskey, and go out of the world upon docthor's stuff!"

"Most folk does that, when they ought to turn ends t'otherwise." James Brown of Grimsby could see how things were going, though his power to aid was restricted by a double turn of rope around him; but a kind hand had given him a pipe, and his manner was to take things easily. "Commander, or captain, or whatever you be, with your king's clothes, constructing a hole in they flints, never you fear, sir. 'Tis medical water, and your own wife wouldn't know you to-morrow. Your complexion will be like a hangel's."

"You d——d rogue," cried Nettlebones, striding up, with his sword flashing in the link-lights, "if ever I had a mind to cut any man down—"

"Well, sir, do it, then, upon a roped man, if the honor of the British navy calleth for it. My will is made, and my widow will have action; and the executioner of my will is a Grimsby man, with a pile of money made in the line of salt fish, and such like."

"Brown, you are a brave man. I would scorn to harm you. Now, upon your honor, are all your puncheons filled with that stuff, and nothing else?"

"Upon my word of honor, sir, they are. Some a little weaker, some with more bilge-water in it, or a trifle of a dash from the midden. The main of it, however, in the very same condition as a' bubbleth out of what they call the spawses. Why, captain, you must 'a lived long enough to know, partiklar if gifted with a family, that no sort of spirit as were ever stilled will fetch so much money by the gallon, duty paid, as the doctor's stuff doth by the phial-bottle."

"That is true enough; but no lies, Brown, particularly when upon your honor! If you were importing doctor's stuff, why did you lead us such a dance, and stand fire?"

"Well, your honor, you must promise not to be offended, if I tell you of a little mistake we made. We heared a sight of talk about some pirate craft as hoisteth his Majesty's flag upon their villainy. And when first you come up, in

279

the dusk of the night—"

"You are the most impudent rogue I ever saw. Show your bills of lading, sir. You know his Majesty's revenue cruisers as well as I know your smuggling tub."

"Ship's papers are aboard of her, all correct, sir. Keys at your service, if you please to feel my pocket, objecting to let my hands loose."

"Very well, I must go on board of her, and test a few of your puncheons and bales, Master Brown. Locker in the master's own cabin, I suppose?"

"Yes, sir, plain as can be, on the starboard side, just behind the cabin door. Only your honor must be smart about it; the time-fuse can't 'a got three inches left."

"Time-fuse? What do you mean, you Grimsby villain?"

"Nothing, commander, but to keep you out of mischief. When we were compelled to beach the old craft, for fear of them scoundrelly pirates, it came into my head what a pity it would be to have her used illegal; for she do outsail a'most everything, as your honor can bear witness. So I just laid a half-hour fuse to three big-powder barrels as is down there in the hold; and I expect to see a blow-up almost every moment. But your honor might be in time yet, with a run, and good luck to your foot, you might—"

"Back, lads! back every one of you this moment!" The first concern of Nettlebones was rightly for his men. "Under the cliff here. Keep well back. Push out those smuggler fellows into the middle. Let them have the benefit of their own inventions, and this impudent Brown the foremost. They have laid a train to their powder barrels, and the lugger will blow up any moment."

"No fear for me, commander," James Brown shouted through the hurry and jostle of a hundred runaways. "More fear for that poor man as lieth there a-lurching. She won't hit me when she bloweth up, no more than your honor could. But surely your duty demandeth of you to board the old bilander, and take samples."

"Sample enough of you, my friend. But I haven't quite done with you yet. Simpson, here, bear a hand with poor Lieutenant Donovan."

Nettlebones set a good example by lifting the prostrate Irishman; and they bore him into safety, and drew up there; while the beachmen, forbidden the shelter at point of cutlass, made off right and left; and then, with a crash that shook the strand and drove back the water in a white turmoil, the Crown of Gold flew into a fount of timbers, splinters, shreds, smoke, fire, and dust.

"Gentlemen, you may come out of your holes," the Grimsby man shouted from his mooring-post, as the echoes ran along the cliffs, and rolled to and fro in the distance. "My old woman will miss a piece of my pigtail, but she hathn't hurt her old skipper else. She blowed up handsome, and no mistake! No more danger, gentlemen, and plenty of stuff to pick up afore next pay-day."

"What shall we do with that insolent hound?" Nettlebones asked poor Donovan, who was groaning in slow convalescence. "We have caught him in nothing. We can not commit him; we can not even duck him legally."

"Be jabers, let him drink his health in his own potheen."

"Capital! Bravo for old Ireland, my friend! You shall see it done, and handsomely. Brown, you recommend these waters, so you shall have a dose of them."

A piece of old truncate kelp was found, as good a drinking horn as need be; and with this Captain Brown was forced to swallow half a bucketful of his own "medical water"; and they left him fast at his moorings, to reflect upon this form of importation.

CHAPTER XXXIII

BEARDED IN HIS DEN

"What do you think of it by this time, Bowler?" Commander Nettlebones asked his second, who had been left in command afloat, and to whom they rowed back in a wrathful mood, with a good deal of impression that the fault was his, "You have been taking it easily out here. What do you think of the whole of it?"

"I have simply obeyed your orders, sir; and if I am to be blamed for that, I had better offer no opinion."

"No, no, I am finding no fault with you. Don't be so tetchy, Bowler. I seek your opinion, and you are bound to give it."

"Well, then, sir, my opinion is that they have made fools of the lot of us, excepting, of course, my superior officer."

"You think so, Bowler? Well, and so do I—and myself the biggest fool of any. They have charged our centre with a dummy cargo, while they run the real stuff far on either flank. Is that your opinion?"

"To a nicety, that is my opinion, now that you put it so clearly, sir."

"The trick is a clumsy one, and never should succeed. Carroway ought to catch one lot, if he has a haporth of sense in him. What is the time now; and how is the wind?"

"I hear a church clock striking twelve; and by the moon it must be that. The wind is still from the shore, but veering, and I felt a flaw from the east just now."

"If the wind works round, our turn will come. Is Donovan fit for duty yet?"

"Ten times fit, sir—to use his own expression. He is burning to have at somebody. His eyes work about like the binnacle's card."

"Then board him, and order him to make all sail for Burlington, and see what old Carroway is up to. You be off for Whitby, and as far as Teesmouth, looking into every cove you pass. I shall stand off and on from this to Scarborough, and as far as Filey. Short measures, mind, if you come across them. If I nab that fellow Lyth, I shall go near to hanging him as a felon outlaw. His trick is a little too outrageous."

"No fear, commander. If it is as we suppose, it is high time to make a strong example."

Hours had been lost, as the captains of the cruisers knew too well by this time. Robin Lyth's stratagem had duped them all, while the contraband cargoes might be landed safely, at either extremity of their heat. By the aid of the fishing-boats, he had learned their manoeuvres clearly, and outmanoeuvred them.

Now it would have been better for him, perhaps, to have been content with a lesser triumph, and to run his own schooner, the Glimpse, further south, toward Hornsea, or even Aldbrough. Nothing, however, would satisfy him but to land his fine cargo at Carroway's own door—a piece of downright insolence, for which he paid out most bitterly. A man of his courage and lofty fame should have been above such vindictive feelings. But, as it was, he cherished and, alas! indulged a certain small grudge against the bold lieutenant, scarcely so much for endeavoring to shoot him, as for entrapping him at Byrsa Cottage, during the very sweetest moment of his life. "You broke in disgracefully," said the smuggler to himself, "upon my privacy when it should have been most sacred. The least thing I can do is to return your visit, and pay my respects to Mrs. Carroway and your interesting family."

Little expecting such a courtesy as this, the vigilant officer was hurrying about, here, there, and almost everywhere (except in the right direction), at one time by pinnace, at another upon horseback, or on his unwearied though unequal feet. He carried his sword in one hand, and his spy-glass in the other, and at every fog he swore so hard that he seemed to turn it yellow. With his heart worn almost into holes, as an overmangled quilt is, by burdensome roll of perpetual lies, he condemned, with a round mouth, smugglers, cutters, the coast-guard and the coast itself, the weather, and, with a deeper depth of condemnation, the farmers, landladies, and fishermen. For all of these verily seemed to be in league to play him the game which school-boys play with a gentle-faced new-comer—the game of "send the fool further."

John Gristhorp, of the "Ship Inn," at Filey, had turned out his visitors, barred his door, and was counting his money by the fireside, with his wife grumbling at him for such late hours as half past ten of the clock in the bar, that night when the poor bilander ended her long career as aforesaid. Then a thundering knock at the door just fastened made him upset a little pyramid of pence, and catch up the iron candlestick.

"None of your roistering here!" cried the lady. "John, you know better than to let them in, I hope."

"Copper coomth by daa, goold coomth t'naight-time," the sturdy publican answered, though resolved to learn who it was before unbarring.

"In the name of the King, undo this door," a deep stern voice resounded, "or by royal command we make splinters of it."

"It is that horrible Carroway again," whispered Mrs. Gristhorp. "Much gold comes of him, I doubt. Let him in if you dare, John."

"'Keep ma oot, if ye de-arr,' saith he. Ah'll awand here's the tail o' it."

While Gristhorp, in wholesome fealty to his wife, was doubting, the door flew open, and in marched Carroway and all his men, or at least all save one of his present following. He had ordered his pinnace to meet him here, himself having ridden from Scarborough, and the pinnace had brought the jolly-boat in tow, according to his directions. The men had landed with the jolly-boat, which was handier for beach work, leaving one of their number to mind the larger craft while they should refresh themselves. They were nine in all, and Carroway himself the tenth, all sturdy fellows, and for the main of it tolerably honest; Cadman, Ellis, and Dick Hackerbody, and one more man from Bridlington, the rest a re-enforcement from Spurn Head, called up for occasion.

"Landlord, produce your best, and quickly," the officer said, as he threw himself into the arm-chair of state, being thoroughly tired. "In one hour's time we must be off. Therefore, John, bring nothing tough, for our stomachs are better than our teeth. A shilling per head is his Majesty's price, and half a crown for officers. Now a gallon of ale, to begin with."

Gristhorp, being a prudent man, brought the very toughest parts of his larder forth, with his wife giving nudge to his elbow. All, and especially Carroway, too hungry for nice criticism, fell to, by the light of three tallow candles, and were just getting into the heart of it, when the rattle of horseshoes on the pitch-stones shook the long low window, and a little boy came staggering in, with scanty breath, and dazzled eyes, and a long face pale with hurrying so.

"Why, Tom, my boy!" the lieutenant cried, jumping up so suddenly that he overturned the little table at which he was feeding by himself, to preserve the proper discipline. "Tom, my darling, what has brought you here? Anything wrong with your mother?"

"Nobody wouldn't come, but me," Carroway's eldest son began to gasp, with his mouth full of crying; "and I borrowed Butcher Hewson's pony, and he's going to charge five shillings for it."

"Never mind that. We shall not have to pay it. But what is it all about, my son?"

"About the men that are landing the things, just opposite our front door, father. They have got seven carts, and a wagon with three horses, and one of the horses is three colors; and ever so many ponies, more than you could count."

"Well, then, may I be forever"—here the lieutenant used an expression which not only was in breach of the third commandment, but might lead his son to think less of the fifth—"if it isn't more than I can bear! To be running a cargo at my own hall door!" He had a passage large enough to hang three hats in, which the lady of the house always called "the hall." "Very well, very good, very fine indeed! You sons of"—an animal that is not yet accounted the mother of the human race—"have you done guzzling and swizzling?"

The men who were new to his orders jumped up, for they liked his expressions, by way of a change; but the Bridlington squad stuck to their trenchers. "Ready in five minutes, sir," said Cadman, with a glance neither loving nor respectful.

"If ever there was an old hog for the trough, the name of him is John Cadman. In ten minutes, lads, we must all be afloat."

"One more against you," muttered Cadman; and a shrewd quiet man from Spurn Head, Adam Andrews, heard him, and took heed of him.

While the men of the coast-guard were hurrying down to make ready the jolly-boat and hail the pinnace, Carroway stopped to pay the score, and to give his son some beer and meat. The thirsty little fellow drained his cup, and filled his mouth and both hands with food, while the landlady picked out the best bits for him.

"Don't talk, my son—don't try to talk," said Carroway, looking proudly at him, while the boy was struggling to tell his adventures, without loss of feeding-time; "you are a chip of the old block, Tom, for victualling, and for riding too. Kind madam, you never saw such a boy before. Mark my words, he will do more in the world than ever his father did, and his father was pretty well known in his time, in the Royal Navy, ma'am. To have stuck to his horse all that way in the dark was wonderful, perfectly wonderful. And the horse blows more than the rider, ma'am, which is quite beyond my experience. Now, Tom, ride home very carefully and slowly, if you feel quite equal to it. The Lord has watched over you, and He will continue, as He does with brave folk that do their duty. Half a crown you shall have, all for yourself, and the sixpenny boat that you longed for in the shops. Keep out of the way of the smugglers, Tom; don't let them even clap eyes on you. Kiss me, my son; I am proud of you."

Little Tom long remembered this; and his mother cried over it hundreds of times.

Although it was getting on for midnight now, Master Gristhorp and his wife came out into the road before their house, to see the departure of their guests. And this they could do well, because the moon had cleared all the fog away, and was standing in a good part of the sky for throwing clear light upon Filey. Along the uncovered ridge of shore, which served for a road, and was better than a road, the boy and the pony grew smaller; while upon the silvery sea the same thing happened to the pinnace, with her white sails bending, and her six oars glistening.

"The world goeth up, and the world goeth down," said the lady, with her arms akimbo; "and the moon goeth over the whole of us, John; but to my heart I do pity poor folk as canna count the time to have the sniff of their own blankets."

"Margery, I loikes the moon, as young as ever ye da. But I sooner see the snuff of our own taller, a-going out, fra the bed-curtings."

Shaking their heads with concrete wisdom, they managed to bar the door again, and blessing their stars that they did not often want them, took shelter beneath the quiet canopy of bed. And when they heard by-and-by what had happened, it cost them a week apiece to believe it; because with their own eyes they had seen everything so peaceable, and had such a good night afterward.

When a thing is least expected, then it loves to come to pass, and then it is enjoyed the most, whatever good there is of it. After the fog and the slur of the day, to see the sky at all was joyful, although there was but a white moon upon it, and faint stars gliding hazily. And it was a great point for every man to be satisfied as to where he was; because that helps him vastly toward being satisfied to be there. The men in the pinnace could see exactly where they were in this world; and as to the other world, their place was fixed—if discipline be an abiding gift—by the stern precision of their commander in ordering the lot of them to the devil. They carried all sail, and they pulled six oars, and the wind and sea ran after them.

"Ha! I see something!" Carroway cried, after a league or more of swearing. "Dick, the night glass; my eyes are sore. What do you make her out for?"

"Sir, she is the Spurn Head yawl," answered Dick Hackerbody, who was famed for long sight, but could see nothing with a telescope. "I can see the patch of her foresail."

"She is looking for us. We are the wrong way of the moon. Ship oars, lads; bear up for her."

In ten minutes' time the two boats came to speaking distance off Bempton

Cliffs, and the windmill, that vexed Willie Anerley so, looked bare and black on the highland. There were only two men in the Spurn Head boat—not half enough to manage her. "Well, what is it?" shouted Carroway.

"Robin Lyth has made his land-fall on Burlington Sands, opposite your honor's door, sir. There was only two of us to stop him, and the man as is deaf and dumb."

"I know it," said Carroway, too wroth to swear. "My boy of eight years old is worth the entire boiling of you. You got into a rabbit-hole, and ran to tell your mammy."

"Captain, I never had no mammy," the other man answered, with his feelings hurt. "I come to tell you, sir; and something, if you please, for your own ear, if agreeable."

"Nothing is agreeable. But let me have it. Hold on; I will come aboard of you."

The lieutenant stepped into the Spurn Head boat with confident activity, and ordered his own to haul off a little, while the stranger bent down to him in the stern, and whispered.

"Now are you quite certain of this?" asked Carroway, with his grim face glowing in the moonlight, "I have had such a heap of cock and bulls about it. Morcom, are you certain?"

"As certain, sir, as that I stand here, and you sit there, commander. Put me under guard, with a pistol to my ear, and shoot me if it turns out to be a lie."

"The Dovecote, you say? You are quite sure of that, and not the Kirk Cave, or Lyth's Hole?"

"Sir, the Dovecote, and no other. I had it from my own young brother, who has been cheated of his share. And I know it from my own eyes too."

"Then, by the Lord in heaven, Morcom, I shall have my revenge at last; and I shall not stand upon niceties. If I call for the jolly-boat, you step in. I doubt if either of these will enter."

It was more than a fortnight since the lieutenant had received the attentions of a barber, and when he returned to his own boat, and changed her course inshore, he looked most bristly even in the moonlight. The sea and the moon between them gave quite light enough to show how gaunt he was—the aspect of a man who can not thrive without his children to make play, and his wife to do cookery for him.

CHAPTER XXXIV

THE DOVECOTE

With the tiller in his hand, the brave lieutenant meditated sadly. There was plenty of time for thought before quick action would be needed, although the Dovecote was so near that no boat could come out of it unseen. For the pinnace was fetching a circuit, so as to escape the eyes of any sentinel, if such there should be at the mouth of the cavern, and to come upon the inlet suddenly. And the two other revenue boats were in her wake.

The wind was slowly veering toward the east, as the Grimsby man had predicted, with no sign of any storm as yet, but rather a prospect of winterly weather, and a breeze to bring the woodcocks in. The gentle rise and fall of waves, or rather, perhaps, of the tidal flow, was checkered and veined with a ripple of the slanting breeze, and twinkled in the moonbeams. For the moon was brightly mounting toward her zenith, and casting bastions of rugged cliff in gloomy largeness on the mirror of the sea. Hugging these as closely as their peril would allow, Carroway ordered silence, and with the sense of coming danger thought:

"Probably I shall kill this man. He will scarcely be taken alive, I fear. He is as brave as myself, or braver; and in his place I would never yield. If he were a Frenchman, it would be all right. But I hate to kill a gallant Englishman. And such a pretty girl, and a good girl too, loves him with all her heart, I know. And that good old couple who depend upon him, and who have had such shocking luck themselves! He has been a bitter plague to me, and often I have longed to strike him down. But to-night—I can not tell why it is—I wish there were some way out of it. God knows that I would give up the money, and give up my thief-catching business too, if the honor of the service let me. But duty drives me; do it I must. And after all, what is life to a man who is young, and has no children? Better over, better done with, before the troubles and the disappointment come, the weariness, and the loss of power, and the sense of growing old, and seeing the little ones hungry. Life is such a fleeting vapor—I smell some man sucking peppermint! The smell of it goes on the wind for a mile. Oh! Cadman again, as usual. Peppermint in the Royal Coast-Guard! Away with it, you ancient beldame!"

Muttering something about his bad tooth, the man flung his lozenge away; and his eyes flashed fire in the moonlight, while the rest grinned a low grin at him. And Adam Andrews, sitting next him, saw him lay hands upon his musketoon.

"Are your firelocks all primed, my lads?" the commander asked, quite as if he had seen him, although he had not been noticing; and the foremost to answer "Ay, ay, sir," was Cadman.

"Then be sure that you fire not, except at my command. We will take them without shedding blood, if it may be. But happen what will, we must have Lyth."

With these words, Carroway drew his sword, and laid it on the bench beside him; and the rest (who would rather use steel than powder) felt that their hangers were ready. Few of them wished to strike at all; for vexed as they were with the smugglers for having outwitted them so often, as yet there was no bad blood between them, such as must be quenched with death. And some of them had friends, and even relatives, among the large body of free-traders, and counted it too likely that they might be here.

Meanwhile in the cave there was rare work going on, speedily, cleverly, and with a merry noise. There was only one boat, with a crew of six men, besides Robin Lyth the captain; but the six men made noise enough for twelve, and the echoes made it into twice enough for any twenty-four. The crew were trusty, hardy fellows, who liked their joke, and could work with it; and Robin Lyth knew them too well to attempt any high authority of gagging. The main of their cargo was landed and gone inland, as snugly as need be; and having kept beautifully sober over that, they were taking the liberty of beginning to say, or rather sip, the grace of the fine indulgence due to them.

Pleasant times make pleasant scenes, and everything now was fair and large in this happy cave of freedom. Lights of bright resin were burning, with strong flare and fume, upon shelves of rock; dark water softly went lapping round the sides, having dropped all rude habits at the entrance; and a pulse of quiet rise and fall opened, and spread to the discovery of light, tremulous fronds and fans of kelp. The cavern, expanding and mounting from the long narrow gut of its inlet, shone with staves of snowy crag wherever the scour of the tide ran round; bulged and scooped, or peaked and fissured, and sometimes beautifully sculptured by the pliant tools of water. Above the tide-reach darker hues prevailed, and more jagged outline, tufted here and there with yellow, where the lichen freckles spread. And the vault was framed of mountain fabric, massed with ponderous gray slabs.

All below was limpid water, or at any rate not very muddy, but as bright as need be for the time of year, and a sea which is not tropical. No one may hope to see the bottom through ten feet of water on the Yorkshire coast, toward the end of the month of November; but still it tries to look clear upon occasion; and here in the caves it settles down, after even a week free from churning. And perhaps the fog outside had helped it to look clearer inside; for the larger world has a share of the spirit of contrariety intensified in man.

Be that as it may, the water was too clear for any hope of sinking tubs deeper than Preventive eyes could go; and the very honest fellows who were laboring here had not brought any tubs to sink. All such coarse gear was shipped off inland, as they vigorously expressed it; and what they were concerned with now was the cream and the jewel of their enterprise.

The sea reserved exclusive right of way around the rocky sides, without even a niche for human foot, so far as a stranger could perceive. At the furthermost end of the cave, however, the craggy basin had a lip of flinty pebbles and shelly sand. This was no more than a very narrow shelf, just enough for a bather to plunge from; but it ran across the broad end of the cavern, and from its southern corner went a deep dry fissure mounting out of sight into the body of the cliff. And here the smugglers were merrily at work.

The nose of their boat was run high upon the shingle; two men on board of her were passing out the bales, while the other four received them, and staggered with them up the cranny. Captain Lyth himself was in the stern-sheets, sitting calmly, but ordering everything, and jotting down the numbers. Now and then the gentle wash was lifting the brown timbers, and swelling with a sleepy gush of hushing murmurs out of sight. And now and then the heavy vault was echoing with some sailor's song.

There was only one more bale to land, and that the most precious of the whole, being all pure lace most closely packed in a water-proof inclosure. Robin Lyth himself was ready to indulge in a careless song. For this, as he had promised Mary, was to be his last illegal act. Henceforth, instead of defrauding the revenue, he would most loyally cheat the public, as every reputable tradesman must. How could any man serve his time more notably, toward shop-keeping, and pave fairer way into the corporation of a grandly corrupt old English town, than by long graduation of free trade? And Robin was yet too young and careless to know that he could not endure dull work. "How pleasant, how comfortable, how secure," he was saying to himself, "it will be! I shall hardly be able to believe that I ever lived in hardship."

But the great laws of human nature were not to be balked so. Robin Lyth, the prince of smugglers, and the type of hardihood, was never to wear a grocer's apron, was never to be "licensed to sell tea, coffee, tobacco, pepper, and snuff." For while he indulged in this vain dream, and was lifting his last most precious bale, a surge of neither wind nor tide, but of hostile invasion, washed the rocks, and broke beneath his feet.

In a moment all his wits returned, all his plenitude of resource, and unequalled vigor and coolness. With his left hand—for he was as ambidexter as a brave writer of this age requires—he caught up a handspike, and hurled it so truly along the line of torches that only two were left to blink; with his right he flung the last bale upon the shelf; then leaped out after it, and hurried it away. Then he sprang into the boat again, and held an oar in either hand.

"In the name of the king, surrender," shouted Carroway, standing, tall and grim, in the bow of the pinnace, which he had skillfully driven through the entrance, leaving the other boats outside. "We are three to one, we have muskets, and a cannon. In the name of the king, surrender."

"In the name of the devil, splash!" cried Robin, suiting the action to the word, striking the water with both broad blades, while his men snatched oars and did the same. A whirl of flashing water filled the cave, as if with a tempest, soaked poor Carroway, and drenched his sword, and deluged the priming of the hostile guns. All was uproar, turmoil, and confusion thrice confounded; no man could tell where he was, and the grappling boats reeled to and fro.

"Club your muskets, and at 'em!" cried the lieutenant, mad with rage, as the gunwale of his boat swung over. "Their blood be upon their own heads; draw your hangers, and at 'em!"

He never spoke another word, but furiously leaping at the smuggler chief, fell back into his own boat, and died, without a syllable, without a groan. The roar of a gun and the smoke of powder mingled with the watery hubbub, and hushed in a moment all the oaths of conflict.

The revenue men drew back and sheathed their cutlasses, and laid down their guns; some looked with terror at one another, and some at their dead commander. His body lay across the heel of the mast, which had been unstepped at his order; and a heavy drip of blood was weltering into a ring upon the floor.

For several moments no one spoke, nor moved, nor listened carefully; but the fall of the poor lieutenant's death-drops, like the ticking of a clock, went on. Until an old tar, who had seen a sight of battles, crooked his legs across a thwart, and propped up the limp head upon his doubled knee.

"Dead as a door-nail," he muttered, after laying his ear to the lips, and one hand on the too impetuous heart, "Who takes command? This is a hanging job, I'm thinking."

There was nobody to take command, not even a petty officer. The command fell to the readiest mind, as it must in such catastrophes. "Jem, you do it," whispered two or three; and being so elected, he was clear.

"Lay her broadside on to the mouth of the cave. Not a man stirs out without killing me," old Jem shouted; and to hear a plain voice was sudden relief to most of them. In the wavering dimness they laid the pinnace across the narrow entrance, while the smugglers huddled all together in their boat. "Burn two blue-lights," cried old Jem; and it was done.

"I'm not going to speechify to any cursed murderers," the old sailor said, with a sense of authority which made him use mild language; "but take heed of one thing, I'll blow you all to pieces with this here four-pounder, without you strikes peremptory."

The brilliance of the blue-lights filled the cavern, throwing out everybody's attitude and features, especially those of the dead lieutenant. "A fine job you have made of it this time!" said Jem.

They were beaten, they surrendered, they could scarcely even speak to assert their own innocence of such a wicked job. They submitted to be bound, and cast down into their boat, imploring only that it might be there—that they might not be taken to the other boat and laid near the corpse of Carroway.

"Let the white-livered cowards have their way," the old sailor said, contemptuously. "Put their captain on the top of them. Now which is Robin Lyth?"

The lights were burned out, and the cave was dark again, except when a slant of moonlight came through a fissure upon the southern side. The smugglers muttered something, but they were not heeded.

"Never mind, make her fast, fetch her out, you lubbers. We shall see him well enough when we get outside."

But in spite of all their certainty, they failed of this. They had only six prisoners, and not one of them was Lyth.

CHAPTER XXXV

LITTLE CARROWAYS

Mrs. Carroway was always glad to be up quite early in the morning. But some few mornings seemed to slip in between whiles when, in accordance with human nature, and its operations in the baby stage, even Lauta Carroway failed to be about the world before the sun himself. Whenever this happened she was slightly cross, from the combat of conscience and self-assertion, which fly at one another worse than any dog and cat. Geraldine knew that her mother was put out if any one of the household durst go down the stairs before her. And yet if Geraldine herself held back, and followed the example of late minutes, she was sure "to catch it worse," as the poor child expressed it.

If any active youth with a very small income (such as an active youth is pretty sure to have) wants a good wife, and has the courage to set out with one, his proper course is to choose the eldest daughter of a numerous family. When the others come thickly, this daughter of the house gets worked down into a wonderful perfection of looking after others, while she overlooks herself. Such a course is even better for her than to have a step-mother—which also is a goodly thing, but sometimes leads to sourness. Whereas no girl of any decent staple can revolt against her duty to her own good mother, and the proud sense of fostering and working for the little ones. Now Geraldine was wise in all these ways, and pleased to be called the little woman of the house.

The baby had been troublous in the night, and scant of reason, as the rising race can be, even while so immature; and after being up with it, and herself producing a long series of noises—which lead to peace through the born desire of contradiction—the mother fell asleep at last, perhaps from simple sympathy, and slept beyond her usual hour. But instead of being grateful for this, she was angry and bitter to any one awake before her.

"I can not tell why it is," she said to Geraldine, who was toasting a herring for her brothers and sisters, and enjoying the smell (which was all that she would get), "but perpetually now you stand exactly like your father. There is every excuse for your father, because he is an officer, and has been knocked about, as he always is; but there is no excuse for you, miss. Put your heel decently under your dress. If we can afford nothing else, we can surely afford to behave well."

The child made no answer, but tucked her heel in, and went on toasting nobly, while she counted the waves on the side of the herring, where his ribs should have been if he were not too fat; and she mentally divided him into seven pieces, not one of which, alas! would be for hungry Geraldine. "Tom must have two, after being out all night," she was saying to herself; "and to grudge him would be greedy. But the bit of skin upon the toasting-fork will be for me, I am almost sure."

"Geraldine, the least thing you can do, when I speak to you, is to answer. This morning you are in a most provoking temper, and giving yourself the most intolerable airs. And who gave you leave to do your hair like that? One would fancy that you were some rising court beauty, or a child of the nobility at the very least, instead of a plain little thing that has to work—or at any rate that ought to work—to help its poor mother! Oh, now you are going to cry, I suppose. Let me see a tear, and you shall go to bed again."

"Oh, mother, mother, now what do you think has happened?" little Tom shouted, as he rushed in from the beach. "Father has caught all the smugglers, every one, and the Royal George is coming home before a spanking breeze, with three boats behind her, and they can't be all ours; and one of them must belong to Robin Lyth himself; and I would almost bet a penny they have been and shot him; though everybody said that he never could be shot. Jerry, come and look—never mind the old fish. I never did see such a sight in all my life. They have got the jib-sail on him, so he must be dead at last; and instead of half a crown, I am sure to get a guinea. Come along, Jerry, and perhaps I'll give you some of it!"

"Tommy," said his mother, "you are always so impetuous! I never will believe in such good luck until I see it. But you have been a wonderfully good brave boy, and your father may thank you for whatever he has done. I shall not allow Geraldine to go; for she is not a good child this morning. And of course I can not go myself, for your father will come home absolutely starving. And it would not be right for the little ones to go, if things are at all as you suppose. Now, if I let you go yourself, you are not to go beyond the flag-staff. Keep far away from the boats, remember; unless your father calls for you to run on any errand. All the rest of you go in here, with your bread and milk, and wait until I call you."

Mrs. Carroway locked all the little ones in a room from which they could see nothing of the beach, with orders to Cissy, the next girl, to feed them, and keep them all quiet till she came again. But while she was busy, with a very lively stir, to fetch out whatever could be found of fatness or grease that could be hoped to turn to gravy in the pan—for Carroway, being so lean, loved fat, and to put a fish before him was an insult to his bones—just at the moment when she had struck oil, in the shape of a very fat chop, from forth a stew, which had beaten all the children by stearine inertia—then at this moment, when she was rejoicing, the latch of the door clicked, and a man came in.

"Whoever you are, you seem to me to make yourself very much at home," the lady said, sharply, without turning round, because she supposed it to be a well-accustomed enemy, armed with that odious "little bill." The intruder made no answer, and she turned to rate him thoroughly; but the petulance of her eyes drew back before the sad stern gaze of his. "Who are you, and what do you want?" she asked, with a yellow dish in one hand, and a frying-pan in the other. "Geraldine, come here: that man looks wild."

Her visitor did look wild enough, but without any menace in his sorrowful dark eyes. "Can't the man speak?" she cried. "Are you mad, or starving? We are not very rich; but we can give you bread, poor fellow. Captain Carroway will be at home directly, and he will see what can be done for you."

"Have you not heard of the thing that has been done?" the young man asked her, word by word, and staying himself with one hand upon the dresser, because he was trembling dreadfully.

"Yes, I have heard of it all. They have shot the smuggler Robin Lyth at last. I am very sorry for him. But it was needful; and he had no family."

"Lady, I am Robin Lyth. I have not been shot; nor even shot at. The man that has been shot, I know not how, instead of me, was—was somebody quite different. With all my heart I wish it had been me; and no more trouble."

He looked at the mother and the little girl, and sobbed, and fell upon a salting stool, which was to have been used that morning. Then, while Mrs. Carroway stood bewildered, Geraldine ran up to him, and took his hand, and said: "Don't cry. My papa says that men never cry. And I am so glad that you were not shot."

"See me kiss her," said Robin Lyth, as he laid his lips upon the child's fair forehead. "If I had done it, could I do that? Darling, you will remember this. Madam, I am hunted like a mad dog, and shall be hanged to your flag-staff if I am caught. I am here to tell you that, as God looks down from heaven upon you and me, I did not do it—I did not even know it."

The smuggler stood up, with his right hand on his heart, and tears rolling manifestly down his cheeks, but his eyes like crystal, clear with truth; and the woman, who knew not that she was a widow, but felt it already with a helpless wonder, answered, quietly: "You speak the truth, sir. But what difference can it make to me?" Lyth tried to answer with the same true look; but neither his eyes nor his tongue would serve.

"I shall just go and judge for myself," she said, as if it were a question of marketing (such bitter defiance came over her), and she took no more heed of him than if he were a chair; nor even half so much, for she was a great judge of a chair. "Geraldine, go and put your bonnet on. We are going to meet your father. Tell Cissy and all the rest to come but the baby. The baby can not do it, I suppose. In a minute and a half I shall expect you all—how many? Seven? —yes, seven of you."

"Seven, mother, yes. And the baby makes it eight; and yesterday you said that he was worth all us together."

Robin Lyth saw that he was no more wanted, or even heeded; and without delay he quitted such premises of danger. Why should he linger in a spot where he might have violent hands laid on him, and be sped to a premature end, without benefit even of trial by jury? Upon this train of reasoning he made off.

Without any manner of reasoning at all, but with fierceness of dread and stupidity of grief, the mother collected her children in silence, from the damsel of ten to the toddler of two. Then, leaving the baby tied down in the cradle, she pulled at the rest of them, on this side and on that, to get them into proper trim of dresses and of hats, as if they were going to be marched off to church. For that all the younger ones made up their minds, and put up their ears for the tinkle of the bell; but the elder children knew that it was worse than that, because their mother never looked at them.

"You will go by the way of the station," she said, for the boats were still out at sea, and no certainty could be made of them: "whatever it is, we may thank the station for it."

The poor little things looked up at her in wonder; and then, acting up to their discipline, set off, in lopsided pairs of a small and a big one, to save any tumbling and cutting of knees. The elder ones walked with discretion, and a strong sense of responsibility, hushed, moreover, by some inkling of a great black thing to meet. But the baby ones prattled, and skipped with their feet, and straggled away toward the flowers by the path. The mother of them all followed slowly and heavily, holding the youngest by the hand, because of its trouble in getting through the stones. Her heart was nearly choking, but her eyes free and reckless, wandering wildly over earth, and sea, and sky, in vain search of guidance from any or from all of them.

The pinnace came nearer, with its sad, cold freight. The men took off their hats, and rubbed their eyes, and some of them wanted to back off again; but Mrs. Carroway calmly said, "Please to let me have my husband."

CHAPTER XXXVI

MAIDS AND MERMAIDS

Day comes with climbing, night by falling; hence the night is so much swifter. Happiness takes years to build; but misery swoops like an avalanche. Such, and even more depressing, are the thoughts young folk give way to when their first great trouble rushes and sweeps them into a desert, trackless to the inexperienced hope.

When Mary Anerley heard, by the zealous offices of watchful friends, that Robin Lyth had murdered Captain Carroway ferociously, and had fled for his life across the seas, first wrath at such a lie was followed by persistent misery. She had too much faith in his manly valor and tender heart to accept the tale exactly as it was told to her; but still she could not resist the fear that in the whirl of conflict, with life against life, he had dealt the death. And she knew that even such a deed would brand him as a murderer, stamp out all love, and shatter every hope of quiet happiness. The blow to her pride was grievous also; for many a time had she told herself that a noble task lay before her—to rescue from unlawful ways and redeem to reputable life the man whose bravery and other gallant gifts had endeared him to the public and to her. But now, through force of wretched facts, he must be worse than ever.

Her father and mother said never a word upon the subject to her. Mrs. Anerley at first longed to open out, and shed upon the child a mother's sympathy, as well as a mother's scolding; but firmly believing, as she did, the darkest version of the late event, it was better that she should hold her peace, according to her husband's orders.

"Let the lass alone," he said; "a word against that fellow now would make a sight of mischief. Suppose I had shot George Tanfield, instead of hiding him soundly, when he stuck up to you, why you must have been sorry for me, Sophy. And Mary is sorry for that rogue, no doubt, and believes that he did it for her sake, I dare say. The womenkind always do think that. If a big thief gets swung for breaking open a cash-box, his lassie will swear he was looking for her thimble. If you was to go now for discoursing of this matter, you would never put up with poor Poppet's account of him, and she would run him higher up, every time you ran him down; ay, and believe it too: such is the ways of women."

"Why, Stephen, you make me open up my eyes. I never dreamed you were half so cunning, and of such low opinions."

"Well, I don't know, only from my own observance. I would scarcely trust myself not to abuse that fellow. And, Sophy, you know you can not stop your tongue, like me."

"Thank God for that same! He never meant us so to do. But, Stephen, I will follow your advice; because it is my own opinion."

Mary was puzzled by this behavior; for everything used to be so plain among them. She would even have tried for some comfort from Willie, whose mind was very large upon all social questions. But Willie had solved at last the problem of perpetual motion, according to his own conviction, and locked himself up with his model all day; and the world might stand still, so long as that went on. "Oh, what would I give for dear Jack!" cried Mary.

Worn out at length with lonely grief, she asked if she might go to Byrsa Cottage, for a change. Even that was refused, though her father's kind heart ached at the necessary denial. Sharp words again had passed between the farmer and the tanner concerning her, and the former believed that his brother-in-law would even encourage the outlaw still. And for Mary herself now the worst of it was that she had nothing to lay hold of in the way of complaint or grievance. It was not like that first estrangement, when her father showed how much he felt it in a hundred ways, and went about everything upside down, and comforted her by his want of comfort. Now it was ten times worse than that, for her father took everything quite easily!

Shocking as it may be, this was true. Stephen Anerley had been through a great many things since the violence of his love-time, and his views upon such tender subjects were not so tender as they used to be. With the eyes of wisdom he looked back, having had his own way in the matter, upon such young sensations as very laudable, but curable. In his own case he had cured them well, and, upon the whole, very happily, by a good long course of married life; but having tried that remedy alone, how could he say that there was no better? He remembered how his own miseries had soon subsided, or gone into other grooves, after matrimony. This showed that they were transient, but did not prove such a course to be the only cure for them. Recovering from illness, has any man been known to say that the doctor recovered him?

Mrs. Anerley's views upon the subject were much the same, though modified, of course, by the force of her own experience. She might have had a much richer man than Stephen; and when he was stingy, she reminded him of that, which, after a little disturbance, generally terminated in five guineas. And now she was clear that if Mary were not worried, condoled with, or cried over, she would take her own time, and come gradually round, and be satisfied with Harry Tanfield. Harry was a fine young fellow, and worshipped the ground that Mary walked upon; and it seemed a sort of equity that he should have her, as his father had been disappointed of her mother. Every Sunday morning he trimmed his whiskers, and put on a wonderful waistcoat; and now he did more, for he bought a new hat, and came to church to look at her.

Oftentimes now, by all these doings, the spirit of the girl was roused, and her courage made ready to fly out in words; but the calm look of the elders stopped her, and then true pride came to her aid. If they chose to say nothing of the matter which was in her heart continually, would she go whining to them about it, and scrape a grain of pity from a cartload of contempt? One day, as she stood before the swinging glass—that present from Aunt Popplewell which had moved her mother's wrath so—she threw back her shoulders, and smoothed the plaits of her nice little waist, and considered herself. The humor of the moment grew upon her, and crept into indulgence, as she saw what a very fair lass she was, and could not help being proud of it. She saw how the soft rich damask of her cheeks returned at being thought of, and the sparkle of her sweet blue eyes, and the merry delight of her lips, that made respectable people want to steal a kiss, from the pure enticement of good-will.

"I will cry no more in the nights," she said. "Why should I make such a figure of myself, with nobody to care for it? And here is my hair full of kinkles and neglect! I declare, if he ever came back, he would say, 'What a fright you are become, my Mary!' Where is that stuff of Aunt Deborah's, I wonder, that makes her hair like satin? It is high time to leave off being such a dreadful dowdy. I will look as nice as ever, just to let them know that their cruelty has not killed me."

Virtuous resolves commend themselves, and improve with being carried out. She put herself into her very best trim, as simple as a lily, and as perfect as a rose, though the flutter of a sigh or two enlarged her gentle breast. She donned a very graceful hat, adorned with sweet ribbon right skillfully smuggled; and she made up her mind to have the benefit of the air.

The prettiest part of all Anerley Farm, for those who are not farmers, is a soft little valley, where a brook comes down, and passes from voluntary ruffles into the quiet resignation of a sheltered lake. A pleasant and a friendly little water-spread is here, cheerful to the sunshine, and inviting to the moon, with a variety of gleamy streaks, according to the sky and breeze. Pasture-land and arable come sloping to the margin, which, instead of being rough and rocky, lips the pool with gentleness. Ins and outs of little bays afford a nice variety, while round the brink are certain trees of a modest and unpretentious bent. These having risen to a very fair distance toward the sky, come down again, scarcely so much from a doubt of their merits, as through affection to their native land. In summer they hang like a permanent shower of green to refresh the bright water; and in winter, like loose osier-work, or wattles curved for binding.

Under one of the largest of these willows the runaway Jack had made a seat, whereon to sit and watch his toy boat cruising on the inland wave. Often when Mary was tired of hoping for the return of her playmate, she came to this place to think about him, and wonder whether he thought of her. And now in the soft December evening (lonely and sad, but fair to look at, like herself) she was sitting here.

The keen east wind, which had set in as Captain Brown predicted, was over now, and succeeded by the gentler influence of the west. Nothing could be heard in this calm nook but the lingering touch of the dying breeze, and the long soft murmur of the distant sea, and the silvery plash of a pair of coots at play. Neither was much to be seen, except the wavering glisten and long shadows of the mere, the tracery of trees against the fading light, and the outline of the maiden as she leaned against the trunk. Generations of goat-moths in their early days of voracity had made a nice hollow for her hat to rest in, and some of the powdering willow dusted her bright luxuriant locks with gold. Her face was by no means wan or gloomy, and she added to the breezes not a single sigh. This happened without any hardness of heart, or shallow contempt of the nobler affections; simply from the hopefulness of healthful youth, and the trust a good will has in powers of good.

She was looking at those coots, who were full of an idea that the winter had spent itself in that east wind, that the gloss of spring plumage must be now upon their necks, and that they felt their toes growing warmer toward the downy tepefaction of a perfect nest. Improving a long and kind acquaintance with these birds, some of whom have confidence in human nature, Mary was beginning to be absent from her woes, and joyful in the pleasure of a thoughtless pair, when suddenly, with one accord, they dived, and left a bright splash and a wrinkle. "Somebody is coming; they must have seen an enemy," said the damsel to herself. "I am sure I never moved. I will never have them shot by any wicked poacher." To watch the bank nicely, without being seen, she drew in her skirt and shrank behind the tree, not from any fear, but just to catch the fellow; for one of the laborers on the farm, who had run at his master with a pitchfork once, was shrewdly suspected of poaching with a gun. But keener eyes than those of any poacher were upon her, and the lightest of light steps approached.

"Oh, Robin, are you come, then, at last?" cried Mary.

"Three days I have been lurking, in the hope of this. Heart of my heart, are you glad to see me?"

"I should think that I was. It is worth a world of crying. Oh, where have you been this long, long time?"

"Let me have you in my arms, if it is but for a moment. You are not afraid of me?—you are not ashamed to love me?"

"I love you all the better for your many dreadful troubles. Not a word do I believe of all the wicked people say of you. Don't be afraid of me. You may kiss me, Robin."

"You are such a beautiful spick and span! And I am only fit to go into the pond. Oh, Mary, what a shame of me to take advantage of you!"

"Well, I think that it is time for you to leave off now. Though you must not suppose that I think twice about my things. When I look at you, it makes me long to give you my best cloak and a tidy hat. Oh, where is all your finery gone, poor Robin?"

"Endeavor not to be insolent, on the strength of your fine clothes. Remember that I have abandoned free trade; and the price of every article will rise at once."

Mary Anerley not only smiled, but laughed, with the pleasure of a great relief. She had always scorned the idea that her lover had even made a shot at Carroway, often though the brave lieutenant had done the like to him; and now she felt sure that he could clear himself; or how could he be so light-hearted? "You see that I am scarcely fit to lead off a country-dance with you," said Robin, still holding both her hands, and watching the beauty of her clear bright eyes, which might gather big tears at any moment, as the deep blue sky is a sign of sudden rain; "and it will be a very long time, my darling, before you see me in gay togs again."

"I like you a great deal better so. You always look brave—but you look so honest now!"

"That is a most substantial saying, and worthy of the race of Anerley. How I wish that your father would like me, Mary! I suppose it is hopeless to wish for that?"

"No, not at all—if you could keep on looking shabby. My dear father has a most generous mind. If he only could be brought to see how you are ill-treated—"

"Alas! I shall have no chance of letting him see that. Before to-morrow morning I must say good-by to England. My last chance of seeing you was now this evening. I bless every star that is in the heaven now. I trusted to my luck, and it has not deceived me."

"Robin dear, I never wish to try to be too pious. But I think that you should rather trust in Providence than starlight."

"So I do. And it is Providence that has kept me out of sight—out of sight of enemies, and in sight of you, my Mary. The Lord looks down on every place where His lovely angels wander. You are one of His angels, Mary; and you have made a man of me. For years I shall not see you, darling; never more again, perhaps. But as long as I live you will be here; and the place shall be kept pure for you. If we only could have a shop together—oh, how honest I would be! I would give full weight, besides the paper; I would never sell an egg more than three weeks old; and I would not even adulterate! But that is a dream of the past, I fear. Oh, I never shall hoist the Royal Arms. But I mean to serve under them, and fight my way. My captain shall be Lord Nelson."

"That is the very thing that you were meant for. I will never forgive Dr. Upandown for not putting you into the navy. You could have done no smuggling then."

"I am not altogether sure of that. However, I will shun scandal, as behooves a man who gets so much. You have not asked me to clear myself of that horrible thing about poor Carroway. I love you the more for not asking me; it shows your faith so purely. But you have the right to know all I know. There is no fear of any interruption here; so, Mary, I will tell you, if you are sure that you can bear it."

"Yes, oh yes! Do tell me all you know. It is so frightful that I must hear it."

"What I have to say will not frighten you, darling, because I did not even see the deed. But my escape was rather strange, and deserves telling better than I can tell it, even with you to encourage me by listening. When we were so suddenly caught in the cave, through treachery of some of our people, I saw in a moment that we must be taken, but resolved to have some fun for it, with a kind of whim which comes over me sometimes. So I knocked away the lights, and began myself to splash with might and main, and ordered the rest to do likewise. We did it so well that the place was like a fountain or a geyser; and I sent a great dollop of water into the face of the poor lieutenant—the only assault I have ever made upon him. There was just light enough for me to know him, because he was so tall and strange; but I doubt whether he knew me at all. He became excited, as he well might be; he dashed away the water from his eyes with one hand, and with the other made a wild sword-cut, rushing forward as if to have at me. Like a bird, I dived into the water from our gunwale, and under the keel of the other boat, and rose to the surface at the far side of the cave. In the very act of plunging, a quick flash came before me—or at least I believed so afterward—and a loud roar, as I struck the wave. It might have been only from my own eyes and ears receiving so suddenly the cleavage of the water. If I thought anything at all about it, it was that somebody had shot at me; but expecting to be followed, I swam rapidly away. I did not even look back, as I kept in the dark of the rocks, for it would have lost a stroke, and a stroke was more than I could spare. To my great surprise, I heard no sound of any boat coming after me, nor any shouts of Carroway, such as I am accustomed to. But swimming as I was, for my own poor life, like an otter with a pack of hounds after him, I assure you I did not look much after anything except my own run of the gauntlet."

"Of course not. How could you? It makes me draw my breath to think of you swimming in the dark like that, with deep water, and caverns, and guns, and all!"

"Mary, I thought that my time was come; and only one beautiful image sustained me, when I came to think of it afterward. I swam with my hands well under water, and not a breath that could be heard, and my cap tucked into my belt, and my sea-going pumps slipped away into a pocket. The water was cold, but it only seemed to freshen me, and I found myself able to breathe very pleasantly in the gentle rise and fall of waves. Yet I never expected to escape, with so many boats to come after me. For now I could see two boats outside, as well as old Carroway's pinnace in the cave; and if once they caught sight of me, I could never get away.

"When I saw those two boats upon the watch outside, I scarcely knew what to do for the best, whether to put my breast to it and swim out, or to hide in some niche with my body under water, and cover my face with oar-weed. Luckily I took the bolder course, remembering their portfires, which would make the cave like day. Not everybody could have swum out through that entrance, against a spring-tide and the lollop of the sea; and one dash against the rocks would have settled me. But I trusted in the Lord, and tried a long, slow stroke.

"My enemies must have been lost in dismay, and panic, and utter confusion, or else they must have espied me, for twice or thrice, as I met the waves, my head and shoulders were thrown above the surface, do what I would; and I durst not dive, for I wanted my eyes every moment. I kept on the darkest side, of course, but the shadows were not half so deep as I could wish; and worst of all, outside there was a piece of moonlight, which I must cross within fifty yards of the bigger of the sentry boats.

"The mouth of that cave is two fathoms wide for a longish bit of channel; and, Mary dear, if I had not been supported by continual thoughts of you, I must have gone against the sides, or downright to the bottom, from the waves keeping knocking me about so. I may tell you that I felt that I should never care again, as my clothes began to bag about me, except to go down to the bottom and be quiet, but for the blessed thought of standing up some day, at the 'hymeneal altar,' as great people call it, with a certain lovely Mary."

"Oh, Robin, now you make me laugh, when I ought to be quite crying. If such a thing should ever be, I shall expect to see you swimming."

"Such a thing will be, as sure as I stand here—though not at all in hymeneal garb just now. Whatever my whole heart is set upon, I do, and overcome all obstacles. Remember that, and hold fast, darling. However, I had now to overcome the sea, which is worse than any tide in the affairs of men. A long and hard tussle it was, I assure you, to fight against the indraught, and to drag my frame through the long hillocky gorge. At last, however, I managed it; and to see the open waves again put strength into my limbs, and vigor into my knocked-about brain. I suppose that you can not understand it, Mary, but I never enjoyed a thing more than the danger of crossing that strip of moonlight. I could see the very eyes and front teeth of the men who were sitting there to look out for me if I should slip their mates inside; and knowing the twist of every wave, and the vein of every tide-run, I rested in a smooth dark spot, and considered their manners quietly. They had not yet heard a word of any doings in the cavern, but their natures were up for some business to do, as generally happens with beholders. Having nothing to do, they were swearing at the rest.

"In the place where I was halting now the line of a jagged cliff seemed to cut the air, and fend off the light from its edges. You can only see such a thing from the level of the sea, and it looks very odd when you see it, as if the moon and you were a pair of playing children, feeling round a corner for a glimpse of one another. But plain enough it was, and far too plain, that the doubling of that little cape would treble my danger, by reason of the bold moonlight, I knew that my only refuge was another great hollow in the crags between the cave I had escaped from and the point—a place which is called the 'Church Cave,' from an old legend that it leads up to Flamborough church. To the best of my knowledge, it does nothing of the kind, at any rate now; but it has a narrow fissure, known to few except myself, up which a nimble man may climb; and this was what I hoped to do. Also it has a very narrow entrance, through which the sea flows into it, so that a large boat can not enter, and a small one would scarcely attempt it in the dark, unless it were one of my own, hard pressed. Now it seemed almost impossible for me to cross that moonlight without being seen by those fellows in the boat, who could pull, of course, four times as fast as I could swim, not to mention the chances of a musket-ball. However, I was just about to risk it, for my limbs were growing very cold, when I heard a loud shout from the cave which I had left, and knew that the men there were summoning their comrades. These at once lay out upon their oars, and turned their backs to me, and now was my good time. The boat came hissing through the water toward the Dovecote, while I stretched away for the other snug cave. Being all in a flurry, they kept no look-out; if the moon was against me, my good stars were in my favor. Nobody saw me, and I laughed in my wet sleeves as I thought of the rage of Carroway, little knowing that the fine old fellow was beyond all rage or pain."

"How wonderful your luck was, and your courage too!" cried Mary, who had listened with bright tears upon her cheeks. "Not one man in a thousand could have done so bold a thing. And how did you get away at last, poor Robin?"

"Exactly as I meant to do, from the time I formed my plan. The Church has ever been a real friend in need to me; I took the name for a lucky omen, and swam in with a brisker stroke. It is the prettiest of all the caves, to my mind, though the smallest, with a sweet round basin, and a playful little beach, and nothing very terrible about it. I landed, and rested with a thankful heart upon the shelly couch of the mermaids."

"Oh, Robin, I hope none of them came to you. They are so wonderfully beautiful. And no one that ever has seen them cares any more for—for dry people that wear dresses."

"Mary, you delight me much, by showing signs of jealousy. Fifty may have come, but I saw not one, for I fell into a deep calm sleep. If they had come, I would have spurned them all, not only from my constancy to you, my dear, but from having had too much drip already. Mary, I see a man on the other side of the mere, not opposite to us, but a good bit further down. You see those two swimming birds: look far away between them, you will see something moving."

"I see nothing, either standing still or moving. It is growing too dark for any eyes not thoroughly trained in smuggling. But that reminds me to tell you, Robin, that a strange man—a gentleman they seemed to say—has been seen upon our land, and he wanted to see me, without my father knowing it. But only think! I have never even asked you whether you are hungry—perhaps even starving! How stupid, how selfish, how churlish of me! But the fault is yours, because I had so much to hear of."

"Darling, you may trust me not to starve, I can feed by-and-by. For the present I must talk, that you may know all about everything, and bear me harmless in your mind, when evil things are said of me. Have you heard that I went to see Widow Carroway, even before she had heard of her loss, but not before I was hunted? I knew that I must do so, now or never, before the whole world was up in arms against me; and I thank God that I saw her. A man might think nothing of such an act, or even might take it for hypocrisy; but a woman's heart is not so black. Though she did not even know what I meant, for she had not felt her awful blow, and I could not tell her of it, she did me justice afterward. In the thick of her terrible desolation, she stood beside her husband's grave, in Bridlington Priory Church yard, and she said to a hundred people there: 'Here lies my husband, foully murdered. The coroner's jury have brought their verdict against Robin Lyth the smuggler. Robin Lyth is as innocent as I am. I know who did it, and time will show. My curse is upon him; and my eyes are on him now.' Then she fell down in a fit, and the Preventive men, who were drawn up in a row, came and carried her away. Did anybody tell you, darling? Perhaps they keep such things from you."

"Part of it I heard; but not so clearly. I was told that she acquitted you and I blessed her in my heart for it."

"Even more than that she did. As soon as she got home again, she wrote to Robin Cockscroft—a very few words, but as strong as could be, telling him that I should have no chance of justice if I were caught just now; that she must have time to carry out her plans; that the Lord would soon raise up good friends to help her; and as sure as there was a God in heaven, she would bring the man who did it to the gallows. Only that I must leave the land at once. And that is what I shall do this very night. Now I have told you almost all. Mary, we must say 'good-by.'"

"But surely I shall hear from you sometimes?" said Mary, striving to be brave, and to keep her voice from trembling. "Years and years, without a word—and the whole world bitter against you and me! Oh, Robin, I think that it will break my heart. And I must not even talk of you."

"Think of me, darling, while I think of you. Thinking is better than talking, I shall never talk of you, but be thinking all the more. Talking ruins thinking. Take this token of the time you saved me, and give me that bit of blue ribbon, my Mary; I shall think of your eyes every time I kiss it. Kiss it yourself before you give it to me."

Like a good girl, she did what she was told to do. She gave him the love-knot from her breast, and stored his little trinket in that pure shrine.

"But sometimes—sometimes, I shall hear of you?" she whispered, lingering, and trembling in the last embrace.

"To be sure, you shall hear of me from time to time, through Robin and Joan Cockscroft. I will not grieve you by saying, 'Be true to me,' my noble one, and my everlasting love."

Mary was comforted, and ceased to cry. She was proud of him thus in the depth of his trouble; and she prayed to God to bless him through the long sad time.

CHAPTER XXXVII

FACT, OR FACTOR

"Papa, I have brought you a wonderful letter," cried Miss Janetta Upround, toward supper-time of that same night; "and the most miraculous thing about it is that there is no post to pay. Oh, how stupid I am! I ought to have got at least a shilling out of you for postage."

"My dear, be sorry for your sins, and not for having failed to add to them. Our little world is brimful of news just now, but nearly all of it bad news. Why, bless me, this is in regular print, and it never has passed through the post at all, which explains the most astounding fact of positively naught to pay. Janetta, every day I congratulate myself upon such a wondrous daughter. But I never could have hoped that even you would bring me a letter gratis."

"But the worst of it is that I deserve no credit. If I had cheated the postman, there would have been something to be proud of. But this letter came in the most ignominious way—poked under the gate, papa! It is sealed with a foreign coin! Oh, dear, dear, I am all in a tingle to know all about it. I saw it by the moonlight, and it must belong to me."

"My dear, it says, 'Private, and to his own hands.' Therefore you had better go, and think no more about it. I confide to you many of my business matters: or at any rate you get them out of me: but this being private, you must think no more about it."

"Darling papa, what a flagrant shame! The man must have done it with no other object than to rob me of every wink of sleep. If I swallow the outrage and retire, will you promise to tell me every word to-morrow? You preached a most exquisite sermon last Sunday about the meanness and futility of small concealments."

"Be off!" cried the rector; "you are worse than Mr. Mordacks, who lays down the law about frankness perpetually, but never lets me guess what his own purpose is."

"Oh, now I see where the infection comes from! Papa, I am off, for fear of catching it myself. Don't tell me, whatever you do. I never can sleep upon dark mysteries."

"Poor dear, you shall not have your rest disturbed," Dr. Upround said, sweetly, as he closed the door behind her; "you are much too good a girl for other people's plagues to visit you." Then, as he saddled his pleasant old nose with the tranquil span of spectacles, the smile on his lips and the sigh of his breast arrived at a quiet little compromise. He was proud of his daughter, her quickness and power to get the upper turn of words with him; but he grieved at her not having any deep impressions, even after his very best sermons. But her mother always told him not to be in any hurry, for even she herself had felt no very profound impressions until she married a clergyman; and that argument always made him smile (as invisibly as possible), because he had not detected yet their existence in his better half. Such questions are most delicate, and a husband can only set mute example. A father, on the other hand, is bound to use his pastoral crook upon his children foremost.

"Now for this letter," said Dr. Upround, holding council with himself; "evidently a good clerk, and perhaps a first-rate scholar. One of the very best Greek scholars of the age does all his manuscript in printing hand, when he wishes it to be legible. And a capital plan it is—without meaning any pun. I can read this like a gazette itself."

"REVEREND AND WORSHIPFUL SIR,—Your long and highly valued kindness requires at least a word from me, before I leave this country. I have not ventured into your presence, because it might place you in a very grave predicament. Your duty to King and State might compel you with your own hand to arrest me; and against your hand I could not strive. The evidence brought before you left no choice but to issue a warrant against me, though it grieved your kind heart to do that same. Sir, I am purely innocent of the vile crime laid against me. I used no fire-arm that night, neither did any of my men. And it is for their sake, as well as my own, that I now take the liberty of writing this. Failing of me, the authorities may bring my comrades to trial, and convict them. If that were so, it would become my duty as a man to surrender myself, and meet my death in the hope of saving them. But if the case is sifted properly, they must be acquitted; for no fire-arm of any kind was in my boat, except one pair of pistols, in a locker under the after thwart, and they happened to be unloaded. I pray you to verify this, kind sir. My firm belief is that the revenue officer was shot by one of his own men; and his widow has the same opinion. I hear that the wound was in the back of the head. If we had carried fire-arms, not one of us could have shot him so.

"It may have been an accident; I can not say. Even so, the man whose mishap it was is not likely to acknowledge it. And I know that in a court of law truth must be paid for dearly. I venture to commit to your good hands a draft upon a well-known Holland firm, which amounts to 78 pounds British, for the defense of the men who are in custody. I know that you as a magistrate can not come forward as their defender; but I beg you as a friend of justice to place the money for their benefit. Also especially to direct attention to the crew of the revenue boat and their guns.

"And now I fear greatly to encroach upon your kindness, and very long-suffering good-will toward me. But I have brought into sad trouble and distress with her family—who are most obstinate people—and with the opinion of the public, I suppose, a young lady worth more than all the goods I ever ran, or ever could run, if I went on for fifty years. By name she is Mistress Mary Anerley, and by birth the daughter of Captain Anerley, of Anerley Farm, outside our parish. If your reverence could only manage to ride round that way upon coming home from Sessions, once or twice in the fine weather, and to say a kind word or two to my Mary, and a good word, if any can be said of me, to her parents, who are stiff but worthy people, it would be a truly Christian act, and such as you delight in, on this side of the Dane-dike.

"Reverend sir, I must now say farewell. From you I have learned almost everything I know, within the pale of statutes, which repeal one another continually. I have wandered sadly outside that pale, and now I pay the penalty. If I had only paid heed to your advice, and started in business with the capital acquired by free trade, and got it properly protected, I might have been able to support my parents, and even be churchwarden of Flamborough. You always told me that my unlawful enterprise must close in sadness; and your words have proved too true. But I never expected anything like this; and I do not understand it yet. A penetrating mind like yours, with all the advantages of authority, even that is likely to be baffled in such a difficult case as this.

"Reverend sir, my case is hard; for I always have labored to establish peaceful trade; and I must have succeeded again, if honor had guided all my followers. We always relied upon the coast-guard to be too late for any mischief; and so they would have been this time, if their acts had been straightforward. In sorrow and lowness of fortune, I remain, with humble respect and gratitude, your Worship's poor pupil and banished parishioner,

"ROBIN LYTH, of Flamborough."

"Come, now, Robin," Dr. Upround said, as soon as he had well considered this epistle, "I have put up with many a checkmate at your hands, but not without the fair delight of a counter-stroke at the enemy. Here you afford me none of that. You are my master in every way; and quietly you make me make your moves, quite as if I were the black in a problem. You leave me to conduct your fellow-smugglers' case, to look after your sweetheart, and to make myself generally useful. By-the-way, that touch about my pleading his cause in my riding-boots, and with a sessional air about me, is worthy of the great Verdoni. Neither is that a bad hit about my Christianity stopping at the Dane-dike. Certes, I shall have to call on that young lady, though from what I have heard of the sturdy farmer, I may both ride and reason long, even after my greatest exploits at the Sessions, without converting him to free trade; and trebly so after that deplorable affair. I wonder whether we shall ever get to the bottom of that mystery. How often have I warned the boy that mischief was quite sure to come! though I never even dreamed that it would be so bad as this."

Since Dr. Upround first came to Flamborough, nothing (not even the infliction of his nickname) had grieved him so deeply as the sad death of Carroway. From the first he felt certain that his own people were guiltless of any share in it. But his heart misgave him as to distant smugglers, men who came from afar freebooting, bringing over ocean woes to men of settlement, good tithe-payers. For such men (plainly of foreign breed, and very plain specimens of it) had not at all succeeded in eluding observation, in a neighborhood where they could have no honest calling. Flamborough had called to witness Filey, and Filey had attested Bridlington, that a stranger on horseback had appeared among them with a purpose obscurely evil. They were right enough as to the fact, although the purpose was not evil, as little Denmark even now began to own.

"Here I am again!" cried Mr. Mordacks, laying vehement hold of the rector's hand, upon the following morning; "just arrived from York, dear sir, after riding half the night, and going anywhere you please; except perhaps where you would like to send me, if charity and Christian courtesy allowed. My dear sir, have you heard the news? I perceive by your countenance that you have not. Ah, you are generally benighted in these parts. Your caves have got something to do with it. The mind gets accustomed to them."

"I venture to think, Mr. Mordacks, on the whole," said the rector, who studied this man gently, "that sometimes you are rapid in your conclusions. Possibly of the two extremes it is the more desirable; especially in these parts, because of its great rarity. Still the mere fact of some caves existing, in or out of my parish, whichever it may be, scarcely seems to prove that all the people of Flamborough live in them. And even if we did, it was the manner of the ancient seers, both in the Classics, and in Holy Writ—"

"Sir, I know all about Elijah and Obadiah, and the rest of them. Profane literature we leave now for clerks in holy orders—we positively have no time for it. Everything begins to move with accelerated pace. This is a new century, and it means to make its mark. It begins very badly; but it will go on all the better. And I hope to have the pleasure, at a very early day, of showing you one of its leading men, a man of large intellect, commanding character, the most magnificent principles—and, in short, lots of money. You must be quite familiar with the name of Sir Duncan Yordas."

"I fancy that I have heard or seen it somewhere. Oh, something to do with the Hindoos, or the Africans. I never pay much attention to such things."

"Neither do I, Dr. Upround. Still somebody must, and a lot of money comes of it. Their idols have diamond eyes, which purity of worship compels us to confiscate. And there are many other ways of getting on among them, while wafting and expanding them into a higher sphere of thought. The mere fact of Sir Duncan having feathered his nest—pardon so vulgar an expression, doctor —proves that while giving, we may also receive: for which we have the highest warrant."

"The laborer is worthy of his hire, Mr. Mordacks. At the same time we should remember also—"

"What St. Paul says per contra. Quite so. That is always my first consideration, when I work for my employers. Ah, Dr. Upround, few men give such pure service as your humble servant. I have twice had the honor of handing you my card. If ever you fall into any difficulty, where zeal, fidelity, and high principle, combined with very low charges—"

"Mr. Mordacks, my opinion of you is too high for even yourself to add to it. But what has this Sir Duncan Yorick—"

"Yordas, my dear sir—Sir Duncan Yordas—the oldest family in Yorkshire. Men of great power, both for good and evil, mainly, perhaps, the latter. It has struck me sometimes that the county takes its name—But etymology is not my forte. What has he to do with us, you ask? Sir, I will answer you most frankly. 'Coram populo' is my business motto. Excuse me, I think I hear that door creak. No, a mere fancy—we are quite 'in camera.' Very well; reverend sir, prepare your mind for a highly astounding disclosure."

"I have lived too long to be astounded, my good sir. But allow me to put on my spectacles. Now I am prepared for almost anything."

"Dr. Upround, my duty compels me to enter largely into minds. Your mind is of a lofty order—calm, philosophic, benevolent. You have proved this by your kind reception of me, a stranger, almost an intruder. You have judged from my manners and appearance, which are shaped considerably by the inner man, that my object was good, large, noble. And yet you have not been quite able to refrain, at weak moments perhaps, but still a dozen times a day, from exclaiming in the commune of your heart, 'What the devil does this man want in my parish?'"

"My good sir, I never use bad language; and if I did my duty, I should now inflict—"

"Five shillings for your poor-box. There it is. And it serves me quite right for being too explicit, and forgetting my reverence to the cloth. However, I have coarsely expressed your thoughts. Also you have frequently said to yourself, 'This man prates of openness, but I find him closer than any oyster.' Am I right? Yes, I see that I am, by your bow. Very well, you may suppose what pain it gave me to have the privilege of intercourse with a perfect gentleman and an eloquent divine, and yet feel myself in an ambiguous position. In a few words I will clear myself, being now at liberty to indulge that pleasure. I have been here, as agent for Sir Duncan Yordas, to follow up the long-lost clew to his son, and only child, who for very many years was believed to be out of all human pursuit. My sanguine and penetrating mind scorned rumors, and went in for certainty. I have found Sir Duncan's son, and am able to identify him, beyond all doubt, as a certain young man well known to you, and perhaps too widely known, by the name of Robin Lyth."

In spite of the length of his experience of the world, in a place of so many adventures, the rector of Flamborough was astonished, and perhaps a little vexed as well. If anything was to be found out, in such a headlong way, about one of his parishioners, and notably such a pet pupil and favorite, the proper thing would have been that he himself should do it. Failing that, he should at least have been consulted, enlisted, or at any rate apprised of what was toward. But instead of that, here he had been hoodwinked (by this marvel of incarnate candor employed in the dark about several little things), and then suddenly enlightened, when the job was done. Gentle and void of self-importance as he was, it misliked him to be treated so.

"This is a wonderful piece of news," he said, as he fixed a calm gaze upon the keen, hard eyes of Mordacks. "You understand your business, sir, and would not make such a statement unless you could verify it. But I hope that you may not find cause to regret that you have treated me with so little confidence."

"I am not open to that reproach. Dr. Upround, consider my instructions. I was strictly forbidden to disclose my object until certainty should be obtained. That being done, I have hastened to apprise you first of a result which is partly due to your own good offices. Shake hands, my dear sir, and acquit me of rudeness—the last thing of which I am capable."

The rector was mollified, and gave his hand to the gallant general factor. "Allow me to add my congratulations upon your wonderful success," he said; "but would that I had known it some few hours sooner! It might have saved you a vast amount of trouble. I might have kept Robin well within your reach. I fear that he is now beyond it."

"I am grieved to hear you say so. But according to my last instructions, although he is in strict concealment, I can lay hands upon him when the time is ripe."

"I fear not. He sailed last night for the Continent, which is a vague destination, especially in such times as these. But perhaps that was part of your skillful contrivance?"

"Not so. And for the time it throws me out. I have kept most careful watch on him. But the difficulty was that he might confound my vigilance with that of his enemies; take me for a constable, I mean. And perhaps he has done so, after all. Things have gone luckily for me in the main; but that murder came in most unseasonably. It was the very thing that should have been avoided. Sir Duncan will need all his influence there. Suppose for a moment that young Robin did not do it—"

"Mr. Mordacks, you frighten me. What else could you suppose?"

"Certainly—yes. A parishioner of yours, when not engaged unlawfully upon the high seas. We heartily hope that he did not do it, and we give him the benefit of the doubt; in which I shared largely, until it became so manifest that he was a Yordas. A Yordas has made a point of slaying his man—and sometimes from three to a dozen men—until within the last two generations. In the third generation the law revives, as is hinted, I think, in the Decalogue. In my professional course a large stock of hereditary trail—so to speak— comes before me. Some families always drink, some always steal, some never tell lies because they never know a falsehood, some would sell their souls for a sixpence, and these are the most respectable of any—"

"My dear sir, my dear sir, I beg your pardon for interrupting you; but in my house the rule is to speak well of people, or else to say nothing about them."

"Then you must resign your commission, doctor; for how can you take depositions? But, as I was saying, I should have some hope of the innocence of young Robin if it should turn out that his father, Sir Duncan, has destroyed a good many of the native race in India. It may reasonably be hoped that he has done so, which would tend very strongly to exonerate his son. But the evidence laid before your Worship and before the coroner was black—black —black."

"My position forbids me to express opinions. The evidence compelled me to issue the warrant. But knowing your position, I may show you this, in every word of which I have perfect faith."

With these words Dr. Upround produced the letter which he had received last night, and the general factor took in all the gist of it in less than half a minute.

"Very good! very good!" he said, with a smile of experienced benevolence.

"We believe some of it. Our duty is to do so. There are two points of importance in it. One as to the girl he is in love with, and the other his kind liberality to the fellows who will have to bear the brunt of it."

"You speak sarcastically, and I hope unfairly. To my mind, the most important facts are these—that poor Carroway was shot from behind, and that the smugglers had no fire-arms, except two pistols, both unloaded."

"Who is to prove that, Dr. Upround? Their mouths are closed; and if they were open, would anybody believe them? We knew long ago that the vigilant and deservedly lamented officer took the deathblow from behind; but of that how simple is the explanation! The most intelligent of his crew, and apparently his best subordinate, whose name is John Cadman, deposes that his lamented chief turned round for one moment to give an order, and during that moment received the shot. His evidence is the more weighty because he does not go too far with it. He does not pretend to say who fired. He knows only that one of the smugglers did. His evidence will hang those six poor fellows, from the laudable desire of the law to include the right one. But I trust that the right one will be far away."

"I trust not. If even one of them is condemned, even to transportation, Robin Lyth will surrender immediately. You doubt it. You smile at the idea. Your opinion of human nature is low. Mine is not enthusiastic. But I judge others by myself."

"So do I," Mr. Mordacks answered, with a smile of curious humor. And the rector could not help smiling too, at this instance of genuine candor. "However, not to go too deeply into that," his visitor continued, "there really is one point in Robin's letter which demands inquiry. I mean about the guns of the Preventive men. Cadman may be a rogue. Most probably he is. None of the others confirm, although they do not contradict him. Do you know anything about him?"

"Only villainy—in another way. Ho led away a nice girl of this parish, an industrious mussel-gatherer. And he then had a wife and large family of his own, of which the poor thing knew nothing. Her father nearly killed him; and I was compelled (very much against my will) to inflict a penalty. Cadman is very shy of Flamborough now. By-the-way, have you called upon poor Widow Carroway?"

"I thank you for the hint. She is the very person. It will be a sad intrusion; and I have put it off as long as possible. After what Robin says, it is most important. I hope that Sir Duncan will be here very shortly. He is coming from Yarmouth in his own yacht. Matters are crowding upon me very fast. I will see Mrs. Carroway as soon as it is decent. Good-morning, and best thanks to your Worship."

CHAPTER XXXVIII

THE DEMON OF THE AXE

The air was sad and heavy thus, with discord, doubt, and death itself gathering and descending, like the clouds of long night, upon Flamborough. But far away, among the mountains and the dreary moorland, the "intake" of the coming winter was a great deal worse to see. For here no blink of the sea came up, no sunlight under the sill of clouds (as happens where wide waters are), but rather a dark rim of brooding on the rough horizon seemed to thicken itself against the light under the sullen march of vapors—the muffled funeral of the year. Dry trees and naked crags stood forth, and the dirge of the wind went to and fro, and there was no comfort out-of-doors.

Soon the first snow of the winter came, the first abiding earnest snow, for several skits had come before, and ribbed with white the mountain breasts. But nobody took much heed of that, except to lean over the plough, while it might be sped, or to want more breakfast. Well resigned was everybody to the stoppage of work by winter. It was only what must be every year, and a gracious provision of Providence. If a man earned very little money, that was against him in one way, but encouraged him in another. It brought home to his mind the surety that others would be kind to him; not with any sense of gift, but a large good-will of sharing.

But the first snow that visits the day, and does not melt in its own cold tears, is a sterner sign for every one. The hardened wrinkle, and the herring-bone of white that runs among the brown fern fronds, the crisp defiant dazzle on the walks, and the crust that glitters on the patient branch, and the crest curling under the heel of a gate, and the ridge piled up against the tool-house door—these, and the shivering wind that spreads them, tell of a bitter time in store.

The ladies of Scargate Hall looked out upon such a December afternoon. The massive walls of their house defied all sudden change of temperature, and nothing less than a week of rigor pierced the comfort of their rooms. The polished oak beams overhead glanced back the merry fire-glow, the painted walls shone with rosy tints, and warm lights flitting along them, and the thick-piled carpet yielded back a velvety sense of luxury. It was nice to see how bleak the crags were, and the sad trees laboring beneath the wind and snow.

"If it were not for thinking of the poor cold people, for whom one feels so deeply," said the gentle Mrs. Carnaby, with a sweet soft sigh, "one would rather enjoy this dreary prospect. I hope there will be a deep snow to-night. There is every sign of it upon the scaurs. And then, Philippa, only think—no post, no plague of news, no prospect of even that odious Jellicorse! Once more we shall have our meals in quiet."

Mrs. Carnaby loved a good dinner right well, a dinner unplagued by hospitable cares; when a woodcock was her own to dwell on, and pretty little teeth might pick a pretty little bone at ease.

"Eliza, you are always such a creature of the moment," Mistress Yordas answered, indulgently; "you do love the good things of the world too much. How would you like to be out there, in a naked little cottage where the wind howls through, and the ewer is frozen every morning? And where, if you ever get anything to eat—"

"Philippa, I implore you not to be so dreadful. One never can utter the most commonplace reflection—and you know that I said I was sorry for the people."

"My object is good, as you ought to know. My object is to habituate your mind—"

"Philippa, I beg you once more to confine your exertions, in that way, to your own more lofty mind. Again I refuse to have my mind, or whatever it is that does duty for it, habituated to anything. A gracious Providence knows that I should die outright, after all my blameless life, if reduced to those horrible straits you always picture. And I have too much faith in a gracious Providence to conceive for one moment that it would treat me so. I decline the subject. Why should we make such troubles? There is clear soup for dinner, and some lovely sweet-breads. Cook has got a new receipt for bread sauce, and Jordas says that he never did shoot such a woodcock."

"Eliza, I trust that you may enjoy them all; your appetite is delicate, and you require nourishment. Why, what do I see over yonder in the snow? A slim figure moving at a very great pace, and avoiding the open places! Are my eyes growing old, or is it Lancelot?"

"Pet out in such weather, Philippa! Such a thing is simply impossible. Or at any rate I should hope so. You know that Jordas was obliged to put a set of curtains from end to end even of the bowling-alley, which is so beautifully sheltered; and even then poor Pet was sneezing. And you should have heard what he said to me, when I was afraid of the sheets taking fire from his warming-pan one night. Pet is unaccountable sometimes, I know. But the very last thing imaginable of him is that he should put his pretty feet into the snow."

"You know him best, Eliza; and it is very puzzling to distinguish things in snow. But if it was not Pet, why, it must have been a squirrel."

"The squirrels are gone to sleep for the winter, Philippa. I dare say it was only Jordas. Don't you think that it must have been Jordas?"

"I am quite certain that it was not Jordas. But I will not pretend to say that it was not a squirrel. He may forego his habitudes more easily than Lancelot."

"How horribly dry you are sometimes, Philippa. There seems to be no softness in your nature. You are fit to do battle with fifty lawyers; and I pity Mr. Jellicorse, with his best clothes on."

"You could commit no greater error. We pay the price of his black silk stockings three times over, every time we see him. The true objects of pity are —you, I, and the estates."

"Well, let us drop it for a while. If you begin upon that nauseous subject, not a particle of food will pass my lips; and I did look forward to a little nourishment."

"Dinner, my ladies!" cried the well-appointed Welldrum, throwing open the door as only such a man can do, while cleverly accomplishing the necessary bow, which he clinched on such occasions with a fine smack of his lips.

"Go and tell Mr. Lancelot, if you please, that we are waiting for him." A great point was made, but not always effected, of having Master Pet, in very gorgeous attire, to lead his aunt into the dining-room. It was fondly believed that this impressed him with the elegance and nice humanities required by his lofty position and high walk in life. Pet hated this performance, and generally spoiled it by making a face over his shoulder at old Welldrum, while he strode along in real or mock awe of Aunt Philippa.

"If you please, my ladies," said the butler now, choosing Mrs. Carnaby for his eyes to rest on, "Mr. Lancelot beg to be excoosed of dinner. His head is that bad that he have gone for open air."

"Snow-headache is much in our family; Eliza, you remember how our dear father used to feel it." With these words Mistress Yordas led her sister to the dining-room; and they took good care to say nothing more about it before the officious Welldrum.

Pet meanwhile was beginning to repent of his cold and lonely venture. For a mile or two the warmth of his mind and the glow of exercise sustained him; and he kept on admiring his own courage till his feet began to tingle. "Insie will be bound to kiss me now; and she never will be able to laugh at me again," he said to himself some fifty times. "I am like the great poet who describes the snow; and I have got some cherry-brandy." He trudged on very bravely; but his poor dear toes at every step grew colder. Out upon the moor, where he was now, no shelter of any kind encouraged him; no mantlet of bank, or ridge, or brush-wood, set up a furry shiver betwixt him and the tatterdemalion wind. Not even a naked rock stood up to comfort a man by looking colder than himself.

But in truth there was no severe cold yet; no depth of snow, no intensity of frost, no splintery needles of sparkling drift; but only the beginning of the wintry time, such as makes a strong man pick his feet up, and a healthy boy start an imaginary slide. The wind, however, was shrewd and searching, and Lancelot was accustomed to a warming-pan. Inside his waistcoat he wore a hare-skin, and his heart began to give rapid thumps against it. He knew that he was going into bodily peril worse than any frost or snow.

For a long month he had not even seen his Insie, and his hot young heart had never before been treated so contemptuously. He had been allowed to show himself in the gill at his regular interval, a fortnight ago. But no one had ventured forth to meet him, or even wave signal of welcome or farewell. But that he could endure, because he had been warned not to hope for much that Friday; now, however, it was not his meaning to put up with any more such nonsense. That he, who had been told by the servants continually that all the land for miles and miles around was his, should be shut out like a beggar, and compelled to play bo-peep, by people who lived in a hole in the ground, was a little more than in the whole entire course of his life he could ever have imagined. His mind was now made up to let them know who he was and what he was; and unless they were very quick in coming to their senses, Jordas should have orders to turn them out, and take Insie altogether away from them.

But in spite of all brave thoughts and words, Master Pet began to spy about very warily, ere ever he descended from the moor into the gill. He seemed to have it borne in upon his mind that territorial rights—however large and goodly—may lead only to a taste of earth, when earth alone is witness to the treatment of her claimant. Therefore it behooved him to look sharp; and possessing the family gift of keen sight, he began to spy about, almost as shrewdly as if he had been educated in free trade. But first he had wit enough to step below the break, and get behind a gorse bush, lest haply he should illustrate only the passive voice of seeing.

In the deep cut of the glen there was very little snow, only a few veins and patches here and there, threading and seaming the steep, as if a white-footed hare had been coursing about. Little stubby brier shoots, and clumps of russet bracken, and dead heather, ruffling like a brown dog's back, broke the dull surface of withered herbage, thistle stumps, teasels, rugged banks, and naked brush. Down in the bottom the noisy brook was scurrying over its pebbles brightly, or plunging into gloom of its own production; and away at the bend of the valley was seen the cot of poor Lancelot's longing.

The situation was worth a sigh, and came half way to share one; Pet sighed heavily, and deeply felt how wrong it was of any one to treat him so. What could be easier for him than to go, as Insie had said to him at least a score of times, and mind his own business, and shake off the dust—or the mud—of his feet at such strangers? But, alas! he had tried it, and could shake nothing, except his sad and sapient head. How deplorably was he altered from the Pet that used to be! Where were now his lofty joys, the pleasure he found in wholesome mischief and wholesale destruction, the high delight of frightening all the world about his safety?

"There are people here, I do believe," he said to himself, most touchingly, "who would be quite happy to chop off my head!"

As if to give edge to so murderous a thought, and wings to the feet of the thinker, a man both tall and broad came striding down the cottage garden. He was swinging a heavy axe as if it were a mere dress cane, and now and then dealing clean slash of a branch, with an air which made Pet shiver worse than any wind. The poor lad saw that in the grasp of such a man he could offer less resistance than a nut within the crackers, and even his champion, the sturdy Jordas, might struggle without much avail. He gathered in his legs, and tucked his head well under the gorse to watch him.

"Surely he is too big to run very fast," thought the boy, with his valor evaporated; "it must be that horrible Maunder. What a blessing that I stopped up here just in time! He is going up the gill to cleave some wood. Shall I cut away at once, or lie flat upon my stomach? He would be sure to see me if I tried to run away; and much he would care for his landlord!"

In such a choice of evils, poor Lancelot resolved to lie still, unless the monster should turn his steps that way. And presently he had the heart-felt pleasure of seeing the formidable stranger take the track that followed the windings of the brook. But instead of going well away, and rounding the next corner, the big man stopped at the very spot where Insie used to fill her pitcher, pulled off his coat and hung it on a bush, and began with mighty strokes to fell a dead alder-tree that stood there. As his great arms swung, and his back rose and fell, and the sway of his legs seemed to shake the bank, and the ring of his axe filled the glen with echoes, wrath and terror were fighting a hot battle in the heart of Lancelot.

His sense of a land-owner's rights and titles had always been most imperious, and though the Scargate estates were his as yet only in remainder, he was even more jealous about them than if he held them already in possession. What right had this man to cut down trees, to fell and appropriate timber? Even in the garden which he rented he could not rightfully touch a stick or stock. But to come out here, a good furlong from his renting, and begin hacking and hewing, quite as if the land were his—it seemed almost too brazen-faced for belief! It must be stopped at once—such outrageous trespass stopped, and punished sternly. He would stride down the hill with a summary veto—but, alas, if he did, he might get cut down too!

Not only this disagreeable reflection, but also his tender regard for Insie, prevented him from challenging this process of the axe; but his feelings began to goad him toward something worthy of a Yordas—for a Yordas he always accounted himself, and not by any means a Carnaby. And to this end all the powers of his home conspired.

"That fellow is terribly big and strong," he said to himself, with much warmth of spirit; "but his axe is getting dull; and to chop down that tree of mine will take him at least half an hour. Dead wood is harder to cut than live. And when he has done that, he must work till dark to lop the branches, and so on. I need not be afraid of anybody but this fellow. Now is my time, then, while he is away. Even if the old folk are at home, they will listen to my reasons. The next time he comes to hack my tree on this side, I shall slip out, and go down to the cottage. I have no fear of any one that pays any heed to reason."

This sudden admirer and lover of reason cleverly carried out his bold discretion. For now the savage woodman, intent upon that levelling which is the highest glory of pugnacious minds, came round the tree, glaring at it (as if it were the murderer, and he the victim), redoubling his tremendous thwacks at every sign of tremor, flinging his head back with a spiteful joy, poising his shoulders on the swing, and then with all his weight descending into the trenchant blow. When his back was fairly turned on Lancelot, and his whole mind and body thus absorbed upon his prey, the lad rose quickly from his lair, and slipped over the crest of the gill to the moorland. In a moment he was out of sight to that demon of the axe, and gliding, with his head bent low, along a little hollow of the heathery ground, which cut off a bend of the ravine, and again struck its brink a good furlong down the gill. Here Pet stopped running, and lay down, and peered over the brink, for this part was quite new to him, and resolved as he was to make a bold stroke of it, he naturally wished to see how the land lay, and what the fortress of the enemy was like, ere ever he ventured into it.

CHAPTER XXXIX

BATTERY AND ASSUMPSIT

That little moorland glen, whose only murmur was of wavelets, and principal traffic of birds and rabbits, even at this time of year looked pretty, with the winter light winding down its shelter and soft quietude. Ferny pitches and grassy bends set off the harsh outline of rock and shale, while a white mist (quivering like a clew above the rivulet) was melting into the faint blue haze diffused among the foldings and recesses of the land. On the hither side, nearly at the bottom of the slope, a bright green spot among the brown and yellow roughness, looking by comparison most smooth and rich, showed where the little cottage grew its vegetables, and even indulged in a small attempt at fruit. Behind this, the humble retirement of the cot was shielded from the wind by a breastwork of bold rock, fringed with ground-ivy, hanging broom, and silver stars of the carline. So simple and low was the building, and so matched with the colors around it, that but for the smoke curling up from a pipe of red pottery-ware, a stranger might almost have overlooked it. The walls were made from the rocks close by, the roof of fir slabs thatched with ling; there was no upper story, and (except the door and windows) all the materials seemed native and at home. Lancelot had heard, by putting a crafty question in safe places, that the people of the gill here had built their own dwelling, a good many years ago; and it looked as if they could have done it easily.

Now, if he intended to spy out the land, and the house as well, before the giant of the axe returned, there was no time to lose in beginning. He had a good deal of sagacity in tricks, and some practice in little arts of robbery. For before he attained to this exalted state of mind one of his favorite pastimes had been a course of stealthy raids upon the pears in Scargate garden. He might have had as many as he liked for asking; but what flavor would they have thus possessed? Moreover, he bore a noble spite against the gardener, whose special pride was in that pear wall; and Pet more than once had the joy of beholding him thrash his own innocent son for the dark disappearance of Beurre and Bergamot. Making good use of this experience, he stole his way down the steep glen-side, behind the low fence of the garden, until he reached the bottom, and the brush-wood by the stream. Here he stopped to observe again, and breathe, and get his spirit up. The glassy water looked as cold as death; and if he got cramp in his feet, how could he run? And yet he could see no other way but wading, of approaching the cottage unperceived.

Now fortune (whose privilege it is to cast mortals into the holes that most misfit them) sometimes, when she has got them there, takes pity, and contemptuously lifts them. Pet was in a hole of hardship, such as his dear mamma never could have dreamed of, and such as his nurture and constitution made trebly disastrous for him. He had taken a chill from his ambush, and fright, and the cold wind over the snow of the moor; and now the long wading of that icy water might have ended upon the shores of Acheron. However, he was just about to start upon that passage—for the spirit of his race was up—when a dull grating sound, as of footsteps crunching grit, came to his prettily concave ears.

At this sound Lancelot Carnaby stopped from his rash venture into the water, and drew himself back into an ivied bush, which served as the finial of the little garden hedge. Peeping through this, he could see that the walk from the cottage to the hedge was newly sprinkled with gray wood ash, perhaps to prevent the rain from lodging and the snow from lying there. Heavy steps of two old men (as Pet in the insolence of young days called them) fell upon the dull soft crust, and ground it, heel and toe—heel first, as stiff joints have it—with the bruising snip a hungry cow makes, grazing wiry grasses. "One of them must be Insie's dad," said Pet to himself, as he crouched more closely behind the hedge; "which of them, I wonder? Well, the tall one, I suppose, to go by the height of that Maunder. And the other has only one arm; and a man with one arm could never have built their house. They are coming to sit on that bench; I shall hear every word they say, and learn some of their secrets that I never could get out of Insie one bit of. But I wonder who that other fellow is?"

That other fellow, in spite of his lease, would promptly have laid his surviving hand to the ear of Master Lancelot, or any other eavesdropper; for a sturdy and resolute man was he, being no less than our ancient friend and old soldier, Jack of the Smithies. And now was verified that homely proverb that listeners never hear good of themselves.

"Sit down, my friend," said the elder of the twain, a man of rough dress and hard hands, but good, straightforward aspect, and that careless humor which generally comes from a life of adventures, and a long acquaintance with the world's caprice. "I have brought you here that we may be undisturbed. Little pitchers have long ears. My daughter is as true as steel; but this matter is not for her at present. You are sure, then, that Sir Duncan is come home at last? And he wished that I should know it?"

"Yes, sir, he wished that you should know it. So soon as I told him that you was here, and leading what one may call this queer life, he slapped his thigh like this here—for he hath a downright way of everything—and he said,

'Now, Smithies, so soon as you get home, go and tell him that I am coming. I can trust him as I trust myself; and glad I am for one old friend in the parts I am such a stranger to. Years and years I have longed to know what was become of my old friend Bert.' Tears was in his eyes, your honor: Sir Duncan hath seen such a mighty lot of men, that his heart cometh up to the few he hath found deserving of the name, sir."

"You said that you saw him at York, I think?"

"Yes, sir, at the business house of his agent, one Master Geoffrey Mordacks. He come there quite unexpected, I believe, to see about something else he hath in hand, and I got a message to go there at once. I save his life once in India, sir, from one of they cursed Sours, which made him take heed of me, and me of him. And then it come out where I come from, and why; and the both of us spoke the broad Yorkshire together, like as I dea naa care to do to home. After that he got on wonderful, as you know; and I stuck to him through the whole of it, from luck as well as liking, till, if I had gone out to see to his breeches, I could not very well have knowed more of him. And I tell you, sir, not to regard him for a Yordas. He hath a mind far above them lot; though I was born under them, to say so!"

"And you think that he will come and recover his rights, in spite of his father's will against him. I know nothing of the ladies of the Hall; but it seems a hard thing to turn them out, after being there so long."

"Who was turned out first, they or him? Five-and-twenty years of tent, open sky, jungle, and who knows what, for him—but eider-down, and fireside, and fat of land for them! No, no, sir; whatever shall happen there, will be God's own justice."

"Of His justice who shall judge?" said Insie's father, quietly. "But is there not a young man grown, who passes for the heir with every one?"

"Ay, that there is; and the best game of all will be neck and crop for that young scamp. A bully, a coward, a puling milksop, is all the character he beareth. He giveth himself born airs, as if every inch of the Riding belonged to him. He hath all the viciousness of Yordas, without the pluck to face it out. A little beast that hath the venom, without the courage, of a toad. Ah, how I should like to see—"

Jack of the Smithies not only saw, but felt. The Yordas blood was up in Pet. He leaped through the hedge and struck this man with a sharp quick fist in either eye. Smithies fell backward behind the bench, his heels danced in the air, and the stump of his arm got wedged in the stubs of a bush, while Lancelot glared at him with mad eyes.

"What next?" said his companion, rising calmly, and steadfastly gazing at Lancelot.

"The next thing is to kill him; and it shall be done," the furious youth replied, while he swung the gentleman's big stick, which he had seized, and danced round his foe with the speed of a wild-cat. "Don't meddle, or it will be worse for you. You heard what he said of me. Get out of the way."

"Indeed, my young friend, I shall do nothing of the sort." But the old man was not at all sure that he could do much; such was the fury and agility of the youth, who jumped three yards for every step of his, while the poor old soldier could not move. The boy skipped round the protecting figure, whose grasp he eluded easily, and swinging the staff with both arms, aimed a great blow at the head of his enemy. Suddenly the other interposed the bench, upon which the stick fell, and broke short; and before the assailant could recover from the jerk, he was a prisoner in two powerful old arms.

"You are so wild that we must make you fast," his captor said, with a benignant smile; and struggle as he might, the boy was very soon secured. His antagonist drew forth a red bandana handkerchief, and fastened his bleeding hands behind his back. "There, now, lad," he said, "you can do no mischief. Recover your temper, sir, and tell us who you are, as soon as you are sane enough to know."

Pet, having spent his just indignation, began to perceive that he had made a bad investment. His desire had been to maintain in this particular spot strict privacy from all except Insie, to whom in the largeness of love he had declared himself. Yet here he stood, promulged and published, strikingly and flagrantly pronounced! At first he was like to sulk in the style of a hawk who has failed of his swoop; but seeing his enemy arising slowly with grunts, and action nodose and angular—rather than flexibly graceful—contempt became the uppermost feature of his mind.

"My name," he said, "if you are not afraid of it, that you tie me in this cowardly low manner, is—Lancelot Yordas Carnaby."

"My boy, it is a long name for any one to carry. No wonder that you look weak beneath it. And where do you live, young gentleman?"

Amazement sat upon the face of Pet—a genuine astonishment, entirely pure from wrath. It was wholly beyond his imagination that any one, after hearing his name, should have to ask him where he lived. He thought that the question must be put in low mockery, and to answer was far beneath his dignity.

By this time the veteran Jack of the Smithies had got out of his trap, and was standing stiffly, passing his hand across his sadly smitten eyes, and talking to himself about them.

"Two black eyes, at my time of life, as sure as I'm a Christian! Howsomever, young chap, I likes you better. Never dreamed there was such good stuff in you. Master Bert, cast him loose, if so please you. Let me shake hands with 'un, and bear no malice. Bad words deserve hard blows, and I ask his pardon for driving him into it. I called 'un a milksop, and he hath proved me a liar. He may be a bad 'un, but with good stuff in 'un. Lord bless me, I never would have believed the lad could hit so smartly!"

Pet was well pleased with this tribute to his prowess; but as for shaking hands with a tenant, and a "common man"—as every one not of gentle birth was then called—such an act was quite below him, or above him, according as we take his own opinion, or the truth. And possibly he rose in Smithies' mind by drawing back from bodily overture.

Mr. Bert looked on with all the bliss of an ancient interpreter. He could follow out the level of the vein of each, as no one may do except a gentleman, perhaps, who has turned himself deliberately into a "common man." Bert had done his utmost toward this end; but the process is difficult when voluntary.

"I think it is time," he now said, firmly, to the unshackled and triumphant Pet, "for Lancelot Yordas Carnaby to explain what has brought him into such humble quarters, and induced him to turn eavesdropper; which was not considered (at least in my young days) altogether the part of a gentleman."

The youth had not seen quite enough of the world to be pat with a fertile lie as yet; especially under such searching eyes. However, he did as much as could be well expected.

"I was just looking over my property," he said, "and I thought I heard somebody cutting down my timber. I came to see who it was, and I heard people talking, and before I could ask them about it, I heard myself abused disgracefully; and that was more than I could stand."

"We must take it for granted that a brave young gentleman of your position would tell no falsehood. You assure us, on your honor, that you heard no more?"

"Well, I heard voices, sir. But nothing to understand, or make head or tail of." There was some truth in this; for young Lancelot had not the least idea who "Sir Duncan" was. His mother and aunt had kept him wholly in the dark as to any lost uncle in India. "I should like to know what it was," he added, "if it has anything to do with me."

This was a very clever hit of his; and it made the old gentleman believe him altogether.

"All in good time, my young friend," he answered, even with a smile of some pity for the youth. "But you are scarcely old enough for business questions, although so keen about your timber. Now after abusing you so disgracefully, as I admit that my friend here has done, and after roping your pugnacious hands, as I myself was obliged to do, we never can launch you upon the moor, in such weather as this, without some food. You are not very strong, and you have overdone yourself. Let us go to the house, and have something."

Jack of the Smithies showed alacrity at this, as nearly all old soldiers must; but Pet was much oppressed with care, and the intellect in his breast diverged into sore distraction of anxious thought. Whether should he draw the keen sword of assurance, put aside the others, and see Insie, or whether should he start with best foot foremost, scurry up the hill, and avoid the axe of Maunder? Pallas counselled this course, and Aphrodite that; and the latter prevailed, as she always used to do, until she produced the present dry-cut generation.

Lancelot bowed to the gentleman of the gill, and followed him along the track of grit, which set his little pearly teeth on edge; while Jack of the Smithies led, and formed, the rear-guard. "This is coming now to something very queer," thought Pet; "after all, it might have been better for me to take my chance with the hatchet man."

Brown dusk was ripely settling down among the mossy apple-trees, and the leafless alders of the brook, and the russet and yellow memories of late autumn lingering in the glen, while the peaky little freaks of snow, and the cold sighs of the wind, suggested fireside and comfort. Mr. Bert threw open his cottage door, and bowing as to a welcome guest, invited Pet to enter. No passage, no cold entrance hall, demanded scrapes of ceremony; but here was the parlor, and the feeding-place, and the warm dance of the fire-glow. Logs that meant to have a merry time, and spread a cheerful noise abroad, ere ever they turned to embers, were snorting forth the pointed flames, and spitting soft protests of sap. And before them stood, with eyes more bright than any flash of fire-light, intent upon rich simmering scents, a lovely form, a grace of dainties—oh, a goddess certainly!

"Master Carnaby," said the host, "allow me, sir, the honor to present my daughter to you, Insie darling, this is Mr. Lancelot Yordas Carnaby. Make him a pretty courtesy."

Insie turned round with a rosy blush, brighter than the brightest fire-wood, and tried to look at Pet as if she had never even dreamed of such a being. Pet drew hard upon his heart, and stood bewildered, tranced, and dazzled. He had never seen Insie in-doors before, which makes a great difference in a girl; and the vision was too bright for him.

For here, at her own hearth, she looked so gentle, sweet, and lovely. No longer wild and shy, or gayly mischievous and watchful, but calm-eyed, firm-lipped, gravely courteous; intent upon her father's face, and banishing not into shadow so much as absolute nullity any one who dreamed that he ever filled a pitcher for her, or fed her with grouse and partridge, and committed the incredible atrocity of kissing her.

Lancelot ceased to believe it possible that he ever could have done such a thing as that, while he saw how she never would see him at all, or talk in the voice that he had been accustomed to, or even toss her head in the style he had admired, when she tried to pretend to make light of him. If she would only make light of him now, he would be well contented, and say to himself that she did it on purpose, for fear of the opposite extreme. But the worst of it was that she had quite forgotten, beyond blink of inquiry or gleam of hope, that ever in her life she had set eyes on a youth of such perfect insignificance before.

"My friend, you ought to be hungry," said Bert of the Gill, as he was proud to call himself; "after your exploit you should be fed. Your vanquished foe will sit next to you. Insie, you are harassed in mind by the countenance of our old friend Master John Smithies. He has met with a little mishap—never mind —the rising generation is quick of temper. A soldier respects his victor; it is a beautiful arrangement of Providence; otherwise wars would never cease. Now give our two guests a good dish of the best, piping hot, and of good meaty fibre. We will have our own supper by-and-by, when Maunder comes home, and your mother is ready. Gentlemen, fall to; you have far to go, and the moors are bad after night-fall."

Lancelot, proudly as he stood upon his rank, saw fit to make no objection. Not only did his inner man cry, "Feed, even though a common man feed with thee," but his mind was under the influence of a stronger one, which scorned such stuff. Moreover, Insie, for the first time, gave him a glance, demure but imperative, which meant, "Obey my father, sir."

He obeyed, and was rewarded; for the beautiful girl came round him so, to hand whatever he wanted, and seemed to feel so sweetly for him in his strange position, that he scarcely knew what he was eating, only that it savored of rich rare love, and came from the loveliest creature in the world. In stern fact, it came from the head of a sheep; but neither jaws nor teeth were seen. Upon one occasion he was almost sure that a curl of Insie's lovely hair fell upon the back of his stooping neck; he could scarcely keep himself from jumping up; and he whispered, very softly, when the old man was away, "Oh, if you would only do that again!" But his darling made manifest that this was a mistake, and applied herself sedulously to the one-armed Jack.

Jack of the Smithies was a trencherman of the very first order, and being well wedded (with a promise already of young soldiers to come), it behooved him to fill all his holes away from home, and spare his own cupboard for the sake of Mistress Smithies. He perceived the duty, and performed it, according to the discipline of the British army.

But Insie was fretting in the conscience of her heart to get the young Lancelot fed and dismissed before the return of her great wild brother. Not that he would hurt their guest, though unwelcome; or even show any sort of rudeness to him; but more than ever now, since she heard of Pet's furious onslaught upon the old soldier—which made her begin to respect him a little —she longed to prevent any meeting between this gallant and the rough Maunder. And that anxiety led her to look at Pet with a melancholy kindness. Then Jack of the Smithies cut things short.

"Off's the word," he said, "if ever I expects to see home afore daylight. All of these moors is known to me, and many's the time I have tracked them all in sleep, when the round world was betwixt us. But without any moon it is hard to do 'em waking; and the loss of my arm sends me crooked in the dark. And as for young folk, they be all abroad to once. With your leave, Master Bert, I'll be off immediate, after getting all I wants, as the manner of the world is. My good missus will be wondering what is come of me."

"You have spoken well," his host replied; "and I think we shall have a heavy fall to-night. But this young gentleman must not go home alone. He is not robust, and the way is long and rough. I have seen him shivering several times. I will fetch my staff, and march with him."

"No, sir, I will not have such a thing done," the veteran answered, sturdily. "If the young gentleman is a gentleman, he will not be afraid for me to take him home, in spite of what he hath done to me. Speak up, young man, are you frightened of me?"

"Not if you are not afraid of me," said Pet, who had now forgotten all about that Maunder, and only longed to stay where he was, and set up a delicious little series of glances. For the room, and the light, and the tenor of the place, began more and more to suit such uses. And most and best of all, his Insie was very thankful to him for his good behavior; and he scarcely could believe that she wanted him to go. To go, however, was his destiny; and when he had made a highly laudable and far-away salute, it happened—in the shift of people, and of light, and clothing, which goes on so much in the winter-time

—that a little hand came into his, and rose to his lips, with ground of action, not for assault and battery, but simply for assumpsit.

CHAPTER XL

STORMY GAP

Snowy weather now set in, and people were content to stay at home. Among the scaurs and fells and moors the most perturbed spirit was compelled to rest, or try to do so, or at any rate not agitate its body out-of-doors. Lazy folk were suited well with reason good for laziness; and gentle minds, that dreaded evil, gladly found its communication stopped.

Combined excitement and exertion, strong amazement, ardent love, and a cold of equal severity, laid poor Pet Carnaby by the heels, and reduced him to perpetual gruel. He was shut off from external commune, and strictly blockaded in his bedroom, where his only attendants were his sweet mother, and an excellent nurse who stroked his forehead, and called him "dear pet," till he hated her, and, worst of all, that Dr. Spraggs, who lived in the house, because the weather was so bad.

"We have taken a chill, and our mind is a little unhinged," said the skillful practitioner: "careful diet, complete repose, a warm surrounding atmosphere, absence of undue excitement, and, above all, a course of my gentle alteratives regularly administered—these are the very simple means to restore our beloved patient. He is certainly making progress; but I assure you, my dear madam, or rather I need not tell a lady of such wonderfully clear perception, that remedial measures must be slow to be truly efficacious. With lower organizations we may deal in a more empiric style; but no experiments must be tried here—"

"Dr. Spraggs, I should hope not, indeed. You alarm me by the mere suggestion."

"Gradation, delicately pursued, adapted subtly, discriminated nicely by the unerring diagnosis of extensive medical experience, combined with deep study of the human system, and a highly distinguished university career—such, madam, are, in my humble opinion, the true elements of permanent amelioration. At the same time we must not conceal from ourselves that our constitution is by no means one of ordinary organization. None of your hedger and ditcher class, but delicate, fragile, impulsive, sensitive, liable to inopine derangements from excessive activity of mind—"

"Oh, Dr. Spraggs, he has been reading poetry, which none of our family ever even dreamed of doing—it is a young man, over your way somewhere. Possibly you may have heard of him."

"That young man has a great deal to answer for. I have traced a very bad case of whooping-cough to him. That explains many symptoms which I could not quite make out. We will take away this book, madam, and give him Dr. Watts—the only wholesome poet that our country has produced; though even his opinions would be better expressed in prose."

But the lad, in spite of all this treatment, slowly did recover, and then obtained relief, which set him on his nimble legs again. For his aunt Philippa, one snowy morning, went into the room beneath that desperately sick chamber, to see whether wreaths of snow had entered, as they often did, between the loose joints of the casement. She walked very carefully, for fear of making a noise that might be heard above, and disturb the repose of the poor invalid. But, to her surprise, there came loud thumps from above, and a quivering of the ceiling, and a sound as of rushing steps, and laughter, and uproarious jollity.

"What can it be? I am perfectly amazed," said Mistress Yordas to herself. "I must inquire into this."

She knew that her sister was out of the way, and the nurse in the kitchen, having one of her frequent feeds and agreeable discourses. So she went to a mighty ring in her own room, as large as an untaxed carriage wheel, and from it (after due difficulty) took the spare key of the passage door that led the way to Lancelot.

No sooner had she passed this door than she heard a noise a great deal worse than the worst imagination—whiz, and hiss, and crack, and smash, and rolling of hollow things over hollow places, varied with shouts, and the flapping of skirts, and jingling of money upon heart of oak; these and many other travails of the air (including strong language) amazed the lady. Hastening into the sick-room, she found the window wide open, with the snow pouring in, a dozen of phial bottles ranged like skittles, some full and some empty, and Lancelot dancing about in his night-gown, with Divine Songs poised for another hurl.

"Two for a full, and one for an empty. Seven to me, and four to you. No cheating, now, or I'll knock you over," he was shouting to Welldrum's boy, who had clearly been smuggled in at the window for this game. "There's plenty more in old Spraggs's chest. Holloa, here's Aunt Philippa!"

Mistress Yordas was not displeased with this spirited application of pharmacy; she at once flung wide the passage door, and Pet was free of the house again, but upon parole not to venture out of doors. The first use he made of his liberty was to seek the faithful Jordas, who possessed a little private sitting-room, and there hold secret council with him.

The dogman threw his curly head back, when he had listened to his young lord's tale (which contained the truth, and nothing but the truth, yet not by any means the whole truth, for the leading figure was left out), and a snort from his broad nostrils showed contempt and strong vexation.

"Just what I said would come o' such a job," he muttered, without thought of Lancelot; "to let in a traitor, and spake him fair, and make much of him. I wish you had knocked his two eyes out, Master Lance, instead of only blacking of 'un. And a fortnight lost through that pisonin' Spraggs! And the weather going on, snow and thaw, snow and thaw. There's scarcely a dog can stand, let alone a horse, and the wreaths getting deeper. Most onlucky! It hath come to pass most ontoimely."

"But who is Sir Duncan? And who is Mr. Bert? I have told you everything, Jordas; and all you do is to tell me nothing."

"What more can I tell you, sir? You seem to know most about 'em. And what was it as took you down that way, sir, if I may make so bold to ask?"

"Jordas, that is no concern of yours; every gentleman has his own private affairs, which can not in any way concern a common man. But I wish you particularly to find out all that can be known about Mr. Bert—what made him come here, and why does he live so, and how much has he got a year? He seems to be quite a gentleman—"

"Then his private affairs, sir, can not concern a common man. You had better ways go yourself and ask him; or ask his friend with the two black eyes. Now just you do as I bid you, Master Lance. Not a word of all this here to my ladies; but think of something as you must have immediate from Middleton. Something as your health requires"—here Jordas indulged in a sarcastic grin—"something as must come, if the sky come down, or the day of Judgment was to-morrow."

"I know, yes, I am quite up to you, Jordas. Let me see: last time it was a sweet-bread. That would never do again. It shall be a hundred oysters; and Spraggs shall command it, or be turned out."

"Jordas, I really can not bear," said the kind Mrs. Carnaby, an hour afterward, "that you should seem almost to risk your life by riding to Middleton in such dreadful weather. Are you sure that it will not snow again, and quite sure that you can get through all the wreaths? If not, I would on no account have you go. Perhaps, after all, it is but the fancy of a poor fantastic invalid, though Dr. Spraggs feels that it is so important, and may be the turning-point in his sad illness. It seems such a long way in such weather; and selfish people, who can never understand, might say that it was quite unkind of us. But if you have made up your mind to go, in spite of all remonstrance, you must be sure to come back to-night; and do please to see that the oysters are round, and have not got any of their lids up."

The dogman knew well that he jeopardized his life in either half of the journey; no little in going, and tenfold as much in returning through the snows of night. Though the journey in the first place had been of his own seeking, and his faithful mind was set upon it, some little sense of bitterness was in his heart, that his life was not thought more of. He made a low bow, and turned away, that he might not meet those eyes so full of anxiety for another, and of none for him. And when he came to think of it, he was sorry afterward for indulging in a little bit of two-edged satire.

"Will you please to ask my lady if I may take Marmaduke? Or whether she would be afeared to risk him in such weather?"

"I think it is unkind of you to speak like that. I need not ask my sister, as you ought to know. Of course you may take Marmaduke. I need not tell you to be careful of him."

After that, if he had chosen for himself, he would not have taken Marmaduke. But he thought of the importance of his real purpose, and could trust no other horse to get him through it.

In fine summer weather, when the sloughs were in, and the water-courses low or dry, and the roads firm, wherever there were any, a good horse and rider, well acquainted with the track, might go from Scargate Hall to Middleton in about three hours, nearly all of the journey being well down hill. But the travel to come back was a very different thing; four hours and a half was quick time for it, even in the best state of earth and sky, and the Royal Mail pony was allowed a good seven, because his speed (when first established) had now impaired his breathing. And ever since the snow set in, he had received his money for the journey, but preferred to stay in stable; for which everybody had praised him, finding letters give them indigestion.

Now Jordas roughed Marmaduke's shoes himself; for the snow would be frozen in the colder places, and ball wherever any softness was—two things which demand very different measures. Also he fed him well, and nourished himself, and took nurture for the road; so that with all haste he could not manage to start before twelve of the day. Travelling was worse than he expected, and the snow very deep in places, especially at Stormy Gap, about a league from Scargate. Moreover, he knew that the strength of his horse must be carefully husbanded for the return; and so it was dusk of the winter evening, and the shops of the little town were being lit with hoops of candles, when Jordas, followed by Saracen, came trotting through the unpretending street.

That ancient dog Saracen, the largest of the blood-hounds, had joined the expedition as a volunteer, craftily following and crouching out of sight, until he was certain of being too far from home to be sent back again. Then he boldly appeared, and cantered gayly on in front of Marmaduke, with his heavy dewlaps laced with snow.

Jordas put up at a quiet old inn, and had Saracen chained strongly to a ringbolt in the stable; then he set off afoot to see Mr. Jellicorse, and just as he rang the office bell a little fleecy twinkle fell upon one of his eyelashes, and looking sharply up, he saw that a snowy night was coming.

The worthy lawyer received him kindly, but not at all as if he wished to see him; for Christmas-tide was very nigh at hand, and the weather made the ink go thick, and only a clerk who was working for promotion would let his hat stay on its peg after the drum and fife went by, as they always did at dusk of night, to frighten Bonyparty.

"There are only two important facts in all you have told me, Jordas," Mr. Jellicorse said, when he had heard him out: "one that Sir Duncan is come home, of which I was aware some time ago; and the other that he has been consulting an agent of the name of Mordacks, living in this county. That certainly looks as if he meant to take some steps against us. But what can he do more than might have been done five-and-twenty years ago?" The lawyer took good care to speak to none but his principals concerning that plaguesome deed of appointment.

"Well, sir, you know best, no doubt. Only that he hath the money now, by all accounts; and like enough he hath labored for it a' purpose to fight my ladies. If your honor knew as well as I do what a Yordas is for fighting, and for downright stubbornness—"

"Perhaps I do," replied the lawyer, with a smile; "but if he has no children of his own, as I believe is the case with him, it seems unlikely that he would risk his substance in a rash attempt to turn out those who are his heirs."

"He is not so old but what he might have children yet, if he hath none now to hand. Anyways it was my duty to tell you my news immediate."

"Jordas, I always say that you are a model of a true retainer—a character becoming almost extinct in this faithless and revolutionary age. Very few men would have ridden into town through all those dangerous unmade roads, in weather when even the Royal Mail is kept, by the will of the Lord, in stable."

"Well, sir," said Jordas, with his brave soft smile, "the smooth and the rough of it comes in and out, accordin'. Some days I does next to nought; and some days I earns my keepin'. Any more commands for me, Lawyer

Jellicoose? Time cometh on rather late for starting."

"Jordas, you amaze me! You never mean to say that you dream of setting forth again on such a night as this is? I will find you a bed; you shall have a hot supper. What would your ladies think of me, if I let you go forth among the snow again? Just look at the window-panes, while you and I were talking! And the feathers of the ice shooting up inside, as long as the last sheaf of quills I opened for them. Quills, quills, quills, all day! And when I buy a goose unplucked, if his quills are any good, his legs won't carve, and his gizzard is full of gravel-stones! Ah, the world grows every day in roguery."

"All the world agrees to that, sir; ever since I were as high as your table, never I hear two opinions about it; and it maketh a man seem to condemn himself. Good-night, sir, and I hope we shall have good news so soon as his Royal Majesty the king affordeth a pony as can lift his legs."

Mr. Jellicorse vainly strove to keep the man in town that night. He even called for his sensible wife and his excellent cook to argue, having no clerk left to make scandal of the scene. The cook had a turn of mind for Jordas, and did think that he would stop for her sake; and she took a broom to show him what the depth of snow was upon the red tiles between the brew-house and the kitchen. An icicle hung from the lip of the pump, and new snow sparkled on the cook's white cap, and the dark curly hair which she managed to let fall; the brew-house smelled nice, and the kitchen still nicer; but it made no difference to Jordas. If he had told them the reason of this hurry, they would have said hard things about it, perhaps; Mrs. Jellicorse especially (being well read in the Scriptures, and fond of quoting them against all people who had grouse and sent her none) would have called to mind what David said, when the three mighty men broke through the host, and brought water from the well of Bethlehem. So Jordas only answered that he had promised to return, and a trifle of snow improved the travelling.

"A willful man must have his way," said Mr. Jellicorse at last. "We can not put him in the pound, Diana; but the least we can do is to provide him for a coarse, cold journey. If I know anything of our country, he will never see Scargate Hall to-night, but his blanket will be a snowdrift. Give him one of our new whitneys to go behind his saddle, and I will make him take two things. I am your legal adviser, Jordas, and you are like all other clients. Upon the main issue, you cast me off; but in small matters you must obey me."

The hardy dogman was touched with this unusual care for his welfare. At home his services were accepted as a due, requiring little praise and less of gratitude. It was his place to do this and that, and be thankful for the privilege. But his comfort was left for himself to study; and if he had studied it much, reproach would soon have been the chief reward. It never would do, as his ladies said, to make too much of Jordas. He would give himself airs, and think that people could not get on without him.

Marmaduke looked fresh and bold when he came out of stable; he had eaten with pleasure a good hot dinner, or supper perhaps he considered it, liking to have his meals early, as horses generally do. And he neighed and capered for the homeward road, though he knew how full it was of hardships; for never yet looked horse through bridle, without at least one eye resilient toward the charm of headstall. And now he had both eyes fixed with legitimate aim in that direction; and what were a few tiny atoms of snow to keep a big horse from his household?

Merrily, therefore, he set forth, with a sturdy rider on his back; his clear neigh rang through the thick dull streets, and kind people came to their white blurred windows, and exclaimed, as they glanced at the party-colored horseman rushing away into the dreary depths, "Well, rather him than me, thank God!"

"You keep the dog," Master Jordas had said to the hostler, before he left the yard; "he is like a lamb, when you come to know him. I can't be plagued with him to-night. Here's a half crown for his victuals; he eats precious little for the size of him. A bullock's liver every other day, and a pound and a half the between times. Don't be afeared of him. He looks like that, to love you, man."

Instead of keeping on the Durham side of Tees, as he would have done in fair weather for the first six miles or so, Jordas crossed by the old town bridge into his native county. The journey would be longer thus, but easier in some places, and the track more plain to follow, which on a snowy night was everything. For all things now were in one indiscriminate pelt and whirl of white; the Tees was striped with rustling floes among the black moor-water; and the trees, as long as there were any, bent their shrouded forms and moaned.

But with laborious plunges, and broad scatterings of obstruction, the willing horse ploughed out his way, himself the while wrapped up in white, and caked in all his tufty places with a crust that flopped up and down. The rider, himself piled up with snow, and bearded with a berg of it, from time to time, with his numb right hand, fumbled at the frozen clouts that clogged the poor horse's mane and crest.

"How much longer will a' go, I wonder?" said Jordas to himself for the twentieth time. "The Lord in heaven knows where we be; but horse knows better than the Lord a'most. Two hour it must be since ever I 'tempted to make head or tail of it. But Marmaduke knoweth when a' hath his head; these creatures is wiser than Christians. Save me from the witches, if I ever see such weather! And I wish that Master Lance's oysters wasn't quite so much like him."

For, broad as his back was, perpetual thump of rugged and flintified knobs and edges, through the flag basket strapped over his neck, was beginning to tell upon his stanch but jolted spine; while his foot in the northern stirrup was numbed, and threatening to get frost-bitten.

"The Lord knoweth where we be," he said once more, growing in piety as the peril grew. "What can old horse know, without the Lord hath told 'un? And likely he hath never asked, no more than I did. We mought 'a come twelve moiles, or we mought 'a come no more than six. What ever is there left in the world to judge by? The hills, or the hollows, or the boskies, all is one, so far as the power of a man's eyes goes. Howsomever, drive on, old Dukie."

Old Dukie drove on with all his might and main, and the stout spirit which engenders strength, till he came to a white wall reared before him, twice as high as his snow-capped head, and swirling like a billow of the sea with drift. Here he stopped short, for he had his own rein, and turned his clouted neck, and asked his master what to make of it.

"We must 'a come at last to Stormy Gap: it might be worse, and it might be better. Rocks o' both sides, and no way round. No choice but to get through it, or to spend the night inside of it. You and I are a pretty good weight, old Dukie. We'll even try a charge for it, afore we knock under. We can't have much more smother than we've gotten already. My father was taken like this, I've heard tell, in the service of old Squire Philip; and he put his nag at it, and scumbled through. But first you get up your wind, old chap."

Marmaduke seemed to know what was expected of him; for he turned round, retreated a few steps, and then stood panting. Then Jordas dismounted, as well as he could with his windward leg nearly frozen. He smote himself lustily, with both arms swinging, upon his broad breast, and he stamped in the snow till he felt his tingling feet again. Then he took up the skirt of his thick heavy coat, and wiped down the head, mane, and shoulders of the horse, and the great pile of snow upon the crupper. "Start clear is a good word," he said.

For a moment he stopped to consider the forlorn hope of his last resolution. "About me, there is no such great matter," he thought; "but if I was to kill Dukie, who would ever hear the last of it? And what a good horse he have been, to be sure! But if I was to leave him so, the crows would only have him. We be both in one boat; we must try of it." He said a little prayer, which was all he knew, for himself and a lass he had a liking to, who lived in a mill upon the river Lune; and then he got into the saddle again, and set his teeth hard, and spoke to Marmaduke, a horse who would never be touched with a spur. "Come on, old chap," was all he said.

The horse looked about in the thick of the night, as the head of the horse peers out of the cloak, in Welsh mummery, at Christmas-tide. The thick of the night was light and dark, with the dense intensity of down-pour; light in itself, and dark with shutting out all sight of everything—a close-at-hand confusion, and a distance out of measure. The horse, with his wise snow-crusted eyes, took in all the winnowing of light among the draff, and saw no possibility of breaking through, but resolved to spend his life as he was ordered. No power of rush or of dash could he gather, because of the sinking of his feet; the main chance was of bulk and weight; and his rider left him free to choose. For a few steps he walked, nimbly picking up his feet, and then, with a canter of the best spring he could compass, hurled himself into the depth of the drift, while Jordas lay flat along his neck, and let him plunge. For a few yards the light snow flew before him, like froth of the sea before a broad-bowed ship, and smothered as he was, he fought onward for his life. But very soon the power of his charge was gone, his limbs could not rise, and his breath was taken from him; the hole that he had made was filled up behind him; fresh volumes from the shaken height came pouring down upon him; his flanks and his back were wedged fast in the cumber, and he stood still and trembled, being buried alive.

Jordas, with a great effort, threw himself off, and put his hat before his mouth, to make himself a breathing space. He scarcely knew whether he stood or lay; but he kicked about for want of air, and the more he kicked the worse it was, as in the depth of nightmare. Blindness, choking, smothering, and freezing fell in a lump upon his poor body now, and the shrieking of the horse and the panting of his struggles came, by some vibration, to him.

But just as he began to lose his wits, sink away backward, and gasp for breath, a gleam of light broke upon his closing eyes; he gathered the remnant of his strength, struck for it, and was in a space of free air. After several long pants he looked around, and found that a thicket of stub oak jutting from the crag of the gap had made a small alcove with billows of snow piled over it. Then the brave spirit of the man came forth. "There is room for Dukie as well as me," he gasped; "with God's help, I will fetch him in."

Weary as he was, he cast himself back into the wall of snow, and listened. At first he heard nothing, and made sure that all was over; but presently a faint soft gurgle, like a dying sob, came through the murk. With all his might he dashed toward the sound, and laid hold of a hairy chin just foundering. "Rise up, old chap," he tried to shout, and he gave the horse a breath or two with the broad-brimmed hat above his nose. Then Marmaduke rallied for one last fight, with the surety of a man to help him. He staggered forward to the leading of the hand he knew so well, and fell down upon his knees; but his head was clear, and he drew long breaths, and his heart was glad, and his eyes looked up, and he gave a feeble whinny.

CHAPTER XLI

BAT OF THE GILL

Upon that same evening the cottage in the gill was well snowed up, as befell it every winter, more or less handsomely, according to the wind. The wind was in the right way to do it truly now, with just enough draught to pile bountiful wreaths, and not enough of wild blast to scatter them again. "Bat of the Gill," as Mr. Bert was called, sat by the fire, with his wife and daughter, and listened very calmly to the whistle of the wind, and the sliding of the soft fall that blocked his window-panes.

Insie was reading, Mrs. Bert was knitting stockings, and Mr. Bert was thinking of his own strange life. It never once occurred to him that great part of its strangeness sprang from the oddities of his own nature, any more than a man who has been in a quarrel believes that he could have kept out of it. "Matters beyond my own control have forced me to do this and that," is the sure belief of every man whose life has run counter to his fellows, through his own inborn diversity. In this man's nature were two strange points, sure (if they are strong enough to survive experience) to drive anybody into strange ways: he did not care for money, and he contemned rank.

How these two horrible twists got into his early composition is more than can be told, and in truth it does not matter. But being quite incurable, and meeting with no sympathy, except among people who aspired to them only, and failed—if they ever got the chance of failing—these depravations from the standard of mankind drove Christopher Bert from the beaten tracks of life. Providence offered him several occasions of return into the ordinary course; for after he had cast abroad a very nice inheritance, other two fortunes fell to him, but found him as difficult as ever to stay with. Not that he was lavish upon luxury of his own, for no man could have simpler tastes, but that he weakly believed in the duty of benevolence, and the charms of gratitude. Of the latter it is needless to say that he got none, while with the former he produced some harm. When all his bread was cast upon the waters, he set out to earn his own crust as best he might.

Hence came a chapter of accidents, and a volume of motley incidents in various climes, and upon far seas. Being a very strong, active man, with gift of versatile hand and brain, and early acquaintance with handicrafts, Christopher Bert could earn his keep, and make in a year almost as much as he used to give away, or lend without redemption, in a general day of his wealthy time. Hard labor tried to make him sour, but did not succeed therein.

Yet one thing in all this experience vexed him more than any hardship, to wit, that he never could win true fellowship among his new fellows in the guild of labor. Some were rather surly, others very pleasant (from a warm belief that he must yet come into money); but whatsomever or whosoever they were, or of whatever land, they all agreed that Christopher Bert was not of their communion. Manners, appearance, education, freedom from prejudice, and other wide diversities marked him as an interloper, and perhaps a spy, among the enlightened working-men of the period. Over and over again he strove to break down this barrier; but thrice as hard he might have striven, and found it still too strong for him. This and another circumstance at last impressed him with the superior value of his own society. Much as he loved the working-man—in spite of all experience of him—that worthy fellow would not have it, but felt a truly and piously hereditary scorn for "a gentleman as took a order, when, but for being a blessed fool, he might have stood there giving it."

The other thing that helped to drive him from this very dense array was his own romantic marriage, and the copious birth of children. After the sensitive age was past, and when the sensibles ought to reign—for then he was past five-and-thirty—he fell (for the first time of his life) into a violent passion of love for a beautiful Jewish maid barely turned seventeen; Zilpah admired him, for he was of noble aspect, rich with variety of thoughts and deeds. With women he had that peculiar power which men of strong character possess; his voice was like music, and his words as good as poetry, and he scarcely ever seemed to contradict himself. Very soon Zilpah adored him; and then he gave notice to her parents that she was to be his wife. These stared considerably, being very wealthy people, of high Jewish blood (and thus the oldest of the old), and steadfast most—where all are steadfast—to their own race of religion. Finding their astonishment received serenely, they locked up their daughter, with some strong expressions; which they redoubled when they found the door wide open in the morning. Zilpah was gone, and they scratched out her name from the surface of their memories.

Christopher Bert, being lawfully married—for the local restrictions scorned the case of a foreigner and a Jewess—crossed the Polish frontier with his mules and tools, and drove his little covered cart through Austria. And here he lit upon, and helped in some predicament of the road, a spirited young Englishman undergoing the miseries of the grand tour, the son and heir of Philip Yordas. Duncan was large and crooked of thought—as every true Yordas must be—and finding a mind in advance of his own by several years of such sallyings, and not yet even swerving toward the turning goal of corpulence, the young man perceived that he had hit upon a prophet.

For Bert scarcely ever talked at all of his generous ideas. A prophet's proper mantle is the long cloak of Harpocrates, and his best vaticinations are inspired more than uttered. So it came about that Duncan Yordas, difficult as he was to lead, largely shared the devious courses of Christopher Bert the workman, and these few months of friendship made a lasting mark upon the younger man.

Soon after this a heavy blow befell the ingenious wanderer. Among his many arts and trades, he had some knowledge of engineering, or at any rate much boldness of it; which led him to conceive a brave idea concerning some tributary of the Po. The idea was sound and fine, and might have led to many blessings; but Nature, enjoying her bad work best, recoiled upon her improver. He left an oozy channel drying (like a glanderous sponge) in August; and virulent fever came into his tent. All of his eight children died except his youngest son Maunder; his own strong frame was shaken sadly; and his loving wife lost all her strength and buxom beauty. He gathered the remnants of his race, and stricken but still unconquered, took his way to a long-forgotten land. "The residue of us must go home," he said, after all his wanderings.

In London, of course, he was utterly forgotten, although he had spent much substance there, in the days of sanguine charity. Durham was his native county, where he might have been a leading man, if more like other men. "Cosmopolitan" as he was, and strong in his own opinions still, the force of years, and sorrow, and long striving, told upon him. He had felt a longing to mend the kettles of the house that once was his; but when he came to the brink of Tees his stout heart failed, and he could not cross.

Instead of that he turned away, to look for his old friend Yordas; not to be patronized by him—for patronage he would have none—but from hankering after a congenial mind, and to touch upon kind memories. Yordas was gone, as pure an outcast as himself, and his name almost forbidden there. He thought it a part of the general wrong, and wandered about to see the land, with his eyes wide open as usual.

There was nothing very beautiful in the land, and nothing at all attractive, except that it commanded length of view, and was noble in its rugged strength. This, however, pleased him well, and here he resolved to set up his staff, if means could be found to make it grow. From the higher fells he could behold (whenever the weather encouraged him) the dromedary humps of certain hills, at the tail whereof he had been at school—a charming mist of retrospect. And he felt, though it might have been hard to make him own it, a deeply seated joy that here he should be long lengths out of reach of the most highly illuminated working-man. This was an inconsistent thing, but consistent forever in coming to pass.

Where the will is, there the way is, if the will be only wise. Bert found out a way of living in this howling wilderness, as his poor wife would have called it, if she had been a bad wife. Unskillful as he had shown himself in the matter of silver and gold, he had won great skill in the useful metals, especially in steel—the type of truth. And here in a break of rock he discovered a slender vein of a slate-gray mineral, distinct from cobalt, but not unlike it, such as he had found in the Carpathian Mountains, and which in metallurgy had no name yet, for its value was known to very few. But a legend of the spot declared that the ancient cutlers of Bilbao owed much of their fame to the use of this mineral in the careful process of conversion.

"I can make a living out of it, and that is all I want," said Bert, who was moderately sanguine still. "I know a manufacturer who has faith in me, and is doing all he can against the supremacy of Sheffield. If I can make arrangements with him, we will settle here, and keep to our own affairs for the future."

He built him a cottage in lonely snugness, far in the waste, and outside even of the range of title-deeds, though he paid a small rent to the manor, to save trouble, and to satisfy his conscience of the mineral deposit. By right of discovery, lease, and user, this became entirely his, as nobody else had ever heard of it. So by the fine irony of facts it came to pass, first, that the squanderer of three fortunes united his lot with a Jewess; next, that a great "cosmopolitan" hugged a strict corner of jealous monopoly; and again, that a champion of communism insisted upon his exclusive right to other people's property. However, for all that, it might not be easy to find a more consistent man.

Here Maunder, the surviving son, grew up, and Insie, their last child, was born; and the land enjoyed peace for twenty years, because it was of little value. A man who had been about the world so loosely must have found it hard to be boxed up here, except for the lowering of strength and pride by sorrow of affection, and sore bodily affliction. But the air of the moorland is good for such troubles. Bert possessed a happy nature; and perhaps it was well that his children could say, "We are nine; but only two to feed."

It must have been the whistling wind, a long memorial sound, which sent him, upon this snowy December night, back among the echoes of the past; for he always had plenty of work to do, even in the winter evenings, and was not at all given to folded arms. And before he was tired of his short warm rest, his wife asked, "Where is Maunder?"

"I left him doing his work," he replied; "he had a great heap still to clear.

He understands his work right well. He will not go to bed till he has done it. We must not be quite snowed up, my dear."

Mrs. Bert shook her head: having lost so many children, she was anxious about the rest of them. But before she could speak again, a heavy leap against the door was heard; the strong latch rattled, and the timbers creaked. Insie jumped up to see what it meant, but her father stopped her, and went himself. When he opened the door, a whirl of snow flew in, and through the glitter and the flutter a great dog came reeling, and rolled upon the floor, a mighty lump of bristled whiteness. Mrs. Bert was terrified, for she thought it was a wolf, not having found it in her power to believe that there could be such a desert place without wolves in the winter-time.

"Why, Saracen!" said Insie; "I declare it is! You poor old dog, what can have brought you out this weather?"

Both her parents were surprised to see her sit down on the floor and throw her arms around the neck of this self-invited and very uncouth visitor. For the girl forgot all of her trumpery concealments in the warmth of her feeling for a poor lost dog.

Saracen looked at her, with a view to dignity. He had only seen her once before, when Pet brought him down (both for company and safeguard), and he was not a dog who would dream of recognizing a person to whom he had been rashly introduced. And he knew that he was in a mighty difficulty now, which made self-respect all the more imperative. However, on the whole, he had been pleased with Insie at their first interview, and had patronized her— for she had an honest fragrance, and a little taste of salt—and now with a side look he let her know that he did not wish to hurt her feelings, although his business was not with her. But if she wanted to give him some refreshment, she might do so, while he was considering.

The fact was, though he could not tell it, and would scorn to do so if he could, that he had not had one bit to eat for more hours than he could reckon. That wicked hostler at Middleton had taken his money and disbursed it upon beer, adding insult to injury by remarking, in the hearing of Saracen (while strictly chained), that he was a deal too fat already. So vile a sentiment had deepened into passion the dog's ever dominant love of home; and when the darkness closed upon him in an unknown hungry hole, without even a horse for company, any other dog would have howled; but this dog stiffened his tail with self-respect. He scraped away all the straw to make a clear area for his experiment, and then he stood up like a pillar, or a fine kangaroo, and made trial of his weight against the chain. Feeling something give, or show propensity toward giving, he said to himself that here was one more triumph for him over the presumptuous intellect of man. The chain might be strong enough to hold a ship, and the great leathern collar to secure a bull; but the fastening of chain to collar was unsound, by reason of the rusting of a rivet.

Retiring to the manger for a better length of rush, he backed against the wall for a fulcrum to his spring, while the roll of his chest and the breadth of his loins quivered with tight muscle. Then off like the charge of a cannon he dashed, the loop of the collar flew out of the rivet, and the chain fell clanking on the paving-bricks. With grim satisfaction the dog set off in the track of the horse for Scargate Hall. And now he sat panting in the cottage of the gill, to tell his discovery and to crave for help.

"Where do you come from, and what do you want?" asked Bert, as the dog, soon beginning to recover, looked round at the door, and then back again at him, and jerked up his chin impatiently, "Insie, you seem to know this fine fellow. Where have you met him? And whose dog is he? Saracen! Why, that is the name of the dog who is everybody's terror at Scargate."

"I gave him some water one day," said Insie, "when he was terribly thirsty. But he seems to know you, father, better than me. He wants you to do something, and he scorns me."

For Saracen, failing of articulate speech, was uttering volumes of entreaty with his eyes, which were large, and brown, and full of clear expression under eyebrows of rich tan; and then he ran to the door, put up one heavy paw and shook it, and ran back, and pushed the master with his nozzle, and then threw back his great head and long velvet ears, and opening his enormous jaws, gave vent to a mighty howl which shook the roof.

"Oh, put him out, put him out! open the door!" exclaimed Mrs. Bert, in fresh terror. "If he is not a wolf, he is a great deal worse."

"His master is out in the snow," cried Bert; "perhaps buried in the snow, and he is come to tell us. Give me my hat, child, and my thick coat. See how delighted he is, poor fellow! Oh, here comes Maunder! Now lead the way, my friend. Maunder, go and fetch the other shovel. There is somebody lost in the snow, I believe. We must follow this dog immediately."

"Not till you both have had much plenty food," the mother said: "out upon the moors, this bad, bad night, and for leagues possibly to travel. My son and my husband are much too good. You bad dog, why did you come, pestilent? But you shall have food also. Insie, provide him. While I make to eat your father and your brother."

Saracen would hardly wait, starving as he was; but seeing the men prepare to start, he made the best of it, and cleared out a colander of victuals in a minute.

"Put up what is needful for a starving traveller," Mr. Bert said to the ladies. "We shall want no lantern; the snow gives light enough, and the moon will soon be up. Keep a kettle boiling, and some warm clothes ready. Perhaps we shall be hours away; but have no fear. Maunder is the boy for snow-drifts."

The young man being of a dark and silent nature, quite unlike his father's, made no reply, nor even deigned to give a smile, but seemed to be wonderfully taken with the dog, who in many ways resembled him. Then he cast both shovels on his shoulder at the door, and strode forth, and stamped upon the path that he had cleared. His father took a stout stick, the dog leaped past them, and led them out at once upon the open moor.

"We are in for a night of it," said Mr. Bert, and his son did not contradict him.

"The dog goes first, then I, then you," he said to his father, with his deep slow tone. And the elderly man, whose chief puzzle in life—since he had given up the problem of the world—was the nature of his only son, now wondered again, as he seldom ceased from wondering, whether this boy despised or loved him. The young fellow always took the very greatest care of his father, as if he were a child to be protected, and he never showed the smallest sign of disrespect. Yet Maunder was not the true son of his father, but of some ancestor, whose pride sprang out of dust at the outrageous idea of a kettle-mending Bert, and embodied itself in this Maunder.

The large-minded father never dreamed of such a trifle, but felt in such weather, with the snow above his leggings, that sometimes it is good to have a large-bodied son.

CHAPTER XLII

A CLEW OF BUTTONS

When Jack o' the Smithies met his old commander, as related by himself, at the house of Mr. Mordacks, everything seemed to be going on well for Sir Duncan, and badly for his sisters. The general factor, as he hinted long ago, possessed certain knowledge which the Middleton lawyer fondly supposed to be confined to himself and his fair clients. Sir Duncan refused to believe that the ladies could ever have heard of such a document as that which, if valid, would simply expel them; for, said he, "If they know of it, they are nothing less than thieves to conceal it and continue in possession. Of a lawyer I could fancy it, but never of a lady."

"My good sir," answered the sarcastic Mordacks, "a lady's conscience is not the same as a gentleman's, but bears more resemblance to a lawyer's. A lady's honor is of the very highest standard; but the standard depends upon her state of mind; and that, again, depends upon the condition of her feelings. You must not suppose me to admit the faintest shadow of disrespect toward your good sisters; but ladies are ladies, and facts are facts; and the former can always surmount the latter; while a man is comparatively helpless. I know that Mr. Jellicorse, their man of law, is thoroughly acquainted with this interesting deed; his first duty was to apprise them of it; and that, you may be quite sure, he has done."

"I hope not. I am sure not. A lawyer does not always employ hot haste in an unwelcome duty."

"True enough, Sir Duncan. But the duty here was welcome. Their knowledge of that deed, and of his possession of it, would make him their master, if he chose to be so. Not that old Jellicorse would think of such a thing. He is a man of high principle like myself, of a lofty conscience, and even sentimental. But lawyers are just like the rest of mankind. Their first consideration is their bread and cheese; though some of them certainly seem ready to accept it even in the toasted form."

"You may say what you like, Mordacks, my sister Philippa is far too upright, and Eliza too good, for any such thing to be possible. However, that question may abide. I shall not move until I have some one to do it for. I have no great affection for a home which cast me forth, whether it had a right to do so or not. But if we succeed in the more important matter, it will be my duty to recover the estates, for the benefit of another. You are sure of your proofs that it is the boy?"

"As certain as need be. And we will make it surer when you meet me there the week after next. For the reasons I have mentioned, we must wait till then. Your yacht is at Yarmouth. You have followed my advice in approaching by sea, and not by land, and in hiring at Yarmouth for the purpose. But you never should have come to York, Sir Duncan; this is a very great mistake of yours. They are almost sure to hear of it. And even your name given in our best inn! But luckily they never see a newspaper at Scargate."

"I follow the tactics with which you succeed—all above-board, and no stratagems. Your own letter brought me; but perhaps I am too old to be so impatient. Where shall I meet you, and on what day?"

"This day fortnight, at the Thornwick Inn, I shall hope to be with you at three o'clock, and perhaps bring somebody with me. If I fixed an earlier day, I should only disappoint you. For many things have to be delicately managed; and among them, the running of a certain cargo, without serious consequence. For that we may trust a certain very skillful youth. For the rest you must trust to a clumsier person, your humble land-agent and surveyor—titles inquired into and verified, at a tenth of solicitors' charges."

"Well," said Sir Duncan, "you shall verify mine, as soon as you have verified my son, and my title to him. Good-by, Mordacks. I am sure you mean me well, but you seem to be very long about it."

"Hot climates breed impatience, sir. A true son of Yorkshire is never in a hurry. The general complaint of me is concerning my wild rapidity."

"You are like the grocer, whose goods, if they have any fault at all, have the opposite one to what the customer finds in them. Well, good-by, Mordacks. You are a trusty friend, and I thank you."

These words from Sir Duncan Yordas were not merely of commonplace. For he was a man of great self-reliance, quick conclusion, and strong resolve. These had served him well in India, and insured his fortune; while early adversity and bitter losses had tempered the arrogance of his race. After the loss of his wife and child, and the breach with all his relatives, he had led a life of peril and hard labor, varied with few pleasures. When first he learned from Edinburgh that the ship conveying his only child to the care of the mother's relatives was lost, with all on board, he did all in his power to make inquiries. But the illness and death of his wife, to whom he was deeply attached, overwhelmed him. For while with some people "one blow drives out another," with some the second serves only to drive home, deepen, and aggravate the first. For years he was satisfied to believe both losses irretrievable. And so he might still have gone on believing, except for a queer little accident.

Being called to Calcutta upon government business, he happened to see a pair of English sailors, lazily playing, in a shady place by the side of the road, at hole-penny. One of them seemed to have his pocket cleared out, for just as Sir Duncan was passing, he cried, "Here, Jack, you give me change of one of them, and I'll have at you again, my boy. As good as a guinea with these blessed niggers. Come back to their home, I b'lieve they are, same as I wish I was; rale gold—ask this gen'leman."

The other swore that they were "naught but brass, and not worth a copper farden"; until the tars, being too tipsy for much fighting, referred the question to Sir Duncan.

Three hollow beads of gold were what they showed him, and he knew them at once for his little boy's buttons, the workmanship being peculiar to one village of his district, and one family thereof. The sailor would thankfully have taken one rupee apiece for them; but Sir Duncan gave him thirty for the three—their full metallic value—upon his pledging honor to tell all he knew about them, and make affidavit, if required. Then he told all he knew, to the best of his knowledge, and swore to it when sober, accepted a refresher, and made oath to it again, with some lively particulars added. And the facts that he deposed to, and deposited, were these:

Being down upon his luck, about a twelvemonth back, he thought of keeping company with a nice young woman, and settling down until a better time turned up; and happening to get a month's wages from a schooner of ninety-five tons at Scarborough, he strolled about the street a bit, and kept looking down the railings for a servant-girl who might have got her wages in her work-box. Clean he was, and taut, and clever, beating up street in Sunday rig, keeping sharp look-out for a consort, and in three or four tacks he hailed one. As nice a young partner as a lad could want, and his meaning was to buckle to for the winter. But the night before the splicing-day, what happened to him he never could tell after. He was bousing up his jib, as a lad is bound to do, before he takes the breakers. And when he came to, he was twenty leagues from Scarborough, on board of his Majesty's recruiting brig the Harpy. He felt in his pocket for the wedding-ring, and instead of that, there were these three beads.

Sir Duncan was sorry for his sad disaster, and gave him ten more rupees to get over it. And then he discovered that the poor forsaken maiden's name was Sally Watkins. Sally was the daughter of a rich pawnbroker, whose frame of mind was sometimes out of keeping with its true contents. He had very fine feelings, and real warmth of sympathy; but circumstances seemed sometimes to lead them into the wrong channel, and induced him to kick his children out of doors. In the middle of the family he kicked out Sally, almost before her turn was come; and she took a place at 4 pounds a year, to disgrace his memory—as she said—carrying off these buttons, and the jacket, which he had bestowed upon her, in a larger interval.

There was no more to be learned than this from the intercepted bridegroom. He said that he might have no objection to go on with his love again, as soon as the war was over, leastways, if it was made worth his while; but he had come across another girl, at the Cape of Good Hope, and he believed that this time the Lord was in it, for she had been born in a caul, and he had got it. With such a dispensation Sir Duncan Yordas saw no right to interfere, but left the course of true love to itself, after taking down the sailor's name—"Ned Faithful."

However, he resolved to follow out the clew of beads, though without much hope of any good result. Of the three in his possession he kept one, and one he sent to Edinburgh, and the third to York, having heard of the great sagacity, vigor, and strict integrity of Mr. Mordacks, all of which he sharpened by the promise of a large reward upon discovery. Then he went back to his work, until his time of leave was due, after twenty years of arduous and distinguished service. In troublous times, no private affairs, however urgent, should drive him from his post.

Now, eager as he was when in England once again, he was true to his character and the discipline of life. He had proof that the matter was in very good hands, and long command had taught him the necessity of obedience. Any previous Yordas would have kicked against the pricks, rushed forward, and scattered everything. But Sir Duncan was now of a different fibre. He left York at once, as Mordacks advised, and posted to Yarmouth, before the roads were blocked with snow, and while Jack o' the Smithies was returning to his farm. And from Yarmouth he set sail for Scarborough, in a sturdy little coaster, which he hired by the week. From Scarborough he would run down to Bridlington—not too soon, for fear of setting gossip going, but in time to meet Mordacks at Flamborough, as agreed upon.

That gentleman had other business in hand, which must not be neglected; but he gave to this matter a very large share of his time, and paid five-and-twenty pounds for the trusty roadster, who liked the taste of Flamborough pond, and the salt air on the oats of Widow Tapsy's stable, and now regularly neighed and whisked his tail as soon as he found himself outside Monk Bar. By favor of this horse and of his own sword and pistols, Mordacks spent nearly as much time now at Flamborough as he did in York; but unluckily he had been obliged to leave on the very afternoon before the run was accomplished, and Carroway slain so wickedly; for he hurried home to meet

Sir Duncan, and had not heard the bad news when he met him.

That horrible murder was a sad blow to him, not only as a man of considerable kindness and desire to think well of every one—so far as experience allows it—but also because of the sudden apparition of the law rising sternly in front of him. Justice in those days was not as now: her truer name was Nemesis. After such an outrage to the dignity of the realm, an example must be made, without much consideration whether it were the right one. If Robin Lyth were caught, there would be the form of trial, but the principal point would be to hang him. Like the rest of the world, Mr. Mordacks at first believed entirely in his guilt; but unlike the world, he did not desire to have him caught, and brought straightway to the gallows. Instead of seeking him, therefore, he was now compelled to avoid him, when he wanted him most; for it never must be said that a citizen of note had discoursed with such a criminal, and allowed him to escape. On the other hand, here he had to meet Sir Duncan, and tell him that all those grand promises were shattered, that in finding his only son all he had found was a cowardly murderer flying for his life, and far better left at the bottom of the sea. For once in a way, as he dwelt upon all this, the general factor became down-hearted, his vigorous face lost the strong lines of decision, and he even allowed his mouth to open without anything to put into it.

But it was impossible for this to last. Nature had provided Mordacks with an admirably high opinion of himself, enlivened by a sprightly good-will toward the world, whenever it wagged well with him. He had plenty of business of his own, and yet could take an amateur delight in the concerns of everybody; he was always at liberty to give good advice, and never under duty to take it; he had vigor of mind, of memory, of character, and of digestion; and whenever he stole a holiday from self-denial, and launched out after some favorite thing, there was the cash to do it with, and the health to do it pleasantly.

Such a man is not long depressed by a sudden misadventure. Dr. Upround's opinion in favor of Robin did not go very far with him; for he looked upon the rector as a man who knew more of divine than of human nature. But that fault could scarcely be found with a woman; or at any rate with a widow encumbered with a large family hanging upon the dry breast of the government. And though Mr. Mordacks did not invade the cottage quite so soon as he should have done, if guided by strict business, he thought himself bound to get over that reluctance, and press her upon a most distressing subject, before he kept appointment with his principal.

The snow, which by this time had blockaded Scargate, impounded Jordas, and compelled Mr. Jellicorse to rest and be thankful for a hot mince-pie, although it had visited this eastern coast as well, was not deep enough there to stop the roads. Keeping head-quarters at the "Hooked Cod" now, and encouraging a butcher to set up again (who had dropped all his money, in his hurry to get on), Geoffrey Mordacks began to make way into the outer crust of Flamborough society. In a council of the boats, upon a Sunday afternoon, every boat being garnished for its rest upon the flat, and every master fisherman buttoned with a flower—the last flowers of the year, and bearing ice-marks in their eyes—a resolution had been passed that the inland man meant well, had naught to do with Revenue, or Frenchmen either, or what was even worse, any outside fishers, such as often-time came sneaking after fishing grounds of Flamborough. Mother Tapsy stood credit for this strange man, and he might be allowed to go where he was minded, and to take all the help he liked to pay for.

Few men could have achieved such a triumph, without having married a Flamborough lass, which must have been the crown of all human ambition, if difficulty crowns it. Even to so great a man it was an added laurel, and strengthened him much in his opinion of himself. In spite of all disasters, he recovered faith in fortune, so many leading Flamborough men began to touch their hats to him! And thus he set forth before a bitter eastern gale, with the head of his seasoned charger bent toward the melancholy cot at Bridlington.

Having granted a new life of slaughter to that continually insolvent butcher, who exhibited the body of a sheep once more, with an eye to the approach of Christmas, this universal factor made it a point of duty to encourage him. In either saddle-bag he bore a seven-pound leg of mutton—a credit to a sheep of that district then—and to show himself no traitor to the staple of the place, he strapped upon his crupper, in some oar-weed and old netting, a twenty-pound cod, who found it hard to breathe his last when beginning to enjoy horse-exercise.

"There is a lot of mouths to fill," said Mr. Mordacks, with a sigh, while his landlady squeezed a brown loaf of her baking into the nick of his big sword-strap; "and you and I are capable of entering into the condition of the widow and the fatherless."

"Hoonger is the waa of them, and victuals is the cure for it. Now mind you coom home afore dark," cried the widow, to whom he had happened to say, very sadly, that he was now a widower. "To my moind, a sight o' more snaw is a-coomin'; and what mah sard or goon foight again it? Captain Moordocks, coom ye home arly. T' hare sha' be doon to a toorn be fi' o'clock. Coom ye home be that o'clock, if ye care for deener."

"I must have made a tender impression on her heart," Mr. Mordacks said to himself, as he kissed his hand to the capacious hostess. "Such is my fortune, to be loved by everybody, while aiming at the sternest rectitude. It is sweet, it is dangerously sweet; but what a comfort! How that large-hearted female will baste my hare!"

CHAPTER XLIII

A PLEASANT INTERVIEW

Cumbered as he was of body, and burdened with some cares of mind, the general factor ploughed his way with his usual resolution. A scowl of dark vapor came over the headlands, and under-ran the solid snow-clouds with a scud, like bonfire smoke. The keen wind following the curves of land, and shaking the fringe of every white-clad bush, piped (like a boy through a comb) wherever stock or stub divided it. It turned all the coat of the horse the wrong way, and frizzed up the hair of Mr. Mordacks, which was as short as a soldier's, and tossed up his heavy riding cape, and got into him all up the small of his back. Being fond of strong language, he indulged in much; but none of it warmed him, and the wind whistled over his shoulders, and whirled the words out of his mouth.

When he came to the dip of the road, where it crosses the Dane's Dike, he pulled up his horse for a minute, in the shelter of shivering fir-trees. "What a cursed bleak country! My fish is frozen stiff, and my legs are as dead as the mutton in the saddle-bags. Geoffrey, you are a fool," he said. "Charity is very fine, and business even better; but a good coal fire is the best of all. But in for a penny of it, in for a pound. Hark! I hear some fellow-fool equally determined to be frozen. I'll go at once and hail him; perhaps the sight of him will warm me."

He turned his horse down a little lane upon the left, where snow lay deep, with laden bushes overhanging it, and a rill of water bridged with bearded ice ran dark in the hedge-trough. And here he found a stout lusty man, with shining red cheeks and keen blue eyes, hacking and hewing in a mighty maze of brambles.

"My friend, you seem busy. I admire your vast industry," Mr. Mordacks exclaimed, as the man looked at him, but ceased not from swinging his long hedge-hook. "Happy is the land that owns such men."

"The land dothn't own me; I own the land. I shall be pleased to learn what your business is upon it."

Farmer Anerley hated chaff, as a good agriculturist should do. Moreover, he was vexed by many little griefs to-day, and had not been out long enough to work them off. He guessed pretty shrewdly that this sworded man was "Moreducks"—as the leading wags of Flamborough were gradually calling him—and the sight of a sword upon his farm (unless of an officer bound to it) was already some disquietude to an English farmer's heart. That was a trifle; for fools would be fools, and might think it a grand thing to go about with tools they were never born to the handling of; but a fellow who was come to take up Robin Lyth's case, and strive to get him out of his abominable crime, had better go back to the rogue's highway, instead of coming down the private road to Anerley.

"Upon my word I do believe," cried Mordacks, with a sprightly joy, "that I have the pleasure of meeting at last the well-known Captain Anerley! My dear sir, I can not help commending your prudence in guarding the entrance to your manor; but not in this employment of a bill-hook. From all that I hear, it is a Paradise indeed. What a haven in such weather as the present! Now, Captain Anerley, I entreat you to consider whether it is wise to take the thorn so from the rose. If I had so sweet a place, I would plant brambles, briers, blackthorn, furze, crataegus, every kind of spinous growth, inside my gates, and never let anybody lop them. Captain, you are too hospitable."

Farmer Anerley gazed with wonder at this man, who could talk so fast for the first time of seeing a body. Then feeling as if his hospitality were challenged, and desiring more leisure for reflection, "You better come down the lane, sir," he said.

"Am I to understand that you invite me to your house, or only to the gate where the dogs come out? Excuse me: I always am a most plain-spoken man."

"Our dogs never bite nobody but rogues."

"In that case, Captain Anerley, I may trust their moral estimate. I knew a farmer once who was a thorough thief in hay; a man who farmed his own land, and trimmed his own hedges; a thoroughly respectable and solid agriculturist. But his trusses of hay were always six pounds short, and if ever anybody brought a sample truss to steelyard, he had got a little dog, just seven pounds weight, who slipped into the core of it, being just a good hay-color. He always delivered his hay in the twilight, and when it swung the beam, he used to say, 'Come, now, I must charge you for overweight.' Now, captain, have you got such an honest dog as that?"

"I would have claimed him, that I would, if such a clever dog were weighed to me. But, sir, you have got the better of me. What a man for stories you be, for sure! Come in to our fire-place." Farmer Anerley was conquered by this tale, which he told fifty times every year he lived thereafter, never failing to finish with, "What rogues they be, up York way!"

Master Mordacks was delighted with this piece of luck on his side. Many times he had been longing to get in at Anerley, not only from the reputation of good cheer there, but also from kind curiosity to see the charming Mary, who was now becoming an important element of business. Since Robin had given him the slip so sadly—a thing it was impossible to guard against—the best chance of hearing what became of him would be to get into the good graces of his sweetheart.

"We have been very sadly for a long time now," said the farmer, as he knocked at his own porch door with the handle of his bill-hook. "There used to be one as was always welcome here; and a pleasure it was to see him make himself so pleasant, sir. But ever since the Lord took him home from his family, without a good-by, as a man might say, my wife hath taken to bar the doors whiles I am away and out of sight." Stephen Anerley knocked harder, as he thus explained the need of it; for it grieved him to have his house shut up.

"Very wise of them all to bar out such weather," said Mordacks, who read the farmer's thoughts like print, "Don't relax your rules, sir, until the weather changes. Ah, that was a very sad thing about the captain. As gallant an officer, and as single-minded, as ever killed a Frenchman in the best days of our navy."

"Single-minded is the very word to give him, sir. I sought about for it ever since I heard of him coming to an end like that, and doing of his duty in the thick of it. If I could only get a gentleman to tell me, or an officer's wife would be better still, what the manners is when a poor lady gets her husband shot, I'll be blest if I wouldn't go straight and see her, though they make such a distance betwixt us and the regulars.—Oh, then, ye've come at last! No thief, no thief."

"Father," cried Mary, bravely opening all the door, of which the ruffian wind made wrong by casting her figure in high relief—and yet a pardonable wrong—"father, you are quite wise to come home, before your dear nose is quite cut off.—Oh, I beg your pardon, sir; I never saw you."

"My fate in life is to be overlooked," Mr. Mordacks answered, with a martial stride; "but not always, young lady, with such exquisite revenge. What I look at pays fiftyfold for being overlooked."

"You are an impudent, conceited man," thought Mary to herself, with gross injustice; but she only blushed and said, "I beg your pardon, sir."

"You see, sir," quoth the farmer, with some severity, tempered, however, with a smile of pride, "my daughter, Mary Anerley."

"And I take off my hat," replied audacious Mordacks, among whose faults was no false shame, "not only to salute a lady, sir, but also to have a better look."

"Well, well," said the farmer, as Mary ran away; "your city ways are high polite, no doubt, but my little lass is strange to them. And I like her better so, than to answer pert with pertness. Now come you in, and warm your feet a bit. None of us are younger than we used to be."

This was not Master Anerley's general style of welcoming a guest, but he hated new-fangled Frenchified manners, as he told his good wife, when he boasted by-and-by how finely he had put that old coxcomb down. "You never should have done it," was all the praise he got. "Mr. Mordacks is a business man, and business men always must relieve their minds." For no sooner now was the general factor introduced to Mistress Anerley than she perceived clearly that the object of his visit was not to make speeches to young chits of girls, but to seek the advice of a sensible person, who ought to have been consulted a hundred times for once that she even had been allowed to open her mouth fairly. Sitting by the fire, he convinced her that the whole of the mischief had been caused by sheer neglect of her opinion. Everything she said was so exactly to the point that he could not conceive how it should have been so slighted, and she for her part begged him to stay and partake of their simple dinner.

"Dear madam, it can not be," he replied; "alas! I must not think of it. My conscience reproaches me for indulging, as I have done, in what is far sweeter than even one of your dinners—a most sensible lady's society. I have a long bitter ride before me, to comfort the fatherless and the widow. My two legs of mutton will be thawed by this time in the genial warmth of your stable. I also am thawed, warmed, feasted I may say, by happy approximation to a mind so bright and congenial. Captain Anerley, madam, has shown true kindness in allowing me the privilege of exclusive speech with you. Little did I hope for such a piece of luck this morning. You have put so many things in a new and brilliant light, that my road becomes clear before me. Justice must be done; and you feel quite sure that Robin Lyth committed this atrocious murder because poor Carroway surprised him so when making clandestine love, at your brother Squire Popplewell's, to a beautiful young lady who shall be nameless. And deeply as you grieve for the loss of such a neighbor, the bravest officer of the British navy, who leaped from a strictly immeasurable height into a French ship, and scattered all her crew, and has since had a baby about three months old, as well as innumerable children, you feel that you have reason to be thankful sometimes that the young man's character has been so clearly shown, before he contrived to make his way into the bosom of respectable families in the neighborhood."

"I never thought it out quite so clear as that, sir; for I feel so sorry for everybody, and especially those who have brought him up, and those he has made away with."

"Quite so, my dear madam; such are your fine feelings, springing from the goodness of your nature. Pardon my saying that you could have no other, according to my experience of a most benevolent countenance. Part of my duty, and in such a case as yours, one of the pleasantest parts of it, is to study the expression of a truly benevolent—"

"I am not that old, sir, asking of your pardon, to pretend to be benevolent. All that I lay claim to is to look at things sensible."

"Certainly, yet with a tincture of high feeling. Now if it should happen that this poor young man were of very high birth, perhaps the highest in the county, and the heir to very large landed property, and a title, and all that sort of nonsense, you would look at him from the very same point of view?"

"That I would, sir, that I would. So long as he was proclaimed for hanging. But naturally bound, of course, to be more sorry for him."

"Yes, from sense of all the good things he must lose. There seems, however, to be strong ground for believing—as I may tell you, in confidence, Dr. Upround does—that he had no more to do with it than you or I, ma'am. At first I concluded as you have done. I am going to see Mrs. Carroway now. Till then I suspend my judgment."

"Now that is what nobody should do, Mr. Mordacks. I have tried, but never found good come of it. To change your mind is two words against yourself; and you go wrong both ways, before and after."

"Undoubtedly you do, ma'am. I never thought of that before. But you must remember that we have not the gift of hitting—I might say of making—the truth with a flash or a dash, as you ladies have. May I be allowed to come again?"

"To tell you the truth, sir, I am heartily sorry that you are going away at all. I could have talked to you all the afternoon; and how seldom I get the chance now, Lord knows. There is that in your conversation which makes one feel quite sure of being understood; not so much in what you say, sir—if you understand my meaning—as in the way you look, quite as if my meaning was not at all too quick for you. My good husband is of a greater mind than I am, being nine-and-forty inches round the chest; but his mind seems somehow to come after mine, the same as the ducks do, going down to our pond."

"Mistress Anerley, how thankful you should be! What a picture of conjugal felicity! But I thought that the drake always led the way?"

"Never upon our farm, sir. When he doth, it is a proof of his being crossed with wild-ducks. The same as they be round Flamborough."

"Oh, now I see the truth. How slow I am! It improves their flavor, at the expense of their behavior. But seriously, madam, you are fit to take the lead. What a pleasant visit I have had! I must brace myself up for a very sad one now—a poor lady, with none to walk behind her."

"Yes, to be sure! It is very fine of me to talk. But if I was left without my husband, I should only care to walk after him. Please to give her my kind love, sir; though I have only seen her once. And if there is anything that we can do—"

"If there is anything that we can do," said the farmer, coming out of his corn-chamber, "we won't talk about it, but we'll do it, Mr. Mordacks."

The factor quietly dispersed this rebuke, by waving his hand at his two legs of mutton and the cod, which had thawed in the stable. "I knew that I should be too late," he said; "her house will be full of such little things as these, so warm is the feeling of the neighborhood. I guessed as much, and arranged with my butcher to take them back in that case; and he said they would eat all the better for the ride. But as for the cod, perhaps you will accept him. I could never take him back to Flamborough."

"Ride away, sir, ride away," said the farmer, who had better not have measured swords with Mordacks. "I were thinking of sending a cart over there, so soon as the weather should be opening of the roads up. But the children might be hankerin' after meat, the worse for all the snow-time."

"It is almost impossible to imagine such a thing. Universally respected, suddenly cut off, enormous family with hereditary hunger, all the neighbors well aware of straitened circumstances, the kindest-hearted county in Great Britain—sorrow and abundance must have cloyed their appetites, as at a wealthy man's funeral. What a fool I must have been not to foresee all that!"

"Better see than foresee," replied the farmer, who was crusty from remembering that he had done nothing. "Neighbors likes to wait for neighbors to go in; same as two cows staring at a new-mown meadow."

CHAPTER XLIV

THE WAY OF THE WORLD

Cliffs snow-mantled, and storm-ploughed sands, and dark gray billows frilled with white, rolling and roaring to the shrill east wind, made the bay of Bridlington a very different sight from the smooth fair scene of August. Scarcely could the staggering colliers, anchored under Flamborough Head (which they gladly would have rounded if they could), hold their own against wind and sea, although the outer spit of sand tempered as yet the full violence of waves.

But if everything looked cold and dreary, rough, and hard, and bare of beauty, the cottage of the late lieutenant, standing on the shallow bluff, beaten by the wind, and blinded of its windows from within, of all things looked the most forlorn, most desolate, and freezing. The windward side was piled with snow, on the crest of which foam pellets lay, looking yellow by comparison, and melting small holes with their brine. At the door no foot-mark broke the drift; and against the vaporous sky no warmer vapor tufted the chimney-pots.

"I am pretty nearly frozen again," said Mordacks; "but that place sends another shiver down my back. All the poor little devils must be icicles at least."

After peeping through a blind, he turned pale betwixt his blueness, and galloped to the public-house abutting on the quay. Here he marched into the parlor, and stamped about, till a merry-looking landlord came to him. "Have a glass of hot, sir; how blue your nose is!" the genial master said to him. The reply of the factor can not be written down in these days of noble language. Enough that it was a terse malediction of the landlord, the glass of hot, and even his own nose. Boniface was no Yorkshireman, else would he have given as much as he got, at least in lingual currency. As it was, he considered it no affair of his if a guest expressed his nationality. "You must have better orders than that to give, I hope, sir."

"Yes, sir, I have. And you have got the better of me; which has happened to me three times this day already, because of the freezing of my wits, young man. Now you go in to your best locker, and bring me your very best bottle of Cognac—none of your government stuff, you know, but a sample of your finest bit of smuggling. Why did I swear at a glass of hot? Why, because you are all such a set of scoundrels. I want a glass of hot as much as man ever did. But how can I drink it, when women and children are dying—perhaps dead, for all I know—for want of warmth and victuals? Your next-door neighbors almost, and a woman, whose husband has just been murdered! And here you are swizzling, and rattling your coppers. Good God, sir! The Almighty from heaven would send orders to have His own commandment broken."

Mr. Mordacks was excited, and the landlord saw no cause for it. "What makes you carry on like this?" he said; "it was only last night we was talking in the tap-room of getting a subscription up, downright liberal. I said I was good for a crown, and take it out of the tick they owes me. And when you come to think of these hard times—"

"Take that, and then tell me if you find them softer." Suiting the action to the word, the universal factor did something omitted on his card in the list of his comprehensive functions. As the fat host turned away, to rub his hands, with a phosphoric feeling of his future generosity, a set of highly energetic toes, prefixed with the toughest York leather, and tingling for exercise, made him their example. The landlord flew up among his own pots and glasses, his head struck the ceiling, which declined too long a taste of him, and anon a silvery ring announced his return to his own timbers.

"Accept that neighborly subscription, my dear friend, and acknowledge its promptitude," said Mr. Mordacks; "and now be quick about your orders, peradventure a second flight might be less agreeable. Now don't show any airs; you have been well treated, and should be thankful for the facilities you have to offer. I know a poor man without any legs at all, who would be only too glad if he could do what you have done."

"Then his taste must be a queer one," the landlord replied, as he illustrated sadly the discovery reserved for a riper age—that human fingers have attained their present flexibility, form, and skill by habit of assuaging, for some millions of ages, the woes of the human body.

"Now don't waste my time like that," cried Mordacks; and seeing him draw near again, his host became right active. "Benevolence must be inculcated," continued the factor, following strictly in pursuit. "I have done you a world of good, my dear friend; and reflection will compel you to heap every blessing on me."

"I don't know about that," replied the landlord. It is certain, however, that this exhibition of philanthropic vigor had a fine effect. In five minutes all the resources of the house were at the disposal of this rapid agent, who gave his orders right and left, clapped down a bag of cash, and took it up again, and said, "Now just you mind my horse, twice as well as you mind your fellow-creatures. Take a leg of mutton out, and set it roasting. Have your biggest bed hot for a lot of frozen children. By the Lord, if you don't look alive, I'll have you up for murder." As he spoke, a stout fish-woman came in from the quay; and he beckoned to her, and took her with him.

"You can't come in," said a little weak voice, when Mr. Mordacks, having knocked in vain, began to prise open the cottage door. "Mother is so poorly; and you mustn't think of coming in. Oh, whatever shall I do, if you won't stop when I tell you?"

"Where are all the rest of you? Oh, in the kitchen, are they? You poor little atomy, how many of you are dead?"

"None of us dead, sir; without it is the baby;" here Geraldine burst into a wailing storm of tears. "I gave them every bit," she sobbed—"every bit, sir, but the rush-lights; and them they wouldn't eat, sir, or I never would have touched them. But mother is gone off her head, and baby wouldn't eat it."

"You are a little heroine," said Mordacks, looking at her—the pinched face, and the hollow eyes, and the tottering blue legs of her. "You are greater than a queen. No queen forgets herself in that way."

"Please, sir, no; I ate almost a box of rush-lights, and they were only done last night. Oh, if baby would have took to them!"

"Hot bread and milk in this bottle; pour it out; feed her first, Molly," Mr. Mordacks ordered. "The world can't spare such girls as this. Oh, you won't eat first! Very well; then the others shall not have a morsel till your mouth is full. And they seem to want it bad enough. Where is the dead baby?"

In the kitchen, where now they stood, not a spark of fire was lingering, but some wood-ash still retained a feeble memory of warmth; and three little children (blest with small advance from babyhood) were huddling around, with hands, and faces, and sharp grimy knees poking in for lukewarm corners; while two rather senior young Carroways were lying fast asleep, with a jack-towel over them. But Tommy was not there; that gallant Tommy, who had ridden all the way to Filey after dark, and brought his poor father to the fatal place.

Mordacks, with his short, bitter-sweet smile, considered all these little ones. They were not beautiful, nor even pretty; one of them was too literally a chip of the old block, for he had reproduced his dear father's scar; and every one of them wanted a "wash and brush up," as well as a warming and sound victualling. Corruptio optimi pessima. These children had always been so highly scrubbed, that the great molecular author of existence, dirt, resumed parental sway, with tenfold power of attachment and protection, the moment soap and flannel ceased their wicked usurpation.

"Please, sir, I couldn't keep them clean, I couldn't," cried Geraldine, choking, both with bread and milk, and tears. "I had Tommy to feed through the coal-cellar door; and all the bits of victuals in the house to hunt up; and it did get so dark, and it was so cold. I am frightened to think of what mother will say for my burning up all of her brushes, and the baskets. But please, sir, little Cissy was a-freezing at the nose."

The three little children at the grate were peeping back over the pits in their shoulders, half frightened at the tall, strange man, and half ready to toddle to him for protection; while the two on the floor sat up and stared, and opened their mouths for their sister's bread and milk. Then Jerry flew to them, and squatted on the stones, and very nearly choked them with her spoon and basin.

"Molly, take two in your apron, and be off," said the factor to the stout fish-woman—who was simply full of staring, and of crying out "Oh lor!"—"pop them into the hot bed at once; they want warmth first, and victuals by-and-by. Our wonderful little maid wants food most. I will come after you with the other three. But I must see my little queen fill her own stomach first."

"But, please, sir, won't you let our Tommy out first?" cried Jerry, as the strong woman lapped up the two youngest in her woolsey apron and ran off with them. "He has been so good, and he was too proud to cry so soon as ever he found out that mother couldn't hear him. And I gave him the most to eat of anybody else, because of him being the biggest, sir. It was all as black as ink, going under the door; but Tommy never minded."

"Wonderful merit! While you were eating tallow! Show me the coal-cellar, and out he comes. But why don't you speak of your poor mother, child?"

The child, who had been so brave, and clever, self-denying, laborious, and noble, avoided his eyes, and began to lick her spoon, as if she had had enough, starving though she was. She glanced up at the ceiling, and then suddenly withdrew her eyes, and the blue lids trembled over them. Mordacks saw that it was childhood's dread of death. "Show me where little Tommy is," he said; "we must not be too hard upon you, my dear. But what made your mother lock you up, and carry on so?"

"I don't know at all, sir," said Geraldine.

"Now don't tell a story," answered Mr. Mordacks. "You were not meant for lies; and you know all about it. I shall just go away if you tell stories."

"Then all I know is this," cried Jerry, running up to him, and desperately clutching at his riding coat; "the very night dear father was put into the pit-hole—oh, hoo, oh, hoo, oh, hoo!"

"Now we can't stop for that," said the general factor, as he took her up and kissed her, and the tears, which had vainly tried to stop, ran out of young eyes upon well-seasoned cheeks; "you have been a wonder; I am like a father to you. You must tell me quickly, or else how can I cure it? We will let Tommy out then, and try to save your mother."

"Mother was sitting in the window, sir," said the child, trying strongly to command herself, "and I was to one side of her, and Tommy to the other, and none of us was saying anything. And then there came a bad, wicked face against the window, and the man said, 'What was it you said to-day, ma'am?' And mother stood up—she was quite right then—and she opened the window, and she looked right at him, and she said, 'I spoke the truth, John Cadman. Between you and your God it rests.' And the man said, 'You shut your black mouth up, or you and your brats shall all go the same way. Mind one thing— you've had your warning.' Then mother fell away, for she was just worn out; and she lay upon the floor, and she kept on moaning, 'There is no God! there is no God!' after all she have taught us to say our prayers to. And there was nothing for baby to draw ever since."

For once in his life Mr. Mordacks held his tongue; and his face, which was generally fiercer than his mind, was now far behind it in ferocity. He thought within himself, "Well, I am come to something, to have let such things be going on in a matter which pertains to my office—pigeon-hole 100! This comes of false delicacy, my stumbling-block perpetually! No more of that. Now for action."

Geraldine looked up at him, and said, "Oh, please, sir." And then she ran off, to show the way toward little Tommy.

The coal-cellar flew open before the foot of Mordacks; but no Tommy appeared, till his sister ran in. The poor little fellow was quite dazzled with the light; and the grime on his cheeks made the inrush of fresh air come like wasps to him. "Now, Tommy, you be good," said Geraldine; "trouble enough has been made about you."

The boy put out his under lip, and blinked with great amazement. After such a quantity of darkness and starvation, to be told to be good was a little too bad. His sense of right and wrong became fluid with confusion; he saw no sign of anything to eat; and the loud howl of an injured heart began to issue from the coaly rampart of neglected teeth.

"Quite right, my boy," Mr. Mordacks said. "You have had a bad time, and are entitled to lament. Wipe your nose on your sleeve, and have at it again."

"Dirty, dirty things I hear. Who is come into my house like this? My house and my baby belong to me. Go away all of you. How can I bear this noise?"

Mrs. Carroway stood in the passage behind them, looking only fit to die. One of her husband's watch-coats hung around her, falling nearly to her feet; and the long clothes of her dead baby, which she carried, hung over it, shaking like a white dog's tail. She was standing with her bare feet well apart, and that swing of hip and heel alternate which mothers for a thousand generations have supposed to lull their babies into sweet sleep.

For once in his life the general factor had not the least idea of the proper thing to do. Not only did he not find it, but he did not even seek for it, standing aside rather out of the way, and trying to look like a calm spectator. But this availed him to no account whatever. He was the only man there, and the woman naturally fixed upon him.

"You are the man," she said, in a quiet and reasonable voice, and coming up to Mordacks with the manner of a lady; "you are the gentleman, I mean, who promised to bring back my husband. Where is he? Have you fulfilled your promise?"

"My dear madam, my dear madam, consider your children, and how cold you are. Allow me to conduct you to a warmer place. You scarcely seem to enter into the situation."

"Oh yes, I do, sir; thoroughly, thoroughly. My husband is in his grave; my children are going after him; and the best place for them. But they shall not be murdered. I will lock them up, so that they never shall be murdered."

"My dear lady, I agree with you entirely. You do the very wisest thing in these bad times. But you know me well. I have had the honor of making your acquaintance in a pleasant manner. I feel for your children, quite as if I was— I mean, ma'am, a very fine old gentleman's affection. Geraldine, come and kiss me, my darling. Tommy, you may have the other side; never mind the coal, my boy; there is a coal-wharf quite close to my windows at home."

These children, who had been hiding behind Mr. Mordacks and Molly (who was now come back), immediately did as he ordered them; or rather Jerry led the way, and made Tommy come as well, by a signal which he never durst gainsay. But while they saluted the general factor (who sat down upon a box to accommodate them), from the corners of their eyes they kept a timid, trembling, melancholy watch upon their own mother.

Poor Mrs. Carroway was capable of wondering. Her power of judgment was not so far lost as it is in a dream—where we wonder at nothing, but cast off skeptic misery—and for the moment she seemed to be brought home from the distance of roving delusion, by looking at two of her children kissing a man who was hunting in his pocket for his card.

"Circumstances, madam," said Mr. Mordacks, "have deprived me of the pleasure of producing my address. It should be in two of my pockets; but it seems to have strangely escaped from both of them. However, I will write it down, if required. Geraldine dear, where is your school slate? Go and look for it, and take Tommy with you."

This surprised Mrs. Carroway, and began to make her think. These were her children—she was nearly sure of that—her own poor children, who were threatened from all sides with the likelihood of being done away with. Yet here was a man who made much of them, and kissed them; and they kissed him without asking her permission!

"I scarcely know what it is about," she said; "and my husband is not here to help me."

"You have hit the very point, ma'am. You must take it on yourself. How wonderfully clever the ladies always are! Your family is waiting for a government supply; everybody knows that everybody in the world may starve before government thinks of supplying supply. I do not belong to the government—although if I had my deserts I should have done so—but fully understanding them, I step in to anticipate their action. I see that the children of a very noble officer, and his admirable wife, have been neglected, through the rigor of the weather and condition of the roads. I am a very large factor in the neighborhood, who make a good thing out of all such cases. I step in; circumstances favor me; I discover a good stroke of business; my very high character, though much obscured by diffidence, secures me universal confidence. The little dears take to me, and I to them. They feel themselves safe under my protection from their most villainous enemies. They are pleased to kiss a man of strength and spirit, who represents the government."

Mrs. Carroway scarcely understood a jot of this. Such a rush of words made her weak brain go round, and she looked about vainly for her children, who had gladly escaped upon the chance afforded. But she came to the conclusion she was meant to come to—that this gentleman before her was the government.

"I will do whatever I am told," she said, looking miserably round, as if for anything to care about; "only I must count my children first, or the government might say there was not the proper number."

"Of all points that is the very one that I would urge," Mordacks answered, without dismay. "Molly, conduct this good lady to her room. Light a good fire, as the Commissioners have ordered; warm the soup sent from the arsenal last night, but be sure that you put no pepper in it. The lady will go with you, and follow our directions. She sees the importance of having all her faculties perfectly clear when we make our schedule, as we shall do in a few hours' time, of all the children; every one, with the date of their birth, and their Christian names, which nobody knows so well as their own dear mother. Ah, how very sweet it is to have so many of them; and to know the pride, the pleasure, the delight, which the nation feels in providing for the welfare of every little darling!"

CHAPTER XLV

THE THING IS JUST

"Was there ever such a man?" said Mr. Mordacks to himself, as he rode back to Flamborough against the bitter wind, after "fettling" the affairs of the poor Carroways, as well as might be for the present. "As if I had not got my hands too full already, now I am in for another plaguesome business, which will cost a lot of money, instead of bringing money in. How many people have I now to look after? In the first place, two vile wretches—Rickon Goold, the ship-scuttler, and John Cadman, the murderer—supposing that Dr. Upandown and Mrs. Carroway are right. Then two drunken tars, with one leg between them, who may get scared of the law, and cut and run. Then an outlawed smuggler, who has cut and run already; and a gentleman from India, who will be wild with disappointment through the things that have happened since I saw him last. After that a lawyer, who will fight tooth and nail of course, because it brings grist to his mill. That makes seven; and now to all these I have added number eight, and that the worst of all—not only a woman, but a downright mad one, as well as seven starving children. Charity is a thing that pays so slowly! That this poor creature should lose her head just now is most unfortunate. I have nothing whatever to lay before Sir Duncan, when I tell him of this vile catastrophe, except the boy's own assertion, and the opinion of Dr. Upandown. Well, well, 'faint heart,' etc. I must nurse the people round; without me they would all have been dead. Virtue is its own reward. I hope the old lady has not burned my hare to death."

The factor might well say that without his aid that large family must have perished. Their neighbors were not to be blamed for this, being locked out of the house, and having no knowledge of the frost and famine that prevailed within. Perhaps, when the little ones began to die, Geraldine might heave escaped from a window, and got help in time to save some of them, if she herself had any strength remaining; but as it was, she preferred to sacrifice herself, and obey her mother. "Father always told me," she had said to Mr. Mordacks, when he asked her how so sharp a child could let things come to such a pitch, "that when he was out of the way, the first thing I was to mind always was to do what mother told me; and now he can't come back no more, to let me off from doing it."

By this time the "Cod with the Hook in his Gills" was as much at the mercy of Mr. Mordacks as if he had landed and were crimping him. Widow Precious was a very tough lady to get over, and she liked to think the worst she could of everybody—which proves in the end the most charitable course, because of the good-will produced by explanation—and for some time she had stood in the Flamburian attitude of doubt toward the factor. But even a Flamburian may at last be pierced; and then (as with other pachydermatous animals) the hole, once made, is almost certain to grow larger. So by dint of good offices here and there, kind interest, and great industry among a very simple and grateful race, he became the St. Oswald of that ancient shrine (as already has been hinted), and might do as he liked, even on the Sabbath-day. And as one of the first things he always liked to do was to enter into everybody's business, he got into an intricacy of little knowledge too manifold even for his many-fibred brain. But some of this ran into and strengthened his main clew, leading into the story he was laboring to explore, and laying before him, as bright as a diamond, even the mystery of ear-rings.

"My highly valued hostess and admirable cook," he said to Widow Precious, after making noble dinner, which his long snowy ride and work at Bridlington had earned, "in your knowledge of the annals of this interesting town, happen you to be able to recall the name of a certain man, John Cadman?"

"Ah, that ah deah," Widow Tapsy answered, with a heavy sigh, which rattled all the dishes on the waiter; "and sma' gude o' un, sma' gude, whativer. Geroot wi' un!"

The landlady shut her firm lips with a smack, which Mordacks well knew by this time though seldom foreclosed by it now, as he had been before he became a Danish citizen. He was sure that she had some good reason for her silence; and the next day he found that the girl who had left her home, through Cadman's villainy, was akin by her mother's side to Mistress Precious. But he had another matter to discuss with her now, which caused him some misgivings, yet had better be faced manfully. In the safe philosophical distance of York from this strong landlady he had (for good reasons of his own) appointed the place of meeting with Sir Duncan Yordas at the rival hostelry, the inn of Thornwick. Widow Precious had a mind of uncommonly large type, so lofty and pure of all petty emotions, that if any one spoke of the Thornwick Inn, even upon her back premises, her dignity stepped in and said, "I can't abide the stinkin' naam o' un."

Of this persistently noble regard of a lower institution Mr. Mordacks was well aware; and it gave him pause, in his deep anxiety to spare a tender heart, and maintain the high standard of his breakfast kidneys. "Madam," he began, and then he rubbed his mouth with the cross-cut out of the jack-towel by the sink, newly set on table, to satisfy him for a dinner napkin—"madam, will you listen, while I make an explanation?"

The landlady looked at him with dark suspicions gathering.

"Joost spak' oot," she said, "whativer's woorkin' i' thah mahnd."

"I am bound to meet a gentleman near Flamborough to-morrow," Mr. Mordacks continued, with the effrontery of guilt, "who will come from the sea. And as it would not suit him to walk far inland, he has arranged for the interview at a poor little place called the Thorny Wick, or the Stubby Wick, or something of that sort. I thought it was due to you, madam, to explain the reason of my entering, even for a moment—"

"Ah dawn't care. Sitha—they mah fettle thee there, if thow's fondhead enew."

Without another word she left the room, clattering her heavy shoes at the door; and Mordacks foresaw a sad encounter on the morrow, without a good breakfast to "fettle" him for it. It was not in his nature to dread anything much, and he could not see where he had been at all to blame; but gladly would he have taken ten per cent off his old contract, than meet Sir Duncan Yordas with the news he had to tell him.

One cause of the righteous indignation felt by the good mother Tapsy, was her knowledge that nobody could land just now in any cove under the Thornwick Hotel. With the turbulent snow-wind bringing in the sea, as now it had been doing for several days, even the fishermen's cobles could not take the beach, much less any stranger craft. Mr. Mordacks was sharp; but an inland factor is apt to overlook such little facts marine.

Upon the following day he stood in the best room of the Thornwick Inn—which even then was a very decent place to any eyes uncast with envy—and he saw the long billows of the ocean rolling before the steady blowing of the salt-tongued wind, and the broad white valleys that between them lay, and the vaporous generation of great waves. They seemed to have little gift of power for themselves, and no sign of any heed of purport; only to keep at proper distance from each other, and threaten to break over long before they meant to do it. But to see what they did at the first opposition of reef, or crag, or headland bluff, was a cure for any delusion about them, or faith in their liquid benevolence. For spouts of wild fury dashed up into the clouds; and the shore, wherever any sight of it was left, weltered in a sadly frothsome state, like the chin of a Titan with a lather-brush at work.

"Why, bless my heart!" cried the keen-eyed Mordacks; "this is a check I never thought of. Nobody could land in such a surf as that, even if he had conquered all India. Landlord, do you mean to tell me any one could land? And if not, what's the use of your inn standing here?"

"Naw, sir, nawbody cud laun' joost neaw. Lee-ast waas, nut to ca' fur naw yell to dry hissen."

The landlord was pleased with his own wit—perhaps by reason of its scarcity—and went out to tell it in the tap-room while fresh; and Mordacks had made up his mind to call for something—for the good of the house and himself—and return with a sense of escape to his own inn, when the rough frozen road rang with vehement iron, and a horse was pulled up, and a man strode in. The landlord having told his own joke three times, came out with the taste of it upon his lips; but the stern dark eyes looking down into his turned his smile into a frightened stare. He had so much to think of that he could not speak—which happens not only at Flamborough—but his visitor did not wait for the solution of his mental stutter. Without any rudeness he passed the mooning host, and walked into the parlor, where he hoped to find two persons.

Instead of two, he found one only, and that one standing with his back to the door, and by the snow-flecked window, intent upon the drizzly distance of the wind-struck sea. The attitude and fixed regard were so unlike the usual vivacity of Mordacks, that the visitor thought there must be some mistake, till the other turned round and looked at him.

"You see a defeated but not a beaten man," said the factor, to get through the worst of it. "Thank you, Sir Duncan, I will not shake hands. My ambition was to do so, and to put into yours another hand, more near and dear to it. Sir, I have failed. It is open to you to call me by any hard name that may occur to you. That will do you good, be a hearty relief, and restore me rapidly to self-respect, by arousing my anxiety to vindicate myself."

"It is no time for joking; I came here to meet my son. Have you found him, or have you not?"

Sir Duncan sat down and gazed steadfastly at Mordacks. His self-command had borne many hard trials; but the prime of his life was over now; and strong as he looked, and thought himself, the searching wind had sought and found weak places in a sun-beaten frame. But no man would be of noble aspect by dwelling at all upon himself.

The quick intelligence of Mordacks—who was of smaller though admirable type—entered into these things at a flash. And throughout their interview he thought less of himself and more of another than was at all habitual with him, or conducive to good work.

"You must bear with a very heavy blow," he said; "and it goes to my heart to have to deal it."

Sir Duncan Yordas bowed, and said, "The sooner the better, my good friend."

"I have found your son, as I promised you I would," replied Mordacks, speaking rapidly; "healthy, active, uncommonly clever; a very fine sailor, and as brave as Nelson; of gallant appearance—as might be expected; enterprising, steadfast, respected, and admired; benevolent in private life, and a public benefactor. A youth of whom the most distinguished father might be proud. But—but—"

"Will you never finish?"

"But by the force of circumstances, over which he had no control, he became in early days a smuggler, and rose to an eminent rank in that profession."

"I do not care two pice for that; though I should have been sorry if he had not risen."

"He rose to such eminence as to become the High Admiral of smugglers on this coast, and attain the honors of outlawry."

"I look upon that as a pity. But still we may be able to rescind it. Is there anything more against my son?"

"Unluckily there is. A commander of the Coastguard has been killed in discharge of his duty; and Robin Lyth has left the country to escape a warrant."

"What have we to do with Robin Lyth? I have heard of him everywhere—a villain and a murderer."

"God forbid that you should say so! Robin Lyth is your only son."

The man whose word was law to myriads rose without a word for his own case; he looked at his agent with a stern, calm gaze, and not a sign of trembling in his lull broad frame, unless, perhaps, his under lip gave a little soft vibration to the grizzled beard grown to meet the change of climate.

"Unhappily so it is," said Mordacks, firmly meeting Sir Duncan's eyes. "I have proved the matter beyond dispute; and I wish I had better news for you."

"I thank you, sir. You could not well have worse. I believe it upon your word alone. No Yordas ever yet had pleasure of a son. The thing is quite just. I will order my horse."

"Sir Duncan, allow me a few minutes first. You are a man of large judicial mind. Do you ever condemn any stranger upon rumor? And will you, upon that, condemn your son?"

"Certainly not. I proceed upon my knowledge of the fate between father and son in our race."

"That generally has been the father's fault. In this case, you are the father."

Sir Duncan turned back, being struck with this remark. Then he sat down again; which his ancestors had always refused to do, and had rued it. He spoke very gently, with a sad faint smile.

"I scarcely see how, in the present case, the fault can be upon the father's side."

"Not as yet, I grant you. But it would be so if the father refused to hear out the matter, and joined in the general outcry against his son, without even having seen him, or afforded him a chance of self-defense."

"I am not so unjust or unnatural as that, sir. I have heard much about this— sad occurrence in the cave. There can be no question that the smugglers slew the officer. That—that very unfortunate young man may not have done it himself—I trust in God that he did not even mean it. Nevertheless, in the eye of the law, if he were present, he is as guilty as if his own hand did it. Can you contend that he was not present?"

"Unhappily I can not. He himself admits it; and if he did not, it could be proved most clearly."

"Then all that I can do," said Sir Duncan, rising with a heavy sigh, and a violent shiver caused by the chill of his long bleak ride, "is first to require your proofs, Mr. Mordacks, as to the identity of my child who sailed from India with this—this unfortunate youth; then to give you a check for 5000 pounds, and thank you for skillful offices, and great confidence in my honor. Then I shall leave with you what sum you may think needful for the defense, if he is ever brought to trial. And probably after that—well, I shall even go back to end my life in India."

"My proofs are not arranged yet, but they will satisfy you. I shall take no 5000 pounds from you, Sir Duncan, though strictly speaking I have earned it. But I will take one thousand to cover past and future outlay, including the possibility of a trial. The balance I shall live to claim yet, I do believe, and you to discharge it with great pleasure. For that will not be until I bring you a son, not only acquitted, but also guiltless; as I have good reason for believing him to be. But you do not look well; let me call for something."

"No, thank you. It is nothing. I am quite well, but not quite seasoned to my native climate yet. Tell me your reasons for believing that."

"I can not do that in a moment. You know what evidence is a hundred times as well as I do. And in this cold room you must not stop. Sir Duncan, I am not a coddler any more than you are. And I do not presume to dictate to you. But I am as resolute a man as yourself. And I refuse to go further with this subject, until you are thoroughly warmed and refreshed."

"Mordacks, you shall have your way," said his visitor, after a heavy frown, which produced no effect upon the factor. "You are as kind-hearted as you are shrewd. Tell me once more what your conviction is; and I will wait for your reasons, till—till you are ready."

"Then, sir, my settled conviction is that your son is purely innocent of this crime, and that we shall be able to establish that."

"God bless you for thinking so, my dear friend. I can bear a great deal; and I would do my duty. But I did love that boy's mother so."

The general factor always understood his business; and he knew that no part of it compelled him now to keep watch upon the eyes of a stern, proud man.

"Sir, I am your agent, and I magnify mine office," he said, as he took up his hat to go forth. "One branch of my duty is to fettle your horse; and in Flamborough they fettle them on stale fish." Mr. Mordacks strode with a military tramp, and a loud shout for the landlord, who had finished his joke by this time, and was paying the penalties of reaction. "Gil Beilby, thoo'st nobbut a fondhead," he was saying to himself. "Thoo mun hev thy lahtel jawk, thof it crack'th thy own pure back." For he thought that he was driving two great customers away, by the flashing independence of too brilliant a mind; and many clever people of his native place had told him so. "Make a roaring fire in that room," said Mordacks.

CHAPTER XLVI

STUMPED OUT

"I think, my dear, that you never should allow mysterious things to be doing in your parish, and everybody full of curiosity about them, while the only proper person to explain their meaning is allowed to remain without any more knowledge than a man locked up in York Castle might have. In spite of all the weather, and the noise the sea makes, I feel quite certain that important things, which never have any right to happen in our parish, are going on here, and you never interfere; which on the part of the rector, and the magistrate of the neighborhood, to my mind is not a proper course of action. I am sure that I have not the very smallest curiosity; I feel very often that I should have asked questions, when it has become too late to do so, and when anybody else would have put them at the moment, and not had to be sorry afterward."

"I understand that feeling," Dr. Upround answered, looking at his wife for the third cup of coffee to wind up his breakfast as usual, "and without hesitation I reply that it naturally arises in superior natures. Janetta, you have eaten up that bit of broiled hake that I was keeping for your dear mother!"

"Now really, papa, you are too crafty. You put my mother off with a wretched generality, because you don't choose to tell her anything; and to stop me from coming to the rescue, you attack me with a miserable little personality. I perceive by your face, papa, every trick that rises; and without hesitation I reply that they naturally arise in inferior natures."

"Janetta, you never express yourself well." Mrs. Upround insisted upon filial respect. "When I say 'well,' I mean—Well, well, well, you know quite well what I mean, Janetta."

"To be sure, mamma, I always do. You always mean the very best meaning in the world; but you are not up to half of papa's tricks yet."

"This is too bad!" cried the father, with a smile.

"A great deal too bad!" said the mother, with a frown. "I am sure I would never have asked a word of anything, if I could ever have imagined such behavior. Go away, Janetta, this very moment; your dear father evidently wants to tell me something. Now, my dear, you were too sleepy last night; but your peace of mind requires you to unburden itself at once of all these very mysterious goings on."

"Well, perhaps I shall have no peace of mind unless I do," said the rector, with a slight sarcasm, which missed her altogether; "only it might save trouble, my dear, if you would first specify the points which oppress your—or rather I should say, perhaps, my mind so much."

"In the first place, then," began Mrs. Upround, drawing nearer to the doctor, "who is that highly distinguished stranger who can not get away from the Thornwick Inn? What made him come to such a place in dreadful weather; and if he is ill, why not send for Dr. Stirbacks? Dr. Stirbacks will think it most unkind of you; and after all he did for dear Janetta. And then, again, what did the milkman from Sewerby mean by the way he shook his head this morning, about something in the family at Anerley Farm? And what did that most unaccountable man, who calls himself Mr. Mordacks—though I don't believe that is his name at all—"

"Yes, it is, my dear; you never should say such things. He is well known at York, and for miles around; and I entertain very high respect for him."

"So you may, Dr. Upround. You do that too freely; but Janetta quite agrees with me about him. A man with a sword, that goes slashing about, and kills a rat, that was none of his business! A more straightforward creature than himself, I do believe, though he struts like a soldier with a ramrod. And what did he mean, in such horrible weather, by dragging you out to take a deposition in a place even colder than Flamborough itself—that vile rabbit-warren on the other side of Bempton? Deposition of a man who had drunk himself to death—and a Methodist too, as you could not help saying."

"I said it, I know; and I am ashamed of saying it. I was miserably cold, and much annoyed about my coat."

"You never say anything to be ashamed of. It is when you do not say things that you should rather blame yourself. For instance, I feel no curiosity whatever, but a kind-hearted interest, in the doings of my neighbors. We very seldom get any sort of excitement; and when exciting things come all together, quite within the hearing of our stable bell, to be left to guess them out, and perhaps be contradicted, destroys one's finest feelings, and produces downright fidgets."

"My dear, my dear, you really should endeavor to emancipate yourself from such small ideas."

"Large words shall never divert me from my duty. My path of duty is distinctly traced; and if a thwarting hand withdraws me from it, it must end in a bilious headache."

This was a terrible menace to the household, which was always thrown out of its course for three days when the lady became thus afflicted.

"My first duty is to my wife," said the rector. "If people come into my parish with secrets, which come to my knowledge without my desire, and without official obligation, and the faithful and admirable partner of my life threatens to be quite unwell—"

"Ill, dear, very ill—is what would happen to me."

"—then I consider that my duty is to impart to her everything that can not lead to mischief."

"How could you have any doubt of it, my dear? And as to the mischief, I am the proper judge of that."

Dr. Upround laughed in his quiet inner way; and then, as a matter of form, he said, "My dear, you must promise most faithfully to keep whatever I tell you as the very strictest secret."

Mrs. Upround looked shocked at the mere idea of her ever doing otherwise; which indeed, as she said, was impossible. Her husband very nearly looked as if he quite believed her; and then they went into his snug sitting-room, while the maid took away the breakfast things.

"Now don't keep me waiting," said the lady.

"Well, then, my dear," the rector began, after crossing stout legs stoutly, "you must do your utmost not to interrupt me, and, in short—to put it courteously—you must try to hold your tongue, and suffer much astonishment in silence. We have a most distinguished visitor in Flamborough setting up his staff at the Thornwick Hotel."

"Lord Nelson! I knew it must be. Janetta is so quick at things."

"Janetta is too quick at things; and she is utterly crazy about Nelson. No; it is the famous Sir Duncan Yordas."

"Sir Duncan Yordas! Why, I never heard of him."

"You will find that you have heard of him when you come to think, my dear. Our Harry is full of his wonderful doings. He is one of the foremost men in India, though perhaps little heard of in this country yet. He belongs to an ancient Yorkshire family, and is, I believe, the head of it. He came here looking for his son, but has caught a most terrible chill, instead of him; and I think we ought to send him some of your rare soup."

"How sensible you are! It will be the very thing. But first of all, what character does he bear? They do such things in India."

"His character is spotless; I might say too romantic. He is a man of magnificent appearance, large mind, and lots of money."

"My dear, my dear, he must never stay there. I shudder to think of it, this weather. A chill is a thing upon the kidneys always. You know my electuary; and if we bring him round, it is high time for Janetta to begin to think of settling."

"My dear!" said Dr. Upround; "well, how suddenly you jump! I must put on my spectacles to look at you. This gentleman must be getting on for fifty!"

"Janetta should have a man of some discretion, somebody she would not dare to snap at. Her expressions are so reckless, that a young man would not suit her. She ought to have some one to look up to; and you know how she raves about fame, and celebrity, and that. She really seems to care for very little else."

"Then she ought to have fallen in love with Robin Lyth, the most famous man in all this neighborhood."

"Dr. Upround, you say things on purpose to provoke me when my remarks are unanswerable. Robin Lyth indeed! A sailor, a smuggler, a common working-man! And under that terrible accusation!"

"An objectionable party altogether; not even desirable as a grandson. Therefore say nothing more of Janetta and Sir Duncan."

"Sometimes, my dear, the chief object of your existence seems to be to irritate me. What can poor Robin have to do with Sir Duncan Yordas?"

"Simply this. He is his only son. The proofs were completed, and deposited with me for safe custody, last night, by that very active man of business, Geoffrey Mordacks, of York city."

"Well!" cried Mrs. Upround, with both hands lifted, and a high color flowing into her unwrinkled cheeks; "from this day forth I shall never have any confidence in you again. How long—if I may dare to put any sort of question—have you been getting into all this very secret knowledge? And why have I never heard a word of it till now? And not even now, I do believe, through any proper urgency of conscience on your part, but only because I insisted upon knowing. Oh, Dr. Upround, for shame! for shame!"

"My dear, you have no one but yourself to blame," her husband replied, with a sweet and placid smile. "Three times I have told you things that were to go no further, and all three of them went twenty miles within three days. I do not complain of it; far less of you. You may have felt it quite as much your duty to spread knowledge as I felt it mine to restrict it. And I never should have let you get all this out of me now, if it had been at all incumbent upon me to keep it quiet."

"That means that I have never got it out of you at all. I have taken all this trouble for nothing."

"No, my dear, not at all. You have worked well, and have promised not to say a word about it. You might not have known it for a week at least, except for my confidence in you."

"Much of it I thank you for. But don't be cross, my dear, because you have behaved so atrociously. You have not answered half of my questions yet."

"Well, there were so many, that I scarcely can remember them. Let me see: I have told you who the great man is, and the reason that brought him to Flamborough. Then about the dangerous chill he has taken; it came through a bitter ride from Scarborough; and if Dr. Stirbacks came, he would probably make it still more dangerous. At least so Mordacks says; and the patient is in his hands, and out of mine; so that Stirbacks can not be aggrieved with us. On the other hand, as to the milkman from Sewerby. I really do not know why he shook his head. Perhaps he found the big pump frozen. He is not of my parish, and may shake his head without asking my permission. Now I think that I have answered nearly all your questions."

"Not at all; I have not had time to ask them yet, because I feel so much above them. But if the milkman meant nothing, because of his not belonging to our parish, the butcher does, and he can have no excuse. He says that Mr. Mordacks takes all the best meanings of a mutton-sheep every other day to Burlington."

"I know he does. And it ought to put us to the blush that a stranger should have to do so. Mordacks is finding clothes, food, and firing for all the little creatures poor Carroway left, and even for his widow, who has got a wandering mind. Without him there would not have been one left. The poor mother locked in all her little ones, and starved them, to save them from some quite imaginary foe. The neighbors began to think of interfering, and might have begun to do it when it was all over. Happily, Mordacks arrived just in time. His promptitude, skill, and generosity saved them. Never say a word against that man again."

"My dear, I will not," Mrs. Upround answered, with tears coming into her kindly eyes. "I never heard of anything more pitiful. I had no idea Mr. Mordacks was so good. He looks more like an evil spirit. I always regarded him as an evil spirit; and his name sounds like it, and he jumps about so. But he ought to have gone to the rector of the parish."

"It is a happy thing that he can jump about. The rector of the parish can not do so, as you know; and he lives two miles away from them, and had never even heard of it. People always talk about the rector of a parish as if he could be everywhere and see to everything. And few of them come near him in their prosperous times. Have you any other questions to put to me, my dear?"

"Yes, a quantity of things which I can not think of now. How it was that little boy—I remember it like yesterday—came ashore here, and turned out to be Robin Lyth; or at least to be no Robin Lyth at all, but the son of Sir Duncan Yordas. And what happened to the poor man in Bempton Warren."

"The poor man died a most miserable death, but I trust sincerely penitent. He had led a sad, ungodly life, and he died at last of wooden legs. He was hunted to his grave, he told us, by these wooden legs; and he recognized in them Divine retribution, for the sin of his life was committed in timber. No sooner did any of those legs appear—and the poor fellow said they were always coming—than his heart began to patter, and his own legs failed him, and he tried to stop his ears, but his conscience would not let him."

"Now there!" cried Mrs. Upround; "what the power of conscience is! He had stolen choice timber, perhaps ready-made legs."

"A great deal worse than that, my dear; he had knocked out a knot as large as my shovel-hat from the side of a ship home bound from India, because he was going to be tried for mutiny upon their arrival at Leith, it was, I think. He and his partners had been in irons, but unluckily they were just released. The weather was magnificent, a lovely summer's night, soft fair breeze, and every one rejoicing in the certainty of home within a few short hours. And they found home that night, but it was in a better world."

"You have made me creep all over. And you mean to say that a wretch like that has any hope of heaven! How did he get away himself?"

"Very easily. A little boat was towing at the side. There were only three men upon deck, through the beauty of the weather, and two of those were asleep. They bound and gagged the waking one, lashed the wheel, and made off in the boat wholly unperceived. There was Rickon Goold, the ringleader, and four others, and they brought away a little boy who was lying fast asleep, because one of them had been in the service of his father, and because of the value of his Indian clothes, which his ayah made him wear now in his little cot for warmth. The scoundrels took good care that none should get away to tell the tale. They saw the poor Golconda sink with every soul on board, including the captain's wife and babies; then they made for land, and in the morning fog were carried by the tide toward our North Landing. One of them knew the coast as well as need be; but they durst not land until their story was concocted, and everything fitted in to suit it. The sight of the rising sun, scattering the fog, frightened them, as it well might do; and they pulled into the cave, from which I always said, as you may now remember, Robin must have come—the cave which already bears his name.

"Here they remained all day, considering a plausible tale to account for themselves, without making mention of any lost ship, and trying to remove every trace of identity from the boat they had stolen. They had brought with them food enough to last three days, and an anker of rum from the steward's stores; and as they grew weary of their long confinement, they indulged more freely than wisely in the consumption of that cordial. In a word, they became so tipsy that they frightened the little helpless boy; and when they began to fight about his gold buttons, which were claimed by the fellow who had saved his life, he scrambled from the side of the boat upon the rock, and got along a narrow ledge, where none of them could follow him. They tried to coax him back; but he stamped his feet, and swore at them, being sadly taught bad language by the native servants, I dare say. Rickon Goold wanted to shoot him, for they had got a gun with them, and he feared to leave him there. But Sir Duncan's former boatman would not allow it; and at dark they went away and left him there. And the poor little fellow, in his dark despair, must have been led by the hand of the Lord through crannies too narrow for a man to pass. There is a well-known land passage out of that cave; but he must have crawled out by a smaller one, unknown even to our fishermen, slanting up the hill, and having outlet in the thicket near the place where the boats draw up. And so he was found by Robin Cockscroft in the morning. They had fed the child with biscuit soaked in rum, which accounts for his heavy sleep and wonderful exertions, and may have predisposed him for a contraband career."

"And perhaps for the very bad language which he used," said Mrs. Upround, thoughtfully. "It is an extraordinary tale, my dear. But I suppose there can be no doubt of it. But such a clever child should have known his own name. Why did he call himself 'Izunsabe'?"

"That is another link in the certainty of proof. On board that unfortunate ship, and perhaps even before he left India, he was always called the 'Young Sahib,' and he used, having proud little ways of his own, to shout, if anybody durst provoke him, 'I'se young Sahib, I'se young Sahib;' which we rendered into 'Izunsabe.' But his true name is Wilton Bart Yordas, I believe, and the initials can be made out upon his gold beads, Mr. Mordacks tells me, among heathen texts."

"That seems rather shocking to good principles, my dear. I trust that Sir Duncan is a Christian at least; or he shall never set foot in this house."

"My dear, I can not tell. How should I know? He may have lapsed, of course, as a good many of them do, from the heat of the climate, and bad surroundings. But that happens mostly from their marrying native women. And this gentleman never has done that, I do believe."

"They tell me that he is a very handsome man, and of most commanding aspect—the very thing Janetta likes so much. But what became of those unhappy sadly tipsy sailors?"

"Well, they managed very cleverly, and made success of tipsiness. As soon as it was dark that night, and before the child had crawled away, they pushed out of the cave, and let the flood-tide take them round the Head. They meant to have landed at Bridlington Quay, with a tale of escape from a Frenchman; but they found no necessity for going so far. A short-handed collier was lying in the roads; and the skipper, perceiving that they were in liquor, thought it a fine chance, and took some trouble to secure them. They told him that they had been trying to run goods, and were chased by a revenue boat, and so on. He was only too glad to be enabled to make sail, and by dawn they were under way for the Thames; and that was the end of the Golconda."

"What an awful crime! But you never mean to tell me that the Lord let those men live and prosper?"

"That subject is beyond our view, my dear. There were five of them, and Rickon Goold believed himself the last of them. But being very penitent, he might have exaggerated. He said that one was swallowed by a shark, at least his head was, and one was hanged for stealing sheep, and one for a bad sixpence; but the fate of the other (too terrible to tell you) brought this man down here, to be looking at the place, and to divide his time between fasting, and drinking, and poaching, and discoursing to the thoughtless. The women flocked to hear him preach, when the passion was upon him; and he used to hint at awful sins of his own, which made him earnest. I hope that he was so, and I do believe it. But the wooden-legged sailors, old Joe and his son, who seem to have been employed by Mordacks, took him at his own word for a 'miserable sinner'—which, as they told their master, no respectable man would call himself—and in the most business-like manner they set to to remove him to a better world; and now they have succeeded."

"Poor man! After all, one must be rather sorry for him. If old Joe came stumping after me for half an hour, I should have no interest in this life left."

"My dear, they stumped after him the whole day long, and at night they danced a hornpipe outside his hut. He became convinced that the Prince of Evil was come, in that naval style, to fetch him; and he drank everything he could lay hands on, to fortify him for the contest. The end, as you know, was extremely sad for him, but highly satisfactory to them, I fear. They have signified their resolution to attend his funeral; and Mordacks has said, with unbecoming levity, that if they never were drunk before—which seems to me an almost romantic supposition—that night they shall be drunk, and no mistake."

"All these things, my dear," replied Mrs. Upround, who was gifted with a fine vein of moral reflection, "are not as we might wish if we ordered them ourselves. But still there is this to be said in their favor, that they have a large tendency toward righteousness."

CHAPTER XLVII

A TANGLE OF VEINS

Human resolution, energy, experience, and reason in its loftiest form may fight against the doctor; but he beats them all, maintains at least his own vitality, and asserts his guineas. Two more resolute men than Mr. Mordacks and Sir Duncan Yordas could scarcely be found in those resolute times. They sternly resolved to have no sort of doctor; and yet within three days they did have one; and, more than that, the very one they had positively vowed to abstain from.

Dr. Stirbacks let everybody know that he never cared two flips of his thumb for anybody. If anybody wanted him, they must come and seek him, and be thankful if he could find time to hear their nonsense. For he understood not the system only, but also the nature of mankind. The people at the Thornwick did not want him. Very good, so much the better for him and for them; because the more they wanted him, the less would he go near them. Tut! tut! tut! he said; what did he want with crack-brained patients?

All this compelled him, with a very strong reluctance, to be dragged into that very place the very same day; and he saw that he was not come an hour too soon. Sir Duncan was lying in a bitterly cold room, with the fire gone out, and the spark of his life not very far from following it. Mr. Mordacks was gone for the day upon business, after leaving strict orders that a good fire must be kept, and many other things attended to. But the chimney took to smoking, and the patient to coughing, and the landlady opened the window wide, and the fire took flight into the upper air. Sir Duncan hated nothing more than any fuss about himself. He had sent a man to Scarborough for a little chest of clothes, for his saddle-kit was exhausted; and having promised Mordacks that he would not quit the house, he had nothing to do except to meditate and shiver.

Gil Beilby's wife Nell, coming up to take orders for dinner, "got a dreadful turn" from what she saw, and ran down exclaiming that the very best customer that ever drew their latch was dead. Without waiting to think, the landlord sent a most urgent message for Dr. Stirbacks. That learned man happened to be round the corner, although he lived at Bempton; he met the messenger, cast to the winds all sense of wrong, and rushed to the succor of humanity.

That night, when the general factor returned, with the hunger excited by feeding the hungry, he was met at the door by Dr. Stirbacks, saying, "Hush, my good sir," before he had time to think of speaking. "You!" cried Mr. Mordacks, having met this gentleman when Rickon Goold was near his last. "You! Then it must be bad indeed!"

"It is bad, and it must have been all over, sir, but for my being providentially at the cheese shop. I say nothing to wound any gentleman's feelings who thinks that he understands everything; but our poor patient, with the very best meaning, no doubt, has been all but murdered."

"Dr. Stirbacks, you have got him now, and of course you will make the best of him. Don't let him slip through your fingers, doctor; he is much too good for that."

"He shall not slip through my fingers," said the little doctor, with a twinkle of self-preservation. "I have got him, sir, and I shall keep him, sir; and you ought to have put him in my hands long ago."

The sequel of this needs no detail. Dr. Stirbacks came three times a day; and without any disrespect to the profession, it must be admitted that he earned his fees. For Sir Duncan's case was a very strange one, and beyond the best wisdom of the laity. If that chill had struck upon him when his spirit was as usual, he might have cast it off, and gone on upon his business. But coming as it did, when the temperature of his heart was lowered by nip of disappointment, it went into him, as water on a duck's back is not cast away when his rump gland is out of order.

"A warm room, good victuals, and cheerful society—these three are indispensable," said Dr. Stirbacks to Mr. Mordacks, over whom he began to try to tyrannize; "and admirable as you are, my good sir, I fear that your society is depressing. You are always in a fume to be doing something—a stew, I might say, without exaggeration—a wonderful pattern of an active mind. But in a case of illness we require the passive voice. Everything suggestive of rapid motion must be removed, and never spoken of. You are rapid motion itself, my dear sir. We get a relapse every time you come in."

"You want me out of the way. Very well. Let me know when you have killed my friend. I suppose your office ends with that. I will come down and see to his funeral."

"Mr. Mordacks, you may be premature in such prevision. Your own may come first, sir. Look well at your eyes the next time you shave, and I fear you will descry those radiant fibres in the iris which always co-exist with heart-disease. I can tell you fifty cases, if you have time to listen."

"D—n your prognostics, sir!" exclaimed the factor, rudely; but he seldom lathered himself thenceforth without a little sigh of self-regard. "Now, Dr. Stirbacks," he continued, with a rally, "you may find my society depressing, but it is generally considered to be elevating; and that, sir, by judges of the highest order, and men of independent income. The head of your profession in the northern half of England, who takes a hundred guineas for every one you take, rejoices, sir—rejoices is not too strong a word to use—in my very humble society. Of course he may be wrong; but when he hears that Mr. Stirbacks, of Little Under-Bempton—is that the right address, sir?—speaks of my society as depressing—"

"Mr. Mordacks, you misunderstood my meaning. I spoke with no reference to you whatever, but of all male society as enervating—if you dislike the word 'depressing'—relaxing, emollient, emasculating, from want of contradictory element; while I was proceeding to describe the need of strictly female society. The rector offers this; he was here just now. His admiration for you is unbounded. He desires to receive our distinguished patient, with the vast advantage of ladies' society, double-thick walls, and a southern aspect, if you should consider it advisable."

"Undoubtedly I do. If the moving can be done without danger; and of that you are the proper judge, of course."

Thus they composed their little disagreement, with mutual respect, and some approaches to good-will; and Sir Duncan Yordas, being skillfully removed, spent his Christmas (without knowing much about it) in the best and warmest bedroom in the rectory. But Mordacks returned, as an honest man should do, to put the laurel and the mistletoe on his proper household gods. And where can this be better done than in that grand old city, York? But before leaving Flamborough, he settled the claims of business and charity, so far as he could see them, and so far as the state of things permitted.

Foiled as he was in his main object by the murder of the revenue officer, and the consequent flight of Robin Lyth, he had thoroughly accomplished one part of his task, the discovery of the Golconda's fate, and the history of Sir Duncan's child. Moreover, his trusty agents, Joe of the Monument, and Bob his son, had relieved him of one thorny care, by the zeal and skill with which they worked. It was to them a sweet instruction to watch, encounter, and drink down a rogue who had scuttled a ship, and even defeated them at their own weapons, and made a text of them to teach mankind. Dr. Upround had not exaggerated the ardor with which they discharged their duty.

But Mordacks still had one rogue on hand, and a deeper one than Rickon Goold. In the course of his visits to Bridlington Quay, he had managed to meet John Cadman, preferring, as he always did, his own impressions to almost any other evidence. And his own impressions had entirely borne out the conviction of Widow Carroway. But he saw at once that this man could not be plied with coarse weapons, like the other worn-out villain. He reserved him as a choice bit for his own skill, and was careful not to alarm him yet. Only two things concerned him, as immediate in the matter—to provide against Cadman's departure from the scene, and to learn all the widow had to tell about him.

The widow had a great deal to say about that man; but had not said it yet, from want of power so to do. Mordacks himself had often stopped her, when she could scarcely stop herself; for until her health should be set up again, any stir of the mind would be dangerous. But now, with the many things provided for her, good nursing, and company, and the kindness of the neighbors (who jealously rushed in as soon as a stranger led the way), and the sickening of Tommy with the measles—which he had caught in the coal-cellar—she began to be started in a different plane of life; to contemplate the past as a golden age (enshrining a diamond statue of a revenue officer in full uniform), and to look upon the present as a period of steel, when a keen edge must be kept against the world, for a defense of all the little seed of diamonds.

Now the weather was milder, as it generally is at Christmas time, and the snow all gone, and the wind blowing off the land again, to the great satisfaction of both cod and conger. The cottage, which had looked such a den of cold and famine, with the blinds drawn down, and the snow piled up against the door, and not a single child-nose against the glass, was now quite warm again, and almost as lively as if Lieutenant Carroway were coming home to dinner. The heart of Mr. Mordacks glowed with pride as he said to himself that he had done all this; and the glow was reflected on the cheeks of Geraldine, as she ran out to kiss him, and then jumped upon his shoulder. For, in spite of his rigid aspect and stern nose, the little lass had taken kindly to him; while he admired her for eating candles.

"If you please, you can come in here," said Jerry. "Oh, don't knock my head against the door."

Mrs. Carroway knew what he was come for; and although she had tried to prepare herself for it, she could not help trembling a little. The factor had begged her to have some friend present, to encourage and help her in so grievous an affair; but she would not hear of it, and said she had no friend.

Mr. Mordacks sat down, as he was told to do, in the little room sacred to the poor lieutenant, and faithful even yet to the pious memory of his pipe. When the children were shut out, he began to look around, that the lady might have time to cry. But she only found occasion for a little dry sob.

"It is horrible, very, very horrible," she murmured, with a shudder, as her eyes were following his; "but for his sake I endure it."

"A most sad and bitter trial, ma'am, as ever I have heard of. But you are bound to bear in mind that he is looking down on you."

"I could not put up with it, without the sense of that, sir. But I say to myself how much he loved it; and that makes me put up with it."

"I am quite at a loss to understand you, madam. We seem to be at cross-purposes. I was speaking of—of a thing it pains me to mention; and you say how much he loved—"

"Dirt, sir, dirt. It was his only weakness. Oh, my darling Charles, my blessed, blessed Charley! Sometimes I used to drive him almost to his end about it; but I never thought his end would come; I assure you I never did, sir. But now I shall leave everything as he would like to see it—every table and every chair, that he could write his name on it. And his favorite pipe with the bottom in it. That is what he must love to see, if the Lord allows him to look down. Only the children mustn't see it, for the sake of bad example."

"Mrs. Carroway, I agree with you most strictly. Children must be taught clean ways, even while they revere their father. You should see my daughter Arabella, ma'am. She regards me with perfect devotion. Why? Because I never let her do the things that I myself do. It is the only true principle of government for a nation, a parish, a household. How beautifully you have trained pretty Geraldine! I fear that you scarcely could spare her for a month, in the spring, and perhaps Tommy after his measles; but a visit to York would do them good, and establish their expanding minds, ma'am."

"Mr. Mordacks, I know not where we may be then. But anything that you desire is a law to us."

"Well said! Beautifully said! But I trust, my dear madam, that you will be here. Indeed, it would never do for you to go away. Or rather, I should put it thus—for the purposes of justice, and for other reasons also, it is most important that you should not leave this place. At least you will promise me that, I hope? Unless, of course, unless you find the memories too painful. And even so, you might find comfort in some inland house, not far."

"Many people might not like to stop," the widow answered, simply; "but to me it would be a worse pain to go away. I sit, in the evening, by the window here. Whenever there is light enough to show the sea, and the beach is fit for landing on, it seems to my eyes that I can see the boat, with my husband standing up in it. He had a majestic way of standing, with one leg more up than the other, sir, through one of his daring exploits; and whenever I see him, he is just like that; and the little children in the kitchen peep and say, 'Here's daddy coming at last; we can tell by mammy's eyes;' and the bigger ones say, 'Hush! You might know better.' And I look again, wondering which of them is right; and then there is nothing but the clouds and sea. Still, when it is over, and I have cried about it, it does me a little good every time. I seem to be nearer to Charley, as my heart falls quietly into the will of the Lord."

"No doubt of it whatever. I can thoroughly understand it, although there is not a bit of resignation in me. I felt that sort of thing, to some extent, when I lost my angelic wife, ma'am, though naturally departed to a sphere more suited for her. And I often seem to think that still I hear her voice when a coal comes to table in a well-dish. Life, Mrs. Carroway, is no joke to bandy back, but trouble to be shared. And none share it fairly but the husband and the wife, ma'am."

"You make it very hard for me to get my words," she said, without minding that her tears ran down, so long as she spoke clearly. "I am not of the lofty sort, and understand no laws of things; though my husband was remarkable for doing so. He took all the trouble of the taxes off, though my part was to pay for them. And in every other way he was a wonder, sir; not at all because now he is gone above. That would be my last motive."

"He was a wonder, a genuine wonder," Mordacks replied, without irony. "He did his duty, ma'am, with zeal and ardor; a shining example upon very little pay. I fear that it was his integrity and zeal, truly British character and striking sense of discipline, that have so sadly brought him to—to the condition of an example."

"Yes, Mr. Mordacks, it was all that. He never could put up with a lazy man, as anybody, to live, must have to do. He kept all his men, as I used to do our children, to word of command, and no answer. Honest men like it; but wicked men fly out. And all along we had a very wicked man here."

"So I have heard from other good authority—a deceiver of women, a skulk, a dog. I have met with many villains; and I am not hot. But my tendency is to take that fellow by the throat with both hands, and throttle him. Having thoroughly accomplished that, I should prepare to sift the evidence. Unscientific, illogical, brutal, are such desires, as you need not tell me. And yet, madam, they are manly. I hate slow justice; I like it quick—quick, or none at all, I say, so long as it is justice. Creeping justice is, to my mind, little better than slow revenge. My opinions are not orthodox, but I hope they do not frighten you."

"They do indeed, sir; or at least your face does; though I know how quick and just you are. He is a bad man—too well I know it—but, as my dear husband used to say, he has a large lot of children."

"Well, Mrs. Carroway, I admire you the more, for considering what he has not considered. Let us put aside that. The question is—guilty or not guilty? If he is guilty, shall he get off, and innocent men be hanged for him? Six men are in jail at this present moment for the deed which we believe he did. Have they no wives, no fathers and mothers, no children—not to speak of their own lives? The case is one in which the Constitution of the realm must be asserted. Six innocent men must die unless the crime is brought home to the guilty one. Even that is not all as regards yourself. You may not care for your own life, but you are bound to treasure it seven times over for the sake of your seven children. While John Cadman is at large, and nobody hanged instead of him, your life is in peril, ma'am. He knows that you know him, and have denounced him. He has tried to scare you into silence; and the fright caused your sad illness. I have reason to believe that he, by scattering crafty rumors, concealed from the neighbors your sad plight, and that of your dear children. If so, he is worse than the devil himself. Do you see your duty now, and your interest also?"

Mrs. Carroway nodded gently. Her strength of mind was not come back yet, after so much illness. The baby lay now on its father's breast, and the mother's had been wild for it.

"I am sorry to have used harsh words," resumed Mordacks; "but I always have to do so. They seem to put things clearer; and without that, where would business be? Now I will not tire you if I can help it, nor ask a needless question. What provocation had this man? What fanciful cause for spite, I mean?"

"Oh, none, Mr. Mordacks, none whatever. My husband rebuked him for being worthless, and a liar, and a traitor; and he threatened to get him removed from the force; and he gave him a little throw down from the cliff— but what little was done was done entirely for his good."

"Yes, I see. And, after that, was Cadman ever heard to threaten him?"

"Many times, in a most malicious way, when he thought that he was not heeded. The other men may fear to bear witness. But my Geraldine has heard him."

"There could be no better witness. A child, especially a pretty little girl, tells wonderfully with a jury. But we must have a great deal more than that. Thousands of men threaten, and do nothing, according to the proverb. A still more important point is—how did the muskets in the boat come home? They were all returned to the station, I presume. Were they all returned with their charges in them?"

"I am sure I can not say how that was. There was nobody to attend to that.

But one of them had been lost altogether."

"One of the guns never came back at all!" Mordacks almost shouted. "Whose gun was it that did not come back?"

"How can we say? There was such confusion. My husband would never let them nick the guns, as they do at some of the stations, for every man to know his own. But in spite of that, each man had his own, I believe. Cadman declares that he brought home his; and nobody contradicted him. But if I saw the guns, I should know whether Cadman's is among them."

"How can you possibly pretend to know that, ma'am? English ladies can do almost anything. But surely you never served out the guns?"

"No, Mr. Mordacks. But I have cleaned them. Not the inside, of course; that I know nothing of; and nobody sees that, to be offended. But several times I have observed, at the station, a disgraceful quantity of dust upon the guns—dust and rust and miserable blotches, such as bad girls leave in the top of a fish-kettle; and I made Charley bring them down, and be sure to have them empty; because they were so unlike what I have seen on board of the ship where he won his glory, and took the bullet in his nineteenth rib."

"My dear madam, what a frame he must have had! But this is most instructive. No wonder Geraldine is brave. What a worthy wife for a naval hero! A lady who could handle guns!"

"I knew, sir, quite from early years, having lived near a very large arsenal, that nothing can make a gun go off unless there is something in it. And I could trust my husband to see to that; and before I touched one of them I made him put a brimstone match to the touch-hole. And I found it so pleasant to polish them, from having such wicked things quite at my mercy. The wood was what I noticed most, because of understanding chairs. One of them had a very curious tangle of veins on the left cheek behind the trigger; and I just had been doing for the children's tea what they call 'crinkly-crankly'—treacle trickled (like a maze) upon the bread; and Tommy said, 'Look here! it is the very same upon this gun.' And so it was; just the same pattern on the wood! And while I was doing it Cadman came up, in his low surly way, and said, 'I want my gun, missus; I never shoot with no other gun than that. Captain says I may shoot a sea-pye, for the little ones.' And so I always called it 'Cadman's gun.' I have not been able to think much yet. But if that gun is lost, I shall know who it was that lost a gun that dreadful night."

"All this is most strictly to the purpose," answered Mordacks, "and may prove most important. We could never hope to get those six men off, without throwing most grave suspicion elsewhere; and unless we can get those six men off, their captain will come and surrender himself, and be hanged, to a dead certainty. I doubted his carrying the sense of right so far, until I reflected upon his birth, dear madam. He belongs, as I may tell you now, to a very ancient family, a race that would run their heads into a noose out of pure obstinacy, rather than skulk off. I am of very ancient race myself, though I never take pride in the matter, because I have seen more harm than good of it. I always learned Latin at school so quickly through being a grammatical example of descent. According to our pedigree, Caius Calpurnius Mordax Naso was the Governor of Britain under Pertinax. My name means 'biting'; and bite I can, whether my dinner is before me, or my enemy. In the present case I shall not bite yet, but prepare myself for doing so. I watch the proceedings of the government, who are sure to be slow, as well as blundering. There has been no appointment to this command as yet, because of so many people wanting it. This patched-up peace, which may last about six months (even if it is ever signed), is producing confusion everywhere. You have an old fool put in charge of this station till a proper successor is appointed."

"He is not like Captain Carroway, sir. But that concerns me little now. But I do wish, for my children's sake, that they would send a little money."

"On no account think twice of that. That question is in my hands, and affords me one of the few pleasures I derive from business. You are under no sort of obligation about it. I am acting under authority. A man of exalted position and high office—but never mind that till the proper time comes; only keep your mind in perfect rest, and attend to your children and yourself. I am obliged to proceed very warily, but you shall not be annoyed by that scoundrel. I will provide for that before I leave; also I will see the guns still in store, without letting anybody guess my motive. I have picked up a very sharp fellow here, whose heart is in the business thoroughly; for one of the prisoners is his twin brother, and he lost his poor sweetheart through Cadman's villainy—a young lass who used to pick mussels, or something. He will see that the rogue does not give us the slip, and I have looked out for that in other ways as well. I am greatly afraid of tiring you, my dear madam; but have you any other thing to tell me of this Cadman?"

"No, Mr. Mordacks, except a whole quantity of little things that tell a great deal to me, but to anybody else would have no sense. For instance, of his looks, and turns, and habits, and tricks of seeming neither the one thing nor the other, and jumping all the morning, when the last man was hanged—"

"Did he do that, madam? Are you quite sure?"

"I had it on the authority of his own wife. He beats her, but still she can not understand him. You may remember that the man to be suspended was brought to the place where—where—"

"Where he earned his doom. It is quite right. Things of that sort should be done upon a far more liberal scale. Example is better than a thousand precepts. Let us be thankful that we live in such a country. I have brought some medicine for brave Tommy from our Dr. Stirbacks. Be sure that you stroke his throat when he takes it. Boys are such rogues—"

"Well, Mr. Mordacks, I really hope that I know how to make my little boy take medicine!"

CHAPTER XLVIII

SHORT SIGHS, AND LONG ONES

Now it came to pass that for several months this neighborhood, which had begun to regard Mr. Mordacks as its tutelary genius—so great is the power of bold energy—lost him altogether; and with brief lamentation began to do very well without him. So fugitive is vivacious stir, and so well content is the general world to jog along in its old ruts. The Flamborough butcher once more subsided into a piscitarian; the postman, who had been driven off his legs, had time to nurse his grain again; Widow Tapsy relapsed into the very worst of taps, having none to demand good beverage; and a new rat, sevenfold worse than the mighty net-devourer (whom Mordacks slew; but the chronicle has been cut out, for the sake of brevity), took possession of his galleries, and made them pay. All Flamborough yearned for the "gentleman as did things," itself being rather of the contemplative vein, which flows from immemorial converse with the sea. But the man of dry hand-and-heel activity came not, and the lanes forgot the echo of his Roman march.

The postman (with a wicked endeavor of hope to beget faith from sweet laziness) propagated a loose report that Death had claimed the general factor, through fear of any rival in activity. The postman did not put it so, because his education was too good for long words to enter into it; but he put his meaning in a shorter form than a smattering of distant tongues leaves to us. The butcher (having doubt of death, unless by man administered) kicked the postman out of his expiring shop, where large hooks now had no sheep for bait; and Widow Tapsy, filled with softer liquid form of memory, was so upset by the letter-man's tale that she let off a man who owed four gallons, for beating him as flat as his own bag. To tell of these things may take time, but time is thoroughly well spent if it contributes a trifle toward some tendency, on anybody's part, to hope that there used to be, even in this century, such a thing as gratitude.

But why did Mr. Mordacks thus desert his favorite quest and quarters, and the folk in whom he took most delight—because so long inaccessible? The reason was as sound as need be: important business of his own had called him away into Derbyshire. Like every true son of stone and crag, he required an annual scratch against them, and hoped to rest among them when the itch of life was over. But now he had hopes of even more than that—of owning a good house and fair estate, and henceforth exerting his remarkable powers of agency on his own behalf. For his cousin, Calpurnius Mordacks, the head of the family, was badly ailing, and having lost his only son in the West Indies, had sent for this kinsman to settle matters with him. His offer was generous and noble; to wit, that Geoffrey should take, not the property alone, but also his second cousin, fair Calpurnia, though not without her full consent. Without the lady, he was not to have the land, and the lady's consent must be secured before her father ceased to be a sound testator.

Now if Calpurnia had been kept in ignorance of this arrangement, a man possessing the figure, decision, stature, self-confidence, and other high attributes of our Mordacks, must have triumphed in a week at latest. But with that candor which appears to have been so strictly entailed in the family, Colonel Calpurnius called them in; and there (in the presence of the testator and of each other) they were fully apprised of this rather urgent call upon their best and most delicate emotions. And the worst of it was (from the gentleman's point of view), that the contest was unequal. The golden apples were not his to cast, but Atalanta's. The lady was to have the land, even without accepting love. Moreover, he was fifty per cent beyond her in age, and Hymen would make her a mamma without invocation of Lucina. But highest and deepest woe of all, most mountainous of obstacles, was the lofty skyline of his nose, inherited from the Roman. If the lady's corresponding feature had not corresponded—in other words, if her nose had been chubby, snub, or even Greek—his bold bridge must have served him well, and even shortened access to rosy lips and tender heart. But, alas! the fair one's nose was also of the fine imperial type, truly admirable in itself, but (under one of nature's strictest laws) coy of contact with its own male expression. Love, whose joy and fierce prank is to buckle to the plated pole ill-matched forms and incongruous spirits, did not fail of her impartial freaks. Mr. Mordacks had to cope with his own kin, and found the conflict so severe that not a breath of time was left him for anybody's business but his own.

If luck was against him in that quarter (although he would not own it yet), at York and Flamborough it was not so. No crisis arose to demand his presence; no business went amiss because of his having to work so hard at love. There came, as there sometimes does in matters pressing, tangled, and exasperating, a quiet period, a gentle lull, a halcyon time when the jaded brain reposes, and the heart may hatch her own mares'-nests. Underneath that tranquil spell lay fond Joe and Bob (with their cash to spend), Widow Precious (with her beer laid in), and Widow Carroway, with a dole at last extorted from the government; while Anerley Farm was content to hearken the creak of wagon and the ring of flail, and the rector of Flamborough once more rejoiced in the bloodless war that breeds good-will.

For Sir Duncan Yordas was a fine chess-player, as many Indian officers of that time were; and now that he was coming to his proper temperature (after three months of barbed stab of cold, and the breach of the seal of the seventy-seventh phial of Dr. Stirbacks), in gratitude for that miraculous escape, he did his very best to please everybody. To Dr. Upround he was an agreeable and penetrative companion; to Mrs. Upround, a gallant guest, with a story for every slice of bread and butter; to Janetta, a deity combining the perfections of Jupiter, Phoebus, Mars, and Neptune (because of his yacht), without any of their drawbacks; and to Flamborough, more largely speaking, a downright good sort of gentleman, combining a smoke with a chaw—so they understood cigars—and not above standing still sometimes for a man to say some sense to him.

But before Mr. Mordacks left his client under Dr. Upround's care, he had done his best to provide that mischief should not come of gossip; and the only way to prevent that issue is to preclude the gossip. Sir Duncan Yordas, having lived so long in a large commanding way, among people who might say what they pleased of him, desired no concealment here, and accepted it unwillingly. But his agent was better skilled in English life, and rightly foresaw a mighty buzz of nuisance—without any honey to be brought home—from the knowledge of the public that the Indian hero had begotten the better-known apostle of free trade. Yet it might have been hard to persuade Sir Duncan to keep that great fact to himself, if his son had been only a smuggler, or only a fugitive from a false charge of murder. But that which struck him in the face, as soon as he was able to consider things, was the fact that his son had fled and vanished, leaving his underlings to meet their fate. "The smuggling is a trifle," exclaimed the sick man; "our family never was law-abiding, and used to be large cattle-lifters; even the slaying of a man in hot combat is no more than I myself have done, and never felt the worse for it. But to run away, and leave men to be hanged, after bringing them into the scrape himself, is not the right sort of dishonor for a Yordas. If the boy surrenders, I shall be proud to own him. But until he does that, I agree with you, Mordacks, that he does not deserve to know who he is."

This view of the case was harsh, perhaps, and showed some ignorance of free-trade questions, and of English justice. If Robin Lyth had been driven, by the heroic view of circumstances, to rush into embrace constabular, would that have restored the other six men to family sinuosities? Not a chance of it. Rather would it treble the pangs of jail—where they enjoyed themselves—to feel that anxiety about their pledges to fortune from which the free Robin relieved them. Money was lodged and paid as punctual as the bank for the benefit of all their belongings. There were times when the sailors grumbled a little because they had no ropes to climb; but of any unfriendly rope impending they were too wise to have much fear. They knew that they had not done the deed, and they felt assured that twelve good men would never turn round in their box to believe it.

Their captain took the same view of the case. He had very little doubt of their acquittal if they were defended properly; and of that a far wealthier man than himself, the Chancellor of the Exchequer of free trade, Master Rideout of Malton, would take good care, if the money left with Dr. Upround failed. The surrender of Robin would simply hurt them, unless they were convicted, and in that case he would yield himself. Sir Duncan did not understand these points, and condemned his son unjustly. And Mordacks was no longer there to explain such questions in his sharp clear way.

Being in this sadly disappointed state, and not thoroughly delivered from that renal chill (which the northeast wind, coming over the leather of his valise, had inflicted), this gentleman, like a long-pendulous grape with the ventilators open, was exposed to the delicate insidious billing of little birds that love something good. It might be wrong—indeed, it must be wrong, and a foul slur upon fair sweet love—to insinuate that Indian gold, or rank, or renown, or vague romance, contributed toward what came to pass. Miss Janetta Upround, up to this time of her life, had laughed at all the wanton tricks of Cupid; and whenever the married women told her that her time would be safe to come, and then she might understand their behavior, they had always been ordered to go home and do their washing. And this made it harder for her to be mangled by the very tribulation she had laughed at.

Short little sighs were her first symptom, and a quiet way of going up the stairs—which used to be a noisy process with her—and then a desire to know something of history, and a sudden turn of mind toward soup. Sir Duncan had a basin every day at twelve o'clock, and Janetta had orders to see him do it, by strict institution of Stirbacks. Those orders she carried out with such zeal that she even went so far as to blow upon the spoon; and she did look nice while doing it. In a word—as there is no time for many—being stricken, she did her best to strike, as the manner of sweet women is.

Sir Duncan Yordas received it well. Being far on toward her futurity in years, and beyond her whole existence in experience and size, he smiled at her ardor and short vehemence to please him, and liked to see her go about, because she turned so lightly. Then the pleasant agility of thought began to make him turn to answer it; and whenever she had the best of him in words, her bright eyes fell, as if she had the worst. "She doesn't even know that she is clever," said the patient to himself, "and she is the first person I have met with yet who knows which side of the line Calcutta is."

The manner of those benighted times was to keep from young ladies important secrets which seemed to be no concern of theirs. Miss Upround had never been told what brought this visitor to Flamborough, and although she had plenty of proper curiosity, she never got any reward for it. Only four Flamburians knew that Sir Duncan was Robin Lyth's papa—or, as they would put it (having faster hold of the end of the stick next to them), that Robin Lyth was the son of Sir Duncan. And those four were, by force of circumstance, Robin Cockscroft and Joan his wife, the rector and the rectoress. Even Dr. Stirbacks (organically inquisitive as he was, and ill content to sniff at any bottle with the cork tied down), by mastery of Mordacks and calm dignity of rector, was able to suspect a lot of things, but to be sure of none of them; and suspicion, according to its usual manner, never came near the truth at all. Miss Upround, therefore, had no idea that if she became Lady Yordas, which she very sincerely longed to be, she would, by that event, be made the step-mother of a widely celebrated smuggler; while her Indian hero, having no idea of her flattering regard as yet, was not bound to enlighten her upon that point.

At Anerley Farm the like ignorance prevailed; except that Mistress Anerley, having a quick turn for romance, and liking to get her predictions confirmed, recalled to her mind (and recited to her husband in far stronger language) what she had said, in the clover-blossom time, to the bravest man that ever lived, the lamented Captain Carroway. Captain Carroway's dauntless end, so thoroughly befitting his extraordinary exploits, for which she even had his own authority, made it the clearest thing in all the world that every word she said to him must turn out Bible-true. And she had begged him—and one might be certain that he had told it, as a good man must, to his poor dear widow—not to shoot at Robin Lyth; because he would get a thousand pounds, instead of a hundred for doing it. She never could have dreamed to find her words come true so suddenly; but here was an Indian Prince come home, who employed the most pleasant-spoken gentleman; and he might know who it was he had to thank that even in the cave the captain did not like to shoot that long-lost heir; and from this time out there was no excuse for Stephen if he ever laughed at anything that his wife said. Only on no account must Mary ever hear of it; for a bird in the hand was worth fifty in the bush; and the other gone abroad, and under accusation, and very likely born of a red Indian mother. Whereas Harry Tanfield's father, George, had been as fair as a foal, poor fellow; and perhaps if the church books had been as he desired, he might have kept out of the church-yard to this day.

"And me in it," the farmer answered, with a laugh—"dead for love of my wife, Sophy; as wouldn't 'a been my wife, nor drawn nigh upon fi' pounds this very week for feathers, fur, and ribbon stuff. Well, well, George would 'a come again, to think of it. How many times have I seen him go with a sixpence in the palm of 's hand, and think better of the king upon it, and worser of the poor chap as were worn out, like the tail of it! Then back go the sixpence into George's breeches; and out comes my shilling to the starving chap, on the sly, and never mentioned. But for all that, I think, like enow, old George mought 'a managed to get up to heaven."

"Stephen, I wish to hear nothing of that. The question concerns his family, not ours, as Providence has seen fit to arrange. Now what is your desire to have done with Mary? William has made his great discovery at last; and if we should get the 10,000 pounds, nobody need look down on us."

"I should like to see any one look down on me," Master Anerley said, with his back set straight; "a' mought do so once, but a' would be sorry afterward. Not that I would hinder him of 's own way; only that he better keep out of mine. Sometimes, when you go thinking of your own ideas, you never seem to bear in mind what my considerations be."

"Because you can not follow out the quickness of the way I think. You always acknowledge that, my dear."

"Well, well. Quick churn spoileth butter. Like Willie with his perpetual motion. What good to come of it, if he hath found out? And a' might, if ever a body did, from the way he goeth jumping about forever, and never hold fast to anything. A nice thing 'twould be for the fools to say, perpetual motion come from Anerley Farm!"

"You never will think any good of him, Stephen, because his mind comes from my side. But wait till you see the 10,000 pounds."

"That I will; and thank the Lord to live so long. But, to come to common-sense—how was Mary and Harry a-carrying on this afternoon?"

"Not so very bad, father; and nothing good to speak of. He kept on very well from the corners of his eyes; but she never corresponded, so to speak— same as—you know."

"The same as you used to do when you was young. Well, manners may be higher stylish now. Did he ask her about the hay-rick?"

"That he did. Three or four times over; exactly as you said it to him. He knew that was how you got the upper hand of me, according to your memory, but not mine; and he tried to do it the very same way; but the Lord makes a lot of change in thirty years of time. Mary quite turned her nose up at any such riddle, and he pulled his spotted handkerchief out of that new hat of his, and the fagot never saw fit to heed even the color of his poor red cheeks. Stephen, you would have marched off for a week if I had behaved to you so."

"And the right way too; I shall put him up to that. Long sighs only leads to turn-up noses. He plays too knuckle-down at it. You should go on with your sweetheart very mild at first; just a-feeling for her finger-tips; and emboldening of her to believe that you are frightened, and bringing her to peep at you as if you was a blackbird, ready to pop out of sight. That makes 'em wonderful curious and eager, and sticks you into 'em, like prickly spinach. But you mustn't stop too long like that. You must come out large, as a bull runs up to gate; and let them see that you could smash it if you liked, but feel a goodness in your heart that keeps you out of mischief. And then they comes up, and they says, 'poor fellow!'"

"Stephen, I do not approve of such expressions, or any such low opinions. You may know how you went on. Such things may have answered once; because of your being—yourself, you know. But Mary, although she may not have my sense, must have her own opinions. And the more you talk of what we used to do—though I never remember your trotting up, like a great bull roaring, to any kind of gate—the less I feel inclined to force her. And who is Harry Tanfield, after all?"

"We know all about him," the farmer answered; "and that is something to begin with. His land is worth fifteen shillings an acre less than ours, and full of kid-bine. But, for all that, he can keep a family, and is a good home-dweller. However, like the rest of us, in the way of women, he must bide his bolt, and bode it."

"Father," the mistress of the house replied, "I shall never go one step out of my way to encourage a young man who makes you speak so lightly of those you owe so much to. Harry Tanfield may take his chance for me."

"So a' may for me, mother—so a' may for me. If a' was to have our Mary, his father George would be coming up between us, out of his peace in churchyard, more than he doth a'ready; and a' comes too much a'ready.— Why, poppet, we were talking of you—fie, fie, listening!"

"No, now, father," Mary Anerley answered, with a smile at such a low idea; "you never had that to find fault with me, I think. And if you are plotting against me for my good—as mother loves to put it—it would be the best way to shut me out before you begin to do it."

"Why, bless my heart and soul," exclaimed the farmer, with a most crafty laugh—for he meant to kill two birds with one stone—"if the lass hathn't got her own dear mother's tongue, and the very same way of turning things! There never hath been such a time as this here. The childer tell us what to do, and their mothers tell us what not to do. Better take the business off my hands, and sell all they turnips as is rotting. Women is cheats, and would warrant 'em sound, with the best to the top of the bury. But mind you one thing—if I retires from business, like Brother Popplewell, I shall expect to be supported; cheap, but very substantial."

"Mary, you are wicked to say such things," Mistress Anerley began, as he went out, "when you know that your dear father is such a substantial silent man."

CHAPTER XLIX

A BOLD ANGLER

As if in vexation at being thwarted by one branch of the family, Cupid began to work harder at the other, among the moors and mountains. Not that either my lady Philippa or gentle Mistress Carnaby fell back into the snares of youth, but rather that youth, contemptuous of age, leaped up, and defied everybody but itself, and cried tush to its own welfare.

For as soon as the trance of snow was gone, and the world, emboldened to behold itself again, smiled up from genial places; and the timid step of peeping spring awoke a sudden flutter in the breast of buds; and streams (having sent their broken anger to the sea) were pleased to be murmuring clearly again, and enjoyed their own flexibility; and even stern mountains and menacing crags allowed soft light to play with them—at such a time prudence found very narrow house-room in the breast of young Lancelot, otherwise "Pet."

"If Prudence be present, no Divinity is absent," according to high authority; but the author of the proverb must have first excluded Love from the list of Divinities. Pet's breast, or at any rate his chest, had grown under the expansive enormity of love; his liver, moreover (which, according to poets, both Latin and Greek, is the especial throne of love), had quickened its proceedings, from the exercise he took; from the same cause, his calves increased so largely that even Jordas could not pull the agate buttons of his gaiters through their holes. In a word, he gained flesh, muscle, bone, and digestion, and other great bodily blessings, from the power believed by the poets to upset and annihilate every one of them. However, this proves nothing anti-poetical, for the essence of that youth was to contradict experience.

Jordas had never, in all his born days, not even in the thick of the snow-drift, found himself more in a puzzle than now; and he could not even fly for advice in this matter to Lawyer Jellicorse. The first great gift of nature, expelled by education, is gratitude. A child is full of gratitude, or at least has got the room for it; but no full-grown mortal, after good education, has been known to keep the rudiments of thankfulness. But Jordas had a stock of it—as much as can remain to any one superior to the making of a cross.

Now the difficulty of it was that Jordas called to mind, every morning when he saw snow, and afterward when he saw anything white, that he must have required a grave, and not got it (in time to be any good to him), without the hard labor, strong endurance, and brotherly tendance of the people of the gill. Even the three grand fairy gifts of Lawyer Jellicorse himself might scarcely have saved him, although they were no less than as follows, in virtue: the tip of a tongue that had never told a lie (because it belonged to a bullock slain young), a flask of old Scotch whiskey, and a horn comfit-box of Irish snuff. All these three had stood him in good stead, especially the last, which kept him wide-awake, and enabled him to sneeze a yellow hole in the drift, whenever it threatened to ingulf his beard. Without those three he could never have got on; but, with all the three, he could never have got out, if Bat and Maunder of the gill had not come to his succor in the very nick of time. Not only did they work hard for hours under the guidance of Saracen (who was ready to fly at them if they left off), but when at length they came on Jordas, in his last exhaustion, with the good horse rubbing up his chin to make him warmer, they did a sight of things, which the good Samaritan, having finer climate, was enabled to dispense with. And when they had set him on his legs again, finding that he could not use them yet, they hoisted him on the back of Maunder, who was strong; and the whole of that expedition ended at the little cottage in the gill. But the kindness of the inhabitants was only just beginning; for when Jordas came to himself he found that his off-foot—as Marmaduke would have called it—the one which had ridden with a northeast aspect, was frozen as hard as a hammer, and as blue as a pistol barrel. Mrs. Bart happened to have seen such cases in her native country, and by her skillful treatment and never-wearying care, the poor fellow's foot was saved and cured, though at one time he despaired of it. Marmaduke also was restored, and sent home to his stable some days before his rider was in a condition to mount him.

In return for all these benefits, how could the dogman, without being worse than a dog, go and say to his ladies that mischief was breeding between their heir and a poor girl who lived in a corner of their land? If he had been ungrateful, or in any way a sneak, he might have found no trouble in this thing; but being, as he was, an honest, noble-hearted fellow, he battled severely in his mind to set up the standard of the proper side to take. For such matters Pet cared not one jot. Crafty as he was, he could never understand that Jordas and Welldrum were not the same man, one half working out-of-doors, and the other in. For him it was enough that Jordas would not tell, probably because he was afraid to do so, and Pet resolved to make him useful. For Lancelot Carnaby was very sharp indeed in espying what suited his purpose. His set purpose was to marry Insie Bart, in whom he had sense enough to perceive his better, in every respect but money and birth, in which two he was before her, or at any rate supposed so. He was proud, as need be, of his station in life; but he reasoned—if the process of his mind was reason—that being so exalted, he might please himself; that his wife would rise to his rank, instead of lowering him; that her father was a man of education and a gentleman, although he worked with his own hands; and that Insie was a lady, though she went to fill a pitcher.

For one happy fact the youth deserved some credit, or rather, perhaps, his youth deserved it for him. He was madly in love with Insie, and his passion could not be of very high spiritual order; but the idea of obtaining her dishonorably never occurred to his mind for one moment. He knew her to be better, purer, and nobler than himself in every way; and he felt, though he did not want to feel it, that her nature gave a lift to his. Insie, on the other hand, began to like him better, and to despise him less and less; his reckless devotion to her made its way; and in spite of all her common-sense, his beauty and his lordly style had attractions for her young romance. And at last her heart began to bound, like his, when they were together. "With all thy faults, I love thee still," was the loose condition of her youthful mind.

Into every combination, however steep and deep be the gill of its quiet incubation, a number of people and of things peep in, and will enter, like the cuckoo, at the glimpse of a white feather, or even without it, unless beak and claw are shown. And now the intruder into Pet's love nest had the right to look in, and to pull him out, neck and crop, unless he sat there legally. Whether birds discharge fraternal duty is a question for Notes and Queries even in the present most positive age. Sophocles says that the clever birds feed their parents and their benefactors, and men ascribe piety to them in fables, as a needful ensample to one another.

Be that as it may, this Maunder Bart, when his rather slow attention was once aroused, kept a sharp watch upon his young landlord's works. It was lucky for Pet that he meant no harm, and that Maunder had contemptuous faith in him; otherwise Insie's brother would have shortly taken him up by his gaiters, and softly beaten his head in against a rock. For Mr. Bart's son was of bitter, morose, and almost savage nature, silent, moody, and as resolute as death. He resented and darkly repined at the loss of position and property of which he had heard, and he scorned the fine sentiments which had led to nothing at all substantial. It was not in his power to despise his father, for his mind felt the presence of the larger one; but he did not love him as a son should do; neither did he speak out his thoughts to anybody beyond a few mutters to his mother. But he loved his gentle sister, and found in her a goodness which warmed him up to think about getting some upon his own account.

Such thoughts, however, were fugitive, and Maunder's more general subject of brooding was the wrong he had suffered through his father. He was living and working like a peasant or a miner, instead of having horses, and dogs, and men, and the right to kick out inferior people—as that baby Lancelot Carnaby had—for no other reason, that he could find, than the magnitude of his father's mind. He had gone into the subject with his father long ago—for Mr. Bart felt a noble pride in his convictions—and the son lamented with all his heart the extent of his own father's mind. In his lonely walks, heavy hours, and hard work—which last he never grudged, for his strength required outlet—he pondered continually upon one thing, and now he seemed to see a chance of doing it. The first step in his upward course would be Insie's marriage with Lancelot.

Pet, who had no fear of any one but Maunder, tried crafty little tricks to please him; but instead of earning many thanks, got none at all, which made him endeavor to improve himself. Mr. Bart's opinion of him now began to follow the course of John Smithies's, and Smithies looked at it in one light only (ever since Pet so assaulted him, and then trusted his good-will across the dark moors), and that light was that "when you come to think of him, you mustn't be too hard upon him, after all." And one great excellence of this youth was that he cared not a doit for general opinion, so long as he got his own special desire.

His desire was, not to let a day go by without sight and touch of Insie. These were not to be had at a moment's notice, nor even by much care; and five times out of six he failed of so much as a glimpse or a word of her. For the weather and the time of year have much to say concerning the course of the very truest love, and worse than the weather itself too often is the cloudy caprice of maiden mind.

Insie's father must have known what attraction drew this youth to such a cold unfurnished spot, and if he had been like other men, he would either have nipped in the bud this passion, or, for selfish reasons, fostered it. But being of large theoretical mind, he found his due outlet in giving advice.

It is plain at a glance that in such a case the mother is the proper one to give advice, and the father the one to act strenuously. But now Mrs. Bart, who was a very good lady, and had gone through a world of trouble from the want of money—the which she had cast away for sake of something better—came to the forefront of this pretty little business, as Insie's mother, vigorously.

"Christophare," she said to her husband, "not often do I speak, between us, of the affairs it is wise to let alone. But now of our dear child Incsa it is just that I should insist something. Mandaro, which you call English Maunder, already is destroyed for life by the magnitude of your good mind. It is just that his sister should find the occasion of reversion to her proper grade of life. For you, Christophare, I have abandoned all, and have the good right to claim something from you. And the only thing that I demand is one—let Inesa return to the lady."

"Well," said Mr. Bart, who had that sense of humor without which no man can give his property away, "I hope that she never has departed from it. But, my dear, as you make such a point of it, I will promise not to interfere, unless there is any attempt to do wrong, and intrap a poor boy who does not know his own mind. Insie is his equal by birth and education, and perhaps his superior in that which comes foremost nowadays—the money. Dream not that he is a great catch, my dear; I know more of that matter than you do. It is possible that he may stand at the altar with little to settle upon his bride except his bright waistcoat and gaiters."

"Tush, Christophare! You are, to my mind, always an enigma."

"That is as it should be, and keeps me interesting still. But this is a mere boy and girl romance. If it meant anything, my only concern would be to know whether the boy was good. If not, I should promptly kick him back to his own door."

"From my observation, he is very good—to attend to his rights, and make the utmost of them."

Mr. Bart laughed, for he knew that a little hit at himself was intended; and very often now, as his joints began to stiffen, he wished that his youth had been wiser. He stuck to his theories still; but his practice would have been more of the practical kind, if it had come back to be done again. But his children and his wife had no claim to bring up anything, because everything was gone before he undertook their business. However, he obtained reproach —as always seems to happen—for those doings of his early days which led to their existence. Still, he liked to make the best of things, and laughed, instead of arguing.

For a short time, therefore, Lancelot Carnaby seemed to have his own way in this matter, as well as in so many others. As soon as spring weather unbound the streams, and enlarged both the spots and the appetite of trout (which mainly thrive together), Pet became seized, by his own account, with insatiable love of angling. The beck of the gill, running into the Lune, was alive, in those unpoaching days, with sweet little trout of a very high breed, playful, mischievous, and indulging (while they provoked) good hunger. These were trout who disdained to feed basely on the ground when they could feed upward, ennobling almost every gulp with a glimpse of the upper creation. Mrs. Carnaby loved these "graceful creatures," as she always called them, when fried well; and she thought it so good and so clever of her son to tempt her poor appetite with them.

"Philippa, he knows—perhaps your mind is absent," she said, as she put the fifth trout on her plate at breakfast one fine morning—"he feels that these little creatures do me good, and to me it becomes a sacred duty to endeavor to eat them."

"You seem to succeed very well, Eliza."

"Yes, dear, I manage to get on a little, from a sort of sporting feeling that appeals to me. Before I begin to lift the skins of any of these little darlings, I can see my dear boy standing over the torrent, with his wonderful boldness, and bright eagle eyes—"

"To pull out a fish of an ounce and a half. Without any disrespect to Pet, whose fishing apparel has cost 20 pounds, I believe that Jordas catches every one of them."

Sad to say, this was even so; Lancelot tried once or twice, for some five minutes at a time, throwing the fly as he threw a skittle-ball; but finding no fish at once respond to his precipitance, down he cast the rod, and left the rest of it to Jordas. But inasmuch as he brought back fish whenever he went out fishing, and looked as brilliant and picturesque as a salmon-fly, in his new costume, his mother was delighted, and his aunt, being full of fresh troubles, paid small heed to him.

For as soon as the roads became safe again, and an honest attorney could enter "horse hire" in his bill without being too chivalrous, and the ink that had clotted in the good-will time began to form black blood again, Mr. Jellicorse himself resolved legitimately to set forth upon a legal enterprise. The winter had shaken him slightly—for even a solicitor's body is vulnerable; and well for the clerk of the weather it is that no action lies against him—and his good wife told him to be very careful, although he looked as young as ever. She had no great opinion of the people he was going to, and was sure that they would be too high and mighty even to see that his bed was aired. For her part, she hoped that the reports were true which were now getting into every honest person's mouth; and if he would listen to a woman's common-sense, and at once go over to the other side, it would serve them quite right, and be the better for his family, and give a good lift to his profession. But his honesty was stout, and vanquished even his pride in his profession.

CHAPTER L

PRINCELY TREATMENT

"This, then, is what you have to say," cried my lady Philippa, in a tone of little gratitude, and perhaps not purely free from wrath; "this is what has happened, while you did nothing?"

"Madam, I assure you," Mr. Jellicorse replied, "that no one point has been neglected. And truly I am bold enough—though you may not perceive it—to take a little credit to myself for the skill and activity of my proceedings. I have a most conceited man against me; no member at all of our honored profession; but rather inclined to make light of us. A gentleman—if one may so describe him—of the name of Mordacks, who lives in a den below a bridge in York, and has very long harassed the law by a sort of cheap-jack, slap-dash, low-minded style of doing things. 'Jobbing,' I may call it—cheap and nasty jobbing—not at all the proper thing, from a correct point of view. 'A catch-penny fellow,' that's the proper name for him—I was trying to think of it half the way from Middleton."

"And now, in your eloquence, you have hit upon it. I can easily understand that such a style of business would not meet with your approbation. But, Mr. Jellicorse, he seems to me to have proved himself considerably more active in his way—however objectionable that may be—than you, as our agent, have shown yourself."

The cheerful, expressive, and innocent face of Mr. Jellicorse protested now. By nature he was almost as honest as Geoffrey Mordacks himself could be; and in spite of a very long professional career, the original element was there, and must be charged for.

"I can not recall to my memory," he said, "any instance of neglect on my part. But if that impression is upon your mind, it would be better for you to change your legal advisers at an early opportunity. Such has been the frequent practice, madam, of your family. And but for that, none of this trouble could exist. I must beg you either to withdraw the charge of negligence, which I understand you to have brought, or else to appoint some gentleman of greater activity to conduct your business."

With the haughtiness of her headstrong race, Miss Yordas had failed as yet to comprehend that a lawyer could be a gentleman. And even now that idea scarcely broke upon her, until she looked hard at Mr. Jellicorse. But he, having cast aside all deference for the moment, met her stern gaze with such courteous indifference and poise of self-composure that she suddenly remembered that his grandfather had been the master of a pack of fox-hounds.

"I have made no charge of negligence; you are hasty, and misunderstand me," she answered, after waiting for him to begin again, as if he were a rash aggressor. "It is possible that you desire to abandon our case, and conceive affront where none is meant whatever."

"God forbid!" Mr. Jellicorse exclaimed, with his legal state of mind returning. "A finer case never came into any court of law. There is a coarse axiom, not without some truth, that possession is nine points of the law. We have possession. What is even more important, we have the hostile instrument in our possession."

"You mean that unfortunate and unjust deed, of a by-gone time, that was so wickedly concealed? Dishonest transaction from first to last!"

"Madam, the law is not to blame for that, nor even the lawyers; but the clients, who kept changing them. But for that, your admirable father must have known that the will he dictated to me was waste paper. At least as regards the main part of these demesnes."

"What monstrous injustice! A positive premium upon filial depravity. You regard things professionally, I suppose. But surely it must have struck you as a flagrant dishonesty, a base and wicked crime, that a document so vile should be allowed even to exist."

Miss Yordas had spoken with unusual heat; and the lawyer looked at her with an air of mild inquiry. Was it possible that she suggested to him the destruction of the wicked instrument? Ladies had done queer things, within his knowledge; but this lady showed herself too cautious for that.

"I know what my father would have done in such a case," she continued, with her tranquil smile recovered: "he would just have ridden up to his solicitor's office, demanded the implement of robbery, brought it home, and set it upon the hall fire, in the presence of the whole of his family and household. But now we live in such a strictly lawful age that no crime can be stopped, if only perpetrated legally. And you say that Mr. More—something, 'Moresharp,' I think it was, knows of that iniquitous production?"

"Madam, we can not be certain; but I have reason to suspect that Mr. Mordacks has got wind of that unfortunate deed of appointment."

"Supposing that he has, and that he means to use his knowledge, he cannot force the document from your possession, can he?"

"Not without an order. But by filing affidavit, after issue of writ in

432

ejectment, they may compel us to produce, and allow attested copy to be taken."

"Then the law is disgraceful to the last degree, and it is useless to own anything. That deed is in your charge, as our attorney, I suppose, sir?"

"By no other right, madam: we have twelve chestfuls, any one or all of which I am bound to render up to your order."

"Our confidence in you is unshaken. But without shaking it we might order home any particular chest for inspection?"

"Most certainly, madam, by giving us receipt for it. For antiquarian uses, and others, such a thing is by no means irregular. And the oldest of all the deeds are in that box—charters from the crown, grants from corporations, records of assay by arms—warrants that even I can not decipher."

"A very learned gentleman is likely soon to visit us—a man of modern family, who spends his whole time in seeking out the stories of the older ones. No family in Yorkshire is comparable to ours in the interest of its annals."

"That is a truth beyond all denial, madam. The character of your ancient race has always been a marked one."

"And always honorable, Mr. Jellicorse. Undeviating principle has distinguished all my ancestors. Nothing has ever been allowed to stand between them and their view of right."

"You could not have put it more clearly, Mistress Yordas. Their own view of right has been their guiding star throughout. And they never have failed to act accordingly."

"Alas! of how very few others can we say it! But being of a very good old family yourself, you are able to appreciate such conduct. You would like me, perhaps, to sign the order for that box of ancient—cartularies—is not that the proper word for them? And it might be as well to state why they happen to be wanted—for purposes of family history."

"Madam, I will at once prepare a memorandum for your signature and your sister's."

The mind of Mr. Jellicorse was much relieved, although the relief was not untempered with misgivings. He sat down immediately at an ancient writing-table, and prepared a short order for delivery, to their trusty servant Jordas, of a certain box, with the letter C upon it, and containing title-deeds of Scargate Hall estate.

"I think it might be simpler not to put it so precisely," my lady Philippa suggested, "but merely to say a box containing the oldest of the title-deeds, as required for an impending antiquarian research."

Mr. Jellicorse made the amendment; and then, with the prudence of long practice, added, "The order should be in your handwriting, madam; will it give you too much trouble just to copy it?" "How can it signify, if it bears our signatures?" his client asked, with a smile at such a trifle; however, she sat down, and copied it upon another sheet of paper. Then Mr. Jellicorse, beautifully bowing, drew near to take possession of his own handwriting; but the lady, with a bow of even greater elegance, lifted the cover of the standing desk, and therein placed both manuscripts; and the lawyer perceived that he could say nothing.

"How delightful it is to be quit of business!" The hostess now looked hospitable. "We need not recur to this matter, I do hope. That paper, whatever it is, will be signed by both of us, and handed over to you, in your legal head-quarters, to-morrow. We must have the pleasure of sending you home in the morning, Mr. Jellicorse. We have bought a very wonderful vehicle, invented for such roads as ours, and to supersede the jumping-car. It is warranted to traverse any place a horse can travel, with luxurious ease to the passengers, and safety of no common description. Jordas will drive you; your horse can trot behind; and you can send back by it whatever there may be."

Mr. Jellicorse detested new inventions, and objected most strongly to any experiment made in his own body. However, he would rather die than plead his time of life in bar, and his faith in the dogman was unlimited. And now the gentle Mrs. Carnaby, who had gracefully taken flight from "horrid business," returned in an evening dress and with a sweetly smiling countenance, and very nearly turned the Jellicorsian head, snowy as it was, with soft attentions and delicious deference.

"I was treated like a prince," he said next day, when delivered safe at home, and resting among his rather dingy household gods. "There never could have been a more absurd idea than that notion of yours about my being put into wet sheets, Diana. Why, I even had my night-cap warmed; and a young woman came, with a blush upon her face, and a question whether I would be pleased to sleep in a gross of Naples stockings! Ah, to my mind, after all, it proves what I have always said—that there is nothing like old blood."

"Nothing like old blood for being made a fool of," his wife replied, with a coarseness which made him shiver, after Mrs. Carnaby. "They know what they are about, I'll lay a penny. Some roguery, no doubt, that they seek to lead you into. That is what their night-caps and stockings mean. How low it is to make a foreground of them!"

"Hush, my dear! I can not bear such want of charity. And what is even worse, you expose me to an action at law, with heavy damages."

The lawyer had sundry little qualms of conscience, which were deepened by his wife's sagacious words; and suddenly it struck him that the new-fangled vehicle which had brought him home so quietly from Scargate had shown a strange inability to stand still for more than two minutes at his side door. So much had he been hurried by the apparent straits of his charioteer that he ran out with box C without ever stopping to make an inventory of its contents—as he intended to do—or even looking whether the all-important deed was there. In fact, he had scarcely time to seal up the key in a separate package, hand it to Jordas, and take the order (now become a receipt) from the horny fist of the dogman, before Marmaduke, rendered more dashing by snow-drift, was away like a thunder-bolt—if such a thing there be, and if it has four legs.

"How could I have helped doing as I have done?" he whispered to himself, uncomfortably. "Here are two ladies of high position, and they send a joint order for their property. By-the-bye, I will just have a look at that order, now that there is no horse to jump over me." Upon going to the day file, he found the order right, transcribed from his own amended copy, and bearing two signatures, as it should do. But it struck him that the words "Eliza Carnaby" were written too boldly for that lady's hand; and the more he looked at them, the more he was convinced of it. That was no concern of his, for it was not his duty, under the circumstances of the case, to verify her signature. But this conviction drove him to an uncomfortable conclusion—"Miss Yordas intends to destroy that deed without her sister's knowledge. She knows that her sister's nerve is weaker, and she does not like to involve her in the job. A very brave, sisterly feeling, no doubt, and much the wiser course, if she means to do it. It is a bold stroke, and well worthy of a Yordas. But I hope, with all my heart, that she never can have thought of it. And she kept that order in my handwriting to make it look as if the suggestion came from me! And I am as innocent as any lamb is of the frauds that shall come to be written on his skin. The duty of attorney toward client prevents me from opening my lips upon the matter. But she is a deep woman, and a bold one too. May the Lord direct things aright! I shall retire, and let Robert have the practice, as soon as Brown's bankruptcy has worn out captious creditors. It is the Lord alone that doeth all things well."

Mr. Jellicorse knew that he had done his best; and though doubtful of the turn which things had taken, with some exclusion of his agency, he felt (though his conscience told him not to feel it) that here was one true source of joy. That impudent, dashing, unprofessional man, who was always poking his vile unarticled nose into legal business, that fellow of the name of Mordacks, now would have no locus standi left. At least a hundred and fifty firms, of good standing in the county, detested that man, and even a judge would import a scintillula juris into any measure which relieved the country of him. Meditating thus, he heard a knock.

CHAPTER LI

STAND AND DELIVER

The day was not far worn as yet; and May month having come at last, the day could stand a good deal of wear. With Jordas burning to exhibit the wonders of the new machine (which had been bought upon his advice), and with Marmaduke conscious of the new gloss on his coat, all previous times had been beaten—as the sporting writers put it; that is to say, all previous times of the journey from Scargate to Middleton, for any man who sat on wheels. A rider would take a shorter cut, and have many other advantages; but for a driver the time had been the quickest upon record.

Mr. Jellicorse, exulting in his safety, had imprinted the chaste salute upon his good wife's cheek at ten minutes after one o'clock; when the clerks in the office with laudable promptitude (not expecting him as yet) had unanimously cast down pen, and betaken hand and foot toward knife and fork. Instead of blaming them, this good lawyer went upon that same road himself, with the great advantage that the road to his dinner lay through his own kitchen. At dinner-time he had much to tell, and many large helps to receive, of interest and of admiration, especially from his pet child Emily (who forgot herself so largely as to lick her spoon while gazing), and after dinner he was not without reasons for letting perhaps a little of the time slip by. Therefore, by the time he had described all dangers, discharged his duty to all comforts, and held the little confidential talk with his wife and himself above recorded, the clock had made its way to half past three.

Mrs. Jellicorse and Emily were gone forth to pay visits; the clerks, shut away in their own room, were busy, scratching up a lovely case for nisi prius; the cook had thrown the sifted cinders on the kitchen fire, and was gone with the maids to exchange just a few constitutional words with the gardener; and the whole house was drowsy with that by-time when light and shadow seem to mix together, and far-away sounds take a faint to and fro, as if they were the pendulum of silence.

"That is Emily's knock. Impatient child! Come back for her mother's gloves, or something. All the people are out; I must go and let her in."

With these words, and a little placid frown—because a soft nap was impending on his eyelids, and yet they were always glad to open on his favorite—the worthy lawyer rose, and took a pinch of snuff to rouse himself; but before he could get to the door, a louder and more impatient rap almost made him jump.

"What a hurry you are in, my dear! You really should try to learn some little patience."

While he was speaking, he opened the door; and behold, there was no little girl, but a tall and stately gentleman in horseman's dress, and of strong commanding aspect.

"What is your pleasure, sir?" the lawyer asked, while his heart began to flutter; for exactly such a visitor had caused him scare of his life, when stronger by a quarter of a century than now.

"My pleasure, or rather my business, is with Mr. Jellicorse, the lawyer."

"Then, sir, you have come to the right man for it. My name is Jellicorse, and greatly at your service. Allow me the honor of inviting you within."

"My name is Yordas—Sir Duncan Yordas," said the stranger, when seated in the lawyer's private room. "My father, Philip Yordas, was a client of yours, and of other legal gentlemen before he came to you. Upon the day of his death, in the year 1777, you prepared his will, which you have since found to be of no effect, except as regards his personal estate, and about one-eighth part of the realty. Of the bulk of the land, including Scargate Hall, he could not dispose, for the simple reason that it had been strictly entailed by a deed executed by my grandfather and his wife in 1751. Under that entail I take in fee, for it could not have been barred without me; and I never concurred in any disentailing deed, and my father never knew that such was needful."

"Excuse me, Sir Duncan, but you seem to be wonderfully apt with the terms of our profession."

"I could scarcely be otherwise, after all that I have had to do with law, in India. Our first object is to apply our own laws, and our second to spread our religion. But no more of that. Do you admit the truth of a matter so stated that you can not fail to grasp it?"

Sir Duncan Yordas, as he put this question, fixed large, unwavering, and piercing eyes (against which no spectacles were any shelter) upon the mild, amiable, and, generally speaking, very honest orbs of sight which had lighted the path of the elder gentleman to good repute and competence. But who may turn a lawyer's hand from the Heaven-sped legal plough?

"Am I to understand, Sir Duncan Yordas, that your visit to me is of an amicable nature, and intended (without prejudice to other interests) to ascertain, so far as may be compatible with professional rules, how far my clients are acquainted with documents alleged or imagined to be in existence,

439

and how far their conduct might be guided by desire to afford every reasonable facility?"

"You are to understand simply this, that as the proper owner of Scargate Hall, and the main part of the estates held with it, I require you to sign a memorandum that you hold all the title-deeds on my behalf, and to deliver at once to me that entailing instrument of 1751, under which I make my claim."

"You speak, sir, as if you had already brought your action, and entered verdict. Legal process may be dispensed with in barbarous countries, but not here. The title-deeds and other papers of Scargate Hall were placed in my custody neither by you nor on your behalf, sir. I hold them on behalf of those at present in possession; and until I receive due instructions from them, or a final order from a court of law, I should be guilty of a breach of trust if I parted with a dog's-ear of them."

"You distinctly refuse my requirements, and defy me to enforce them?"

"Not so, Sir Duncan. I do nothing more than declare what my view of my duty is, and decline in any way to depart from it."

"Upon that score I have nothing more to say. I did not expect you to give up the deeds, though in 'barbarous countries,' as you call them, we have peremptory ways. I will say more than that, Mr. Jellicorse—I will say that I respect you for clinging to what you must know better than anybody else to be the weaker side."

The lawyer bowed his very best bow, but was bound to enter protest against the calm assumption of the claimant.

"Let us leave that question," Sir Duncan said; "the time would fail us to discuss that now. But one thing I surely may insist upon as the proper heir of my grandfather. I may desire you to produce for my inspection that deed in pursuance of his marriage settlement, which has for so many years lain concealed."

"With pleasure I will do so, Sir Duncan Yordas (presuming that any such deed exists), upon the production of an order from the Court either of King's Bench or of Common Pleas."

"In that case you would be obliged to produce it, and would earn no thanks of mine. But I ask you to lay aside the legal aspect; for no action is pending, and perhaps never will be. I ask you, as a valued adviser of the family, and a trustworthy friend to its interests—as a gentleman, in fact, rather than a mere lawyer—to do a wise and amicable thing. You can not in any way injure your case, if a law case is to come of it, because we know all about the deed already. We even have an abstract of it as clear as you yourself could make, and we have discovered that one of the witnesses is still alive. I have come to you myself in preference to employing a lawyer, because I hope, if you meet me frankly, to put things in train for a friendly and fair settlement. I am not a young man; I have been disappointed of any one to succeed me, and I wish to settle my affairs in this country, and return to India, which suits me better, and where I am more useful. My sisters have not behaved kindly to me; but that I must try to forgive and forget. I have thought matters over, and am quite prepared to offer very liberal terms—in short, to leave them in possession of Scargate, upon certain conditions and in a certain manner."

"Really, Sir Duncan," Mr. Jellicorse exclaimed, "allow me to offer you a pinch of snuff. You are pleased with it? Yes, it is of quite superior quality. It saved the life of a most admirable fellow, a henchman of your family—in fact, poor Jordas. The power of this snuff alone supported him from freezing —"

"At another time I may be highly interested in that matter," the visitor replied, without meaning to be rude, but knowing that the man of law was making passes to gain time; "just at present I must ask you to say yes or no. If you wish me to set my offer plainly before you, and so relieve the property of the cost of a hopeless struggle—for I have taken the opinion of the first real property counsel of the age—you will, as a token of good faith and of common-sense, produce for my inspection that deed-poll of November 15, 1751."

Poor Mr. Jellicorse was desperately driven. He looked round the room, to seek for any interruption. He went to the window, and pretended to see another visitor knocking at the door. But no help came; he must face it out himself; and Sir Duncan, with his quiet resolution, looked more stern than his violent father.

"I think that before we proceed any further," said the lawyer, at last sitting down, and taking up a pen and trying what the nib was like, "we really should understand a little where we are already. My own desire to avoid litigation is very strong—almost unprofessionally so—though the first thing consulted by all of us naturally is the pocket of our client—"

"Whether it will hold out, I suppose." Sir Duncan Yordas departed from his dignity in saying this, and was sorry as soon as he had said it.

"That is the vulgar impression about us, which it is our duty to disdain. But without losing time upon that question, let me ask, what shall I put down as your proposition, sir?"

"There is nothing to put down. That is just the point. I do not come here with any formal proposition. If that had been my object, I would have brought a lawyer. What I say is that I have the right to see that deed. It forms no part of my sisters' title-deeds, but even destroys their title. It belongs to me, it is my property, and only through fraud is it now in your hands. Of course we can easily wrest it from you, and must do so if you defy me. It rests with you to take that risk. But I prefer to cut things short. I pledge myself to two things —first, to leave the document in your possession; and next, to offer fair and even handsome terms when you have met me thus fairly. Why should you object? For we know all about it. Never mind how."

Those last three words decided the issue. Even worse than the fear of breach of trust was the fear of treason in the office, and the lawyer's only chance of getting clew to that was to keep on terms with this Sir Duncan Yordas. There had been no treason whatever in the office; neither had anything come out through the proctorial firm in York, or Sir Walter Carnaby's solicitors; but a note among longheaded Duncombe's papers had got into the hands of Mordacks. Of that, however, Mr. Jellicorse had no idea.

"Sir Duncan Yordas, I will meet you as you come," he said, with his good, fresh-colored face, as honest as the sun when the clouds roll off. "It is an unusual step on my part, and perhaps irregular. But rather than destroy the prospect of a friendly compromise, I will strain a point, and candidly admit that there is an instrument open to an interpretation which might, or might not, be in your favor."

"That I knew long ago, and more than that. My demand is—to see it, and to satisfy myself."

"Under the circumstances, I am half inclined to think that I should be disposed to allow you that privilege if the document were in my possession."

"Now, Mr. Jellicorse," Sir Duncan answered, showing his temper in his eyes alone, "how much longer will you trifle with me? Where is that deed?"

Mr. Jellicorse drew forth his watch, took off his spectacles, and dusted them carefully with a soft yellow handkerchief; then restored them to their double sphere of usefulness, and perused, with some diligence, the time of day. By the law which compels a man to sneeze when another man sets the example, Sir Duncan also drew forth his watch.

"I am trying to make my reply as accurate," said the lawyer, beginning to enjoy the position as a man, though not quite as a lawyer—"as accurate as your candor and confidence really deserve, Sir Duncan. The box containing that document, to which you attach so much importance (whether duly or otherwise is not for me to say until counsel's opinion has been taken on our side), considering the powers of the horse, that box should be about Stormy Gap by this time. A quarter to four by me. What does your watch say, sir?"

442

"The deed has been sent for, post-haste, has it? And you know for what purpose?"

"You must draw a distinction between the deed and the box containing it, Sir Duncan. Or, to put it more accurately, betwixt that deed and its casual accompaniments. It happens to be among very old charters, which happen to be wanted for certain excellent antiquarian purposes. Such things are not in my line, I must confess, although so deeply interesting. But a very learned man seems to have expressed—"

"Rubbish. Excuse me, but you are most provoking. You know, as well as I do, that robbery is intended, and you allow yourself to be made a party to it."

This was the simple truth; and the lawyer, being (by some strange inversion of professional excellence) honest at the bottom, was deeply pained at having such words used, as to, for, about, or in anywise concerning him.

"I think, Sir Duncan, that you will be sorry," he answered, with much dignity, "for employing such language where it can not be resented. Your father was a violent man, and we all expect violence of your family."

"There is no time to go into that question now. If I have wronged you, I will beg your pardon. A very few hours will prove how that is. How and by whom have you sent the box?"

Mr. Jellicorse answered, rather stiffly, that his clients had sent a trusty servant with a light vehicle to fetch the box, and that now he must be half way toward home.

"I shall overtake him," said Sir Duncan, with a smile; "I have a good horse, and I know the shortcuts. Hoofs without wheels go a yard to a foot upon such rocky collar-work."

Without another word, except "Good-by," Sir Duncan Yordas left the house, walked rapidly to the inn, and cut short the dinner his good horse was standing up to. In a very few minutes he was on Tees bridge, with his face toward the home of his ancestors.

It may be supposed that neither his thoughts nor those of the lawyer were very cheerful. Mr. Jellicorse was deeply anxious as to the conflict which must ensue, and as to the figure his fair fame might cut, if this strange transaction should be exposed and calumniated by evil tongues. In these elderly days, and with all experience, he had laid himself open, not legally perhaps, but morally, to the heavy charge of connivance at a felonious act, and even some contribution toward it. He told himself vainly that he could not help it, that the documents were in his charge only until he was ordered to give them up, and that it was no concern of his to anticipate what might become of them.

His position had truly been difficult, but still he might have escaped from it with clearer conscience. His duty was to cast away drawing-room manners, and warn Miss Yordas that the document she hated so was not her own to deal with, but belonged (in equity at least) to those who were entitled under it, and that to take advantage of her wrongful possession, and destroy the foe, was a crime, and, more than that, a shabby one. The former point might not have stopped her; but the latter would have done so without fail, for her pride was equal to her daring. But poor Mr. Jellicorse had felt the power of a will more resolute than his own, and of grand surroundings and exalted style; and his desire to please had confused, and thereby overcome, his perception of the right. But now these reflections were all too late, and the weary brain found comfort only in the shelter of its night-cap.

If a little slip had brought a very good man to unhappiness, how much harder was it for Sir Duncan Yordas, who had committed no offense at all! No Yordas had ever cared a tittle for tattle—to use their own expression—but deeper mischief than tattle must ensue, unless great luck prevented it. The brother knew well that his sister inherited much of the reckless self-will which had made the name almost a by-word, and which had been master of his own life until large experience of the world, and the sense of responsible power, curbed it. He had little affection for that sister left—for she had used him cruelly, and even now was imbittering the injury—but he still had some tender feeling for the other, who had always been his favorite. And though cut off, by his father's act, from due headship of the family, he was deeply grieved, in this more enlightened age, to expose their uncivilized turbulence.

Therefore he spurred his willing horse against the hill, and up the many-winding ruggedness of road, hoping, at every turn, to descry in the distance the vehicle carrying that very plaguesome box. If his son had been there, he might have told him, on the ridge of Stormy Gap (which commanded high and low, rough and smooth, dark and light, for miles ahead), that Jordas was taking the final turn, by the furthest gleam of the water-mist, whence the stone road labored up to Scargate. But Sir Duncan's eyes—though as keen as an eagle's while young—had now seen too much of the sun to make out that gray atom gliding in the sunset haze.

Upon the whole, it was a lucky thing that he could not overtake the car; for Jordas would never have yielded his trust while any life was in him; and Sir Duncan having no knowledge of him, except as a boy-of-all-work about the place, might have been tempted to use the sword, without which no horseman then rode there. Or failing that, a struggle between two equally resolute men must have followed, with none at hand to part them.

When the horseman came to the foot of the long steep pull leading up to the stronghold of his race, he just caught a glimpse of the car turning in at the entrance of the court-yard. "They have half an hour's start of me," he thought, as he drew up behind a rock, that the house might not descry him; "if I ride up in full view, I hurry the mischief. Philippa will welcome me with the embers of my title. She must not suspect that the matter is so urgent. Nobody shall know that I am coming. For many reasons I had better try the private road below the Scarfe."

CHAPTER LII

THE SCARFE

Jordas, without suspicion of pursuit, had allowed no grass to grow under the feet of Marmaduke on the homeward way. His orders were to use all speed, to do as he had done at the lawyer's private door, and then, without baiting his horse, to drive back, reserving the nose-bag for some very humpy halting-place. There is no such man, at the present time of day, to carry out strict orders, as the dogman was, and the chance of there being such a one again diminishes by very rapid process. Marmaduke, as a horse, was of equal quality, reasoning not about his orders, but about the way to do them.

There was no special emergency now, so far as my lady Philippa knew; but the manner of her mind was to leave no space between a resolution and its execution. This is the way to go up in the world, or else to go down abruptly; and to her the latter would have been far better than to halt between two opinions. Her plan had been shaped and set last night, and, like all great ideas, was the simplest of the simple. And Jordas, who had inklings of his own, though never admitted to confidence, knew how to carry out the outer part.

"When the turbot comes," she said to Welldrum, as soon as her long sight showed her the trusty Jordas beginning the home ascent, "it is to be taken first out of the car, and to my sister's sitting-room; the other things Jordas will see to. I may be going for a little walk. But you will at once carry up the turbot. Mrs. Carnaby's appetite is delicate."

The butler had his own opinion upon that interesting subject. But in her presence it must be his own. Any attempt at enlargement of her mind by exchange of sentiment—such as Mrs. Carnaby permitted and enjoyed—would have sent him flying down the hill, pursued by square-toed men prepared to add elasticity to velocity. Therefore Welldrum made a leg in silence, and retreated, while his mistress prepared for her intended exploit. She had her beaver hat and mantle ready by the shrubbery door—as a little quiet postern of her own was called—and in the heavy standing desk, or "secretary," of her private room she had stored a flat basket, or frail, of stout flags, with a heavy clock weight inside it.

"Much better to drown the wretched thing than burn it," she had been saying to herself, "especially at this time of year, when fires are weak and telltale. And parchment makes such a nasty smell; Eliza might come in and suspect it. But the Scarfe is a trusty confidant."

Mistress Yordas, while sure that her sister (having even more than herself at stake) would approve and even applaud her scheme, was equally sure that it must be kept from her, both for its own sake and for hers. And the sooner it was done, the less the chance of disturbing poor Eliza's mind.

The Scarfe is a deep pool, supposed to have no bottom (except, perhaps, in the very bowels of the earth), upon one of the wildest head-waters of the Tees. A strong mountain torrent from a desolate ravine springs forth with great ferocity, and sooner than put up with any more stabs from the rugged earth, casts itself on air. For a hundred and twenty feet the water is bright, in the novelty and the power of itself, striking out freaks of eccentric flashes, and even little sun-bows, in fine weather. But the triumph is brief; and a heavy retribution, created by its violence, awaits below. From the tossing turmoil of the fall two white volumes roll away, with a clash of waves between them, and sweeping round the craggy basin, meet (like a snowy wreath) below, and rush back in coiling eddies flaked with foam. All the middle is dark deep water, looking on the watch for something to suck down.

What better duty, or more pious, could a hole like this perform, than that of swallowing up a lawyer; or, if no such morsel offered, then at least a lawyer's deeds? Many a sheep had been there ingulfed, and never saluted by her lambs again; and although a lawyer by no means is a sheep (except in his clothing, and his eyes perhaps), yet his doings appear upon the skin thereof, and enhance its value more than drugs of Tyre. And it is to be feared that some fleeced clients will not feel the horror which they ought to feel at the mode pursued by Mistress Yordas in the delivery of her act and deed.

She came down the dell, from the private grounds of Scargate, with a resolute face, and a step of strength. The clock weight, that should know time no more, was well imbosomed in the old deed-poll, and all stitched firmly in the tough brown frail, whose handles would help for a long strong cast. Towering crags, and a ridge of jagged scaurs, shut out the sunset, while a thicket of dwarf oak, and the never-absent bramble, aproned the yellow dugs of shale with brown. In the middle was the caldron of the torrent, called the "Scarfe," with the sheer trap-rock, which is green in the sunlight, like black night flung around it, while a snowy wreath of mist (like foam exhaling) circled round the basined steep, or hovered over the chasm.

Miss Yordas had very stanch nerves, but still, for reasons of her own, she disliked this place, and never came near it for pleasure's sake, although in dry summers, when the springs were low, the fury of the scene passed into grandeur, and even beauty. But a Yordas (long ago gone to answer for it) had flung a man, who plagued him with the law, into this hole. And what was more disheartening, although of less importance, a favorite maid of this lady, upon the exile of her sweetheart, hearing that his feet were upside down to hers, and that this hole went right through the earth, had jumped into it, in a lonely moment, instead of taking lessons in geography. Philippa Yordas was as brave as need be; but now her heart began to creep as coldly as the shadows crept.

For now she was out of sight of home, and out of hearing of any sound, except the roaring of the force. The Hall was half a mile away, behind a shoulder of thick-ribbed hill; and it took no sight of this torrent, until it became a quiet river by the downward road. "I must be getting old," Miss Yordas thought, "or else this path is much rougher than it used to be. Why, it seems to be getting quite dangerous! It is too bad of Jordas not to see to things better. My father used to ride this way sometimes. But how could a horse get along here now?"

There used to be a bridle-road from the grounds of Scargate to a ford below the force, and northward thence toward the Tees; or by keeping down stream, and then fording it again, a rider might hit upon the Middleton road, near the rock that warned the public of the blood-hounds. This bridle-road kept a great distance from the cliffs overhanging the perilous Scarfe; and the only way down to a view of the fall was a scrambling track, over rocks and trunks, unworthy to be called a foot-path. The lady with the bag had no choice left but to follow this track, or else abandon her intention. For a moment she was sorry that she had not been satisfied with some less troublesome destruction of her foe, even at the risk of chance suspicions. But having thus begun it, she would not turn back, and be angry with her idle fears when she came to think of them.

With hereditary scorn of second thoughts she cast away doubt, and went down the steep, and stood on the brow of sheer rock, to recover her breath and strength for a long bold cast. The crag beneath her feet was trembling with the power of the flood below, and the white mist from the deep moved slowly, shrouding now, and now revealing, the black gulf and its slippery walls. For the last few months Miss Yordas had taken very little exercise, and seldom tasted the open air; therefore the tumult and terror of the place, in the fading of the sky and darkening of the earth, got hold of her more than they should have done.

With the frail in her right hand, poised upon three fingers (for the fourth had been broken in her childhood), she planted the sole of her left foot on the brink, and swung herself for the needful cast.

A strong throw was needful to reach the black water that never gave up anything: if the bag were dropped in the foaming race, it might be carried back to the heel of the fall. She was proud of her bodily strength, which was almost equal to that of a muscular man, and her long arm swelled with the vigor of the throw. But just when the weight should have been delivered, and flown with a hiss into the bottomless abyss, a loose flag of the handle twisted on her broken finger. Instead of being freed, the bag fell back, struck her in the chest, and threw her back, for the clock weight was a heavy one. Her balance was lost, her feet flew up, she fell upon her back, and the smooth beaver cloak began sliding upon the slippery rock. Horrible death was pulling at her; not a stick nor a stone was in reach of her hands, and the pitiless crags echoed one long shriek above all the roar of the water-fall. She strove to turn over and grasp the ground, but only felt herself going faster. Her bright boots were flashing against the white mist—a picture in her mind forever—her body was following, inch by inch. With elbow and shoulder, and even hair coils, she strove to prolong the descent into death; but the descent increased its speed, and the sky itself was sliding.

Just when the balance was inclining downward, and the plunge hanging on a hair's-breadth, powerful hands fell upon her shoulders; a grating of a drag against the grain was the last thing she was conscious of; and Sir Duncan Yordas, having made a strong pull, at the imminent risk of his life, threw back his weight on the heels of his boots, and they helped him. His long Indian spurs, which had no rowel, held their hold like a falcon's hind talon; and he drew back the lady without knowing who she was, having leaped from his horse at her despairing scream. From his knowledge of the place he concluded that it was some person seeking suicide, but recoiling from the sight of death; and without another thought he risked his life to save.

Breathless himself—for the transit of years and of curry-powder had not improved his lungs—he labored at the helpless form, and laid it at last in a place of safety.

"What a weight the lady is!" was his first idea; "it can not be want of food that has driven her, nor of money either; her cloak would fetch a thousand rupees in Calcutta. And a bag full of something—precious also, to judge by the way she clings to it. Poor thing! Can I get any water for her? There used to be a spring here, where the woodcocks came. Is it safe to leave her? Certainly not, with her head like that; she might even have apoplexy. Allow me, madam. I will not steal it. It is only for a cushion."

The lady, however, though still in a stupor, kept her fingers clinched upon the handle of the bag; and without using violence he could not move them. Then the stitching of the frail gave way, and Sir Duncan espied a roll of parchment. Suddenly the lady opened large dark eyes, which wandered a little, and then (as he raised her head) met his, and turned away.

"Philippa!" he said, and she faintly answered "Yes," being humbled and shaken by her deadly terror, and scarcely sure of safety yet, for the roar and the chasm were in sight and hearing still.

"Philippa, are you better? Never mind what you were thinking of. All shall be right about that, Philippa. What is land in comparison with life? Look up at me. Don't be afraid to look. Surely you know your only brother! I am Duncan, who ran away, and has lived for years in India. I used to be very kind to you when we were children, and why should I alter from it now? I remember when you tumbled in the path down there, and your knee was bleeding, and I tied it up with a dock leaf and my handkerchief. Can you remember? It was primrose time."

"To be sure I do," she said, looking up with cheerfulness; "and you carried me all the way home almost, and Eliza was dreadfully jealous."

"That she always was, and you not much better. But now we are getting on in life, and we need not have much to do with one another. Still, we may try not to kill one another by trumpery squabbles about property. Stay where you are for a moment, sister, and you shall see the end of that."

Sir Duncan took the bag, with the deed inside it, returned in three steps to the perilous shelf, and with one strong hurl sent forth the load, which cleft the white mist, and sank forever in the waves of the whirlpool.

"No one can prosecute me for that," he said, returning with a smile, "though Mordacks may be much aggrieved. Now, Philippa, although I can not carry you well, from the additions time has made to you, I can help you home, my dear; and then on upon my business."

The pride and self-esteem of Miss Yordas had never been so crushed before. She put both hands upon her brother's shoulders, and burst into a flood of tears.

CHAPTER LIII

BUTS REBUTTED

Sir Duncan Yordas was a man of impulse, as almost every man must be who sways the wills of other men. But he had not acted upon mere impulse in casting away his claim to Scargate. He knew that he could never live in that bleak spot, after all his years in India; he disliked the place, through his father's harshness; he did not care that any son of his, who had lain under charge of a foul crime, and fled instead of meeting it, should become a "Yordas of Scargate Hall," although that description by no means involved any very strict equity of conduct. And besides these reasons, he had another, which will appear very shortly. But whatever the secondary motives were, it was a large and generous act.

When Mrs. Carnaby saw her brother, she was sure that he was come to turn her out, and went through a series of states of mind natural to an adoring mother with a frail imagination of an appetite—as she poetically described it. She was not very swift of apprehension, although so promptly alive to anything tender, refined, and succulent. Having too strong a sense of duty to be guilty of any generosity, she could not believe, either then or thereafter, that her brother had cast away anything at all, except a mere shred of a lawsuit. And without any heed of chronology—because (as she justly inquired), what two clocks are alike?—she was certain that if he did anything at all to drive off those horrible lawyers from the house, there was no credit due to any one but Pet. It was the noble way Pet looked at him!

Pet, being introduced to his uncle, after dinner, when he came home from fishing, certainly did look nobly at him, if a long stare is noble. Then he went up to him, with a large and liberal sniff, and an affable inquiry, as a little dog goes up to a big one. Sir Duncan was amused, having heard already some little particulars about this youth, whose nature he was able to enter into as none but a Yordas could rightly do. However, he was bound to make the best of him, and did so; discovering not only room for improvement, but some hope of that room being occupied.

"The boy has been shockingly spoiled," he said to his sister Philippa that evening; "also he is dreadfully ignorant. None of us are very great at scholarship, and never have much occasion for it. But things are becoming very different now. Everybody is beginning to be expected to know everything. Very likely, as soon as I am no more wanted, I shall be voted a blockhead. Luckily the wars keep people from being too choice, when their pick goes every minute. And this may stop the fuss, that comes from Scotland mainly, about universal distribution—or some big words—of education. 'Pet,' as you call him, is a very clever fellow, with much more shape of words about him than ever I was blessed with. In spelling I saw that he was my master; and so I tried him with geography, and all he knew of India was that it takes its name from India rubber!"

"Now I call that clever of him," said Miss Yordas; "for I really might have forgotten even that. But the fatal defect in his education has been the want of what you grow, chiefly in West India perhaps—the cane, Duncan, the sugar-cane. I have read all about it; you can tell me nothing. You suck it, you smoke it, and you beat your children with it."

"Well," said Sir Duncan, who was not quite sure, in the face of such authority, "I disremember; but perhaps they do in some parts, because the country is so large. But it is not the ignorance of Pet I care for—such a fault is natural and unavoidable; and who is there to pick holes in it? The boy knows a great deal more than I did at his age, because he is so much younger. But, Philippa, unless you do something with him, he will never be a gentleman."

"Duncan, you are hard. You have seen so much."

"The more we see, the softer we become. The one thing we harden against is lying—the seed, the root, and the substance of all vileness. I am sorry to say your Pet is a liar."

"He does not always tell the truth, I know. But bear in mind, Duncan, that his mother did not insist—and, in fact, she does not herself always—"

"I know it; I am grieved that it should come from our side. I never cared for his father much, because he went against me; but this I will say for him, Lance Carnaby would sooner cut his tongue out that put it to a lie. When I am at home, my dealings are with fellows who could not speak the truth if they tried for dear life, simply through want of practice. They are like your lower class of horse-dealers, but with infinitely more intelligence. It is late to teach poor Pet the first of all lessons; and for me to stop to do it is impossible. But will you try to save further disgrace to a scapegrace family, but not a mean one?"

"I feel it as much as you do—perhaps more," Miss Yordas answered, forgetting altogether about the deed-box and her antiquary. "You need not tell me how very sad it is. But how can it be cured? His mother is his mother. She never would part with him; and her health is delicate."

"Stronger than either yours or mine, unless she takes too much nourishment. Philippa, her will is mere petulance. For her own good, we must set it aside. And if you agree with me, it can be done. He must go into a marching regiment at once, ordered abroad, with five shillings in his pocket, earn his pay, and live upon it. This patched-up peace will never last six months. The war must be fought out till France goes down, or England. I can get him a commission; and I know the colonel, a man of my own sort, who sees things done, instead of talking. It would be the making of Lancelot. He has plenty of courage, but it has been milched. At Oxford or Cambridge he would do no good, but simply be ruined by having his own way. Under my friend Colonel Thacker, he will have a hard time of it, and tell no lies."

Thus it was settled. There was a fearful outcry, hysterics of an elegant order, and weepings enough to produce summer spate in the Tees. But the only result was the ordering of the tailor, the hosier, the boot-maker, and the scissors-grinder to put a new edge upon Squire Philip's razors, that Pet might practice shaving. "Cold-blooded cruelty, savage homicide; cannibalism itself is kinder," said poor Mrs. Carnaby, when she saw the razors; but Pet insisted upon having them, made lather, and practiced with the backs, till he began to understand them.

"He promises well; I have great hopes of him," Sir Duncan said to himself. "He has pride; and no proud boy can be long a liar. I will go and consult my dear old friend Bart."

Mr. Bart, who was still of good bodily strength, but becoming less resolute in mind than of yore, was delighted to see his old friend again; and these two men, having warm, proud hearts, preserved each other from self-contempt by looking away through the long hand-clasp. For each of them was to the other almost the only man really respected in the world.

Betwixt them such a thing as concealment could not be. The difference in their present position was a thing to laugh at. Sir Duncan looked up to Bart as being the maker of his character, and Bart admired Sir Duncan as a newer and wiser edition of himself. They dispatched the past in a cheery talk; for the face of each was enough to show that it might have been troublous—as all past is—but had slidden into quiet satisfaction now, and a gentle flow of experience. Then they began to speak of present matters, and the residue of time before them; and among other things, Sir Duncan Yordas spoke of his nephew Lancelot.

"Lancelot Yordas Carnaby," said Bart, with the smile of a gray-beard at young love's dream, "has done us the honor to fall in love, for ever and ever, with our little Insie. And the worst of it is that she likes him."

"What an excellent idea!" his old friend answered; "I was sure there was something of that sort going on. Now betwixt love and war we shall make a man of Pet."

As shortly as possible he told Mr. Bart what his plan about his nephew was, and how he had carried it against maternal, and now must carry it against maiden, love. If Lancelot had any good stuff in him, any vertebrate embryo of honesty, to be put among men, and upon his mettle (with a guardian angel in the distance of sweet home), would stablish all the man in him, and stint the beast. Mr. Bart, though he hated hard fighting, admitted that for weak people it was needful; and was only too happy so to cut the knot of his own home entanglements with the ruthless sword. For a man of liberal education, and much experience in spending money, who can put a new bottom to his own saucepan, is not the one to feel any despair of his fellow-creatures mending.

Then arose the question, who should bell the cat, or rather, who should lead the cat to the belling. Pet must be taken, under strong duress, to the altar—as his poor mother said, and shrieked—whereat he was to shed his darling blood. His heart was in his mouth when his uniform came; and he gave his sacred honor to fly, straight as an arrow, to the port where his regiment was getting into boats; but Sir Duncan shook his grizzled head. "Somebody must see him into it," he said. "Not a lady; no, no, my dear Eliza. I can not go myself; but it must be a man of rigidity, a stern agent. Oh, I know! how stupid of me!"

"You mean poor dear Mr. Jellicorse," suggested Mrs. Carnaby, with a short hot sob. "But, Duncan, he has not the heart for it. For anything honest and loyal and good, kind people may trust him with their lives. But to tyranny, rapine, and manslaughter, he never could lend his fine honorable face."

"I mean a man of a very different cast—a man who knows what time is worth; a man who is going to be married on a Sunday, that he may not lose the day. He has to take three days' holiday, because the lady is an heiress; otherwise he might get off with one. But he hopes to be at work again on Wednesday, and we will have him here post-haste from York on Thursday. It will be the very job to suit him—a gentleman of Roman ancestry, and of the name of Mordacks."

"My heart was broken already; and now I can feel the poor pieces flying into my brain. Oh, why did I ever have a babe for monsters of the name of Mordacks to devour?"

Mordacks was only too glad to come. On the very day after their union, Calpurnia (likewise of Roman descent) had exhibited symptoms of a strong will of her own.

Mordacks had temporized during their courtship; but now she was his, and must learn the great fact. He behaved very well, and made no attempt at reasoning (which would have been a fatal course), but promptly donned cloak, boots, and spurs while his horse was being saddled, and then set off, with his eyes fixed firmly upon business. A crow could scarcely make less than fifty miles from York to Scargate, and the factor's trusty roadster had to make up his mind to seventy. So great, however, is sometimes the centrifugal force of Hymen, that upon the third day Mr. Mordacks was there, vigorous, vehement, and fit for any business.

When he heard what it was, it liked him well; for he bore a fine grudge against Lancelot for setting the dogs at him three years ago, when he came (as an agent for adjoining property) to the house of Yordas, and when Mr. Jellicorse scorned to meet an illegal meddler with legal matters. If Mordacks had any fault—and he must have had some, in spite of his resolute conviction to the contrary—it was that he did not altogether scorn revenge.

Lives there man, or even woman, capable of describing now the miseries, the hardships, the afflictions beyond groaning, which, like electric hail, came down upon the sacred head of Pet? He was in the grasp of three strong men— his uncle, Mr. Bart, worst of all, that Mordacks—escape was impossible, lamentation met with laughter, and passion led to punishment. Even stern Maunder was sorry for him, although he despised him for feeling it. The only beam of light, the only spark of pleasure, was his royal uniform; and to know that Insie's laugh thereat was hollow, and would melt away to weeping when he was out of sight, together with the sulky curiosity of Maunder, kept him up a little, in this time of bitter sacrifice.

Enough that he went off, at last, in the claws of that Roman hippogriff—as Mrs. Carnaby savagely called poor Mordacks—and the visitor's flag hung half-mast high, and Saracen and the other dogs made a howling dirge, with such fine hearts (as the poor mother said, between her sobs) that they got their dinners upon china plates.

Sir Duncan had left before this, and was back under Dr. Upround's hospitable roof. He had made up his mind to put his fortune, or rather his own value, to the test, in a place of deep interest to him now, the heart of the fair Janetta. He knew that, according to popular view, he was much too old for this young lady; but for popular view he cared not one doit, if her own had the courage and the will to go against it. For years he had sternly resisted all temptation of second marriage, toward which shrewd mothers and nice maidens had labored in vain to lead him. But the bitter disappointment about his son, and that long illness, and the tender nursing (added to the tenderness of his own sides, from lying upon them, with a hard dry cough), had opened some parts of his constitution to matrimonial propensities. Miss Upround was of a playful nature, and teased everybody she cared about; and although Sir Duncan was a great hero to her, she treated him sometimes as if he were her doll. Being a grave man, he liked this, within the bounds of good taste and manners; and the young lady always knew where to stop. From being amused with her, he began to like her; and from liking her, he went on to miss her; and from missing her to wanting her was no long step.

However, Sir Duncan was not at all inclined to make a fool of himself herein. He liked the lady very much, and saw that she would suit him, and help him well in the life to which he was thinking of returning. For within the last fortnight a very high post at Calcutta had been offered to him by the powers in Leadenhall Street, upon condition of sailing at once, and foregoing the residue of his leave. If matters had been to his liking in England, he certainly would have declined it; but after his sad disappointment, and the serious blow to his health, he resolved to accept it, and set forth speedily. The time was an interlude of the war, and ships need not wait for convoy.

This had induced him to take his Yorkshire affairs (which Mordacks had been forced to intermit during his Derbyshire campaign) into his own hands, and speed the issue, as above related. And part of his plan was to quit all claim to present possession of Scargate; that if the young lady should accept his suit, it might not in any way be for the sake of the landed interest. As it happened, he had gone much further than this, and cast away his claim entirely, to save his sister from disgrace and the family property from lawyers. And now having sought Dr. Upround's leave (which used to be thought the proper thing to do), he asked Janetta whether she would have him, and she said, "No, but he might have her." Upon this he begged permission to set the many drawbacks before her, and she nodded her head, and told him to begin.

"I am of a Yorkshire family. But, I am sorry to say that their temper is bad, and they must have their own way too much."

"But, that suits me; and I understand it. Because I must have my own way too."

"But, I have parted with my inheritance, and have no place in this country now."

"But, I am very glad of that. Because I shall be able to go about."

"But, India is a dreadfully hot country; many creatures tease you, and you get tired of almost everything."

"But, that will make it all the more refreshing not to be tired of you, perhaps."

"But, I have a son as old as you, or older."

"But, you scarcely suppose that I can help that!"

"But, my hair is growing gray, and I have great crow's-feet, and everybody will begin to say—"

"But, I don't believe a word of it, and I won't have it; and I don't care a pin's head what all the world says put together, so long as you don't belong to it."

CHAPTER LIV

TRUE LOVE

About a month after Sir Duncan's marriage, when he and his bride were in London, with the lady's parents come to help, in the misery of outfit, a little boy ran through a field of wheat, early in the afternoon, and hid himself in a blackthorn hedge to see what was going on at Anerley. Nothing escaped him, for his eyes were sharp, being of true Danish breed. He saw Captain Anerley trudging up the hill, with a pipe in his mouth, to the bean field, where three or four men were enjoying the air, without any of the greedy gulps produced by too great exertion of the muscles; then he saw the mistress of the house throw wide a lattice, and shake out a cloth for the birds, who skipped down from the thatch by the dozen instantly; and then he saw Mary, with a basket and a wooden measure, going round the corner of the house, and clucking for the fowls to rally from their scratching-places. These came zealously, with speed of leg and wing, from straw-rick, threshing-floor, double hedge, or mixen; and following their tails, the boy slipped through the rick-yard, and tossed a note to Mary with a truly Flamburian delivery.

Although it was only a small-sized boy, no other than the heir of the "Cod-fish," a brighter rose flew into Mary's cheeks than the master-cock of all the yard could show upon comb or wattle. Contemptuous of twopence, which Mary felt for, the boy disappeared like a rabbit; and the fowls came and helped themselves to the tail-wheat, while their mistress was thinking of her letter. It was short and sweet—at least in promise—being no more than these few words: "Darling, the dike where first we met, an hour after sunset."

Mary never doubted that her duty was to go; and at the time appointed she was there, with firm knowledge of her own mind, being now a loving and reasonable woman. It was just a year since she had saved the life of Robin; and patience, and loneliness, and opposition, had enlarged and ennobled her true and simple heart. No lord in the land need have looked for a purer or sweeter example of maidenhood than this daughter of a Yorkshire farmer was, in her simple dress, and with the dignity of love. The glen was beginning to bestrew itself with want of light, instead of shadows; and bushy places thickened with the imperceptible growth of night. Mary went on, with excitement deepening, while sunset deepened into dusk; and the color of her clear face flushed and fleeted under the anxious touch of love, as the tint of a delicate finger-nail, with any pressure, varies. But not very long was she left in doubt.

"How long you have been! And oh, where have you been? And how much longer will you be?" Among many other words and doings she insisted chiefly on these points.

"I am a true-blue, as you may see, and a warrant-officer already," he said, with his old way of smiling at himself. "When the war begins again (as it must—please God!—before many weeks are over), I shall very soon get my commission, and go up. I am quite fit already to command a frigate."

Mary was astonished at his modesty; she thought that he ought to be an admiral at least, and so she told him; however, he knew better.

"You must bear in mind," he replied, with a kindly desire to spare her feelings, "that until a change for the better comes, I am under disadvantages. Not only as an outlaw—which has been upon the whole a comfort—but as a suspected criminal, with warrant against him, and reward upon him. Of course I am innocent; and everybody knows it, or at least I hope so, except the one who should have known it best."

"I am the person who should know it best of all," his true love answered, with some jealousy. "Explain yourself, Robin, if you please."

"No Robin, so please you, but Mr. James Blyth, captain of the foretop, then cockswain of the barge, and now master's mate of H. M. ship of the line Belleisle. But the one who should have trusted me, next to my own love, is my father, Sir Duncan Yordas."

"How you are talking! You have such a reckless way. A warrant-officer, an arrant criminal! And your father, Sir Duncan Yordas, that very strange gentleman, who could never get warm! Oh, Robin, you always did talk nonsense, when—whenever I would let you. But you should not try to make my head go round."

"Every word of it is true," the young sailor answered, applying a prompt remedy for vertigo. "It had been clearly proved to his knowledge, long before the great fact was vouchsafed to me, that I am the only son of Sir Duncan Yordas, or, at any rate, his only son for the present. The discovery gratified him so little, that he took speedy measures to supplant me."

"The very rich gentleman from India," said Mary, "that married Miss Upround lately; and her dress was all made of spun diamonds, they say, as bright as the dew in the morning. Oh, then you will have to give me up; Robin, you must give up me!"

Clasping her hands, she looked up at him with courage, keeping down all sign of tears. She felt that her heart would not hold out long, and yet she was prouder than to turn away. "Speak," she said; "it is better to speak plainly;

you know that it must be so."

"Do I? why?" Robin Lyth asked, calmly, being well contented to prolong her doubts, that he might get the benefit thereafter.

"Because you belong to great people, and I am just a farmer's daughter, and no more, and quite satisfied to remain so. Such things never answer."

"A little while ago you were above me, weren't you? When I was nobody's son, and only a castaway, with a nickname."

"That has nothing to do with it. We must take things exactly as we find them at the time."

"And you took me as you found me at the time; only that you made me out so much better. Mary, I am not worthy of you. What has birth to do with it? And so far as that goes, yours is better, though mine may seem the brighter. In every other way you are above me. You are good, and I am wicked. You are pure, and I am careless. You are sweet, and I am violent. In truth alone can I ever vie with you; and I must be a pitiful scoundrel, Mary, if I did not even try to do that, after all that you have done for me."

"But," said Mary, with her lovely eyes gleaming with the glittering shade of tears, "I like you very much to do it—but not exactly as a duty, Robin."

"You look at me like that, and you talk of duty! Duty, duty; this is my duty. I should like to be discharging it forever and a day."

"I did not come here for ideas of this kind," said Mary, with her lips as red as pyracanthine berries; "free trade was bad enough, but the Royal Navy worse, it seems. Now, Robin dear, be sensible, and tell me what I am to do."

"To listen to me, and then say whether I deserve what my father has done to me. He came back from India—as you must understand—with no other object in life, that I can hear of (for he had any quantity of money), than to find out me, his only child, and the child of the only wife he ever could put up with. For twenty years he had believed me to be drowned, when the ship he sent me home in to be educated was supposed to have foundered, with all hands. But something made him fancy that I might have escaped; and as he could not leave India then, he employed a gentleman of York, named Mordacks, to hunt out all about it. Mordacks, who seems to be a wonderful man, and most kind-hearted to everybody, as poor Widow Carroway says of him with tears, and as he testifies of himself—he set to work, and found out in no time all about me and my ear-rings, and my crawling from the cave that will bear my name, they say, and more things than I have time to tell. He appointed a meeting with Sir Duncan Yordas here at Flamborough, and would have brought me to him, and everything might have been quite happy. But in the mean while that horrible murder of poor Carroway came to pass, and I was obliged to go into hiding, as no one knows better than you, my dear. My father (as I suppose I must call him) being bound, as it seems that they all are, to fall out with their children, took a hasty turn against me at once. Mordacks, whom I saw last week, trusting myself to his honor, tells me that Sir Duncan would not have cared twopence about my free-trade work, and so on, or even about my having killed the officer in fair conflict, for he is used to that. But he never will forgive me for absconding, and leaving my fellows, as he puts it, to bear the brunt. He says that I am a dastard and a skulk, and unworthy to bear the name of Yordas."

"What a wicked, unnatural man he must be!" cried Mary. "He deserves to have no children."

"No; I am told that he is a very good man, but stiff-necked and disdainful. He regards me with scorn, because he knows no better. He may know our laws, but he knows nothing of our ways, to suppose that my men were in any danger. If I had been caught while the stir was on, a gibbet on the cliff would have been set up, even before my trial—such is the reward of eminence—but no Yorkshire jury would turn round in the box, with those poor fellows before them. 'Not guilty, my lord,' was on their tongues, before he had finished charging them."

"Oh, I am so glad! They have been acquitted, and you were there to see it!"

"To be sure. I was in the court, as Harry Ombler's father. Mr. Mordacks got it up; and it told on the jury even more than could have been expected. Even the judge wiped his eyes as he looked at me, for they say he has a scapegrace son; and Harry was the only one of all the six in danger, according to the turn of the evidence. My poor eyes have scarcely come round yet from the quantity of sobbing that I had to do, and the horrible glare of my goggles. And then I had a crutch that I stumped with as I sighed, so that all the court could hear me; and whenever I did it, all the women sighed too, and even the hardest hearts were moved. Mr. Mordacks says that it was capital."

"Oh, but, Robin, how shocking, though you make me laugh! If the verdict had been otherwise—oh, what then?"

"Well, then, Harry Ombler had a paper in his hand, done in printing letters by myself, because he is a very tidy scholar, and signed by me; the which he was to read before receiving sentence, saying that Robin Lyth himself was in York town, and would surrender to that court upon condition that mercy should be warranted to the prisoners."

"And you would have given yourself up? And without consulting me about it!"

"Bad, I admit," Robin answered, with a smile; "but not half so bad as to give up you—which you calmly proposed just now, dear heart. However, there is no need for any trouble now, except that I am forced to keep out of sight until other evidence is procured. Mordacks has taken to me, like a better father, mainly from his paramount love of justice, and of daring gallantry, as he calls it."

"So it was, and ten times more; heroic self-devotion is a much more proper term."

"Now don't," said Robin. "If you make me blush, you may guess what I shall do to hide it—carry the war into the sweet land of the enemy. But truly, my darling, there was very little danger. And I am up for a much better joke this time. My august Roman father, who has cast me off, sails as a very great Indian gun, in a ship of the line, from Spithead, early in September. The Belleisle is being paid off now, and I have my certificate, as well as lots of money. Next to his lass, every sailor loves a spree; and mine, instead of emptying, shall fill the locker. With this disgusting peace on, and no chance of prize-money, and plenty in their pockets for a good spell ashore, blue-jackets will be scarce when Sir Duncan Yordas sails. If I can get a decent berth as a petty officer, off I go for Calcutta, and watch (like the sweet little cherub that sits up aloft) for the safety of my dear papa and mamma, as the Frenchmen are teaching us to call them. What do you think of such filial devotion?"

"It would be a great deal more than he deserves," Mary answered, with sweet simplicity. "But what could you do, if he found out who you are?"

"Not the smallest fear of that, my dear. I have never had the honor of an introduction. My new step-mother, who might have been my sweetheart if I had not seen somebody a hundred times as good, a thousand times as gentle, and a million times as lovely—"

"Oh, Robin, do leave off such very dreadful stories! I saw her in the church, and she looked beautiful."

"Fine feathers make fine birds. However, she is well enough in her way; and I love her father. But, for all that, she has no business to be my step-mother; and of course it was only the money that did it. She has a little temper of her own, I can assure you; and I wish Sir Duncan joy of her when they get among mosquitoes. But, as I was going to say, the only risk of my being caught is from her sharp eyes. Even of that there is not much danger, for we common sailors need not go within hail of those grandees, unless it comes to boat-work. And even if Miss Janetta—I beg her pardon, Lady Yordas—should chance to recognize me, I am sure she would never tell her husband. No, no; she would be too jealous; and for fifty other reasons. She is very cunning, let me tell you."

"Well," cried Mary, with a smile of wisdom, "I hope that I may never live to be a step-mother. The way those poor things get abused—"

"You would have more principle, I should hope, than to marry anybody after me. However, I have told you nearly all my news, and in a few minutes I must be off. Only two things more. In the first place, Mordacks has taken a very great fancy to me, and has turned against my father. He and Widow Carroway and I had a long talk after the trial, and we all agreed that the murder was committed by a villain called 'John Cadman,' a sneak and a skulk, whom I knew well, as one of Carroway's own men. Among other things, they chanced to say that Cadman's gun was missing, and that the poor widow can swear to it. I asked if any one had searched for it; and Mordacks said no, it would be hopeless. I told them that if I were only free to show myself and choose my time, I would lay my life upon finding it, if thrown away (as it most likely was) in some part of that unlucky cave. Mordacks caught at this idea, and asked me a number of questions, and took down my answers; for no one else knows the cave as I do. I would run all risks myself, and be there to do it, if time suited. But only certain tides will serve, even with the best of weather; and there may be no such tide for months—I mean tide, weather, and clear water combined, as they must be for the job. Therefore I am not to wait, but go about my other business, and leave this to Mordacks, who loves to be captain of everything. Mr. Mordacks talked of a diving-bell, and some great American inventions; but nothing of the kind can be used there, nor even grappling-irons. The thing must not be heard of even, until it has been accomplished. Whatever is done, must be done by a man who can swim and dive as I can, and who knows the place almost as well. I have told him where to find the man, when the opportunity comes for it; and I have shown my better father, Robin Cockscroft, the likely spot. So now I have nothing more to do with that."

"How wonderfully you can throw off cares!" his sweetheart answered, softly. "But I shall be miserable till I know what happens. Will they let me be there? Because I understand so much about tides, and I can hold my tongue."

"That you have shown right well, my Mary; but your own sense will tell you that you could not be there. Now one thing more: here is a ring, not worthy—although it is the real stuff—to go upon your precious hand, yet allow me to put it on; no, not there; upon your wedding finger. Now do you know what that is for?"

"For me, I suppose," she answered, blushing with pleasure and admiration; "but it is too good, too beautiful, too costly."

"Not half good enough. Though, to tell you the truth, it can not be matched easily; any more than you can. But I know where to get those things. Now promise me to wear it, when you think of me; and the one habit will confirm the other. But the more important part is this, and the last thing for me to say to you. Your father still hates my name, I fear. Tell him every word I have told you, and perhaps it will bring him half way round. Sooner or later he must come round; and the only way to do it is to work him slowly. When he sees in how many ways I have been wronged, and how beautifully I have borne it all, he will begin to say to himself, 'Now this young man may be improving.' But he never will say, 'He hath no need of it.'"

"I should rather think not, you conceited Robin, or whatever else I am to call you now. But I bargain for one thing—whatever may happen, I shall never call you anything else but Robin. It suits you, and you look well with it. Yordas, indeed, or whatever it may be—"

"No bargain is valid without a seal," etc., etc. In the old but ever-vivid way they went on, until they were forced to part, at the very lips of the house itself, after longing lingerings. The air of the fields was sweet with summer fragrance and the breath of night; the world was ripe with soft repose, whose dreams were hope and happiness; and the heaven spread some gentle stars, to show mankind the way to it. Then a noble perfume strewed the ambient air with stronger presence, as the farmer, in his shirt sleeves, came, with a clay pipe, and grumbled, "Wherever is our Mary all this time?"

CHAPTER LV

NICHOLAS THE FISH

Five hundred years ago there was a great Italian swimmer, even greater than our Captain Webb; inasmuch as he had what the wags of the age unjustly ascribe to our hero, that is to say, web toes and fingers. This capable man could, if history be true, not only swim for a week without ceasing (reassuring solid nature now and then by a gulp of live fish), but also could expand his chest so considerably that it held enough air for a day's consumption. Fortified thus, he explored Charybdis and all the Liparic whirlpools, and could have found Cadman's gun anywhere, if it had only been there. But at last the sea had its revenge upon him, through the cruel insistence of his king.

No man so amphibious has since arisen through the unfathomed tide of time. But a swimmer and diver of great repute was now living not far from Teesmouth. That is to say, he lived there whenever the state of the weather or the time of year stranded him in dry misery. Those who have never come across a man of this description might suppose that he was happy and content at home with his wife and growing family, assuaging the brine in the delightful manner commended by Hero to Leander. But, alas! it was not so at all. The temper of the man was very slow to move, as generally happens with deep-chested men, and a little girl might lead him with her finger on the shore; and he liked to try to smell land flowers, which in his opinion were but weeds. But if a man can not control his heart, in the very middle of his system, how can he hope to command his skin, that unscientific frontier of his frame?

"Nicholas the fish," as his neighbors (whenever, by coming ashore, he had such treasures) contemptuously called him, was endowed from his birth with a peculiar skin, and by exercise had improved it. Its virtue was excessive thickness—such as a writer should pray for—protected also by powerful hairiness—largely admired by those with whom it is restricted to the head.

Unhappily for Nicholas, the peremptory poises of nature struck a line with him, and this was his line of flotation. From perpetual usage this was drawn, obliquely indeed, but as definitely as it is upon a ship of uniform displacement—a yacht, for instance, or a man-of-war. Below that line scarcely anything could hurt him; but above it he was most sensitive, unless he were continually wetted; and the flies, and the gnats, and many other plagues of England, with one accord pitched upon him, and pitched into him, during his short dry intervals, with a bracing sense of saline draught. Also the sun, and the wind, and even the moon, took advantage of him when unwetted.

This made his dry periods a purgatory to him; and no sooner did he hear from Mr. Mordacks of a promising job under water than he drew breath enough for a ten-fathom dive, and bursting from long despair, made a great slap at the flies beneath his collar-bone. The sound was like a drum which two men strike; and his wife, who was devoted to him, hastened home from the adjoining parish with a sad presentiment of parting. And this was speedily verified; for the champion swimmer and diver set forth that very day for Bempton Warren, where he was to have a private meeting with the general factor.

Now it was a great mistake to think—as many people at this time did, both in Yorkshire and Derbyshire—that the gulf of connubial cares had swallowed the great Roman hero Mordacks. Unarmed, and even without his gallant roadster to support him, he had leaped into that Curtian lake, and had fought a good fight at the bottom of it. The details are highly interesting, and the chronicle might be useful; but, alas! there is no space left for it. It is enough, and a great thing too, to say that he emerged triumphant, reduced his wife into very good condition, and obtained the due mastery of her estates, and lordship of the household.

Refreshed and recruited by the home campaign, and having now a double base for future operations—York city with the fosse of Ouse in the east, and Pretorian Hill, Derbyshire, westward—Mordacks returned, with a smack of lip more dry than amontilladissimo, to the strict embrace of business. So far as the needs of the body were concerned, he might have done handsomely without any business; but having no flesh fit to weigh against his mind, he gave preference to the latter. Now the essence of his nature was to take strong views; not hastily—if he could help it—nor through narrow aspect of prejudice, but with power of insight (right or wrong), and stern fixity thereafter. He had kept his opinion about Sir Duncan Yordas much longer than usual pending, being struck with the fame of the man, and his manner, and generous impulsive nature. All these he still admired, but felt that the mind was far too hasty, and, to put it in his own strong way, Sir Duncan (whatever he might be in India) had been but a fool in England. Why had he cast away his claim on Scargate, and foiled the factor's own pet scheme for a great triumph over the lawyers? And why condemn his only son, when found with such skill and at heavy expense, without even hearing both sides of the tale? Last, but not least, what induced him to marry, when amply old enough to know better, a girl who might be well enough in her way, but had no family estate to bring, was shrewdly suspected of a cutting tongue, and had more than once been anything but polite to Geoffrey Mordacks?

Although this gentleman was not a lawyer, and indeed bore a tyrannous hate against that gentle and most precious class, he shared the solicitor's just abhorrence of the word "farewell," when addressed to him by any one of good substance. He resolved that his attentions should not cease, though undervalued for the moment, but should be continued to the son and heir— whose remainder in tail subsisted still, though it might be hard to substantiate —and when his cousin Lancelot should come into possession, he might find a certain factor to grapple him. Mr. Mordacks hated Lancelot, and had carried out his banishment with intense enjoyment, holding him as in a wrench-hammer all the way, silencing his squeaks with another turn of the screw, and as eager to crack him as if he were a nut, the first that turns auburn in September.

This being the condition of so powerful a mind, facts very speedily shaped themselves thereto, as they do when the power of an eminent orator lays hold of them and crushes them, and they can not even squeak. Or even as a still more eminent 'bus driver, when the street is blocked, and there seems to be no room for his own thumb, yet (with a gentle whistle and a wink) solves the jostling stir and balk, makes obstructive traffic slide, like an eddy obsequious, beside him and behind, and comes forth as the first of an orderly procession toward the public-house of his true love.

Now if anything beyond his own conviction were wanted to set this great agent upon action, soon it was found in York Summer Assizes, and the sudden inrush of evidence, which—no matter how a case has been prepared— gets pent up always for the Bar and Bench. Then Robin Lyth came, with a gallant dash, and offered himself as a sacrifice, if needful, which proved both his courage and his common-sense in waiting till due occasion demanded him. Mordacks was charmed with this young man, not only for proving his own judgment right, but also for possessing a quickness of decision akin to his own, and backing up his own ideas.

With vigor thus renewed by many interests and motives, the general and generous factor kept his appointment in Bempton Warren. Since the distressing, but upon the whole desirable, decease of that poor Rickon Goold, the lonely hut in which he breathed his last had not been by any means a popular resort. There were said to be things heard, seen, and felt, even in the brightest summer day, which commended the spot to the creatures that fear mankind, but not their spectres. The very last of all to approach it now would have been the two rollicking tars who had trodden their wooden-legged watch around it. Nicholas the fish was superstitious also, as it behooved him well to be; but having heard nothing of the story of the place, and perceiving no gnats in the neighborhood, he thankfully took it for his short dry spells.

Mr. Mordacks met him, and the two men were deeply impressed with one another. The diver admired the sharp, terse style and definite expression of the factor, while the factor enjoyed the large ponderous roll and suggestive reservations of the diver. For this was a man who had met great beings, and faced mighty wonders in deep places; and he thought of them more than he liked to say, because he had to get his living.

Nothing could be settled to a nicety between them, not even as to pounds, shillings, and pence. For the nature of the job depended wholly upon the behavior of the weather; and the weather must be not only at its best, but also setting meekly in the right direction at the right moment of big springtide. The diver was afraid that he might ask too little, and the factor disliked the risk of offering too much, and possibly spoiling thereby a noble nature. But each of them realized (to some extent) the honesty of the other, and neither of them meant to be unreasonable.

"Give and take, is what I say," said the short man with the monstrous chest, looking up at the tall man with the Roman nose; "live and let live. Ah! that's it."

Mr. Mordacks would have said, "Right you are," if that elegant expression had been in vogue; but as that brilliance had not yet risen, he was content to say, "Just so." Then he added, "Here you have everything you want. Madam Precious will send you twice a day, to the stone at the bottom of the lane, a gallon of beer, and victuals in proportion. Your duty is to watch the tides and weather, keep your boat going, and let me know; and here I am in half an hour."

Calpurnia Mordacks was in her duty now, and took her autumn holiday at Flamborough. And though Widow Precious felt her heart go pitapat at first sight of another Mrs. Mordacks, she made up her mind, with a gulp, not to let this cash go to the Thornwick. As a woman she sighed; but as a landlady she smiled, and had visions of hoisting a flag on her roof.

When Mordacks, like a victorious general, conqueror of this Danish town, went forth for his evening stroll to see his subjects and be saluted, a handsome young sailor came up from the cliffs, and begged to have a few quiet words with him. "Say on, my lad; all my words are quiet," replied the general factor. Then this young man up and told his tale, which was all in the well-trodden track of mankind. He had run away to sea, full of glorious dreams—valor, adventure, heroism, rivers of paradise, and lands of heaven. Instead of that, he had been hit upon the head, and in places of deeper tenderness, frequently roasted, and frozen yet more often, basted with brine when he had no skin left, scorched with thirst, and devoured by creatures whose appetites grew dainty when his own was ravening.

"Excellent youth," Mr. Mordacks said, "your tale might move a heart of flint. All who know me have but one opinion. I am benevolence itself. But my balance is low at my banker's."

"I want no money, sir," the sailor answered, simply offering benevolence itself a pipeful of tobacco from an ancient bit of bladder; "I have not got a farthing, but I am with good people who never would take it if I had it, and that makes everything square between us. I might have a hatful of money if I chose, but I find myself better without it, and my constitution braces up. If I only chose to walk a league sou'west, there would be bonfires burning. But I vowed I would go home a captain, and I will."

"Ha!" cried Mr. Mordacks, with his usual quickness, and now knowing all about everybody; "you are Mr. John Anerley, the son of the famous Captain Anerley."

"Jack Anerley, sir, till better times; and better they never will be, till I make them. But not a word to any one about me, if you please. It would break my mother's heart (for she doth look down upon people, without asking) to hear that Robin Cockscroft was supporting of me. But, bless you, I shall pay him soon, a penny for a guinea."

Truth, which struggles through the throng of men to get out and have a little breath sometimes, now and then succeeds, by accident, or the stupid misplacement of a word. A penny for a guinea was as much as Robin Cockscroft was likely ever to see for his outlay upon this very fine young fellow. Jack Anerley accepted the situation with the large philosophy of a sailor; and all he wanted from Mr. Mordacks was leave to be present at the diving job. This he obtained, as he promised to be useful, and a fourth oar was likely to be needed.

It was about an hour before noon of a beautifully soft September day, when little Sam Precious, the same boy that carried Robin Lyth's note to Mary, came up to Mr. Mordacks with a bit of plaited rushes, the scytale of Nicholas the fish, who was happy enough not to know his alphabet. The factor immediately put on his hat, girded himself with his riding sword and pistol belt, and told his good wife that business might take him away for some hours. Then he hastened to Robin Cockscroft's house, after sending the hostler, on his own horse, with a letter to Bridlington coast-guard station, as he had arranged with poor Carroway's successor.

The Flamborough fishermen were out at sea; and without any fuss, Robin's boat was launched, and manned by that veteran himself, together with old Joe and Bob, who had long been chewing the quid of expectation, and at the bow oar Jack Anerley. Their orders were to slip quietly round, and wait in the

Dovecote till the diver came. Mordacks saw them on their way; and then he strode up the deserted path, and struck away toward a northern cove, where the diver's little boat was housed. There he found Nicholas the fish, spread out in all his glory, like a polypod awash, or a basking turtle, or a well-fed calf of Proteus. Laid on his back, where the wavelets broke, and beaded a silver fringe upon the golden ruff of sand, he gave his body to soft lullaby, and his mind to perfect holiday. His breadth, and the spring of fresh air inside it, kept him gently up and down; and his calm enjoyment was enriched by the baffled wrath of his enemies. For flies, of innumerable sorts and sizes, held a hopeless buzz above him, being put upon their mettle to get at him, and perishing sweetly in the vain attempt.

With a grunt of reluctance he awoke to business, swam for his boat, and embarking Mr. Mordacks, pulled him across the placid bay to the cave where his forces were assembled.

"Let there be no mistake about it," the factor shouted from the mermaids' shelf, having promised his Calpurnia to keep upon dry land whenever the water permitted him; "our friend the great diver will first ascertain whether the thing which we seek is here. If so, he will leave it where it is until the arrival of the Preventive boat. You all understand that we wish to put the matter so that even a lawyer can not pick any hole in the evidence. Light no links until I tell you. Now, Nicholas the fish, go down at once."

Without a word the diver plunged, having taken something between his teeth which he would not let the others see. The watery floor of the cavern was as smooth as a mill-pond in July, and he plunged so neatly that he made no splash; nothing but a flicker of reflection on the roof, and a lapping murmur round the sides, gave token that a big man was gone into the deep. For several minutes no one spoke, but every eye was strained upon the glassy dimness, and every ear intent for the first break of sound.

"T' goop ha' got un," cried old Robin, indignant at this outrage by a stranger to his caves, "God niver mahd mon to pree intil 's ain warks."

Old Joe and Bob grunted approbation, and Mordacks himself was beginning to believe that some dark whirlpool or coil of tangles had drowned the poor diver, when a very gentle noise, like a dabchick playing beneath a bridge, came from the darkest corner. Nicholas was there, inhaling air, not in greedy gulps and gasps, like a man who has had no practice, but leisurely encouraging his lungs with little doses, as a doctor gives soup to a starved boat crew. Being hailed by loud voices, he answered not, for his nature was by no means talkative; but presently, with very little breach of water, he swam to the middle, and asked for his pipe.

"Have you found the gun?" cried Mordacks, whose loftiest feelings had subsided in a quarter of a minute to the business level. Nicholas made no reply until the fire of his pipe was established, while he stood in the water quite as if he were on land, supporting himself by nothing more than a gentle movement of his feet, while the glow of the touch-paper lit his round face and yellow leather skull-cap. "In coorse I has," he said at last, blowing a roll of smoke along the gleaming surface; "over to yon little cornder."

"And you can put your hand upon it in a moment?" The reply was a nod and another roll of smoke. "Admirable! Now, then, Joe, and Bob the son of Joe, do what I told you, while Master Cockscroft and our nimble young friend get the links all ready."

The torches were fixed on the rocky shelf, as they had been upon the fatal night; but they were not lit until Joe and his son, sent forth in the smaller boat to watch, came back with news that the Preventive gig was round the point, and approaching swiftly, with a lady in the stern, whose dress was black.

"Right!" cried Mr. Mordacks, with a brisk voice ringing under the ponderous brows of rock. "Men, I have brought you to receive a lesson. You shall see what comes of murder. Light the torches. Nicholas, go under, with the exception of your nose, or whatever it is you breathe with. When I lift my hand, go down; and do as I have ordered you."

The cavern was lit with the flare of fire, and the dark still water heaved with it, when the coast-guard boat came gliding in. The crew, in white jerseys, looked like ghosts flitting into some magic scene. Only the officer, darkly clad, and standing up with the tiller-lines in hand, and the figure of a woman sitting in the stern, relieved their spectral whiteness.

"Commander Hardlock, and men of the coastguard," shouted Mr. Mordacks, when the wash of ripples and the drip of oars and the creak of wood gave silence, "the black crime committed upon this spot shall no longer go unpunished. The ocean itself has yielded its dark secret to the perseverance of mankind, and the humble but not unskillful efforts which it has been my privilege to conduct. A good man was slain here, in cold blood slain—a man of remarkable capacity and zeal, gallantry, discipline, and every noble quality, and the father of a very large family. The villain who slew him would have slain six other harmless men by perjury if an enlightened English jury had been fools enough to believe him. Now I will show you what to believe. I am not eloquent, I am not a man of words; my motto is strict business. And business with me is a power, not a name. I lift my hand; you wait for half a minute; and then, from the depths of this abyss, arises the gun used in the murder."

475

The men understood about half of this, being honest fellows in the main, and desiring time to put heads together about the meaning; but one there was who knew too well that his treacherous sin had found him out. He strove to look like the rest, but felt that his eyes obeyed heart more than brain; and then the widow, who had watched him closely through her black veil, lifted it, and fixed her eyes on his. Deadly terror seized him, and he wished that he had shot himself.

"Stand up, men," the commander shouted, "until we see the end of this. The crime has been laid upon our force. We scorn the charge of such treachery. Stand up, men, and face, like innocent men, whatever can be shown against you."

The men stood up, and the light of the torches fell upon their faces. All were pale with fear and wonder, but one was white as death itself. Calling up his dogged courage, and that bitterness of malice which had made him do the deed, and never yet repent of it, he stood as firmly as the rest, but differed from them in three things. His face wore a smile; he watched one place only; and his breath made a noise, while theirs was held.

Then, from the water, without a word, or sign of any hand that moved it, a long gun rose before John Cadman, and the butt was offered to his hand. He stood with his arms at his sides, and could not lift them to do anything. Neither could he speak, nor make defense, but stood like an image that is fastened by the feet.

"Hand me that," cried the officer, sharply; but instead of obeying, the man stared malignantly, and then plunged over the gun into the depth.

Not so, however, did he cheat the hangman; Nicholas caught him (as a water-dog catches a worn-out glove), and gave him to any one that would have him. "Strap him tight," the captain cried; and the men found relief in doing it. At the next jail-delivery he was tried, and the jury did their duty. His execution restored good-will, and revived that faith in justice which subsists upon so little food.

CHAPTER LVI

IN THE THICK OF IT

One of the greatest days in all the history of England, having no sense of its future fame, and being upon a hostile coast, was shining rather dismally. And one of England's greatest men, the greatest of all her sons in battle—though few of them have been small at that—was out of his usual mood, and full of calm presentiment and gloomy joy. He knew that he would see the sun no more; yet his fear was not of that, but only of losing the light of duty. As long as the sun endures, he shall never see duty done more brilliantly.

The wind was dropping, to give the storm of human fury leisure; and while a sullen swell was rolling, canvas flapped and timbers creaked. Like a team of mallards in double column, plunging and lifting buoyant breasts to right and left alternately, the British fleet bore down upon the swan-like crescent of the foe. These were doing their best to fly, but failing of that luck, put helm alee, and shivered in the wind, and made fine speeches, proving that they must win the day.

"For this I have lived, and for this it would be worth my while to die, having no one left, I dare say now, in all the world to care for me."

Thus spake the junior lieutenant of that British ship, the Victory—a young man after the heart of Nelson, and gazing now on Nelson's face. No smarter sailor could be found in all that noble fleet than this Lieutenant Blyth, who once had been the captain of all smugglers. He had fought his way up by skill, and spirit, and patience, and good temper, and the precious gift of self-reliance, failing of which all merit fails. He had always thought well of himself, but never destroyed the good of it by saying so; and whoever praised him had to do it again, to outspeak his modesty. But without good fortune all these merits would never have been successes. One of Robin's truest merits was that he generally earned good luck.

However, his spirits were not in their usual flow of jocundity just now, and his lively face was dashed with care. Not through fear of lead, or steel, or wooden splinter, or a knock upon the head, or any other human mode of encouraging humanity. He hoped to keep out of the way of these, as even the greatest heroes do; for how could the world get on if all its bravest men went foremost? His mind meant clearly, and with trust in proper Providence, to remain in its present bodily surroundings, with which it had no fault to find. Grief, however—so far as a man having faith in his luck admits that point—

478

certainly was making some little hole into a heart of corky fibre. For Robin Lyth had heard last night, when a schooner joined the fleet with letters, that Mary Anerley at last was going to marry Harry Tanfield. He told himself over and over again that if it were so, the fault was his own, because he had not taken proper care about the safe dispatch of letters. Changing from ship to ship and from sea to sea for the last two years or more, he had found but few opportunities of writing, and even of those he had not made the utmost. To Mary herself he had never once written, knowing well that her father forbade it, while his letters to Flamborough had been few, and some of those few had miscarried. For the French had a very clever knack just now of catching the English dispatch-boats, in most of which they found accounts of their own thrashings, as a listener catches bad news of himself. But none of these led them to improve their conduct.

Flamborough (having felt certain that Robin could never exist without free trade, and missing many little courtesies that flowed from his liberal administration), was only too ready to lament his death, without insisting on particulars. Even as a man who has foretold a very destructive gale of wind tempers with the pride of truth the sorrow which he ought to feel for his domestic chimney-pots (as soon as he finds them upon his lawn), so Little Denmark, while bewailing, accepted the loss as a compliment to its own renowned sagacity.

But Robin knew not until last night that he was made dead at Flamborough, through the wreck of a ship which he had quitted a month before she was cast away. And now at last he only heard that news by means of his shipmate, Jack Anerley. Jack was a thorough-going sailor now, easy, and childish, and full of the present, leaving the past to cure and the future to care for itself as might be. He had promised Mr. Mordacks and Robin Cockscroft to find out Robin Lyth, and tell him all about the conviction of John Cadman; and knowing his name in the navy and that of his ship, he had done so after in-and-out chase. But there for the time he had rested from his labors, and left "Davy Jones" to send back word about it; which that Pelagian Davy fails to do, unless the message is enshrined in a bottle, for which he seems to cherish true naval regard.

In this state of things the two brothers-in-law—as they fully intended to be by-and-by—were going into this tremendous battle: Jack as a petty officer, and Robin as a junior lieutenant of Lord Nelson's ship. Already had Jack Anerley begun to feel for Robin—or Lieutenant Blyth, as he now was called —that liking of admiration which his clear free manner, and quickness of resource, and agreeable smile in the teeth of peril, had won for him before he had the legal right to fight much. And Robin—as he shall still be called while the memory of Flamborough endures—regarded Jack Anerley with fatherly affection, and hoped to put strength into his character.

However, one necessary step toward that is to keep the character surviving; and in the world's pell-mell now beginning, the uproar alone was enough to kill some, and the smoke sufficient to choke the rest. Many a British sailor who, by the mercy of Providence, survived that day, never could hear a word concerning any other battle (even though a son of his own delivered it down a trumpet), so furious was the concussion of the air, the din of roaring metal, and the clash of cannon-balls which met in the air, and split up into founts of iron.

No less than seven French and Spanish ships agreed with one accord to fall upon and destroy Lord Nelson's ship. And if they had only adopted a rational mode of doing it, and shot straight, they could hardly have helped succeeding. Even as it was, they succeeded far too well; for they managed to make England rue the tidings of her greatest victory.

In the storm and whirl and flame of battle, when shot flew as close as the teeth of a hay-rake, and fire blazed into furious eyes, and then with a blow was quenched forever, and raging men flew into pieces—some of which killed their dearest friends—who was he that could do more than attend to his own business? Nelson had known that it would be so, and had twice enjoined it in his orders; and when he was carried down to die, his dying mind was still on this. Robin Lyth was close to him when he fell, and helped to bear him to his plank of death, and came back with orders not to speak, but work.

Then ensued that crowning effort of misplaced audacity—the attempt to board and carry by storm the ship that still was Nelson's. The captain of the Redoubtable saw through an alley of light, between walls of smoke, that the quarter-deck of the Victory had plenty of corpses, but scarcely a life upon it. Also he felt (from the comfort to his feet, and the increasing firmness of his spinal column) that the heavy British guns upon the lower decks had ceased to throb and thunder into his own poor ship. With a bound of high spirits he leaped to a pleasing conclusion, and shouted, "Forward, my brave sons; we will take the vessel of war of that Nielson!"

This, however, proved to be beyond his power, partly through the inborn absurdity of the thing, and partly, no doubt, through the quick perception and former vocation of Robin Lyth. What would England have said if her greatest hero had breathed his last in French arms, and a captive to the Frenchman? Could Nelson himself have departed thus to a world in which he never could have put the matter straight? The wrong would have been redressed very smartly here, but perhaps outside his knowledge. Even to dream of it awakes a shudder; yet outrages almost as great have triumphed, and nothing is quite beyond the irony of fate.

But if free trade can not be shown as yet to have won for our country any other blessing, it has earned the last atom of our patience and fortitude by its indirect benevolence at this great time. Without free trade—in its sweeter and more innocent maidenhood of smuggling—there never could have been on board that English ship the Victory, a man, unless he were a runagate, with a mind of such laxity as to understand French. But Robin Lyth caught the French captain's words, and with two bounds, and a holloa, called up Britons from below. By this time a swarm of brave Frenchmen was gathered in the mizzen-chains and gangways of their ship, waiting for a lift of the sea to launch them into the English outworks. And scarcely a dozen Englishmen were alive within hail to encounter them. Not even an officer, till Robin Lyth returned, was there to take command of them. The foremost and readiest there was Jack Anerley, with a boarder's pike, and a brace of ship pistols, and his fine ruddy face screwed up as firm as his father's, before a big sale of wheat "Come on, you froggies; we are ready for you," he shouted, as if he had a hundred men in ambush.

They, for their part, failed to enter into the niceties of his language—which difficulty somehow used never to be felt among classic warriors—yet from his manner and position they made out that he offered let and hinderance. To remove him from their course, they began to load guns, or to look about for loaded ones, postponing their advance until he should cease to interfere, so clear at that time was the Gallic perception of an English sailor's fortitude. Seeing this to be so, Jack (whose mind was not well balanced) threw a powder-case amongst them, and exhibited a dance. But this was cut short by a hand-grenade, and, before he had time to recover from that, the deck within a yard of his head flew open, and a stunning crash went by.

Poor Jack Anerley lay quite senseless, while ten or twelve men (who were rushing up, to repel the enemy) fell and died in a hurricane of splinters. A heavy round shot, fired up from the enemy's main-deck, had shattered all before it; and Jack might thank the grenade that he lay on his back while the havoc swept over. Still, his peril was hot, for a volley of musketry whistled and rang around him; and at least a hundred and fifty men were watching their time to leap down on him.

Everything now looked as bad as could be, with the drifting of the smoke, and the flare of fire, and the pelting of bullets, and of grapnel from coehorns, and the screams of Frenchmen exulting vastly, with scarcely any Englishmen to stop them. It seemed as if they were to do as they pleased, level the bulwarks of English rights, and cover themselves with more glory than ever. But while they yet waited to give one more scream, a very different sound arose. Powder, and metal, and crash of timber, and even French and Spanish throats at their very highest pressure, were of no avail against the onward vigor and power of an English cheer. This cheer had a very fine effect. Out of their own mouths the foreigners at once were convicted of inferior stuff, and their two twelve-pounders crammed with grapnel, which ought to have scattered mortality, banged upward, as harmless as a pod discharging seed.

In no account of this great conflict is any precision observed concerning the pell-mell and fisticuff parts of it. The worst of it is that on such occasions almost everybody who was there enlarges his own share of it; and although reflection ought to curb this inclination, it seems to do quite the contrary. This may be the reason why nobody as yet (except Mary Anerley and Flamborough folk) seems even to have tried to assign fair importance to Robin Lyth's share in this glorious encounter. It is now too late to strive against the tide of fortuitous clamor, whose deposit is called history. Enough that this Englishman came up, with fifty more behind him, and carried all before him, as he was bound to do.

CHAPTER LVII

MARY LYTH

Conquests, triumphs, and slaughterous glory are not very nice till they have ceased to drip. After that extinction of the war upon the waves, the nation which had won the fight went into general mourning. Sorrow, as deep as a maiden's is at the death of her lover, spread over the land; and people who had married their romance away, and fathered off their enthusiasm, abandoned themselves to even deeper anguish at the insecurity of property. So deeply had England's faith been anchored into the tenacity of Nelson. The fall of the funds when the victory was announced outspoke a thousand monuments.

From sires and grandsires Englishmen have learned the mood into which their country fell. To have fought under Nelson in his last fight was a password to the right hands of men, and into the hearts of women. Even a man who had never been known to change his mind began to condemn other people for being obstinate. Farmer Anerley went to church in his Fencible accoutrements, with a sash of heavy crape, upon the first day of the Christian year. To prove the largeness of his mind, he harnessed the white-nosed horse, and drove his family away from his own parish, to St. Oswald's Church at Flamborough, where Dr. Upround was to preach upon the death of Nelson. This sermon was of the noblest order, eloquent, spirited, theological, and yet so thoroughly practical, that seven Flamborough boys set off on Monday to destroy French ships of war. Mary did her very utmost not to cry—for she wanted so particularly to watch her father—but nature and the doctor were too many for her. And when he came to speak of the distinguished part played (under Providence) by a gallant son of Flamborough, who, after enduring with manly silence evil report and unprecious balms, stood forward in the breach, like Phineas, and, with the sword of Gideon, defied Philistia to enter the British ark; and when he went on to say that but for Flamborough's prowess on that day, and the valor of the adjoining parish (which had also supplied a hero), England might be mourning her foremost [Greek word], her very greatest fighter in the van, without the consolation of burying him, and embalming him in a nation's tears—for the French might have fired the magazine—and when he proceeded to ask who it was that (under the guiding of a gracious hand) had shattered the devices of the enemy, up stood Robin Cockscroft, with a score of equally ancient captains, and remembering where they were, touched their forelocks, and answered—"Robin Lyth, sir!"

Then Mary permitted the pride of her heart, which had long been painful with the tight control, to escape in a sob, which her mother had foreseen; and pulling out the stopper from her smelling-bottle, Mistress Anerley looked at her husband as if he were Bonaparte himself. He, though aware that it was inconsistent of her, felt (as he said afterward) as if he had been a Frenchman; and looked for his hat, and fumbled about for the button of the pew, to get out of it. But luckily the clerk, with great presence of mind, awoke, and believing the sermon to be over, from the number of men who were standing up, pronounced "Amen" decisively.

During the whole of the homeward drive Farmer Anerley's countenance was full of thought; but he knew that it was watched, and he did not choose to let people get in front of him with his own brains. Therefore he let his wife and daughter look at him, to their hearts' content, while he looked at the ledges, and the mud, and the ears of his horse, and the weather; and he only made two observations of moment, one of which was "gee!" and the other was "whoa!"

With females jolting up and down, upon no springs—except those of jerksome curiosity—conduct of this character was rude in the extreme. But knowing what he was, they glanced at one another, not meaning in any sort of way to blame him, but only that he would be better by-and-by, and perhaps try to make amends handsomely. And this, beyond any denial, he did as soon as he had dined, and smoked his pipe on the butt of the tree by the rick-yard. Nobody knew where he kept his money, or at least his good wife always said so, when any one made bold to ask her. And even now he was right down careful to go to his pot without anybody watching; so that when he came into the Sunday parlor there was not one of them who could say, even at a guess, where he last had been.

Master Simon Popplewell, gentleman-tanner (called out of his name, and into the name of "Johnny," even by his own wife, because there was no sign of any Simon in him), he was there, and his good wife Debby, and Mistress Anerley in her best cap, and Mary, dressed in royal navy blue, with bars of black (for Lord Nelson's sake), according to the kind gift of aunt and uncle; also Willie, looking wonderfully handsome, though pale with the failure of "perpetual motion," and inclined to be languid, as great genius should be in its intervals of activity. Among them a lively talk was stirring; and the farmer said, "Ah! You was talking about me."

"We mought be; and yet again we mought not," Master Popplewell returned, with a glance at Mrs. Deborah, who had just been describing to the company how much her husband excelled in jokesomeness. "Brother Stephen, a good man seeks to be spoken of, and a bad one objects to it, in vain."

"Very well. You shall have something for your money. Mary, you know where the old Mydeary wine is that come from your godfathers and godmothers when you was called in baptism. Take you the key from your mother, child, and bring you up a bottle, and brother Popplewell will open it, for such things is beyond me."

"Well done, our side!" exclaimed the tanner; for if he had a weakness it was for Madeira, which he always declared to have a musky smack of tan; and a waggish customer had told him once that the grapes it was made of were always tanned first. The others kept silence, foreseeing great events.

Then Mr. Popplewell, poised with calm discretion, and moving with the nice precision of a fine watchmaker, shed into the best decanter (softly as an angel's tears) liquid beauty, not too gaudy, not too sparkling with shallow light, not too ruddy with sullen glow, but vivid—like a noble gem, a brown cairngorm—with mellow depth of lustre. "That's your sort!" the tanner cried, after putting his tongue, while his wife looked shocked, to the lip of the empty bottle.

"Such things is beyond my knowledge," answered Farmer Anerley, as soon as he saw the best glasses filled; "but nothing in nature is too good to speak a good man's health in. Now fill you up a little glass for Mary; and, Perpetual Motion, you stand up, which is more than your machines can do. Now here I stand, and I drink good health to a man as I never clapped eyes on yet, and would have preferred to keep the door between us; but the Lord hath ordered otherwise. He hath wiped out all his faults against the law; he hath fought for the honor of old England well; and he hath saved the life of my son Jack. Spite of all that, I might refuse to unspeak my words, which I never did afore, if it had not been that I wronged the man. I have wronged the young fellow, and I am man enough to say so. I called him a murderer and a sneak, and time hath proved me to have been a liar. Therefore I ask his pardon humbly; and, what will be more to his liking, perhaps, I say that he shall have my daughter Mary, if she abides agreeable. And I put down these here twenty guineas, for Mary to look as she ought to look. She hath been a good lass, and hath borne with me better than one in a thousand would have done. Mary, my love to you; and with leave all round, here's the very good health of Robin Lyth!"

"Here's the health of Robin Lyth!" shouted Mr. Popplewell, with his fat cheeks shining merrily. "Hurrah for the lad who saved Nelson's death from a Frenchman's grins, and saved our Jack boy! Stephen Anerley, I forgive you. This is the right stuff, and no mistake. Deborah, come and kiss the farmer."

Mrs. Popplewell obeyed her husband, as the manner of good wives is. And over and above this fleeting joy, solid satisfaction entered into noble hearts, which felt that now the fruit of laborious years, and the cash of many a tanning season, should never depart from the family. And to make an end of any weak misgivings, even before the ladies went—to fill the pipes for the gentlemen—the tanner drew with equal care, and even better nerve, the second bottle's cork, and expressed himself as follows:

"Brother Steve hath done the right thing. We hardly expected it of him, by rights of his confounded stubbornness. But when a shut-up man repenteth, he is equal to a hoyster, or this here bottle. What good would this 'a been without it was sealed over? Now mark my words. I'll not be behind no man when it comes to the right side up. I may be a poor man, a very poor man; and people counting otherwise might find themselves mistaken. I likes to be liked for myself only. But the day our Mary goes to church with Robin Lyth she shall have 500 pounds tied upon her back, or else my name's not Popplewell."

Mary had left the room long ago, after giving her father a gentle kiss, and whispering to Willie that he should have half of her twenty guineas for inventing things; which is a most expensive process, and should be more highly encouraged. Therefore she could not express at the moment her gratitude to Squire Popplewell; but as soon as she heard of his generosity, it lifted a great weight off her mind, and enabled her to think about furnishing a cottage. But she never told even her mother of that. Perhaps Robin might have seen some one he liked better. Perhaps he might have heard that stupid story about her having taken up with poor Harry Tanfield; and that might have driven him to wed a foreign lady, and therefore to fight so desperately. None, however, of these perhapses went very deeply into her heart, which was equally trusting and trusty.

Now some of her confidence in the future was justified that very moment almost, by a sudden and great arrival, not of Jack Anerley and Robin Lyth (who were known to be coming home together), but of a gentleman whose skill and activity deserved all thanks for every good thing that had happened.

"Well! I am in the very nick of time. It is my nature," cried Mr. Mordacks, seated in the best chair by the fire. "Why? you inquire, with your native penetration. Simply because in very early days I acquired the habit of punctuality. This holding good where an appointment is, holds good afterward, from the force of habit, in matters that are of luck alone. The needle-eye of time gets accustomed to be hit, and turns itself up, without waiting for the clew. Wonderful Madeira! Well, Captain Anerley, no wonder that you have discouraged free trade with your cellars full of this! It is twenty years since I have tasted such wine. Mistress Anerley, I have the honor of quaffing this glass to your very best health, and that of a very charming young lady, who has hitherto failed to appreciate me."

"Then, sir, I am here to beg your pardon," said Mary, coming up, with a beautiful blush. "When I saw you first I did not enter into your—your—"

"My outspoken manner and short business style. But I hope that you have come to like me better. All good persons do, when they come to know me."

"Yes, sir; I was quite ashamed of myself, when I came to learn all that you have done for somebody, and your wonderful kindness at Bridlington."

"Famously said! You inherit from your mother the power and the charm of expression. And now, my dear lady, good Mistress Anerley, I shall undo all my great merits by showing that I am like the letter-writers, who never write until they have need of something. Captain Anerley, it concerns you also, as a military man, and loyal soldier of King George. A gallant young officer (highly distinguished in his own way, and very likely to get on, in virtue of high connection) became of age some few weeks back; and being the heir to large estates, determined to entail them. I speak as in a parable. My meaning is one which the ladies will gracefully enter into. Being a large heir, he is not selfish, but would fain share his blessings with a little one. In a word, he is to marry a very beautiful young lady to-morrow, and under my agency. But he has a very delightful mother, and an aunt of a lofty and commanding mind, whose views, however, are comparatively narrow. For a hasty, brief season, they will be wroth; and it would be unjust to be angry with them. But love's indignation is soon cured by absence, and tones down rapidly into desire to know how the sinner is getting on. In the present case, a fortnight will do the business; or if for a month, so much the better. Heroes are in demand just now; and this young gentleman took such a scare in his very first fight that he became a hero, and so has behaved himself ever since. Ladies, I am astonished at your goodness in not interrupting me. Your minds must be as practical as my own. Now this lovely young pair, being married to-morrow, will have to go hunting for the honey in the moon, to which such enterprises lead."

"Sir, you are very right," Squire Popplewell replied; and, "That is Bible truth," said the farmer.

"Our minds are enlarged by experience," resumed the genial factor, pleasantly, and bowing to the ladies, who declined to say a word until a better opportunity, "and we like to see the process going on with others. But a nest must be found for these young doves—a quiet one, a simple one, a place where they may learn to put up with one another's cookery. The secret of happiness in this world is not to be too particular. I have hit upon the very place to make them thankful by-and-by, when they come to look back upon it —a sweet little hole, half a league away from anybody. All is arranged—a frying-pan, a brown-ware tea-pot, a skin of lard, a cock and a hen, to lay some eggs; a hundredweight of ship biscuits, warranted free from weevil, and a knife and fork. Also a way to the sea, and a net, for them to fish together. Nothing more delightful can be imagined. Under such circumstances, they will settle, in three days, which is to be the master—which I take to be the most important of all marriage settlements. And, unless I am very much mistaken, it will be the right one—the lady. My little heroine, Jerry Carroway, is engaged as their factotum, and every auspice is favorable. But without your consent, all is knocked on the head; for the cottage is yours, and the tenant won't go out, even under temptation of five guineas, without your written order. Mistress Anerley, I appeal to you. Captain, say nothing. This is a lady's question."

"Then I like to have a little voice sometimes, though it is not often that I get it. And, Mr. Mordacks, I say 'Yes.' And out of the five guineas we shall get our rent, or some of it, perhaps, from Poacher Tim, who owes us nigh upon two years now."

The farmer smiled at his wife's good thrift, and, being in a pleasant mood, consented, if so be the law could not be brought against him, and if the young couple would not stop too long, or have any family to fall upon the rates. The factor assured him against all evils; and then created quite a brisk sensation by telling them, in strict confidence, that the young officer was one Lancelot Yordas, own first cousin to the famous Robin Lyth, and nephew to Sir Duncan Yordas. And the lady was the daughter of Sir Duncan's oldest friend, the very one whose name he had given to his son. Wonder never ceased among them, when they thought how things came round.

Things came round not only thus, but also even better afterward. Mordacks had a very beautiful revenge of laughter at old Jellicorse, by outstripping him vastly in the family affairs. But Mr. Jellicorse did not care, so long as he still had eleven boxes left of title-deeds to Scargate Hall, no liability about the twelfth, and a very fair prospect of a lawsuit yet for the multiplication of the legal race. And meeting Mr. Mordacks in the highest legal circles, at Proctor Brigant's, in Crypt Court, York, he acknowledged that he never met a more delightful gentleman, until he found out what his name was. And even then he offered him a pinch of snuff, and they shook hands very warmly without anything to pay.

When Robin Lyth came home he was dissatisfied at first—so difficult is mankind to please—because his good luck had been too good. No scratch of steel, no permanent scorch of powder, was upon him, and England was not in the mood to value any unwounded valor. But even here his good luck stood him in strong stead, and cured his wrong. For when the body of the lamented hero arrived at Spithead, in spirits of wine, early in December, it was found that the Admiralty had failed to send down any orders about it. Reports, however, were current of some intention that the hero should lie in state, and the battered ship went on with him. And when at last proper care was shown, and the relics of one of the noblest men that ever lived upon the tide of time were being transferred to a yacht at the Nore, Robin Lyth, in a sad and angry mood, neglected to give a wide berth to a gun that was helping to keep up the mourning salute, and a piece of wad carried off his starboard whisker.

This at once replaced him in the popular esteem, and enabled him to land upon the Yorkshire coast with a certainty of glorious welcome. Mr. Mordacks himself came down to meet him at the Northern Landing, with Dr. Upround and Robin Cockscroft, and nearly all the men, and entirely all the women and children, of Little Denmark. Strangers also from outlandish parts, Squire Popplewell and his wife Deborah, Mrs. Carroway (with her Tom, and Jerry, and Cissy, and lesser Carroways, for her old aunt Jane was gone to Paradise at last, and had left her enough to keep a pony-carriage), and a great many others, and especially a group of four distinguished persons, who stood at the top of the slide, because of the trouble of getting back if they went down.

These had a fair and double-horsed carriage in the lane, at the spot where fish face their last tribunal; and scarcely any brains but those of Flamborough could have absorbed such a spectacle as this, together with the deeper expectations from the sea. Of these four persons, two were young enough, and two not so young as they had been, but still very lively, and well pleased with one another. These were Mrs. Carnaby and Mr. Bart; the pet of the one had united his lot with the darling of the other; for good or for bad, there was no getting out of it, and the only thing was to make the best of it. And being good people, they were doing this successfully. Poor Mrs. Carnaby had said to Mr. Bart, as soon as Mr. Mordacks let her know about the wedding, "Oh, but, Mr. Bart, you are a gentleman; now, are you not? I am sure you are, though you do such things! I am sure of it by your countenance."

"Madam," Mr. Bart replied, with a bow that was decisive, "if I am not, it is my own fault, as it is the fault of every man."

At this present moment they were standing with their children, Lancelot and Insie, who had nicely recovered from matrimony, and began to be too high-spirited. They all knew, by virtue of Mr. Mordacks, who Robin Lyth was; and they wanted to see him, and be kind to him, if he made no claim upon them. And Mr. Bart desired, as his father's friend, to shake hands with him, and help him, if help were needed.

But Robin, with a grace and elegance which he must have imported from foreign parts, declined all connection and acquaintance with them, and declared his set resolve to have nothing to do with the name of "Yordas." They were grieved, as they honestly declared, to hear it, but could not help owning that his pride was just; and they felt that their name was the richer for not having any poor people to share it.

Yet Captain Lyth—as he now was called, even by revenue officers—in no way impoverished his name by taking another to share it with him. The farmer declared that there should be no wedding until he had sold seven stacks of wheat, for his meaning was to do things well. But this obstacle did not last long, for those were times when corn was golden, not in landscape only.

So when the spring was fair with promise of green for the earth, and of blue for heaven, and of silver-gray upon the sea, the little church close to Anerley Farm filled up all the complement of colors. There was scarlet, of Dr. Upround's hood (brought by the Precious boy from Flamborough); a rich plum-color in the coat of Mordacks; delicate rose and virgin white in the blush and the brow of Mary; every tint of the rainbow on her mother's part; and gold, rich gold, in a great tanned bag, on behalf of Squire Popplewell. His idea of a "settlement" was cash down, and he put it on the parish register.

Mary found no cause to repent of the long endurance of her truth, and the steadfast power of quiet love. Robin was often in the distance still, far beyond the silvery streak of England's new salvation. But Mary prayed for his safe return; and safe he was, by the will of the Lord, which helps the man who helps himself, and has made his hand bigger than his tongue. When the war was over, Captain Lyth came home, and trained his children in the ways in which he should have walked, and the duties they should do and pay.

THE END.

Hopelessly Devoted

"Don't worry – I've got somewhere in mind that I think you'll like," Rick went on, to her relief. Then he kissed her again, still very gently, his hand reaching under her mass of hair to find her neck. His touch was electric. Jessie could feel herself trembling.

"Good night, firebrand," whispered Rick. "See you soon."

That night, as she fell at last into a feverish sleep, Jessie began to dream that she was diving from a high rock into a vast lake, and something was telling her that she was about to plunge in far too deep.

Point Romance

Hopelessly Devoted

Amber Vane

SCHOLASTIC

Scholastic Children's Books
7–9 Pratt Street, London NW1 0AE, UK
a division of Scholastic Publications Ltd,
London ~ New York ~ Toronto ~ Sydney ~ Auckland

First published by Scholastic Publications Ltd, 1995

Copyright © Amber Vane, 1995

ISBN 0 590 13101 X

Typeset by TW Typesetting, Midsomer Norton, Avon
Printed by Cox & Wyman Ltd, Reading, Berks.

All rights reserved

10 9 8 7 6 5 4 3 2 1

The right of Amber Vane to be identified as the author
of this work has been asserted by her in accordance with the
Copyright, Designs and Patents Act, 1988.

This book is sold subject to the condition that it shall not,
by way of trade or otherwise, be lent, resold, hired out, or
otherwise circulated without the publisher's prior consent
in any form of binding or cover other than that in which it
is published and without a similar condition, including this
condition, being imposed upon the subsequent purchaser.

1

The stage was in darkness. An expectant hush filled the air. Then a single spotlight picked out a lone figure. It was Jessie's big moment.

For twenty minutes the band had been pelting out their usual wild brand of indie-rock. "Not exactly heavy metal," Toby, the bass player, would say. "More sort of aluminium, our style is."

"Crushable, recyclable, very green," Jessie would add.

"Don't forget the touch of brass." That was Hazel, Jessie's best friend, who played saxophone and was always trying to get the rest of them to show some interest in jazz.

The four members of *Thunderball* had been friends for so long that they practically talked in code. If Jessie or Hazel thought a boy was a bit of a nerd they always called him a Martin, because of a really sad case who'd been in their class at primary school. Geoff, the drummer, would occasionally complain of having a bad case of the

Number 29s. That meant his parents were giving him a hard time, and dated back to the week when he and Toby had had a competition to see who could be most irritating to their families. Geoff had proudly scored 29 different shouting matches in a single week and was still reigning champion.

Now the four had left school and had just started A-level courses at the Sixth Form College in Amberley, a small town near Birmingham where they all lived. And tonight they were making their college début at the Saturday night talent evening.

"Talent!" Geoff had exclaimed in disgust. "What a cruddy idea! You won't catch me plonking around some kiddy hall doing my party piece for a bunch of losers with nowhere better to go than some spotty teenage version of Butlins. Out of season."

Toby had sighed, his freckled nose wrinkling in consternation, a worried frown on his slightly plump, slightly comical face.

"Yes, well, it's OK for you to scoff," he'd reasoned. "Clever scientists don't really need to be performers, do they. You only need to know how, not why."

It was a familiar argument. Geoff and Hazel were good at science, Toby and Jessie at the arts, and their slanging matches about which was more useful had intensified now because Geoff had got such brilliant GCSEs that the others were secretly in awe of him and felt it was their duty to put him down as much as possible to prevent him getting too swanky.

Toby had managed to persuade Geoff that he owed it to his friends to turn up at the talent-spotting evening, even though the college had misguidedly called it "Reach for the Stars" so Geoff had instantly dubbed it "Topple Over and Die". Jessie had long thought that Geoff had to act hard and cynical because he was physically so weedy that if a football came flying in his direction and someone yelled, "*Kick!*" he'd blink behind his Ben Elton-style glasses and say, "Why?" with a puzzled look on his face.

But Geoff was a good friend. He knew it was important for the others to make an impact in the first week. Jessie was taking Theatre Studies and Music for A-levels, and Toby was doing Theatre Studies, Music and Computer Studies, so they both wanted to take part in as many performances as they could, and for that they needed to be seen. Hazel couldn't have cared less about being picked for shows. But she was just as keenly interested in being seen – preferably by as many boys as possible. Hazel regarded boys as her area of special interest and would have done A-level flirting if she hadn't felt so qualified to teach it.

"Just think of the effect you're going to have on all the new girls," she'd pointed out cunningly to Geoff. "It'll be your big chance to impress all the ones who don't know you yet. There you'll be, beating the daylights out of all those drums with such masterful passion – they'll be falling over themselves to get near you."

Privately, Geoff was rather hoping that she was right. He was shy with girls and usually covered his embarrassment by being very quiet and looking very bored. So although he pretended to be putting himself out to help the other members of the band he was secretly pleased at the chance to shine without having to speak.

And it was fortunate that they had turned up. The theatre was packed, but not many students had come forward to offer their talents. There had been five attempts at stand-up comedy – brave rather than funny. Three girls had performed a few numbers as a singing trio, with their own backing track. And there had been a whole string of rappers, of course, some of them pretty good.

But there was no doubt as soon as *Thunderball* took to the stage that they were the hit of the evening. Jessie, dressed in a tight leather mini-skirt and matching black waistcoat, had beaten and whammed her guitar into wild, siren-like wails and screeching riffs for song after song. Responding to the appreciative yells from the audience, she'd stamped her black thigh boots up and down the stage, screaming out the lyrics in harmony with Hazel's searing saxophone.

They'd been through a few well-known chart numbers and a few more songs Toby had written for them. But the sound had been consistently loud, relentless and aggressive. Now there was silence. You could hear the audience wondering what was coming next. The spotlight was on Jessie. Her dark, tangled hair had broken free of the knotted scarves that had tied it back and now framed her flushed face.

For a few seconds she stood quite still, her

guitar hanging round her waist, her arms by her sides. Then she looked up and began to sing in a pure, sweet, unaccompanied contralto. It was an old Beatles number, "You've Really Got a Hold on Me," but the way Jessie was treating it, it might have been a hymn rather than an insistently suggestive piece of rock and roll.

I don't like you, but I love you
Seems that I'm always thinking of you...

At the first chorus Hazel joined her in a close harmony, the two girls standing together, filling the theatre with the droning chant: *You've really got a hold on me*. After the first electrifying verse the girls spun round, grabbed their instruments, and the whole band launched into heavy rock once again.

There was thunderous applause, whistles, even screams. And then they were into their final number. This was Geoff's cue for a dramatic drum solo – the one he was hoping would somehow give him a little much-needed sex appeal. Hazel and Jessie managed to snatch a few moments to swap notes as he crashed into his crescendo.

"I feel as if my whole past is flashing before me," Hazel whispered. "I've already seen four people I've been out with ... and three of them I was hoping I'd never see again."

Jessie could barely hear her over Geoff's frenzied crashes. But then, she wasn't really paying much attention. She was squinting out through the stage lights at a tall, attractive figure

5

standing in the aisle very near the front. He was dark and good-looking with brooding eyes and a casual slouch which was all the more noticeable because even though it was September he was dressed in a white suit. Jessie saw that he was holding a notebook. She nudged Hazel.

"Look! A talent scout!" she hissed.

"Talk about talent!" Hazel smacked her lips appreciatively. "He's the only thing that comes close in the whole place."

The girls were so busy ogling him that they almost forgot their cues for the close of the number. Toby had to remind Jessie by kicking her subtly in the foot. But Toby was never very subtle. His kick sent her reeling into Hazel, and the two of them nearly skittered right off the stage. They tried to pretend it was all part of the act, but Jessie noticed the dishy guy in the white suit scribbling in his notebook, and somehow she was sure he'd noticed the mad scramble up on stage.

After the lights had come on and the show was over they were bombarded. Even Geoff had attracted some interest, and was busily showing a couple of girls how to do a drum roll. Hazel, as usual, was surrounded by admirers. She was very blonde, very skinny and very pretty and never had trouble attracting boyfriends. It was getting rid of them that always caused her problems. Even now, the four exes were all somewhere in the circle round her and she was managing to chat to several others over the general chaos. Toby was always very popular, too. Jessie thought girls must like him because he wasn't a threat to them.

He was great fun and very easy to get on with – but with his boyish looks, rueful smile, freckles and rather solid build he wasn't exactly a turn-on. More of a brother figure.

Jessie was about to join Toby, who was laughing with a group of friends, when she felt a tap on her shoulder. She turned round and froze. It was as if the whole theatre had fallen silent and she was alone again in the spotlight. For there, standing right behind her, was the talent scout. Close up, he was even more gorgeous. He was very tanned with a strong, chiselled face and eyes which looked appraisingly straight at her.

"That was quite some performance," he said at once. "Especially the acrobatics at the end."

"Oh, I'm glad you enjoyed that," Jessie answered as glibly as she could. "We practised it for ages."

"Your timing was magnificent," the talent scout went on. She still couldn't tell if he was joking. But she didn't care, either. She just wanted to carry on talking to him and feeling his eyes on her.

"I'm Rick Meade," he said, extending his hand to her.

"Jessica Mackenzie," she mumbled, aware only of the sensation of his firm hand shaking hers, then holding it just a little longer before releasing it. "Er … why have you been taking notes all evening?"

"Oh, I'm a reporter," he explained. "For the *Amberley Herald*. I thought I'd do a story on this 'Reach for the Stars' thing, but quite honestly it was a bit of a wash-out until you came on. I was just about to leave, actually."

"You mean – you're going to write about us? In the newspaper?" Jessie was so agog with excitement that she forgot to look casual. Rick laughed.

"I might. I mean, it's not often you get a sexy singer and mean guitarist and brilliant gymnast all in one person, is it?"

Jessie looked crestfallen. Obviously he had noticed their undignified slip-up in that last number and he was going to make fun of them. But then he spoke again. "You really do have a great voice, you know. Do you always sing so aggressively? I would have thought you're much better suited to ballads – softer things."

"Oh, I do a bit of everything really," Jessie answered vaguely. Her heart was beating wildly and she badly wanted to say something witty and pert to make him laugh, only her tongue seemed to be freezing up in her mouth. "When we're *Thunderball* we tend to do the heavier repertoire. But I'm interested in musicals and classic rock and a bit of country. My friend Hazel prefers jazz. And our bass player, Toby – he's into weird contemporary stuff that he composes on computer."

"I'd love to hear you singing something gentler," Rick said, his voice sounding like a caress. "You've got a wonderful velvet quality."

Jessie found herself becoming tongue-tied again and was furious. How come she could banter away for hours with practically anybody, but with the one decent-looking, half-way attractive guy she'd encountered all year she'd suddenly turned to jelly?

"Watch out for the smooth-talker," whispered a voice in her ear. It was Geoff, sidling up behind her. "Any minute now he'll be trying to take you away from all this."

She swung round to glare at him. He was grinning. Toby was with him.

"Come on, Jess – we're off to the bar before it closes."

Jessie loved her friends dearly. But at that moment she wished they were on the other side of the planet. Why couldn't they just disappear and let her get on with being enchanted by this dazzling stranger?

"You remind me of a singer called Grace Hari – do you know her?" Rick was saying. Know her! Grace Hari was a singer-songwriter who was just breaking into the big time with her own band. She was Jessie's hero – especially as she had come from the same town.

Jessie nodded enthusiastically. "I think she's great."

"I've got a couple of tickets to see her on tour next Saturday. Do you fancy coming?"

Jessie nearly squeaked with joy. He was asking her out – on a dream date, to see her favourite singer. She tried to sound nonchalant. "Isn't she appearing in Coventry?" she asked.

"No problem," he answered airily. "We'll drive. I'll pick you up around seven and we'll be in plenty of time. OK?"

Jessie floated after the others, and was still in a daze when Hazel handed her a Coke.

"So who was the talent scout?" Hazel demanded. "Looked like you were being spotted for something." Jessie told the others who he was and Toby gave a whistle.

"A reporter! Just you make sure you're nice to him, Jessie, and do everything he says. Because if he gives us a good review it'll be the launch of our careers into stardom."

Jessie wasn't listening. She was thinking about those dark, searching eyes, the feel of his hand closing round hers. And she was wondering how on earth she was going to get through the days and nights until she could be with him again.

2

When Jessie came down to earth the next day, she realized that her date with Rick was going to present a few problems. First of all, how was she going to persuade her mother to let her drive off to Coventry with a complete stranger?

"Tricky," agreed Hazel over the phone that morning. "It's a language problem really. We say dishy, they say dangerous. We say exciting, they say…"

"Dangerous," supplied Jessie with a sigh. "I think I'm going to have to start working on her right away."

"You've got practically a week," said Hazel hopefully. "You'll think of something. What are you going to wear?"

Jessie sighed again. "That's my even worse problem. I don't know. What would you wear for the hottest date imaginable?"

Hazel considered. "Well, remember Mark who bought me a drink last night? The OK-looking one with glasses? He's taking me to Trampoline on Friday – you know, that new disco. I'll probably go shiny – my pink satin jeans and top, the one that shows lots of midriff. I like to drive them crazy."

Jessie giggled. Hazel always knew how to cheer her up. But that didn't help her to solve any of her problems.

But she needn't have worried. The following evening the *Amberley Herald* carried Rick's account of the Sixth Form College talent night. He was disappointed in the general standard but raved about "the inventive student rock scratch band *Thunderball,* which stole the show." He didn't even allude to the fact that two members had very nearly rocketed off the stage. Best of all were his final remarks.

"There was some genuine raw musical promise here – I wasn't surprised to learn that several of the band are music students. The one to watch is the lead singer and guitarist Jessica Mackenzie who has yet to discover the right environment for her luscious voice."

"Oh, Jessie!" breathed her mum proudly. "Fancy someone saying that about you – in the news-paper! I'm going to buy up every copy. Gran would love one, and all the aunties..."

"Please, Mum!" protested Jessie's younger brother Dan. "Don't let it go to her head even more than it has already, or she'll swell up and explode. Come on, Jess, confess. How much did you pay him?"

Jessie was tempted to hit him, as she usually did when he was irritating, which was about eighty per cent of the time. But he'd given her a cue that was just too convenient to miss.

"Actually, I didn't have to pay him," she said casually, "as long as I agreed to go out with him. He's taking me to see Grace Hari..."

It worked! Mum had already decided that he must be a charming young man to have written such lovely things about her daughter. She was even quite impressed that he was actually going to take her out in a car. Now Jessie had to work out how she was going to make it through the rest of the week without bursting.

By Saturday evening she'd worked herself up to fever pitch. She spent hours getting ready, threading red and silver beads into her unruly shock of long, tangly curls. She'd decided to wear her favourite black velvet leggings with a sexy red and black top borrowed from Hazel. It flashed with beads and sequins and revealed quite an expanse of midriff – Hazel's favourite area.

When the front door bell rang, she crept downstairs nervously. If Mum saw her she was bound to disapprove. She'd never actually said: "You're not going out like that!" but this could always be the first time. She managed to get to the door undetected, but when she opened it there was Toby lounging on the step. He looked her up and down gravely, then said: "You're never going out like that!"

"What do you mean?" Jessie snapped crossly. "Since when have you been a prude? And anyway, what are you doing here?"

"Very nice, Miss Hospitality," sniffed Toby. "You

certainly know how to make a boy feel wanted. In answer to your questions, I think I'll take them backwards. I'm here to sort out a little software problem with your resident genius." Jessie remembered that Toby and Dan were working together on some terribly complicated computer game. One of the most irritating things about her brother was that he was so good at things like that.

"As for being a prude," Toby went on, "I think you're missing the point. Look, Jessie, you're going out with a nice fancy guy, right? You want to impress him, right? You want to look sophisticated, right?" Jessie nodded, wondering what he was leading up to. "So why – why are you dressed up like a Barbie Doll? This outfit qualifies you for the cover of *Sugar*. And that, by the way, is what I mean."

He followed her into the house, picking an apple from the fruit dish as he went. "OK," conceded Jessie. "What do you suggest, since you've just appointed yourself my personal style consultant?"

Toby looked at her carefully for a few moments. "Have you got a black jacket? A shiny one, preferably."

Jessie didn't have, but she knew someone who did. She raced up to her mother's wardrobe and reappeared a few minutes later wearing a soft white shirt with a black silk jacket. "How does it look?" she asked anxiously.

Toby shook his head. "Take it off."

Jessie panicked. "Make your mind up!" she said crossly. "I thought you said I needed a jacket."

"I did," Toby said calmly. "Take the shirt off. Then put the jacket back on."

The minute Jessie tried his idea she admitted, reluctantly, that he was right. The jacket looked great with nothing underneath, falling softly over her tight leggings. And when Rick turned up a few minutes later, she could tell from his appreciative gaze that the look was perfect.

His car was a battered Metro that rattled alarmingly as soon as he got into fourth gear.

"It's a bit noisy," he shouted above the roar of the engine, "but it's all I can afford at the moment." He explained that he was working for the paper for a year before going to university. "I do quite a lot of routine work in the office and whenever I can I try to do some reporting. They usually let me do the rock music because I'm the only person there who's actually been to any gigs since Bob Dylan toured England. The first time."

Jessie laughed and began to relax. Rick was great company, and kept her in fits with his stories about working at the newspaper.

"Obituaries are the worst," he said. "People can be so unreasonable about them. I had to edit two the other day. One was about a woman who'd set up the first local family planning clinic about a hundred years ago and the other was about some Baroness who kept a bird sanctuary. It wasn't my fault the pictures got mixed up..."

By the time they'd taken their seats in the auditorium Jessie was beginning to feel she was in a dream. Rick was gorgeous-looking, he was fun, he was out there in the real world – and here she was by his side, sparkling with excitement as he took her hand and whispered: "One day it'll be you up on that stage. I bet you…"

Grace Hari gave a spectacular performance, and by her third encore Jessie's hands were sore with clapping. Everything had been so perfect she couldn't believe there were more treats in store. Then Rick said casually, "Come on, quick, or we'll never make it."

"Make it where?" said Jessie, bewildered.

"Backstage, of course," said Rick. "I'm going to see if I can get a couple of quotes from her." Jessie was speechless. She was actually going to meet Grace Hari!

Somehow, Rick managed to talk his way backstage to the dressing room. Somehow, there was Grace herself, smiling at them. Rick put his arm round Jessie and introduced her. "She's a singer too," he announced. Jessie was embarrassed.

"Well, not really, only a bit," she blurted out. "Not compared with you. You've been my favourite singer ever since I first heard you on the radio years ago and you did that old Sade number."

"Oh, I still love that," said Grace, obviously pleased. She was quite willing to chat to Jessie and answer all her questions about the music she chose and the songs she wrote. She wished her luck in her career as they said goodbye.

"Well done, Jessica Mackenzie, girl reporter," said Rick as they clambered back into the car. "You did all the work for me – and thanks to you I've got some great quotes."

"But I was only asking her what I wanted to know," Jessie blushed.

"Exactly," Rick explained. "That's the whole art of interviewing. You just have to make sure that what you want to know is the same as what your readers want to know. You did very well."

On the way home Jessie chatted happily to Rick, telling him about her first impressions of college, her A-levels, her friends.

"It seems such a long time ago that I was doing all that," he said. "I finished A-levels last year and then spent a year travelling round Europe which is a lot more fun than doing exams. But then, there weren't any girls like you when I was at school." By now, he'd pulled up outside the house and stopped the car. "You're quite something, Jessie," he said softly, turning to look at her. "You're talented, funny and…" He reached a hand to her chin and turned her face towards him. "And you've got the sexiest lips I've ever seen." With that, he bent down and kissed her – a long, lingering kiss that sent darts of pleasure shooting through her.

"Am I going to see you again?" he asked gently. She nodded, unsure of what to say. She'd been out with boys before, of course – she'd been kissed by quite a few. But no one had ever made her feel so dizzy with joy and at the same time so uncertain about every move.

"Good. I'll call you – and we'll go out for dinner. Anywhere special you'd like to go?" Another surge of panic washed over her. She had no idea what to suggest, since the only restaurants she'd been to

17

were the local Indian curry houses, and the posh Italian one where Mum and Dad occasionally took the family for birthdays. Somehow neither of those seemed right.

"Don't worry – I've got somewhere in mind that I think you'll like," Rick went on, to her relief. Then he kissed her again, still very gently, his hand reaching under her mass of hair to find her neck. His touch was electric. Jessie could feel herself trembling.

"Good night, firebrand," whispered Rick. "See you soon."

That night, as she fell at last into a feverish sleep, Jessie began to dream that she was diving from a high rock into a vast lake, and something was telling her that she was about to plunge in far too deep.

3

When Rick picked her up on the following Wednesday to take her out for dinner she had no idea what to expect. Would it be one of those places with endless courses where you had to know which knives and forks to use? What if there were snails or mussels or anything else that she'd no idea how to eat?

She was even more alarmed when she realized they were going all the way to Birmingham. He led her into a very tiny, very loud café, full of people he seemed to know who greeted him across the wails of a live Flamenco guitarist. He told her it was a tapas bar and gave her one of his amused glances when she looked blank.

"A tapas bar," he repeated. "You order lots of little snacks and share them. It's Spanish."

It was impossible to enjoy the food that evening because it was all so strange. Rick took charge of the ordering and seemed to enjoy explaining everything to her. "Let's have some tortilla – it's

19

nice, like cold omelette. And with that, let's see, some mushrooms, a bit of seafood salad..." Jessie let him get on with it and tried to get used to the idea of dipping into a lot of strange little dishes without having much idea what was in any of them.

She stared round at everyone else. They were all engaged in animated conversations – laughing, waving their bread in the air, toasting each other. She had the distinct feeling that she was the only one who didn't feel at home in this noisy, friendly little restaurant. And yet she wanted desperately to be part of it all – part of this crowd, that was clearly where Rick belonged.

The following Saturday night, Jessie lay sobbing uncontrollably, the pile of screwed-up tissues mounting all round her. Next to her on the sofa, Rick was regarding her with a look of puzzled disbelief. On the TV in front of them, Meg Ryan was driving through the night, electrified by the lonely tones of Tom Hanks.

"I'm sorry," Jessie burbled through her tears. "I don't know how many times I've seen *Sleepless in Seattle*, but it always gets to me!"

"I just don't believe you sometimes," Rick said affectionately. "One minute you're a fairly normal human being. Then you get up on stage and become a wild Amazon with a voice like a police siren bumping into a cattle truck. And then all of a sudden you're little Pollyanna who cries at a junky piece of Hollywood nonsense."

"I don't think it's nonsense," protested Jessie

hotly. "It just happens to be one of my favourite films of all time. And I had hoped it would be a romantic moment watching it with you."

"Ah, well, if romantic moments are what you're after, you've come to the right guy." Rick pulled her lazily towards him and kissed her, his arms tightening round her. "I'll show you romantic – forget Tom Hanks!"

Jessie snuggled towards him, still sniffing. There was something very comforting about being in his arms, sinking into his kisses, accompanied by the sentimental screenplay on the TV. She was sorry that Rick didn't share her love of slushy movies. It was the first sign of any difference between them. She adored tear-jerkers. He liked tough action films. She liked reading romantic novels. He preferred lean American thrillers. But then, she told herself, there was no rule that said you both had to have the same taste in everything. And besides – Rick seemed to find the differences rather endearing.

"There's so much to show you, Jessie," he'd say. "There's a whole world out there that I can introduce you to." It was almost as if he looked forward to teaching her the things he knew – as if he relished being more worldly and more experienced.

"I'm not a child, you know," Jessie protested, when he'd first said that, earlier that week. "Why are you so keen to treat me like one?"

A shadow passed over Rick's face. "Of course you're not," he said, scowling. "But you're not exactly a woman, either. At least, you're still young enough and sweet enough for me to trust you."

"What do you mean?" demanded Jessie, still feeling insulted. Then, suddenly, light dawned. "You're talking about someone else, aren't you? Some other woman?"

"There was someone," Rick admitted, his face creased with bitterness. "She was a woman all right. Louise. She was gorgeous, sophisticated, knew exactly what she was doing and where she was going... And she forgot to tell me I wasn't part of the big life plan."

Jessie looked at him expectantly, and after a pause he continued.

"I don't want to talk about it, Jess. Let's just say that I had a few illusions shattered, that's all. Tough can be cruel, strong can be selfish, and a woman who likes to be in charge is really just a woman who likes to grind you under her heel. In Louise's case her very expensive, two-tone stiletto heels which can be very painful. Especially when some other guy could afford to buy them for her..."

He looked into Jessie's eyes and cupped her chin in his hand.

"I'm not going to make that mistake again," he said, kissing her very softly. "You're different, Jess. This time, with you – it's like looking at the world through new eyes, your eyes. And I want to be the one to open them..."

Jessie wasn't completely satisfied. She resented Rick's assumption that she was so very young and naive. But at the same time she was flattered that

22

this gorgeous, hunky guy had chosen her. And she was intrigued by him, too – he was so much more experienced than she was, in every way.

"I don't know how you can be so innocent," he was saying now, holding his face close to hers. "So innocent and yet so inviting..." Then he was kissing her again, more passionately, pulling her down beside him and enfolding her in his arms.

Jessie's arms had crept round his neck and she felt as though she was melting into his long, passionate kisses. It was as if their lips were welded together so that they were one mouth, one endless embrace. Now they were lying side by side, and Rick's hand moved slowly, expertly down her back, urging her closer to him.

She froze. This was too much, too fast. And it scared her. She wanted to stop him but couldn't think of the words. But Rick had sensed that she had become tense, and gently released his hand.

"Like I said," he murmured. "There's so much I want to show you. But all in your own time." Then he kissed her tenderly, and casually got up to make some coffee.

It was something she was going to have to get used to, Jessie thought. One minute she felt happy and comfortable with Rick. Then suddenly she'd tense up and become tongue-tied and confused. She'd tried to explain it to Hazel, but it was difficult to find the words.

"He's lovely, you know," she began one lunch-time in the canteen.

"But demanding?" suggested Hazel, who was always keen to get down to basics.

"No, not exactly demanding. More like – sophisticated."

"Sophisticated!" repeated Hazel. "You mean, he takes you to expensive places."

"No – not exactly. I mean, he acts sophisticated."

"You mean – he doesn't do elephant jokes and he doesn't make his ice-cream into soup before eating and he doesn't do all those boy noises?"

"No, not exactly…"

"Oh, for heaven's sake!" Hazel burst out, infuriated. "If you say *no, not exactly* one more time, I'll stop being your friend and I'll tell the whole of our year that you've got a complete run of Kylie Minogue singles and I'll … I'll phone up Rick myself and find out just how supercool he really is!"

"Well, I wouldn't exactly say supercool," answered Jessie. Hazel whopped her over the head with her yogurt spoon.

"You really are hopeless, Jess the mess," she taunted. "I'd say you just don't know when to enjoy the moment. You've got this immaculately dishy boyfriend, he's gorgeous, he's clever, he's got a car, he likes you, he doesn't seem to have any obvious vices. So why look for problems? Just accept the fact that he's older than you. You should be flattered."

Jessie let it go then. She knew that Hazel was right. She did worry too much. It would be much better to relax and have fun, like Hazel always did. Even now she was launching into the tale of her latest romantic disaster.

"So what do you do when you happen to be seeing two people at the same time and they both happen to use the same launderette? At least, I didn't really think either one of them would have any cause to use a launderette, but that's what you get for not thinking ahead. I was doing the washing for my mum and I'd asked Mark to come along to help. How was I to know that Clive would be doing the washing for his mum the very same Saturday morning in the very same place? Bad luck, bad timing, that's me all over…"

"Why did it matter?" asked Jessie, enjoying the story.

"It probably wouldn't have," reflected Hazel. "Only the last time I'd seen Clive I'd spilt a chocolate milkshake down his Nirvana T-shirt, so I said I'd wash it. So I did. And he just happened to walk in as I was taking it out of the machine, and he recognized it and swiped it off me and said he'd be able to dry it himself, thank you very much. Mark just stared at him with his mouth open and he looked a bit huffy and walked out and now I've got all this explaining to do…"

"That'll teach you to get them to do chores with you," giggled Jessie.

"No, the moral is I should never have offered to wash the shirt," mused Hazel. "Anyhow, I don't suppose you and Rick have time to do boring things like go to the launderette. What've you been up to, anyway? I haven't seen you properly for at least a week, and all you've told me about is that time you went to see Grace Hari, you jammy doughnut."

"Well, we haven't exactly established a routine or anything," Jessie said casually. "Last week we went out for a meal." She waited for Hazel's reaction and noticed she looked suitably impressed. "It was quite a nice place, actually – Spanish. We had to drive to Birmingham. Not bad at all..."

She just couldn't find a way to tell Hazel how she'd really felt that evening – how awkward and out of her depth. So instead, she decided to impress her.

"It was a tapas bar," she was saying now to Hazel. "You know – you order lots of little snacks and share them. Really delicious. I enjoyed it." Well, she had enjoyed being with Rick and allowing him to help her to all the different dishes, even feeding her the odd forkful of strange salads and spicy sausages.

"It's like going into a different world, being with him," she said dreamily.

"Lucky old you," Hazel said. "So what else is new?"

Jessie remembered something Rick had mentioned just the other day. Apparently some of the local Amberley businesses were getting together to fund a Christmas pantomime to raise money for charity.

"They're auditioning next Monday," he'd told her. "And I think you and your friends should go along. The idea is to be a showcase for local talent and they're hoping for lots of young people to take part."

Jessie looked at him curiously. "A pantomime? Doesn't sound your sort of thing at all."

"You'd be surprised," retorted Rick. "I happen to be very fond of pantomimes. Besides … my paper is one of the sponsors, and they've asked me to be involved in the music. At least," he amended his rather sweeping claim, "the paper's music editor John Bottrell is going to direct the music and I'm supposed to help. Anyway, it's going to be fun. I know a few people who are going to be involved and I reckon you stand a good chance of getting a part. It's high time you did more with that voice of yours than let it scream."

Jessie was surprised and rather offended. Rick had never scoffed at what she did before. He'd been impressed when he first heard her singing with the band. She decided to ignore the remark. After all, he genuinely seemed to believe in her and wanted her to do well. Now she mentioned the pantomime to Hazel.

"Oh, right – there's a poster about it on the bulletin board," Hazel said. "It's going to be *Cinderella*, surprise, surprise."

"Well, we might as well go along and check it out," said Jessie. "How about the boys? Do you think they'll be interested?"

"Interested in what?" enquired a familiar voice beside her. Toby and Geoff had appeared, and sat down with the hot dogs, crisps and cans of Coke that they called lunch.

"We were thinking about auditioning for the charity pantomime."

"No way," said Geoff immediately. "Count me out. Absolutely not. I'm a no-wig, no-tights sort of guy. I'm a drummer, not a buffoon."

27

"I'm a buffoon," volunteered Toby cheerfully. "And I even quite like tights. Besides, I'll do anything for a break into showbiz. Count me in."

"You just don't know what you'll be missing," Hazel warned Geoff. "All those gorgeous girls in the chorus line, just waiting to be swept off their feet." She suddenly looked all eager and excited. "Who knows – maybe I'll strike lucky this time and meet my very own Prince Charming."

4

The Town Hall theatre was thronging: crowds of young people milled round the auditorium, some slouching in jeans and baggy jumpers, others limbering up in leotards. No one knew what was going on or what would be expected of them.

Hazel had brought her saxophone.

"I'm hopeless at acting, you know I am," she explained to Jessie. "I was wondering if they needed a horn section for the band."

Toby and Jessie had worked up a couple of audition pieces each, as they were always being advised to do by their Theatre Studies teacher. All round them people were declaiming, practising dancing steps, reading intently.

Eventually a distinguished looking man with greying hair and a very tanned face appeared on the stage. He was wearing jeans that looked as if someone had ironed them for him and a well-worn, very expensive, Aran sweater. He looked familiar – but Jessie wasn't sure whether she'd seen him at the supermarket or on television.

"Good evening," he began, in deep, resonant tones. "My name's Michael Wayne and I'm the director of this season's Amberley spectacular." A murmur swept through the theatre. Michael Wayne was an actor – not a household name, exactly, but he was relatively well-known. Jessie remembered now where she'd seen him – in a TV sitcom earlier that year. He'd played a businessman who'd been made redundant and become a house-husband instead, and she'd thought he was quite good.

"Now I'm sure you're all wondering how we're going to choose the cast for this production, especially as I believe it's the first time Amberley has attempted such a venture. Well, the various sponsors of the show and the members of the Amberley Council Arts Subcommittee have agreed that this is to be a local event, by and for the community. And they are very keen to involve as many young people as possible..."

As he went on to explain how they would be auditioning and what they were looking for, Jessie felt a familiar hand on her waist. It was Rick, who'd sidled up next to her.

"Recognize him?" he whispered. She nodded. "He's local," Rick explained. "He and his wife live in Crampton village. She's about to have a baby so he's decided not to take on any touring for the rest of the year. That's why he's agreed to take on the pantomime..."

The auditioning seemed to go terribly slowly,

and it soon became clear that it would stretch into the following evening as well. Jessie began to feel rather weary. As she sat back sipping water, she noticed that Rick had joined a group of slightly older people who were hanging round near the stage. She recognized one or two of them from the tapas bar. She also recognized a rather glamorous-looking girl with shiny auburn hair glossed into a bob, and immaculate make-up.

It was Candida Manley, who'd been in the year above her at school. Jessie's mother was quite friendly with Candida's so she'd known her for a long time. And all that time, Candida had been ahead of her in every way. When Jessie took up horse-riding, Candida owned her own pony. When Jessie and her friends were still playing with Barbie dolls, Candida was getting make-up kits for Christmas. She was the first girl to go on holiday without her parents, the first girl to go out with a college boy – when she was only fifteen.

Jessie had never got to know her very well, but she always saw her as impossibly lucky: confident, worldly, and somehow in a different league from the rest of them. They hadn't seen each other since Candida left school the previous year, but she knew from her mother's regular bulletins that for the past year Candida had been working at the Rialto, a big hotel on the outskirts of the town.

Candida must just have said something amusing, because Rick was roaring with laughter and she was looking very coy and pretty as if she didn't quite understand why. When Candida was called up on stage it was clear that she'd made a big hit with Michael Wayne, too. He couldn't take his eyes off her.

She'd chosen a monologue from a rather difficult modern play, but followed it with a chirpy little song and dance which Jessie thought must be an old Music Hall number. It was funny and well done, and there was no mistaking the enthusiasm in the director's voice when he thanked her. Rick looked appreciative, too, Jessie noticed with a pang.

Then he was beside her again. "What are you going to do?" he wanted to know. "I hope you're going to show off that voice properly. I mean, Jess, you know I'm a big fan of new music. But just this once, how about something with a melody?"

"You sound like my dad!" retorted Jessie. Then she grinned. "I think you might get a bit of a surprise." And he did. Because when it was her turn to take the stage Jessie launched into an old country number, "Love Letters in the Sand", accompanied approvingly by the rather dejected pianist sitting at the edge of the stage.

She was about to go on to her rehearsed speech, from *Romeo and Juliet*, but Michael Wayne stopped her

"That was nice – very nice," he said. "Look, dear – can you do an American accent? A Southern accent, I mean?"

"Why, I sure ca-an, honey," drawled Jessie at once. "Now you have a nice day, y'all, d'you hear me?"

Michael Wayne laughed. "Not bad, not bad, young lady," he said. "I think you've given me an idea. I'll be in touch later."

32

"Good girl," said Rick, thumping her on the back. "What did I tell you? Melody!"

Jessie was beginning to feel like everybody's youngest sister – she'd been called girl, dear and young lady all in the space of five minutes. But somehow she couldn't summon up much indignation. She felt too happy and excited.

Then it was Toby's turn. He'd obviously made up his mind to play the clown in a big way. He'd chosen "I Wanna Be Like You" from *The Jungle Book*, and sang it with his back to the audience, swaying his hips suggestively and ending with a flourish in which he coquettishly turned his head, looking back over his shoulder and fluttering his eyelashes. He followed that up with a reading from an Enid Blyton book, which he managed to spice up so that even the most innocent escapades of the Famous Five on their Treasure Island sounded rather suggestive. He was a huge hit.

Jessie felt fairly sure that she and Toby had been a success. And there was no doubt at all that Candida was going to land a plum part. Apart from them, Jessie thought that there were just a handful of really good players: a couple of other very funny boys, a few older people from the amateur dramatic society, and some people from the year above her at college. But there were to be more auditions the following evening, and Hazel was going to try out for the band the next day, too.

"Come on, we need a drink!" urged Toby, flinging one arm round Jessie and the other round Hazel. "It's tough work getting to the top."

Jessie's face fell. Rick had offered to drive her

home. As far as she was concerned, there was no contest. She thought about inviting him to come out with the rest of the gang, but she was too late. He was making his way towards her now. He nodded to the others, and told Toby what a brilliant performance he'd given. Then he took Jessie firmly by the arm.

"We really must be off," he said briskly. "Good night, stars." And before she knew what was happening he'd steered her out of the theatre and round the corner to where his car was parked. He drove for a few minutes and pulled up outside a row of tall houses which had been turned into flats.

"Time for you to meet some of my friends," he announced. They climbed up to the very top of the house to what was very obviously a shared flat, shared by boys. It wasn't exactly tidy, and as they went past the open kitchen door Jessie couldn't help noticing the teetering pile of washing up stacked by the sink.

Rick led her into a cramped living-room. There were mattresses on the floor instead of proper furniture and about eight people were squeezed together, some drinking coffee, others wine. Candida was there, of course, and she waved cheerily at Jessie and Rick.

"Hi," she greeted them warmly. "I really enjoyed your singing tonight, Jessica – I bet you've landed a good part."

"You both have," added someone else from the corner of the room. "Although I'm willing to bet it won't be the best part."

"Oh, no – I think you'll find that's reserved for a real star," added someone else, handing round a bowl of crisps.

"They mean Miriam Wayne," Rick explained.

"Who?" Jessie demanded, puzzled.

"She's Michael Wayne's daughter – from his first marriage. I think she sort of comes as part of the package."

From then on, the conversation was dominated by gossip about the pantomime and who else might be in for favours from the famous director. Everyone started to shout out wild suggestions – from Jessie's old headmistress (who scored 99 on the unlikely scale) to Mrs Willoughby, who ran the garden centre and who rather prided herself on her ability to recite the whole of *The Ancient Mariner* off by heart, which she had attempted to do for her audition.

Soon Jessie was settled on one of the mattresses, a cup of coffee in her hand and someone's feet poking into her side. She was beginning to get used to the slightly dreamlike feeling that so often accompanied outings with Rick. His friends weren't that much older than she was – two or three years at most. But there seemed to be a world of difference, somehow, between her sheltered life and this bohemian, casual existence they all shared.

How did Candida manage it? she wondered enviously. She seemed perfectly at home sprawled on a bean bag, arguing spiritedly about whether the Rolling Stones were finally to old to cut it. In fact, Candida was one of those people who always managed to fit in. And the more confident she seemed, the more awkward and out of place Jessie felt.

"How are you doing, sunshine?" whispered Rick after a while. "Do you want to go?" She nodded gratefully. It could be a bit of a strain looking relaxed all the time. Wistfully, she thought of Toby and Hazel and the rest of their friends who'd all headed straight for the Wimpy Bar. Life was so much less complicated with them.

Then Rick took her arm and led her out of the room, his friends smiling as they said goodbye. It was great that they accepted her – and great to be seen by them all as his girlfriend. And greatest of all was the moment they arrived home and he took her in his arms.

"You did so well tonight," he murmured. "I was really proud of you – I know you're going to get a good part and do it brilliantly. And we're all going to have such a good time..."

Jessie wasn't sure quite what he meant by "all" – but as his lips met hers and she began to melt into his kisses, she ceased to care...

A few days later, Michael Wayne called another meeting at the theatre – but this time it was by invitation only. Toby, Hazel and Jessie were all invited and tried to look casual as the announcements of the cast list were made. Toby was to be an Ugly Sister, playing alongside another boy from their college called Peter. To no one's surprise, Miriam Wayne was Cinderella, and someone none of them had seen before was Prince Charming. Candida was chosen to be Buttons.

"Well, she's got the legs for it, hasn't she?" commented Toby rather meanly. Jessie wondered if he was saying that to make her feel better, just in case she didn't land such a good part.

But he needn't have worried. To her amazement, she was given the part of the Fairy Godmother.

"It was your song that gave me the idea," explained Michael Wayne. "I want you to play the part as a Southern Belle – very down home and country. I think it could be hilarious."

There was going to be a chorus line and a small band. Hazel looked pleased when the music director asked if she would play saxophone for them.

"I knew Geoff would be sorry," she remarked later. "The band gets a bird's eye view of the chorus."

"Why? You're not going to be a flying orchestra are you?" asked Toby.

"No, silly. I mean, when the bird's still on the ground – looking up skirts."

"OK – congratulations all of you," the director was saying. "I'm delighted we've got such a strong cast – we're certainly going to show what Amberley is made of. And, most important, I know we're going to give lots of pleasure to lots of people this Christmas. But a word of warning. We haven't much time to get the show together. It's mid-September now, we open the week before Christmas. That's just three months, folks – and I know you're all busy people with work to do, so all our rehearsals have to be at evenings and weekends until the final couple of weeks. So I want your commitment, I want lots of hard work, I want you to take it seriously – because you're in showbiz now."

Everyone cheered and laughed excitedly. Even Mrs Willoughby was beaming. She was going to play the Ugly Sisters' mother. Jessie felt so happy that she very nearly hugged her. Instead, she turned to hug Rick, who swung her in the air.

"Now the fun is really going to begin," he said. And right then, she couldn't have agreed with him more.

5

The chips were sizzling dangerously as Jessie turned over the sausages and prepared to crack the eggs. A towel was wound round her wet hair and she wore nothing but a huge stripy bathrobe. She'd already had one disaster when chip fat flew on to the white satin shirt she'd been planning to wear that evening. Now it was draped over a chair recovering from her emergency anti-stain operations. She'd decided to take no chances from now on.

She'd promised Mum that she'd feed her brother Dan and his friend Andy before she went out that evening. "I know you'll be out yourself later, but your dad and I are going to meet in town after work and go to a film. I'd just feel happier if I knew they'd had something decent to eat."

Jessie didn't mind, really. Her parents deserved a night out and she quite enjoyed being in charge, even though it wasn't very restful. Every few minutes a tousled head would appear round the kitchen door with another request.

"Are you sure you're making enough chips?"

"Can we borrow your video – the Kevin Costner one? Where do you keep it – under your pillow?"

"Quick! Andy's hurt himself! He's bleeding to death!"

Actually that had been a bit of a panic. Andy had been showing Dan how to use all the attachments to his Swiss Army Knife and his finger had somehow slipped on the gadget for taking stones out of horses' hooves. A deep gash between his thumb and forefinger was spurting blood and he looked very pale as he trailed after Dan into the kitchen.

Jessie had taken action immediately, vaguely remembering a First Aid course she'd done at school. She'd grabbed a clean teatowel, folded it into a thick pad, and pressed it hard on the wound. After a minute or so she'd told Andy to carry on pressing hard.

"It'll stop the bleeding eventually," she told him. "Now, why don't you sit quietly in the living-room and watch your video for a bit. Try and hold your arm up a bit, that'll help to stop the bleeding as well."

She'd felt a little less calm when she returned to the kitchen to find the chips sizzling so furiously that they were sending out sparks of burning oil, which was when her beautiful new shirt got spattered. She'd dabbed the spots carefully with stain remover, left it to dry, rushed upstairs for the bathrobe, then rushed down again to check on Andy's cut hand.

"I don't know," she muttered as she carefully

dressed it and put on a plaster. "No one would think that tonight I was going on a dream date to a posh dinner party. I should be bathing in asses' milk, not tending to the needs of two teenage toddlers."

"Oh, not Rick the Card again," teased Dan. He'd taken to calling Rick various versions of cards and card games ever since Rick had taught him a very complicated card trick. He'd gone from "Rick the Trick" to "Rick the Card Trick" to "The Card".

"Don't call him that!" said Jessie automatically.

"OK, how about your Trump Card?" suggested Dan.

"Or the Joker," added Andy helpfully, beginning to cheer up.

"What d'you think you'll get to eat at the posh dinner party then?" enquired Dan. "Caviare? Oysters? Lobster?" he mused, rapidly running out of exotic foods.

"Well definitely not sausage, egg and chips," Jessie told them briskly. "Which reminds me..."

Secretly Jessie had been wondering exactly the same thing. She was hoping desperately that she wouldn't be confronted with anything too unfamiliar. She still hadn't quite recovered from the tapas bar. But what did people give you to eat when they invited you for dinner? Her experience was rather limited. She and Hazel had occasionally cooked up spaghetti bolognaise for the gang, followed by mountains of chocolate ice-cream. And when her mum had friends over, it was usually for something really simple like stew – or turkey, of course, for Christmas.

41

Jessie sighed as she scooped out the chips and piled them on to plates for the boys. It was so exciting to be going round with Rick, meeting his friends, being accepted as part of the gang. But there was a kind of anxiety about it all, too. This evening, for example, they'd be visiting Sue and Eddie, who were both students at Wolverhampton University and lived together in a little flat in town. It all sounded incredibly glamorous to Jessie. She wondered if she and Rick would ever get to the stage where they'd be living together, in a little flat, with their own sofa and a fridge full of fancy cheeses and beer and loads of spices to cook with...

She was just putting the tomato ketchup on the table and saying, "Here you are, the main course with a bit of food on the side," when the doorbell rang. Dan rushed to answer it.

"It's the King of Hearts," he chortled, very pleased with himself.

Jessie squawked. "What are you doing here? You're much too early."

"Oh, they let me go early because I'd achieved the work of six men already," Rick explained airily. "I knew you'd be pleased." Unperturbed, Rick strode into the kitchen. As usual, Jessie's heart gave a little flip when he peered round the door. He was such a stunning-looking guy. Her stunning-looking guy.

He looked her up and down, from her wet hair down to the stripy bathrobe and on down to the old trainers with the holes in the toes.

"Why, Miss Mackenzie," he said, putting on an

American accent. "I never realized. You're so gorgeous without your clothes on."

Jessie tried to look casual. "Tell you what, boys," she said at once, "why don't you take your supper into the living-room and carry on with your video?"

As soon as they'd left, Rick took her in his arms and ran his hands down her back.

"Mmm..." he murmured. "I like what you're wearing under this flattering robe." Then he kissed her and Jessie felt the familiar, melting sensation as they stood locked together in a long embrace. Then he gently held the lapels of the bathrobe, and for a moment she panicked that he might pull them apart. But he didn't. He just looked deep into her eyes.

"You don't know how gorgeous you are, do you Jess?" he said quietly. And then he quickly pushed her away. "Go on, you'd better start getting ready. We'll have to leave in an hour. I know – I'll help you dry your hair."

Rick carefully dried and brushed her hair, a strand a time, while she sat at the kitchen table doing her make-up and feeling blissfully happy. It felt so comfortable when they were alone like this. Rick managed to make simple things like hair-drying and doing make-up seem even more intimate than kissing. She wondered if this was what living together would be like? Perhaps she'd be able to tell by watching Sue and Eddie.

She was relieved when dinner turned out to be spaghetti. It made her feel at home – even though the sauce was a little spicier and more foreign-tasting than anything she and Hazel had ever attempted, and even though it was served with real Parmesan cheese you had to grate yourself, and a salad full of different kinds of lettuce with a very tangy dressing; even though they were eating off a bare, gnarled table with candles in bottles which flickered excitingly and made everyone look dark and mysterious. Sue was very friendly and asked her all about her A-level course and the pantomime. She was studying English and really seemed interested in what Jessie was telling her.

"I don't know," she said, "it doesn't seem any time since I was at Sixth Form College, but you seem to be having much more fun than we did. I'd have loved the chance to do all that acting. I suppose you must be in the final year, too. How do you find the time?"

"Oh, no – I've only just started," Jessie explained. "I joined the college last month."

Eddie laughed. "You dirty old cradle snatcher!" he teased Rick. Jessie felt awful – embarrassed and angry at the same time. But Rick didn't seem at all put out.

"Oh, she's mature for her age," he said casually. "And she's a quick learner." Everyone laughed, then Sue poured some more red wine and started asking Jessie about which Shakespeare plays she'd be studying. Soon Jessie was deep into a discussion of *Antony and Cleopatra* and enjoying herself far more than she'd imagined possible.

After the main course there was fresh fruit and chocolate. Then someone suggested a game of Scrabble.

"Tell you what, Jessie," suggested Eddie. "Since we did all the hard work preparing dinner, why don't you go and make the coffee."

Jessie felt rather like a condemned woman as she made her way into the kitchen. Her heart sank when she saw a glass jug poised on a glass machine on the cluttered worktop. Next to it was a packet of coffee beans. Coffee beans! She'd never made real coffee in her life and had no idea how to go about it. She remembered Eddie's quizzical smile as he'd spoken to her and felt sure it was all part of some awful test to see if she was good enough for Rick.

For what seemed like several hours, but was probably a couple of minutes, Jessie stood motionless in the kitchen, completely at a loss. She was just deciding to make some instant, accompanied by a few gurgling noises like in the TV commercial, when Rick appeared in the doorway.

"I thought as much," he said triumphantly. "It's rotten of Eddie to have put you on the spot like this. Look, let's make the coffee together. I think I'm going to enjoy showing you."

He showed her how to grind the beans by standing behind her and guiding her hands. Then he walked her over to the jug, still close behind her, and together they prepared the coffee, touching all the time. While it was brewing and make its satisfying little popping noises, he turned her to face him.

"You really are an ingénue," he whispered, brushing her lips with his.

Jessie knew he meant she was naive and

innocent. She'd come across the term at college. But she played along with him.

"A what?" she asked, opening her eyes wide. "Did you say genius? Thanks very much."

"Sometimes I just think you're a witch," he said. And then, once again, she was in his arms and they were kissing so hard that nothing and no one else existed in the whole world.

"As long as you can make this kind of magic, who cares if you're hopeless in the kitchen?" he whispered fondly.

"That's not fair," retorted Jessie. "Just because I haven't made coffee before doesn't make me hopeless." She remembered how Rick had walked in on her earlier that evening, dishing up supper. "I can do a mean egg and chips, and my sausages are unbeatable." But Rick just laughed fondly. Jessie got the feeling he enjoyed thinking of her as helpless and impractical. And somehow, the more he liked it, the more incompetent she seemed to get.

"Look, I'll go back to the others and you bring in the coffee as if you'd done it all yourself," he suggested. Jessie was sure that no one would be fooled for a minute, but she agreed and busied herself putting cups and saucers on a tray.

No one took much notice of her when she slipped back into the living-room. They were setting out the Scrabble and arguing over who would keep score. Jessie carefully began pouring the coffee and handing it round. As she passed a cup to Eddie, Rick looked up and said indulgently: "See how well she's doing!"

At that moment Jessie's hand jerked involuntarily and the cup went shooting out of her hand. Coffee scattered everywhere and the cup smashed. Somehow, a jagged piece flew into her hand and blood began to spurt from a nasty cut.

"Oh, dear – you poor thing," said Sue at once, fussing over her.

"I'm OK," muttered Jessie, overcome with embarrassment. "I – I just don't know what happened. I'm really sorry about the cup."

"Don't worry," Sue reassured her. "We've got loads. Look, I'll mop up and Rick, you see to Jess. What a nasty cut!"

Jessie could hardly believe what was happening. Just a couple of hours ago she'd been briskly and calmly mopping up Andy's wounded hand and dishing out supper. Now here she was again – only this time, she was the clumsy one with the cut hand. And Rick was treating her as if she was Andy's age, only younger.

"It's OK, don't worry," soothed Rick, carefully dabbing at the cut with a length of toilet paper.

"Look, I just need a cloth to press on it and I'll be fine," Jessie tried to say. But no one was taking any notice. So she tried again. "Just leave me alone and I'll be fine!" she shouted. Sue looked sympathetic. Eddie looked amused. Rick put his arm round her.

"My little firebrand," he said affectionately. "I think perhaps we should go."

As he was driving her home he glanced at her curiously. "You seem a bit upset, sweetheart. Is it the pain?"

Jessie took a deep breath. "No. It's not that. It's

just that I wish you wouldn't treat me like a kid sister or something. I'm not totally helpless, you know."

Rick looked astonished. "Of course you're not. You're a terrific singer. And an OK guitarist." He paused and grinned. "And a world class kisser. It's just that you can be a little bit clumsy, darling, where practical matters are concerned. Don't worry, it's not so terrible. In fact, I think it's very sweet indeed."

"I do wish you'd stop calling me sweet all the time," Jessie retaliated crossly. "Sometimes I think you want to make out that I'm hopeless just to make you look good. What's your problem – didn't you have any sisters?"

"As a matter of fact, no I didn't," replied Rick lazily, refusing to get offended. "But this has nothing to do with gender, you know. My mother happens to be a world class fuse-mender, so maybe I get it from her. I can't help it if I'm more practical than you are. When it comes to some things, I'm completely helpless."

Once again, the evening ended with a kiss that sent Jessie's senses reeling, leaving her with her usual mixture of delirious happiness and obscure anxiety. She lay awake for ages that evening, wishing she was in Rick's arms. And wishing that the two of them were the last people left on earth.

6

Jessie stood on stage, her hands on her hips, staring in genuine wonder at the pouting girl facing her. Miriam Wayne was someone who was used to getting her own way and it wasn't going down very well.

"I just think this whole lizard and mouse thing is so corny," she whined. "Couldn't we … like … do a new spin on the story? I mean it is a pantomime, isn't it? How about we get a lot of homeless people and give them jobs as coachmen and things? Or – I know – we've got a whole lot of travellers squatting in the garden and I have to go and turn them into servants!"

"Can you believe this kid?" Candida whispered to Jessie. "I mean, talk about spoilt! If we're not careful we'll have Prince Charming agreeing to fund a help clinic for people Cinderella doesn't like the look of!"

Jessie couldn't help agreeing with Candida. Miriam was outrageously spoilt and her suggestions

were insulting as well as absurd. But she felt a little awkward when Candida badmouthed her. Jessie wondered if it was because she could so easily imagine Candida saying awful things about her, too.

"She goes to that posh girls' school in Birmingham," Candida went on. "So she probably thinks she's doing us all a big favour slumming it in the sticks."

Michael Wayne sighed in a long-suffering sort of way. He treated Miriam much more like a difficult starlet than like his own teenage daughter. Jessie supposed that was because he'd split up from his first wife years before, when Miriam was only eight, and he only saw her occasionally.

"It's a pantomime, luvvie," he explained wearily. "A traditional form of Christmas entertainment. People want lizards and mice and coachmen and pretty frocks. It's the way it is. Now just try the scene again – with a little bit of pathos this time, OK, honey bunch?"

He had drawn up a strict timetable for rehearsals. You only had to show up for your own scenes for the first month and for Jessie that meant Tuesday and Thursday evenings – along with Toby and his Ugly Sister and Candida, who was Buttons. And Cinderella, of course. Michael called them his Kitchen Cabinet because so many of their scenes together took place in the kitchen.

Jessie's mum, who was terribly proud of her, was also worried that the pantomime might get in the way of her studies. So she'd made a firm rule, which Jessie had had to agree to, that she must be

in by eleven o'clock during the week. Otherwise, no pantomime. They were only into the second week and already Jessie was finding her curfew a terrible restriction.

"It's even worse than Cinderella's," she complained. "Couldn't you make it midnight – it's more traditional." But her mother just laughed and shook her head.

"I'm sorry, Jessie, but Cinderella didn't have A-levels to think about. And maybe if she had she wouldn't have had to count on meeting a rich man to take care of her."

But that was no comfort to Jessie, who knew she was missing out on all the fun the others had after rehearsals. Even now, while she was busy trying to turn Cinderella into a beautiful princess, she could see Candida and Rick sitting in the stalls, having a really good laugh about something. "Probably me," she told herself gloomily, trying for the umpteenth time to wave her magic wand.

"Michael, does it *have* to be a magic wand?" she asked suddenly, trying not to sound like Miriam. "I mean, I am supposed to be a country Fairy Godmother. How about a whip?"

"Brilliant!" Michael snapped his fingers excitedly. He loved what he called flashes of inspiration. Now he turned to Rick and John Bottrell. "Could we have a sort of hoe-down riff and a crack of the whip when she first appears? Then every time she transforms something, there's another crack of the whip?"

"That is just so unfair!" complained Miriam, as

Rick and John began to confer. "How come country and western Fairy Godmothers with whips are allowed if we're supposed to be so traditional?"

"Now, now dear," intervened Mrs Willoughby unexpectedly. "What you need to know about the theatre is the director knows best. It may just be that some ideas are better than others." She sniffed disapprovingly. "And I for one certainly could never have supported a production which was uncharitable enough to mock the poor, particularly at Christmas."

"So I'm stuck with lizards and mice," muttered Miriam, obviously unable to know when she'd lost. Michael, however, was staring at her with a gleam in his eye.

"You're giving me a great idea!" he declared. Everyone else looked apprehensive. Michael seemed to have so many sudden ideas, most of which entailed changes to the script or the music if not the whole storyline.

"I want you to try being a modern Cinderella," he said, thinking aloud. "You behave like any teenager who's grounded, then the Fairy Godmother appears and you think she's gross, and you refuse to collect all those lizards and rats and things because you don't touch slimy creatures and nothing's going to make you." Miriam looked even sulkier, and drew in her breath as if she was about to speak. But he stopped her.

"Perfect! I want you to look exactly like that! Curl your lips even more, that's right, and give a kind of shudder every time there's a mention of reptiles."

"Well, maybe he does know how to manage that brat of his after all," Candida shrugged at the end of the rehearsal. "Coming out for a coffee, Jess?"

Jessie shook her head regretfully. "I can't. I've got to get home."

And even though Rick took her arm and led her away, even though he drove her home and kissed her as sweetly and as passionately as ever, Jessie couldn't help feeling miserable. As he drove off she was sure he was making straight for the all night coffee bar to meet Candida and the others. And who knew where he got to all the other weekday nights when she was stuck at home studying? She'd never liked to ask him directly, but she was sure that he was out clubbing, at least sometimes. And it was a world where she just didn't belong...

She adored the pantomime, though – and at the very next rehearsal she realized just what an opportunity Michael had given her. Rick and John had worked out a wonderful fast country hoedown for the band to play as she appeared, cracking her magic whip. And to announce the fact that she was the Fairy Godmother they'd written a song for her which was the theme tune of the whole show. The chorus went:

It's the magic – the magic of love
A love that has to be true
And if you – if you truly believe
Then one day it will happen to you.

Jessie was to sing it as a solo when she first

appeared; then as a duet with Candida, as Buttons, to cheer him up after Cinders has gone to the ball. And then finally with the whole cast at the end when she'd transformed Cinderella into a princess for the last time. She loved the hammy country style that Michael had suggested, and it suited the song perfectly.

As well as that, though, Michael had invented an entirely new comic sequence involving Cinderella's revulsion at the idea of all the reptiles. He'd decided to create a couple of giant rats who would try to get the audience to help them escape. Since Cinderella was refusing to have anything to do with them, it was up to the Fairy Godmother to catch them.

"Oh, but we're not gonna get caught, are we?" they'd say to the children, leading up to a traditional: "Oh, yes you are/Oh, no we're not!" exchange. Finally, they'd creep up behind Jessie, who would be asking the children if they'd seen those wretched rats anywhere. With any luck, they'd have a lot of roars of: "They're behind you!" and Jessie would have to keep turning round and losing them. She was thrilled – she'd never thought she'd get to play real pantomime slapstick.

"But darling, what's Cinderella without the transformation scene?" Michael pointed out. He explained that most of the money supplied by the sponsors would be spent on costumes and special effects. The most important costume, of course, was Cinderella's ballgown. The most important effects were the Fairy Godmother's magic, which turned the heroine from a ragged scullery maid into a ravishing princess.

Jessie worked harder than she'd ever worked at the rehearsal that evening. Out of nowhere, it seemed, Michael had produced two rats, a couple of boys called Philip and Graham who Jessie recognized from college. Michael really knew a lot about stagecraft and spent ages teaching the three of them how to move and work together to create the best comic suspense. By the end of the evening they were all hoarse with laughter. "How am I going to keep a straight face when we do the real thing?" Jessie wanted to know, still giggling.

"You'll be amazed," Michael told her. "Once they're in their costumes they won't be these two clowns any more, they'll be rats. Trick number one: you won't be able to see their faces. Trick number two: if you do your bit properly you won't see them at all until the end of the routine."

Exhausted, Jessie went to find Rick, who'd long since finished that evening's music session, held in a nearby hall, and was sitting at the back of the theatre, engrossed in a thriller.

"*The Ice House*," she read over his shoulder, making him jump. "By Minette Walters. Why are you so keen on murder and violence? It's not healthy."

Rick shrugged. He was mad about whodunnits and couldn't understand why Jessie found them so off-putting. "You'd enjoy them, you know, once you got into them. This one's really gripping..."

"How's the music going?" Jessie wanted to know as they left the theatre together.

"Not bad," he said. "We've had to hire in a banjo player and steel guitar just for your country number. But I was saying to Candy that maybe we should play down the country style for your duet."

A dart of anxiety shot through Jessie. "Oh, what was she doing at the band rehearsal?" she asked, trying to sound casual.

"She wanted some extra singing practice because she knew she wouldn't be needed while you were playing with the rats," replied Rick – almost too quickly, Jessie thought. "She's not a natural singer like you, Jess," he added, as if to make her feel better. "She's sensible enough to know that, so she's decided to come along to band rehearsals whenever she can. Of course, she can't always make it because she has to work late quite a bit."

Jessie changed the subject abruptly. She couldn't help being jealous of Candida and her relaxed, easygoing manner when she was around Rick and his friends. But she knew it was best not to let him know how she felt.

"How's Hazel doing?" she asked. Rick grinned.

"Your mate Hazel is unbelievable," he said. "All that energy! I'm amazed she ever manages to stop talking long enough to put the sax in her mouth, let alone play it. But she's good, when she lays off flirting with the rest of the musicians and puts her mind to it."

Suddenly Jessie realized how much she missed talking to Hazel. Of course they saw each other at college quite a bit. But they hadn't had a proper talk for a couple of weeks at least, and they hadn't been out anywhere for ages. Jessie had been too bound up with Rick to go anywhere or do anything that didn't involve him. And somehow that always seemed to mean going out as a couple or getting together with his friends.

What she needed, she told herself, was a good long girls' evening where they could have a laugh and a gossip and then get down to some real talking. Maybe Hazel would know why falling in love felt so much like going on the biggest ride in Blackpool: fast, high, dizzying, frightening – and the most exhilarating, ecstatic adventure in the world.

7

Jessie and Hazel were slouching in the kitchen, idly waiting for their Pop Tarts to pop. It was Saturday morning and they'd planned a marathon day out.

"How long do we need in the shopping centre?" wondered Jessie. "There's masses I want to look at but I've only got enough for..." she counted her money for the sixth time. "Well, maybe one top. And a Big Mac. And some more hair beads. How about you?"

"I need some jeans and a present for my mum," Hazel was saying. Then the doorbell rang and they both stopped talking. They overheard Jessie's mother answering the door, and then a very strident voice wafted through the hall.

"Sorry to bother you on a Saturday morning, dear, when you must be so busy. But I was just dropping by to see about the raffle tickets for the Charity barn dance next week. You did promise to take a few off my hands..."

"It's Mrs Manley!" Jessie hissed. "Stuck-up Candida's even more stuck-up mother."

"I don't think Candida's all that stuck-up really," whispered Hazel reasonably. "Is she your mum's friend?"

"Well, they know each other," Jessie replied. "But I wouldn't say they're friends exactly. It's just that she's always getting involved in these charity events and sitting on committees and things and that means she needs all the suckers she can get her hands on to help her with the dirty work." Footsteps, and the strident voice, grew louder.

"I don't mean my mum's a sucker," Jessie corrected herself. "But she's got a problem with saying no. Just wait and see."

Mrs Mackenzie, looking harrassed but wearing a brave smile, showed her visitor into the kitchen. She was wearing a pair of jeans and a T-shirt with a big slogan on it proclaiming: DULL WOMEN HAVE IMMACULATE HOUSES. Mrs Manley looked immaculate, in a crisp beige suit and high heels, even though it was nine o'clock on Saturday morning.

"Hello, girls!" she greeted them with a gushing smile. "How are you? My Candida's been telling me all about you and how hard you're all working on the pantomime." She turned to Jessie's mum. "So good for them to have something focused to do in their spare time, isn't it? I do think it's marvellous of Michael Wayne to take on such a worthwhile project. I mean, they are only amateurs, it's not as if it's going to bring him any glory, is it?" Then she simpered a little. "Although of course little Candy is rather exceptionally talented. And naturally your Jessie is a very nice singer…"

Hazel kicked Jessie under the kitchen table. Jessie got the hint at once.

"Er … well, we really must be going," she muttered. "So much to do…"

"Just like my Candida, always in a rush," commented Mrs Manley. "Mind you, of course it's very different for her now with this job she's got. She's so busy there, I don't know how they ever managed without her. Just think, she's only been there a year but they're talking about promotion, you know. And the hours she has to work! She's late home most evenings. And then there's the night shift. She has to leave home at eleven o'clock some nights, and she even goes off to work after her rehearsals. I don't know how she does it, I really don't. 'Bye dears," she added as the girls got up to leave.

Jessie's mother grinned at them but didn't say anything. She didn't have a chance. Mrs Manley was in full flow.

"So you'll get rid of as many tickets as you can for me, won't you, dear, and bring the leftovers to the dance. You are coming, aren't you? Oh, and by the way, we're doing a little Harvest Festival Fair for the Senior Citizens next month…"

"What a monster!" fumed Hazel, as soon as they were out of the house.

"It's amazing, isn't it?" mused Jessie. "That someone so horrible could be involved in so many good works. I wonder why she does it?"

"Boredom," said Hazel at once. "She obviously doesn't have enough to do so she's picked on charity work to get rid of all that energy. Imagine having to be grateful to her!"

"S'pose so," answered Jessie. "Anyway, imagine having her for a mother!"

"Wow, yes," agreed Hazel. "The way she was bragging you'd think that hotel couldn't run without her precious daughter. Anyway, she was talking rubbish."

Jessie felt a dart of anxiety. "What do you mean?"

"Oh, you know – saying Candida had to do all that overtime. I mean, she's always hanging around after rehearsals and going for coffee with the gang. She comes to band rehearsals sometimes and never seems in that much of a hurry. So I reckon her mother must be kidding herself. She certainly wants to believe her darling daughter is queen bee."

"No wonder Candida's so full of herself," said Jessie.

"I wouldn't say that, really," said Hazel. "I think you're a bit hard on her, you know, Jess. She always seems to want to be friendly with you."

They'd reached the bus stop by now, so Hazel turned and looked hard at her friend.

"You're not jealous, are you? Just 'cos she gets on with Rick?"

Jessie blushed at once. " 'Course not," she replied quickly. "Well – not exactly jealous, anyway..." she added, not quite able to lie so glibly to her best friend. She was glad when the bus came and Hazel was immediately distracted by the sight of three boys from the year above them at college, all sitting together at the back and waving at them. So for the rest of the journey they sat and chatted with the boys which, as Hazel remarked later, was a very good start to the day.

It was always fun shopping with Hazel, and Jessie realized how long it had been since they'd had one of their marathon outings. First of all they tried on hats – lots of hats. Jessie was very tempted by a red beret but Hazel thought she looked much better in a black velvet boater with a huge brim and a feather at the back. They very nearly bought a couple of wigs after trying every one in the shop, and then moved on to exercise wear.

"Such gorgeous colours," sighed Jessie, wriggling out of a red, purple and yellow leotard. "Pity we don't have a gym to go with it."

By lunchtime they were exhausted, and flopped down at McDonalds, their arms full of parcels. Hazel had bought a pair of black jeans and a matching jacket which, she pointed out defensively, was such a bargain that she was actually saving money. And she'd used a similar argument on Jessie, who'd fallen in love with a black and white full-length skirt which sparkled with beading and sequins.

"You'll get much more wear out of it if you get it now," she reasoned. "There's the whole winter ahead of us, so if you buy that skirt it'll save you getting any other party things. Provided you get a couple of different tops to go with it..."

After they'd been happily munching their hamburgers for a few minutes, Hazel began to tell Jessie about her latest boyfriend fiasco.

"It's Luke – the guitarist in the band. You must have seen him!"

"Of course I have," said Jessie. "He looks nice." Not as nice as Rick, of course. But Luke was good-looking in a quiet sort of way. "What's the problem?"

Hazel sighed. "I think I've frightened him off. You see, he's awfully quiet. And he works in the music shop in town, so he doesn't know the same gang as me, really, and for some reason when he sees me being friendly with people he kind of gets the wrong idea."

Jessie couldn't help laughing. "You mean the right idea, surely."

"I don't think that's very nice," retorted Hazel. "I can't help being sociable, can I? He should be able to tell the difference between good honest flirting and – and..."

"Good dishonest flirting?" suggested Jessie. Hazel giggled good-humouredly, but Jessie could tell she was worried.

"I went out with him once and it was lovely," she explained. "We really got on well, and I thought he liked me. In fact, I still think he likes me. But he hasn't asked me out again and I've decided it must be because he thinks I've got all these other boyfriends, even though I haven't."

"Why don't you ask *him* out?" suggested Jessie.

"I've thought about that," Hazel told her. "But I'm worried that might frighten him even more. I think I'm going to have to tread very carefully. I mean, he even goes all quiet and sulky when I mess around with your Rick. And quite frankly, Jessie, the whole world chats up Rick all the time and you don't mind, do you?"

Jessie went quiet. Of course she knew Rick was very popular. She'd seen him laughing and flirting often enough. But she couldn't help feeling a pang when her best friend pointed it out to her.

"Well, not really," she conceded. "I know what he's like. And most of the time it's fine. But just sometimes it really gets to me…"

"You don't know how lucky you are," Hazel said. "You've got this gorgeous bloke who's crazy about you. You should be flattered that everyone fancies him and you're the one he's chosen."

"Oh, I know. I am!" Jessie assured her. "I've nothing to complain about. He's great – we're really happy…" She longed to pour out her heart to Hazel – to try and untangle the mess of emotions winding round her heart. How could she explain the sneaking anxiety, the moments of panic and insecurity that seemed to go hand in hand with the excitement and joy of being with Rick?

"Maybe it's just the way I am," she said lamely. "I guess I sometimes feel a bit out of my depth. It doesn't matter to him that he's so much older than me – but I think it matters to his friends. They make me feel so…"

"You worry too much," Hazel told her, as usual.

"Believe me, Jess, the more you fret, the more you drive them away. My advice is just to enjoy Rick. Have fun. Don't go looking for tragedies. And maybe you shouldn't spend every single moment with him, either. Sure, he probably goes out without you sometimes, but that's only healthy. You should do the same."

"Well I am, aren't I?" reasoned Jessie. "We're all going bowling tonight, aren't we?"

"Hmm – but that's only because Rick's working tonight. I bet you'd never have come out with us if you could have had him."

Jessie knew that Hazel was right, and she felt ashamed. She didn't believe you should neglect your friends when you started going out with someone. But she couldn't deny that was what she'd been doing.

"You're right," she said, slurping down her milkshake. "I've got far too obsessed with him. And I'm really looking forward to tonight. I know, let's go swimming this afternoon so that we're really fit and ready to take on the boys!"

As they marched out of the shopping centre arm in arm, loaded down with carrier bags, Jessie felt much happier. It was great being with friends, she decided. Maybe a night out with the gang was just what she needed, to help her make sense of the madness of being in love with Rick Meade.

8

It was Jessie's turn to bowl and she was bounding with confidence. She stood poised and calm,
gently testing the weight of the speckled ball. It
was about right. She narrowed her eyes at the
pins and took aim. Then rolled. The ball flew
down the centre of the alley knocking down five,
then six, then a seventh skittle.

"Great!" yelled Hazel. "Now just concentrate
and you can put us in the lead!"

There were three of them on each side. With
Hazel and Jessie was a girl called Jane, who had
turned up with Geoff. He'd been looking rather
smug since they'd met up, as if he was dying to
show her off but didn't want anyone to think he
was making a fuss about actually having a girlfriend for once. She was small and thin, with very
short hair and big glasses with red frames. Jessie
liked her at once; she smiled a lot, but in a
friendly rather than a nervous way.

"I hope you're not going to be too brilliant," she'd

said when Geoff introduced them. "I'd never been bowling before only –" she dropped her voice so that only the girls could hear – "Geoff took me last night, to show me how to do it so I wouldn't make a fool of myself." They all laughed then, and Jessie couldn't help envying her. Why couldn't she just admit when she was hopeless at something, or new to something, like Jane did?

Toby and Geoff had also brought along Philip, one of the rats in the pantomime, who was in the same science group as Geoff. He was a rather earnest person who was so thrilled to be included in their company that all he wanted to do was please them all. So it was Philip who was sent to get more drinks, Philip who had to organize their bowling lane and get it changed when the computer went down. Privately Jessie thought he was a bit wet to keep agreeing to do the dirty work, but she couldn't help liking him. And the more she smiled at him the more anxious he seemed to do things for her.

"Have you met him before?" whispered Jane, as they started marking up their names for the start of the game. Jessie noticed that Geoff had called himself KING KONG and Jane was JANE. Hesitantly, she put down CLEOPATRA for herself, and Philip immediately decided he was ANTONY. So when it was Toby's turn he carried on the joke and called himself ASP. Hazel ignored everyone else as usual and decided on MADONNA.

"Yes, I know him a bit," Jessie whispered back to Jane. "We're in a pantomime together. Why?"

"Why?" repeated Jane, pushing her glasses way

up into her forehead for maximum effect. "Because he fancies you like crazy, that's why. I've never seen anyone make it so obvious."

"Well, I hadn't noticed," Jessie replied. "And even if it was true, he'd be wasting his time. I've got a boyfriend already. He's coming to meet me later."

At that moment, Philip asked anxiously: "Have you chosen a ball yet, Jessie? You need to make sure you pick the right weight you know. Do you want any help?"

"Oh, my hippy aunt!" groaned Hazel. "And she says she hasn't noticed!"

Toby was the first to bowl, for the boys' team. He was in high spirits, even by his standards, and spent ages posing with the ball, giving his impression of Mike Atherton, and another of Fred Flintstone, before finally sending it straight down the lane in a perfect strike.

"Yess!" yelled the three boys, clenching their fists and thumping each other on the back. Toby and Philip did a quick dance routine, as the two rats from the pantomime, until people on the other lanes started staring at them. "They're not with me," Geoff started muttering to no one in particular. "This doctor sort of asked me to look after them and he never came back..."

By this time Jessie had laughed so much she was beginning to hurt. She'd forgotten how good it was just to let yourself have fun without having to worry about anything. She felt so relaxed with the gang – even with poor Philip, who was watching Jane anxiously. It would be his turn soon, and he clearly hadn't decided whether to try and win for his team or lose to help the girls.

Jane obviously had no such doubts. She picked up the heaviest ball, walked up to the edge of the lane and chucked it with all her might. Five of the pins went down. She repeated the action for her second throw, and knocked down another two.

"Well done," the girls called, and she grinned at them, clearly not that bothered about who was going to win. She sauntered over to Geoff and planted a casual kiss on his cheek. "Had a good teacher, you see," she explained, and he tried not to look too pleased in case anyone noticed.

Philip managed to score exactly the same number as Jane, which Jessie thought was very tactful, if he'd done it on purpose. She couldn't quite believe that, though. No one went to the lengths of not winning at bowling, however much they fancied someone.

Now it was her turn, and she'd already floored seven skittles. There were three to go. Again, she held the ball in front of her, trying to measure the distance with her eyes. She gave a little skip this time as she bowled the ball, aware of several pairs of eyes focusing on her every movement. The ball smashed into the remaining three pins – and they were down!

Now it was the girls' turn to cheer. Philip was despatched for more Cokes and crisps while Hazel and Geoff took their turns. Toby glanced at the score. "Hmm," he commented. "Looks like the asp is stinging Cleopatra, Madonna is chasing

Antony, King Kong has made off with Jane and, let's see now, we're slightly ahead – but that's only the first round. By the end of the evening, you girls should be well and truly slaughtered, proving once again that there are some things you just don't do as well as we do, and why not just admit it?"

"Oh, what have we here," Jane taunted him. "Surely not an old-fashioned sexist man? I thought they were extinct."

"There was a danger of that," added Jessie. "So they opened a zoo for a few remaining examples of the species. And they called it…"

"Amberley Sixth Form College!" shouted Hazel.

"Oh, so that's where they keep them, is it?" said Jane innocently. "You see I don't know very much about men because I go to Bailey Girls' High and they don't tell us anything. And I didn't know they still had sexists. What are they like?"

"Well," said Jessie, scratching her head. "The ones at our college all have to practise these habits that were disappearing from modern male behaviour. Like talking with their mouths full and burping a lot and telling jokes about their mothers."

"And they've all learned how to pretend that there are some things they're better at than girls," added Hazel, pointing at Toby, who obediently put on a really macho expression, stuck out his hips and said: "Yeah, and we get advanced lessons in how to call girls chicks and babes."

"And be careful if one of them tells you that you've got a beautiful mind," said Geoff, slipping his arm round Jane. "Because we're only after one thing, you know."

Everyone was in fits of giggles by now, especially Jessie, who was almost speechless with laughter. "And they're doing an experiment with some of the species," she gasped, in between guffaws. "They're teaching them to open doors for girls and offer to buy them drinks."

At that moment, Philip returned with a teetering tray of Cokes and crisps. "Well, I hope you all wanted salt and vinegar because that's what you're getting. The drinks are on me, guys." He looked puzzled as the other five collapsed in hoots of laughter.

"What did I say?" he asked. "I only said I'd buy the drinks. Gosh, you lot must have weird minds."

"Beautiful minds!" shouted the girls, now in hysterics.

They carried on the game in a manic mood. Everyone was relaxed, even Philip. Jessie was having the time of her life, and her high spirits showed in her bowling. On her next turn she scored two straight strikes and was so pleased with herself that she leapt into the air and ended up doing the splits, then she pretended she was stuck, and everyone had to grab a bit of her and hoist her up again.

Towards the end of their third game, it was Jessie's go once more. Flushed with success, she lifted the ball and carefully took aim. She was about to roll it straight down the alley when a familiar voice behind her said: "Good – I've made it in time to see you making a strike!"

It was Rick, of course. At the sound of his voice Jessie jerked the ball out of her hand and sent it skeetering into the gutter. Her heart began its usual racing, as the pleasure of seeing him mingled with a sudden awkwardness. Just a few moments ago she had felt so relaxed and care-free, laughing and joking with the gang. Now Rick had arrived the atmosphere had instantly changed.

"Wow, you've jinxed her!" exclaimed Jane, who'd never met any of them before but was always happy to speak her mind. "She was playing brilliantly till you arrived."

"Nah, you're just saying that," quipped Rick. "Typical – blaming the man for the woman's inadequacies."

"Never mind, mate," said Geoff happily. "She's got a beautiful mind." And they all laughed, except for Rick, who gave him a long, puzzled look, and Jessie herself. She suddenly wanted to leave as quickly as possible. Somehow the jokes didn't seem as funny, now that she was seeing them through Rick's eyes.

"Well sorry, gang, we've got to be going," she said brightly. "It was my last go anyway, so it won't make any difference to the score. See you."

Once they were alone in Rick's car, she felt happier. He was telling her all about how he was supposed to have been reviewing a couple of bands that evening, but the night editor had rung him on the mobile phone to say he had to go to the scene of a car accident. They hadn't been able to contact another reporter, so Rick was given the story.

"I was a bit worried, I must admit," he was saying. "I didn't know how I'd cope with all the carnage. But once you've got a job to do you just have to get on with it, even though it's not very nice. You just can't allow yourself to get upset."

Jessie thought that was quite good advice for her at the moment. Just do your job of being a fun girlfriend, don't get too involved, she told herself. But at the same time, she was thinking what a fascinating person Rick was, so full of ideas and experiences, and with so much to give.

He drove out of town for a couple of miles, eventually turning down a little track into the woods. There, he stopped the car and turned off the lights. "At last, I've got you to myself," he whispered, taking her in his arms. Then his lips found hers, and all the familiar, dizzying sensations coursed through her as she melted into him, wanting the hungry, urgent kisses to go on for ever and ever.

At last he held her gently away from him and looked into her eyes.

"I want you, Jess," he said softly. "You know that, don't you?" She nodded, her pulse racing with excitement and fear, too.

"I care too much to rush you," he carried on. "But one day, when you're ready, I'm going to make love to you."

"Rick, I – I do want to," she stammered. "It's just that…"

"I know. I know you're young and it's a big step,"

he said. "I understand. But Jessie, sometimes there's this gulf between us, and I think that it'll only go away once we become real lovers. Do you know what I mean?"

Jessie nodded, but didn't trust herself to say anything. Could it be that Rick was right? If they made love, really made love, would all the awkwardness and confusion really disappear? She remembered how his arrival had made her foul up that last throw at the bowling alley. Was his presence so exciting that she couldn't concentrate on anything else? Or was it just because he always made her feel nervous?

She giggled, and he raised an eyebrow. "What?"

"Oh, nothing really," she said. "I was just wondering if my bowling average would improve if we ever slept together." He shook his head wonderingly.

"Mad, totally barmy," he said affectionately. "How ever did I get mixed up with this crazy teenager?" And he kissed her once again, before they drove home.

9

Jessie swaggered on to the stage for the eighteenth time that evening and declared, rather wearily: "Cinderella, you *shall* go to the ball!" It wasn't as though she was saying it wrong or anything – although she was well aware that by about take eight she'd lost some of the conviction she'd been trying to bring to the most famous lines in the whole show. But you couldn't really keep up a Meryl Streep level of acting when everyone round you was measuring up the stage for puffs of dry ice, counting in the lighting and practising whipcracks and thunderbolts.

Besides, Jessie was preoccupied. It was her birthday this Saturday, October 31, and she was going to have a party. Her mother had already set the ground rules: she and her friends would have to do the catering; no one was allowed in the bedrooms; she supposed they could make Hallowe'en decorations if they had to, but nothing that would stain. And although she didn't mind a little alcohol as well as soft drinks, she definitely meant a little, and that was that.

Jessie had joyously settled for all the conditions because in return her mum and dad had agreed to stay out of the way until midnight. Hazel and Toby were taking charge of the food and decorations. Rick had undertaken to provide the music.

"I can't help with the preparations, hon," he'd warned her. "I'd like to obviously, but I'm working all day. I'll be there for the start, though – with the hottest tapes in town."

Jessie sighed. She knew Rick worked hard, but she couldn't help minding his attitude sometimes. He enjoyed his job so much he never seemed to regret the time he spent away from her. "Won't you miss me?" she'd asked him once, when he'd had to work on a Sunday. She'd instantly regretted her words. He'd looked at her strangely and then shrugged. "I don't see it that way. Work is work. You are you. In fact, I'm surprised you'd come out with something like that."

Jessie had looked hurt so he'd tried to explain. "The reason I was attracted to you in the first place is that you're so full of energy and talent," he said. "You're always doing things – playing in bands, singing, acting... You're your own person Jess, and I like that. I like it very much..." Then, naturally, he'd pulled her towards him and kissed her doubts away. "So let's enjoy each other – not tie each other down..."

Now, as she cracked her whip yet again and began to weave her magic on poor, tattered Cinderella, she made up her mind to be as independent and as carefree as she had been when she first got involved with Rick. And that meant showing him that she was relaxed about him and not the least bit possessive. Which meant, in turn, that she'd better be very careful about who she invited to the party.

"OK, OK – I think we've got it," Michael declared in a rather harassed voice. "Now let's just run through the rest of that kitchen scene. Cinders, over here. Buttons? Where's Buttons got to?"

"I'll go and find her," volunteered Jessie. She was fairly sure that Candida would be lounging around somewhere backstage. After a quick search she found her in one of the dressing rooms, lying on a sofa reading a paperback that Jessie recognized. *The Ice House* by Minette Walters. It was the book Rick had been raving about not long ago. This was her big moment, Jessie told herself. Don't be jealous, don't start inventing problems. Prove what a nice, easygoing person you are.

"Michael wants you for a kitchen rehearsal," she said to Candida. Then she took a deep breath. This was it. "Oh, and by the way, I'm having a party on Saturday night and I'd like you to come."

Candida looked pleased – really pleased. "That's great Jessie, I'd love to!" she said at once. "Come on, let's get back to the pouting primadonna on stage. I swear if I had a half pint of lager for every time Cinderella fluffed her lines I'd be able to open a brewery by now."

Jessie laughed. "Maybe you could get the parts other beers don't reach!"

She was gratified when Candida burst into raucous giggles, but deep down, even though she didn't want to, she was wondering whether Candida had accepted the invitation not because of her but because of Rick. Then she told herself sternly to stop torturing herself, and for the rest of the evening she threw herself into hard work.

The following evening Toby, Geoff, Jane and Hazel were sprawled over her bedroom floor making lists. "Lots of French bread and cheese, pickles, crisps, peanuts," Toby said, writing furiously. "What else do people eat?"

"Sausages," suggested Jane. "I'll do those if you like. I'll put them on cocktail sticks. Actually, I like putting things on cocktail sticks. How about cheese and pineapple – or olives and ham?"

"I know, let's do bacon and fruit pastilles on sticks," said Hazel, and everyone started inventing even nastier combinations.

"Black pudding and Turkish Delight!"

"Spam and orange sorbet!"

"Mars bar pieces with spaghetti and catfood!"

That, of course, was Dan, who'd sneaked into the room licking a home-made ice lolly.

Jessie groaned. "Who said you could come in?"

He grinned. "No one actually asked me, but I can always tell when I'm needed. I mean, you're going to want someone to do the décor, aren't you?"

"Oh, no!" snapped Jessie at once. "I know all about you and fake blood. And I remember the year you beheaded yourself. And the time you made your eyeballs fall out. And I'm warning you now – don't even think about it!"

Dan looked wounded. "I wasn't going to suggest anything remotely like that," he protested. "I was simply offering myself for heavy duty carrying, lifting and pumpkin carving. Oh, and a little light trick-or-treating, naturally."

"You mean, if people don't give you treats you might bite them on the neck at midnight," suggested Toby, who'd always had a soft spot for Dan.

"Something like that," agreed Dan. "Or I might just keep a list of who's getting off with who and kind of brandish it as I go round with my sack."

"The little brother from hell," muttered Jessie as the others started laughing.

"Tell you what," suggested Hazel. "Why don't we do all the shopping on Friday after college, and then go out for a pizza?"

Jessie was about to find an excuse to say no. She always saved Friday evenings for Rick. Then she remembered that he was going to Birmingham that night to see some bands for the paper. He was going to try to write his reviews the next day in between all the other stories that were piled up for the Saturday shift.

"And because it'll be your very last day of being Sweet Sixteen, we'll treat you!" declared Toby.

"Wow – shopping in the supermarket!" Geoff said to Jane. "I told you that if you stuck with me I'd drive you into the fast lane." Jessie wanted to hug him. It was obvious that he was still so besotted with Jane that falling in the mud with her after a wild day cleaning drains would have had its attractions. And he was glad to be able to show her off to his friends, too. If only she could feel that carefree about Rick...

As she saw them to the front door she heard a loud, unmistakable voice echoing from the kitchen. The door opened.

"I really must be going now, dear," Mrs Manley was saying, or rather booming. "Thanks so much for agreeing to take on the Meals on Wheels for me next week. I don't know what I'd do without you, I really don't. And Candida's no help at all now, of course. Do you know, she's got to spend all of tonight at that hotel, then there's a rehearsal on Thursday, and then on Friday she's got to work all day, come home and then go back again! Working on a Friday night! I suppose they've discovered that they can't do without her, but honestly, I'm sure they're exploiting the poor girl. Oh, hello!" She suddenly noticed the gang loitering in the hallway.

"Hello, dears – all ready for the party? Candida's told me all about it. You're not actually dressing up though, are you?"

"Oh, no," Jessie answered. "It's come as you please." But she couldn't help adding: "Although you can tell Candida she can be a witch if she wants to," and they all fell about laughing as Mrs Manley said her goodbyes and swept off home.

Toby, Jessie and Jane did most of the shopping. Geoff and Hazel were inclined to pounce on anything that took their fancy and had to be kept in check.

"Well, why can't we have chocolate and hazelnut spread sandwiches?" they'd demand. Or: "Hey, look – economy size sacks of toffee popcorn. We need some. It's a bargain!" Eventually they settled on a sensible amount of party food that would be easy to prepare, and piled it into Jessie's father's car. He was waiting patiently for them outside the supermarket, an anxious look on his usually placid face.

"What's up, Mr Mackenzie?" asked Toby. "It's not us, is it?"

"Oh, no – it's not the party I'm worried about. It's the birthday present. As of tomorrow, this car is under threat."

"Yup," beamed Jessie. "I'm getting a course of driving lessons – and you'd think they'd be pleased, wouldn't you?"

"I got that for my birthday," put in Geoff helpfully. "And you don't have to worry about a thing, Mr Mackenzie. Young people today are very good with mechanical things."

"Yes, that dent hardly shows now, does it?" added Jane, and they all muffled their giggles as Jessie's father turned pale.

They spent most of the evening at the pizza restaurant planning the party and gossiping about the guests.

"Did you invite Miriam?" Toby wanted to know. Jessie nodded.

"I did in the end. I thought it would be mean not to. She'd only hear about it from the others. Practically the whole cast is coming."

"I know," suggested Hazel. "Why don't you tell

her it's fancy dress? Then she can turn up as a vampire, we'll be in ordinary clothes, she'll say why did you tell me to wear fancy dress and we can all say: 'What's the problem? You're not *in* fancy dress!'"

"Let's play Consequences," suggested Toby suddenly. "Everybody write down a man's name and then pass on your paper to the next person..."

Soon they were all engrossed in dreaming up unlikely venues for romance, and even more unlikely opening lines. They rocked with laughter as they took it in turns to read out the final ridiculous outcomes: Madonna and Paddy Ashdown, Hugh Grant and the Queen.

The last one was Jessie's. Everyone looked expectantly at her as she began to read aloud. "Count Dracula met Enid Blyton at Jessie's birthday party. He said: You *shall* go to the ball. She said: I'm washing my hair tonight. The consequence was: they invented a new pizza topping. And the world said..."

"I like a full-blooded man," suggested Jane.

"Everyone had a bite," put in Geoff.

"Even Timmy the Dog!" added Hazel.

"She wanted a happy ending but he just wanted to drink her dry," said Toby quietly.

Jessie stared at him, horrified. It was as if he could read her soul, her innermost fears. How could Toby possibly understand so clearly her worries about Rick?

"Stupid game," she said lightly. "Probably what happened was that she ordered garlic bread, he disintegrated and nobody got a goodnight kiss."

It was nearly eleven o'clock by the time they left the restaurant and it was fairly quiet outside, even though they were in the centre of town.

"I promised you life would be an adventure with me, didn't I?" Geoff said to Jane, carrying on his usual joke, which she didn't seem to mind at all. "That's what I love about this town – bright lights, excitement, always on the go. You will tell me if it gets too fast for you, won't you?"

"How could I ever get enough if it?" replied Jane. "I mean, with any luck we might catch the last bus together. It's all so indescribably romantic!"

The others were straggling along the High Street, joking about what a one-horse town Amberley was – and dreaming about the day when they'd all get out. But Jessie had gone silent. As they passed the next set of lights she'd noticed a little green Fiat Uno, parked up a side street. She knew the car. She'd have recognized it anywhere. It belonged to Candida. But Mrs Manley had distinctly said that Candida was working at the hotel all Friday night – and the hotel was miles out of town.

Jessie's mind was racing painfully. Just down the road were the offices of the *Amberley Herald*. Could she be meeting Rick there? she wondered wildly. But that was a crazy thought. It was much more likely that she was at the Peacock Disco. Or even at the Belvedere Hotel just on the corner, which ran a Friday night disco. Jessie tried to stem the flow of her thoughts. Why should she be jumping to crazy conclusions like this? It was none of her business what Candida got up to, and her heart certainly had no right to be beating so wildly.

But an insistent little voice inside her kept reminding her that Candida had lied to her mother and said she was at work, when in fact she was in town. She'd lied before, too – Jessie remembered Hazel scoffing at Mrs Manley's claim that her beloved daughter worked so hard, so many evenings. Then, with another pang, she remembered the book Candida had been so engrossed in at the rehearsal – the book Rick had so enjoyed.

When they'd said their good nights and Jessie had gone home, she promised herself that she wouldn't allow her suspicions to get in the way of her birthday. She must simply bury all the treacherous thoughts and concentrate on having fun.

After all, she comforted herself as she snuggled into bed, Rick would be with her tomorrow night – no one else. It would be full of her friends, she'd be at the very centre of attention and everything would be perfect.

10

Jessie woke up ridiculously early the next morning, aware of a bubble of excitement deep inside her. Even though she was now seventeen, Jessie got just as thrilled about her birthday as she had when she was seven. She opened her eyes a fraction and gave a squawk. There was a strange shape on the bed. At first she thought it was a giant tarantula. Then she told herself not to be so stupid, it must be the family cat, Harold. On closer inspection she realized it *was* a giant tarantula, but not a real one. This one was made of an old bowler hat, its legs constructed of coat hangers covered in black tights. Attached to it was a long piece of black cord.

Cautiously Jessie slid out of bed and tugged at the cord. Nothing happened. It was attached to something heavy – outside her room. She followed the cord to the door, out into the passageway and down to the bottom of the stairs where it was attached to a huge box covered in black paper. She pulled the string that was tied round it, opened the top flaps, and out popped a second tarantula attached to a spring. Pinned to it was a crudely scrawled message: *LOOK INSIDE*.

Inside was a smaller box, inside that a smaller one. She was down to her tenth box before she finally got to two small white envelopes. The first contained a computer-designed birthday card from Dan, with two tickets for a Meat Loaf concert tucked inside. The second was heavier. When she ripped it open she found a card from her parents, and a key. It was the key to her father's car. Yippee! That meant that not only was he buying her the promised set of driving lessons. He was also prepared to let her use his beloved Volvo after all!

Suddenly there was a tremendous crash in the kitchen and Dan came rushing out.

"Get back to bed!" he ordered. "You're spoiling everything! You're supposed to be asleep!" So Jessie snuggled back into bed, and a few minutes later Dan appeared with a tray of rather soggy toast, a cup of tea, with only a bit slopped in the saucer, and a glass of what looked like orange juice. "Actually it's Buck's Fizz, orange juice and champagne," he explained. "Happy birthday."

And then her parents appeared with their own glasses of Buck's Fizz, and toasted her seventeenth birthday. "This is so great!" she said, quite overcome. "Why are you being so nice to me?"

"Because we're hoping that if we're really, really nice you'll take care of the house tonight," said her mum.

"And that you'll take care of my car when you start driving it," added her dad.

"And that you'll let me come to the party and help out," piped up Dan hopefully. Jessie laughed. "Er – yes, yes and yes!" she said. "You can come to the party provided you do the decorations, pass round food and drink, do all the washing-up, don't tell any elephant jokes, don't tell any light bulb jokes and don't tell anyone any stories at all about me as a child."

Dan looked crestfallen. "Just one light bulb joke?" he pleaded. Jessie fixed him with a long stare.

"No jokes. No stories. Actually, could you manage not to talk at all?" But Dan had already sped out of the room, shouting:

"Just going to start the pumpkins. I'm going to make them all look like Mr Pratt our technology teacher."

After that, the day was one long hectic rush. Hazel arrived at about ten o'clock and presented Jessie with a huge pair of earrings. One was a silver moon with an owl, the other was a silver star with a cat.

"I thought you'd appreciate something witchy," she explained. "It'll sort of match what I'm wearing." She produced a slinky black all-in-one cat suit, which she was planning to wear with black bat earrings.

The girls spent the morning clearing the living-room, pushing back all the furniture and removing anything that looked as though it might be fragile. Dan was merrily carving out pumpkins and singing along to Radio One.

After lunch, Toby and Geoff arrived. When Jessie opened the front door they stood on the porch, waiting.

"Er – the others are just parking," Geoff said.

"Others?" asked Jessie. Then she saw Jane making her way up the path with Philip. She looked questioningly at the boys.

"He wanted to come," Geoff explained. "And we thought another pair of hands couldn't do any harm…"

They all crowded into the kitchen and handed Jessie her presents. Geoff gave her some removable tattoos, Jane a friendship bracelet, and Philip a set of juggling balls.

"Oh, that's just what I need!" she exclaimed, and started practising right away, as the others bustled round making sandwiches, cutting up vegetables and arranging glasses.

The only disappointment was Toby's present. He just handed her a copy of *Just Seventeen* as he pecked her cheek. She tried to cover up how hurt she felt by rushing round maniacally, telling everyone else what to do. But she was surprised at how much she ached inside. After all, it was her seventeenth birthday. He was one of her closest friends. Surely he could have managed more than a tatty old teenage magazine?

It was only later, when everyone except Hazel had gone home to change, that Jessie found his real present. Hazel had brought her party things with her so that they could get dressed together. While she was in the bathroom washing her hair

Jessie lay on her bed browsing through the magazine. A little package was tucked between the pages. It was beautifully wrapped in shiny silver paper. Intrigued, she opened it. Nestling in a bed of red tissue paper was a little silver brooch in the shape of a guitar. It was so intricately made that each string was moulded in a shiny finish, and tiny jewels sparkled across the body. She gasped. The brooch was exquisite. And expensive. And more than that, it was a very intimate gift. Who better than Toby knew how she'd slogged to master the lead guitar and how much it meant to her to be a player as well as a singer? It was a true badge of friendship. Somehow, she didn't know why, her eyes filled with tears.

Jessie was wearing black leggings and a very glamorous black velvet top with long, voluminous sleeves which fell in soft folds from her elbows, but cut so that her shoulders were bare. Carefully, she pinned the brooch to her chest but didn't mention it, and Hazel barely glanced at it. She was too busy helping her to thread silver and black beads into her hair, which looked great with the new earrings.

"Ooh, you look so Goth!" exclaimed Dan. "Wanna borrow any fake blood for your lips!"

"You both look very nice," commented her mum. "Exotic – but nice. I do think girls are so, um, individual these days, don't you, Bill?"

Jessie's dad grunted, looking anxious. "You won't let anyone go near my records, will you, love?"

Jessie laughed. "No, Dad, I promise no one will

89

filch your Elvis collection or any of your Swinging Blue Jeans forty-fives. Don't worry – Rick's bringing some party tapes he's made specially, and I've got loads of good cassettes, without having to plunder your musical antiques."

Finally she managed to bundle her parents out of the door, as Toby and the others arrived. They all stood in the middle of the living-room, surveying their work. Dan's pumpkins were arrayed in a row along the windowsill, lit by candles. There were masks, bats and spiders hanging from the ceiling and Dan and Toby had managed to set up a flickering light show against one wall.

"Oh, it's lovely!" Jane said approvingly. "Very *Homes and Gardens*. Why don't you persuade your mum to keep it like this?"

Geoff put on a tape of disco music. "I declare this party officially open!" he said, and to Jessie's amazement he grabbed Jane and actually started dancing with her. Jessie hadn't even known he could dance. Up until now he'd always refused on principle. Toby grabbed Hazel and started jiving with her – a routine they'd been practising for hours. That left Jessie and Philip.

He gave her a shy grin, then took her hands and began to dance. He was surprisingly good. Jessie found herself being led round the floor, half jiving, half disco-dancing, one minute being pulled into his arms and the next being flung in a spin round the room. As the track finished he steered her towards him, threw her to one side, then the other, and ended with both arms round her waist.

Flushed with the exertion of the dance as well

as the general excitement, Jessie wasn't sure what to say to him. But at that moment the bell rang, someone flung open the door, there was the sound of chattering and laughing ... the party had begun.

For the first half-hour or so Jessie was so busy greeting her friends, making sure people were offered drinks and had someone to talk to, that she couldn't think at all. Then she started to wonder about Rick. He'd promised to be there by eight and now it was eight-thirty. Where could he be? Surely he'd come soon on this of all days?

She tried to fling herself into the mood of the party, chatting and laughing, darting from group to group, her eyes glittering dangerously, her cheeks flushed. The more she tried not to worry about Rick, the more wildly she'd joke and tease, giggle and show off.

Everyone else seemed to be having a great time. Geoff and Jane were gazing into each other's eyes all the time and feeding each other peanuts. Toby seemed to be flirting with four girls from college all at the same time. Hazel's face was a mask of ecstasy. Her elusive guitarist, Luke, had finally shown up and she was doing everything she could to show him she cared.

Someone found her dad's Beatles collection and put it on for fun. Immediately she and Toby grabbed Hazel, who'd already grabbed Luke, and they began a dazzling impromptu display of rock and roll dancing. The four of them finished up collapsed in a heap on the floor, while everyone else clapped and whistled. Then the next track of the record came on. It was her absolute favourite, the song she'd sung at the talent night when she'd first met Rick. "*I don't like you, but I love you,*" droned the Fab Four.

Geoff and Jane were locked in a dance that was more of an embrace. Hazel was wrapped round Luke. Almost before she'd realized it, Jessie found she was dancing again, this time with Philip. He'd taken her in his arms and was holding her close. He really was a good dancer. Even as her thoughts strayed to Rick and the anxious knot tugged inside her, she was aware of Philip's strong body guiding her round the floor, aware of his breath very close to her neck.

"You're terrific, Jessie," he whispered. "I wish you'd let me get close to you." Jessie was about to retort that she had a boyfriend already. That Philip must be crazy to think she'd go out with anyone else when she had the greatest-looking, most interesting, most fabulous guy anyone could ever want. That he actually had a cheek coming on to her when he'd seen her with Rick, her Rick.

Then she glanced at the clock over the mantel-piece. It was nine-thirty! A flash of panic struck her, quickly followed by something quite new. Anger. It was like a white flame, burning yet cold at the same time. It was her birthday party – and her own boyfriend hadn't even bothered to turn up! How could he treat her like this?

She turned to Philip and looked him in the eyes. He was good-looking in a mild, unthreatening sort of way. A soft lock of hair fell boyishly into his eyes and strong white teeth protruded slightly from full, sensitive lips. Not exactly sexy, she thought, but he's OK. He likes me. He's a great dancer. And he's here.

Jessie didn't say anything but she allowed him to lead her into the kitchen for a drink, and then, quite naturally, out of the back door into the garden. He took her hand as they made their way down the little path to her dad's vegetable patch.

She was glad that Philip didn't seem to want to talk. Anything they said would have been confusing. But she liked the feeling of his strong hand holding hers, and the look of longing in his eyes as, very tentatively, very slowly, he bent his head to hers in a long, gentle kiss. Jessie closed her eyes, feeling him trembling as their mouths touched and melded together. He was so sweet, so young – and so very different from stylish, sophisticated Rick, who always knew what he was doing, what move he was making and what she was thinking. This was different and she decided to enjoy it.

A little while later she gently pulled away from him.

"I have to get back to the party," she whispered, and hand in hand they slipped into the kitchen and then into the living-room, which was now riotous with loud laughter and even louder music.

At about ten-thirty some late guests arrived – Candida, with Michael Wayne, and his daughter Miriam.

"Sorry we're late, darling," carolled Candida. "I had to work until nine, and Michael and Miriam were out of town doing family things all day so they said they'd pick me up at the Malibou." There was something hollow about the way she said it. For a start, Jessie knew she couldn't stand Miriam, and it just didn't make sense for the three of them to be together. And she didn't believe Candida when she said she'd been working late, because she so often said it. And it was so often a lie.

But she ushered them in anyway, waved them towards the food and drink in the kitchen, and turned to Philip even more defiantly. The music was back in the mid-90s, but it was sexy and slow and she melted into his shoulders, her face resting against his chest as they danced, her eyes closed against the raging pain and anger inside her.

It was nearly eleven o'clock when the bell rang again. As Toby opened the front door the music stopped. Jessie opened her eyes, her arms still round Philip's neck, and saw Rick standing on the porch, dishevelled and harassed. It was like being bathed in sunlight. A laser of happiness beamed through her, dispersing all the hurt and anger.

She glided towards him, leaving Philip alone in the centre of the room. Rick grabbed her hand.

"Jessie, darling – I'm so sorry. I couldn't get away, I was on a story the other side of town. It was a police raid and I managed to get into the car with them for the final bust. There was no way I could get a message to you... But you know how much I wanted to be with you – you know I'd never let you down... Here!"

He pulled a small package from his pocket and handed it to her. "Happy birthday, Sweet Seventeen," he said. She opened it, her hands shaking, to find an exquisite black enamel box painted with white and silver flowers. Inside was a silver bracelet, a linked chain of hearts. She gasped. Rick loved her – he must love her!

Someone was letting loose a cascade of balloons, and everyone was shouting, "Happy birthday!" She was in Rick's arms, her heart bursting with happiness. The music was turned up, the party was jumping, her friends were cheering her and, best of all, the boy she loved was kissing her. In that moment of perfect triumph she had completely forgotten all about Philip, who stood in the shadows abandoned, his face a mask of hurt and betrayal, as everyone danced and laughed the whole night away.

11

It was the morning after the party and Jessie was cruising along the road, her face wreathed in smiles. Not exactly cruising, she corrected herself, glancing at the mirror yet again, but at least she was driving. She'd lived here all her life: skateboarded down these roads, roller-bladed down them, biked along them, been driven through them. Now, at last, she was at the wheel – and it felt great.

"OK, then, love," her father cautioned nervously. "You're doing fine, just fine. Perhaps if you could slow down just a *little* bit more when you come to the junction." Jessie slammed on the brakes and the car shuddered to a standstill with a shriek of protest. She grinned at her dad triumphantly.

"Like that?" she demanded.

"Er – not quite," he said faintly. "What I think you're going to have to learn is a certain amount of, well, you could call it subtlety. Driving needs to be smooth and gradual, like—"

Taking very little notice of her father, Jessie had signalled left and was now merrily jerking the car round the corner in little leaps.

"—horse riding!" gasped her dad. "I was trying to say that good driving is like handling a champion mare. Only in your case," he muttered, "it's more like a bucking bronco at a Wild West Show."

"Oh, come on, Dad," teased Jessie, swerving round a parked car and waving jauntily at a couple of classmates who stood on the pavement staring at her. "It's only my first time. Give me a break!"

Mr Mackenzie couldn't hide his relief when the promised hour was up and they were back in the kitchen drinking coffee. But he was gallant enough to smile proudly when his wife came in and demanded:

"Well? How did she do? No scratches I hope!"

"Of course not," he boomed robustly. "She's doing very well indeed. A born driver, our Jess."

"Yup – born to drive people mad!" added Dan, who'd slipped into the kitchen to concoct one of the deadliest-looking milkshakes Jessie had ever seen.

"You shut up!" she retorted indignantly. "I'm a great driver! Much better than you'll ever be. At least I know the difference between right and left!"

"So do I, sewer brain!" snapped Dan. In his left hand he was holding his revolting-looking combination of milk, bananas, peanut butter and chocolate ice-cream. In his right, he carried a computer magazine.

"OK, what's the time then?" said Jessie. Dan tipped his wrist to glance at his watch and the milkshake splattered to the floor.

"See!" taunted Jessie. "Your right hand doesn't know what your left hand is doing. And you don't either!"

Both their parents were laughing too much to make a fuss about the mess. They were good like that, Jessie thought, suddenly feeling rather guilty. Other parents would have gone mad. She fetched a cloth and was helping Dan to mop up the floor when the doorbell rang.

Jessie opened the door to see Toby shuffling on the doorstep. She smiled. "Thank goodness someone normal is here," she said loudly. "I'm having a bit of trouble in the kitchen with a lunatic."

Toby smiled back and popped his head round the kitchen door to say hello. Jessie thought he looked uncomfortable but she couldn't quite work out why. He'd squeezed into the kitchen to help Dan, who was vaguely brandishing a mop. They were punching each other the way they usually did, but his heart didn't seem to be in it.

"I came round to see if you needed a hand clearing up the party," he said.

"Oh, we did all that this morning, didn't we, Jess?" said Mrs Mackenzie. "But it was very nice of you to think of that, Toby. Look, why don't we get out of your way and leave you in peace."

That was another nice thing about her parents, Jessie thought fondly. They knew when they weren't wanted.

Eventually the floor was cleaned, Dan was

98

despatched upstairs to perform an impossible feat on the computer, and Toby and Jessie were alone.

"I didn't thank you properly for the brooch," she said shyly, pouring him some coffee. "It's – it's gorgeous! I really love it..."

"That's OK," muttered Toby. "Thing is, Jess..." He was looking even more uncomfortable now, and Jessie was getting curious. Of all the people she knew, Toby was the one least likely ever to feel embarrassed. But he did now.

"It's about last night," he began.

"The party? But it was great, wasn't it? Didn't you enjoy it?"

"Oh, yeah – 'course I did. Everyone did. Or almost everyone..."

"What are you talking about?" Jessie wanted to know. She was genuinely puzzled.

"I'm talking about Philip," Toby burst out. Surprised, Jessie noticed that he was looking quite angry. "You know, Philip – my friend. Geoff's friend. Your supposed friend!"

"Well. What about him?" Jessie suddenly began to feel uneasy.

"Look, I bet you're going to say it's none of my business, but I'm going to carry on anyway," said Toby, gazing intently into his coffee. "I think you behaved pretty shabbily last night and it's not like you. At least, it's not like the person you used to be, before you took up with Rick the Slick. Now, I'm not so sure."

Jessie stared at him, an icy feeling creeping very slowly up her back. Until this moment she'd forgotten all about Philip. Now, like a video being rewound, she remembered how angry she'd felt at Rick – and how inviting Philip had been. She blushed as she remembered how she had nestled in his arms, and blushed even deeper as she replayed the scene in the garden, the long, lingering kiss.

She was speechless. How could she have led Philip on like that? Then she closed her eyes and shook her head. At the time it had all seemed perfectly logical. Of course she'd abandoned him the moment Rick arrived. It just proved that he meant nothing to her – that she'd been making do with him until the real man in her life appeared. But not for a moment had she considered how Philip felt about it all.

"I don't know what you're making such a fuss about," she mumbled now to Toby. "Philip knew all along that I was going out with Rick."

"Yes, but you hardly behaved as if you were going out with him – or anyone else," snapped Toby.

"Oh, yeah! So what were you doing – spying on me?" Jessie knew she was shouting at Toby because he was right. She hated being in the wrong.

"I didn't need to," he replied icily. "Whatever you were doing, it was in full view of everyone." He really did sound disgusted – as if he despised her. Jessie hated the very idea of that – even more than she hated having hurt Philip. Even more than she hated being wrong.

"Oh, get real!" she said, trying to sound as cool as possible. "All I was doing was flirting a little. What's so wrong with that?"

Toby gave her a long, curious look. "Oh, so that's what you were doing was it? Well, as long as you're satisfied it was all innocent fun there's nothing more I can say." Jessie was desperate now. Toby sounded so cold, so adult. It was almost like being told off by a teacher or something. She felt herself beginning to cry.

"OK, OK – I'm sorry," she muttered, not very graciously. "I s'pose I was a bit – um – thoughtless. Have you spoken to Phil at all?"

"Not exactly," Toby shrugged. "Geoff and Jane gave him a lift home last night and he was very quiet. You really humiliated him, Jess – and you must know how keen he is on you…"

Jessie nodded. It was all too obvious, suddenly, how badly she'd treated him.

"What d'you think I should do?"

"Well – what do *you* think you should do?" asked Toby gently. Now it was like being in the headmaster's study; he was pulling all the same tricks.

"Talk to him?" whispered Jessie, not much liking the idea. Toby nodded.

"You've got to, hon," he said gently. "You owe it to him. And besides – think how awful it would be for you both, acting in the pantomime with all this stuff going on between you."

By now, Jessie really was crying, and Toby was melting a little bit. "OK, OK – maybe I was coming on a bit too strong. Come here," he said. He put a brotherly arm round her and hugged her. "It'll be fine as long as you sort it out. Now then, I wonder how Dan's doing with his Citadel of Gold?"

Toby stayed for lunch, and spent a couple of

hours with Dan, poring over the computer. At about four o'clock he appeared in the door of Jessie's bedroom. She was sprawled on the bed listening to Meat Loaf and doing her homework.

"Fancy going to the pics tonight?" Toby asked. "Geoff wants to see some Mexican thing with lots of challenging subtitles. But Jane and Hazel were going on about Harrison Ford for some reason."

The old, familiar guilt and confusion spread over her. "Sorry, I can't tonight," she said. "I've got a date." Toby's face darkened very slightly, but he simply shrugged and said:

"Don't worry. Another time. See you..."

For a few moments after he'd left, Jessie felt sad. It was as if she was turning her back on her old life and her old friends, even though she knew it was silly to think that way. She wondered if that empty feeling was worse today because of Philip. It was a shock to think how badly she'd treated him, without even realizing it.

But very soon, her thoughts turned to Rick, and the evening ahead, and all her doubts and sadness began to evaporate. Last night she'd gone from the very depths of despair, when she thought he wasn't going to show up, to the heights of happiness – when he'd arrived with that lovely bracelet, taken her in his arms, and kissed her so passionately in front of the whole party.

That, she knew, had been a turning point in their relationship. He'd signalled to her how much she meant to him. Now, tonight, it would be her turn to show how much she cared.

By the time Rick turned up that evening, all

thoughts of Philip had been banished. Jessie was bubbling with excitement. She knew, she just knew, that tonight was going to be special and would herald the start of a new phase in their relationship. She'd dressed carefully – in her favourite black jeans, but with a fabulous new red jacket, and a red and black skinny jumper underneath.

It was as if her clothes reflected her new sense of hope. Rick clearly appreciated the way she looked. The moment he saw her he gave a low whistle. "You look good enough for the Ritz!" he said at once. "Which is a shame, because that's not exactly what I had in mind for tonight."

Once they were in the car he said casually: "How about coming over to my place? I'm going to cook you the best omelette and chips you've ever had in your life."

"As long as you don't expect me to make the coffee afterwards," said Jessie at once. They both laughed.

Then Rick added quietly: "Oh, no – that's not what I was expecting at all." The way he said it sent shivers of anticipation right through her. Rick must have sensed how differently she felt about him now – he knew as surely as she did that now she was ready to give herself to him totally and completely.

When they arrived at his untidy, cluttered flat he fetched a bottle of wine and two glasses. "I don't believe I've really wished you a happy birthday yet," he said, pulling her to him. "I really wanted to get to the party in time to join in the singing and everything. If it hadn't been for that story, and then the drink..."

"What drink?" she asked. "I thought you came straight to the party."

"Well, more or less," he said, looking uncomfortable. "But listen, those cops had been really good to me, letting me in on the action. The least I could do was buy them a drink later on, to thank them. I got away as soon as I could, of course."

Jessie felt a tiny part of her happiness trickling away. Surely, if he really loved her, he'd have rushed straight to her birthday party no matter what? But she told herself not to be so self-centred. Obviously his work was important. So she decided to play it cool.

"Where did you go?" she asked.

"Oh, the Malibou, I think," he said vaguely. "Yes, that's where it was."

Jessie's heart gave a leap. Wasn't that the bar where Candida said she'd been, earlier that evening, before she and Michael and Miriam had turned up at the party?

But at that moment, Rick began to kiss her, and all her doubts fled away.

"You are so gorgeous," he murmured. "When I saw you at the party last night, looking so fabulous, surrounded by all your friends, I felt like the luckiest guy in the world."

He looked deep into her eyes and she felt herself melting with pleasure. "It was great last night," he said softly. "But being alone with you is far, far better."

He poured a glass of wine for each of them, and

104

they clinked glasses solemnly as he said: "Happy birthday. I want you to have the best year yet." He led her to the sofa and they sat side by side, sipping their wine. The mood between them was electric. Jessie could barely trust herself to speak, she felt so full of love and desire and confusion.

Rick took her hand very gently. "I love you, Jess – you know that." She nodded, her heart pounding with joy. "Are you ready to love me?" She nodded. It was true. More than anything she wanted to be truly his and to make him belong to her.

He kissed her again, a long, intimate kiss full of desire.

"Are you sure?" She nodded again. "Then let's skip those omelettes," he whispered. "I'm going to take you to bed."

12

"What did you want to say to me, Jess?" Philip was gazing at her with eager eyes which made her heart sink. This wasn't going to be easy.

It was Monday lunchtime. Jessie had left a note on Philip's locker first thing in the morning, asking him to meet her at The Hungry Potato, a snack bar near the college, but not near enough to be a regular haunt among the students. Jessie had chosen it because she didn't want anyone eavesdropping on her big apology. Now, with Philip sitting opposite her, she realized he may have had other ideas about why she'd picked somewhere so discreet.

She took a deep breath. "Philip, I owe you an apology," she blurted out. "I shouldn't have behaved the way I did at the party."

"Correction," he put in. "You shouldn't have behaved the way you did at the end of the party. Up until then I had no complaints at all." He took her hand. "It was the most fantastic evening," he said softly. "You're great, Jessie."

"No – no, I'm not," she interrupted. The conversation was going all wrong, somehow. "Look, Philip – you know I'm going out with Rick. That's why I shouldn't have been with you in the first place."

"Oh, I see," he said, as if the whole truth had just dawned on him. "Of course – you must've felt terrible. Everything had been going so well with us but then, with Rick turning up like that, you had no choice. The party was no place to tell him it was all over." He was actually beaming now. "I must admit I felt pretty terrible when you left me standing like that and went off with Rick. I wasn't sure what to make of it, so I thought I'd give you a couple of days to decide what you were going to do. Now I can see how selfish I was being – obviously you needed time to get straight."

Jessie tried to interrupt again but he silenced her. "It's OK, really – I understand. When you're ready, I'll be waiting for you and you've no idea how happy I'm going to make you."

For a moment, at his words, Jessie remembered the night before, when she'd lain in Rick's arms, in Rick's bed. As he was about to make love to her he'd whispered: "I'm going to make you so happy, darling – I want so much to make you happy…" She sighed. It was no good thinking about that now, when here was Philip, convinced that she was about to dump Rick for him. How could this be happening?

"You're making this very difficult for me," she said awkwardly. "Philip, it's not the way you think at all. I'm not leaving Rick. Actually…" she blushed, as more moments from the previous evening flashed before her. "Actually, we're more together now than we've ever been. That's what I've been trying to tell you. That's why I wanted to apologize."

Philip was very quiet suddenly. "So you don't feel anything for me at all?"

"Oh, of course I do! I'm really fond of you. And – if you'll forgive me for leading you to expect any more than that, I hope we'll always be –"

"No! Don't say it!" he rasped. "I don't want to hear you say 'just good friends'. That's not what I want and you know it."

"I'm sorry," Jessie whispered weakly. "I didn't mean to hurt you…"

"Well, don't kid yourself!" Philip snapped. "I don't break that easily. Sure, I fancied you. When you offered yourself on a plate I wasn't going to turn you down. But since you turned out to be just a little tease I'm recovering very fast. See you at rehearsal."

He got up and stalked out, leaving Jessie staring at her baked potato. A couple of tears squeezed down her face. But she knew that she wasn't really sad. Just angry that she'd behaved wrongly. And Philip wasn't really angry, either. He was just doing his best to cover up his sadness. What a mess, she reflected.

But very soon, she'd pushed all thoughts of Philip to the very back of her mind. That afternoon Rick was picking her up from college and giving her a driving session. Her father was paying for a course of ten lessons, but that really wasn't enough to get her through her test, so she was determined to get as much practice as she could with anyone who was prepared to take her.

Her heart leapt as Rick drew up outside the college and got out of the car. He made a point of kissing her there and then, right outside the gates. She was pleased, but a bit embarrassed, too. Toby and Geoff were sauntering past them, and she was worried that Philip might be in the vicinity too. That was all she needed.

But it was good to see Rick again after what had happened the evening before.

"How's my girl?" he asked tenderly. "My own girl." Then, very elaborately, he led her round to the driver's side of his bashed-up little car and opened the door with a bow. "It's all yours, babe," he said, putting on an American accent. "Let's hit the road."

At first things went quite well. Jessie remembered what her father had told her about looking in the mirror before driving off, and gently easing the car from gear to gear. At least, that was the theory. In practice, she found that each gear change was rather jerky, and every time the car gave a bounce it seemed to emit a hiccuping noise as well. Rick tensed at every shudder.

"Careful," he said. "We're not at the Dodgems now, you know. This is a car, and I'd be grateful if you'd drive it. Not abuse it!"

Jessie rattled round a corner and ground to a rather shaky halt.

"OK, OK," she snapped. "I am only a beginner, you know. It's only my second ever go. I thought you knew that!"

"Yes, all right," he said, without much grace. "I'll try and bear that in mind. Come on, let's see if you can get slowly up this hill, using your clutch control."

He was trying to be nice, Jessie could tell. But she knew he was tense, and she suddenly remembered something her mother had once told her.

"Never let a boyfriend teach you driving, fishing or card games," she'd advised. "Your father gave me a driving lesson once, and by the end of it we'd practically broken off the engagement!"

Jessie wished she'd remembered that advice in time to avoid all this. The more Rick tried to be patient, the more she could tell he was irritated. The more tense he was, the more anxious she became. And her anxiety made her very nervous at the wheel. Time after time she'd slam on the brakes, or make the tyres squeak, or stall the engine.

At last, she decided she'd had enough. She drove home as smoothly as she could manage, which wasn't very smoothly at all really. To crown it all, something went wrong as she attempted to pull up outside the house and the engine stalled.

"What happened there?" she asked, surprised.

To her relief, Rick stopped looking worried. Instead, he burst out laughing.

"You nutter!" he said affectionately. "I might have known you'd get into a spin doing something straightforward like driving. You're amazing. You can do all these things that other people find difficult, like playing the guitar and singing. But give you a simple, practical task – and you completely fall apart."

"That's not true!" she protested. "My dad thought I was pretty good when we went out yesterday."

"Your dad thinks you know how to make the sun shine," responded Rick. He ruffled her hair. "Matter of fact, you probably do know how to do that." And he kissed her, right there in front of the house. Once again, like so many times before, Jessie felt her annoyance and her anxiety melt away in the sweetness of his kisses, the excitement that coursed through her when they were together.

"Are you coming to rehearsal tonight?" she asked, as she started to get out of the car.

"Er – no, not tonight. I'm going to be with the band. But on Thursday we're going to start full musical rehearsals. So I hope you've got your routines into shape."

That evening, Jessie arrived at the theatre in some trepidation. They were due to go over the transformation scene yet again, which meant that she'd have to face Philip. Would he still be angry with her? Would he even be prepared to act with her now?

She needn't have worried. Michael Wayne was striding around the stage looking vaguely flustered as he often did. "Right, where's the Fairy Godmother? Where's Cinderella? And where are all the reptiles and rodents?"

"That just about describes me!" said Philip, sidling up to her. "I've been more of a rat than the

111

part I'm playing. I'm sorry I walked out on you today, Jess – and I accept your apology."

Jessie was so relieved that she did a little dance on the stage, ending up with a dozen cartwheels.

"Fairy Godmother! Will you please stop being upside down!" yelled Michael. "Dancing is fine, if you want to incorporate it. The singing's going to be fine. The whip is fine. But cartwheels – they are simply not fine. Fairy godmothers do not cartwheel. Fairy godmothers stay the right way up. Get it? Got it? Good!"

Jessie and Philip started to giggle, and from then on their scene went well. There was the usual happy muddle over the performance with the rats. Everyone knew their positions, and everyone knew that if they didn't keep to them then there was a danger that they wouldn't be behind each other at the right moment. But they all tended to overact and show off. The more the rats misbehaved the more Jessie would screech in her Southern drawl:

"We-ell, I'll be darned. Them thar ra-ats think they can slither away from me but let me tell you – they can't!"

"Oh, yes, we can!" yelled the rats.

Jessie turned her back to the imaginary audience and wiggled her hips exaggeratedly. "Oh, no, they ca-an't!" she shrieked, bending down so that her head was between her legs.

"OK, OK!" laughed Michael. "Have it your own way. It's good, it's funny, I'm bored with it, I'm bored with the whole transformation. Let's have a change. Where's Buttons?"

Everyone looked round. Miriam went backstage to look for Candida but came back looking puzzled.

"She's not anywhere," she said. The now familiar shadow crept over Jessie. And the feeling was confirmed by Michael who said, looking exasperated: "Oh, I suppose she's with the band again, getting even more singing practice."

And getting in even more time with Rick, thought Jessie. She was cross with herself for feeling so jealous. She was the one he loved, wasn't she? She was the one he'd made love to. There couldn't be anything between him and any other girl now.

But still she couldn't quite suppress the nagging doubts that clouded her happiness. For the rest of the rehearsal her spirits were low and somehow the lines she was speaking didn't seem funny any more.

"What's the matter with you?" demanded Miriam crossly as, for the seventh time in a row, Jessie forgot to stand back, arms raised, for the change of dress. They hadn't actually practised this scene properly, with the dry ice. Michael said that could wait for the dress rehearsal. But what was meant to happen was that while the dry ice swirled round the stage, Miriam would rush into the wings, put on her ball gown, and rush back in time for the spotlight to beam away from Jessie and on to her. It was, naturally, her favourite moment in the whole show and she hated Jessie for spoiling it.

"I suppose you're worried about your precious

boyfriend getting all matey with Little Miss Buttons," she said cattily.

" 'Course I'm not," Jessie retorted. "I'm actually worried more about the lizards and the rats. Come on, let's do it one more time." And, as bravely as she could, she did her very best to shout out her comic lines, while inside a knot of worry was winding all round her heart and threatening to break it.

13

The college gym was empty – except for two figures, one leaning against the other at a precarious angle. The upright one was Jessie. The other, tilted in a straight line as if drunk, so that his head reached just below her shoulder, was Toby. They were quite still, frozen like statues.

"Hold it, hold it, hold it – OK stop!" he said after a few moments. He slithered up again and gave her a triumphant grin. "That was fine – much better!" he added. "Now, four or five more times and it's a roll, as they say in showbiz."

Jessie groaned. "Slave driver!" she accused him. "I thought it was a little help you were offering, not a gruelling night of personal Olympic training! Anyhow, I thought you said I was doing all right."

"You are, you're fine." Toby looked at her appraisingly, his nose wrinkling as it often did when he was thinking hard. "At least, most of it's fine. I just can't figure out why you seem to be having such trouble with this one routine. It's not as if it was particularly difficult, but I get this sense that your body is refusing to perform properly for you, as if you were inhibited about something. And that's definitely not like you."

Jessie flushed and felt alarmed. Toby knew her too well, that was the trouble. She'd asked him to go through the dance routines with her because they hadn't been going too well. And last night's rehearsal had almost been a disaster.

This was the only choreographed dance that she had to do in the show, apart from a few very easy slapstick routines with the mice and rats and lizards. Although she hadn't had any formal dance training she hadn't expected to have any problems. Inside her, she knew it wasn't the dancing that was the problem at all really. It was her partner. Toby, as usual, had got right to the heart of what was bothering her.

Michael had decided that when the Fairy God-mother and Buttons had their touching scene together, after Cinderella had swept off to the ball in the magic coach, they should add a little dance to the duet they sang together. Jessie had never quite got used to the toned-down version of the song. She much preferred the raunchy country style that she used when she first appeared to Cinderella. She resented having to make it prettier for Candida, who had a pretty voice but nothing like as strong as Jessie's.

As far as Jessie was concerned, that was hard enough. Now she had to perform a jolly little dance during the musical break of the song –

which involved stepping arm in arm with the one girl in the world she really didn't feel like hugging. Even worse, the whole thing ended with Buttons, straight as a poker, tilting across the stage as if falling to the ground, and landing instead on her shoulder. And last night she'd felt herself rebelling. Every time they tried the dance and Candida began to fall towards her she'd panic. At one point she stepped backwards so that instead of landing on her, Candida collapsed on to the floor.

"What is the matter with you, Jess?" she'd demanded crossly, rubbing her side. "It's perfectly easy. At least, it is for anyone who knows anything about dancing."

Michael ran his hands wildly through his hair, looking exasperated. "Look, love," he began patiently, "we're not asking a great deal. Just relax, let Candy fall down towards you and at the moment of impact you can support her from behind. That way you won't need to worry about the impact."

The more he advised her and Candida taunted her the more stiff and awkward she became. It was terrible. And it would have been even worse if Toby hadn't been there. Michael called a five minute break and then said, quite threateningly for him, that they would have one more go at the dance routine and he expected it to go smoothly.

Jessie sat slumped backstage, sipping hot chocolate from a flask and feeling miserable. She just wasn't used to messing things up. It was so galling! This whole scene was meant to be the

Fairy Godmother consoling Buttons because the girl he loved had no feelings for him at all. She'd rushed off in all her finery without even saying goodbye to him. In fact, the Fairy Godmother could barely bring herself to touch Buttons because he – or rather she – may well be stealing her own boyfriend!

"You're getting into a panic over nothing," said a gentle voice beside her. It was Toby, who crouched down, took her drink without asking, and helped himself to a few sips of the hot chocolate. "Look, if you try to relax for the last part of the rehearsal, I'll go through the whole thing with you tomorrow if you want."

Jessie brightened at once. "Would you? Would you really? That'd make all the difference." Then she looked crestfallen. "But how am I going to get through it tonight? I'm hopeless – I really am. Maybe we should just drop the dance. The song's OK."

"Don't be crazy," said Toby. "It's a pantomime. You've got to have a dance. But try not to take it all so seriously. You've got a great character there – just carry on thinking you're the Queen of the Silver Dollar, forget about yourself, and whatever you do forget that Buttons is really Candida. That's what real actors do."

"Don't you mean Candy?" snarled Jessie viciously. She hated it when people like Michael called her that. It was as if they were part of her magic circle. Most of all, she hated it when Rick called her that.

"Come on, Jess, she's not so bad," said Toby. "I

reckon she's just a bit off with you because you give off these terrible unfriendly vibes. You need to loosen up, you know." He pulled her to her feet and squeezed her hand. "But if you can't manage that, just stick with the acting. She's a lovelorn kitchen boy and you are a country mama who can steer horses and kill rabbits and make apple pie..." He tailed off then, but Jessie was laughing and beginning to feel much better.

So, with Toby's help, she'd managed to get through the dance. It wasn't brilliant. She was still rather stiff and inhibited. But she got the steps more or less right, she put her arm round Candida's waist without flinching and she even managed to catch her at the right place at the end.

It was quite late by then and Jessie was exhausted. She was also feeling anxious. Rick was due to pick her up at the theatre and drive her home. She was very glad he hadn't been there to witness her appalling performance during the dance, but now she was beginning to look round anxiously and the usual knots were forming in her stomach.

She had pinned so many hopes, more than she'd even realized, on the idea that if only she and Rick became lovers then everything would be perfect. She wouldn't be plagued by jealousy and doubts and he, in turn, would have no reason even to look at other girls. She would be all he needed or wanted. So far, though, very little had changed. He loved her, she was sure he did. But, if anything, she felt even more unsure than she had before.

Suddenly, all the lights went out. There was a hush, followed by shouts and a hubbub of voices. And seconds later the whole auditorium was alight with darting sequins of fire. At first Jessie was dazzled by the flashing lights and general chaos. Then it dawned on her. Of course! Tonight was Bonfire Night, and the lights were sparklers. Very soon Rick was beside her, thrusting more sparklers into her hands as he kissed her.

"Let's light up the place first," he whispered. "Then I'm going to take you home so we can light up the night." Jessie shivered with excitement and pleasure. This new phase of their love affair was full of promise and adventure. Rick was loving, sexy and considerate. Yet still she couldn't banish the foolish doubts that pricked her in a thousand places, just as the sparklers were stinging the darkness.

Everyone was milling around the stage and the theatre. Michael was shouting rather nervously that they should be careful, that he wasn't sure if the theatre was insured for this kind of thing. But no one took much notice. They were having fun and sparklers, after all, were indoor fireworks.

They cast a rather eerie light over the place. No one quite looked like themselves, and as everyone was playing with the sparklers, writing their names in the air and waving them above their heads, you only occasionally caught glimpses of people's faces. Jessie spotted Toby, laughing and teasing some of the girls in the cast. And Hazel, who'd arrived with Luke at the same time as Rick. The two of them seemed to be getting on very well and were kissing as they linked arms, their faces bathed in the glow of the sparklers.

Once Jessie saw Candida's face, lit by what looked like a bouquet of fire. Rick was holding the sparklers and saying something in her ear. Candida was nodding and laughing, her face glowing strangely in the unreal white dancing lights.

At that moment there was a sudden flare, turning the white light to bright orange. Candida's raucous laugh became a piercing scream. A spark had somehow caught a strand of her hair, and set it alight. Like a fuse, the flame shot right up to the top of her head. There were a few seconds of confusion. But that was all. Rick came to the rescue. He simply pulled out a handkerchief and damped the flame with it, hardly seeming even to rush. His calm action put out the fire at once, and seemed to soothe Candida, who collected herself quickly, and smiled adoringly at Rick.

"OK, OK – that's enough!" Michael was instantly by her side, his face contorted with anxiety and irritation. "You're all right, aren't you? You're sure you're all right?" he asked her. Then, his arms flapping in all directions, he suddenly started shouting at everyone. "That's enough! I knew something like this would happen. Come on, everyone – let's wrap it up here. Next rehearsal, Sunday night. And don't forget, it's our first rehearsal with the band."

A very short while later, Jessie was in Rick's arms, in his bed. He was making love to her, and she was clinging to him, her every thought and all her desires wrapped up in this moment of longing and loving. Yet even as he murmured her name, and whispered how much he wanted her, an unwelcome picture flashed into her mind. Even at that moment, she remembered Rick, standing close to Candida, the two of them laughing, Candida gazing up at him adoringly as he rescued her from the flames.

Now, with Toby's arm round her shoulders, and hers round his waist as they stepped through the dance routine yet again, Jessie found herself reliving those strange, tormented thoughts. The joy and ecstasy of being with Rick; the torture of wondering about Candida. And, yet again, she tripped and stepped on Toby's toe.

"Look, you're not trying," he said, pretending she'd really hurt him. He hopped round the gym a few times faking agony. "Let's do the song again, then go into the routine. I'm not giving up until you're perfect, so you might as well make an effort."

He rewound the tape in the little portable music centre, until the place where the band struck up for Jessie's theme tune.

It's the magic – the magic of love
A love that has to be true
And if you – if you truly believe
Then one day it will happen to you.

They were standing arm in arm as they harmonized the chorus. Toby was a good, strong singer, and Jessie thought the song had never sounded quite so good. It was so nice to be singing with him that she found it quite easy to put her arm round him, and lead him into the simple dance steps that had been giving her so much trouble.

Strangely, Jessie was sorry when the finale was over. They'd held their pose, and now Toby was straightening up and moving away from her.

"See, I told you it was easy," he said gruffly. "You shouldn't have any problems if you do it like that."

"I think I know the trick," she told him triumphantly. "I'll just pretend it's you pressing up against me instead of Candida, and I'll be fine." She gave him a bright, flirty smile. "I might even enjoy it."

Toby didn't look at her. He was busy packing away the ghetto blaster. "Yeah, well, anything that turns you on," he muttered. "Just remember I'm here if you need me." Jessie felt oddly sad as she and Toby wandered home that evening and he gave one of his funny waves at her door. She just couldn't work out why.

14

Jessie had begun to settle into a new routine. There was college every day of course, and rehearsals on Tuesdays and Thursdays, as well as at the weekends. She saw Rick most weekends and at least twice during the week, though she still had her eleven o'clock curfew except on Saturdays. Rick was always teasing her about it.

"I wish you wouldn't go on about my Cinderella complex!" she'd complain. He'd usually just nuzzle her neck or kiss her tenderly, and say affectionately: "It's only because I can never get enough of you. Why can't you just tell your mum that I'll promise you get to bed on time, as long as you're with me?"

Jessie would always laugh along with him but at the same time she felt uncomfortable. Most evenings that they spent together they would end up making love and she would feel closer and closer entwined with him, almost as if they were the same person, the same body. But then he'd drive her home, leaving her rather forlornly on her front doorstep, and off he'd cruise on his own, living a late night life while she battled with delayed homework and early nights. She couldn't help wondering where he went afterwards and who he saw but she had decided not to ask or probe. Rick hated the idea of being cross-questioned, as he put it. She just had to pretend that everything was fine.

The worst times were always after rehearsals. Jessie was convinced that Rick would be back with Candida the minute he'd dropped her home. She had no proof, of course, she just felt it. And she'd pick up on every little hint, every possible nuance, and interpret it as more evidence that there was something going on between them.

Her insecurity and all her suspicions came to a head one Thursday evening towards the end of November. It was the very first rehearsal with the band. Before that, they'd had to make do with tapes. So this was an important moment, especially as it was the first time Rick had heard the duet performed by Jessie and Candida.

Jessie had made up her mind that she just had to make the scene a success. And at first all her hard work seemed to be paying off. She remembered everything Toby had taught her – singing heartily with Candida, gazing at her fondly just as a Fairy Godmother should do, dancing the jaunty little steps arm in arm, and forcing herself to relax for that last moment, when Buttons fell across the stage and landed just beneath her chin. She thought she'd really pulled it off.

Then Rick's icy voice cut through the auditorium. "It doesn't work!" he announced. "That duet is going to have to change."

"What – what do you mean?" stammered Jessie.

"Well, for a start, your voices aren't balanced properly. Candy's too quiet, you're too screechy, you're just not balanced properly."

"Oh, no!" Candida murmured in Jessie's ear. "I knew it! It's because my voice isn't as strong as yours. I'm too reedy!"

Privately, Jessie agreed with her. But that didn't seem to be what Rick meant at all.

"You're just going to have to tone it down, Jess," he said. "Harmonies don't work if one voice dominates the other. And besides..." This was the bit that really hurt her. "Besides, you're coming on far too strong. Try and bring out the melody, a bit more like Candy does. I want this sweet and lilting, OK?"

Jessie was scarlet with humiliation. How could Rick have criticized her like that? And how could he prefer Candida's anaemic little performance to her own full-blooded one? But there was nothing she could do or say – not in front of the whole cast, and certainly not in front of Candida.

She just had to stay on stage, suppressing all her natural power and strength in order to match Candida's soft, pretty little voice.

Later, she tried to tackle Rick about it. "I don't know why you had to be so horrible," she said. "It wasn't as if I was all that bad. You could have talked about it afterwards or something..."

But Rick couldn't see why she was so upset. "I

thought you'd want to be treated like a professional," he said. "You wouldn't catch a real performer making a fuss about a simple little direction."

"It wasn't a simple direction!" she stormed. "You just told me I was rubbish in front of everyone. OK, so maybe you do think I'm vulgar and over the top and not sweet-sounding enough. Well, I'd far rather be me and too loud than some other people who are subtle and boring and can't even hold down a tune!"

She didn't really mean to criticize Candida so directly, but she'd been genuinely stung at Rick's comparison between them. She wondered whether he'd defend Candida now, against her spiteful words. But all he said was:

"OK, sorry, love. I didn't mean to put you down. Let's talk about the weekend—"

He broke off, his face a picture of guilt. "Oh, no – I forgot! I'm on assignment this weekend. I'll be in Manchester until Sunday at the earliest. But I can come and pick you up and we can spend the evening at my place."

"Oh, no we can't!" rejoined Jessie, still smarting from their row. "As a matter of fact I won't be around on Sunday night. We've got a gig, a proper gig with real loud music and I'm going to sing properly for once, the way I want to! And no one's going to tell me to tone it down because guess what? People like it the way I do it. Right?"

Rick looked rather astonished at her outburst, but he grinned good-humouredly.

"I keep telling you, you're talented in lots of

ways. I love the way you sing in the band, it's great. Tell you what, I'll give you a ring when I get back from Manchester and we'll spend some time together before your gig. Some real quality time." He kissed her tenderly and she melted against him. So what if he made her feel unsure of herself sometimes? It was worth it, for all the good times. After all, lots of girls would give anything for a guy like Rick, she told herself. Someone who couldn't wait to get her alone, to kiss her and make love to her.

The Sunday night gig, at a youth club near the college, was their first for ages. The pantomime was eating into everyone's time so they'd only managed one quick rehearsal and they weren't adding any new numbers to the repertoire. They'd arranged to meet at six o'clock, two hours early, so that they could practise one more time and get the sound right.

By early afternoon Jessie was in her now familiar state of confusion. She was looking forward to the gig. As she lay in the bath, letting rip with all her favourite numbers, she realized how much she'd missed the pure, unadulterated high of being on stage and belting out loud, heavy, wild rock.

But her excitement was mingled with anxiety. She wanted to see Rick. She needed him – needed to know that everything was all right between them after that stinging row. If only he'd get back early – if only he'd ring now to say he'd be over right away because he couldn't bear to be parted from her for another moment.

But he didn't. Two o'clock ticked slowly by ... three o'clock came and went. Jessie brushed her hair obsessively and piled it into an even wilder style than usual, with silver scarves and spikes. Then she squeezed into a new, shiny black mini-dress that looked like leather when she was on stage, but felt like satin.

It was four-thirty when Rick finally showed up. Jessie flung a big coat over her band clothes and rushed out of the house as soon as she saw his car. As she opened the passenger door Rick grinned: "Not so fast, Miss Daisy. I thought you were supposed to be the driver round here."

Jessie was a little disappointed. Of course, she was pleased to get any practice she could, since she was only getting two professional lessons a week. But she'd had a rather different idea about how they were going to spend this precious time together. And she'd hoped Rick had been thinking along the same lines.

And of course, because it was Rick sitting next to her, watching her every move, she kept making mistakes – jerking the little Metro in a series of bumps and gear crashes until he finally lost patience.

"I thought you said you'd done three-point turns!" he snapped.

"I did – I can do them really well with my teacher," she protested.

"Some teacher," he sneered. "Seems to me you don't know the very first rule."

"Which is?" demanded Jessie, unsuccessfully attempting to restart the engine.

129

"If you want to impress your boyfriend, don't mess with his clutch!" he retorted. "Come on, Jess, let's go home. I want three kisses for every time you stall my engine." Then he grinned and ruffled her hair affectionately. "I keep telling you, love – stick to what you're good at. It doesn't matter if your driving's a bit dodgy as long as you can set me on fire the way you do."

"You don't have to be so patronizing," protested Jessie furiously. But then he leant over and kissed her, and her anger evaporated away as it always did.

"Let's go back to the flat," he whispered. Jessie looked at her watch and gasped. It was half-past five. "I've got to get to the gig," she said.

"Oh, come on – just a quick coffee," urged Rick. "I'll get you to the gig, don't worry."

When they arrived at the flat, Jessie slipped off her coat. Rick took one look at her and drew in his breath sharply. "That is some dress," he murmured, pulling her into his arms. His hands slid down the shiny, skin-tight fabric, snaking along the contours of her body. "Oh, God, Jessie – you are so sexy!" he groaned, covering her face with hot, searching kisses.

"Rick – I can't," Jessie protested. "I told you – I've got to get to the gig by six." But Rick simply held her even tighter, his body pressing urgently against hers as his hands roamed up and down her back. There was just one brief moment of doubt, as Jessie remembered the others, waiting for her at the youth club. She should really be there first, because it was her turn to set up the sound system. And in any case, they were relying on her for the final practice.

But somehow, as she twined her arms round Rick's neck and sank into his scorching embrace, nothing seemed to matter but his passion, his desire, his overwhelming need for her.

It was nearly two hours later when Jessie finally arrived at the club. "I'm sorry everyone – I'm really sorry!" she panted as she rushed in. The other three were on stage and Toby was singing. He stopped abruptly at her arrival, his face a mask of fury.

"Oh, don't worry," he spat. "We were managing perfectly without you. After all, we're beginning to get used to the kind of person you've become. But don't think you can stay in this band if you can't even bother to show up on time."

Hazel looked worried, Geoff embarrassed. Toby was so angry that he couldn't even shout at her. He just quickly told her the running order of the songs and ignored her when she tried to apologize for being so late.

She played her heart out for the next two hours. It was the best way of drowning out her anguish about Rick. And she was trying to make up to the others for letting them down so badly.

She went really crazy during their final number, which was a very beaty version of "Baby Come Back" – she played a wild guitar solo, then gyrated round the stage to Hazel's screaming saxophone. As they screeched out the final notes, the audience burst into a frenzy of clapping, whistling and stamping.

Afterwards, though, there was still a definite frost in the atmosphere and Toby was still studiously ignoring her.

"Look – I really am sorry, I couldn't help it," she tried to say. But Toby shook her hand off his shoulder and refused to be placated, even though Jessie went out of her way to do more than her usual share of coiling up the wires of the sound system and putting away speakers and instruments.

"Coming for a coffee?" said Hazel, the peacemaker, when it was time to leave. Jessie took one forlorn look at her three best friends, now ranged against her. She shook her head sadly.

"Not tonight – I don't somehow think I'm wanted." And no one tried to come after her as she made her own, lonely way into the deserted street.

When she got home that evening, she popped her head round the living-room door to say good evening. Sitting next to her mother on the sofa was Mrs Manley, her hand full of a sheaf of documents.

"Hello, dear," she said with an ingratiating smile. "Just the person I wanted to see. I was showing your mother these sponsor forms, they're to raise money for the local hospice. All you need to do is go without your favourite foods for a month, and you get people to sponsor you per item per week. So you see someone could pick chocolate, or butter or something and put down, say, a pound for every week that you did without it. Isn't it a marvellous idea?"

"As long as no one suggests I do without my own creature comforts," added Jessie's dad, pouring himself a whisky. Mrs Manley shot him a disapproving look.

"I'm asking your mother if she'll help out by distributing a few of the forms among her circle, which," she added with a little sniff, "is rather different from my own. And it would be simply wonderful if you could help out too, dear. I'm trying to get my Candida involved and of course she'd love to but she is just so busy these days. That hotel is working her all hours. Next Thursday she has to leave work for rehearsal, then go back to the hotel for the night shift. Honestly…"

But Jessie didn't hear the rest of the monologue. A piercing pain shot through her. She remembered so clearly what Candida had been saying last time she'd seen her. Michael had asked if everyone would be available for the following week's rehearsals because they'd be concentrating on the songs. Candida had said: "I'll be there all day if you need me, we're having such a slack time. Two conferences have been cancelled for next week – if I'm not careful they won't be needing me at all."

So she'd been lying! She wasn't working late at all. In fact, she was working less than usual. So where was she going after rehearsal on Thursday? And where would Rick be after he'd dropped her off home at eleven o'clock?

15

Jessie lay awake all night, fretting about what she'd heard and going over the same pattern of thoughts again and again. So what if Candida was lying to her mother? Why was that any business of hers? Then unwelcome images would flash into her mind of Rick's face close to Candida's; his hand putting out the flame of her hair; the two of them laughing together.

Then Jessie would remember the good times with Rick: the way they laughed together; their passionate love-making that afternoon, when he'd told her over and over again how much he wanted her; the way he looked at her when she was singing…

And that, of course, reminded her of how quick he was to attack her singing these days, and how anxious to protect Candida. It all seemed to piece together so neatly, she tormented herself. Then she became outraged, at the thought of how only this evening she had betrayed her friends, nearly

wrecked their gig, broken the most basic trust –
for a man who probably wasn't even being faithful
to her.

And as she tossed and turned in the darkness,
assailed by the crossfire of her tortured thoughts,
Jessie knew she would never have any peace of
mind until she knew for sure what was going on
between Rick and Candida, and why Candida was
telling all her lies.

By the next day, Jessie had made a plan. It was
wild and hazardous, but it was the best she could
think of and it gave her a sense of purpose which
would help propel her through the next four days
until she could carry it out.

But they were four very difficult days. Jessie
felt as though she was in a daze most of the time,
drifting through her days at college without really
taking much in. It was as though she was in the
grip of an obsession. All she could think about was
her plan for finding out the truth – a plan so
secret she couldn't even tell her best friends. And
she wasn't even sure how many of those she had
left.

"Seeing Rick this week then?" Hazel asked one
day.

"Er, no – not till Thursday," replied Jessie.

"What's up? Have you two had a row or something?" Hazel asked curiously.

"No, of course not," snapped Jessie. "What d'you
mean?"

"Oh, come off it, I am supposed to be your best
friend, Jess. So I sort of notice when you're not
right. Shall we begin with Sunday night?"

Jessie looked wary. "Look, I've said I'm sorry about that. I know I let you down badly."

Hazel sighed. "I didn't bring this up to get at you. I'm worried, that's all. It's just not like you to behave like this. And I want to help. So shoot!"

Jessie felt tears dart to her eyes. She so longed to pour out her heart to Hazel. But this time, she knew she had to keep her secret to herself. So she decided to hint at some of what was troubling her.

"Oh, I suppose this pantomime is getting to be a bit of a strain," she admitted. "You see, when Rick first saw me I was singing with the band and he really seemed to be impressed. Now, with this song I have to do, he's so critical of me..."

"Oh, well, everyone knows why that is," scoffed Hazel. "It's because Candida can't keep up with you. Your voice is so much better. It's obvious to all of us in the band."

Jessie looked at her sharply. "Does she practise that much with the band, then?" she asked at once.

"Well, she did for a while," said Hazel. "But now you come to mention it, she hasn't been around that much for rehearsals lately... Hey, wait a minute, Jessie – you're not still jealous of Candy are you? I thought we'd gone through all that ages ago."

Jessie forced a watery smile. "Oh, no – of course not. Not really. I just, er, just wondered why everything has to be adjusted for her – even if it makes the show worse, that's all."

"It won't make it worse," said Hazel. "You're both good, but the song won't sound right unless your voices are balanced. Honestly, Jess, that's all there is to it. Rick's crazy about you, not Candy. So cool out, will you?"

But Jessie couldn't cool out. She went through her days in a dream, her eyes glittering strangely, her face hot and feverish. And each night she lay awake, plotting and fretting as the day of reckoning drew nearer.

"Are you OK, love?" her mum asked at breakfast on Wednesday morning. "You're looking very flushed. Sure you're not coming down with something?"

Exhausted and shivery after a string of anxious days and sleepless nights, Jessie looked at her mother blankly for a few moments.

"Erm, nothing really," she muttered. Then she thought better of it. "Actually, Mum, I'm not feeling all that great. Didn't sleep too well…"

"You've been working too hard, dear," said her mother, looking worried. "All your studies, and the pantomime on top of everything. Look, I'm not going in to work today. Why not stay at home with me and have a rest? You'll make yourself ill if you don't let up a little."

So Jessie allowed herself to stay in bed all morning and be spoiled by her mother. In the afternoon, she said brightly: "I'm feeling ever so much better now, Mum. And you know what would really cheer me up?"

"What, darling?" asked her mother, who was sipping a cup of tea and catching up with *Neighbours*.

"How about giving me some driving practice?"

Jessie suggested. "It's ages since I had a go of Dad's car, and it's so much nicer than the driving school old wreck."

With the Volvo waiting tantalizingly just outside the house, she was all too aware that a bit of extra practice was just what she needed. Jessie's dad had been away for a few days and had left the car. So she gazed cajolingly at her mother and added: "Besides, it'd be lovely to have you sit with me for a change. Everyone else is so critical."

She was right, too. It did cheer her up to be in the driving seat, with her mother chattering away next to her. Mum was great like that, she reflected. She just assumed you knew what you were doing and let you get on with it. It was almost like driving without anyone at all breathing down her neck. At the end of their outing Jessie was feeling much more confident about her driving, and much happier, too, about everything she'd decided to do the very next day.

"I may not be here when you get home tonight," her mother said the following evening as Jessie was getting ready to leave. Great! she thought, pinning her beloved guitar brooch to her jacket collar.

"Oh, really?" she remarked, trying to sound bored. "Will Dan be OK?"

"He'll be fine. I'll just be distributing a few more of those wretched sponsor forms. I wish I'd never agreed to help out."

At the rehearsal, Jessie was quiet and tense. For most of the evening they were rehearsing some of the ball scenes which didn't involve her.

Rick was vaguely helping out with the music although he didn't really have a lot to do either. So Jessie sat in the stalls, watching him, wondering about him, feeling strangely detached from him now that she was so close to finding out whether he was cheating on her.

She and Candida were only needed tonight for the finale, when the whole ensemble gathered on stage to sing a reprise of *The Magic of Love*. Still feeling as if she was watching herself going through the motions, Jessie acted and sang more forcefully than usual, grabbing Candida by the waist and joining in the general upbeat spirit of the chorus. Toby was right, she thought. It really does work, imagining that you are someone else.

"You're awfully quiet tonight, hon," remarked Rick, as people started to leave. "You OK? I mean, do you fancy going out for a coffee or something? Haven't seen you for so long – I've really missed you this week."

"Well, I am a bit tired," admitted Jessie. "Would you mind if we didn't go anywhere? I think I just need to get home and have an early night."

She could have sworn that a look of relief passed fleetingly over his face. Of course! she thought triumphantly. If he gets me home early that leaves him more time to get back to Candida! Everything was beginning to piece together now.

She was silent as Rick drove her home. He kept glancing at her, looking concerned. It was only just after half-past ten when he pulled up outside her house. "You're sure you're OK?" he asked tenderly. Jessie nearly laughed out loud at his audacity. He actually sounded concerned, as if he really cared about her. Little did he realize how she'd seen through all his tricks, his lies, his deceit.

Well, he wasn't the only one who could put on an act. She turned to him and smiled sweetly. "I'll be fine, as long as I get a good night's sleep," she said. Then she leaned over and kissed him caressingly on the lips. "Maybe you should get to bed early yourself," she added lightly, while inside she was thinking scornfully: *Yes, that's exactly what you'll be doing, you and Candida. Only tonight, you're going to be found out once and for all!*

After she left him and let herself into the house, everything went surprisingly smoothly. Her mother was still out, which was very convenient. As an extra precaution, she deliberately picked a fight with Dan about who was going to use the bathroom first, and made a great display of having to get to bed. By five to eleven Dan was in bed, her mother hadn't come home, her father, of course, was still away. It was very easy to slip downstairs and out of the front door. Not even the cat noticed she was gone.

She did experience one or two qualms as she let herself into her father's precious Volvo and slid into the driver's seat. He'd been so trusting to give her that special key of her own. She had a momentary qualm – then quashed it. How could anything be more important than her moment of discovery – her unmasking of Rick and his terrible deceit?

She tuned the radio to her favourite pirate

station and popped a bag of pear drops into the glove compartment. Might as well make myself at home, she thought.

Jessie loved the feeling of power that filled her as she started the engine and began to drive down the street. It was so exciting to be in charge, completely in charge, with no one telling her what to do. And, even better, she had a mission to accomplish.

A few minutes later she was pulling into Candida's road. There was the big double-fronted house. There was Candida's little green car. And – yes! There was Candida herself, at spot on eleven o'clock, carefully closing the front door and stepping down the path. She took for ever to strap herself into the car and start the engine. At least, it seemed that way to Jessie, skulking just a few yards behind her in the darkness. But eventually, Candida pulled away from the kerb, unaware of the dark, silent shadow behind her.

Jessie was so tense that she could only think about one thing: keeping on Candida's tail, following her through the quiet back roads and on to the main highway until all her secrets were uncovered.

When they reached the open road, Candida quickened her pace. Jessie did, too. They were driving along the main road that led out of town and towards the hotel. Jessie felt a momentary panic. Suppose she really was going to work? Suppose all her suspicions had been madly, crazily wrong – and Candida was simply off to do her job, just as she'd told her mother she was.

Then, suddenly, she signalled left. Jessie, just a short distance behind her, did the same. Candida turned into a side road and drove a very short distance before she pulled up outside a pub. A tall, rangy figure emerged from the shadows and right up to Candida's car. Candida leant over to open the passenger door. He bent down and, with a blinding flash of anguish and fury, Jessie saw them lock into a long kiss.

And that was the last thing she saw before the sudden bang, the tinkle of glass, the heavy jolt ... and then everything turned black.

16

"Jessie! *Jessie! Are you all right?*" Through the blackness and then the dizziness as she began to return to consciousness, Jessie was aware of a familiar voice calling her name anxiously over and over again. Confused and sick, she tried to open her eyes, then quickly closed them again as the world seemed to rotate precariously round her. Something was wrong. She knew that deep voice – would have known it anywhere. But why wasn't it Rick's voice? Where was Rick?

"Rick…" she murmured weakly.

"He's not here," said the voice. "Look at me, Jessie, and tell me you're OK." With great difficulty Jessie forced her eyes open and found herself gazing into the pale, worried face of Michael Wayne!

Horror washed over her in huge waves. It must be a nightmare, she thought wildly. She was still only half awake, and only slowly began to piece together what must be happening. There were so many awful things that her addled brain decided to deal with them one at a time, in order of importance.

"My dad's car!" she managed to moan. "Have I – has it…?"

"Don't worry about it," soothed Michael. "You're OK, that's the most important thing."

Jessie suddenly became very agitated – so much so that she began to forget the pain in her head and the sick feeling that engulfed her.

"What do you mean, don't worry?" she demanded, sounding almost like her old self. "How can I not worry? I wish I'd been hurt, anything, just so long as the car ends up in one piece." And then, quite suddenly, she burst into tears – great wracking sobs which only reminded her of the terrible mess she was in.

"It's not bad, honestly," Michael soothed her. "Just a buckled bumper."

"Really?" sniffed Jessie eventually, her tears beginning to dry up.

"Oh, and … erm … a couple of head lamps," Michael added. She burst into tears all over again.

"Look, Jessie, I think we'd all better have a little talk, don't you?" suggested Michael wearily. He disappeared for a moment, then returned to the car and made Jessie move into the passenger seat. "Coffee first," he announced. "Then I rather think we've all got some explaining to do."

He was silent as he drove back to the main road, on the tail of Candida's little green car, and then to the hotel. Disjointed thoughts raced through

Jessie's mind. What was he doing with Candida? Where was Rick? And what, oh what, was she going to say to her father about his beloved car? And about the trust she had broken so violently?

The first thing she noticed as Michael led her into the coffee bar in the hotel was the cool, almost icy figure sitting waiting for them. Candida was gazing intently at a menu and barely glanced up as they joined her. Jessie was puzzled. But then, everything about this ghastly night was rather unreal.

"Now, how are you feeling, Jessie?" asked Michael gently.

Jessie gulped. "Not bad," she conceded. "I – I don't actually feel ill or anything, just a bit shaken up."

"Well, you certainly had us worried," said Michael heartily. "Didn't she, Candy?" Jessie winced involuntarily. She so hated it when people used that silly name for Candida. Especially, tonight, when she was being anything but sweet and cuddly. More like sorbet, Jessie thought to herself.

Candida gave a slight, imperceptible shrug. Jessie got the distinct impression that if anyone had been worried about her, even for a second, it probably hadn't been Candida. A scuff mark on her new boots would have worried her more. Or a slight change in the weather.

"Anyway, I'm fairly sure it's nothing very serious," Michael continued, still desperately trying to sound cheerful. "I think you just fainted from shock, and it always feels terrible afterwards. But you're not concussed or anything.

Thank goodness you were wearing your safety belt or you might have done yourself a bit more damage. Not that you were going very fast... But driving straight into the back of a stationary vehicle isn't exactly recommended in *The Highway Code*, you know."

"I know," agreed Jessie dolefully. "I've been reading it every night in bed, studying for the test."

"You – er... What did you say?" Michael looked aghast.

"Yes, that's part of the problem," Jessie said tonelessly. "I'm still a learner. And apparently it says in *The Highway Code* that they specially don't recommend driving into the back of stationary vehicles if you haven't passed your test."

Michael's face had turned from pale to sheet white. Candida's expression had not changed at all.

"I think it's time we ordered the coffee," she drawled.

They sat for a while in tense silence. Then, when the coffee arrived, Michael said:

"Right, time for some straight talking. What were you doing driving along that country lane all by yourself, late at night, without, it transpires, a licence?"

Jessie took a deep breath, and then blurted out the truth. The whole truth. How she'd begun to suspect that Rick was more interested in Candida than in her. How she began to piece together all the evidence until she became quite convinced that they were seeing each other secretly, late at night, having a torrid, passionate affair.

"It was driving me crazy," she wept, the tears

146

splashing into her coffee. "I just got fixed on this one idea that I had to catch them in the act and prove that I was right. It sounds stupid, I know it does." She looked earnestly at Candida, whose face was now even more an expressionless mask. It was hardly inviting, but Jessie plunged on regardless. "I'm sorry, Candida, I really am. I can see I got it all wrong. And I should never have gone spying on you."

"Think nothing of it," Candida remarked drily, sipping her espresso. Jessie was furious with her for acting so calmly in the middle of such a drama. A little bit of her was rather impressed, too.

"Well, er – I think after all that," said Michael, obviously distressed, "we owe you a bit of an explanation, too." He looked anxiously at Candida but her face remained blank.

"Jessie, I wouldn't want – well, neither of us would want this to go any further, as I'm sure you'll understand," he blustered. "But as you can see –" He waved rather ineffectually towards Candida. Jessie stared at them, first one and then the other, as light after light began to dawn.

Of course! Candida had been lying to her mother, but not because she was seeing Rick. It was Michael she was seeing. Michael she was hanging around for after rehearsals. Michael she was waiting for, all those evenings she chose to spend with the band. Jessie suddenly remembered the night of her party – how Candida had arrived with Michael, late at night...

"You know how it is," Michael confided. "You can't explain love, it's just that magic something that happens between two people. You see, Jessie, I took on the pantomime because I was going to be at home for a while and because I really wanted to give something back to this community, after all it had given to me."

Jessie vaguely realized that he was talking as if he was reading one of those advertisements you have to sit through at the cinema before you get to the film. But maybe, she thought, just maybe, he was trying to tell her something important.

"Between you and us," he continued in a confiding tone, "I wasn't all that happy about the baby. I mean, obviously, I couldn't have been that happy or I wouldn't have started –" He broke off, then, and gave Candida a really soppy look that reminded Jessie of the look Rick sometimes gave her when they were out together with a bunch of his friends. It was a sweet, adoring look – but somehow she'd never quite trusted it, and always preferred him to be argumentative and teasing and sexy and silly, the way he was when they were alone. Fleetingly, she wondered if Candida felt irritated by the look, but then she squashed the thought. Candida, she reminded herself, simply didn't have feelings.

"Anyway, I got involved with the pantomime and of course I was knocked sideways by all you talented luvvies." He flashed a smile. Jessie, obediently, attempted a smile in return. After all, she told herself guiltily, he was her director.

"But then this – this gorgeous vision turned up," he went on, turning to Candida. She looked bored. Jessie looked interested – she couldn't help it.

"I'm a man of the world, you know," he explained condescendingly. Jessie again remembered things that Rick had said, to show her how much more he knew about the world than she did, than she ever could. She smiled, helplessly.

"So I fell in love," Michael finished simply. "Or, to be accurate, we fell in love. It was wrong, we knew it was. But when something like that hits you, like a thunderbolt, like a flash from the sky, you can't resist. It would be wicked to resist, I think, in a way." Jessie continued to smile, her face frozen. But privately she was thinking that he was laying it on a bit thick. Surely he could have just said he fancied Candida like mad and couldn't resist her?

"And now we're in so deep," he explained earnestly. "We can't stop, Jessie. Can we, darling?" Candida performed another of her immaculate shrugs, and turned her attention to the dark chocolate mints which had arrived with the second round of coffees.

"So we'd both be very grateful indeed if we kept this as a little secret between the three of us," Michael was saying. Jessie had so many new thoughts whirling round her head that she was finding it difficult to concentrate on anything. But through the blur she was aware that Michael was explaining how difficult this all was; how his wife was expecting a baby and although it was Candida he really loved, of course he did, well he just couldn't afford to upset poor Marjorie at a time like this. Jessie even thought she heard him muttering about what bad publicity it would be, if it ever came out that he'd been seeing another woman while his wife was pregnant.

"I'm sorry?" she said. "You're worried about *publicity*?"

Michael didn't seem to notice the irony in her voice.

"Naturally," he nodded. "I'm known as a family man, after all. My biggest telly appearance was playing the husband in *Love Letters*. It could ruin me."

Jessie was amazed that he could so callously admit that his image, his public image, could be more important to him than honesty in his private life. She stared at him, open-mouthed, her own pressing problems temporarily forgotten.

Michael clearly misunderstood the appalled look on her face.

"So I'd really do a great deal to avoid any, er, unpleasantness," he went on. "This car business, for example. Why don't you let me handle it, Jessie? Your father will be in bed by now, won't he?" Jessie stared at him dumbly, feeling rather out of control.

"He's away until tomorrow," she whispered.

"Right, here's what we'll do," said Michael quickly. "I'm going to tell him everything is my fault. I needed the car desperately tonight because – um – because mine broke down and I had to be on a TV programme in Birmingham. People always think that being on TV is an emergency... So I persuaded you to lend the car to me, and unfortunately I had a little argument with, let's see, the BBC car park gate. That sounds nice and glamorous, doesn't it? And of course I'll get it mended, it'll be good as new, I'll see to that…"

Feeling shaken and bemused, Jessie allowed Michael to drive her home. She slipped upstairs, exhausted, knowing that the next day a whole fabric of lies would be put in motion, just to protect the guilty: Michael, who'd betrayed his pregnant wife; Candida, who, without any regard to that fact that he was married, had entered into a full-blown affair with him; and Jessie herself. A criminal, she reminded herself, as she tossed and turned on her pillow, her face burning and her heart pounding. She had broken the law; broken the trust of her father; risked lives, in the pursuit of her mad, groundless obsession. And now she was about to allow Michael to make everything all right again – to paint over all the cracks – just so that all three of them could carry on with their lies and deceit.

As she sank at last into a fevered sleep, Jessie wondered if she could really go through with it. Should she let Michael put his plan into action? And if she did, would she really be able to live with herself afterwards? The last thought of all, as she drifted into her troubled dreams, was of Rick. Rick had turned out to be blameless in all this misery. He'd been telling her the truth all along. So when his chiselled face, his familiar smile, his long, lean body flashed into her mind, why didn't she feel the old surge of happiness and warmth? Why, instead, was there a shadow where all that joy used to be?

17

"*Jessie! Jessie, are you all right?*" The insistent voice penetrating through her troubled dreams startled her into confused consciousness. Where had she heard those words before? Memories of the tinkle of glass, the blackness, the awful sick feeling flashed back to her in a jumble. Was she still slumped at the wheel of her dad's car? Was it Rick's voice urgently calling her name? No, of course, it hadn't been Rick, had it? But it certainly didn't sound like Michael...

Jessie forced open her eyes to see her mother's anxious face close up to hers, her mother's hand smoothing away her hair and touching her burning cheek.

"Hello, Mum," Jessie mumbled rather blearily. At once, her mother's face cleared and she smiled with relief.

"At last!" she said. "I've been trying to wake you for ages. It's way past getting up time, and I couldn't get a peek out of you." She peered suspiciously at her daughter with that special mother kind of look. "Hmm … as I thought. You're not well, are you, love? I thought you hadn't quite recovered after you took the day off on Wednesday. You looked a bit peaky then, but now –" She reached over and laid a cool, practised hand on Jessie's forehead. "Definitely flu," she pronounced, and rushed off to fetch the thermometer. "I knew it, I just knew it…"

Jessie lay back on the pillows, watching the room spin round. So that was it! She was ill. Maybe all those memories were feverish nightmares, she thought in a wild moment of optimism. Maybe she'd been delirious, and none of it had really happened at all. But no – she knew she wasn't all that ill. It had been real all right – the drive through the night on Candida's tail, the shock of seeing that kiss, the crash, and then the realization that it wasn't Rick Candida had been seeing at all, but Michael…

After Jessie's mum took her temperature and gasped worriedly at the verdict she'd given her a hot drink and some aspirins.

"Try and get some sleep now, love," she advised in that special gentle voice that took Jessie way back to her childhood, when a word and a kiss from Mum could fix just about anything. "Your dad's coming home from his conference this afternoon," she added. "See if you can get a bit better to welcome him back."

If only she knew! thought Jessie, her head pounding as if it was going to crack in two. Just the thought of her father and what she had done to him was enough to send her fever sky high!

All morning, she drifted in and out of a troubled sleep, terrified of what the day would bring. At lunchtime, her mother arrived with some soup on a tray.

"That actor Michael Wayne rang this morning," she announced excitedly. "You know, dear, the one who's helping out with your pantomime. He wants to know when your father will be home. Said he'd like to pop in and talk to him this evening. Strange," she mused. "I wouldn't have put him down as someone who'd be all that keen on double glazing. And he sounded as if it was quite urgent, too…"

Jessie sat up at once, startled. "Oh, it's not about the double glazing!" she blurted out. "At least – well, I'm fairly sure it wouldn't be that." She found her voice tailing away and her mother looking at her strangely. She knew it was her moment to speak, but somehow she just couldn't. Instead, she began coughing – at first, to cover her confusion, and then for real, such dry, wracking coughs that her mother became quite alarmed and forgot, for the moment, what Jessie had been saying.

Word seemed to have got around, as if by E-mail, that Jessie was ill. The doorbell kept ringing all afternoon. First, a panting, anxious Hazel arrived, rushing on her bike in between lessons at college.

"Are you really ill?" she demanded, getting to the point at once, as she usually did. "Or is this what those of us in the know like to call an emotional ailment?" To her immense shock, Jessie burst into wild, uncontrollable tears.

"What is it, Jess? It's not Rick, is it?" Even at the height of a drama, Hazel found it difficult to suppress her curiosity. And for once, for the first time in ages, Jessie found herself talking to her best friend – really talking, the way best friends should. She told her everything – about how jealous she'd been of Candida, her master plan to find out the truth, and then, finally, the quite unexpected secret she'd uncovered. Hazel was speechless, her eyes as wide as CDs.

"Wow!" she kept saying in a breathy voice. "Wow! Oh, Jessie, that's amazing. But you know I did keep trying to tell you she wasn't seeing Rick. She's OK, honestly. I like her." Jessie remembered how silent and cool Candida had been last night, even when Michael was saying how much she meant to him. She'd hardly glanced in his direction, and she certainly hadn't said a word to Jessie.

"Anyway," added Hazel, who always liked to look on the bright side. "It's turned out pretty well, hasn't it? I always knew Rick was nuts about you, and only you. And now you've proved it, haven't you?"

Jessie shook her head sadly. "Not really," she croaked, exhausted from the combination of flu, tears and anguish. "I've proved he's not seeing Candida. But I still don't know where I stand with him, Hazel. And it's really hard…"

Hazel gave her a hug, and thrust a magazine and a Mars bar into her hands.

"Look, I keep telling you – don't worry, everything's fine. I mean – you don't even have to do any explaining about the car, do you? Michael's going to get you off the hook. Get well again and you'll soon realize how lucky you are."

Soon after she'd gone a whirlwind appeared in her doorway. It was Dan, just home from school.

"Hi, you don't mind if I don't get too close, do you?" he greeted her. "Yuk! It's true! You really have got the plague! Mum! Mum! Quick, she's got great purple blotches all over her and some of them are bursting and blue kind of stuff is spurting out…!"

"OK, OK! I don't care if you are doing the Tudors and Stuarts this term, that wasn't very funny!" rasped poor Jessie. "What do you want? Why are you here? No reason? Good, then get out. I mean, you wouldn't want to catch your death in here, would you?"

"Nothing, no, course not!" squealed Dan merrily. "Did you ever see *The Killing of Sister George*? No? Pity. So true to life. Oh, by the way, you don't mind if I send this by air mail, do you, as I'm too sensitive to get close to the dying." A large, blue envelope whizzed into the room and on to Jessie's pillow as he scooted away.

Sighing impatiently at the awfulness of little brothers, and hers in particular, she tore open the envelope. Inside was a beautiful picture of an old-fashioned circus, alight with performing elephants, dancing horses, clowns, lions, the flying trapeze… Who could it be from? She squinted for a few seconds at the terrible handwriting before she managed to make any sense of it.

Get well soon! We need you back in the ring. Love, Toby.

She should have been pleased, or at least relieved. Toby hadn't spoken to her at all since the night of the gig, and she'd begun to worry that maybe he never would again. So this peace offering should have cheered her up. But for some reason, the fever she supposed, tears were rolling down her cheeks again, and she was sobbing into her pillow. Why was everything such a mess, just when it should all be so great? She'd just dozed into another fitful sleep when she was awoken by yet another interruption, the sound of voices downstairs. Her stomach turned over as she managed to make out her father's bluff, cheerful tones as well as a deeper, richer voice which boomed through the ceiling. Michael Wayne!

Painfully, her head still throbbing, Jessie forced herself out of bed and on to the landing. Her legs were rather wobbly so she sat at the top of the stairs and listened to the snatches of conversation which wafted her way.

"So very sorry to cause you inconvenience," Michael was saying. "I wanted to come and talk to you right away. You see I was in quite desperate straits last night. I had to go to Pebble Mill after our rehearsal…" Jessie could hear him explaining how he'd had to rush to do an interview at the BBC and his car had broken down.

"You really mustn't blame Jessie, Mr Mackenzie," Michael was saying in his most charming, seductive voice. "She was acting on the most generous of motives, truly she was."

"But if she wanted to lend you the car, why didn't she ask me?" That was Jessie's mum, sounding very puzzled.

"Oh, she tried," Michael assured her expertly. "At that particular time of the evening you were out, and I was, you see," now his voice was apologetic, and very suave, "I was in the most frightful hurry."

"It's true I was out for a bit," Jessie's mother agreed uncertainly. "But only for a very little while, giving out those forms. Why on earth didn't she mention it later on when she got home?" There was just a little pause, and then she answered her own question. "Of course, I was forgetting," she said, sounding relieved. "She wasn't well. She still isn't well, not at all well. She must have flopped into bed with that awful temperature, poor love."

Jessie knew she should be feeling pleased that the story seemed to be working, but she couldn't help feeling uncomfortable. It was as if she was allowing Michael to make a fool of her parents, as well as tell lies on her behalf. As she crept shamefully back to bed she could hear Michael explaining smoothly how sorry he was to have damaged the bumper. How he'd had it all sorted out, at his own expense of course. It was perfectly all right now, but he hadn't liked to deceive them, that was why he'd had to come and straighten it all out there and then.

"Hey!" hissed Dan from her door. "Is that him? *The* Michael Wayne? Can I get his autograph, do you think? Do you suppose if I went down now and had a word with him he'd give me some advice about how to get copyright for my computer songs?"

"Dan – just shut up, will you," groaned Jessie wearily. She didn't even have the spirit for her usual level of insult. The most irritating thing about Dan right now was that he may be a pain in the neck, but he was a relatively innocent, well-meaning pain in the neck. While she was steeped in dishonesty and sleaze. "Shut up and get to bed and give me a break!"

"OK, OK! Chill out, sister. Anyone would think you were ill or something." He put his head round the door daringly. "Or maybe you're just sick at heart." And off he slithered, leaving Jessie shivering in her bed, wretched with fever and guilt.

It wasn't long before the voices calmed down and the front door opened and shut, after a brief exchange of courtesies. A few minutes later Jessie heard her father's familiar footfall creaking up the stairs and into her room.

"Daddy!" she cried weakly. And then she was in his arms, sobbing like a baby all over again.

"It's OK, love," he kept saying as he hugged her. "Don't fret. You were silly to lend Mr Wayne the car but it's OK, he's explained everything. There's no need to get so upset." He held her for a very long time as she sobbed her heart out.

At last, her face still buried in his strong, comfortable shoulder, Jessie realized she couldn't allow the lies to go on. This was her dad, after all. And unless she came clean now, things would never be quite the same between them again. She'd always carry with her the knowledge that she'd deceived him.

So as her tears began to dry and the sobs and the coughs subsided, she managed to whisper in a very small voice: "Dad – Dad there's something I've got to tell you." And once she started blurting out her story, it seemed as if she was never going to stop.

18

"It wasn't quite the way Michael told it," she began hesitantly, quaking inside. Her father was looking at her expectantly and she nearly backed out. Then, heart in mouth, she said quietly: "I don't know how to tell you this, Dad, but I know I've got to." She took a deep breath, and once she'd started she gabbled out the whole story, stopping only to gulp down her tears and cough out her sobs.

"I know, love," her father said simply, when she'd finished.

"What?" she gasped. "What d'you mean?"

"I knew he was covering up," her father explained wearily. "I was just waiting for you to tell me yourself."

"But – but how?" she stammered, amazed. After all, she had decided to come clean because she couldn't bear the deceit. Not because she'd had any idea at all that her father had seen through the whole thing.

He reached into his pocket and brought out a packet of pear drops. "Not what I normally carry in the passenger seat," he explained drily. Then he scrabbled in the other pocket and produced the little guitar brooch that Toby had given her, the one she always wore for good luck.

"It was under the driver's seat," he told her. "But your mother had seen you pinning it on for rehearsal last night. You're not very good at lying, love, are you?" She'd shaken her head, then, silent with shame and embarrassment.

"Don't you want to hear the rest of what happened?" she'd finally whispered.

"No, I've heard enough," her father said quietly. "But there may be more you need to say to me."

Jessie forced herself to look into his eyes, and she didn't like what she saw. Her kind, easy-going father was staring at her with an expression she'd never seen before: cold, icy contempt.

"Dad?" she whispered, barely able to speak. "Oh, Dad, I'm sorry. I think I must have been crazy to do what I did. I – I suppose you'll never trust me again, will you?"

"Well, what would you feel if you were me?" he asked sternly. It was an old trick that he'd often used before. He even sometimes asked her what punishment she thought she deserved. Now she thought hard before answering.

"I'd be really angry about the car and about me driving without a licence," she admitted. "In fact, I'd probably have me locked up or put in a mental hospital or something... But I think I'd be glad that I'd told the truth."

His face softened. "Well, I think maybe I'm getting my little girl back after all," he said gently. "Jessie, I think you know how serious this is, and I think you're suffering, aren't you? This fever of yours – I get the feeling it's tied up with that Rick of yours, and whatever has got into you has driven you to this madness."

Jessie nodded, her eyes filling with tears.

"But at least you've come clean and told me the truth. Because the one thing I couldn't bear is lies. And I suppose it must have taken some courage to own up to last night's bag of tricks."

She nodded again, and noticed that some of the ice in his eyes was beginning to melt. And then he was hugging her, and she was crying again and whispering, "I'm sorry, Dad, I'm really, really sorry," over and over again. "I don't know what got into me," she sobbed. "I suppose I was just so hung up about Rick I lost all my senses."

Her father kissed her head very softly. "Well, at least you trust me enough to tell me the truth. You didn't try to blame this flu thing, did you? You didn't even think of pretending you'd done all this because you weren't well. I can give you credit for that. And I do believe you're sorry. Anyway, thanks to your director chappie the car's going to be fine. And most important of all, no one was hurt. So one way and another I've a good deal to be thankful for."

Warmth and relief were flooding through Jessie. At least the lies were over now, and her father still loved her. "You do know why you felt so ill after your little bump, don't you?" he added. "It's just a touch of flu. The doctor was quite adamant that there were no signs of concussion, not even a bruise. Thank goodness you were wearing your safety belt."

"You – you mean you actually checked with the doctor?" Jessie was beginning to feel as if she must be in a dream again.

Her father nodded. "Well, we knew you must have been involved somehow, so we had to check up. I'm just very, very glad you decided to come out with the truth, all on your own." He hugged her again before getting up to leave her. When he got to the doorway he turned round again.

"Oh, and by the way," he said. "Next time you decide to abscond with my Volvo, do remember that I object very strongly to having the radio tuned to that pirate station. That was the biggest give-away of all."

She managed a watery smile. "I'll remember to make it Radio Two next time, then you'll never pin it on me." Registering his smile, she continued hopefully: "So – so you'll forgive me? We can forget it ever happened?"

"Oh, sure," her dad replied kindly. "You're grounded till the end of the year, but apart from that, everything's just fine."

Of course Jessie felt much, much better now. But she was still unwell, still very guilty, and still in a state of turmoil about all that had happened. More than anything, she found herself thinking about Rick. Where was he now? Surely, if he really loved her, he'd have found out by now that she wasn't well, and flown to her side?

Later that day, she couldn't be sure when, the doorbell chimed into her anxious fretting, and a visitor was invited into the house. She heard footsteps climbing up the stairs and her door was opened.

"Someone to see you," said her mum softly.

And in walked, of all people ... Candida herself, bearing a little bouquet of roses and a basket of goodies from the Body Shop.

"Hi," she said awkwardly. "I heard you weren't well, and I really –" She turned round to make sure that Jessie's mum had left the room and closed the door behind her. Then her face changed dramatically – from polite and embarrassed to fierce and intent.

"Jessie, I really, really need to talk to you!" she hissed. Jessie could only stare at her in astonishment. She was beginning to think she'd had a few too many surprises lately. But this was the most unexpected yet. Cool, cold, icy Candida was gripping her urgently by the wrists, her cheeks red, her eyes glistening with tears.

"You see, you're the only one who knows. I've been keeping it to myself for so long, and it's just getting so hard. Jessie, what do you think? You saw us together! I'm not cross, really I'm not! I know I was a creep last night, but that was only because I was so upset. You see, Michael wants it all to be a secret, but – but I love him so much. I was glad you found us, honestly I was. It made it seem more real, somehow. Less of a dream. And I couldn't say anything because I knew it would only make him angry or something. So tell me, how did it look to you?"

Jessie had never seen Candida emotional or passionate. It was a completely new side of her. And she couldn't help responding to it.

"Well, it looked to me as if he was crazy about you," Jessie began, moved by the look of hope and gratitude in Candida's eyes. And as she heard herself speak, she remembered all the times that Hazel had used exactly the same words to her – about Rick. She, too, had always found them comforting. But at the same time, she'd never really quite believed her. After all, how could anyone, even a friend, really know what was going on between two lovers.

"It certainly looked that way," she corrected herself. "But I'm not the person to ask. I mean – I hardly know either of you..."

"Yes, but that doesn't matter," Candida interrupted her urgently. "You know about us, and you're the only one who does. You've got to tell me—"

Suddenly, Jessie felt wise – weary, but wise. "You've no idea how much I'd like to make you feel better," she said slowly. "But it's much better to tell you the truth. And that is that only you know how it is between you. Nothing anybody on the outside can tell you means anything at all. So – why are you asking me?"

And now it was Candida who had tears streaming down her face, as she began to pour out her heart to Jessica. How she hadn't meant to get involved with Michael – of course she hadn't. She wasn't very proud of the fact that she was seeing a married man. But then, he'd been so insistent – so sure of himself. He'd told her his marriage was over. The baby was a mistake, and he'd be leaving as soon as he could, but he wasn't going to do that before it was born.

Then she was sobbing even more uncontrollably. "I believed him!" she cried. "I thought he loved me! He came on so strongly to start with. He was irresistible."

"You must have been very flattered," Jessie put in faintly.

Candida gave her a strange look. "Why did you say that?" she snapped.

"Oh, only because I know exactly how you must have felt," Jessie replied. She felt a mysterious affinity with Candida, which made her reach out and squeeze the other girl's arm. "He must have seemed like the perfect man for you – except he's not, is he?"

Candida shook her head sadly. "No, I guess not. These last few weeks have become hell, you know. At first, he was desperate to be with me – he'd do all the running, be wherever I wanted him to be, arrange everything round me. But it's not like that any more. I have to hang around waiting for him after rehearsals, and pretend to my mum that I'm working. And then there are all those maybe nights. You know – he might be able to get away, he might not, I have to wait for the phone to ring. I have to pretend not to mind if he can't make it. I suppose I'm just kidding myself that I really matter to him..."

She'd been talking as if to herself, but then she

seemed to remember Jessie and gave her a penetrating look. "But it's hardly the same between you and Rick, is it? I mean, I know I flirted with him a little, but that was only to put everyone off the scent, because Michael was so paranoid about being found out."

"He seemed pretty jealous about the two of you," Jessie couldn't help remarking.

Candida shrugged. "Oh, well, that's men for you. But Rick's sweet. And it's obvious that he cares for you, Jess. I mean, I'm sorry if I made it look like anything was happening between us, but I didn't mean it that way. He's so crazy about you!"

"Yes, well, I'm sure you're right, and I'm really, really sorry I behaved the way I did," Jessie burst out. It was true. She suddenly liked Candida very much indeed. In fact, she felt as though the two of them had been through something very, very similar. And that was why Candida's assurances about Rick meant no more to her than Hazel's, no more to her than her own could possibly mean to Candida. When it came to love, only two people could know the truth.

"Thanks for coming to see me," Jessie said warmly. "I really do appreciate it. And, er – your secret, it won't go any further."

"No, it definitely won't," Candida assured her grimly. "Because it isn't going to be one any more. I'm finishing with him, Jessie. You've made me realize just what a fool I've been, and I'm not going to put up with it any longer."

For some reason, Jessie finally drifted into a

long, peaceful sleep after Candida had gone. Everything, somehow, seemed to be falling into place. And when she woke up, she felt so much better that she managed to get up and make her way very carefully and slowly downstairs that afternoon.

Her mum had gone to work; Dan was out. She was alone, bundled in blankets on the sofa, when her next visitor arrived. It was Rick!

"Jessie! I'm so sorry. I had no idea you'd been ill. I was out of town on a story and I was going to ring you the minute I got back but then I just ran into Hazel down town and she told me, so I rushed on over."

He scrabbled in the shoulder bag that he'd flung on to an armchair. "Here, I've brought something to cheer you up."

Triumphantly he handed Jessie a tattered plastic bag. Inside were two tapes, one a blues compilation and the other the latest Grace Hari album. Typical! Jessie thought bitterly. Fancy giving music tapes to someone with flu. As if her head wasn't pounding enough already!

Then she softened. It was sweet of Rick to get the tapes for her, even if they were probably freebies from work. And after all, he hadn't known then that she was ill.

So she smiled, and melted, and then she was in his arms again, the old familiar longing flooding through her. The tingle ran down her spine as his lips pressed against hers. The shiver of excitement as he wrapped her in a long, passionate embrace. There was no doubt about it, Rick was a gorgeous guy. But now, for the first time ever, something had changed.

As he lifted his face from hers and gazed deep into her eyes, she realized what it was. For some reason, probably because of all that had happened since they'd last been together, all that she'd suffered, worried about, thought about, fretted about, she wasn't asking herself the same questions any more. She wasn't really wondering any longer how much he loved her, or whether he loved her at all.

Suddenly, instead, she found that she was wondering how much *she* loved *him*. Or even if she'd ever really loved him at all.

19

It was never quite the same again between Jessie and Rick, although it took her a little while to realize what had changed. They still saw each other regularly. They even went to bed together and he was as loving and as indulgent as ever. It wasn't Rick, after all, who had changed. It was Jessie. Instead of regarding Rick as someone to look up to, to learn from, to please – she had started to see him as an equal. And somehow just a little of the shine had begun to wear off.

It all became clear on the day of the Dress Rehearsal, a few weeks later. There had been a mad scramble to get everything ready by the beginning of December. Most of the costumes had been hired, but a team of helpers, including some unlucky mothers, had been roped in to put together the rest and to make any last-minute additions. Another team had painted backcloths and scenery, but key members of the cast had been put in charge of collecting extra props for particular scenes.

Miriam, of course, had opted for the ball scene, and had had a wonderful time scouring second hand shops and the attics of various aunts in search of gilt-legged chairs, fans, feathers and general glitter.

Jessie – typically, she thought sardonically – was allocated the kitchen. At first she'd thought it very boring, but in the end she'd amassed an array of extraordinary items that would give the kitchen scenes character and even humour. She was particularly fond of an old Women's Liberation poster belonging to her mother. It was a huge picture of a dustpan and brush and it proclaimed in stark black letters: HOUSEWORK IS DRUDGERY. Jessie thought it would look hilarious pinned above the mantelpiece where Cinders would sit scrubbing and weeping.

She'd found a broom, of course, but she was also very proud of a very ancient Hoover donated by her grandmother, who hadn't ever had the heart to throw it away. "I always thought it belonged in a museum, dear," she'd said. "But I suppose the stage is just as fitting. Oh, and you might as well have this while you're about it."

"This" turned out to be a very heavy old pair of bronze kitchen scales. Jessie loved them. They were huge, and came with their own set of weights. When Michael saw them he was delighted. "We'll put something silly on them, just to get the audience in the right mood!"

"How about the heavy side is women's work and the light side is men's work," suggested Hazel.

"Too political," Toby said at once. "How about a

172

bunch of lizards? That would sort of imply that they were a normal part of kitchen equipment."

"No, I think there should be a great big red heart which is heavier than all the weights," put in Miriam.

"Or the heavy heart is a woman's and the light one is a man's." That, of course, was Candida. She said it lightly enough but Jessie, glancing at Michael, saw him flush with embarrassment, or it might have been annoyance.

"No, it'll have to be onions," he declared, clearly anxious to change the subject. "And we could put in a few jokes about tears, and smelly breath."

"Yes, maybe the Fairy Godmother could offer Buttons a packet of Polos to solve his most intimate problems," quipped Toby. And they'd all laughed.

But the Dress Rehearsal was to be the first time that everything – backdrops, lighting, props and, of course, costumes – would be brought together on stage for the whole performance. They'd set aside a whole Sunday. Everything was to be brought to the theatre first thing in the morning, and Michael had said they should be ready for the performance by late afternoon.

The final turning point for Jessie came that morning, soon after she'd arrived at the theatre in a state of high excitement. Everyone was laughing and chattering as backcloths began to be lowered and raised, costumes appeared as if from nowhere, and in all corners of the auditorium there was frantic activity.

Rick was going through the final score with the

band. Jessie was doing a mad warm-up routine with Candida. Suddenly Michael announced: "OK, props on stage please."

Jessie's hand shot to her mouth as she let out a horrified gasp. "Oh, no! You're not going to believe this. I've forgotten them."

"You what?" said about a dozen people at once.

"I'm sorry," she said. "I really am. I don't know how I could have done anything so stupid. I guess I had other things on my mind last night..."

She shot a pleading glance over at Rick. He knew exactly what she meant. They'd been together the night before, and they'd made love. He'd dropped her home late and she'd rushed to bed, tortured by her usual turmoil of emotions. So surely he'd help her out of this mess now.

"Typical!" he said in a lazy voice that managed to be cutting at the same time. "You're hopeless, Jessie, you really are. I'm amazed you remembered to turn up at all. In fact, it's fairly extraordinary that you know which planet you're on. You certainly seem to be occupying a different one from the rest of us."

There was an awkward silence as everyone waited, astonished. There was no mistaking the cruelty of Rick's words, even though he'd tried to make them sound, as usual, like a big brother teasing a favourite little sister.

Jessie could feel the blood draining from her face. Her first reaction was to flinch with humiliation, as she had done so often in the past when he had criticized her. But then something else took over – a pure, white anger at Rick. How

174

dare he put her down in front of everyone like that? How dare he put her down at all? She wasn't incompetent or forgetful, not really. She just seemed to be that way when she was with Rick. He expected it. Almost, she realized suddenly, he wanted it.

"What did you say?" she demanded icily. The room froze.

"Oh, come off it, Jess – haven't you caused enough problems?" he said lightly. She knew he was trying to pretend that this was just an affectionate little tiff. But she wasn't going to let him get away with it. Not this time.

She walked slowly and purposefully towards him. It seemed to take for ever, especially as everyone in the world was watching her.

"You really do have a problem, you know that, Rick?" she spat. "You're not better than anyone else, or cleverer or cooler. You're just a professional put-down! And I can't for the life of me see any reason why I should put up with it any longer."

Rick flushed with embarrassment. "Don't make a scene, hon," he said uncomfortably. "You're just upset that you forgot the props and held everyone up. So why don't you just run along and get them and we'll all chill out."

"No problem," she said in a very quiet voice. "I'll go and fetch them now. It won't take long... And by the way, you patronizing piece of, of ... of pond weed!" She cast Rick a look of cold contempt. "Don't you ever, ever speak to me like that again. Understood?"

And she flounced past everyone and out of the

door, her heart racing but her head held high. Angry and upset, she charged down the road with such force and purpose that it was a few minutes before she became aware of footsteps running after her and a voice calling her name. It was Toby, who finally caught up with her, panting heavily.

"Jessie, couldn't you hear me shouting at you?" he demanded between breaths. "I'm coming with you. I – er – I thought you might have too much to carry."

Jessie thought she had never in her life been so pleased to see anyone. It had been tough walking out of that theatre alone. What she needed now was a friend. Toby was far too tactful to mention Rick, or the awful scene. He just chatted about the Dress Rehearsal as though nothing much had happened and Jessie quickly found herself relaxing. It was always fun, being with Toby.

They managed to get a bus back to her house, where the props were stored, and it wasn't long before they were on their way back again, staggering under the weight of her eccentric assortment. Toby carried the weights balanced precariously on his shoulders, a broom in one hand and a large clock in the shape of a fried egg in the other. Jessie had the vacuum cleaner, a large teatowel bearing the legend "A Present From Blackpool", and three large plastic jars. One said Bread, one said Sugar, and the third one said Flowers.

"Where did you get that?" demanded Toby, intrigued.

"Oxfam shop," gasped Jessie, concentrating on balancing everything at the same time.

"You mean – someone actually owned them?" Toby started laughing. "I think there must be some crazy person somewhere who invents things like that just so that people will give them away … and then eventually they'll end up where they belong, in pantomimes."

"Oh, no, I think what it is is that nasty things have to be made so you can give them to people you don't like," said Jessie. And while they waited at the bus stop they played a game, thinking up suitable presents for undesirable people.

"A calculator that plays God Save the Queen when it gives you the answer – that's for Mr Robbs," said Toby. Mr Robbs was his Maths tutor.

"Bath salts that smell of onions – for Miriam," said Jessie.

"Oh, yeah – and how about your friend Candida?" asked Toby boldly.

Jessie blushed. "Well – actually she is my friend," she admitted. "I like her. I didn't use to but I do now."

At that moment the bus arrived. The conductor took one look at the pile of strange objects on the pavement. "Upstairs," he said curtly.

"But – but there's rather a lot…" protested Jessie.

"And they're quite heavy," added Toby.

"You're lucky I'm letting you on at all," replied the conductor, unimpressed.

Somehow, they managed to get everything upstairs with them, and by the time they flopped into their seats they were laughing uncontrollably.

People were giving them some very strange glances – and they could both perfectly well see that they made a very odd pair indeed.

They were still giggling when the bus arrived at the nearest stop to the theatre, and they both scrambled down the stairs with all their clutter. Toby was so weighed down that he hurtled down the stairs and right off the bus, straight into Jessie, so that they ended up sprawled over the pavement in a tangle of kitchen equipment.

"You OK?" asked Toby as he pulled her to her feet. She nodded, then noticed that he hadn't removed his hand. Then she noticed she didn't really want him to. They were standing very close, then he was pulling her towards him. And right there, in the street, surrounded by all the crazy kitchen props, he kissed her.

It was a gentle kiss. Almost the kiss of a friend. But at the touch of his lips an electric charge rushed through her. And then it was over. He gave her a hug, and muttered: "Come on – better hurry up with these." Then he immediately tripped over a wire which had escaped from the Hoover, and this time Jessie had to pull him to his feet. They were both giggling now, but there was something else in the air. Something that Jessie had never noticed before.

"Hey – you two need any help?" Geoff and Jane appeared from round the corner.

"We thought we'd offer to help, since we're kindly making up the audience this evening," explained Jane.

"And they sent us off to look for you," Geoff said,

and then stopped in amazement as he took in the clutter around them. "You're mad! You brought this lot on the bus? Totally, completely barmy!"

In the end they spread the load between the four of them, chattering and laughing as they swayed down the road in a crazy crocodile line. As they made their way into the back door of the theatre, Jessie reached out for Toby's hand and squeezed it hard.

"Thanks," she whispered. "You're a real pal."

"Jessie…" Toby said, his hand still firmly in hers.

"What?" Her heart was pounding as their eyes locked together. It seemed very quiet, in that dark empty corridor, and for some reason she was holding her breath.

"Oh, nothing," Toby answered quickly. "It was nothing. Any time you need a – a helping hand, you know where to come."

Then he pulled his hand away from hers and hurried away from her and into the crowd backstage. For a moment or two Jessie stood and watched him disappear round the corner. Then she followed, wondering why she suddenly felt so utterly bereft.

Jessie never knew how she managed to get through the Dress Rehearsal that day. She tried to act as if nothing had happened, of course, but she couldn't help noticing that Rick was icily ignoring her and that just made her react with even more determined cheerfulness. She threw herself into the show, bounding round the stage with such abandon that Michael had to tell her to calm down and save herself for the real thing. And all along, deep inside she was in turmoil.

At the end of the rehearsal Rick approached her grimly. "Lift home?" he offered. Numbly, Jessie nodded and followed him out to the car. He drove in silence, his jaw set sternly. Once, Jessie reflected, she would have been thrown into paroxysms of anguish at this display of cold rejection. Now, it didn't really bother her.

"So – aren't you even going to say good night?" she asked lightly. "Or should I say, goodbye."

Rick was about to turn into her road. Instead, he put his foot down and continued along the road which led out of town. He said nothing until they reached the open countryside. Then he turned into a side road, and again down a track. He stopped the car.

"Jessie, I'm sorry," he said unexpectedly. "You were right. I should never have said those things to you today and I don't blame you for what happened."

Once again, Jessie surprised herself. She should have been flooded with happiness, overcome with gratitude that Rick was willing to forgive her outburst. But all she felt was a kind of distant triumph.

"Well, that's big of you," she started to say. But he stopped her.

"No – let me finish. I wanted to say that although I can understand why you reacted like that, I just didn't expect it. It wasn't like you. I didn't recognize you."

Suddenly, as he spoke, Jessie felt a flash of understanding. "It's her, isn't it?" she said, surprising herself with her own certainty. He glanced at her.

"What are you talking about?" he demanded. As he spoke, Jessie knew her instincts were right.

"Louise," she said softly. "You just couldn't take it when I stood up to you today. Because that's the kind of thing she used to do, isn't it?"

Rick's face darkened with pain as he stared straight ahead. It was beginning to rain, and the windscreen was misting up. Jessie knew, without a doubt, that this was the end for them. But instead of feeling sadness, she felt calm and certain. She reached out for Rick's hand and squeezed it.

"I think maybe I'm not the person you wanted me to be," she said gently.

Slowly, he turned to face her. His eyes were tender, and he smiled – the old, charming smile. "Maybe not – but you are a great person, a wonderful person. The sexiest Fairy Godmother who's ever cast a spell on me."

Jessie smiled back, suddenly fond of Rick. "You know, in the end you'd have got sick of having a passive, hopeless, clinging female hanging round your neck," she teased him. "I reckon you don't really want someone to dominate, any more than you want to be dominated by the Louises of the world. Next time, why not go for an equal?" As she spoke, she thought with a pang of Toby. Already, Rick was beginning to seem far away, like a stranger.

"I guess this is the end for us, isn't it?" he whispered. When she nodded, he squeezed her hand, then started the car and began to drive her home again.

Outside her house, he pulled her towards him and kissed her lips very gently. "I'll never forget you, Jess," he said quietly. "These last few months, with you – it's been great. Hasn't it?"

"It's been like a dream," Jessie assured him with a gentle smile. But as she slipped out of the car and made her way to the front door, she was overcome with relief that it was over, it was finally all over. Now she was herself again. And she was free.

20

There was a sudden crack of a whip, the band burst into a country hoedown, and a full-blooded Tennessee twang announced merrily: "Cinderella – you *shall* go to the ball!"

Jessie had rehearsed this bit so often that she positively relished her first appearance in the show, slapping her hands on her thighs and beaming heartily at the audience. There was an astonished ripple of laughter. She waited for a few seconds longer than usual, before declaiming: "I am your Fairy Godmother!" When the audience laughed even louder she turned to them indignantly and added a few extra lines of her own.

"Oh, so there's some folk out there don't believe me, huh?" Her scornful eyes swept the packed auditorium. "We-ell, ladies and gentlemen, let me tell y'all a thang or two. I most certainly am a Fairy Godmother, and anyone don't believe me I'll see you outside after the show and we'll have a little shooting contest, shall we?"

Jessie could hardly believe that the show was really happening at last. It had only been three months – but they had been the most eventful, the most wonderful, and the most difficult months of her life in so many ways that she felt like a completely different person now. In fact, she felt very different from the person she had been even three days ago: the three days since the Dress Rehearsal.

Nothing much had happened since then, at least, not outwardly. But inside Jessie had been going through such a churning turmoil of thoughts and emotions that those three days had felt like a lifetime.

She'd gone to college as usual. As usual she'd snatched a quick lunch in the canteen with Hazel, and listened to the latest instalment of her now budding romance with Luke. She hadn't seen Toby, except for one brief glimpse when she'd been coming out of the Social Studies class and seen him going into the library. Her stomach had flipped at the sight of him. She didn't know whether she was relieved that they hadn't come face to face. Or heartbroken.

"So – have you made it up with Rick?" Hazel demanded, with her usual tact.

"Oh, no," Jessie answered with a shrug. "We're definitely finished. Thank goodness!"

Hazel, who had a sixth sense when it came to romantic attachments, immediately pounced. "There's someone else, isn't there?" She peered closely into her friend's eyes. "You'd never have

184

stood up to Rick before. I knew something must have changed you in a big way."

Jessie sighed. "I don't think it's quite as simple as that," she began.

"Oh, for heaven's sake!" Hazel interrupted. "That's you all over, isn't it? How come life is simple for the rest of us, just not you? How come I can say I'm hungry and you have to say you're torn between wanting the sandwich and worrying about whether the ham is fresh and what kind of pickle they used. How come I can say I fancy someone but you have to analyse the difference between infatuation and lust, just fancying or fancying like mad, simple attraction and fatal attraction. Oh, and while we're on the subject, how come I can just say I love someone and you have to ponder on about whether it's really love, or being in love, or falling in love, or just loving like you do a friend…?"

"Well, that's just the point," Jessie put in while Hazel took a breath. "It's Toby."

Hazel fell silent. "Wow," she said. "See your point." She wasn't silent for long, though. "Has anything happened?" she asked eagerly.

Jessie shook her head. "Not really. I don't even think he knows."

Hazel snorted. "You might as well have your head in a bucket, Jessica Mackenzie. Toby's in love with you. I mean, he loves you. I mean, he's very attracted to you. He thinks you're nice. He – oh, what's the point, right first time, he's in love with you. Always has been. It's not complicated, Jess. It's simple."

"How – how do you know?" stammered Jessie.

"Well it's obvious," Hazel said pityingly. "To anyone except you, anyhow. Toby is nuts about you. If you feel the same way you just have to tell him."

After that, Jessie floated through the next few days until the first performance of the pantomime. She found herself piecing together all the clues which suddenly began to make sense. The way Toby always helped to choose her clothes – even for dates with Rick. The beautiful brooch he'd given her for her birthday, hidden in that copy of *Just Seventeen* so that no one would guess how he felt about her. His anger at her treatment of Philip. Could that have been his own jealousy about her? Then she remembered all his acts of kindness. How he'd always helped her out: at school, in the band, during the pantomime when she'd got into such a mess. There was that card he'd sent when she was ill ... and then the Dress Rehearsal. She relived for the thousandth time the charge that had shot through her when their hands had touched...

Rick had not attempted to get in touch with her after they'd agreed to break up. And she hadn't wanted him to. She was amazed at her own calmness. It wasn't as if Rick had changed at all. But she had. And that was why she had been able to stand up to him in that blaze of anger. The spell had finally been broken, and at last she was herself again.

But all that had been set aside on Saturday for the first real performance of the show. Everyone had been in a state of high excitement from early that morning, bustling round the theatre in frantic last-minute panic and getting in each other's way.

"People, people," shouted a harassed Michael Wayne. "Calm down everyone. Now, if this was the West End, you wouldn't be here at all. You'd be home, asleep, conserving your energy. I can remember the last time I played in a pantomime. It was Alice in Wonderland. I was Tweedledum and my very good friend Alex was Tweedledee. We were so keen to conserve our energies that we went for a little relaxing drink or two in the very acceptable little watering hole on the corner..." He smiled dreamily at the memory, his mood suddenly serene. "...Very nearly missed our call," he went on. "Nice little thing playing the dormouse had to come and find us..."

He remembered where he was and called everyone to order, glancing anxiously over to where Candida was busily sewing a few extra buttons on to her jacket. She'd decided that you couldn't ever have enough of them if you were playing Buttons.

She didn't even look up, and Jessie noticed that Philip seemed to be hovering very close. She did a double take. He wasn't just hovering – he was actually sewing a few buttons on himself!

But there was no time for speculation. It was as if all emotional attachments had been put on hold for the day, while everyone concentrated on their one big collective passion. Jessie felt a sudden rush of panic when Rick sauntered in. Although she didn't love him any more, she couldn't help feeling sad that their break-up had been so bitter and so very public.

But, much to her relief, he just waved casually at her. Feeling more cheerful, she waved back and grinned. Despite everything, she was fond of him. And then there was suddenly no time to think about anything except the show. She threw herself into practising the transformation of Cinderella one more time. Rick was equally busy, running through the score with the band. Hazel and Luke were busy, too – so busy that they showed up rather late, looking flustered and very pleased with themselves. But as soon as they arrived, they too were caught up in the rush of activity and chaos.

"I'm – I'm a bit nervous," whispered Miriam to Jessie. She was surprised. Miriam very rarely confessed to having any feelings at all. She wasn't the sort to admit weaknesses. Jessie looked at her closely. She seemed very young suddenly – and vulnerable. Jessie gave her a sudden hug.

"You're going to be great!" she said warmly. 'You're a wonderful actress, you know – but I think we'd better do the dress thing one more time, and then the lizards and rats. But don't be too disgusted. I want you to save your best disgust for the afternoon!"

And then the time began to rush by much too fast. The cast had squeezed into their costumes, their faces glistened with grease paint, the theatre was filling up with the screams and chatter of five hundred children and assorted adults. Jessie was desperate to peep through the curtain and catch a glimpse of the audience. But Michael had forbidden any of them to do that. He said it brought bad luck.

Now here she was on stage, thoroughly enjoying herself. "HE'S BEHIND YOU!" the children were shrieking in delight. Philip dodged to her left as she swung round. Then dodged the other way as she swung again. The audience roared and screamed. At last, she managed to turn all the reptiles and rodents into coachmen and horses and turned her attention to Cinderella. She cracked her whip, the stage filled with dry ice as a filmy curtain descended. The band struck up a gentle few bars and Jessie sang one haunting verse of the theme song, knowing that behind that curtain Miriam was frantically scrambling into her ballgown.

It worked! The audience gasped in wonder as the ice receded, the curtain was lifted, and there was Cinderella, sparkling and glittering, ready for the ball. After she'd swept out in her carriage, Jessie's heart began to pound again. She'd enjoyed everything so far, but the next scene was the big test. She was alone with Buttons, and they were about to perform the duet that had given her so many nightmares.

"Cheer up, Buttons," she said cheerfully. "Ain't no woman worth that amount of tears. And who knows. If the magic can happen to her, maybe it can happen to you, too." Then she and Candida linked arms. She glanced down. Candida was smiling at her. She even managed a wink. The band was urging them into their routine.

Suddenly, Jessie wasn't on stage in front of a packed audience. She was back in the empty gym. The arm round her waist was Toby's. The steps were the steps he'd taught her. Before she knew it the song and dance were over, the audience was cheering.

"We've never done it that well," Candida was whispering triumphantly in her ears.

As the curtain fell for the end of Act One, Jessie found herself tripping backstage, straight into the arms of Toby. He'd been standing in the wings waiting for her, his face rouged and spattered with beauty spots, a cascade of bright red hair coiled into a beehive, his purple and yellow gown plumped up with pillows. He towered over her thanks to his ten-centimetre stilettos.

"I told you you'd be fine," he said, holding her arms as if to steady her. Jessie knew with sudden clarity that she didn't want him to let go.

"I had to pretend it was you up there," she whispered. "That's what made it OK." For another long moment they stared into each other's eyes, oblivious to the bustle going on around them. Their faces moved closer together, very slowly. Jessie was willing him with all her might to kiss her. But as his lips were about to touch hers he suddenly pulled away.

"What can I be thinking of?" he squawked in his Ugly Sister voice. "It would just ruin my make-up and heaven knows that would never do!"

They all sailed through the rest of the show. Everyone seemed to be on a high as they realized how all the drudgery, the hard work, the

190

repetitive grind of rehearsals was now paying off. There was a wonderful feeling of togetherness as they all gathered on stage for the final number.

"And if you – if you truly believe
Then one day, one day,
One day it will happen to you!"

Jessie, at the front of the stage, hand in hand with Miriam and Candida, could just about glimpse Hazel and Luke, side by side in the orchestra pit, their eyes locked as they played the familiar strains. There were Geoff and Jane, clapping in time in the front row. It was almost as if the song was coming true.

When they had taken their final curtain call, to tumultuous cheers and screams of applause, they all crowded into the wings, hugging each other and kissing their congratulations.

"Well done, chaps," Michael effused, passing everyone glasses of champagne and orange juice. "I knew you'd pull out all the stops." He looked a little awkward as he handed Candida her glass, but she just smiled, and kissed him lightly on the cheek before turning away to someone standing right behind her. Jessie could barely prevent herself from gawping. Because the person with Candida, putting his arm protectively round her shoulders, was Philip. And as Candida turned to him, Jessie caught a glimpse of her face, transformed, shining with happiness.

"Whoever would have thought it," said a familiar voice hehind her. "Love's young dream, just where you wouldn't have expected it." It was Rick, grinning his most sardonic grin. Then he added, more seriously: "You sang like an angel tonight."

Once again, Jessie was astonished to find that she was able to hear that voice, see that face, without the slightest frisson. "Glad to see you finally took my advice about toning it down for the duet," he added. She just smiled – a friendly, no-hard-feelings sort of smile, and he ruffled her hair in a big-brotherly gesture. "Fancy coming out for dinner?" he added. "I was thinking of the tapas bar…"

Hazel tugged her arm. "We're all going for a pizza at The Park Inn," she said. "Coming?"

"OK," Jessie answered, flashing Rick a rueful smile. He shrugged, and left.

In the crowded dressing-room she quickly changed back into her leggings and boots and was scrubbing at the last remnants of greasepaint when Toby appeared in the doorway, looking rather pale.

"That blusher just isn't working for you," she remarked lightly as she joined him.

"I've decided to go for the natural look," he answered. But he wasn't smiling, and his voice sounded strained. They made their way out of the theatre in silence. By the time they reached the street Jessie knew he was waiting for a signal from her. So she slipped her hand into his.

"Jessie!" he began. Then she was in his arms and at last his lips found hers and he was kissing her with an intensity that made her senses reel. Hazel and Luke sauntered by arm in arm, followed by Geoff and Jane, Miriam, Philip – the whole crowd. And still Toby was holding her as though he would never let her go. Gazing wonderingly into each other's eyes, barely able to take in what was happening to them, they were locked, for that moment, in a perfect fusion of passion and tenderness. And somehow, cradled in his warmth, her whole being melting into his embrace, Jessie knew that she'd finally come home where she belonged.

Point Romance

If you like Point Horror, you'll love Point Romance!

Are you burning with passion and aching with desire? Then these are the books for you! Point Romance brings you passion, romance, heartache, . . . and *love*.

Available now:

First Comes Love:
To Have and to Hold
For Better, For Worse
In Sickness and in Health
Till Death Do Us Part
Last Summer, First Love:
A Time to Love
Goodbye to Love
Jennifer Baker

A Winter Love Story
Jane Claypool Miner

Two Weeks in Paradise
Spotlight on Love
Denise Colby

Saturday Night
Last Dance
New Year's Eve
Summer Nights
Caroline B. Cooney

Cradle Snatcher
Kiss Me, Stupid
Alison Creaghan

Two-Timer
Lorna Read

Summer Dreams, Winter Love
Mary Francis Shura

The Last Great Summer
Carol Stanley

Lifeguards:
Summer's Promise
Summer's End
Todd Strasser

Crazy About You
French Kiss
Robyn Turner

Look out for:

Russian Nights
Robyn Turner

Point Romance

Look out for this heartwarming Point Romance
mini series:

First Comes Love
by Jennifer Baker

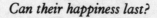

Can their happiness last?

When eighteen-year-old college junior Julie
Miller elopes with Matt Collins, a wayward and
rebellious biker, no one has high hopes for a
happy ending. They're penniless, cut off from
their parents, homeless and too young. But no
one counts on the strength of their love for one
another and commitment of their vows.
Four novels, *To Have and To Hold*, *For Better
For Worse*, *In Sickness and in Health*, and *Till
Death Do Us Part*, follow Matt and Julie through
their first year of marriage.
Once the honeymoon is over, they have to deal
with the realities of life. Money worries,
tensions, jealousies, illness, accidents, and the
most heartbreaking decision of their lives.
Can their love survive?

Four novels to touch your heart . . .

Point Romance

Caroline B. Cooney

The lives, loves and hopes of five young girls appear in this dazzling mini series:

Anne – coming to terms with a terrible secret that has changed her whole life.

Kip – everyone's best friend, but no one's dream date . . . why can't she find the right guy?

Molly – out for revenge against the four girls she has always been jealous of . . .

Emily – whose secure and happy life is about to be threatened by disaster.

Beth Rose – dreaming of love but wondering if it will ever become a reality.

Follow the five through their last years of high school, in four brilliant titles: *Saturday Night, Last Dance, New Year's Eve,* and *Summer Nights*

Dare you unlock...

THE SECRET DIARIES

Dear Diary...

When Joanna starts at her new school, she suddenly has a lot to write about in her diary. For one thing, she's fallen madly in love...

I'm not sure I want to write this down, Diary...

But then she finds her love leads her to write about other things. Betrayal and danger. Maybe even murder...

At least I know my secret will be safe with you. Though you wouldn't think safety was a big concern of mine. Not after I got involved in such terrible things...

Discover Joanna's shocking secrets in
The Secret Diaries by Janice Harrell:

I Temptation
II Betrayal
III Escape

·PATSY KELLY·
INVESTIGATES

When Patsy starts work at her uncle's
detective agency, her instructions are very
clear. Do the filing. Answer the phone.
Make the tea. *Don't* get involved in any
of the cases.

But somehow Patsy can't help
getting involved...

And it's not just the cases she has to worry
about. There's Billy, too. Will she ever work
out what she *really* feels about him...?

·PATSY KELLY·
INVESTIGATES

Anne Cassidy

Look out for:

A Family Affair
The End of the Line